BOOKS BY JUDITH MICHAEL

Deceptions
Possessions
Private Affairs
Inheritance
A Ruling Passion

Judith Michael

A Ruling Passion

A NOVEL

POSEIDON PRESS

New York   London   Toronto   Sydney   Tokyo

Poseidon Press
Simon & Schuster Building
Rockefeller Center
1230 Avenue of the Americas
New York, New York 10020

POSEIDON PRESS is a registered trademark
of Simon & Schuster Inc.

POSEIDON PRESS colophon is a trademark
of Simon & Schuster Inc.

Designed by Levavi & Levavi
Manufactured in the United States of America

1   3   5   7   9   10   8   6   4   2

Library of Congress Cataloging in Publication Data

Michael, Judith.
A ruling passion : a novel / Judith Michael.
p.   cm.
I. Title.
PS3563.I254R85   1990
813'.54 —dc20   89-25484
                                             CIP

ISBN 0-671-64891-8

for
Rebecca, Ysabel, Daniel and Levi—
the new generation

Part One

Chapter
1

alerie heard the small cough in the plane's engine and turned from her view of the forest three thousand feet below to look at Carlton, beside her in the pilot's seat. He was scowling. "Did you hear that?"

"What?" He glanced at her, his scowl deepening. "Hear what?"

"The engine coughed."

"I didn't hear it. Could be some condensation in the gas line." He flicked switches on the instrument panel to turn on the fuel pumps, then withdrew again into his own thoughts.

"Are you sure? It didn't sound like it."

"Since when are you a pilot?" he said impatiently. "Everything's fine. The plane checked out when we flew up here and that was only four days ago."

"Well, if it's not the plane, what is it? What's wrong, Carl? You've barely said a word since we left this morning; you rushed us out to fly home, three days before we planned to, and you won't tell me why."

"I said you and the others could stay; you didn't have to come with me. I didn't even want you."

"I know," she said wryly. "Why do you think I insisted on coming? Are you running off to some mysterious woman I should know about?"

He muttered something she could not make out above the engine noise.

"Well, what's a little silence between friends?" she murmured and turned away from him. Behind her, their friends Alex and Betsy Tarrant were talking together, occasionally trying to draw out the third passenger, a young woman named Lilith Grace, who seemed lost in her own world, gazing out the window or sitting perfectly still, with her eyes closed. Left to herself, Valerie looked at her faint reflection in the cockpit window against the dull gray sky. Her heavy tawny hair and hazel eyes beneath dark brows were like a transparent picture through which she saw the hills and valleys of the Adirondack forest, its dense, dark-green pines mounded with snow. She looked at herself critically. Not bad for thirty-three. Too good to sit back and smile agreeably while her husband fooled around with— The engine coughed again. And then it stopped. One wing dipped toward the earth.

They were all thrown sideways against their seat belts. Betsy Tarrant screamed.

Carlton was hunched forward. "Hold on—" he said, but at that moment the other engine went out. The noise stopped as if a knife had cut across it. In the sudden awful silence, the plane began to lose altitude. "Christ . . . both of—"

"Carl!" shouted Alex Tarrant. Betsy was screeching.

". . . can't be fuel . . . had plenty . . ."

Valerie gripped her hands, watching him.

He leaned down, turning the fuel selectors to switch tanks, then straightened up and tried to restart the engines. When nothing happened, a look of incredulity flashed across his face. "What the fuck . . ."

"Help!" Betsy was screaming. "Do something!"

Carlton leaned forward again, his hands shaking, and trimmed the plane for a glide. The only sound was the rush of the wind past their wings as the plane swept over the forest, dropping five hundred feet a minute. Once in the glide, he tried again to start the engines. "Start, you mothers . . . come on, come on. . . . Fucking son of a bitch. . . . *Start.*" He tried again, his body straining forward as if he could push the engines to life. "Shit!" he exploded after a few minutes. "Must have flooded the bastards; how the hell they'll start in time now . . ."

Valerie saw panic in his eyes. Betsy was screaming; Alex cursed in a low shaking voice. Lilith Grace had not made a sound.

"Radio," Carlton muttered. "No, no time. Later—on the ground...

"Listen," he shouted, "we're going to land it. There's a lake up ahead..." His voice shook. "Put your heads down, arms over your heads.... *Everybody do it!*" He was turning off the fuel and electrical systems, except for the battery, which would give them full flaps for landing.

"There's a road!" Valerie cried, but it swept away beneath them. They dropped lower, the treetops racing past. Half a minute later the trees gave way and they were over the snow-covered expanse of a frozen lake. "This is it!" Carlton shouted. "Hold on!"

Valerie hunched her body as the plane plowed into the deep snow. She had braced for a crash, but instead there was an eerie silence. The light plane skimmed through the powdery snow with a steady hiss, making its own blizzard. Inside, no one made a sound; they were rigid with fear. It seemed they would go on that way forever, a terrifying skid into the eternity of that white blizzard, but then the plane reached the far bank. It plowed into the pine forest, shearing off the wing and fuselage beside Carlton, and at last came to a shuddering stop. The sound of the crash reverberated in the still forest and slowly faded away. Silence enveloped them.

"Alex?" Betsy whimpered. "Valerie? Carl? I hurt. My head hurts..."

"Wait," Alex said. "I can't do anything..." There was no sound from Lilith Grace.

Valerie flexed her arms and legs. Her neck ached and her muscles felt wrenched, but she could move. I'm all right, she thought, and felt a rush of wild exhilaration. *I'm alive; I made it; I'm all right.* "Hey, pilot," she said, turning to Carlton. "That was a terrific—" Her words ended in a scream. "Carl!"

He was slumped forward and lying half out of the plane, held by his seat belt over the jagged opening where the metal had been torn away. "Oh, God, no, no," she breathed. She tore open her seat belt and leaned over him. His head was covered with blood; blood ran over his closed eyes. "Carl!" she cried. "Carl!"

She smelled smoke.

"Fire!" Alex shouted. "Christ, I can't move— Val, help me!"

"Valerie!" He and Betsy were shouting at her. Their voices rang through the white silence. Smoke came from the engine on the plane's remaining wing.

Out. Get out. Get everyone out. She shivered in the icy air that filled the plane. "Just a minute, Alex." She fought her way down the narrow aisle. The plane was tilted to the left, where the wing had sheared off, and she struggled to get past the twisted seats and over Betsy's legs, slipping on sections of the Sunday newspaper and debris that had flown about the cabin. She glanced at Lilith Grace, who lay pale and deathlike in her seat, her eyes closed. *In a minute; not yet.* She reached past her to the coats and jackets they had piled there before taking off, and pulled on her full-length sable coat and the fur-lined leather gloves she found in the pocket. *I need help with Carl; I don't know if I can get him out alone. Alex. Have to get Alex out, and then . . .*

She squeezed through the narrow aisle to Alex, sitting behind Carl, and frantically tugged at the bent metal that pinned him in. It tore her gloves and she clenched her teeth as blood oozed through the rips, but she went on; Alex was helping her with his good hand, and in a minute he shouted, "Okay!" and pulled his legs free.

"Me!" cried Betsy, in the seat across the aisle from him. "What about me?"

"First Carl," Valerie said. "Alex, I need your help."

"If I can. . . . Christ, Val, I can't move my arm . . ."

"Get to the ground," she said. "I'll push him out to you."

"Right." He went to the door at the back. "Can't get to it; she's in the way," he said. "Get her out . . ."

"Damn it!" Valerie went to Alex, who was pushing Lilith's slumped form away so he could unlatch the door. The tilt of the plane brought the door almost to ground level and he stepped out while Valerie unfastened the girl's seat belt. "I'm going to push her out," she said. Alex held out his good arm as they eased Lilith through the door. She fell the last few inches, landing face down in the snow.

"She's okay," Alex said as he turned her over. He wiped snow from her face. "Go on, get Carl." He dragged Lilith a few feet with his one arm, then walked along the outside of the plane as Valerie moved up the aisle to Carlton. She released his seat belt, and when Alex stood on the other side of the gaping hole in the cockpit she threw her sable coat over the jagged edge and swung Carlton's legs over it. Slowly she rolled his body to Alex, but he could not hold him with one arm and they both fell. Valerie cried out and threw herself from the plane to help them. In the trampled snow, churned-up pine needles were slippery, and she staggered as she helped Alex to his feet.

"Can't carry him," Alex said. "Pull him . . ."

"Come on." Taking Carlton by the hands, they dragged him through hip-deep snow, stumbling beneath his dead weight, slipping and getting up, to a tree a good distance from the plane. Valerie held him while Alex packed down a wide circle in the snow, and they leaned him, half sitting, against the trunk.

"Help *me!*" screamed Betsy. On the far side of the plane, the engine had burst into flames. Flames engulfed the wing and the ground below where fuel had spilled. Valerie ran back, Alex just behind her, dodging the ripped trees that lay at crazy angles, and the small pieces of luggage that had been thrown from the storage bins in the wings and torn open by the impact; their clothes were flung everywhere. Slipping in the snow, her wool pants soaked and clinging to her legs, Valerie reached the plane and began to climb in.

She's gone. The empty space beside the plane registered in her mind and she looked down. Lilith Grace was gone. Valerie stared at the trampled snow. "Where did she go?" she asked Alex. "Did you see her?"

"Hurry *up!*" Betsy cried. "The wing's on fire!"

With one more bewildered look at the empty space in the snow, Valerie climbed all the way into the plane. Alex followed and they began to pull at a twisted seat back that pinned Betsy down.

"Hurry up!" Betsy shrilled. "We're going to blow up! Valerie, do something! I can't move my leg! And Alex can't carry me and you're not strong enough!"

"Then I'll just have to scare the hell out of you." Valerie leaned against one of the bent seats, taking ragged breaths. "I'm sick of you thinking only about you. I'll help you if you shut up and move your ass, otherwise you're on your own and you can burn with the plane for all I care. Come on, we're in a hurry."

Betsy was staring at her. "You're crazy. Help me!" She began to push the seat clamping her down.

Valerie and Alex bent over her and in a short time had her free. Valerie's hands were freezing, sticky with blood inside her leather gloves, and she could barely work her fingers. "You'll have to make it back on your own," she said to them, so tired she sounded indifferent. "I'll be right there."

She grabbed the suitcases and coats in the back of the plane and threw them out, then collected the sections of the Sunday newspaper and a first-aid kit from the cockpit, and carried them to the small group under the trees. They were silent, lying or sitting in the space of packed-down, bloody snow. Valerie knelt beside Carlton.

"He's alive," Alex said. "But unconscious."

"Alive," Valerie breathed. His head wound was still bleeding and she pressed her scarf against it, to stop the flow. At that minute the plane exploded.

A huge whoosh, like the leading edge of a tornado, burst to the skies and they felt a rush of hot wind. "My God!" said Alex, awed by the spectacle. The sound rocked the forest, echoing in the trees. Bits of burning debris fell around them, and frantically they stamped them out. "Your coat!" Betsy cried, grabbing a flaming ember from Valerie's sable as Valerie snatched another from Betsy's hair. The noise faded. Awed, they watched the burning pyre. "We just made it," Alex said. "Barely made it..."

In that moment, Valerie became terrified. *We're going to die here.*

Carlton groaned. Betsy was crying.

I can't think about dying; I don't have time. She took a disinfectant-soaked cloth from the first-aid kit and cleaned Carlton's face, and the skin around the ugly wound in his head. It was still bleeding and she wrapped it tightly with gauze. The bandage would not lie properly and she looked at Betsy. "I don't know anything about this. Do you?"

"No." Betsy was suddenly subdued; her voice shook. "We always hired nurses or..."

The story of my life, Valerie thought. When I needed something, I bought it. In a lifetime of luxury, she had never learned first aid. She kept wrapping the gauze, desperate to stop the bleeding, and soon the crimson spot that had soaked through the first layers was no longer visible. Still, Valerie kept winding. How thick should a bandage be? Thick enough to make me feel good, she thought, and a small wild laugh trembled on her lips. She pressed them together. "Alex, we've got to look for Lily Grace."

"I should have broken a leg," he said ruefully.

"Betsy, I brought paper for a fire. You get us some firewood."

"I won't. My leg won't move and my head hurts. I can't do anything."

"You can crawl. Pull dead twigs and branches off the trees; they're all around. We'll use whatever you get."

"We need more than paper," Alex said. "We need kindling. Whatever Betsy finds will be wet."

"Dead branches," Valerie said. "And if they're not enough..." She picked up some of the clothes scattered about. "We'll burn blouses and shirts. Keep the sweaters and socks and jackets; we can wear layers to keep warm."

"We won't be here that long!" Betsy cried. "Someone will come!"

Valerie's terror returned, making her breathless. "We have to look . . ." She struggled through her terror to form words. ". . . for Lily . . ."

Alex led the way into the forest. "Look for footprints," he said. "We won't be here long, you know. Anyone flying overhead will see the plane burning."

"I hope so. How many people fly over the Adirondacks on a Monday in January?"

"God knows. Did Carl file a flight plan?"

"I don't know. He usually doesn't when we fly back during the day. It's less than three hours to Middleburg . . ." Her voice trailed away. *It used to be less than three hours; now it's forever.*

"Val?" Alex was looking worriedly at her.

"I'm sorry."

They walked in the gray light that filtered through the trees. "Lily!" Alex called. "Lily! Lily!"

After half an hour, exhausted, they turned back, guiding themselves by the burning plane and the small fire burning now beneath the tree. And when they reached the group sitting around it, Lily Grace was there, beside Carlton, her hand on his forehead. "I'm sorry you had so much trouble because of me," she said.

Her voice was high and cool, like a pure stream, and her face was luminous. There was something compelling about her, and the others seemed mesmerized. Betsy was sitting so close she was almost leaning against her. Her eyes, Valerie thought: ecstatic, but somehow sad. My God, she thought immediately, what a ridiculous idea; the cold must be getting to me. No one looks like that. But Lily Grace did, and Valerie knew she had not been fanciful. Pale, with white-blond hair and dark-blue eyes, and young—she could have been fourteen or twenty-four—she sat in that dull winter landscape and seemed untouched by it. As she was untouched by the crash. There was not a mark on Lily Grace.

Valerie remembered that she had been introduced as a minister when she arrived at their vacation house only two days before. "My friend, Reverend Lilith Grace," Sybille had said, introducing her. "She has a television ministry." They had all been amused. Well, who knows? Valerie thought. Maybe she knows something I don't know.

"Val!" Carlton was trying to lift his head. "Val!"

"Here," Valerie said. She sat beside Carlton and kissed his cold lips. "I'm here, Carl." Lily seemed to melt away.

"Listen." He opened his eyes, trying to focus them on her. "Couldn't do it." His voice was urgent, but the words were mumbled and Valerie leaned over him. "Sorry, Val. Mean it: sorry! Never meant to hurt you. Tried to keep it. Now you'll know I— Shit, lost control, lost . . . *lost it!*"

"Carl, don't, don't blame yourself," she said. "You did your best, you were wonderful. You brought us down and we're alive. And you shouldn't talk; you should rest until we can get you out of here."

He went on as if she had not spoken. "Never meant to get you into this. Said I'd . . . take care of you. Remember? Christ . . . thought I'd fix it . . . get started again. Too late. Sorry, Val, sorry, sorry . . ."

His voice faded, his eyes closed and he began to roll his head slowly from side to side. "Don't know how the hell . . . Acted like water in the tanks. . . . But—both tanks? Never had any before." A long groan tore from him. "Didn't check. Too much hurry to take off. Stupid fucking mechanic should've reminded me. Can't trust . . ." Suddenly his face tightened in a deep frown. His eyes flew open and he raised his head, looking about wildly. "Not my fault! No accident! Listen! Couldn't be . . . both tanks! Flew up here . . . fine! Right, Val? Right? Water in both tanks! Fuck it, should have thought she might . . ."

His head fell back against the tree. "Should have thought of that . . . sorry." His eyes closed again. His breathing was harsh and slow.

Valerie bent over him and touched his face. "He's so cold," she said. She turned to the others. "Do you know what he was talking about?"

They shook their heads. "I couldn't understand him," Alex said. A spasm of pain crossed his face. "Any painkillers in your handy little kit?"

"Oh, yes, of course. And we'll make you a sling." She opened the first-aid kit and they helped each other, cleaning cuts and scratches, fashioning a sling for Alex's arm, winding Ace bandages around Betsy's hugely swollen leg. Valerie watched her own busy hands, clumsy but getting more skilled with each turn of the bandage, and wondered how she could be doing this. She had no idea. Since the plane crashed, she had not thought about any of it; she moved and planned one step at a time, never asking how she knew what to do next, or how she was able to do it. *A new Valerie. What a pity if I die before I get to know her.*

She sat beside Carlton, watching his restless sleep, while Alex and Lily Grace kept the fire going, sending sparks shooting to the treetops each time they added more wood. They all helped each other to put on extra clothes. They waited for a plane to fly overhead. The hours passed.

By afternoon, with the sun lower in the sky, the air grew colder.

Carlton's breathing was raspy, and so slow Valerie found herself holding her own breath, waiting for him to take another one. She looked at the others, sitting in a kind of stupor, except for Lily Grace, who was deep in some sort of meditation. "I'm going for help," Valerie said. She heard herself say it without surprise, though she had not planned it. "Carl will die if we don't get him to a hospital. There's a road not too far from here; I saw it when we were coming down; it shouldn't take me long to find someone."

Betsy Tarrant stared at her. "You'll get lost! Or freeze to death!"

Valerie looked at Alex. "Can you think of anything else?"

"It's only three-thirty; someone could still fly over. And what about search planes? They must be looking for us; we were due in Middleburg a long time ago."

"If Carl didn't file a flight plan they won't know where to look. They would have if the ELT was working, but they haven't come, so—"

"ELT?" Lily asked, looking up.

"Emergency Locator Transmitter. It's in the plane somewhere—was in the plane—the tail, I think. It sends out some kind of signal that search planes can follow. If it was working, we would have been found."

Valerie touched Carlton's face. His skin was pasty in the firelight. "I don't think anybody's coming to find us and I'm not going to sit here and watch Carl die." She picked through the pile of clothes they had gathered and found an extra pair of ski mittens and fur-lined waterproof boots. She put on three pairs of socks and then the boots. She found her sable hat and put it on, and tied a cashmere scarf around her face, leaving only her eyes exposed. "The newest style," she said lightly. "Today here, tomorrow in *Vogue*." She paused to steady her voice. She didn't want to leave. The small group around the leaping fire seemed like home and security. Beyond them, the forest was dark and forbidding. She took a long breath. "I'll be back with help as soon as I can. Stay together and wait for me."

As she turned, Lily Grace said quietly, "God go with you."

"Thank you," Valerie said, thinking she would rather have the Forest Service.

"Good luck!" Alex called.

"Don't get lost!" Betsy shouted. "Don't freeze! Hurry back!" Valerie shook her head in wonder. Betsy never changed. In a way it was comforting to know there was something predictable in that forest.

Within a few minutes, the fire and the smoldering hulk of the plane were indistinct glows behind her as she walked across the frozen lake, following the path made by the plane. Small clouds scudded across the fading sky; a half moon was rising above nearby hills. I'll have some light, Valerie thought.

She walked across the lake, swinging her arms to keep warm in the icy wind that whistled across the flat expanse, and images darted through her mind, as vivid as paintings against the dark forest. Summer camp when she was little, learning to swim and play tennis and ride; Western dude ranches when she was in her teens, learning to shoot, riding in rodeos and competitions, sneaking out to meet boys after lights out. The counselors at camp had taught her how to use the sun, moon and stars for direction. I should have paid less attention to boys, she thought, and more to the moon and stars.

On the other side of the lake she was in the forest again, out of the wind. But hidden beneath the deep snow were roots and branches and small bushes that wrapped themselves around her like tentacles and held her fast. Sometimes she found a crusted place in the snow and walked on top of it, taking a few long strides, but then the crust broke and she sank in, up to her knees or waist, trying to tread through the snow as if she were swimming.

She was freezing, and exhausted, and her legs were so heavy she could barely lift them to take another step. Then, suddenly, she was too warm, and she stopped walking and began to take off her coat. *No, what am I doing? My God, I've gone crazy; I'd freeze to death.* She pulled the coat tightly around her and went on. She wondered what Betsy would say if she'd frozen; would she be pleased because she'd been proven right or furious because Valerie had let her down by dying? She started to laugh, but the sound in the silent forest had a wild ring to it and she cut it off. *Walk. Don't think. Walk north; that's where the road was. Walk. Walk.*

She walked. She tripped and fell into banks of snow, and pushed herself out of them, groaning with the weight of her wet fur coat. And then she walked on, too tired to fight off the unbidden images that drifted in and out of her mind: the warm depths of her French-provincial bed in their warm sprawling mansion in Middleburg; the warm glossy coats of the horses she raised; the warm yielding cushions of the chintz sofa in her dressing room; the warm softness of her Finnish rug beneath her bare feet as she dressed in front of her warm fireplace; the warm ballrooms where she danced, whirling past her friends in silk and lace.

I should be on the road by now. It couldn't be this far. Unless I missed it.

She was famished; then, oddly, not hungry at all; then hungry again. She ate snow by the handful and it made her think of meringue on a baked alaska; she heard a bird and thought about roast pheasant; a scattering of pinecones reminded her of truffles, shiitake mushrooms, mounds of caviar, foie gras on toast...*Stop it. Just walk. One foot, then the other. Walk.*

Daylight was gone; the forest was dark. She walked with her hands held in front of her, navigating from tree to tree. Her feet were numb, her hands were numb, ice coated the inside of her cashmere scarf where her breath had frozen. She leaned against a tree. *I have to rest; just for a minute; then I'll go on.* She slid down the trunk, asleep. When she fell over in the snow, she woke with a jerk. *No! Get up! Stand up!*

But it was so pleasant to stay there, curled up in the warm embrace of the snow. *Just for a few minutes. I need it, I need to rest; then I'll find the road*...She started up wildly. "The road!" Her voice was high and frail in the silent forest. "I've got to find the road...can't go to sleep. I'll die if I go to sleep. Carl will die. I can't sleep."

She forced herself to stand up, groaning aloud. Her eyes were still closed. "I can't do it," she said aloud. "I can't go any farther. I'll never find the road. It's too far. I'm so tired. I can't do it."

God go with you.
Good luck.
Please come back.
Don't get lost!
Too late. Sorry, Val, sorry...

She heard their voices rising about her as clearly as if they stood beside her in the dark forest. And suddenly a swift rush of energy swept through her as it had in the plane when she knew she was alive. *They all need me. They're all depending on me.* No one had ever depended on her: it was a new and powerful feeling. *They need me.* The energy seeped away, but the knowledge was there: they were depending on her; they were waiting for her. They had no one else. And she walked.

The moon rose higher in the sky; soon it shone into the forest, turning the snow silver, as if it were lit from within. Valerie walked, her breath coming in harsh gasps, her muscles heavy and aching, her eyes burning as she strained to see in the shimmering glow that made the black pine trees seem to dance and shrink and swell until sometimes she was not sure whether she was going forward or back. The walking was harder now, and it took her a while to realize she was going uphill. *The road was near a hill.* The image flashed in her mind:

the road had been cut between two small hills. *I'm almost there.* She raised one foot and put it down, then pulled up the other foot and put it down, treading through the snow, fighting to move forward up the rise, against the backward pull of her weight.

She thought of a night she and Carlton had gone square dancing with friends. Four couples held hands in a circle, pulling each other as they danced to the left and the right. She heard the country violin that rose to the rafters, sending their small circle spinning faster and faster, this way and that. She sang the tune the violin had played, her voice threadlike in the cold air, and she felt her feet grow light, skipping and tapping against the wooden floor as her skirt flew out. It was warm; the lights shone on the brightly dressed couples, the men in jeans and plaid shirts, the women in gingham and ruffles. "What a wonderful dance!" Valerie cried, her hands outstretched to hold the hands of her friends.

Her coat hung open; her body cringed against the cold. "Where am I? Where am I? Dear God, what's happening to me?" She began to cry. "Coat," she told herself. "Close my coat." She pulled it around her. "Now walk. Just walk."

She took a step, then another, and suddenly there was nothing beneath her. Her foot came down into space, her body followed it, and then she was rolling, tumbling, sliding down the other side of the rise. Her face was in the snow, her eyes and mouth were full of it, her coat had flown open and branches clawed at her, snatching the cashmere scarf from her face. But at the bottom of the rise was the road.

She landed on its hard, snowpacked surface and huddled there, a small, wet mound beneath a soaked, bedraggled sable coat. Very slowly she stood up, brushing snow from her face and body. *The road. The road. The road.* She swayed in the center of it. She'd done it; she was there.

But the road was empty and she had to keep walking, not caring this time which direction she went. It was easier now, with no deep snow, but her feet still felt too heavy to lift and she lurched with each step. She walked until the sky was turning gray, and the moon disappeared. And that was when a young man named Harvey Gaines, who had driven all night to reach the town where he would begin a new job with the Forest Service, found her staggering along the road, her lips so stiff she could not speak.

"Don't talk," he said, and bundled her into his jeep, hurtling down the road to a farmhouse where lights were burning. The couple who came to the door took one look at Valerie and brought her to the fire. "Don't talk," they said. "Thaw yourself out."

"Four others," Valerie said; it was barely a whisper. "A lake, south of the road where you found me. We crashed. There's a fire..."

"Got it," Harvey Gaines said briskly and went to the telephone while Valerie sat wrapped in blankets, drinking hot chocolate and letting the heat seep into her until she began, slowly, to feel warm. But she still felt nothing in her feet, and when the police arranged for a helicopter to fly her to the hospital in Glens Falls she could not walk.

Later that morning the Tarrants and Lily Grace were brought out by helicopter and flown to the hospital where Valerie was waiting for them.

And the body of Carlton was there, too. He had died three hours after she set off through the forest.

The State Police came. Valerie saw them in the hospital sunroom, where she sat on a wicker loveseat beside a wall of windows, soaking up the sunlight. Her feet, painful and tingling now, were resting on a hassock beneath a light blanket. Her hands were bandaged, the soreness in her muscles was like a huge throbbing ache on top of the bruises from the crash, and she could barely move. She told the police the story of their flight, from the time Carlton rushed them out of their vacation house for the trip to Virginia to the time she left them to get help. "He said it wasn't an accident," she said. "We were only there four days and the plane was fine on the way up. He said—"

"Why was he in such a hurry to leave?" they asked.

"I don't know. Business, I suppose. He was an investment counselor. He said—it was very strange—he said it was done on purpose. Both fuel tanks having water, he meant; he said it never happened before. And then he said something about a woman."

"What?"

"He said, 'I should have thought she might.'"

"Might what?"

"I don't know."

"Probably meant his plane. People call airplanes 'she.' Like boats."

"I suppose so," Valerie said slowly.

Her mother arrived the next morning. They sat together, holding hands. "I never imagined I could lose you," Rosemary Ashbrook said. "Your poor feet...what will happen to them?"

"We don't know yet." Valerie felt the flash of fear that came every time she thought about frostbite. She was trying to believe that Carlton was gone, and then she had to face the truth of what might happen to her feet. I won't be an invalid, she thought. I'd rather die.

"Poor Carl," Rosemary said. "I was so fond of him. And I relied on him; what will we do now? I don't know anything about my money; he did it all."

"Dan will do it for a while, until we find someone else. Carl took care of mine too, you know. I feel so stupid; I don't know a thing."

"Well, I'll let you take care of it. I just can't think about money; I never could. Poor Valerie, what a terrible time for you. And the police were here! What did they want to know?"

"A lot that I couldn't answer." Valerie closed her eyes briefly, trying to understand what it meant that Carl was gone. She felt helpless. So much unfinished, so much dangling... "I really didn't know much about Carl. But why should I? Three years married and about to be divorced."

"Valerie!"

"Well, we were trying to work things out—that's why we came up here. Carl thought a few days away from everything would make us romantic and forgetful. I don't think he really thought so, though; he was so worried about something at home he couldn't have put anything together, much less a marriage. And we'd never had the kind of passion you'd need to bring love back. And he had someone else, you know."

"He couldn't have! He adored you!"

"No, he didn't. I'm not sure what Carl felt about me. Or about anything. We were friends—we were always friends more than lovers—but lately we were hardly talking. He was so involved in something, and of course someone else..."

The next morning, very early, Lily Grace came to Valerie's room. "If you need comfort, I'd like to help you."

Valerie gave a small smile. "You can pray I don't lose my feet or toes from frostbite; I could use some intervention there. But I want to think about Carl by myself. I have a lot of sorting out to do. I hope you understand that."

"Of course." Lily looked at her thoughtfully. "I've never been married. But I think the death of a spouse would be like losing a part of yourself, even if your marriage was filled with doubts and silence."

Valerie returned her look. "How old are you, Lily?"

"Twenty-one. Twenty-two next week."

"And you saw that Carl and I had doubts and silence."

"It seemed clear to me." She smiled with a radiance that embraced Valerie. "I understand a great deal; it is a divine gift. You have a gift, too. I saw it in the forest: the way you knew what had to be done, and did it, at great risk to yourself. You have a strong sense of purpose and direction and you gave us our lives. I don't know how to thank you, but I'll pray for you. I'll pray that you do your sorting out and give yourself as much life as you gave us, and also that you don't have serious frostbite."

She kissed Valerie on both cheeks and left the room. And that was the last anyone saw of her. Sometime during the night she walked out of the hospital, alone. No one knew where she went. I'd like to see her again, Valerie thought, even though she knew Lily had been wrong about one thing: never in her life had Valerie Sterling had a strong sense of purpose or direction; for thirty-three years she had simply drifted wherever pleasure took her.

But I helped everyone after the crash; I got them out of the forest. That was a new Valerie. But I don't know what I should do next. Or what I want to do.

The next morning Valerie and the others were flown to Lenox Hill Hospital in New York. Two days later, Valerie's doctor allowed a young reporter, who had followed her from Glens Falls, to interview her. He brought a photographer. "How did you feel?" the reporter asked. "Did you worry about wild animals? How did you know which direction to go? Were you ever lost? Have you had survival training? Did you pray a lot? What did you think about?"

"Putting one foot in front of the other," said Valerie.

"She thought about saving the people she'd left behind," her mother said firmly. "That was what kept her going: knowing they'd die without her. She was freezing and exhausted and she'd just about collapsed when that young man found her, but she wouldn't let herself give up. She's a genuine heroine."

Those words, on the front page of the Glens Falls *Times* with Valerie's picture, were seen by editors in New York and Long Island, who sent their own reporters and photographers. This time Valerie gave her own answers. She thought the reporters foolish for romanticizing that awful night, but they were so serious she patiently repeated her story, answering all their questions except those about Carlton.

Television reporters and cameramen arrived, crowding into the hospital sunroom. All three networks, and CNN and the Enderby Broadcasting Network, because Valerie not only provided the kind of human-interest story they always looked for, she also was sensational on television. Her beauty was captivating, even with the scratches and bruises that were just beginning to heal; her voice was low, warm and polished, and her vivid face showed every emotion as she described again and again the whole experience, from the crash landing on the lake to her rescue by Harvey Gaines.

And with the Enderby Broadcasting Network came Sybille Enderby. "You're such a celebrity!" she said to Valerie, holding her hand as she bent down to kiss her cheek. "We never thought you'd be a star on my television network, did we?" She brought a chair close to Valerie. Her black hair was intricately braided into a chignon, and her pale-blue eyes looked like mother-of-pearl against her dark olive complexion. She wore cashmere trimmed with fur. "Tell me about Carl."

Valerie shook her head. "I can't talk about him."

"I just can't believe it. I was with him, with both of you, just a few days ago at Lake Placid. I was so glad Lily wanted to stay on when I had to get home; I thought you'd enjoy each other. Carl thought she was so unusual. And now he's gone. Could he talk after you crashed? What did he say?"

Valerie sighed. Sybille never could let go of anything. As far back as college, she never swerved from a goal she had set herself. "I won't talk about Carl," she said firmly. "Maybe someday, but not now."

"Well . . . but you will call me, won't you, if you want to talk? After all, I knew Carl. Not well, but he was a friend."

"I know. Have you talked to Lily Grace? She disappeared from the hospital in Glens Falls; is she all right?"

"She's fine. She's back home and singing your praises. You were a bigger hit with her than I ever was, and I was the one who gave her a job."

Valerie's eyebrows rose. "I wasn't trying to be a hit. I was trying to survive."

After that visit, Sybille telephoned often from her home in Washington, urging confidences that Valerie was not ready to give. Her other friends were more interested in the drama of the crash and her struggle through the forest. They visited all during Valerie's second week in the hospital, bringing news of the social life in New York and Washington and Virginia, telling her the parties weren't the same without her.

And later, when Valerie's brief stardom had faded and her days were quieter, flowers and a note arrived from Nicholas Fielding. It had been more than twelve years since they were together at college, and they had seen each other only once since then, but, reading his brief note in his sprawling handwriting, she remembered with perfect clarity the clasp of their bodies in the creaky bed in his apartment in Palo Alto, and the way he had touched her cheek, just once, when she told him she didn't want to see him again.

Last of all, Daniel Lithigate, Valerie's lawyer, arrived. She was in the sunroom, with Rosemary. "Terrible thing," Lithigate said, kissing Valerie with nervous little pecks. "Knew him all my life; I can't imagine not seeing him on the polo field and in the club, drinking bourbon and telling the rest of us how we should have played the game. I remember when we were kids he'd do the same thing on the softball field. Did I ever tell you about the time—we were, oh, maybe eleven or twelve—I got so mad at him I took my bat and—"

"Dan." Valerie looked up at him. "You're stalling. Sit down so I can look at you. I don't need stories about Carl; I need to know how much money I have. Not a lot of details, just the general picture."

"Right." He sat in a wicker armchair. "You don't know too much about Carl's affairs."

"I don't know anything; you know that. He was the executor of my father's estate and he's handled our portfolios, Mother's and mine, ever since. Why else would I ask you?"

"Right." Lithigate paused. "Valerie—" He ran a thumb along his nose, pushing up his gold-rimmed glasses; they promptly slid down again. "There's a problem. Something I'd never have imagined of Carl. The most incredibly imprudent behavior..."

"What does that mean?" Valerie remembered Carlton's anxiety; the way they had rushed back; his distraction the past few weeks. "What is it?"

He wiped his forehead and his nose. "He lost badly, you see, in the stock market. Very badly, I'm afraid."

"How badly? Dan, *how badly?*"

"About fifteen million dollars. But—"

"Fifteen million dollars?"

Lithigate cleared his throat. "Right. In the market. But that isn't... there's more, you see. We assume he tried to recoup his losses. We don't have any idea how, and of course we can't ask—"

"Dan."

"Right. He borrowed, you see, on everything: your houses, your apartment in New York, your horses and paintings and antiques—he borrowed on all of it and then he converted your bonds to cash. That gave him approximately another thirteen million dollars."

Valerie tried to focus on his earnest brown eyes behind the gold-rimmed glasses. "Everything we had." Her voice was a whisper. "And where is it?"

"Well, you see, that's it. We don't know." Once again his glasses slid down his perspiring nose, and he tore them off, looking at her myopically. "There's no trace of it, Valerie. There's no trace of any of it. Everything is gone."

<h1 style="text-align:center">*Chapter*
2</h1>

alerie Ashbrook and Sybille Morgen were in their third year of college when they met Nicholas Fielding. Valerie met him first, standing in line at a bookstore on the Stanford University campus shortly after Christmas. He was a graduate student, older, at twenty-five, than most of her friends, tall, thin, raw-looking, wearing a rumpled jacket and mismatched socks, his light-brown hair shaggy from the latest attempt by one of his roommates to cut it. But his strong, angular features and deep voice made him seem more forceful than the other men she knew. There was a tension and spring to his step that made him seem eager to meet whatever lay ahead, as if he found the whole world wonderfully interesting and was open to whatever came into his life. In that crowded bookstore Valerie came into his life, and as soon as they had bought their books they strolled across the campus to sit on the grass in the hazy California sun, and talk.

"I don't know what I want to do," Valerie replied impatiently when he asked the question for the third time. "Do I get a black mark if I don't decide right away?"

He smiled. "I just can't imagine not knowing where I'm going or how I'm going to get there."

"Oh, I'll know one of these days," she said. "I'll have a revelation, or fall in love, or someone will make me an offer I can't refuse, and then I'll know just where I'm going. But why should I be in a hurry when I'm having so much fun along the way?"

Nick smiled again, but his eyes were thoughtful as he gazed at her. She was so lovely he didn't want to look anywhere else. Her tawny hair, heavy and wild, glinted copper in the sunlight, looking as if it had never known a comb. Her almond-shaped eyes beneath dark level brows were auburn or hazel—he would have to look more closely to be sure—and her mouth was wide and warm, the corners faintly turning down when she was not speaking: a beautiful mouth, but stubborn. Dressed in jeans and a white turtleneck sweater, she was almost as tall as he, and she walked lightly, like a dancer. She had a look of wealth and privilege in the confident way she held her head, the ease of her walk, as if she knew traffic would stop for her, and the serene assuredness of someone who is aware that people notice her and find much to admire and little to criticize. She gestured as she talked, and shifted her position on the grass; everything about her was vivid and alive, filled with energy and the promise of excitement, and Nick wanted to sit with her this way, with the sun shining and the world relaxed, forever.

"I suppose I could get a new one if there's a problem," she said mischievously.

He started. "A new what?"

"Whatever you've decided I need after that long inspection."

Quickly he looked down, then back at her. "I'm sorry. I was thinking how beautiful you are; you don't need a new anything. I suppose you get tired of hearing that."

"Oh, now and then it's still nice to hear." She smiled with faint mockery and began to stand up. "But there is something I need. I'm starving and it's almost lunchtime. There's a marvelous Italian place not far from here. Shall we go?"

He hesitated. "I don't eat lunch. But I'll have a cup of coffee with you."

"Everyone eats lunch. Didn't your mother bring you up to eat three good meals a day?"

"I don't eat out," he said evenly. "But I'd like to have a cup of coffee with you."

"Oh. Well, but I'm paying," Valerie said casually. "I invited you, after all."

He shook his head. "I wouldn't let you do that."

"Why not?" She looked at him, smiling, her eyes challenging. "Too untraditional? Too hard on your manhood?"

Startled, he hesitated again, then grinned at her. "You've got it. I don't think I'd survive the shock of seeing a woman pick up the check. And I don't think my father would survive if I told him I'd done it."

Her eyes were bright. "And your mother?"

"She'd probably wish she'd been born in your generation, so she could have been more independent."

Valerie laughed. "I'd like to meet your mother. I'd like to buy her lunch. Come on; next time we'll figure out something else, but today I'm treating."

Nick put his hand on her arm to stop her as she turned away, and looked into her eyes. Hazel, he decided, with flecks of auburn; as changeable as a summer sky. They looked at each other for a long moment; then he forced himself to move away. "I'm hungry, too," he said, and they went to lunch.

The next time he made lunch in his apartment, on the second floor of a private home a few blocks from the campus. While Nick worked in the kitchen, Valerie roamed through the rooms, furnished with a few pieces of furniture, a scattering of cotton rugs, posters taped to the walls, and dozens of floor pillows. "I can't believe it's so neat. Three men on their own and not even a sock on the floor. It's unreal."

"You're right, it is. We cleaned this morning."

"What did you bribe them with?"

He chuckled. "They did it on their own. They were so amazed that I finally had a girl, they wanted to make sure nothing went wrong."

From the doorway, she watched him heat olive oil in a frying pan with onions and garlic, stir in mushrooms and tomatoes and spices, and then pour it over the pasta. His movements were practiced and deliberate; his hand went directly to what he needed; he moved neatly from refrigerator to counter to stove top. He seemed to keep a watchful eye on everything he did, Valerie thought. He was the most careful man she had ever met.

They sat at a scarred pine table overlooking the backyard and Nick poured Chianti into two jelly glasses. "Welcome," he said, raising his and touching it to Valerie's. "I'm glad you're here."

She sipped the wine. It was harsh and she put down her glass, then quickly picked it up again, hoping he hadn't noticed. If that was all he could afford, she'd drink it. But next time she'd bring the wine.

"Why were your roommates surprised?" she asked as they ate. "No man who cooks like this would be left alone very long; you must know dozens of girls."

He smiled. "A few. I'm better with computers than people. And I don't advertise my cooking."

"It's a good thing; otherwise I'd have to stand in line, and I don't stand in line for anything. Is that what you're studying? Computers?"

"Computer design and programs."

"Computers," she echoed. "Well, we'll find lots of other things to talk about. I've seen them, but I don't understand them."

"You will someday."

"Don't hold your breath. I'm really not much interested in those kinds of things."

"Those kinds of things are going to change your life. In ten years, by 1984, maybe earlier, you're going to find them everywhere; there isn't any part of your life they won't touch."

"Sex," she said promptly. "Will that be safe?"

He smiled. "As far as I can tell. But it's probably the only thing, and if you don't understand how computers work or how they're used—"

"Goodness, you're so serious." She shrugged. "I fly in airplanes and drive my car and live in an air-conditioned house, and I can't explain how any of those things work. Come to think of it, I do know how electricity works and I still don't understand it. And then I see a computer screen with all those words coming and going, from nowhere to nowhere, and it's just too much. I'd rather call it magic."

"Terrible idea," said Nick. "I can predict what a computer will do; I can manipulate it and control it. I couldn't do that with magic."

"Of course not; if you could, it wouldn't be magic. What do you do when something wonderful and magical happens in your life? You refuse to believe in it? Or trust it?"

"I don't even know what that means. It sounds like mythology. I wouldn't bet on it."

"What do you bet on? Science?"

"Every time."

Valerie sighed. "It doesn't sound like a lot of fun."

"Fun." He repeated it thoughtfully. Their eyes met.

"You'll figure it out," she said. "I'll help you."

He grinned at her. "Every engineering student dreams of a moment like this."

"I can arrange an endless supply of them," she said. "I do it with magic. How about starting tomorrow? I'm going riding at a friend's ranch in Los Verdes. Would you like to come?"

"I'm not much of a rider; I'd slow you down."

"You wouldn't let yourself. You like to lead."

His eyebrows rose. "So do you."

"Then we'll ride together; the best way."

He chuckled and refilled their wine glasses. She had barely tasted hers. "Where did you learn to ride?"

"On our farm. My mother wanted horses for atmosphere. She thinks they belong on a farm the way chintz furniture belongs in the farmhouse and velvet drapes in our apartment. But she never learned to ride, so she got the atmosphere and I got the horses."

Nick was looking at her curiously. "I wouldn't have guessed you were from a farm."

She laughed. "I'm from New York. That's where the velvet drapes are. The farm is a weekend place. It's wonderful. Have you been to the Eastern Shore?"

"No."

She studied him. "Or to any part of Maryland?"

"No. Or the East Coast. Or the Midwest. Or the South. I like the West and I wanted to get to know it, really know it, so I've spent my summers hitching all through it, doing odd jobs and getting to know people."

Valerie thought again of the way he cooked: deliberate and controlled. "Not Europe either?" she asked.

"No. That's for when I start earning money. Tell me about your farm. How big is it?"

"About twelve hundred acres, I think; I can't keep track of the parcels my father buys and sells. We have a manager who runs it, and we grow corn and soybeans, and we have a huge vegetable garden; I think we feed half the town of Oxford from it. There are lovely woods with trails that my father had cut years ago so they look natural and quite wild sometimes, and of course a pool, and my mother made a croquet green a few years ago. When she and her friends play they look like a watercolor in a nineteenth-century novel. And the house sits on a rise overlooking Chesapeake Bay, so if we don't sail in one of the regattas we can watch them from the terrace. It's the perfect antidote to New

York. And Paris and Rome, for that matter; sometimes we come back to the farm from Europe, to unwind before we go to New York. One of these days you'll come for a visit. You'll love it." She watched him frown. "Is something wrong?"

"No. It's just that I'm having culture shock."

There was a brief pause. "No, you're not," she said evenly. "You've been around; you know there's a lot of money in the world, and you know how people spend it. You're just surprised because I have more than you thought I had, and now you have to re-evaluate me." She stood and began to clear the table. "Take your time."

He watched her stack dishes in the sink. "When did you last do the dishes?"

"Ten years ago," she said calmly. "At camp. But I'm always willing to adapt to a strange culture."

He burst into laughter. Everything is fine, he thought. We have so much to learn from each other and we'll get past our differences and we'll get along. We'll be together. He was surprised at how good that made him feel. He got up to make the coffee. "When did you say we're going riding?" he asked.

Valerie Ashbrook, of Park Avenue and Oxford, Maryland, was born to silk and sable, private schools, personal maids, and leisurely visits to friends in South American mansions, French châteaux, Spanish castles, Italian villas and the last few privately owned palaces in England. She did everything early, winning tennis matches, ski races and spelling bees from the time she was eight, putting her horses through intricate paces when she was ten, getting the lead in school plays as a freshman in high school. She was a superb dancer and converted one of the barns on Ashbrook Farm to a ballroom; if a week went by without an invitation to a ball or a square dance she gave her own. She could have excelled in mathematics, but she was too lazy; science bored her because every experiment had to be repeated. She collected art and tried her hand at painting, but soon discovered she had only enough talent to make it a hobby. She loved to read but had no library because she gave her books to others who would enjoy them. She never learned to cook, thinking it a waste of time when she could hire others who did it so well. She hated inexpensive wines. There was always a young man wanting to make love to her.

When she was in high school her mother insisted she balance her parties and good times with volunteer work for organizations in New York and Maryland. So, with her friends who also had been volunteered by their mothers, she spent a few hours each week working on balls, auctions and other fund-raisers for everything from the New York Public Library to cancer research. It all came under the name of Good Works, but it also was one long party, and from that came something even better: when she was a high-school senior, she was asked to appear for two minutes on an early-evening newscast on Maryland television to talk about a program to raise funds for a new maritime museum. She was young and lovely and poised beyond her years, and everyone thought she was sensational. Later, when she entered Stanford, society families in San Francisco and Palo Alto, who knew her parents, called her a few times to speak for them when a producer of an early-evening or noon news program offered a minute or two to publicize a good cause.

"I don't do it very often," Valerie told Nick as they arrived at the Palo Alto television station a week after their lunch in his apartment. They had not gone riding after all; at the last minute he had been called in to his part-time job in the engineering department, to fill in for someone else. "I'd love to do more because it's such a blast, but there's not a lot of free time for good causes on television. Anyway, I don't have time; I'm too busy with school."

"You might manage to find time if they asked you more often," he said.

She laughed. "You're right; I really love doing it, but I'm not going to camp on their doorstep and beg for more. I'm hardly a professional and I'm certainly not going to make it my life's work."

"Why not?" Nick asked.

She looked at him. "I don't know. I haven't thought about it. I haven't thought about any kind of life's work; I told you that. Anyway, nobody's telling me I'm the ideal television personality—good Lord, do you think that would be a compliment or a put-down? I just do favors for friends, or friends of my parents, and what happens, happens. It's all fun and it can't do any harm."

They walked into the studio and she led him to a folding chair at the side of the large, bare room. "You can sit here and watch. We're just taping a short pitch; it won't take long."

He watched her greet the cameraman and a young woman who stood nearby, wearing headphones and carrying a clipboard. Valerie stepped up to a shabbily carpeted platform, where she sat in an armchair turned at an angle to hide a long tear in the fabric. Beside her was a table with a vase of drooping flowers.

"Are there any fresh flowers?" she asked. She ran the cord from a tiny black microphone under her sweater, then clipped the microphone to her collar. "These ought to be tossed."

"We'll get something else," said the woman with the headphones, and a moment later replaced the flowers with a contorted, vaguely modern bronze sculpture with one long protuberance.

"Two dogs in a moment of passion?" Valerie guessed. "Or a couple of horses fighting over a feedbag. Or one horse and a dog, mismated."

The cameraman was laughing. "A student made it. Dropped it off this morning so you could show it when you talk about the exhibit at the art center. I like it; it's got a certain something."

"It's got a lot of bronze," Valerie said. "But it's better than dying flowers. I'm ready if everyone else is."

The spotlights came on, flooding the set in a white wash that bleached and flattened everything beneath it. Nick understood why Valerie had worn makeup, especially on her eyes and cheeks, with bright-red lipstick, and a vivid dress of coral silk: under those lights, what was exaggerated seemed natural. As a cameraman focused the single camera on her, she read through the script twice from the Tele-PrompTer, once for practice, another time for an engineer in the control room to check the voice level of her microphone. Then the woman with the headphones gave a signal and the taping began.

This time, as Valerie read the script, Nick alternately watched her in front of him, and on a television set to his right, fascinated by the effect of the lights and the camera: on the screen, she looked heavier; a slight difference between her right and left eyelids became apparent; shadows from the downlighting made her shoulders seem rounded. It was all new to Nick, and he reached for the pad of paper in his jacket pocket and scribbled some notes to be stored with dozens of others he had written at various times about things that interested him. Someday he'd have time to go through them and think about all the intriguing tidbits of information he'd collected.

The lights went down, Valerie unclipped the microphone and pulled the cord down beneath her sweater. She came to Nick. "What did you think?"

"It was unreal." He looked from her to the camera. "You sat there and talked to a lens that's like a black hole swallowing everything up, but on the screen you looked like you were talking to me and I was your best friend. How the hell do you do that?"

"I don't know. Some people are better at it than others. I'm one of the good ones."

"You must have done something," he insisted. "Imagined a face in front of you, a real person inside the lens . . . How else could you be so damned *sincere?*"

She laughed. "You can fake sincerity, Nick. It's called making love to the camera and it isn't all that hard, at least not for me. If you're on top of what you're saying, and if you know what people want from you, you can make them believe almost anything. Oh, here's Sybille. Have you two met?"

"No." He held out his hand.

"Sybille Morgen, Nicholas Fielding," said Valerie. "Sybille's at Stanford, too; she works here part time."

"A good place to work," Nick said, feeling the strong grip of Sybille's hand.

"The best, at least while I'm in college." She looked up at him with the most astonishing pale-blue eyes he had ever seen; it was as if she were memorizing everything about him. "It's a good place to learn. It won't make my reputation, but it can't break it, either."

"I hope you find a place to make it," he said.

"I intend to." She turned to Valerie. "I checked the tape; it's fine."

"Good, we can go to dinner." Valerie took Nick's arm. "I'll see you next month; isn't that when you're doing the antique-car show?"

"Two months. I'll send you a note." She looked at Nick. "Come again, whenever you like. We love to show off."

"I'd like that." He watched the cameraman roll the camera to another platform where a long curved desk stood before a world map and a smaller map of Palo Alto with weather arrows on it. "I don't know anything about television and I'd like to."

"Call me; we'll do a tour. Both of you, if you like," she added to Valerie. "Though you'd probably be bored."

"I'm never bored in a television station," Valerie said lightly. "At least not so far. And I like to watch you work, Sybille; you're so good."

"I'll expect you, then," Sybille said to Nick, and he was aware that it was the second time she had talked past Valerie, just to him. "If you want to see anything special, let me know in advance." She walked away and Nick watched her, admiring the decisiveness of her stride; she walked as if she were determined to make up in assertiveness what she lacked in stature. She was striking, with a face one would not forget; about Valerie's age, he thought, with heavy black hair held with an elastic band, a firm mouth, and rounded cheeks. But it was her eyes that Nick remembered: startlingly pale blue against her olive complexion, close together, heavy-lidded, guileless-looking, but alert, a combination that made it impossible to guess what she was thinking.

"Have you known her long?" he asked Valerie as they drove in her car toward the campus.

"Most of my life. She's from Baltimore, and when we're at the farm her mother is my mother's dressmaker. She comes down from Baltimore one day a week, early morning to midnight, or later, doing fittings, because that's where the wealthy clients live, and Sybille's always tagged along, ever since she was a baby. Am I buying dinner or are we splitting it?"

"It's already made at home. If you don't mind. How come she came all this way to school?"

"She told my mother she wanted Stanford and nothing else, because if I chose it it must be the best. Can you imagine me as a role model? Anyway, she was so wild to come here my parents loaned her money for four years' tuition; I think she barely makes it by working at the station."

"Where's her father?"

"Dead, I think." She swerved to the curb. "I want to stop here for a minute, and buy some wine."

"I have wine."

"I know, but I want to contribute something and wine seems to be your weak point. The only one I've found. So far."

He laughed. "Make it white, then; we're having veal."

She bought four bottles of Chablis and he was silent until they left the store. "How are we dividing up four bottles of wine?"

"We're having some left for next time."

He smiled as he put the wine in the car. "Can you make a salad?"

"I never have. Why?"

"I like the idea of our making dinner together."

"I don't think you really want me in your kitchen, but I'll try."

"Good enough."

In the kitchen, he poured two glasses of wine, put the rest in the refrigerator and took out salad ingredients. Valerie stood beside him and began tearing the greens into pieces. "Did your mother teach you to cook?"

"No, my father." He was measuring wild rice but glanced at her in time to see her quick look of surprise. "My mother is a secretary in a real estate office; she used to cook when she got home from work, but after awhile my father took over. She still cooks on weekends."

"So your father cooks after work?"

"During it, is more like it. He has a workshop in the garage and he's in and out of the house all day long." He put a pot of water on the stove and turned on the gas. "He's an inventor."

"An inventor! Of what? Something I've heard of?"

"Probably not. He's patented some tools that are used in automobile manufacture, and a new method for emulsifying paint—" He met her eyes. "Nothing you'd be likely to hear about."

"Nope," she said cheerfully. "But I'm impressed."

"He is impressive." Nick stared unseeing at the pot, waiting for it to boil. "He never gives up, he swallows a thousand discouragements and keeps going, he loves to share his successes but he keeps his failures to himself. He's very smart and endlessly optimistic and he's a realist with a sense of humor. I've always wondered how he manages to be all those things at once."

"You love him very much," Valerie said.

Nick turned at the wistful note in her voice, but she was looking down, at the red pepper she was slowly cutting into tiny dice. He started to tell her to stop, that the pieces were too small already, but he caught himself and watched her for a moment, feeling a rush of protectiveness that took him by surprise. Crazy, he thought. She was enormously wealthy, with beauty and charm, energy, a quick wit, friends in every part of the world, as many men, probably, as she wanted—how could anyone resist her?—and a taste for high living that she had the means to satisfy. And he was feeling protective. But there had been that note in her voice...

She glanced up. "Don't you?" she asked.

"Yes," he said, realizing how long he had been silent. "I love him very much. He's been my lodestar all my life. Even when I hated it that he failed so often, or when he embarrassed me, I couldn't imagine having another father or wanting to follow anyone else."

Valerie was watching him; her hands were still. "Embarrassed?"

"Sure, didn't your parents ever embarrass you? My mother and father would come to school for parents' night or something like it, and all the parents, including my mother, would listen to the teachers talking about our classes, but my father would go around telling anyone who'd listen about his inventions—the ones that failed and the ones that were going to revolutionize modern life and make his fortune, though he said his real goal wasn't money but to make life better for everyone. I wanted him to shut up, but of course I couldn't tell him that; I just went off to a corner and quietly died, as teenagers often do when they're with their parents."

Valerie laughed. "But why did he keep on, if he failed so often?"

Nick looked at her oddly. "Because inventing was what he did; it was his life. It still is. And because he's always sure he'll be successful the next time. Would you give up if you failed at something?"

"It depends on how hard I'd have to work at it. I might not quit right away, but after awhile I'd do some serious rethinking. Is your father happy?"

"Yes," he said without hesitation. "He still dreams of doing something that would have a real impact on history, but he's just about decided I'll be the one to do that while he keeps on doing what he does, the best way he can."

"It sounds so organized," Valerie said. "Like a relay race."

"We're doing what we both want," Nick said shortly. She gave him a swift look, then turned back to her salad, and in a few minutes held out the wooden bowl for his inspection. "You're very neat," he said, gazing at the red and yellow peppers and hearts of palm all cut the same, minuscule size.

"Not really; I'm really very messy. I always need someone to follow me around and clean up after me. But I didn't want you to be ashamed of having me in your kitchen." She looked at the salad bowl. "I must say it looks odd, not like any salad I've ever had; maybe I was concentrating too much. I was hoping it would earn me at least a couple of points."

Nick took the bowl from her and placed it on the counter. He put his arms around her. "I'd never be ashamed of having you here, or anywhere close to me." As Valerie's arms came around him, his lips brushed hers. "And I'm not keeping score. Are you?"

She shook her head. Her mouth opened beneath his and she forgot the salad, forgot that brief shortness in his voice, forgot his seriousness that sent little shivers of doubt through her whenever they were together. His mouth covered hers, she tasted the smooth wine on his tongue, and she gave herself up to the feel of him, the strength that had attracted her when they met, and his openness, so intriguingly different from the people in her life.

He pulled back to look at her, but she kept her arms around him. "Are you worried about burning our dinner?" she asked.

A slow smile lit his face. "It could wait for hours."

"Then let it."

He bent to her again, his mouth finding hers as his hands curved over her body. The silk of her dress felt electric beneath his palms and fingertips; he was alive with the feel of her, the small quiver that went through her when he unbuttoned the front of her dress, the scent and sounds and touch of her.

They turned to the sofa, but Valerie stopped as she took in its narrow Scandinavian lines: a thin piece of foam on a wooden slab, with a wooden back and arms. "Maybe your bedroom?" she asked.

Nick chuckled. " A little better, but not a lot."

"It has a bed. That's better."

He held out his hand and she took it and they walked down the short hallway. "Oh, wait." Valerie stopped him again. "Your roommates."

"They won't be here; Bill is out of town and Ted is at his girl's place."

"Musical chairs," she said with a laugh, and led him into his room. In the stark light of an angled hi-tech lamp, it seemed crowded, though it held only a single bed not much wider than the sofa in the living room, a tall, old-fashioned bureau, and an ancient rolltop desk with a swivel chair. A fine Zapotec rug almost covered the floor, and books were everywhere, on the floor, on the furniture, on the windowsills. Nick swept a pile off the bed, turned the lamp to the wall to soften its glare, and drew Valerie to him. "If you close your eyes, you can pretend it's the Ritz."

"I don't want the Ritz. You wouldn't be there."

"Not yet," he agreed and kissed her, his hands sliding her dress off her shoulders. He undressed her smoothly, easily, and Valerie felt a flash of relief that he was not, after all, inexperienced. There were times when he could have fooled me, she thought wryly, but the thought was fleeting; he had pulled off his clothes and they were holding each other, skin touching skin, the full lengths of their bodies curving together, the pounding of his heart feeling to Valerie as if it were her own. She met his eyes and they lay together on the bed.

"Valerie," Nick murmured; his voice was deep, saying her name slowly, sensuously, as if he were tasting it, as if he were breathing it. "You are so incredibly beautiful." His lips slid slowly along her throat to her breasts, kissing them, drawing the nipples up with his tongue, and then, together, they discovered each other with hands and mouths and twined legs, every touch and every movement a way of drawing out their discoveries, Nick looking down into Valerie's eyes, then Valerie looking down upon him, laughing at the tight maneuvers required on his monastic bed. "Making love to you is a real cliffhanger," she said mischievously as she barely stopped herself from falling off the edge. "I'm never sure where I'll be dangling next."

Momentarily unnerved, Nick's hands stilled, and he looked at her through half-closed eyes. He was the one who felt unsure. None of the women he had known had laughed and joked in bed, and he had always been as serious and silent as they. It was as if they all had learned some rule that said lightheartedness could never be part of romance and passion.

He'd taken it for granted. Now he wondered if Valerie's laughter meant she was bored, and laughed to spice up the moment. Or perhaps she never took anything seriously, no matter what it was. Damn it, she'll take me seriously, he thought, and, at that moment, Valerie bent over him.

"No thinking allowed," she said. "Maybe later, but not now. Now is for this." She kissed him with a long, slow kiss, her tongue moving in a lazy dance with his. "And this." Her tongue moved to the hollow of his throat in small circles that burned into him. She could feel the heat of his skin on her lips and beneath her hands and breasts as she brushed against him while moving her tongue in slow circles down his body. She loved the feel of him; he was more muscular than she had thought, and his skin was almost as smooth as a boy's. An athlete's body, she thought, and a brain that thinks too much.

She gave a low laugh that whispered against him like a warm spring breeze. "What?" he asked.

She looked up at him. "I'm having such a wonderful time."

He laughed, as much startled as pleased. Of course she wasn't bored; he'd never really thought so. But, damn it, he wanted her to concentrate on him and on their lovemaking. Roughly, he lifted her and laid her back on the bed. He held her firmly, his mouth caressing the length of her body as hers had caressed him, his tongue probing in strokes that drew her up, all her senses, all her feelings, to a single point that was the place where they met: his tongue, her flesh, their pleasure. The only sounds were their breathing, and the whispering of their names.

And when he was inside her it was as if they had always known this was how they would be together. Valerie met his eyes and laughed deep in her throat as she drew his mouth to hers, and Nick knew it was all right, it was perfect, because this joining was only one of so many they already had made between them, so many ways they already were a part of each other, and Valerie's laughter was essential to that, to the joy they found together and could not contain, and would always have. He would learn to laugh with her, he thought, and never again desire her silence.

When at last they lay still, Nick kissed her smiling lips and closed eyes, and she held his face between her hands, bringing his mouth once more to hers. "I knew we didn't need the Ritz," she murmured.

In a moment, he sat up beside her. He looked about the tiny room, then back to Valerie's slim form, curved like an ivory flower on the rumpled bed, her tawny hair fanned out around her slender face. He was jubilant and keyed up with anticipation, because he had found exactly what he wanted, and now everything was possible.

"We'll get to the Ritz too, one of these days," he said, "just to see if it makes a difference." He leaned down and kissed her breast. "I'm going to the kitchen, to put together our dinner." He grinned. "Better than a dinner: it's a feast." From a dresser drawer he took a striped pajama top and handed it to her. "The new oversize look. You'll be spectacular in it; you're spectacular in everything. Then we'll eat, and talk about what we're going to do tomorrow." He pulled on his robe and paused in the doorway. "And every tomorrow after that," he added and then he was gone.

Chapter
3

ybille left the station late and drove back to the
campus through the Palo Alto traffic with the
recklessness of a native. In fact she didn't feel at
home in California any more than she did any
other place, even Baltimore, where she'd grown
up. She had always wanted to live somewhere else, the Eastern Shore
where her mother's rich clients lived, or New York, or California. But
when she got to Palo Alto, she didn't want that either; she wanted to
live in the hills where the wealthy were. Never once had she found a
place where she felt she belonged.

She parked her car in an illegal but unobtrusive spot near her apartment, front end in, so the KNEX-TV sticker in her back window
would be visible and look official. She always parked in this small spot,
ever since her second year when she moved to an attic apartment in a
private home just off campus, cleaning house in exchange for her rent.
The parking place was in the alley, just big enough for her microscopic
Fiat, and she had never gotten a ticket. Luck or skill, Sybille thought
as she locked the doors. Not that it really matters which it is; I need
both.

Her dress for the evening was laid out on the bed; she had ironed it that morning before going to class. Her shoes stood below the narrow, slitted skirt; her underclothes were on the bed nearby; and the scent of gardenia filled the room. She had bought herself a corsage.

Valerie had told her most of the women wouldn't have flowers since it wasn't a black-tie dinner, but it was Sybille's first party off campus, and she was so excited she had to do something extravagant. So she bought one gardenia and wore it pinned to the short emerald-green jacket that went with her green-and-gold dress. Her mother had made the dress for a special occasion; this was the first time she would wear it. She stood before the small mirror over the bureau, turning and twisting to see all parts of herself. It always bothered her that she wasn't tall and willowy. Stand tall, she told herself. Head high. I'm Valerie Ashbrook's guest and I'm going to dinner at the home of Thos Carlyle, who owns KNEX-TV and probably has no idea I work for him, and I'll be meeting people who are really important. And if I do things right, someday I'll be invited there on my own, not because Valerie thought I was a charity case. I'll be invited because I'll be as important as the rest of them.

Precisely at seven o'clock she was in front of the house, where Valerie had said she would pick her up. She stood there, near the curbing, feet together, head high, for twenty minutes, until a black limousine pulled to a smooth stop beside her and Valerie opened the back door. "Goodness, you're prompt."

"Did I get the time wrong?" Sybille gave a swift glance at the dark-blue velvet interior of the car, and instantly memorized it. A small bar and telephone were at one side, a television set was on the other. Valerie, she saw, was wearing black, simpler than her own dress, more stylish, more sophisticated. "I thought you said seven."

"I did; I'm late. Somehow I couldn't get myself organized."

"Oh." No apology, Sybille noted, and wondered if that was the way Valerie always behaved. She saw so little of her on campus, and she knew none of her friends; maybe all of them were casual about things like being on time. Even the invitation to the party had been casual; they had run into each other in the library a few days before and when Sybille mentioned KNEX, Valerie said she knew the owner. "He and his wife are giving a dinner party and they told me to bring a friend; would you like to meet him?" Just that easily, Sybille was on the guest list for Thos Carlyle's dinner.

The driver drove toward the hills. "I thought you drive a Mercedes sports car," Sybille said. "Is this your limousine?"

"Lord, no, who wants a boat like this? This is Thos's. He doesn't like the idea of young ladies driving up to the hills alone at night, especially me, since he and my parents are so close. He probably told them he'd keep an eye on me, and he's such a gallant gentleman, I don't argue."

"But why would you?" Sybille asked. "It's wonderful."

"Well, for one thing, we go at the driver's speed, instead of mine. Tell me what's happening at the station. I heard someone got fired."

"He wasn't fired, he's going to the network. It's the greatest thing in the world for him. How do stories get around so fast? It only happened a couple of days ago."

"Oh, this place is so small, and people love to be bearers of news, good or bad. Is that something you want—to go to the network?"

"Of course; what else would I want? It's where everything happens. All the things I'm doing are to get there as fast as I can."

Valerie stirred in her seat, uncomfortable, as always, with intensity. "How can you have it so settled? All laid out, like a roadmap. Nick is like that; he's got it all figured out, where he's going, how he's going to get there, what he'll do when he's there. He's not as fierce about it as you are, but both of you sound sort of like sergeants: charge the hill, don't look left or right until you get to the top. Don't you ever relax and just have a good time?"

"You're jealous," Sybille said shrewdly.

There was the briefest pause, then Valerie laughed. "Guess again. I'm not an onward-and-upward type."

Sybille glanced out the window. They were in the hills overlooking Palo Alto, winding up slopes covered with the lush green and brilliant gardens of March. It was hard to believe, she thought, that by late summer, weeks of dry weather would have turned all this to a pale yellow-brown. She looked at the houses they passed, sprawling cedar and stone, set into the hills, and wondered what Valerie thought of them. Did these magnificent houses look small and ordinary to her? Did she think about living up here; about how free someone would feel with a house on one of these hills, looking down on the town and the peninsula, all the way to the bay? Or did she think it was just another nice neighborhood, not nearly as exciting as some of the others she could choose from, anywhere in the world?

Everything she wants, she gets, Sybille thought.

"I've been waiting for you and Nick to come to the station," she said, turning back to Valerie.

"We've talked about it; we just haven't had time. Maybe when I do the pitch for the antique-auto show."

"That's next week."

"I'll tell him about it." The limousine followed a curve in the road. "It's just a few minutes from here; let me tell you about some of the people you'll be meeting." Valerie listed some names with brief descriptions, and Sybille stored them away. "It's not fair to throw them at you all at once, but you'll sort them out when you're there."

"I'll remember," Sybille said. "Thanks." She tried to think of other words, other ways to thank Valerie for the evening. Why was it so hard for her to be grateful to Valerie? It always had been, from the time they met, when they were five and Valerie asked her if she wanted to go for a swim in their pool. "Will Nick be here tonight?" she asked, to break her silence.

"No, he has to work. It's just as well; he doesn't much like these dinners. This is the third time in the last two weeks he's turned me down when I've invited him."

"Is this really good, the two of you? More than just dating, I mean. Really...close?"

Valerie's eyebrows rose, and with a sinking feeling Sybille knew she had committed a serious blunder: she had no right to ask such a question. It would be a long time before Valerie confided in her again, even a little bit. "This is the house," Valerie said as the limousine turned into a driveway. She glanced at Sybille. "My God, you look as if you're going to the dentist. Listen, these are just nice ordinary people; you're not afraid of them, are you?"

"No, of course not. I just don't do this very often."

"You'll be terrific," Valerie said, and her voice was so natural Sybille knew she wasn't faking to make her feel better. "You're very pretty and you've got a lot to talk about and there's something about you...Nick saw it; he said you were strong and very sure of what you want. People like that, especially men. You'll be fine, really; you haven't got a thing to worry about."

Sybille felt a rush of gratitude. "Thanks."

"Let's go, then," Valerie said, and Sybille followed her out of the car. Just believe her, she told herself; why would she lie? But Sybille had never been able to accept a compliment gracefully. She always wondered if there was a catch somewhere.

She followed Valerie with her usual quick step. "Have a good time," Valerie said at the door and Sybille nodded, but still, as she walked into the large room fear gripped her, especially when Valerie disappeared right after introducing her to their hostess. Sybille watched her move among the guests as comfortably as if she were on the campus, and she thought angrily that she had no right to leave her alone; she should have stayed at her side. Valerie was always like that: swinging wildly from generosity and praise to total thoughtlessness. She did just what she felt like at the moment without concern for what was past or what lay ahead.

While Valerie was the center of attention, Sybille stood at the edges of groups, listening to conversations, smiling when others laughed, always looking intently at the speaker as if she were the one being spoken to. In that way she spent the evening, saying almost nothing while the guests stood about the living room, having drinks, and then sat at three round granite-topped tables for dinner. She watched, she listened, she took note of dresses, gestures and mannerisms, and the anecdotes about television and local and national politics that filled the conversation, giving her her first view from the inside. It was the most exciting evening she'd ever known, and it showed her exactly what had been missing in her plans for the future. Now she expected not only to become wealthy and powerful in television, but also to be part of the life of powerful people.

"Thank you," she said to Valerie at eleven o'clock when the limousine stopped in exactly the same spot it had picked her up only a few hours before.

"I'm glad you could come," Valerie replied. "I hope you had some fun; you were awfully quiet."

"I was watching, and learning a lot. You don't have to worry about me, Valerie. I had the most fun I've ever had in my life."

Nick pulled ahead of Valerie, his horse flying as they reached the crest of a rise and began the downward run. He hadn't ridden in years and was rediscovering the exhilaration of it, the unbridled energy and sense of freedom that swept over him with the wind. He bent low over the horse's sleek neck, and so it was the flying hoofs of Valerie's horse he saw first as she caught and passed him, shouting something he could not hear. She looked back at him, laughing as she turned her horse toward the hills, increasing the distance between them. But Nick, urging his horse on, caught her and then they rode side by side. The matched energy of their horses and the thrill of their speed flowed between them like an embrace, and when at last they stopped, Valerie moved her horse close to his. "It's like making love, don't you think? Like we were inside each other."

"Not quite." He grinned at her. "As I recall, there's a distinct difference."

"Well, but not in essence. We were riding each other just now, weren't we? In a mystical sense, anyway: I felt so much a part of you."

She could always surprise him. As far as Nick could tell, she took nothing as seriously as he took almost everything, but then she would come up with quirky, interesting ideas that showed she'd thought about things in an almost analytical way. But Valerie wasn't analytical; everybody knew that. She was spoiled and willful and restless. She was also absolutely captivating, which had nothing to do with how serious she was, but had everything to do with why he spent so much of his time thinking about her. This morning he had missed a class to ride with her—she had missed one, too, but she brushed it aside—and he had two papers to finish, and a project at work that would keep him up most of the night. But he barely thought about any of that; he was completely absorbed by the warm, hazy day, the excitement of riding, the fascination of Valerie.

"No mystical sense?" she said mockingly, when his silence stretched out. "I should have known; it must be as forbidden as magic in your book of rules."

"I'm open to it," he said. "A scientist is always willing to listen."

"Oh, you want proof. How dreary. Do you know what I love best about riding? Cutting loose from everything. The whole world goes by in a blur, all pale and misty, and the only thing that's real is me, but I'm totally different. I'm my own universe: pure space, pure movement. As if time disappears and there's only speed and eternity. Now, how does a scientist feel about that?"

"He feels he should have been a poet," Nick said quietly. "I may have felt something like that when we were riding, but those weren't the ideas that came to me."

"Well, they're yours now," Valerie said carelessly. "You can do what you want with them. We'd better start back; I have a paper due tomorrow and we're rehearsing the first act of *Misalliance* tonight."

"Before or after dinner?"

"During, I guess; it's called for six-thirty. It's going to be a contest between Shaw's dialogue and our corned-beef sandwiches. Do you want to watch?"

"They don't want an audience, do they?"

"The star gets to bend the rules. If you want to watch, you can watch."

"Another night, then; I'd like to. I'll be working most of tonight."

She sighed. "Nose to the grindstone," she murmured, and rode off, leaving him behind.

But she rode at an easy pace and soon Nick was beside her. Their horses moved in tandem, their bodies rose and fell in a matched rhythm, and they were content to ride that way, without speaking, sharing their smiles as the perfect afternoon slid slowly past.

They were only a mile from the ranch where they would return the horses when they heard a harmonica and an accordion playing a lively tune, and the shrieks and laughter of children. "Let's go see," Valerie said, and, following the sounds, they came to a carnival on the outskirts of Los Verdes. There seemed to be hundreds of children milling about, and a few adults who stood out like tall weeds in a field of waving grass. "Oh, lovely," Valerie said and, jumping down, tied her horse to a fencepost with a loose knot. "Nick, come on; don't you love these?"

"It's been a long time." He'd said the same thing about riding when she first invited him. So many rediscoveries, he thought as he tied up his horse. And discoveries too. Forgotten were the papers due the next day, the rehearsal that evening, Nick's job. They wandered hand in hand through the carnival, tossing horseshoes, shooting at moving ducks, fishing for prizes in wooden barrels, playing miniature golf and skittles. They rode the ferris wheel twice, watched the delight in the eyes of children on the merry-go-round and the miniature train, and then, at the far end of the carnival, they came upon a puppet show.

Valerie grabbed Nick's hand. "I don't believe it; it's just like the one I had when I was growing up." They stood behind a crowd of children sitting cross-legged on the grass, and Valerie gazed at the little theater almost hungrily. "It was all glittery like this one, only with gold spangles instead of silver. When I turned on the stage lights, the gold was like stars and everything was a fairyland." She laughed softly, caught in her memories. "My cousins and I used to make up plays and put them on for the family, until the plots got so gruesome nobody would watch. Sometimes we couldn't watch them, either; we'd scare ourselves so much we wouldn't do it again for weeks. But we always came back and made another one even more awful. Isn't it amazing how children love to terrify themselves with the worst that might happen? I can't imagine why; I refuse to think about those things now. It's much better to think everything will always be gold spangles that look like stars. I wonder if it's still in the basement on the farm. If I ever have children, I'd love to see what they do with it; there must be thirty puppets there, just waiting to be brought to life."

On the small stage, two puppets were playing Ping-Pong. *"If* you have children?" Nick asked.

"Oh, I suppose I will someday. I haven't given it much thought. Not for a long time, anyway; I wouldn't have them if all I'd do is give them to somebody else to bring up, and I'm not about to let some kids take up all my time right now." She caught a glimpse of his curious look before he masked it. "I'm only twenty!" she exclaimed. "Why do you keep expecting me to make all these decisions? I'm not ready. Anyone who has children ought to be settled and wise, and I'm not. Not yet, anyway. Oh, look, what a clever idea!"

One of the puppets had taken a wild swipe at the Ping-Pong ball and sent it sailing out to the audience. With shrieks of glee, the children grabbed at it; a little girl snatched it and hugged it to herself. When the children looked back at the stage, the puppets were quarreling. "Look what you did! You lost the ball!" "I didn't! You hit it wrong and it bounced off my paddle!" "I hit it right! You didn't know how to hit it back!" *"I* hit it right! You hit it wrong!" *"You* hit it wrong!" "Listen, dummy, there's two ways to do things: my way and the wrong way. That's all!"

The children were laughing and jumping up and down and Nick and Valerie looked at each other. "The reason nations go to war," he murmured, and she laughed. "It's a lesson in power politics."

But in a minute the puppets were reconciled. "Maybe there *is* another right way besides mine," said the one who had called his friend a dummy. "But it's an awful nuisance, having to learn two ways." "That's okay," said the other. "A little nuisance isn't so bad if it means we can play together without fighting all the time."

"Moral for the day," Nick said as he and Valerie walked back the way they had come. "But it's not power politics, as we know it."

"No. It's not even marriage as we know it."

He gave her a swift glance. "Then what was that play about?"

"A love affair," she said, laughing. "Couldn't you tell? It's the only time two people really work at being on their best behavior. There are the horses; my God, it's so late, let's see how fast we can get back."

"In a minute." Nick put his arm around her and brought her to him to kiss her. They stood for a long moment beneath the tree. Music and the laughter of children drifted to them, the air was fragrant with sunlight and flowering shrubs, and they held each other close, their breaths mingling.

"I like that," Valerie said when they moved a little apart and smiled at each other. "What inspired it?"

"A wonderful day. And I wanted to be on my best behavior."

She laughed. "But I expect that of you. Otherwise this would be a very unsatisfactory affair. Come on, we're going to race back."

By the time they reached the ranch, their horses neck and neck, Valerie was thinking about the play she would rehearse that night; she had forgotten the puppets. But Nick never forgot them. Because that afternoon was the first time he knew he wanted to marry her—and that he could not ask her because she would turn him down. That afternoon was the first of many afternoons and evenings he would tell himself that she wasn't ready yet; he would have to wait for just the right time.

A college campus is its own world, almost as separate from the larger world as if it were tucked into itself behind a high wall. Even without a wall, a visitor notices changes the instant the Stanford boundary is crossed. The light is softer, sifting down on students strolling, sprawling, and embracing; it glows along the harmonious curves of sandstone buildings with arches and red tile roofs surrounding serene quadrangles and lining long walks. The clamor of the city fades away, even the bicycling students seem reflective, and it is easy to believe that here the hustle of the marketplace takes a backseat to the pursuit of knowledge, perhaps even of wisdom.

Nick had loved it from the moment his parents first drove him to the campus seven years earlier, helping him move his few possessions into his dormitory room, and giving him words of advice as urgently as if it were the last chance they would ever have. As soon as they left, he went for a walk, studying a map to learn his way around the campus, memorizing names of buildings, watching soccer practice, envying the couples walking hand in hand across the grass, wandering through the library stacks and running his hands along the shelves of books. He wanted to read them all.

He never lived at home again. For most of the year he stayed on campus, studying and holding down one job or another, sometimes two at a time. One month every summer he hitchhiked the West, from Oregon and Washington to Arizona and New Mexico, photographing, making notes, reading Indian and Western lore. Most often he went alone. One summer he was joined by a girl he thought he loved, but the closeness proved too much for them. Another summer two friends from his soccer team went along, one of them providing a car, and the three of them explored the rifts and ranges of Wyoming on what became one of the best trips Nick ever took. But his friends graduated the following spring, and that summer he once again took off alone, this time bicycling past the fantastic rock formations that ran the length of Baja California. And that was a great trip, too, solitude having its own pleasures. He had never been afraid of being alone.

When he came back to the campus, whether from a trip through the West or from visiting his parents, it was always with a feeling of coming home. It was where he belonged.

When he told that to Sybille, she stared at him in surprise. She had led him and Valerie on a tour of KNEX and then they had driven in Valerie's sports car to a Chinese restaurant in Palo Alto for dinner. "You can't think college is like home; it's more like a stopping place on the way to the rest of your life."

"Nick builds nests," Valerie said, "even if he's on the way somewhere. It's amazing how good he is at it; I couldn't begin to do what he does."

"You just need a few lessons in homemaking," Nick said with a grin. "Which I will be glad to supply."

"Too late; I'm far too old to learn. Why don't I teach you how to hire servants?"

"Too rich for my budget, and all my dusting and cooking skills would atrophy." He caught a glimpse of Sybille's wistful eyes, and felt guilty for excluding her. "We were talking about Stanford," he said, turning to her. "What's wrong with it?"

"It's not just Stanford; it's any college. It takes forever to get through it, and it doesn't have what I want; what is there to like?"

Nick watched the waiter spread plum jam and shredded meat and vegetables on pancakes, then roll them up. "What do you want?" he asked.

She hesitated. "A lot of things." She wished Valerie weren't there; she would have liked to talk to Nick alone. "To be noticed. To make people know I'm here. Most people I know are so *satisfied;* they don't have that awful ache to be as big and as high—" She broke off and dropped her eyes, her face flushed with embarrassment.

Valerie, who couldn't bear unhappiness, said quickly, "In television? As what? Producer?"

"Maybe, to start." Sybille raised her eyes and saw that they weren't laughing at her. "But that's only a first step. I'm going to be on camera—anchor of a news show, and then with my own show, interviews or something, I'm not sure yet, and I'll do it all: write it, produce it, star in it." She sat back as the waiter set a plate with a large rolled pancake before her. "One thing I won't do is be a big wheel at a little nothing station like KNEX."

"Why not?" Valerie asked curiously.

Sybille looked at her as if she were a slow student. "Because I want the things I don't have now; the things everybody wants. Money. Power. Fame."

Valerie shook her head. "Not me. At least I don't want power and fame. Too much work and not enough fun, and you have to keep fighting off everybody who wants to take them away from you. I can't imagine getting involved in that."

"That's because you've always had money and you're used to getting what you want. It's pretty damned easy to pretend you don't want something when you've already got it and you know you're going to get more without even trying."

"Hey," Valerie said mildly. "It's not worth fighting over."

"I'm sorry," said Sybille, ducking her head and again flushing nervously. "I get too excited. But it means an awful lot to me."

"To get what you don't have?"

"To get everything I want."

"That's a tall order," Nick observed quietly. He had been watching them, aware that others in the restaurant were doing the same, envying him, he thought. They were so striking together: Valerie fair and stunningly beautiful, Sybille dark and intriguing, with those astonishingly pale, almost exotic eyes; Valerie in jeans and an emerald-green silk blouse, Sybille neat and decorous in a black skirt and white sweater; Valerie relaxed, casual, self-confident, Sybille alternating between embarrassment and intense, strained forcefulness.

They were so different he wondered at any friendship between them, even a sporadic and casual one. He had seen Sybille's swift survey of Valerie when they first arrived at the television station, and he had known that Valerie, while she probably was aware of what Sybille was wearing, was far less interested than Sybille was in her. Sybille listened more closely to Valerie than Valerie listened to her; now and then she made a gesture identical to one of Valerie's; she never let her thoughts drift from the conversation as Valerie sometimes did. She gave the impression of a student memorizing everything for some future test.

"I'm not afraid of tall orders," she said to Nick, "as long as there's something for me to win." She gazed at him with a long, measuring look. Her blue eyes were like jewels, he reflected, filled with promise without revealing what the promise was. An interesting woman with a drive to succeed that he could understand because it matched his own. Beneath the table, he took Valerie's hand in his, grateful for having found his fixed star, infinitely happier now than when he had been searching and experimenting with different women, even women who piqued his interest as much as Sybille Morgen did. "What about you?" she was asking. She had been fumbling with her chopsticks, trying to pick up a piece of chicken; now she put them aside as if she had had enough to eat and looked at Nick. "You're in school so you can get what you want, aren't you? Tools for when you leave. Why else would you spend all these years waiting for something real to happen?"

Nick felt a flash of pity, wondering how a woman who did not think her surroundings were real, and who ached to be something different, could ever be content. "I came here to learn," he said, then smiled broadly. "Sounds hopelessly dull, doesn't it?"

"Not for a scientist," Valerie said lightly.

"What about scientists who like puppet shows?" he demanded.

"They're redeemed. Not dull at all. But still," she added ironically, "to come to college to *learn* . . . how very quaint."

Sybille was watching them again, holding her breath as she saw Nick's eyes when he looked at Valerie. Nick glanced at her, and, in confusion, she picked up her chopsticks again. She tried to fit them between her fingers and thumb. Damn it, she thought; Nick and Valerie make it look so easy. It's one of those things that come with money, and time to play around in restaurants, learning stupid things like eating with two sticks of wood. But she resisted asking for a fork; she struggled and after a while began to figure out how it was done. But in the struggle she missed some of the conversation, and when Nick glanced at her she said quickly. "That can't be all you came here for: learning."

"True," he conceded. "I also came to find Valerie, though I didn't know her name or what she'd look like until three months ago."

"Well, but seriously, what else?" Sybille asked impatiently.

"I guess nothing else," he said simply, wondering what it would take to make her laugh. "I'm happiest when I'm finding things I didn't know yesterday. There's a lot I want to do and I'm looking forward to doing it when I finish here in a couple of months and get a job, but I haven't spent the past seven years just preparing for it, and nothing else."

"What kind of job?"

"The same kind I'm doing now: designing computers, writing programs..."

"That's what I said: you're getting your credentials, like the rest of us. It's like running an obstacle course before we can get to the real starting gate; people out there think it's important, but it doesn't have anything to do with the real world."

"It's not that complicated." Nick smiled, still admiring her determination, but wishing she were less shrill. She's like I was, he thought, before Valerie taught me to relax. "I just wanted a few years of being a student. There are men my age making fortunes up and down this valley, from San Francisco to Monterey, with or without college degrees, and I could have had a shot at it anytime, but I wanted this first. It's probably the last time in my life I'll be able to concentrate on me and learning what I want. I always had the idea that was what a college was for. I'll make my fortune when the time comes; I'm not worried about that."

Sybille stared at him. "Not worried," she echoed. "You're so sure."

"I'll make sure. I'll do what I have to and I'll make sure."

He sounds like me, Sybille thought. Why is he with Valerie when it's me he's like? Then, as if she remembered that she had not won her argument, she returned to it. "You'll make sure because you'll have your credentials. And because you've met people here who might help you. Though mostly you have to help yourself, because you can't count on other people being interested in you. Valerie, I'm right, aren't I? You want to go into the theater and this is a way for you to get started."

"Not really," Valerie said. She toyed with her chopsticks, looking bored, Nick thought. "I don't think about the stage as a career; it's too confining. I might do amateur productions now and then, but that's probably about all."

Sybille was staring at her. "Then why did you come to college?"

It was Valerie's turn to look at Sybille as if she were slow. "Why not? It's something new, like going to Africa or India, but I'd already done that. Besides, everybody goes to college; it's the next step after high school."

Nick chuckled and raised his glass of Chinese beer in a toast to each of them. "To the academic life."

"You can have your little jokes," Valerie said serenely. "I like to learn as much as anybody does, I just *do* it instead of talking about it. And I'm having a good time."

"Well, of course I like it, too," said Sybille. "It's just not—" She stopped. She couldn't convince them; they were too set in their ideas.

Valerie touched her glass to Nick's. "To a good time, and lots of ways to have it."

"Together," he said, his eyes holding hers.

"Maybe." She looked across the table, at Sybille. "How about this? Ten years from now, the three of us will be raising our glasses to drink to Sybille Morgen, nationally famous star of her own television show."

"I'll drink to that," Sybille said, and the three of them drank, each to a different toast.

Valerie sat beside the window, daydreaming, while the professor flourished his chalk at the blackboard and worked out the intricacies of a chemical formula. She could tolerate science better now than before she met Nick—in fact, sometimes she was surprised to find herself enjoying it—and she kept herself awake through the dull parts by pretending it was Nick's voice she was hearing, which wasn't so hard since he sounded faintly lecturing when he helped her with her homework.

She was thinking about him a lot these days, more than she had thought about any other man. She wondered why. He wasn't the sexiest man she knew, nor the most handsome or daring; he hadn't traveled and didn't seem in a hurry to catch up with her; he didn't have the money to join her in the jaunts she took with friends, sailing, water skiing, going to parties and nightclubs, driving around the peninsula looking for things to do; he hadn't been able to get away from work to go with her the two weekends she'd flown to New York and had wanted him to come to meet her parents; and he was so damned serious about everything!

That was the worst of all, she thought. Her hand was moving smoothly over her notebook, copying the formula and its solution, but her thoughts were with Nick. The truth was, he may not have been the sexiest or the most handsome or anything else, but he was the most consuming man she had ever known: when they were together she was entirely with him, never drifting off into daydreams or fantasies the way she did with other people, and when they were apart the memory of him filled her thoughts and wrapped around her just the way he did when they lay in his bed.

But then there was his intensity, his drive to do everything he set out to do, even if it was just an afternoon ride through the fields or a part-time job on campus, or the work he was planning for the future.

Always, deeply a part of him, there was that seriousness and control, that concentration that even she couldn't count on breaking.

She couldn't understand it or share it, and yet she couldn't get him out of her mind. How could she feel this way about someone she couldn't understand? It was beginning to make her nervous. She was getting restive too. They were together so much now, studying together, eating together, spending the night together when his roommates were away, that it was beginning to feel like a marriage. She hadn't met a new man for four months, and she was spending less time with her women friends. It didn't seem to bother Nick that he wasn't meeting new women, and, though he still saw his friends, Valerie came first. He seemed settled for life. The thought made her quiver with alarm.

I'm too young for this, she thought. I'm not supposed to get involved with anybody for years.

But I'm not really that involved with him; not at all. It's like a shipboard romance; it will end when we leave here. Probably before.

The professor ended the lecture, and Valerie looked at her notebook. It was covered, in her slightly erratic handwriting, with numbers, diagrams, notes, even the title of a magazine article they were to read before the class met again. It seemed she had taken down the contents of an entire hour without hearing a word of it. From his mouth to my hand, she thought with a laugh; I wonder if Nick will think that's an achievement or a distinct flaw in my character.

Damn it, she thought, the first thing I think about is telling Nick. I'm always doing that lately. She left the building, pausing in the shadowed loggia to let her eyes adjust to the bright April sun. Every time something happens that's funny or surprising or just plain interesting I can't wait to tell him. Well, this time I'll skip it. There's absolutely no reason to tell Nick Fielding everything that happens to me; I have my own life and I refuse to open all of it to anybody.

"So I wrote for the whole hour," she said at dinner that night in his apartment. "Took wonderful notes and never heard a word of his lecture. I was thinking of other things."

Nick chuckled. "You should think about going into politics. If you can think one thing and write another—better yet, say another—you're the perfect candidate."

"I wouldn't like that. I'd rather do my faking in my personal life; it's more honest."

They laughed and Nick poured their coffee and then cut the cake Valerie had brought from the bakery. She watched him, loving the look of his hands: smooth, tanned, long thin fingers. She remembered the feel of his fingers inside her and began to want him again. She never seemed to get enough of him in bed. I thought about that in class today, she recalled.

I also decided not to tell him I took notes without hearing the lecture. I was so sure I wasn't going to tell him. She picked up her fork and toyed with her slice of cake. Somehow it didn't seem important now. She felt so warm and good, being there, watching him move about his kitchen, thinking about going to bed with him and discovering again his tenderness and forcefulness that always seemed new to her, she couldn't recall her perfectly good arguments against getting too involved.

There seemed to be a big difference between what she thought when they were apart and what she did when they were together. I'll have to sort that out one of these days, she thought. But there's no rush; after all, it's all going to end when we leave Stanford, so why do anything now, when I'm having such a wonderful time and he's so much fun to tell things to?

Although that's just the problem. He's becoming a habit that might be awfully hard to break.

Chapter
4

ybille looked down at the closed eyes and open mouth of Terence Beauregard the Third, news director of KNEX-TV, whose overweight nude body bulged between her legs. "Nice," he said, his breath coming in little bursts. "Nice, nice, nice..." She shut him out by closing her eyes. She couldn't stand to look at a man who was in her bed. Instead, she concentrated on her own rhythm, impaling herself on him, rising and sliding slowly down, listening to his breathing to decide when to move faster and when to go slow.

She supported herself on her hands on either side of his broad face and when she lowered herself she brushed her nipples against his chest because that always got him excited. He let her do it all, and she listened to the sounds he made and moved faster, willing him to do what she wanted, until he shouted out and gripped her buttocks with both hands, shuddered beneath her, and finally lay still.

He was still breathing quickly as she slid off him and sat crosslegged on her bed. "Nice," he said, his eyes still closed. "Real nice, sweetie." Sybille waited for what she would feel next, and it came as certainly as it always did: first she felt empty, then lonelier than ever, and finally furiously angry.

He didn't give a damn who was on top of him. He didn't bother to look at her; he didn't say her name once the whole time. Maybe he didn't remember it. He would see her at the television station the next day and act as if he'd never been inside her. She was anonymous to him.

As he was to her, she thought. But that didn't matter. She could not bear to be invisible.

But then he surprised her. She had been about to send him home, as she always did with whoever had been in her bed, so she could spend the rest of the evening once more in control of her life, but he put out his hand. "Have to talk about that newscast you did today. Lots of problems with it."

Sybille froze. "Problems?"

"Dull." He opened his eyes and heaved himself to a sitting position. "It's a noon newscast; people getting lunch, coming and going, on the run... it's gotta move or you lose 'em. What you want, you want personal stuff. Little stories. Moments, somebody called 'em; you know, little stories all strung together. Nobody wants to see just a flood, for Christ's sake—water in the fields and voice-over talking about crop damage—Jee-sus—people want to see other people. Mostly suffering. Family in a boat, lost everything but the clothes they're wearing; river dragged for bodies; little kid on a roof, crying, waiting to be rescued by a helicopter; dog drowned... whatever. Moments. Give people what they want."

"But the big news was the loss of the crops—"

"Fuck the crops. Fuck the news. Nobody cares. They want stories, sweetie. Moments. How many times I have to say that?" He stood beside the bed and ran a finger around her breast. "You're good and you're tough; you'll figure it out. I've got plans for you, you know. We got any beer in the house?"

We? Sybille took a long breath. He had plans for her; he could help her. "Sure." She wrapped her seersucker robe around her and tied it tightly. "I'll see you in the kitchen."

The kitchen was in a corner on the other side of a blanket she had hung to screen her bed and dresser, and she could hear him dressing as she took beer from the refrigerator. She debated taking out cheese and crackers, and then decided against it. There was no need to coddle him.

He was with her in a few minutes, tucking his shirt into his pants.

"Speaking of moments," he said, opening a bottle of beer, "I'll give you a great one. Can't use it, but it's great." He sat on a straight wooden chair and stretched out his legs. "There's this crazy woman in Sunnyvale, worth maybe a couple hundred million—her daddy was in oil and her hubby was in gas—and she calls the president of Stanford one day and says she wants to give him fifty mill for a new engineering building, because her daddy and hubby were both engineers. But, and there has to be a but if you want a great story, there's got to be an ape house too."

"A what?"

"Don't interrupt, sweetie; just absorb. This is a *moment* I'm giving you. She has a whole bunch of apes—raises 'em or breeds 'em or whatever—and her favorite is named Ethelred the Unready...you know who he is? Or was?" Sybille shook her head. "King of England back in the Dark Ages; she likes the name, God knows why. Anyway, she's giving her millions so the university can build the Ethelred Engineering Building and Ape House—don't laugh, sweetie, this is serious stuff, fifty mill is always dead serious—so her apes'll have a home after she dies. I guess she's getting on, somewhere around ninety, maybe more. Great story, right? 'Course we can't do anything with it."

He finished his beer and opened another bottle. "Somebody else might," he said casually, gazing at the bottle opener, "but I can't because I promised."

Sybille sat down opposite him. "Promised?"

"The person who gave me the story. She told me in confidence."

"Who is she? How do you know her?"

"I don't know her. I was in bed with her."

Sybille bit her lip. "Who is she?"

"Somebody's wife. Her husband's at the university; he's been in on the meetings."

She gave him a long look. "I don't believe a word of it. It's crazy."

He shrugged. "World's full of crazy people. Good thing, too, or TV news'd be out of business."

"Not this crazy," she said stubbornly. "Stanford wouldn't do it."

"Listen, sweetie; you like the story?"

"Of course I like it; it's terrific. But it's not true."

"Well." He gazed at his beer. "It's half true. She did say it. With a smile. Seems they were negotiating about her fifty mill and couldn't agree on some things about how to build the building, and she said if they didn't agree pretty soon, the only way she'd give the money was if

Stanford built a home for Ethelred and her other apes. Something like that. She even made a sketch of it, gave it to the v-p of the university for a souvenir." He sighed. "Nice little story. A good news writer could get some mileage from it. Enough to jazz up a newscast. Enough to get the attention of somebody from the network who might be watching."

Sybille looked at him sharply. "And then what?" she asked.

"Well, who knows? I've been told—confidential again; God, I'm giving you all these juicy secrets tonight; must have been something you did earlier—somebody's told me I might be tapped for the network; they're keeping an eye on the station. And then... who knows? I don't think I'd want to leave my best producer here if I moved to New York."

There was a long silence. "Well, it won't work, though." He gave a deep, elaborate sigh. "I did promise. Guess I'd better swear you to secrecy, too." They exchanged a look. "Promise?" he asked.

"Of course," Sybille said easily.

He gave a broad smile, finished his beer and looked around for another. "That's all there is," Sybille said. "And I have an awful lot of homework to do."

"*Do* you, now." He drummed his fingers on the table. "Thursday I won't be expected home till ten."

She nodded. "All right."

"Buy some more beer," he said, and walked to the door.

"Terry," Sybille said as he opened it. "What's the name of the lady with the apes?"

He frowned deeply. "Of course it's a secret."

"Of course."

"Ramona Jackson," he said. "Of Sunnyvale."

"And the vice-president? The one who got the sketch as a souvenir?"

"Oldfield."

"Thanks."

He put his finger to his mouth, winked, and left without closing the door. Sybille closed and locked it. Then she went to her desk and wrote down the Ramona Jackson story, to make sure she didn't forget any details.

"'Papa,'" Valerie said from the center of the stage, looking hungrily at the muscular airplane pilot. "'Buy the brute for me.'"

"God, lady, you look like you're about to swallow me," said Rob Segal, who played the pilot. He cringed, and the others on stage burst out laughing.

"I like it," said the director. "Hypatia devours every man she sees, the ones she wants, anyway. You really hit it, Val; it was perfect."

Valerie made a deep curtsy. "It's not hard, once you figure out that none of Shaw's heroines is truly lovable."

"Neither was Shaw," said Rob Segal, and grinned at her. She smiled back and held his eyes until the director appeared at her side. He discussed the final scene again, and Valerie nodded, but her gaze moved past him to take in the stage, partially furnished with the set it would have on opening night, only a week away. She liked being there. She loved make-believe, especially when she could share it with people who loved it as much as she. That was why she liked the theater. On stage, they lived a fantasy and they convinced audiences to do the same: hundreds of people sharing the same make-believe because, for that little while, it seemed real. Of course *Misalliance* was more farfetched than a lot of plays, even silly in places, but it was fun and Hypatia Tarleton was a delicious role.

And Rob Segal, who looked like a Greek god, hadn't taken his eyes off her for the whole rehearsal.

"How about something to eat?" he asked as the cast began to leave. "A bunch of us are going for Mexican food."

Regretfully, Valerie shook her head and gestured toward the shadowy seats beyond the front of the stage. "I've got a date."

"Yeh, I've seen you and him around. I just thought, maybe, you know, some variety." His hand brushed her arm as he turned. "We've been rehearsing, you know, for ages, and I've been wanting to ask you out ... well, anyway. Next time, maybe, if you can cut loose."

"I can cut loose anytime I please," Valerie said coldly.

"Right," he said hastily. "I mean ... sure. I just meant you might, you know, feel you had to, you know, because you've been going together for a long time. I'd understand that. I mean, I'd understand, you know, if that was what you meant. Listen." He scribbled on her copy of *Misalliance*. "You could call me, we could go out or whatever. Just, you know, do something. God, Val, you are so *great;* you're so *smooth*. So anyway, I just thought we could get together, you know? Without the whole cast and everything. So if you want to call me we could, you know, have a good time. Right?"

"Right," Valerie said, amused by his torrent of words. "I'll see you tomorrow. At rehearsal." She left the stage and went to the eighth row of the theater, where Nick sat, his arms folded, watching. "Ready," she said. "Is it a good day for a picnic? It feels like an eternity since I saw the sun."

"It's perfect. Like you." He uncoiled his long body from the narrow seat and stood beside her. "You were terrific up there."

"Thank you, sir. It was better today than yesterday. I almost feel ready for an audience."

"You had one today; I wanted to cheer, but I thought I'd better not remind anybody I was here." He started to tell her how she had dominated the stage, her poise and confidence as magnetic as her beauty; her sense of fun making Hypatia a delight instead of simply a spoiled girl. But he changed his mind. She often seemed restless when he paid her compliments, especially if they sounded extravagant. "You were good with the pilot, the one who thought you were about to swallow him. The two of you made a good pair."

"Thanks." She smiled, thinking about Rob as they left the theater building and came into the cloudless May afternoon. Sunlight filtered through palm trees and slanted across the buff-colored university buildings, turning them a soft gold. "What a wonderful day. I can't believe I've been cooped up every afternoon with this play, missing most of the spring. Let's run."

They ran across the grass like children, skirting flower beds and sculptures and clusters of trees, dodging other students, until they came to the parking lot where Valerie had left her car. "Better," she said, breathless and laughing. Exhilarated, she put her arms around Nick and kissed him. "I can't bear to stand around all day, doing things in bits and pieces. It always seems like nothing is happening."

He kissed her eyes and mouth and the tip of her nose. "Are you sure you want to go to the Baylands?"

"Yes! I've never been there and you promised a million birds. You promised a picnic too. Do we have food in your backpack?"

"We do. A feast. Are you driving or am I?"

"You. You know the way."

In the car she settled back and let out a long sigh. "Freedom. We've been rehearsing too long. Weren't you bored today?"

"I'm never bored watching you. And I learned something. You and Hypatia are two of a kind."

"Oh, no." She glanced at him. "How?"

"Hypatia wants to have things happen."

There was a pause. "You mean when she says she wants to get married, only it's not for love but to have something happen. But I'm not like that; I'd never get married just to have something happen, and you know it. If that's the only way you think we're alike, you're not being very scientific, my learned friend."

"What about buying whatever you want? That's Hypatia in a nutshell. Or she asks her papa to do it for her."

"But I don't buy men and I wouldn't ask my papa to buy me one. Come on, Nick, you know I wouldn't."

"You're right. I do know it. Hold on, I have to decide where we turn, somewhere along here..."

He was trying to shift the conversation, she thought. He got in deeper than he wanted, and now he doesn't want to talk about it anymore. Which is fine with me. But he does think I buy too many things, and keep looking for things to happen. Once he said my ruling passion was pleasure. Well, what if it is? Why can't he just accept me for what I am, instead of *thinking* so much? She studied him, his face absorbed and stern as he looked for landmarks. She loved it when he drove her car; she loved it when he took charge. He definitely acted older than the other men she knew, including Rob Segal, who was, she had to admit it, very young. But, still, Rob was charming, in spite of being young, or maybe because of it, and he was the most gorgeous man she had ever known. He would be like a cool, shady hollow after the bright heat of Nick Fielding.

They drove in silence until they reached the yacht harbor at the end of Embarcadero Road and Nick parked the car. "We'll come back," he said, leaving his pack on the seat. "No picnicking around here."

"What is around here?" Valerie asked, shading her eyes and looking at what seemed to be desolate marshland on both sides.

"I told you: birds. Come on, the place closes in an hour."

Hand in hand they walked past the duck pond and through the Nature Center to a railed boardwalk that seemed to float a few feet above the marsh. Walking along it, Valerie began to see the life around her. At first she had to strain, but as her eyes sharpened she began seeing more, until suddenly everything was alive. A mouse swam through silvery-green water plants; insects crawled along the red-orange parasite that grew on the plants; waterfowl threaded their way through tall cordgrass; and schools of fish sped by in military formation. All around the marsh, black-crowned herons guarded their nests, white-tailed kites and marsh hawks wheeled above, coming in low to snatch insects from the surface of the water, soaring up and out, then turning and diving again and again to the bay.

Nick identified the birds, but Valerie barely heard him. Names weren't important. What held her was the enchantment of the scene: vividly feathered birds flying in formation or in separate circles, the brilliant iridescence of sunlit insects, the muted colors of fish in the dim water, the hum and whispers and cries of the marsh. She was silent until they had turned and walked back and were almost at the car. "I've never seen anything like it," she said. "It's been here all this time and I never knew it. And it's so incredibly beautiful, so different . . ."

"Stick around," he said lightly, to disguise how moved he was: he had never thought she would be so excited or, by her excitement, make him love her more than he thought possible. "There's lots more where this came from."

She did not respond. Nick saw that she was looking out the window on her side of the car, catching a last glimpse of the marshes as they drove away. Not now, he told himself. It's not the time to talk about marriage. But damn it, it never seems like the right time, and she's excited now and happy and why the hell shouldn't I . . . ?

He glanced at Valerie again. Wait, an inner voice said. At least wait for the picnic, when you can really talk.

He couldn't wait; the words tumbled out. "I think we should get married." But his voice was wrong: it was choked and sounded abrupt, almost hard, and he cleared his throat to say it again, more softly, with all the love he felt, when, suddenly, a pickup truck appeared in their lane, coming straight at them as it passed a passenger car. Nick swerved to the shoulder, heart pounding, cursing the truck driver, his knuckles white as he gripped the wheel. The car skidded, kicking up sprays of gravel; a tree branch struck the roof and scraped across Valerie's window with a metallic whine. "Son of a bitch," Nick said through gritted teeth as the truck moved back to its own lane. He turned the wheel and they were back on the road, bucking as the tires caught on the blacktop. The truck was out of sight behind him; the passenger car the truck had passed had driven serenely on. Valerie had not made a sound.

His face grim, breathing hard, Nick turned off at the first intersection and pulled to a stop on the grass at the edge of the road. "Are you all right?" he asked.

"I'm great," Valerie said. "You were terrific. That was really unbelievable."

His eyebrows drew together as he gazed at her. "You weren't afraid?"

"Oh, sure, but that's part of it, isn't it? Everything seems more important when you're afraid. Really incredible."

He shook his head. "As long as something is happening."

"There are times when it's good to have things happen," she said coolly. She sat straight. "Is this where we're having our picnic?"

"It's not the place I planned. Valerie, I'm sorry. This is a hell of a way to propose to a lady one loves. If I'd done it before, I'm sure I'd have done better, but this is my first—"

"Well, I predict it won't be your last," she said.

"Why not?" he asked. "If that's an answer, it's a lousy way to give one."

"I thought it was a nice way, and, yes, it is an answer." Valerie put her hand on his. "Nick, I don't want to talk about this. We've been having such a good time—four, almost five, lovely months—don't ruin it."

"I didn't think I was ruining anything."

"Oh for heaven's sake, you sound like a sulky little boy."

"Sorry," he said tightly, and started the car.

"Well, that wasn't nice, and I apologize, but really, Nick, you do sound awfully young when you get that way."

"When I get what way?"

"Oh, all solemn and pushy. I don't want to marry you, Nick. I don't want to marry anybody right now. I've told you that a few thousand times, about, but you haven't listened. You just want your own way."

"And you want yours."

"Well, that's true." She laughed and leaned across to kiss him. "We're both so stubborn. But we do have fun. Can't we forget all this and just go on the way we've been doing? That's not so awful, is it?" She settled back in her seat and gazed at his stony profile. "What's in your backpack for our picnic? Did you whip up something special?"

He shook his head. "I didn't have time; I just bought some bread and cheese and fruit." He put the car in gear and drove back to the main road. It was the wrong time, he thought. Next time I won't rush into it. There's a whole future at stake; that's worth some patience. Valerie is right: we're having a wonderful time; there's no need to change anything now. I'll wait for a better time.

He did not let himself think that a better time might never come.

Sybille had begun as a receptionist at KNEX-TV in her first year at Stanford; later she became a secretary. By her third year she was an assistant producer. She also became a scriptwriter one busy morning when the noon news writer became ill and she neatly took over, getting a script to the anchor team who read it on camera before anyone realized she had done it. She was good—she wrote quickly and her sentences were sharp and dramatic—and after that she wrote scripts for newscasts and local programs, in addition to her work as assistant producer. Every job taught her something else about the station and, though her memory seemed infallible, she stored the information in precise outlines in a set of notebooks she kept and read at night in bed.

The only purchase she made for her furnished attic apartment was a large-screen television set, and she sat in front of it for hours, writing criticisms of programs, ideas for new shows, commercials, promotions, even station breaks. Usually she watched late at night, after going out with men and women she had met in class or at work, or after having someone in her bed. She went out or brought someone home every night, because she could not bear to be alone. If she planned carefully, she could fill most of her waking hours, and when she had to be alone—when everyone else left, or she couldn't stand whoever she had brought home to bed another minute—then she turned on the television set and it was almost as good as having someone there. At least, she did not have to listen to silence.

What filled her thoughts and took most of her energy was her work. Every time she walked into KNEX-TV—five days a week, four hours a day—she knew it was where she belonged. The station pulled her deep inside its fascination and wonder, making her an insider who sent words and pictures to hundreds of thousands of people who had no idea what went on behind the scenes. She knew she didn't really belong, because she was still a student, not a full-time professional, but no one made fun of her, and most of them even helped her learn. Even if they didn't, it wouldn't matter. This was where she wanted to be.

Her desk was one of many in a large newsroom crowded with Teletype machines, file cabinets, typewriters on rolling stands, coffee machines and water coolers. Along one wall was a curved desk used by the news teams; behind it was a mural of the Bay Area with Palo Alto in the center. The desk was empty most of the time; the work of putting together the newscast was done at the writers' and producer's desks.

"Syb, honey, there's a white space in the middle of my script," said Dawn Danvers, one half of the early evening news team. She was blond and sparkling, with surprised eyebrows and a wide smile, and she wore silks and suedes on the air. "If you don't give me something to say, it's gonna be awful quiet when we go on."

"I'm waiting for a story," Sybille replied distantly. She detested Dawn Danvers, who was nothing but a big smile and an empty head. "Story and film, two minutes with a ten-second lead; it should be here within an hour."

"An hour! Honey, that only gives me a half hour to study it; you wouldn't do that to me, I know you wouldn't. You find me another story real quick."

Sybille gave her a brief look. "I was told to go with this one."

"Well, but if you don't have it you don't have it. Anyway, this is your show, and they'll go with whatever you have; they think you're wonderful, you know that. Get a backup; have something ready, just in case. Come on, honey, give me a break."

Sybille clenched her teeth. Don't call me honey, she said silently.

"Come on, honey, make something up, for God's sake! I don't care what you do; just don't ever give me a script with white space in it! Otherwise I get this nervous stomach and I can't stand it; I can't stand being sick. Okay? *Okay?* I want an answer!"

Don't order me around, Sybille said furiously to herself. Her hands were shaking and she gripped the edge of her desk. "I can write another story, and you can study it, but we won't use it."

"We'll use it if I want to. I'll make sure of that. Thanks, honey, you're a blessing. Oh, and make sure it's dynamite. I love to read the juicy ones."

Sybille watched her as she left the newsroom. Bitch, she fumed silently. Rich and pretty—well, fairly pretty, if you like vacuous blondes, and she expects everybody to bend over backward to make her life easier. Like Valerie. They're two of a kind: they want what they want and the hell with everybody else.

She sat down at her typewriter. Dawn Danvers wants a story in a hurry. She wants a juicy one. And she'll make sure we use it.

Well, I can give her just what she wants.

She reached into the bottom drawer of her desk and pulled out a pile of handwritten notes, and a sketch. She would have liked more time to gather details, and she didn't have the film she wanted for it, but she couldn't pass up this perfect chance. She smiled as she began to type. I'll give her something that will make her reputation. And my future.

For the next fifteen minutes she wrote steadily. She really had a lot, she thought, especially after getting the sketch. That had been the scary part: slipping into Lawrence Oldfield's office while the cleaning crew was next door, rifling through the file marked "Jackson," and grabbing the drawing and getting out. She'd wanted to stay and read the whole file—all those letters and memoes, staring at her, filled with secret information!—but she couldn't; she had to leave before the maids came in to turn out the lights and lock the door. But it was all right, she thought, typing rapidly. She had enough. She had her story.

When she was through, she skimmed the story quickly, making a few revisions. Then, gathering the pages together, she went to the film library and found some stock film. An hour and a half later, Dawn Danvers read the story on the air in her sweetly modulated voice, while Sybille watched from the control room.

"Stanford University has a new sweetheart, KNEX learned today: the Sunnyvale Sweetheart, they may be calling her, or the Engineering Angel, or, better yet, the Benefactress We All Go Ape Over."

A film of Sunnyvale appeared on the screen, the camera closing in on a residential area of large homes.

"Heiress Ramona Jackson, ninety-one, has lived in Sunnyvale all her life. The daughter of a prominent oilman and the widow of an oil and gas engineer, she's dreamed for years of giving an engineering building to Stanford in memory of her husband and father. But Ms. Jackson has another dream too, and she's decided to bring both of her dreams to Stanford University."

The film of Sunnyvale gave way on the screen to shots of the ape house at the San Francisco Zoo. Sybille would have preferred film of Ramona Jackson's apes, but there was no time. Dawn talked sweetly on.

"For the past fifteen years Ms. Jackson has provided a home and companionship to a number of apes, teaching them sign language and etiquette in comfortable surroundings that make them seem like members of her family. Lately, it appears she's become concerned about their care when she's no longer here, especially that of her favorite ape, Ethelred, named for an ancient king of England."

The Stanford campus appeared on the screen, the camera moving past classroom buildings to the engineering building.

"According to a high-ranking Stanford official, Ms. Jackson has promised fifty million dollars to the University for the construction of the Ethelred Engineering Building and Ape House." A small giggle teetered on the edge of Dawn's ambrosial lips, but was quickly squelched. On the screen, the engineering building was replaced by the drawing Sybille had lifted from Oldfield's file, a boldly sketched cartoon of a lively monkey perched on the tower of a structure that had "Engineering" scribbled over the door. "Ms. Jackson sketched her dream building for university officials, perhaps to give the architects a head start. Other details have not been released, but in the past, Lyle Wilson, chairman of the engineering department, has been quoted as saying work in the areas of electronic and optical and computer engineering would be expanded if funds were available. And of course there will be a home for the apes."

The blond prettiness of Dawn Danvers once again filled the screen. "It's a sweetheart of a day for Stanford and it's good news for Palo Alto and the whole Bay Area. The only question we have is whether the administration will let us nonacademics visit the Ethelred Engineering Building and Ape House. It's so much closer, you know, than the San Francisco Zoo." She paused and smiled. "That's all for this evening; network news is next; we'll see you tomorrow. Thanks for joining us."

She held her smile while her co-anchor said good night and the red light on his camera went off and they knew the commercial was rolling. "That is the *damndest* story," Dawn said to her co-anchor, and they talked about it for a minute and then forgot it. It was just one of so many that they read and never thought much about, even while they were reading them. It was amusing, but there was no reason to remember it.

But others did. They paid attention, they talked about it, and they remembered it.

"Not true," Nick said, watching Dawn Danvers tell the story of Ramona Jackson. He was making dinner and Valerie was watching him. "God damn it, it was a joke!"

"What was a joke?" she asked idly. They had spent the afternoon in bed, the first time in almost a month they had had his apartment to themselves for more than an hour or two, and she was feeling slow and lazy as she sipped her wine. She had barely glanced at the newscast.

"Listen," Nick said and she heard Dawn say, ". . . let us nonacademics visit the Ethelred Engineering Building and Ape House. It's so much closer, you know, than the San Francisco Zoo."

"Ape house? What's that about?"

"That was the joke," he said. "But the jackass who wrote that newscast doesn't know it. How the hell did they get hold of it? And where did they get that cartoon? That was another joke."

"I wonder if Sybille had something to do with it," Valerie said. "She writes one of their newscasts; I don't remember which. What did you mean about it being a joke?"

Nick leaned against the counter, arms folded. "There's a terrific lady in Sunnyvale named Ramona Jackson, over ninety, full of energy and humor, and she's giving Stanford a chunk of money for a new engineering building. It took her a while to decide—in fact, she was leaning toward Cal Tech—but Lyle Wilson, the chairman of engineering, put on a six-month courtship and convinced her to give it to us. I got in on it when he brought three of us to dinner with her one night; he wanted to show off his top graduate students and have us talk about our projects. Lyle worked like crazy for this building, and a few of us helped him; we made a film of what the department had done in the past, we put together picture books and reports...but mainly it was Lyle. He worked for a solid six months and it paid off."

"But what about the apes?"

"Monkeys. I don't know who started calling them apes. She has four pet monkeys in her greenhouse and nobody in her family will promise to take care of them. She'll probably give them to the zoo or something, I don't know what she'll do, but at a meeting with her lawyer and university lawyers, and some university people—one of them was a vice-president—Lyle told me when they were disagreeing over details, she said if it kept dragging on she might make the gift contingent on a home for her monkeys, named after the oldest. Who is called Ethelred the Unready, God knows why. She drew a quick sketch and gave it to the vice-president and they all laughed and went on talking."

"And that's the story that was on the news?"

"Straight. As if it's absolute truth."

"Well, but so what? It's their problem, isn't it? When the real story comes out, they'll look like idiots and they'll have to apologize, and that will be that."

"I don't know." He began to pace around the small kitchen. "She's a very proud lady. Her family's lived here for four generations and she spends a lot of time worrying about reputations, hers and all the Jacksons', living and dead. She's got a good sense of humor, but how upset is she going to be over this? She could be a laughingstock, and if that makes Cal Tech look better to her all of a sudden... *God damn it.*" He picked up an orange and slammed it into the sink, splitting it open. "Lyle's been as excited as a kid over this building; all of us have. We feel like we've been part of it; almost as if we're leaving a legacy when we go." He took a few more paces. "I'll have to call him; he may want us to meet with her again. Try to calm the troubled waters."

Valerie was looking at the split orange, her eyebrows raised. "You're getting awfully worked up, Nick; you can't be sure any of that will happen. It was just one newscast, after all; probably nobody watched, and even if they did they wouldn't remember—"

"They'll remember. Money always makes people remember, and this is a hell of a lot of money. God damn son of a bitch—"

"Oh, stop it," Valerie said. "I hate it when you get all wound up like this. We haven't had this much time together for ages and now you'll brood over something that has nothing to do with us and be thoroughly unpleasant and that's not what I expected for tonight."

Nick stopped pacing and gazed at her. "Well, I guess this isn't what I expected, either. I didn't expect you to say this has nothing to do with us right after I've told you how I feel about it. I didn't expect you to tell me I shouldn't get all wound up about a mess that bothers the hell out of me and could hurt a man I admire, who's worked damned hard for this building. But that doesn't seem to matter to you. What the hell does matter to you? Fun, right? The campus doesn't matter. I don't matter—"

"You would if you'd just relax and have a good time! How can I say you matter to me when you're always making a fuss about something or other that I don't care about at all? The other day you had to go to some meeting about campus politics or something, and you belong to a dozen committees—"

"Two, but who's counting?" He paused, then took a deep breath. "Come on, Valerie, can we have a truce? It seems like we're always quarreling lately and it always comes from nowhere—one minute everything's wonderful and the next there's a battlefield. I never know what's going to set us off and I'd like to put an end to it."

Valerie nodded slowly. "Maybe we should."

Alarmed, he stared at her. "That isn't what I meant."

"I know it isn't. But do you know when we started quarreling? When you started talking about getting married. Ever since then, you've been impatient and critical and not nice the way you used to be."

"I could say the same about you. I'm sorry I jumped the gun and asked you to marry me, but I don't know why that would make us quarrel and snipe at each other, do you?"

She shook her head.

"Well, I apologize for my part in it. You know I'd never hurt you if I could help it. And I don't mean to criticize you—"

"Don't," Valerie said. There was such tenderness in his eyes when he looked at her that her heart sank. *Oh, God, what am I doing? I don't deserve him.* But then she thought, Damn it, I'm tired of thinking that! I'm tired of feeling he's better and nobler and smarter than I am. I'd love to be with somebody who's a little dumb, just for awhile. Rob, or somebody like him; somebody who doesn't demand anything.

She felt miserable. All she wanted was to get out of Nick's apartment, get away from him, be alone for a while.

She stood up, and Nick quickly put his hand on her arm. "You're not going, you can't be. What the hell is going on, do you know?"

"A lot, I guess. I'm going, Nick; I'll call you, or something, but I don't want to talk anymore."

"But I do. Listen, Valerie darling, you can't leave with everything up in the air. It doesn't make any sense—a few quarrels—that's no reason to walk out. My God, you know how much I love you, how much I want for the two of us...I can't imagine not being with you and I know it's not what you want—"

"Yes it is." She drew back from him, quivering to get away. "Don't you understand? I do want it. Everything is so damned intense around here, it's like living in a hothouse! We have so much fun, Nick, I've told you and told you, but you just won't leave it alone. It isn't enough for you. You have to make everything into a dramatic production, and the only place I can handle that is on the stage when I know it's make-believe."

"That's not—"

"Don't talk, just listen for a minute! You're so good at talking, you can always outargue me, but this time just be quiet. Will you?"

He nodded and Valerie felt like crying. She wanted to put her arms around him and kiss away the pain in his eyes and kiss the sadness from his wonderful mouth that had given her such pleasure, but she fought against herself and took a step toward the door. "Remember the day we were at the Baylands and I was so excited? There's so much that I don't know yet...I thought I'd seen it all, you know, I've been all over Europe and Asia and India and this country, and I figured I'd seen pretty much everything. But I haven't always looked in the right places. You taught me that and I have a lot of plans, and I'm not going to mess them up by being tied down with a family or anything ordinary or predictable. I don't want to know what I'll be doing tomorrow! Can't you understand that? You understand so much about me, it's one of the things I love best about you. I'm asking you to understand this. I want to do whatever I want, and go where I want, and meet people and go out with them and not have to worry about hurting your feelings—or anybody's feelings. I want to have a good time without feeling guilty about it. I don't think that's a lot to ask. And I've told you all this before; I hardly kept it a secret."

"No, you didn't, but you liked—"

"You said you'd listen and not interrupt!"

"I listened. Now it's my turn. You've liked everything about me that you're busy trashing. You liked having somebody take care of you, drive your car, help you with your homework, listen when you wanted to talk... You liked it that I was older than your friends. You liked it when I was dramatic because it made it seem as if something was happening. You liked knowing I wasn't thrilled when you batted your eyes at that asshole who played the pilot in the—"

"I never batted my eyes!"

"The hell you didn't. You play with people, Valerie, and you know it. You're spoiled and self-centered and restless—"

"Why do you want me, then?" Her eyes blazed at him. "What's wrong with being restless at twenty? When do I get to have fun, if not now? You're right, I like having somebody do things for me, and it was nice that you were older because you weren't always flying off somewhere the way—"

"The way you do."

"I don't! I've been here for five months, with you, remember? I just can't stand it that you're always standing over me, waiting for me to make decisions. I don't want to make any more decisions than I have to, not for a long time, and I wish you'd let me be the way I am and not keep trying to change me!"

She had reached the door and opened it and instantly Nick was beside her. "I don't want to change you. I love you for what you are; I have from the day I met you."

"That's not true." She looked at him steadily. "You had an idea of what we'd be like together, or what we ought to be like together, sort of like writing one of your computer programs. You thought you knew what would work best and that's how you wanted us to be. Me especially. You think I spend too much on clothes and go to too many parties and don't pay enough attention to my grades and—"

"But those are little things that don't matter. What I love about you is your spirit and your—"

"Oh, *spirit*. All that means is I'm easier to talk to and better in bed than one of your computers. You've got this *image* of me, Nick, and I can't live up to it. I don't even want to. I want to do my own thing in my own way and I can't do that when I'm with you. I guess I can't . . . I'm not always sure."

"If you're not sure, then give us time. Why would you destroy what we've built for the past five months?"

"Because I feel not good enough and guilty and . . . smothered!" She shook her head sharply. "I'm sorry, Nick, but I don't want to see you anymore."

"Don't say that!"

"I have to. I don't want to see you at all. I've thought about it—"

"You haven't thought about it! Not until today!"

"I've thought about it for a long time. I just didn't tell you."

"You thought about it while you were making love to me?"

"They don't have anything to do with each other. I loved making love to you."

"*You can fake sincerity.* That's what you said that day at the television station. That's it, isn't it? Making love to the camera, you called it. Is that like making love to me? You said it wasn't hard, at least for you, because if you knew what people wanted you could make them believe almost anything."

"Oh, damn it, Nick, I hate it when people tell me what I said a long time ago. I don't even remember it."

She was fighting her feelings again. She couldn't bear the stunned look on his face; her hands trembled with the desire to hold him so she could kiss him and wipe out everything they had said. But she fought it off. "Goodbye, Nick. I hope"—she made an awkward gesture, trying to find a good word on which to end—"you find somebody better than me."

She turned and stepped through the door, out of his apartment, for the last time. "Valerie," Nick said quietly. She turned and he touched her cheek with his hand, holding it gently along the length of her face. "Goodbye, my love," he said, very softly, and then he was the one who closed the door.

Chapter
5

veryone beamed, clustering around her with con-
gratulations and little pats on her arm. The morn-
ing after the Ramona Jackson broadcast, Sybille
felt like a heroine. She was the center of attention,
the star of the station. She had scooped every
newspaper and radio and television station in the Bay Area.

"Hell of a lucky break," said one of the directors, his arm casually
around Sybille's shoulders.

"Lucky, hell," scoffed someone else, "Sybille *found* that story!"

"Well, whatever," the director said. "But how come it didn't leak? A
ton of money, a nutty old bat like Ramona Jackson, apes in the attic—
how the hell did they keep it under wraps?"

The others shrugged; they didn't know. When Terence Beauregard
the Third heard the question, he dismissed it with a wave of his hand.
"You never know when or how a story's gonna break. You just have to
be ready. The way our little Sybille is. Always ready."

They drifted back to work, but the story was revived when Laurence
B. Oldfield, vice-president of the university, issued a statement. "The
story about an engineering and ape building at Stanford is ridiculous,

absolutely false, and defamatory. The university is consulting with its attorneys on possible future action."

"Well, what would you expect them to say?" they shrugged in the newsroom of KNEX-TV.

The news editor of the *Palo Alto Times-Crier* called and was switched to Sybille's phone. "Details," he begged her. "I haven't got any. Terrific story, if it's true, but Jackson isn't answering her door or her phone, and the university's saying no comment and I'm stuck. What can you give me?"

"Nothing," Sybille said coolly; she didn't know yet what she would do with the story, but one thing she wouldn't do was give it to anyone else, especially anyone who thought it might not be true. "We're still working on it for a follow-up; I don't have any more than you heard last night." She hung up, but the telephone rang again, and then again and again, throughout the morning, as reporters from newspapers and television stations in San Jose, San Francisco, Oakland, Los Angeles and the wire services called in. Sybille fended them off, while excitement coursed through her. She had her scoop and everyone knew. Everyone thought she was wonderful, and no one was criticizing her for anything.

Midmorning, Beauregard called Sybille into his office. "Quite a story. Congratulations."

"Thank you. I owe it to you."

"Well, yes indeed, some of it you do indeed."

Sybille's look sharpened. "All of it."

"*All of it?* The drawing? Where'd that come from?"

"I found it. But I wouldn't have known anything about it if you hadn't told me. It's because of you, Terry—"

"Found it where?"

"I can't tell you."

"You'll tell me."

Sybille shook her head. "You wouldn't ask me to reveal my sources."

He stared at her through narrowed eyes. "And the stuff she teaches them? Sign language and etiquette? Where'd you get that?"

There was barely a pause. "One of my sources."

"Who?"

"I can't tell you, Terry. I can't reveal—"

"To me you can."

"Not even to you."

He was glaring at her. "Where'd you get the quote from Lyle Wilson about the projects they want to work on?"

"The *LA Times*. They did a story on engineering in California."

"So you did do some research."

"Of course."

"And you have reliable sources."

"As reliable as yours."

He shot out of his chair. "What the hell does that mean? How the fuck do you know who I talk to?"

"I don't! I only meant...It doesn't mean anything, Terry; I didn't mean to upset you."

"Who's upset? I just like to know what's going on. You got that? No games, no surprises. You got that?"

"Yes."

"So who told you about sign language and etiquette? Where'd you get the drawing?"

Sybille shook her head.

"Okay, little lady, but you just remember, it's on your head."

"Not just mine! Terry, I have the station behind me!"

"As much as we can. As *much* as we *can*."

"You told me the station always stands behind its people!"

"As *much* as we *can*."

She sat very still. "You gave me the story, Terry."

He let out an elaborate sigh. "Sounds like we're back where we started, sweetie. I gave you a cute *story* I said we couldn't use." His telephone rang and he answered it. "Okay," he said. "Hold him half a minute, then I'll talk to him." He replaced the receiver. "Oldfield," he said to Sybille. "V-p of the university; thinks he's a fucking tiger. Don't worry; I'll cover for you." He shook his head in mock amazement. "What a little wonder you are, shaking Stanford up the way you did. And the network's looking at us, too, I hear." He walked around his desk. "Just keep in touch, okay, before you write about apes anymore." He gave her rear end a firm pinch and scooted her out the door.

"Okay," he said to his secretary, and picked up his telephone.

"Where'd it come from?" Oldfield demanded. "Who's this 'high-ranking university official'? There isn't one and you know it. You made it up. It's false, it's damaging to the university, and we want to know where it came from and what you're going to do about it."

"It came from an impeccably reliable source," Beauregard said easily. He sat back in his chair, prepared to enjoy himself. He closed his eyes and pictured Laurence B. Oldfield's wife Marjorie lying beneath him, making little sounds of excitement, and then, later, chattering away as they lay together and he asked questions about the university, especially about the delicious little story she'd gotten from her husband about Ramona Jackson and her apes. "*Impeccably* reliable," he repeated to Oldfield. "We're not irresponsible, you know, Larry; we're the best there is." He gave a modest cough. "As for what we're going to do about it, I'd say at the moment not a thing. We might do some poking around for a follow-up, but I'm not even sure of that right now. We're looking into it, of course; that's our job, too."

"Looking into it," repeated Oldfield furiously. "You fucking well might have looked into it before you put it on the air."

My, my, thought Beauregard, such language from a university official.

"—legal department," Oldfield was saying. "They're looking at our options. You're all at risk, you know; every damn one of you who worked on that newscast—*and whoever broke into my office and stole private papers from my files*—but I'm not waiting for the lawyers; I'm telling you right now we're demanding a public retraction and apology. On that same news show, read by the same woman, what's her name, the blonde, explaining that none of the story was true—"

"None of it?" repeated Beauregard slyly. "Larry, did she say fifty million?"

"That's not the issue!"

"Did she say she wanted the university to take care of her apes?"

"Monkeys. It was a joke."

"Monkeys? Well, we'll definitely issue a correction on that; we shouldn't have said apes if it was monkeys. But, a joke? You want us to tell our viewing audience that Ms. Jackson joked about monkeys when making her donation to the university? And drew a cute little cartoon?"

"We're demanding that you tell your viewing audience the story was distorted, parts of it were fabricated, your sources were wrong...you figure out how to say it; you must have had plenty of practice if this is an example of how you work."

"Well, now, we think we work pretty well around here," Beauregard said comfortably. "We'll make that correction about the apes, Larry, but unless you give me evidence of other errors, that's about all we'll do, as far as I can see."

"In addition," said Oldfield as if Beauregard had not spoken, "we want to know the source of that story, or sources, assuming there are any. I doubt it, but if you don't give us names we'll take it that you made it up. You and this Morgen woman, the producer, and whoever wrote it. We have a right to those names and I want them now. One of them broke into my office and I want to know who it was!"

"Hold on there, Larry. You're throwing around a lot of accusations, and I don't want to hear them. How do you know somebody broke in? Your office is open a lot of the time, right? I don't think you want to accuse my staff of illegalities when you don't have any facts. As for your rights, with all due respect, you have no right to any names, not one. We couldn't put on a responsible newscast—"

"There was nothing responsible about that newscast!"

"—if we couldn't promise confidentiality to our sources to protect them from frivolous lawsuits, for God's sake, just because they're courageous enough to tell the truth—"

"It was a lie!"

"—so of course you understand that as a dedicated journalist, I could never even consider—"

"Bullshit."

"Well." There was a silence. "I won't give you those names, Larry; you didn't really expect me to. What the hell would you do with them anyway? The story's out."

"Get them to retract it. You know damn well that's what we'd do with them."

"Well, maybe they would and maybe they wouldn't. Come on, Larry, what the hell, this is a little story, a wrinkle; it doesn't hurt you a damn bit. It maybe shook up your stuffy academics, but that's—"

"She's talking about withdrawing the money!" Oldfield sucked in his breath. "That's off the record, God damn it, if you use it I'll nail you on it."

"I don't believe it. Why would she? What's she going to do with all that dough, for Christ's sake?"

"Give it to Cal Tech or Berkeley. They were on her list from the beginning, until Lyle Wilson talked her out of it."

"Why?"

"Because some people don't have your thick hide, you bastard! She didn't like being made a fool of!"

"Well, what the hell, she was sweet-talked once, she can be again. Talk to your guy Wilson. Maybe he's screwing her; he can do it in bed."

There was a silence. "I want a retraction," said Oldfield tightly. "Tonight. On that same newscast."

"Sorry, Larry, you won't get it."

"Then you'll hear from our lawyers," Oldfield snapped, and slammed down the telephone.

My, my, thought Beauregard, a little excitement around here for a change. But his face was thoughtful as he hung up and swiveled his chair to look through the glass wall of his office at the newsroom, and Sybille, at her desk. She'd sounded convincing. She probably had her sources; she knew it was one thing to jazz up a story and a whole different ball game to make something up out of whole cloth, or to steal a document. She'd done a nice job, produced a nice little story; she'd just better be covered. She was damn good; he'd hate to have to get rid of her.

Valerie and Rob Segal left the theater building and walked across the quadrangle. He took her hand, enthusiastically squeezing her fingers until she jerked them away. "Hey!" he exclaimed as she quickened her stride. "Something I said?"

She shook her head. "I don't want to be late for class."

"Well, neither do I, but we can be friendly while we walk, okay?"

"I just don't feel like it," Valerie said shortly and kept walking.

"Jesus," he muttered. "How'm I supposed to know what's coming next with you..." They walked in silence to a long, low classroom building fronted by wide steps where students sprawled, reading, eating, and talking in small groups. Valerie threaded her way among them and Rob followed, glowering. "We still on for tonight?"

"I suppose," she said and walked into the cool dimness of the building.

"Jesus," said Rob again, louder this time, but before he could say more Valerie had darted ahead.

"Sybille!" she cried. "I haven't seen you for so long! How are you?"

Sybille's eyes brightened as Valerie ran to her. "Oh, Valerie, I was hoping I'd see you. So many things have been happening...yesterday was the most incredible day of my life, practically..."

"Good, you can tell me all about it. I'm so bored I'd love to hear about something happening. What was it?"

Sybille looked curiously at Rob, hovering nearby. "If you're busy I can tell you another time."

"Of course I'm not busy." Valerie turned to Rob. "Six-thirty?"

He nodded. "Right."

"I'll see you then." She took Sybille's arm. "How about a lemonade, or something?"

"You have a class," Rob blurted.

"Well, actually, not for an hour," Valerie said calmly. "Do you have a class?" she asked Sybille.

"No," Sybille said, erasing her history class from her thoughts.

"Then let's go."

Ignoring Rob as easily as Valerie did, Sybille turned and they walked back across the square and past a quadrangle to the Student Union. "It's too beautiful to go inside," Valerie said, and they took a table on the terrace. "Now tell me about your incredible day. I need a fun story; everything is so dull lately."

"I didn't know you were dating other boys," Sybille said.

"Well, now you know."

"But you're still dating Nick."

"No." Valerie was rummaging in her book bag for her wallet, so Sybille could not see her face. "I decided marriage wasn't for me."

Sybille gasped. "You were *married*? I didn't know...when were you..."

"No, of course not." She paused. Oh, what the hell, she thought; she's so awfully anxious, and she's harmless. "But going with Nick is about as close to being married as you can get. He doesn't date; the word isn't in his vocabulary. He *mates*. It got to be too much and I broke it off. Lemonade," she said to the waitress, then stared moodily at her spoon. "I wish people weren't so *busy*," she said. "They're always doing and planning and working, and then talking about what they're doing and planning and working on. It makes me nervous. And they always expect me to listen and nod and look enthusiastic, as if I'm a cheering section or crew on a boat...or a wife."

"Well," Sybille said after a moment of silence. "I guess I shouldn't tell you what I've been doing and working on."

"Oh." Valerie looked up and smiled, the warm, generous smile that always made others forget how wrapped up in herself she had been only a moment before. "That wasn't nice of me; I totally ignored you and you were so excited about your incredible day. Say you forgive me, and then tell me all about it."

"Of course I forgive you, don't be silly. If you really want to hear what happened..." Valerie nodded, so intent on her now that Sybille felt as if she were the only person in the world Valerie cared about. "It's something that happened at the station, just yesterday, well, actually the day before but everything sort of developed yesterday; everybody made it seem so terrific..."

As soon as she heard the name Ramona Jackson, Valerie wished she could stop Sybille in midsentence. She didn't want to hear about it. It brought back that whole awful evening with Nick; their angry quarrel still echoed in her mind. But she'd let herself in for it and she couldn't hurt Sybille by cutting her off.

"I saw it," she said when Sybille finished. "I wondered if you'd had anything to do with it. It's a crazy story." She paused. Maybe she could get Sybille to talk about something else. "How do you put together a story like that? Do you interview everyone?"

"Sometimes. I didn't on this one; I trusted the person who told me about it."

"Did you? Such an odd story. You didn't check it with other people?"

"I didn't have to! You get to know when you have to and when you don't. This guy who told me was sleeping with the wife of somebody at the university. A vice-president," she added wildly, not caring whether it was true or not. "Terry said I was fantastic for finding that story and he'd bring me with him if he went to the network."

"You found it yourself?"

"Of course I did. I found that sketch too; no one helped me. I brought them to Terry and he loved the whole thing and told me to go ahead with it. It was one of his *moments* he's always talking about."

"Moments?" Valerie was listening intently, and Sybille felt herself expand.

"Human interest. Moments in people's lives that an audience can identify with. Things that are more interesting than facts and figures about crop damage or pollution or even a new building. This story made the new building mean something to people, and it was so good it didn't need much to make it perfect: it was funny, and still part of a serious story. When I finished with it, it had a little bit of everything."

Valerie's interest was piqued. "What does that mean: it didn't need much to make it perfect? You have to use what you have."

"We do our best with what we have," Sybille corrected, as if she were the teacher. "Most news is so dull you have to work on it to grab people's interest."

"Invent it, you mean."

"No, of course not." She studied Valerie to see if she were baiting her and decided she wasn't. "Not invent. Just write it in a way that makes people pay attention. If you know what you're doing you can put a quote in a different context, give it a new slant, a new emphasis, add a little color, maybe a few details, and then you've got something that will keep your audience from wandering off somewhere. And they don't care; they don't even remember it five minutes after it's over. But you do. You know that for two minutes and thirty seconds you had a perfect piece, and if you wrote and produced it, you remember it. And so do the professionals. That's how reputations are made."

Valerie nodded. She was getting bored again; tired of Sybille's slightly pompous intensity and energy. She pushed her lemonade away. It was awful; it had no flavor. Nothing had any flavor lately; everything was flat and dull and dreary. I want Nick, she thought. I want to talk to him, and hear him laugh. I want to laugh with him. I want to see his eyes light up when I say something he likes. I want to lie underneath him and on top of him. I want him to hold me.

She couldn't believe it; she'd never let herself get into such a mess before. And it was beginning to look as if she wasn't going to have much fun, or be interested in anybody, or even enjoy a glass of lemonade, until she got herself out of it. But for right now she was really very bored with talk about television. She fastened her book bag and stood up. "Congratulations. I'm glad you're so set there. It's nice to see people making a success of things."

"Wait, I'll walk with you," Sybille said. "Are you going to class?"

"I suppose."

"So am I."

They walked back the way they had come. "Rob seems nice," Sybille said. "He's incredibly handsome."

Valerie sighed. "Rob is a little boy dressed up like a college student dressed up like a fabulously successful salesman, which he'll be one of these days."

"He didn't seem to be selling you on anything."

"I'm a tough customer. What about this Terry character you talked about?"

"What about him?"

"I don't know. Something in your voice. Is he somebody special?"

"I hate him. I have to work for him." Sybille stopped walking. "I'm going this way; I'm going to the library. I'll see you around."

"I thought you had a class."

"Yes, but I need a book. See you." She walked away, almost scurrying across the pavement.

Valerie shook her head. All I did was ask about Terry, whoever he is, and she got her back up. She's probably sleeping with him. But how was I supposed to know he was a sacred cow and I couldn't even ask a question about him?

She walked on, alone, scuffing the brick path with her moccasins.

Two whole days since I've seen Nick. We haven't been apart for two whole days since January. Five months.

It wasn't the two days that was bothering her as much as knowing she would not see him again. That was it: she couldn't bear the thought of not seeing him anymore. She gave a kick to a stone in her path and sent it careening into a tree trunk. *Damn it.* Why is everything so complicated?

The bell for her class rang and she turned to enter the building. But she stopped in the loggia. I can't. I can't sit in class and listen to what English poets said about love and desire. I'd rather hear what Nick says about it. I'd rather he showed me what he feels about it. I'm tired of missing him. All I have to do is call him and he'll ask me to come to dinner and everything will be fine.

She turned and almost ran across the campus, waving at friends who called to her, but going on until she reached her dormitory. She shared a suite with three other girls, each of them in a private room off the living room. No one was there when she arrived, but she went into her own room anyway. She shut the door and sat on the edge of her bed and reached for the telephone. But she could not pick it up.

He won't be home; he works all day today. Well, but I could call him at work. He doesn't like to be bothered at work. But he'd be glad to hear from me. He'd be glad to hear me say...

What? What will I say to him?

She lay back on her bed and stared unseeing out the window. I'd say I want him and I want us to be the way we were before. No more. No less. And he'll say the same things he's already said. And I'll say the same things. And we'll be where we were before. And I'll get mad at him and forget how much I missed him. And then we'll be fighting.

I don't want any of that. But I want Nick.

My God, I am very mixed up about this guy.

She leaped off the bed and paced around her room, finally going into the living room and standing beside the window, shaded by a towering palm tree that swayed slightly in the breeze. There's nothing I can do but forget him. I can't call him; I can't write to him; he'd be more impossible than ever if I did that. He wouldn't think I'd come back to have a good time; he'd think I'd given in. He'd think we were on our way to the altar.

He'd be so serious.

Damn it, why did I have to fall in love with someone who doesn't know how to play?

Oh, no, I'm not in love with him, she told herself swiftly and firmly. I've just let myself get involved; I've let him take up too much space in my life.

It will be a long time before that happens again, with anybody.

She picked up her books and walked back across the campus, to her classroom. She'd be late, but that didn't matter so much. Right now it would be better to think about whatever the English poets said about love and desire than to think about Nick. Maybe poetry would calm her down.

But poetry didn't do it, and neither did anything else all that long day, and by the time she returned to her room she was tense and angry at herself and wanting something to happen. In her mailbox was a note from Rob, reminding her that he'd see her at six-thirty. She crumpled it up. He was so young. And uncomplicated. And deadly dull. She wanted something dramatic, and Rob wasn't it.

Also in her mail was a telephone message from Andy Barlow, a lawyer in Palo Alto who was a friend of her father's, inviting her to a dinner party for that night. She called him back. "We just decided to get together," he said. "Very casual, mostly university people. I saw your folks the other day in New York and told them I'd be keeping an eye on you. Say you'll come."

"I'll come," said Valerie. It was better than Rob. And by the time she arrived at the Barlows' house she had almost succeeded in pushing away the memory of Rob's anger when she broke their date, and all thoughts of Nick. She concentrated on having a good time.

"Valerie, I'd like you to meet Laurence Oldfield," said Andy Barlow as he took her about the room, and she smiled and held out her hand.

"I don't often meet students at dinner parties," Oldfield said, holding her hand, struck by her beauty and a poise seldom found in students. Money, Oldfield thought, and these off-campus dinner parties, friends of her parents, connections, influence. But she was also a good listener, as he discovered in the hour before dinner when they had cocktails on the terrace. Answering her questions, he found himself talking about his grown children, his sailboat, his work at the university, and his much-younger wife who was restless and dissatisfied and wanted to travel around the world.

"I promised her we would when I retire," he said. By now they were at the dinner table and he was ignoring his soup to talk to Valerie. His wife Marjorie was at the other end of the table. "That's only three more years, and I'm doing my best to make them easy. No scandals, no conflicts, no messes to leave my successor."

"There must be some scandals at Stanford," said Valerie challeng-ingly. "Even if they're little ones."

Oldfield smiled and shook his head. "We don't allow them. It's hard enough to run a university these days without someone coming along and muddying the waters."

"But there's a lady named Ramona Jackson," said Valerie innocently. She took a sip of chowder and looked up to see Oldfield's startled eyes. She was so bored; she thought maybe she could shake him up a little. "That's such an odd story," she said brightly. "And quite charming."

"Charming?"

"Well, poor thing, she's worried about her pets. Most people are so selfish they don't worry about anyone, but here she is, about to make a magnificent gift that will make her admired, in a way even immortal, and she makes it contingent on a place for her pets, forever. I think that's charming."

Oldfield was frowning. "How much do you know about that story?"

"Just a few things, really. I saw part of it on television, and a woman I know was the producer of the newscast; in fact, she wrote the story. I understand a lot of people thought it was very well done."

"Well done," Oldfield echoed flatly.

"I suppose it was, for what it was trying to do. Get people's atten-tion, give them some human interest in the context of a more serious story..."

"Bullshit. I'm sorry, please forgive me, I shouldn't talk that way to a lovely dinner companion. But that's jargon and I don't like it. This woman, the producer, Sybille Morgen, isn't that right?—her name was on the credits at the end of the show, though I didn't know she was the writer as well—this woman did incalculable damage to the univer-sity, and that's a little more than human interest."

"What kind of damage? You won't get the money for the new build-ing?"

"We're not sure yet."

"Then it's not incalculable."

"Well. Not yet. But it could be. We have to look at the worst possi-ble scenario."

Valerie finished her chowder. "It wasn't malicious. I'm sure no one at that station wants to hurt Stanford."

"Of course it was malicious. The story wasn't true; it was created because somebody had it in for us, and got to us by making a fool of an old lady who worries about what people will say if her blouse is buttoned the wrong way."

"Oh, that's nonsense." Valerie watched one of the maids take away her soup bowl and replace it with a watercress salad. She picked up her fork. She wished she were somewhere else. All this seemed so unimportant. Nick thought it was important. But Nick wasn't here. "Sybille was worried about an audience. That's all. She doesn't care about Stanford; she cares about ratings. And she told me she didn't make it up; she got it from someone who's supposedly sleeping with the wife of a university vice-president—it's really a grubby little story," she added, seeing Oldfield's mouth fall open and make little gasping sounds. "Anyway, even if Sybille did slant it, add color, whatever she did, it wasn't to hurt Stanford, it was to keep her audience awake. And I'm sure she didn't do anything unethical; she wouldn't do that. She's very serious about her work. And she works harder than anyone I know. She told me she went out and found that drawing by herself; no one helped her. That takes a lot of dedication, if you ask me. Excuse me." Her dinner companion on her right was claiming her attention, and Valerie turned to him with relief, instantly forgetting Sybille and Ramona Jackson.

Oldfield did not move. He stared at his watercress salad, numbed by the revelation that the source for the story, whose name he had demanded from Beauregard, was probably himself. And then, a spark of excitement flickered through his numbness. Because he had had another revelation. That Sybille Morgen had known from the first she was distorting that story; that Sybille Morgen had been the one who broke into his office and stole the drawing. And he had a most respectable witness to testify to all of it.

One week later, Sybille Morgen was called before the university Disciplinary Committee for a hearing on the theft from Laurence Oldfield's office. She sat in her bed in her small apartment, reading and rereading the notification, and waited for Beauregard to call, to tell her he would stand by her, provide a lawyer, give evidence that she acted on orders from him, do whatever was necessary to save her. But the hours stretched out and the telephone was silent. On my own, she thought bitterly. It's always the same. No one cares about me; no one will help. Well, fuck them. They have no right to ask me anything. All they want to do is make me crawl because I showed how stupid they are. They can have their hearing without me. They can play their little games by themselves; I won't have anything to do with them. I don't need them. I don't need any of them.

The Disciplinary Committee met without Sybille, and concluded that her refusal to accept their authority, and thus the authority of the university, meant she was not willing to be a member of their community. And for that reason, their recommendation was that she be expelled.

Two days later, Sybille was notified of her expulsion. And the next day, Terence Beauregard the Third, as soon as he heard about it from Laurence B. Oldfield, fired her from KNEX-TV for violating the public trust by distorting a story and then willfully broadcasting it on a news show which she produced.

Chapter
6

ybille's eyes were downcast as she stood beside her chair. "Everything changed at once; it all just... fell apart." She filled Nick's plate from a steaming chicken casserole. "I'd been going out with someone from the station and that ended, and so did school, and my job..." Hastily, she looked up and smiled, a small, brave smile. "But I found another one, almost right away—it's only a salesclerk, but it means I can pay rent so I won't lose my apartment—and everything's going to be fine. Is the chicken all right? I didn't even ask you if you like chicken, or if you'd rather have something else."

"I like chicken, and everything is fine," he said. He had been watching her closely, puzzled by her nervousness. She was wearing a white sundress, her hair was tied back with a white ribbon, and she looked young and defenseless; virginal, he thought, and prettier than he had remembered. "In fact, it's wonderful. You're a good cook."

"I love to cook. But not when I'm alone; it just makes me more lonely. It's always better when I do it for someone else."

"Like a lot of other things," he said quietly, and raised his glass. "To a great cook."

She flushed. "You can't really know that; one dinner..."

"Plus the sample I had last week when you dropped your box of cookies outside the engineering building." He grinned. "The crumbs were terrific. That was a lucky break."

"Dropping the cookies?"

"Our meeting each other that way. Not too many people other than engineers get to that part of the campus."

Sybille nodded. "Yes, it was lucky."

"Especially since you'd left Stanford a few weeks earlier." He refilled their wine glasses. "Were you looking for me?"

She hesitated, then gave him a wistful smile. "You're too quick for me. I thought I was being so clever."

"Why bother?" he asked. "If you wanted to see me, why didn't you call me and tell me so?"

She shook her head. "I couldn't do that."

He waited, but she said nothing more. "Why couldn't you?"

"Because you might have said no. You might have said you weren't interested; or you might have lied and said you were busy, so you wouldn't sound rude; or you might have said yes even if you didn't mean it, because you felt sorry for me—"

"And I might have said yes because I was intrigued and flattered that you'd called me. Do you always think up scenarios that make you sound undesirable?"

She flushed again. "If I do, it's not because I want to."

"I'm sorry," he said. "That wasn't kind of me. I hope the time comes when you're sure enough of yourself to—" He stopped. It wasn't his place to talk to her like that. "Anyway," he added lightly, "I thought modern women were past worrying about such things. Or at least they understand that men have those worries, too, and equality means sharing the worry. If it doesn't mean that, it ought to. Whatever it is, I do prefer honesty."

"So do I," she said swiftly. Her face had cleared. "Maybe next time I'll surprise you, and call you for another dinner."

"Unless I do first." He watched her reach over to the kitchen counter and bring a salad bowl to the table. Her apartment was so tiny almost everything was within arm's reach. They were sitting at a small round table near a blanket hung to screen her bed and a low dresser. She had done nothing to make the attic apartment inviting; it was clean but spartan, with a few posters on the wall, bare wood floors, and shades but no curtains on the two dormer windows. A large television set dominated the room. It was a lot like the apartment he and his roommates shared, Nick reflected; an interim place until they could make a real home. "Tell me about your family," he said.

"Oh." She sat back, shrugging slightly. "There isn't much to tell. My father died before I was born...he was an Air Force test pilot and he was killed when his plane crashed. Just that morning he'd sent my mother eighteen roses for her birthday, one for each year, and then she never saw him again. They were married on her seventeenth birthday in a little church in the countryside, in Virginia; my mother had run away from home to marry him because her parents were insisting she marry someone else, and they hadn't spoken since then, so she didn't even call them when my father was killed; she just pretended they'd died, too, and when I was born it was just the two of us. And we had no money then, either; there was something wrong about my father's insurance, so we had nothing."

Nick was fascinated. First she said there wasn't much to tell and then she spun a fairy-tale fantasy that any young girl would love to believe. He was sure she didn't believe it, either. But what difference did it make? If the truth about her family was too painful to talk about, let her have her fantasy. We all need a pretty story now and then, he thought, to replace memories we'd rather forget.

"What did your mother do when you were born?" he asked.

"Became a dress designer. We lived in Baltimore and she didn't want to work in an office because she didn't have anyone to leave me with. So she became a designer, first in Baltimore and then on the Eastern Shore where the money was. One of her customers helped me with a loan so I could come to Stanford."

Nick remembered Valerie saying Sybille's mother was a seamstress, not a designer; she'd also said it was her father who gave Sybille the money for college. But Sybille wasn't going to mention Valerie. And neither would Nick. It's much better that way, he thought, fighting against the hollow feeling of loss that swept through him every time he thought of her. Don't bring her in; don't think about her. There's no reason to.

"Why Stanford?" he asked. "It's not strong in television."

"I know, but I'll learn when I'm working in it. Everyone will teach me. They'll tell themselves they shouldn't, because they'll think I'm a threat, but they will anyway because they love to show off how much they know."

Nick smiled, but he was a little repelled by the sting of her words. "But why Stanford?" he asked again.

"Oh, no special reason. I'd heard a lot about it; it sounded better than the others."

She had chosen it because Valerie did. Valerie had told him that too. And he was sure that had something to do with it. "But why did you leave before you'd graduated? Even before the end of your junior year."

Sybille looked at her hands. "I didn't leave. I was expelled."

"You were *what*?"

She kept her eyes down. "One of my newscasts at KNEX had a report about the university that wasn't true. I thought it was true—I'd never, never have used it if I hadn't thought so—but it was somebody's idea of a joke and—"

"You're talking about the apes and the engineering building."

Her eyes came up and met his; their pale-blue intensity gave him a jolt. "I suppose everybody's laughing about it."

"No one is laughing," he said flatly. "There was nothing to laugh about; it could have been very bad for the university. I didn't know that was your doing."

Her lower lip caught between her teeth. "It was. It was all my fault. I should have checked it out. It was the kind of story that should be double- and triple-checked and I knew it. But I heard it from someone who said he was there and heard it all, and we were always looking for colorful stories..." She twisted her hands together and waited for Nick to say something. But the silence drew out. Sybille's lower lip began to quiver. "And then I was fired."

"Fired," Nick repeated. He was stunned. As angry as he was at her irresponsibility, and her confession that she had known she was being careless, it wasn't cause to expel her, he thought, or to fire her. Unless someone needed a scapegoat and Sybille was it: young, and a woman.

But still, he could not believe it. "How could they expel you? Universities almost never expel students. They discipline them, or suspend them; they do everything they can to avoid—"

"Don't, please don't!" Tears ran down her cheeks. "I can't talk about it, I can't even think about it. I can't bear it, it hurts so much, I can't, I can't..."

"I'm sorry," Nick said. "Of course we won't talk about it if you don't want to."

There was a long silence. Sybille's tears stopped. She took a deep breath. "I was proud of that news show. It was mine, at least when they let me produce it, and I did a good job, everyone said so. That meant more to me than anybody could imagine. It was all I had to make me feel happy with myself." She saw Nick's swift look. "I mean, I'm happiest in my work, when I feel I'm getting where I want to be. I want so much; sometimes I feel like I'm going to explode with wanting... That probably sounds silly to you, but I really can't stand the waiting because I know what I want and I'm willing to do anything to get it, but things are so slow, people are so slow. And then things happen. When I got the job at the station I felt as if my life had really started, I was finally moving, not just standing still in college being *young*. And then it was gone. I made one little mistake, that's all, and they took everything away from me. Just when I was beginning to think I was really special, going to Stanford, being a television producer, they took it all away. They don't care about ripping up people's lives, getting them fired and kicked out of school, they're so *smug*—"

Her face was almost ugly with anger. Abruptly, she went to the sink and turned on the water. "I forgot to make the coffee." Her voice was choked. "I'm sorry; I'm usually a lot more efficient..."

Nick followed her and put his arms around her, stilling her hands as he held her against him. Her head barely reached his chin and he leaned his cheek on her black hair. "You're very special," he said quietly. "You're a special person, and I don't believe any of this is going to stop you. I think you'll get what you want. You'll learn from what happened and you'll use it, but you won't let it hold you back."

Sybille turned within his arms and looked up at him. "How can you say that? You don't know me."

"Not yet, but I can guess that much." He smiled, watching her face change as he did. She was so hungry for approval; hungry for a smile, a friendly comment, a word of praise. Hungry for love. He ached for her neediness. It affected him even more strongly after months of being close to Valerie's supreme self-confidence, the laughter with which she faced the world...

Once again he pushed away the image of Valerie, angry at himself for weakness. He had always believed he could control his feelings and focus his attention; those were his strengths. But he hadn't found a way to keep Valerie from his thoughts, even though he told himself each day, each night, that she was not the woman for him and, obviously, he wasn't the man for her.

"And I'll know you much better after we call each other for dinner a few times," he said to Sybille. "We can take turns." He smiled again. "We're going to get to know each other very well."

Sybille reached up and brought his face to hers. Briefly he was surprised at her assertiveness, but he forgot it in the yielding softness of her mouth. It opened beneath his; her tongue met his with something like coy reluctance before submitting to his demanding one. Her body seemed to flow and curve into the shape of his; her arms embraced him as if clinging for support.

But as yielding as she was, there was something devouring in her, and instinctively Nick pulled away, breaking the kiss. Instantly, her face clouded over.

"I want to get to know you," he said gently, thinking with a flash of humor that, traditionally, that wasn't the man's line. And as he thought it, he knew he could have shared that moment of humor with Valerie but that Sybille would not find it amusing. Still, at that moment, even her lack of humor seemed beguiling to him; he was sure it came from being young and vulnerable, and deeply hurt, and having no one on whom to rely. If she had security, she would find laughter.

He could not escape the tug of so much need.

And there was something else that drew him powerfully to her: she had the same singleminded determination about work that he had, the determination that had annoyed Valerie. Sybille wouldn't be annoyed; she would understand it.

She was interesting, intelligent, and attractive; she shared his feelings about work; and she had powerful needs. It was an irresistible combination, he thought, and promised himself he would go slowly. He put his arm around her and held her to him. "How about that coffee?" he asked.

By the beginning of June, the university had emptied out. The school year was over and the summer session had not yet begun; the campus seemed to sleep. In the stillness, Sybille walked from one end of the campus to the other. Except for her brief visit to the engineering building, when she had found Nick and invited him to dinner, it was the first time she had been back since being expelled three weeks earlier, and she felt more of an outsider than ever. It was as if she were allowed on these sacred grounds only when everyone else was gone.

"The hell with them," she said aloud. "The hell with everybody."

She sat cross-legged beneath a cypress tree near the administration building. Not quite everybody. Not Nick Fielding, who was warm and smart and sexy and interested in her, even though he still hadn't been in her bed and they'd been together three evenings since their first dinner. But she wouldn't push it. She'd let him set the pace, however peculiar it seemed; there was plenty of time, as long as he stayed sympathetic and protective. She knew that was what attracted him right now, more than her body or her brains, even more than her cooking, though he'd mentioned more than once how nice it was to have someone cook for him.

Not that she wanted to be known as a cook; it was low on her list. But it was nice having a man eat at her table, and she'd found that she could cook a whole dinner while her thoughts went their own way: to finding another job in television; to Nick, and where the two of them were going; to Nick and Valerie and why they'd broken up.

What if Valerie had dropped him? I don't want Valerie's leavings, she thought. I've already been through that: all those years when her mother gave me clothes Valerie was tired of, and I had to smile and be grateful. They were fantastic clothes and I looked wonderful in them after my mother altered them—from tall, slim Valerie to short round Sybille always trying to lose weight—but they weren't mine. They were always Valerie's, and I hated them.

If Valerie dumped Nick, I don't want him.

"Sybille?" A shadow fell across Sybille's knees and she looked up, shading her eyes.

"Lenore," she said and folded her arms as if in self-protection. She'd been hoping she would see someone she knew, but at the same time she was afraid. She wanted to know what people were saying about her, but she didn't really want to hear it. And now she would, because Lenore was a part-time secretary in the personnel office and an expert in gossip.

"I heard about your troubles," said Lenore, sprawling beside her. She was tall and angular, a perennial student always a few months from finishing her degree, with a long, melancholy face that made her a natural for the dissemination of bad news. "Bad news," Lenore said, shaking her head. "A lot of bad feelings all over the place."

"About me," Sybille said.

"Sure, but you aren't the only one. There's been plenty to go around."

"I didn't hear anything. I'm so out of it..."

They were magic words; Lenore could not resist a listener who knew nothing. She stretched her long legs in front of her and leaned against the cypress tree. "Well. First off, Jackson withdrew the money. Said she'd give it someplace where she'd be taken seriously. Much tearing of hair, guzzling of tranquilizers, saying of prayers, until she calmed down. They told her you were gone and you'd never be allowed to darken our door again—and what's-his-name at KNEX, the guy you worked for, was also gone, booted out—"

"Oh!" Sybille cried. There was some justice after all.

"—because he was executive producer and ultimately responsible for what got on the air and so on and so forth. So all the baddies were punished and there was Jackson holding her money in her hot little fist and the powers that be convinced her it was best to give it to the university and give herself the happiness of giving it. Something like that. So she did."

There was a pause. "That's all?" Sybille asked.

"Hardly; it keeps on bubbling away. The president blames the mess on Larry Oldfield, and Larry blames it on your boss, former boss, and your former boss is mad at that gorgeous creature who does television once in awhile, you've seen her around, Valerie Ashbrook, because he heard from Larry that she spilled the beans about you at a dinner party and they used what she said to get rid of your former boss. By the way, *did* you make it up? I've heard so many versions, you wouldn't believe..."

Lenore's melancholy voice droned on and on, but Sybille had stopped listening. Valerie. *Valerie.* Rage swept through her. *We have a witness.* That's what Oldfield had told her when he called her into his office. *Someone who knows you were perfectly aware of the true story but distorted it, manufactured parts of it, for your own purposes. It was out-and-out fraud and we can prove it and you have forfeited all rights to be a part of our university community.*

Valerie. The name pounded inside her, and an image flashed from her memory: Sybille and Valerie sitting at a table on the terrace of the Student Union, and Valerie listening—so damned sweet and friendly—egging Sybille on to talk about the way she wrote that story. I was so excited, Sybille thought, and she was so interested, and I told her everything. That bitch. She probably thought it was all very funny, something to gossip about so she could be the center of attention.

Her hand closed around a rock and she clenched her fingers against its cold roughness. That bitch, that bitch, that bitch.

...spilled the beans at a dinner party. Oh, that made it worse. One of those parties in town. The kind Valerie had condescended to take her to. Once. Only once.

Valerie. Valerie on camera, relaxed, smiling, stunning, as Sybille never would be. Valerie walking across the campus as if she owned it. Valerie with her hand in Nick's. Valerie in Nick's bed.

But not anymore.

From now on he'll be in my bed. I'll make him forget her; I'll make him forget everyone but me. Maybe she did drop him, but it doesn't matter because she'll want him back one of these days, but she won't have a hope in hell, because he won't want her. Ever again.

But that wasn't all. She was going to make that bitch pay for what she'd done. Once she'd admired her, envied her and wanted to be like her, and for awhile she'd been so happy because they were equals: students on the same campus. But that was over. She didn't admire Valerie Ashbrook or want to be like her. There's nothing to admire, nothing, nothing, she raged silently. She's stupid and thoughtless. She never thinks of anyone but herself and her own pleasure. Dinner parties, gossip, chattering away, passing on stories people tell her in confidence, and if somebody gets hurt by it, what does Valerie care? She acts like there are hordes of servants following behind her, ready to clean up any mess she makes.

"Not this one, damn it," Sybille muttered, forgetting Lenore. She raised her hand, still clenched around the rock, and, with a snap of her wrist, flung the rock away. She won't be able to clean up this mess, because I'll never forget it. And I'm going to destroy her.

I'll find a way to make her lose everything she has; make her know what it's like to be poor and on the outside. I don't care how long it takes, I'll find a way to do it.

She sprang up. "I have to go. Thanks for telling me everything.... I'm late; I have so much to do, I'll see you around..."

She strode away, almost running. So much to do. Find another job. Find people who can help. Read and study; watch other people and find their weak points. Learn and learn and learn to find the fastest way to the top.

Figure out how to pay back Valerie.

Call Nick.

"I hoped you'd hang around after you got your Ph.D.," said Lyle Wilson. He put his hand on Nick's shoulder. "With your ambition, in a few years you'd be ready to take over the place. Then I'd retire and play the gentleman."

Nick laughed. "Not for a long time. Anyway, you know what I want, Lyle, and I can't do it if I'm working in a university."

Lyle sighed. "All that energy. What about security? Don't tell me there's no pretty girl wanting to get married and settle down. I tell you, *she'd* like it if you stayed put. How many fellas graduate and they already have a great job and their future taken care of?"

Nick smiled. "Nobody wants to get married, and right now a little mystery in my future sounds just fine." He picked up a box filled with the possessions that had filled his desk for the past three years. "I've enjoyed it here," he said simply, taking a last look around. He was surprised by a brief flash of panic. He was leaving everything that was familiar, a place where he was known and respected, where he knew the rules and had gained a measure of authority, and he was going into a world of unknowns where he had no authority, no assurances, and no money.

But as quickly as it came, the panic was gone. He was doing what he wanted: starting on the road he and his father had talked and dreamed about, to make Nicholas Fielding the best in his field, the most powerful and influential—and wealthy.

He would also be getting away from Stanford and the memories that dogged him. And he would be going alone; he was not planning his future around anyone else. He'd tried that, and gotten stung, and he wasn't about to do it again. He had too much to do and he didn't know how long it would take him, but he did know he'd do it best, and fastest, alone.

He was turning to leave when the telephone rang. Automatically, he answered it. "Hi," Sybille said. Her voice was husky and caressing; different from the last time he had seen her, the week before. "I don't remember whose turn it is to call, but I hope you can come to dinner tonight."

"I'd like that," he said, smiling, and when they had set a time and he hung up, he was still smiling. He admired the easy way she had invited him, even though it was still hard for her. There was so much to admire in Sybille, Nick thought. There was much to pity, especially her aloneness and lack of humor, but there was more to admire.

And because he admired her, and liked her, he knew he had to tell her, right away, his plans for the future. He hadn't told anyone but his parents about the company he and Ted McIlvain, one of his roommates, would be starting next month in San Jose, but now he thought he owed it to Sybille, because she depended on him so much. And that night, as they sat over coffee, he told her.

"San Jose!" she cried, as if it were on another planet instead of a few miles away. "But why? Everything you want to do you can do right here!"

"We might, but Ted's aunt has a house there that's empty, and she's letting us have it for a year. So what we save on rent we'll put into the company. Besides, San Jose is where the customers are. It's only a short drive away," he said gently.

She shook her head. "It's not the miles. It's the differences. You'll look out the window and see different places; you'll be meeting different people; you'll be thinking about different kinds of work and different kinds of excitement. Palo Alto won't be real for you anymore, and neither will I."

Once again he was struck by her cold, biting intelligence. *Palo Alto won't be real for you* . . . It was true; he knew it. When he had come to Palo Alto, he had felt a distancing from his home, his hometown, even his family. They were no longer permanent parts of the life he was making for himself. He knew he would never live with them again.

He glanced around Sybille's apartment. It was small and drab, but it was familiar. He put his hand on hers. "We'll find each other. If that's what we want, we'll manage it."

"*Is* it what we want?" Her voice, still with that new huskiness, had turned wistful. "You know just where you're going and how you're going to get there, and you'll do it all, I know you will; but I'm still trying to find a way out of here." Her lip was quivering and she held it between her teeth as she turned her hand to clasp Nick's. "It isn't your fault that I'm in this mess; you've been wonderful to me. I know how much you have to do, and you want to do it fast; you don't want to be stuck with someone who's . . . lost . . . her way . . ."

Her head was bent. The smooth line of her neck trembled slightly, as if awaiting a blow. Nick's heart contracted. He laid his hand on her neck and caressed her warm skin, his fingers moving beneath the loose collar of her blouse to her shoulder.

A long, shuddering sigh escaped Sybille. "I wish . . ." she said almost inaudibly.

"What?" Nick asked. His hand tightened on her shoulder and he turned her to him.

" . . . I was stronger and better. We could be together . . . and help each other. . . . I'd like to help you . . ."

Nick brought her face up to his and kissed her, his mouth opening hers, his hand moving beneath her blouse.

"No!" Sybille exclaimed. She pulled away, pushing back her chair so sharply it fell over. "You can't, I won't let you—!" She took agitated steps around the small room. "You have a straight shot to where you want to be, you have everything going for you, and I'm not going to hold you back. You'd hate me for clinging—"

"I'd never hate you." Nick stood beside her and put his arm around her shoulders to walk her firmly with him to her bed. "You're a strong, fine woman; you don't cling, and if you feel you've lost your way maybe I can help you find it."

She looked up at him, her eyes wide. "If you really mean that . . ."

He bent to kiss her again. "One of these days you'll stop doubting yourself."

"Maybe . . . with your help . . ." Sybille murmured. She searched his face, then smiled with more delight than he had ever seen in her. "I'm so glad . . ." she said, the word lingering in a sigh, and then, still looking at him, she unbuttoned her blouse.

They undressed swiftly and lay on her bed. Her body was small and compact, her breasts pointed, like a young girl's, and her olive skin was soft and moist. Her eyes were closed and she did not speak or even smile; her face was absorbed, as if she were concentrating. Someone should teach her to smile, Nick thought, and laugh and joke . . .

Damn it, he cried silently, and bent over Sybille as she moved beneath him. "Look at me," he commanded.

Surprised, her eyes flew open, but just as swiftly closed. She could not look at him and she hated him for demanding it. It should have been enough for him that he was in her bed and that she'd make sure he was satisfied.

She felt his weight and the heat of his skin; her hands moved over his body and she arched beneath him, and then, at the perfect moment, she opened her legs. "Mine," she said, but it might have been only a sigh, it was so low, like a single note beneath the thunder of an orchestra. She gripped Nick's narrow hips between her thighs as if to show him how strong she could be, and guided him into her. And it was all right, better than usual, because she liked him and, so far, he had treated her better than anyone she'd known. I might even enjoy it, she thought.

For a long time, she had tried to enjoy being in bed with a man; she'd tried so hard to feel the waves of pleasure she read about and could sometimes give herself. But nothing ever happened. No matter how she moved or what fantasies she conjured, nothing happened. Maybe with Nick, she thought. It was almost a prayer. Then she stopped thinking and let her body move on its own, skillfully sensuous, not aroused but wet enough to do what it had to do to the last shuddering breath, and do it so perfectly no one had ever guessed that she wasn't the least bit involved.

When they lay quietly, Nick held her and she turned her face to his shoulder, her lips brushing his skin. But in a moment, tears ran from beneath her eyelids and Nick felt them.

"Sybille, what is it?" He tilted her face and searched it. "What is it now?" he asked and there was a thread of impatience in his voice.

"Nothing. I'm sorry, there's nothing wrong. You're wonderful. I love being with you, I love you—" She caught her breath and tried to look away, but Nick held her firmly and she met his eyes, seeing him blurred through her tears.

"Go on," he said.

"I love you," she repeated, her voice low. "But it won't work, our being together: it's the wrong time. If we'd met a year from now, when you have your company started . . . well, but we didn't. And you're right to go to San Jose, you're right to do everything you can for yourself; you shouldn't be thinking about me. I'll be fine, you know; I know what I want, and I'll go after it the same way you're doing. I can't stay here, either; I should be in Los Angeles or New York." She brushed away the last tear that had not yet dried. "I was just feeling lonely because this was so wonderful, being with you to-night, it's always wonderful, but I'd never try to stop you from leaving, because you don't need me right now."

Nick gazed at her for a long moment. A few minutes earlier he had been astonished at her passion, and grateful for it, because he had known then that he could feel more for her than pity and admiration. Now he felt it all: his heart ached for her loneliness and lack of confidence; he admired her courage and her determination; and he knew there were fires within her that he could free. He would teach her to love and laugh and to be sure of herself. He tightened his arm around her. "You'll come with me," he said.

Sybille drew in her breath, then shook her head, a tiny frown between her eyes. "You mustn't say that. Men say things in bed they don't mean."

"Oh, for God's sake," he said impatiently. "I don't know which men you've been in bed with but if you think I'm in a weakened condition, limp with gratitude, you've got me wrong." He grinned at her. "I won't change my mind."

Her eyes were fixed on his. "If you're sure . . . I couldn't stand it if you weren't . . ."

"Sybille." He turned her to him and repeated her name, his voice caressing it. "Sybille, I want you to come with me. I can't leave you. You said it yourself: we'll be together; we'll help each other."

She was holding her breath. She closed her eyes and let it out slowly. Little by little her muscles loosened until she lay completely relaxed within Nick's embrace, her hand on his chest, her lips touching the hollow of his throat. With another sigh, she gave herself over to him. "Yes," she whispered.

Nick felt a sudden shock as the enormity of it struck him. He willed it away and turned his head to kiss her forehead. "I love you, Sybille," he said.

A week later, in a simple ceremony in the office of a Palo Alto judge, Nicholas Fielding and Sybille Morgen were married.

They moved to San Jose and settled into a small house on the southern edge of the city. Since the house belonged to Ted McIlvain's aunt, and the two men were setting up their company in the family room, Ted moved in, too. He took over the upstairs, with its two small bedrooms and bath, while Sybille and Nick settled into a larger bedroom and bath downstairs. The three of them shared the living room, dining room and kitchen. "I'm sorry we have to start out this way," Nick said. "It won't be long before we have our own place. That's a promise."

Sybille ran her fingers along the chipped Formica dining table. Valerie would take one look at this place and walk out. If Valerie had a new husband, she'd never share a house with anybody. Valerie would never let a stranger squeeze her into a bedroom and one bathroom, with or without a new husband.

And Nick wouldn't ask her to. He wouldn't have done this to her in the first place. If Valerie was his wife, he would have found some other way.

But Valerie wasn't his wife. Valerie was gone and Sybille was Mrs. Nicholas Fielding. And Sybille was the woman to whom Nick was making promises.

"It's all right," she said, moving into his arms. She reached up to kiss him, exulting in the tightening of his arms about her. He wanted her. And he would forget Valerie.

He'll forget her long before I do.

She spoke against his lips. "As long as we have each other, we don't need a grand house."

"But you'll have one," he promised. "You'll have everything you want."

"I know," Sybille said. And beneath the sounds of Ted moving furniture upstairs, they went to their bedroom, and Nick turned the lock with a loud click.

Holding him later, as they lay on the rumpled bed, Sybille began to think there was an advantage in having three of them there. With his work and his partner all in one place, Nick would find it natural to work long hours; he wouldn't be making a lot of demands on his wife. He'd leave her alone, but she wouldn't be alone in the house; she wouldn't have to worry anymore about filling her hours with other people, other sounds. And I'll be working, too, she thought. Tomorrow I'll be sure to find a job in a San Jose television station. It would all be fine. They'd have no trouble sharing the house, they'd have no trouble being married. And they'd be happy.

The house was narrow, on a narrow lot, with brown grass in front and back, a tilting, emaciated palm near the driveway, and a large window in the living room looking into an identical window in an identical house across the street. The rooms were painted an odd shade of mustard which glowed with an eerie incandescence in the light from the streetlamp in front of the house. Sybille and Nick bought white bed sheets and hung them as curtains, but, even though that diffused the light, still they looked strangely unearthly to each other and it was always a little startling when one of them looked up and wondered, briefly, who that oddly hued stranger was.

The three of them arranged their few pieces of furniture, put away their mismatched dishes and utensils, and shelved the cartons of books they had hauled from Palo Alto, with their furniture, in a rented van. For a week, as they cooked their first dinners in the large kitchen, they tripped over the ripped linoleum and each other, but soon they began to find their own spaces. And each night after dinner, Nick and Ted went back to work, and much later, Sybille and Nick went to their room, and Ted went to his.

"You're sure you're all right here?" Nick asked as he reached for her in bed.

"I'm fine," she said. "I'm happy."

He believed her. She had not complained about the house after their first day there; and she no longer talked about not being really important in his life. Even the mustard walls had become a joke between them. But still, Nick knew there was a restlessness in Sybille always simmering below the surface, and two weeks after they had moved in, when they had turned out the light in their bedroom, she lay tense beside him, turning and turning until, finally, she slid out of bed.

"Can I help?" he asked.

"No, I'm just not sleepy. I think I'll read through my television notebooks for awhile. I usually do, at night. You go to sleep; I'll read in the living room."

He raised himself on his elbow, watching her in the light from the street. "You're worried about finding a job."

"Yes. But it's all right; I'll get over it." She picked up one of the notebooks on the bureau. "I just have to talk myself out of worrying. I'll find something. Good night, Nick."

He lay back. Talk herself out of worrying. It was amazing, he thought, that that strength was always there, even when she was insecure in so many other ways. And she would talk herself out of it; he was sure of it. And she would get a job, and be the success she always vowed to be. He did not doubt that any more than she did.

The next morning, Nick and Ted left early to buy equipment for their workshop. But Sybille had left even earlier. And that day she found a job at the largest television station in San Jose.

Now, she thought; finally, this minute, my life really begins.

Chapter
7

hey were so busy they almost never saw each other. Nick and Ted had formed a consulting company named Omega Computing Services, and they spent their days helping companies install and operate new computer systems. The rest of the time they worked in the office they had set up in the family room; evenings and weekends, through lunch, often through dinner, they put together proposals to attract new customers, wrote computer programs for the customers they had, improved the programs they'd already installed, and tossed ideas back and forth for ways to use computers that no one had yet thought of. When their minicomputer at home could not handle the complex programs they were writing, they rented time on a mainframe computer in downtown San Jose, and, since it was cheaper to rent time at night, they would begin after dark, often working until morning, when they would install the new program in a customer's company and teach office workers how to use it. By the time they returned home, late in the day, they were too tired even for dinner, and they disappeared into their bedrooms for a rare full night's sleep.

And all the while, Sybille was moving up at KTOV, always moving up. Before coming to San Jose, she had written to the president of KNEX in Palo Alto, suggesting she would expose Terence Beauregard's sexual activities unless he wrote her a letter of reference. After a week of silence he had sent her one that was tepid, but better than she had expected. Still, the day she arrived at her new job, she was defiant and fearful, and her fear was with her until she realized that no one connected her with the Ramona Jackson story. From then on, it was as if that whole scandal had never occurred. She was a part of KTOV, starting fresh.

She worked from early morning to late at night, twelve or fourteen hours at a stretch, listening, watching, soaking up information, finding ways to use everything she already knew to impress those she worked for. She wasn't trying to be liked; she wanted to be respected and admired, she wanted to be noticed, she wanted to be on camera. But that was not what they wanted from her. "You're too good to be on camera," they said. "Good producers are hard to come by and you're one of the best. And that's where we want you." They increased her salary and gave her a bigger desk in the newsroom. Putting her on the other side of the camera was out of the question.

Sybille thought about quitting. But no other station in the valley could compare with KTOV. I'll make them change their mind, she vowed. I'll produce whatever they want me to, and when I have enough influence, they'll give me what I want. They'll have to.

Within a year, she was writing and producing the noon news five days a week, and producing the ten-o'clock news on weekends. And she was creating a new program that would be hers to produce and direct if it was approved.

She was working at such a high pitch that for the first time in years she needed no diet to keep her weight down. Every morning before dawn, she exercised for an hour; just before she went to work she had a cup of coffee with Nick and Ted, and then she forgot about eating until dinner. That was at nine, or later, either at the station or at home, brought in by one of the three of them, or cooked by Nick. They didn't much care what it was; they were too busy to pay attention to food.

For Sybille, thoughts of everything but work dropped away the minute she stepped through the glass front door of KTOV. The station sat on a small rise on the eastern edge of San Jose. A network affiliate, it reached the electronics whiz kids who were creating what was already being called Silicon Valley; and the Mexican-Americans whose parents had come north a generation or two earlier to settle on the fertile land; and the Californians whose families had been there since the Gold Rush, and talked about the old days, when you could drive from San Francisco to Monterey without seeing a single shopping mall or fast-food drive-in. KTOV reached them all, and because it was aggressive and innovative and it successfully targeted each group, it was the fastest-growing and richest station in the valley. It was the perfect place for someone driven by ambition.

At the early hour when Sybille walked in the front door, the receptionist had not arrived, the secretaries were not due for some time, and no visitors or talk-show guests had appeared. She walked through the silent lobby and hushed corridors, almost trembling with excitement. She felt she owned everything around her, from the greenroom to the makeup rooms, from the control room to the main studio, high-ceilinged, with four semicircular sets permanently in place for the news and weather, a cooking show, a cozy afternoon talk show, and a Sunday-afternoon entertainment hour. She had a right to be there. She belonged.

Because it was on top, there was an air of excitement everywhere in the KTOV building, not felt by outsiders, but as real and powerful to Sybille as a current running through her blood. Much of the time she barely noticed Nick's long days and weekends; she was engrossed in her work at the station or at a desk she had set up in a corner of their bedroom. She liked knowing that Nick and Ted were just a few feet away, in the family room, but they did not see each other until a break came in their work or one of them decided it was time to eat.

Sometimes Sybille emerged first, to suggest dinner or just to wander around the cluttered family room that was the office, workshop and research lab for Omega Computing Services. Huge flow charts were tacked to the walls; reams of computer printouts were strewn over a long table made from a door balanced across two file cabinets. A large computer, its glowing numbers and letters seeming to dance on its dark screen, sat on an identical table nearby. A rolling stool and a typist's chair found in the storeroom of the engineering building at Stanford rolled from one table to the other. Nearby was a Ping-Pong table with two scarred paddles and a sagging net, the scene of fierce competitions. A coffeepot stood beside two Mickey Mouse mugs; cardboard doughnut boxes were filled with notes and sketches; and in a corner a pencil lay forgotten beneath dusty cobwebs.

Sybille would watch the men absently, still thinking about her own work; or she would peer at their printouts, trying to decipher the program language, or gaze in bewilderment at the rows of equations on the computer screen. She knew vaguely what Nick did all day as a consultant, and she knew that their goal was to expand four- or five- or sixfold as rapidly as possible, to hire a staff and move into new quarters and then expand even more. She knew it all, but she could not understand what they wrote.

"It's a foreign language," she said. But she did not ask him to explain it. When he tried, the numbers and symbols swelled and swayed dizzyingly in front of her; she just wasn't interested enough to work at understanding them. So she glanced at Nick's work, surprised at its mysteries, and then asked about dinner. The three of them usually ate right there, shoving papers aside to make a clear space on one of the worktables, and then Sybille would go back to her desk to work on the next day's schedule, or the new program she was creating that she would soon present to the station manager and the news director, for their approval.

On the nights when he was home, Nick came to her after midnight and led her to bed. As tired as they both were then, they were buoyed up by an energy that fed on what they had done all day, and thoughts of tomorrow. Nick was instantly aroused, as soon as they lay together, and it was the closest Sybille ever came to the kind of intense peak of feeling she had once dreamed of. It was as much exhaustion and the excitement of their separate lives as passion, but they did not know that. While it lasted, they thought it was love.

Valerie doesn't have anything like this.

The thought came to Sybille at odd moments, like flashes of lightning, so bright it blocked out everything else. Then it would be gone. But other thoughts of Valerie would appear at any time, her image dimmed by Sybille's unabated fury, but still there, intruding. *Where is she? What is she doing?*

She knew a little bit, from talking to her mother, who still sewed for Valerie's family. She had spent a year in Europe after college, and then traveled around the world. Somewhere along the way, she had married Kent Shoreham, someone from Boston whose parents knew Valerie's parents. She and Kent divided their time between Maryland's Eastern Shore and New York, where they had bought an apartment on Fifth Avenue. That was all Sybille's mother knew.

It was enough for Sybille, for now. All she could do was keep track of Valerie until she found a way for them to meet again. And then... She didn't know. But she would, when she had time to think, and to plan.

She wanted to learn to ride horseback, knowing Nick had shared that with Valerie, but it was too expensive, and so, temporarily, she gave it up. But she did take up skeet shooting, another of Valerie's sports, and she was so good, her aim so steady and her eye so sharp, that her score was better than Valerie's ever had been. Valerie doesn't have the patience, she thought, to become an expert at anything.

I have Nick, Sybille thought; I have my job, I have my shooting. She repeated it at night before she fell asleep. In every way she was superior to Valerie.

When she learned she was pregnant she bought a few new clothes and managed to squeeze in a doctor's appointment once a month; otherwise nothing in her life changed. In February she hired a nanny. And in March, Chad was born.

For a few days, Sybille let herself relax, backing off from the relentless pace she had kept for nearly two years, to sit at the window, staring at the heavy clouds above the houses across the street, thinking about how this might affect her plans.

"That's an astonishing kid," Nick said, sitting beside her a week after Chad was born. "Did you see him smile?" And even through her absorption, Sybille heard the pride and elation in his voice.

"He's very handsome," she said. "He looks like you."

Nick grinned. "I thought so, too. But he has your mouth. Lucky kid; it's a very kissable mouth."

She shook her head. "I don't see any of me in him; he's much more like you. He'll probably use a computer before he learns to talk."

She did not nurse Chad; she had no time. "I'll be at the station all day and if I don't get my sleep at night I won't be worth a thing at my job."

"Don't go back for awhile," Nick said. "They've given you two months off; why not take it?"

"Without pay."

"We don't need it. Don't think about it."

"It's all right, Nick. I'm doing what I want to do."

When Chad was two weeks old, she turned him over to the nanny and returned to the station and her usual fourteen-hour days. At the end of a month she was too tired even to go out to dinner.

"You weren't ready," Nick said. "Take a few months off, starting today." They were lying in bed on a Sunday morning, the radio playing softly, Chad asleep in a crib nearby. Now and then a shaft of sunlight pierced the clouds and reached across the room to touch their bed. Nick felt the beauty of the moment and put his arm around Sybille. "I told you when Chad was born: we can afford it. Ted and I are getting clients faster than we can take care of them."

"No," she said.

He was silent. There was probably nothing he could say to convince her, but her exhaustion had alarmed him and so he tried once more. "It wouldn't hurt to take some time off; it wouldn't even slow you down. Enjoy Chad for a little while; you don't have to have everything at once."

"Why not?" she snapped. "*You* want it all; why shouldn't I? You know how many things are happening for me, why should I give any of it up? What for? A baby who doesn't care who feeds him as long as somebody does?"

"You were the one who wanted a baby," Nick said, his voice puzzled. "I thought we should wait a couple of years more, but you wouldn't. Why not, if all you wanted to do was work?"

"I wanted both," Sybille retorted.

"Why?" he said again. "You're happier at work than you are with Chad."

She looked at him sharply. "Are you saying I don't love my own son?"

"I'd never say that. But you don't seem comfortable with him. You close up, somehow; you're not open—"

"Not loving," she said flatly.

"Of course you love him. I don't doubt that."

"You do," she insisted. "You think I don't love him, that I shut him out. That's what you said."

"Not quite." He pulled back to look at her. "Do you care about him? Do you want to be close to him? You've never made any secret of what you've wanted, and it sure as hell isn't a child." She was silent, but her rigid body told him how angry she was. "Sybille, look at me! You're not home enough to be anything of a mother. When you are here, you pay damn little attention to Chad; you even have trouble holding him for very long. You get tired, or bored, or you start thinking of all the other things you could be doing. You—"

"You're doing it again!" she said furiously. "Saying I don't love him!"

"Tell me I'm wrong!"

"Every mother loves her baby! You make me sound like a monster!"

The word struck Nick. "I don't mean to. But I'd like to hear you tell me you love Chad."

"God damn you, you know I do!"

"I wish I did. I don't know what I know. I watch you with him and there isn't any—" He stopped, then shrugged. "Even when you hold him it looks like you're keeping him at arm's length. It bothers me. He needs a mother, you know."

"He has a nanny!"

"He also has a mother, and he needs her."

"You're trying to make me feel guilty!"

"Not guilty, Sybille; loving! But that can't be forced, can it? He's part of you, but there's nothing in you reaching out to him." He saw the darkness of her face and would have stopped, but he was too angry. "I suppose I could understand that your work is more important to you than anything else—I'd have trouble understanding it, but I'd try—but what made you insist on having this baby? You're too self-centered to take care of him; you're an infant yourself, all wrapped up in yourself with not an inch of compassion or interest in anyone else. . . . What the hell got into you to have a baby when you don't—"

"Because Valerie doesn't have one!" she blurted out.

A shaft of sunlight brushed the bed, then vanished as clouds piled up. The baby sighed. The room was very still.

Nick pulled his arm from beneath Sybille's shoulders and sat up. The room seemed to shrink around him, like a prison.

"I didn't mean it!" She was sitting beside him, her eyes alarmed. "I mean she doesn't want one. Or she—oh, I don't know—we used to talk about having babies, we talked a lot, and she said she didn't want any . . . she didn't like them . . ." Her voice ran down. She and Valerie had never talked about having children. They had never talked about anything personal. "Anyway, it's not important . . . we have Chad and that's what counts, isn't it?" Her eyes filled with tears. "You're right, I'm not very good with him, but I don't know what to do. . . . I'm sure I can learn, I want to, you know, but I've been so scared. . . . I can't imagine how some people just pick up a baby and know what to do right away; don't they worry about smothering them or crushing them or something like that . . . ?"

Bitterness welled up in Nick. Of all that he had learned about his wife, he had never guessed that she harbored such envy. Who was she, this woman he had married, that she could be so deeply obsessed, and let it control so fundamental a part of her life as the birth of a child? His bitterness became anger; he was furious at himself for not seeing what must have been there from the beginning. Suddenly, overwhelmingly, he wanted to get out of there, before he could discover how much else he did not know about her. But Chad slept on the other side of the room, and Nick could not move.

"Nick, listen to me." Sybille's hand was on his arm. "Are you listening? I don't know what to do!"

He heard the plea in her voice, and knew it was genuine. Tears trembled in it. He looked searchingly into her face, and she returned his look steadily. She had never been afraid, he thought; she always met trouble head on. "I'll learn; I promise I will," she said, her voice warm now, caressing, still a little unsteady. "I want you to be proud of me and I can learn anything if I try; remember you said that once?"

Slowly, he nodded. He took her hand and forced himself to pretend nothing had changed between them. And nothing had, he thought, except that now he saw more clearly. "I'm sure you'll learn," he said quietly. "You and Chad are going to get along wonderfully."

And neither of them observed that that was an odd way to describe a mother and her son.

The nanny was named Elena Garcia. She was thirty-one, round and rosy-cheeked; she had raised nine younger brothers and sisters, and, more than anything in the world, she longed for a bed all to herself. Suddenly, with her new job, she had not only a bed but a whole room, one of those on the second floor vacated by Ted McIlvain, who had moved out when Omega Computing Services began making money. Ecstatically, Elena explored her room, Chad's room across the hall, and the bathroom, used by no one but herself. From that moment, she loved Chad for making this possible, and she made him the center of her life.

"Have a nice day together," Sybille said, handing Chad back to Elena. She still couldn't get the hang of holding him. It was easier now that he was seven months old and could hold himself straight—she'd been terrified of the way his head flopped around the first month—but seven months meant he was much heavier, a real burden now that she'd exercised and dieted back to ninety-five pounds. He squirmed a lot, too, and sometimes he would screw up his face and start to scream, for no reason in the world that Sybille could fathom, transformed in an instant from a pleasant baby to an inhuman creature in such agony that all she wanted to do was give him to someone who could solve whatever problems he had. And it seemed that Elena always could.

"I don't know what time I'll be back," Sybille said. She picked up

her car keys and briefcase and went to the door. "I left money on the
kitchen counter for groceries; don't forget to ask Mr. Fielding if he
wants something special for dinner before you go shopping."

She opened the door, but something—Elena's silence, perhaps—
made her turn back. Chad was asleep, rosy and beautiful, a tiny fist
tucked under his chin. Sybille met Elena's eyes, then crossed the room
and bent to rest her cheek briefly on Chad's. It was velvety and fragrant, like an opening flower; she was always amazed at the softness of
his skin. "Don't let him get sunburned," she said, and touched her
cheek to his once again before walking swiftly to the door, and out of
the house.

From that moment she forget Chad and Elena; she forgot Nick; she
forgot how much she hated their small house, shabby and crowded
and in a poor neighborhood that she detested, with large families,
roaming dogs and cats, and even a tethered goat a few houses down.
She forgot it all, because this was the day her program was to be
broadcast for the first time.

She had developed and produced it; she had convinced the station
executives to allow her to make two pilot episodes, and the station had
used the pilots to sign up sponsors for thirteen weeks. Then she had
taped four more programs, and tonight, as one of the new shows
premiering throughout September, "The Hot Seat" would be shown
at six-thirty, following the local news.

There was nothing left for her to do: the program was on tape and
her part was done. There was nothing to do but watch the hours crawl
past. She sat in the control room during the noon news and tried to do
her job while excitement churned inside her and she had to swallow
through the dryness of her throat. Because it wasn't just excitement; it
was fear too: that even though the pilot had gotten good reviews, no
one would like tonight's program, critics would tear it to pieces,
viewers would flick their remote controls to other channels. And she
had other fears: that a devastating earthquake would strike just before
six-thirty and her half hour would be given to news of the disaster. Or,
if not an earthquake, the crash of a jumbo jet, terrorists in Miami, the
death of the President, a nuclear war. Any of them would knock "The
Hot Seat" out of its hard-won slot and she would have to go through
another week of agonized waiting.

But of course nothing like that would happen. The show would go
on at the proper time and it would be an instant success. Her name
would become known; she would have something to show when she

went to bigger stations in bigger cities; she would step from here to more powerful positions. And she would have something with which to bargain when she demanded her own show, that she would produce and host. It all began tonight.

Tonight, she thought, my life really begins.

And then, at last, for the first time in months she left the station early and went home. "Come and watch something with me," she said to Nick, taking a pen from his hand and laying it down. He was standing at one of the long tables, writing notes on a spread sheet, one hand holding a Ping-Pong ball that his thumb rolled rhythmically across his palm. His body was tense with coiled energy, and his eyes, when he turned to her, were distant.

"Watch something?" he echoed. He brought her into focus. "What time is it?"

"After six. I want you to watch a new program on television." She tugged at his hand like a child with a reluctant parent. "It's mine, I wrote it and produced it, and it's starting tonight. And I want us to watch it together. Nick, are you listening?"

He frowned then. "Yours," he said slowly. "New programs take months. You haven't mentioned it."

"I couldn't, not until I knew it would really happen. I can't bear to talk about things that might not work out, you know that. Oh, Nick, don't start something; I'm telling you about it now, aren't I? I want us to share it." She looked up at him. "Nick, I can't watch it alone."

He saw the tension in her face. "Of course you can't. You shouldn't." He reminded himself that it took both of them to keep their marriage going. Sybille had been trying; he had watched her. She was better with Chad; she was making an effort to be caring and loving even though it was clear to Nick that she had trouble being a caring and loving person, with anyone, and probably always would.

Still, she had been trying to be closer to Chad and to him, ever since that terrible Sunday morning in bed. For days after that, they had barely spoken; it had been a kind of separation. Then, little by little, it faded to the background. Living in the same house, it was hard not to talk, and soon they were talking about Chad and then the house and their jobs, and finally it was almost as if they had forgotten, and everything was the same as before.

He put his arm around her. "If you have a new show, it should be a family affair. Come on; we'll get Chad. For the first time, the Fieldings are going to watch television together. Maybe we'll make popcorn."

She looked at him to see if he were making fun of her, but his eyes and his smile were warm. "Thank you," she said huskily; her throat was dry with fear.

Nick brought Chad from his room upstairs and held him against his chest, while his other arm held Sybille. They watched the end of the local news and the commercials at the half hour. And then, in bold jagged letters, "The Hot Seat" splashed across the screen. Sybille's body clenched into a tense knot.

On the screen, two men and a woman sat in brown leather armchairs at a round table, notepads and pencils before them. In a red leather chair sat a balding young man wearing horn-rimmed glasses and a somber tie that clutched a high, starched collar. A circle of white light pinpointed the red leather chair.

"The hot seat," murmured Nick.

Sybille smiled.

"The Hot Seat," said a deep voice as the camera moved in to the group at the table, then panned slowly around it, pausing at each of the three interrogators and the young man in the red leather chair. "The toughest place in San Jose. Where there's no hiding. No room for pretense. No escape." The camera pulled back, showing the whole group. "The Hot Seat. A discussion among equals where the truth will be found, because our questioners ask all the questions you, our audience, would ask if you were in their seats. No holds barred."

The announcer introduced the interrogators and the man in the hot seat. "Wilfred Broome, Republican candidate for the U.S. Senate. We'll begin our discussion with Morton Case."

Case was short and round, with cheerful eyes and rosy cheeks. His voice was like syrup. "Mr. Broome, thirteen years ago you led several demonstrations at the University of California in Berkeley. Today you come down hard on demonstrators—"

"That was a long time ago." Broome's smile did not reach his eyes. "It has nothing to do with this election."

"Or with you?" asked the other man at the table.

"Nothing to do with me *today*," Broome said, his smile becoming complicitous, man to man. "We all had our salad days; you know how it is. I went through mine—wild oats, and all that—but it didn't last; I came to my senses when I realized"—his shoulders went back, his chin came up, and his words rolled out—"I could not risk destroying the fabric of our society, the very beliefs and ethics and morals I revered and vowed to cherish and protect—"

"The kind of morals that led you to be sued for child support by a woman whose baby you fathered?"

The woman who had dropped the question into the middle of Broome's sentence looked at him with raised eyebrows.

"What the—" Broome's eyes darted to the camera, then away. The muscles of his face were drawn. "You can't bring up—" He ran a hand over his cheeks and tightened his lips to a thin line. "That was a long time ago. The past. Nothing to do with me."

"But you were the father," one of them said.

"I was a kid—!" exclaimed Broome.

"You were thirty-one." Suddenly the pace quickened. "Eight years ago—"

"You were running a business—"

"And giving speeches on American morality—"

"Mothers shouldn't work, you said, to protect the family—"

"Ban abortions, you said, to protect the family—"

"While you were getting an elementary-school teacher from Santa Cruz pregnant."

"I never—hey, what is this, I didn't—"

"You aren't paying child support today?"

"Yes! No! I'm helping a young woman who was in trouble!" Silence fell over the table. The three interrogators let the silence stretch out. Broome stretched his lips. "This is ridiculous. I won't sit here and let you dredge up the past—"

Case pointed over Broome's shoulder. "The door is behind you, Mr. Broome. You don't have to talk about anything. You don't have to be in the Hot Seat. We'd regret your departure, and our viewers would, too, but we don't try to keep embarrassed guests against their will."

Nick leaned forward as if pulled toward the screen. He didn't like Broome, he hated everything he stood for, but there were accepted ways to question candidates and this was not one of them. He felt Broome's helpless fury so keenly it was as if he too were squirming in that bright light.

"Isn't it *incredible*?" Sybille asked. "It works; it really works. Oh, Nick, isn't it wonderful?"

He looked at her. Her face was as bright as as child's, her eyes shining, her moist lips parted. She was breathing rapidly, as if she were at the height of sexual pleasure. He drew back and stood up. Chad hung over his arm, wide-eyed, turning his head to watch the television screen.

"Where are you going?" Sybille cried. "You haven't seen all of it!"

"It's just more of the same, isn't it?" He lifted Chad to his shoulder. "Twisting the knife. They aren't interested in ideas or information; all they're interested in is making him squirm. I don't find that amusing. I don't think many people will."

"You're wrong," she said. "Everybody loves to watch people squirm. How many people really want ideas and information? They'd rather see someone slip on a banana peel or get whacked in the rear with a paddle or be made a fool of. What do you think 'Candid Camera' was about? Someone once told me nobody cares about news; they want human interest. Well, this is the best kind of human interest. The kind that makes viewers feel superior to the fool on the screen."

She watched Morton Case ask three rapid-fire questions in a row. "When we were showing the pilot to Wooster Insurance, trying to sell them on sponsoring it, the president of the company said I'd have been in the first row of the Colosseum, watching the Christians being thrown to the lions."

Nick felt his heart contract. "Did you take that as a compliment?"

She met his eyes. "He meant it as one. He told me he likes tough people. He bought this show because he knew I'd deliver."

"Meaning you wouldn't get soft."

"Exactly. That's what you meant, wasn't it, when you told me you loved my determination?"

"Not quite." Chad began chewing on his knuckle, and with relief Nick said, "I'm going to get this young man some food."

"What *did* you mean when you said that?"

"I meant I loved it that you refused to be defeated, that you weren't afraid to try again, that you always picked yourself up from a setback and kept going. That has nothing to do with getting ahead by appealing to the side of people that likes to watch Christians thrown to the lions. I didn't know that was a side of you, either." He turned to go, then paused. "I should congratulate you. It's not easy to get a new program on the air. You've done wonders in a very short time. I hope you're pleased."

"Of course," Sybille said automatically. She felt cold. Her delight in her program was oozing away beneath Nick's hard voice, and she hated him for it. She looked at him as he stood in the doorway, holding his son as naturally as he held a pencil at his desk. He was good at whatever he did, she thought, everything came easily to him, and it rankled her especially with Chad. Nick hadn't ever been a father, he didn't even have younger brothers or sisters, but he'd helped with

Chad's delivery as calmly as if he'd been trained for it, and, from the first time he held that tiny form in the hospital, he had handled him and cared for him with a casual authority Sybille couldn't hope to compete with, and a pleasure she couldn't understand.

Chad knew that his father was more comfortable with him than his mother was, and he was mean about it, Sybille thought. Seven months old and he had a mean streak, squirming and kicking and crying when she held him and then grinning and making odd singing noises as soon as he was in Nick's arms. It was as if they'd fallen in love with each other, those two, and she was the outsider.

"Of course I'm pleased," she said. "I'm going to make people notice me. That's what this is all about." She turned her back on both of them and stared at the screen. "I'm sorry you won't watch it with me. You said you would. And we don't do so many things together these days."

"Whatever we do," Nick said as he left, "it won't be watching that show."

The warm spring day that Nick and Ted moved Omega Computing Services from the family room to the garage was a red-letter day. At the time, they joked about it—"Doesn't look like progress to me," Nick said, "banished to the garage"—but in fact it was a leap forward that would take them, in less than five years' time, to triumphs and fortunes greater than any they had ever dreamed of.

They were at the beginning of a revolution. Only a few people, in the early 1970s, glimpsed the future that would be transformed by computers; Nick was one of them. He knew, when they changed the name of their company to Omega Computer, that they had nothing but room to grow.

Computers themselves had been around since the 1940s, but they were primitive things: big and slow, used mostly by universities for mathematical calculations, and by big corporations to handle large amounts of data. But by 1974, the year Nick and Sybille moved to San Jose, the first successful microprocessor had appeared: an integrated circuit etched on a tiny chip of silicon. The chip, barely a quarter of an inch square, did the same work that until then had taken five thousand separate transistors. And that chip would transform not only the computer industry, but a piece of California: the stretch of land from San Francisco south to Monterey, already dubbed Silicon Valley.

It was there, in small towns and fields lush with vineyards and artichoke fields—soon to become industrial parks and cities blurring into each other along traffic-clogged highways—that growing numbers of young inventors plunged into the world of computers. In homes and offices, garages, basements and family rooms, they scribbled ideas, assembled circuits, and stared for hours at terminal screens; they sat in coffee shops late at night debating possibilities, drawing circuit diagrams and making programming notes on the backs of envelopes; they sat in silent rooms, thinking in new languages.

What they wanted was clear to them: to solve any problem, cut through any conundrum, organize any chaos so swiftly and with such clarity that the messy world would seem neat.

Most of them, in their casual, laid-back style, would have said it differently: that they were turned on by computers and wanted to see what they could do; or they liked being part of revolutions; or they wanted a piece of the big money they were sure was there to be made; or they wanted to help humanity with new technology.

Among them, Nick was an oddity. He was too normal to be accepted by the freaks whose whole world lay between a keyboard and its terminal; he was too ambitious to fit in with those who were in it only for one thing, whether it was fun, or excitement, or a sense of accomplishment, or for the good of humanity.

Sybille didn't understand what he wanted, though he had tried to explain it to her. "I love the fun of it," he said. "It's a game: like kids writing letters to each other in secret codes, or solving puzzles they've made up."

"It doesn't sound very grown-up," she said.

He grinned at her. "It's not. We're all little kids with a new toy and we keep making the new toy better."

"You don't mean that."

"Why not? If work can be fun, why not?"

"Because it's serious."

"Work?"

"Everything. Work, getting what you want, handling people, being married . . . And you do work hard, I've watched you; you take off and play Ping-Pong, but the rest of the time you're not having fun; you're hard at work."

"Games can take as much concentration as work; why not make it as much fun as we can?"

"Because then you won't get anywhere."

She couldn't risk lightheartedness, he thought, and a brief memory came to him of someone who could, even in making love. "I'm willing to give it a chance," he said. "And if I have a good time and still make myself the biggest in this business, would you be convinced?"

She shrugged. "It wouldn't matter. I have to live my own way; I can't live yours."

So they went separate ways, and Nick shared the hard work and the sense of play with Ted and others who became his friends in those first years of Omega Computing. But besides the fun, the excitement of discovery, the pleasures of work, it was ambition that drove him: the compulsion to do more, expand their company from the garage to its own building, make his reputation, make his fortune, start a second company, start a third . . . there was no end to what he expected of himself.

And he was getting there faster than most. Already he and Ted were known as the top consultants in the valley; they were the ones called in first, and called back when companies wanted to expand.

Then, after only two years, everything changed. One day they were following current technology, showing others how to use it; the next they were making inventions of their own. They moved to the front of the crowd, and stayed there.

They found only a handful of others already there, among them two young men named Wozniak and Jobs, working in another garage in a city not far from San Jose. They started a company called Apple Computer. With Nick's Omega Computer, and a few others, they helped make the revolution that created the era of modern computers.

It was when they began their own inventions that Nick and Ted moved from the family room to the garage. It all started with a new client: a chain of twenty-six high-priced women's-sportswear shops called Pari's of Pebble Beach, that stretched up and down the West Coast, from Carmel south to San Diego and north to Vancouver. Pari Shandar, forty-nine, shrewd, small, darkly exquisite, had built the chain by herself in the fifteen years since her husband left her for a younger woman. Energetic and curious, Pari welcomed each new idea that caught her attention. Two years earlier Nick had helped her set up a computer system for her accounts payable and receivable, her payroll, and the mailing list that was a key to her success, since it was a closely guarded list of wealthy women throughout the world, including her native India.

"Now I think you can help me again," she said to Nick as they sat in her fringed silk and velvet parlor. She lived alone in a stone castle perched above the Pacific on Seventeen Mile Drive in Pebble Beach. A high stone wall protected her from the tourists who drove along the looping road to see the ocean and the cypresses, the famous golf courses and the huge homes. The crash of the surf could be heard through her open windows, and the cries of gulls soaring against a silver-blue sky. Otherwise it was very quiet and secluded, the rooms filled with Indian and American art, the atmosphere warm, a little heavy, like an embrace.

Pari poured tea into translucent porcelain cups and moved a plate of small cakes closer to Nick. "This is what I want: to know what is the inventory in my shops every day. Now, we count sweaters, skirts, jackets and so on by hand three times a year—and we must close the shops early to do this. It would be so much better to know every day what items have sold so we can adjust our main inventory list. Is this clear?"

Nick nodded. "You want reports at the end of each workday on what was sold that day in each of your twenty-six stores, and you want it done automatically. You probably want it removed automatically from your inventory list at the same time."

She looked startled. "Is that possible? Is any of it possible? When I told this idea to someone, he said it could not be done."

"It can be done, but it has problems. This is what we can do right now." Leaning forward, he sketched on a pad of paper, turning it so Pari could read it with him. He drew swiftly, surely, but part of his mind was distracted, aware of her perfume, the rustle of the silk dress she wore, the gleam of her ebony hair, fastened in a neat bun at her neck. The prim hairstyle belied the seductive perfume and that soft whisper of silk that made a man think of bare limbs and soft skin, the curves and taut muscles of an embrace—

"But what are these arrows?" Pari asked. Her eyes were on his drawing, but there was a small smile on her lips, and Nick knew that somehow she had known what he was thinking.

"How the system could work for you." He kept his voice level. "Your clerk rings up a sale—a cashmere sweater, say, at a hundred dollars—"

"Try two or three hundred," said Pari with a gentle laugh.

His eyebrows rose. He had never bought Sybille a cashmere sweater. Lately he hadn't bought Sybille anything at all. "All right. The clerk enters the code for that sweater in the cash register, and when it's entered it's automatically recorded, with the sweater size, style and price, and anything else you want, on a magnetic tape recorder—"

"One in each store?"

"Yes." He met her eyes. She was watching him more than she was watching his pencil. There was a tiny mole below her left eye: a dark fleck that made her skin seem even smoother. He had never noticed it before. He knew if he moved slightly, his arm would brush hers.

He wrenched his eyes down, to his diagram. "After the shops close, the tape recorders play back the information through the telephone system to your main computer in Monterey. The cashmere sweater—and all the other items sold in the shop—is deleted from the inventory stored in the main computer; it's also printed in a list of items sold that day in each of your shops. So you have a fresh inventory, updated from the day before, and a list of sales in twenty-six stores."

Now she too was looking at the diagram, nodding her head. "Perfect. Perfect. When can I have it? What will it cost? Ah, but it will save me so much, I can afford to spend... well, we will see how much I can afford to spend." She put her hand on his arm. "Nicholas, I need to know what it will cost and how soon you can have it in my shops. That is, if you give me a price I can manage."

Her hand burned on his arm, each of her fingers like a small flame curled around his sleeve. But he smiled at her sudden wariness about money. "I can't promise anything yet; I want to work on how we'd put it together. There are problems in connecting the magnetic recorders with the telephone system. No one's come up with a good way to get all that information stored and transmitted. You don't want us to install another minicomputer to do it; it's too expensive, it takes up too much room, and it doesn't have the speed we want. What we need is something small and fast, uncomplicated, low-cost, very reliable..."

"Like a team of workers in Bombay," said Pari with a laugh. "Perhaps that is what I really need: my family could send me a team and I would give each of them a pen and a telephone. Unless you have something that will do the work of a dozen people, maybe even a hundred."

Nick looked at her. "Or five thousand," he said slowly.

"Oh, no, I could not possibly need so many. We are a small chain ... But that is not what you meant."

"No." Tapping his pencil on the table, he absentmindedly ate a piece of cake, then took another. "I could build you a computer, just a printed circuit board, really... combining microprocessors into a custom-made board... small enough to fit in a desk drawer—well, maybe a small cabinet; it has to have a power supply—and then we'd program it... we'd need a keyboard, but that's no problem; we might even have a video screen so we could see the commands while we're putting them in..."

He looked at Pari and smiled, a wide, gleeful smile. It was the smile of a child who had suddenly made a discovery that changed forever the look and shape of the world.

"We could program it to do the whole job," he said, taking another piece of cake. "Convert the information from the cash registers to signals that are stored on a tape recorder and then transmit them over the phone lines. Incredibly simple, really. Your own specialized micro-computer. Cheaper and smaller than anything on the market. Probably faster too."

Pari was watching him. She had no idea what a microprocessor was, or a microcomputer; custom circuit board had no meaning for her. But she understood cheaper, she understood smaller and faster, and she understood what it meant when a man had that absorbed, rapt look of discovery on his face. She trusted it; she trusted Nick. The talk in the valley was that no one saw possibilities as quickly as Nick Field-ing; no one put together programming concepts with such brilliance; and no one else had a partner like Ted McIlvain, with his superb electronic skills.

"Very good," Pari said firmly. "Tell me how much money you need to build these special micro-whatevers. I want them."

Nick barely heard her. "It could probably do other things." He ate another piece of cake. "It would already be converting information and transmitting it—why not do four jobs? Or a dozen? What would be the limit? Why should there be a limit at all?"

"Nicholas," Pari said, "would you like more cake?"

He looked at the plate. "My God, did I do that?"

"You did. Would you like more? Or something else? Dinner, per-haps?"

"No. Thanks, Pari, but we have a project to finish tonight." The diagram drew him, and his glance returned to it. "It's an idea; no-body's done it. Of course there would have to be a limit. But I don't know what it would be. Or what would determine it. We'd have to build—"

"But later, yes? Right now, before you get involved in anything else, you are going to build this custom board and whatever else for me. You are, aren't you, Nick? I must have it soon."

He laughed. "An hour ago you hadn't even thought of it."

"But now I see how badly I need it. I do not need this other thing you started talking about."

"I was talking about a computer small enough to fit on your desk and do anything you want to do."

"But as soon as you build my custom board, what more would I need?"

"I don't know." He looked past her, through the window. The sky was still bright; it was April and the cypress trees were moving gently in a warm sea breeze. "We don't know all the possibilities of anything until we've built it. But the possibilities... all the possibilities..." His eyes were still on the sky, and it was a moment before he turned back to her, and stood up. "I'll build yours first, Pari, I promise."

She nodded gravely. "Thank you." She stood with him, the top of her head just at his shoulder level. "It is not good to interfere with a man's work, and I would be accommodating if you insisted; but, you see, I have my own work, and it is all I have."

Abruptly, Nick thought of Sybille, who showed no signs, ever, of being accommodating. Would she also say her work was all she had?

Of course she would. Because even though she had tried to be caring and loving, and he had tried to help her, the premiere of "The Hot Seat" had changed their marriage permanently. From that time on, without pretense, they had let all feelings of closeness dwindle and die. Sybille was where she had been when he met her: she had only her work.

"I'm sorry," Pari said, searching his face. "What have I said?"

"It's not you," Nick said quietly. "My own thoughts got in the way. I appreciate your being accommodating, but it won't be necessary; we'll start on this tomorrow." He took her hand. She swayed toward him and he bent to kiss her forehead, breathing in her heady scent. She was so close the warmth of her body seemed to embrace him, and desire surged through him with a force that made him dizzy. When she lifted her face to his, her lips slightly parted, Nick brought her into his arms, his mouth covering hers and opening it wider, his hunger so fierce it made his tongue a weapon.

Gently but very firmly, Pari broke free. "We should go slowly," she said. Her eyes smiled, but Nick felt her words as small stabs of reproach.

"I'm sorry," he muttered. Through the raging of his desire, longing filled him, so deep and bitter he felt like weeping. "I don't usually..." Floundering, he blundered on. "I really am sorry."

"Oh, Nicholas." He saw the slight shake of her head and the tender amusement in her eyes, and he felt very young. I'm twenty-eight, he thought; Pari is forty-nine. It would have made no difference at all, and he had not even thought of it in his overwhelming desire for her, but he wondered what amused her: his youthful clumsiness or the inexperience of a man who had never before strayed from his marriage bed.

It did not matter. What struck Nick at the moment was that he was, in fact, ready to betray Sybille and he felt no anguish over it. He felt nothing. That may have jolted him enough to make his floundering worse, because it said far more about his marriage than about either youth or inexperience or clumsiness.

He took Pari's hands in his. "That was foolish of me; you deserve better. I want to make love to you, Pari. I'll wait until you tell me you want me, but you must know how much I want...how much I need..." He cleared his throat. "I suppose that sounds very young to you."

She shook her head gently. "Why would it sound young? We all have wants and needs, and if we cannot satisfy them one day, we hold them in abeyance for...another time?"

He smiled, grateful to her, appreciating her tact. "I hope so. I hope I'll be welcome if I come back."

"Dear Nicholas, you will always be welcome here."

He took a deep breath. He might still stay. They would talk and have dinner together, and probably spend the night in her bed. But Pari had said what she wanted and he would not try to change her mind. Because she was right: it was better to go slowly. I already rushed once when I shouldn't have, he thought. Rushed off with Sybille before I'd figured out whether I could try again with Valerie. Before I'd even been alone long enough to think things through. I felt so goddam sorry for myself I couldn't wait; I had to—

He caught himself. Never before had he thought their marriage had been a mistake from the beginning. They'd had some good times; he had thought he loved her. After all, he hadn't been attracted to Pari when he first worked for her, a year earlier; he and Sybille had been close then. Or so busy they hadn't paid much attention to how close they were. Or how far apart.

"Nicholas, you said you wanted to get home early."

He smiled wryly. "You're right." Leaning down, he kissed her cheek. "Thank you for being here. I'll call you about the computer as soon as I have a breakdown of costs. Give us a few days." And then he left the velvet and silk room and made the two-hour drive north to San Jose, along the ocean, as afternoon faded into night and the sand dunes and orchards and fields of feathery artichoke plants disappeared into blackness. All the way home, he thought only about computers and inventory and hookups between magnetic recorders and the telephone system. It was easier than thinking about Sybille.

But she was there when he walked in, talking to Ted in the brightly lit kitchen, pacing as she talked. "It's just that nothing changes," Nick heard her say as he closed the living-room door behind him and stood in the darkness. "The show is an absolute success—no one dares refuse to be on it; either they don't have the guts to admit they're afraid or they think they'll be the first to make fools of the interrogators—and we get piles of mail—"

"Not all flattering," Ted interjected.

"It doesn't matter. Mail means viewers. They can send hate mail and we'll love them for it as long as they keep watching. We've knocked out the other channels in that half hour; it doesn't matter what they put on, we always beat them. And the cooking show is good. Nothing like 'The Hot Seat,' but it gets better each month."

"What cooking show?"

"Oh, something I put together on ethnic cooking, just to let everyone know how versatile I am; nothing important."

"You get a lot of mail on that too," Nick said, coming into the kitchen. He laid his cheek briefly against Sybille's forehead.

She gave him a perfunctory pat on his arm. Her eyebrows shot up. "Good heavens." She followed him as he went to the refrigerator, and put her nose to his jacket, sniffing audibly. "*Isn't* that nice? A little much, but very classy; I'd guess it cost a king's ransom. Or a queen's. Computers make strange bedfellows, is that how you'd put it? If you're getting a drink, make me one, too."

"What would you like?" Nick asked evenly.

"Scotch and soda. Light on the soda. Have you spent the whole day in bed with her or did you do a little business on the side?"

Ted pushed back his chair. "I'll be in the garage."

"Don't go," Sybille said. "If he's screwing your clients, you ought to know about it; he's your partner, after all."

"He's my friend too, and if there's anything I need to know, he'll tell me."

When he left, the kitchen was silent, except for the clink of ice cubes as Nick filled two glasses. "Are you worried about Ted or about yourself?" he asked, handing a drink to Sybille.

She shrugged. "What difference does it make? You'll do what you want. You always do."

"What does that mean?"

"It means we came to this damn town because you wanted to; we moved into this shack because you wanted to; we stay in this lousy neighborhood because you want to. You know I want to go to New York; you've known it since we got married, but you've never, never thought about moving there. You want to be here. That's all that matters."

Nick gazed at her. "You haven't mentioned New York since you started work at the station. You said this was the right place for you; you were learning so much you'd need later."

"In New York. 'Later' meant New York, and you knew it."

He nodded. "Probably."

"Well, I've learned it. There's no reason for me to stay here anymore."

"Except that you have a husband and a son who live here and I can't leave right now. Everything Ted and I are building is based on our reputation here; it wouldn't make any sense to go somewhere else and start from scratch."

"Who said I have a husband? I have someone who's screwing his way up and down the California coast...damn you, how could you! Doesn't it mean anything to you that we're married? I've never even thought about anyone else since I met you! I see a lot of men at work and I don't want to go to bed with any of them, not one of them! But you come home smelling like a whorehouse and expect me to talk about staying here, no matter what, just because you want to. That's what you want, isn't it? Somebody who cleaves to you and doesn't ask questions."

Nick finished his drink. The ice-filled glass chilled his palm. "But you don't want to cleave to anyone, do you?"

She was at the refrigerator, taking out the soda, refilling her glass. "Do you want another drink?"

"Fine."

"Were you in bed with her all day?"

"Would it change anything if I was?"

"It might." She handed him his drink. "No wife likes her husband to play around. That's probably the reason we haven't been getting along. Isn't it? You've been too busy thinking about other women to think about me. That would explain everything, wouldn't it? Anyway, I have a right to know."

Involuntarily, Nick smiled slightly. "We haven't claimed very many rights in this marriage. Are you sure you want to start now?"

"Don't be clever; you know I hate it. I want to know what you were doing today."

"Talking about a computer system for a chain of clothing stores."

"I don't believe you."

"I know. Sybille, if I said we'd move to New York tomorrow, would that make you happy?"

She frowned, looking for the catch. "You know it's what I want. I can't stay here; it's too small and far away from everything, and they won't give me what I want. You don't have to stay here, either. Whatever it is you're doing, you can do it in New York as well as here. There are a few chains of clothing stores in New York, you know. And we'd have places to go at night, things to do—we'd be completely different in New York! If we could just get out of this awful place everything would be better—we'd have a wonderful time—it would be like a honeymoon. We've never even had a honeymoon."

"And when would we be with Chad?"

"Oh." She made a gesture. "As much as we are now. Elena would come with us, of course; they're crazy about each other."

Nick took a drink. "Chad and I are staying here," he said. "You're right about this house; we definitely need a bigger one, with a yard for him to play in, and a school that he can walk to when he's ready, and Omega somewhere else. But we're not leaving San Jose. At least not for a few years. I don't know what will happen later, but right now everything I've got is here and I'm not throwing it away."

"Everything you've got? Not if I go to New York. Then you wouldn't have a wife here."

Nick gazed at her. "That's right."

Sybille flushed darkly. "You don't mean that. We're married. You chose me instead of—anyone else. You're not going to break us up; I won't let you. Nick, listen. We're good together; we need each other. We just haven't had enough time together; that's why I want to go to New York. Everything will be fine there; we'll be starting fresh; we can pretend we're in college and just starting out. Nick? Are you listening?"

He was looking beyond her, at the dark window. "We're not good together." His voice was flat and hard. "You don't enjoy sex; I'm not sure you ever did. And we don't need each other. You don't care what I do in my work and I don't like what you do in yours. There's nothing left, Sybille, and I can't see any reason to pretend there is."

"It's that woman!" she cried. "You spend the day in bed with her and then you come back and tell me you want a divorce! You never said anything about a divorce before!"

"I never let myself think about it before. For God's sake, Sybille, are you happy with me?"

·

"I'm happy when things are good. When we're really together. We *are* good together, damn it, and I do like sex! I love it! I don't know what you're talking about, I don't know what made you say that. Nick, listen to me!" She came to him and put her hands on his shoulders, her body pressed to his. "You can't pretend we're not good together; we have been, lots of times. You can't just throw that away."

"That's it?" he asked contemptuously. "A successful fuck is what I'm supposed to hang on to?"

Her hands dropped away. "I didn't say that was all; I said—"

"I heard what you said."

She stamped her foot. "I keep Chad. You can get out if you want to—if you think I give a damn, you're wrong—but you're not taking—"

"Chad stays with me. Don't make any mistake about that; he goes where I go. You don't care about him, you never have, and you're not going to use him now to bargain with. I'll get out tonight if you want me to, and Chad goes with me."

"He stays here! No judge in the world would let you take a child from his mother!"

Nick gazed at her without answering, and angrily she stared back. But then her gaze flickered and her eyes fell.

"Please," she said. She looked at him again and he saw panic in her eyes. "Nick, don't leave me. I need you. I've always needed you. I like knowing you're my husband; I like being married to you. I can't stand the idea of starting again, just me, and everybody else in couples, knowing they have somebody waiting for them at night. . . . Stay with me, Nick, I'll try to change; just tell me what you don't like and I'll change it. I can do what I decide to do; you know that. You admire that. Don't kick me out, Nick; I've been kicked out before; I can't stand it. *Don't leave me.*"

"I'm sorry," Nick said. The hardness had gone from his voice; instead a deep, weary sadness was there, and when Sybille heard it she knew it was over.

"*Damn you.*" Her breath rasped. "I told you how I really felt—I practically got down on my knees to you! You don't care about me any more than your girlfriend does! Both of you, going to bed, betraying me, tearing up my life . . . Damn you to hell, both of you!"

Nick started to repeat that he had not gone to bed with Pari, but then it struck him that Sybille had not meant Pari. She was not speaking about the present, but about the past. And he was silent.

Sybille tightened her lips. "You'll pay for me to go to New York.

You'll pay for me to live there until I find a job. When I'm settled, I'll send for Chad."

Nick knew it was her way out: she could not admit, to herself or him, that she did not want Chad, especially in New York. He let it pass. If she needed to believe she would send for Chad, he would not contradict her. "Let me know when you're settled," he said. He took a checkbook and pen from his inside pocket. "I can give you a thousand now, and five thousand by tomorrow afternoon; we'll have to talk about how much you think you'll need to live on."

"A lot," she said flatly. "I'll need a lot."

"I'll do what I can." Nick wondered, as he said it, if he meant money or making a life with his son. Both, he told himself. Starting right now. "For tonight, we'll go to Ted's," he said abruptly, and without another word he went upstairs, to wake Chad and Elena, and leave the house, and his marriage, behind.

Chapter

8

t the studios of the Enderby Broadcasting Network overlooking Trinity Church in lower Manhattan, they had heard of Sybille Fielding. "Smart
and tough," Quentin Enderby told his executive
staff when he showed them tapes of "The Hot
Seat." "Knows what she wants and isn't afraid to get her hands dirty
going after it. A nice change from all these pale pusillanimous peddlers
of piddling pap and pablum."

The executives smiled. They were expected to smile at Enderby's
alliterative phrases, and they always did, even when the phrases were
turned on them. But they did not smile a few months later when he
hired Sybille Fielding and named her executive producer of "World
Watch," WEBN's weekly news roundup that had never had good ratings. And there were no smiles when Enderby led her through the
offices and studios on the fifteenth floor of the Enderby Building,
making introductions.

"They'll adjust," he told her as he led her to a glassed-in cubicle
after the last cold handshake. "It's impressive how much people can
adjust to when they're getting paid well."

"It would make things easier if they do," Sybille said.

He raised an eyebrow. "But if they don't you'll manage? You're not chasing after popularity."

She shook her head, then looked up at him. "I want them to know I'm here. And I want you to approve of me."

He was fascinated by the intensity of her ice-blue eyes, set off by her smooth olive skin and heavy black hair. He had already noted her prettiness, and her compact figure, small but curving in the right places, neat and orderly in a severe, tailored gray suit. Now he saw again, as he had seen in their interviews before he hired her, that her eyes were as searching as beacons, and he wondered whether her controlled body and the tightness of her mouth hid ruthlessness or passion. *I want them to know I'm here.* It would be amusing to watch her make sure they did. Enderby was interested to discover in himself a flicker of sexual curiosity. It took a lot, lately, to arouse him.

"It's too early to talk about approval," he said. "But you do interest me."

Sybille's eyes became alert; she met his eyes in a long look, then turned away with a visible effort, as if forcing herself. "This is a wonderful office."

He gave a cursory glance at the cubicle. "It's functional, which is all anyone gets around here. The linocut behind the desk is a Picasso; that'll impress about two people out of a thousand."

"It impresses me." She stood beside the desk chair, wanting to sit in it, but holding back until Enderby was gone. "I didn't expect an office right away; I thought first you'd want me to prove what I could do."

"While working out of a closet? Don't be asinine. I don't have any truck with people who short-change themselves or get cute with false modesty. Either you're good and you know it or you're not and you won't be around very long. You have a reputation for being tough and good; if you really are, you make damn sure people know it the minute they meet you. Don't ever give anybody a chance to reach any conclusion about you but the one you want. Remember that."

Sybille was frowning. She contemplated him through hooded eyes, trying to figure him out. He was tall and broad, with stooped shoulders and a deeply lined face, and his hair stood out from his head in a frizzed yellow-white aureole like raveling steel wool that quivered when he spoke. He had a loud voice, and his fingers were gnarled. He walked with a goldheaded cane and dressed in tweeds and bow ties, like a British country squire.

Sybille had looked him up before she came to New York to be

interviewed by him, and she knew he was seventy-seven, from a wealthy Canadian family, all of them dead. He had been divorced four times and widowed once, and had no children. He had started the Enderby Broadcasting Network to cash in on television when it was new, but had never built a network: he owned only WEBN, an independent station once powerful but lately so low in the ratings no one took it seriously. And he was reluctant to spend a lot of money rebuilding it.

Which is why he hired a twenty-three-year-old producer from a small station in California, Sybille thought. And a woman. That saved him twenty-five percent right away.

But she hadn't argued about salary; she had no choice She told herself it was temporary; there was no way she would be satisfied for long with less than a man would make.

Don't ever give people a chance to reach any conclusion about you but the one you want. This was the first conclusion: no one would ever look at her again and think she came cheap.

"I'll remember," she said to Enderby. "That's good advice. Thank you."

Surprise showed in his eyes. "I'll be damned. A generous response." There was a pause. Reluctantly, he turned to the door. "Get familiar with the place. If you have questions, call anyone you like; they'll think more of you the more demanding you are. Be definitively decisive and demanding." He watched her, waiting for her smile, but none came. Instead she looked puzzled. "'World Watch' editorial meeting tomorrow at eight," he growled. "I'll expect to hear your ideas for whipping it into shape." Halfway through the door, he turned back. "Have you found a place to live?"

Sybille nodded shortly, her body tense with the desire to sit at her desk.

"Where is it?"

"On Thirty-fourth Street."

"Where on Thirty-fourth Street?"

"The Webster Apartments."

"Never heard of it."

"It was recommended to me."

"Any problems with it?"

"No. It's fine."

He nodded and took another step.

"Thank you again," Sybille said, her voice warmer now that he was really leaving. "I won't disappoint you."

"It will be easier if you don't," he said, echoing her own words of a few minutes earlier, and he closed the door behind him.

She let out her breath with a little explosion. Son of a bitch. Old, mean, nasty. The worst kind to work for: the kind she couldn't predict.

But at least he was gone. Now, at last, she could settle into her own chair and survey her own office. Even she couldn't pretend it was big or handsome, but it was her first, and the desk, though the wood was scratched and had cigarette burns in it, had a dark, masculine look that pleased her. Two office chairs were squeezed on the other size of the desk, facing her.

Behind the desk, next to the Picasso linocut, a small window looked across Broadway at the spire of Trinity Church. Sybille swiveled to look at it. The cross at its tip and its arched stained-glass windows at treetop level, in the midst of looming office buildings, made it look to her like a picture postcard. The church made her uncomfortable. It seemed wrong for New York: small and graceful, almost delicate. She wanted everything to be the tallest, the largest, the boldest, the fastest, the noisiest. The most important city in the world. The most reward-ing. The place where success meant more than anywhere else.

The place where Valerie lived.

The day before, she had taken a bus all the way up Madison Avenue and then walked over to Fifth Avenue, to the building where her mother had told her Valerie and Kent Shoreham had bought an apart-ment. She stood on the opposite side of the avenue, gazing at it in the crisp November sun. Behind her was the Metropolitan Museum of Art, its broad steps stretching across the front of the building, the grandeur of its pillars making even the trees of Central Park seem small and friendly. And in front of her was the grandeur of Valerie's build-ing, made of sedate gray stone with tall paned windows. An awning stretched from the carved wooden doors to the street, and two uni-formed doormen with glossy hats and white gloves blew imperious whistles that made taxis come to heel.

Sybille stared at the building, envying Valerie for living there, hat-ing the sleek people who came and went while she watched, their heels clacking arrogantly on the sidewalk, their furs gleaming, even the two dogs one of them was walking looking fat and smug. She had read about such buildings, and seen them in movies and on television, but she had never stood before one; she had never known anyone who lived in one. She watched the people come and go, knowing they hadn't the faintest idea she was there and wouldn't have cared if they did know. Envy and anger burned in her; she thought it must be radiating out, across the street, and scorching everyone there. But they never looked up; she was invisible.

Not for long. Pretty soon they'll know I'm here. I'll live in that building, or one just like it. I'll be that bitch's neighbor.

She walked up and down in front of the museum, inspecting Valerie's building from different angles, jostled by the Sunday crowds and the activity around her. On the expanse of sidewalk, someone was displaying strands of glass jewelry on a white cloth; nearby, two rickety tables were stacked with books for fifty cents apiece; at the corner of the museum steps a gangly man in a dark jacket, dark pants and a stocking cap had set up a small table and was playing a shell game with two tourists while his friend kept a lookout for police. On the steps, a tall figure swayed to the rhythm of his saxophone and the beat of two tomtoms and a steel drum being played by three teenage boys.

Sybille stood among the swirling crowds, watching all the performances. It would make good television, she thought; audiences would like it. Her eye saw everything framed within the borders of a television screen.

She stopped beside an aproned man with a drooping mustache and bought a hot pretzel with mustard, biting into its doughy saltiness as she walked. But then she threw it onto an overflowing trashcan. You wouldn't catch Valerie Shoreham chewing on a pretzel while she walked on the street.

Suddenly Valerie and her apartment building seemed impossibly remote. Sybille's fury grew: why was everything so difficult? She turned and walked rapidly away, ignoring the bus stop where a crowd waited. She didn't want to wait: she wanted to move.

But as she strode down the avenue, her anger lessened. The sidewalks were crowded, traffic was heavy, and the city's energy flowed around her, flowed through her, until she began to feel she could do anything she wanted. New York was everything she had expected it to be, fast and furious, the place for her, the place to be unencumbered and unattached.

She was young and ambitious and divorced. It had been very easy —much smoother and faster than she had thought a divorce could go, because there was nothing to quarrel over. Nick had no property and no expectations of any that she could see; it was obvious to her that he would always be a failure, like his father. There was no trouble over Chad either. Nick had custody and she had visitation rights whenever she wanted. And maybe more, she told herself. *I can get a judge to give me my son whenever I want him. No judge would refuse me if I* tell him my husband talked me into giving up my baby and now I want him back. I can do that anytime. But for now I'm free.

The first few days in New York, she repeated it to herself wherever she was: in her apartment, in her office, walking in the streets. No one nagged at her for attention or listening or *caring*. She'd been so afraid of being divorced and alone, but now she woke up every morning with a sense of being cut loose from everything that had ever made demands on her. She didn't miss Nick. She thought she had missed him in the first weeks after he moved out, but in truth what she really missed was thinking of herself as part of a couple. And she thought she had missed Chad, but in fact what she had missed was thinking of herself as a mother. The truth was, she didn't miss anything.

She felt most free when she walked home from work. Her first days in the Enderby Building she stayed late each evening to avoid running the cold gauntlet that had greeted her when Enderby made his introductions, and so each evening she reached the street alone, and walked alone, the bite of the chill air against her face making her feel combative and excited. Striding through Greenwich Village and then into Chelsea, she quickened her pace so the bustling people about her would know she was one of them, not a tourist. She glanced at dilapidated buildings and renovated ones as if she had seen them all her life; she casually skirted the heaps of clothing and overflowing bags that turned out to be people asleep in doorways or across heating vents in the sidewalk; she thought briefly of Nick and Chad, telling herself of course she would see them often; and then she let them slip from her thoughts. She had worked for Quentin Enderby for three days and she had an editorial meeting in the morning: that was what she had to think about.

She had stayed up much of the night, preparing for it, sure it would be high-powered and demanding compared to the meetings in Palo Alto and San Jose, and when she took her seat at a little before eight o'clock in the morning she was tense and alert. She told herself no one expected her to know everything on the first day, but still her hands shook. She had to prove herself, and Enderby would be there. As president, he never attended editorial meetings, but this morning, to see what she could do, he would sit at the head of the table. And he had told her how he felt about first impressions.

Six men and two women sat at a long table strewn with newspapers and wire reports, discussing the lead stories, deciding what they would feature that week on "World Watch." In a few minutes, Sybille began to relax. After half an hour she knew she had nothing to worry about.

They dealt more heavily with international events and less with local ones than she was used to, but otherwise everything was the same. She was smarter than everyone else, just as she had been in California. She would stand out here just as she had stood out there. Everything was going to be fine.

Enderby picked up a glass of ice water and drained it. "Sybille is going to give us the benefit of her worldly wit and wisdom to make 'World Watch' more watched." Everyone but Sybille chuckled. She watched them with contempt. "We're waiting," Enderby snapped.

Her notes were in her briefcase; she left them there. It was more impressive to speak without them. "I've seen six weeks of 'World Watch' tapes. Every program has been the same: too slow, too solemn, too tame. I kept waiting for something I could love or hate or talk back to, and there wasn't anything. It all went past me like a fog, words and words, and pictures that every other newscast uses, and a set design I can't even remember." She met the hostile eyes that were focused on her, then she looked at Enderby. He was leaning back in his chair, eyes closed, hands folded on his chest, their age spots dark and splotchy against his white shirt. Like a corpse, Sybille thought. Except that he was smiling. Coolly she returned every look around the table. This was what Quentin Enderby wanted.

"I have a few ideas. Of course we'll need dozens to get this show where it should be, but this is a start. Make the backdrop a huge world map like the ones they have in kindergartens, bright colors, big letter-ing, dark lines for countries' borders, and so on. Every time a news item is introduced we'll light up the place where it happened. Most people haven't the faintest idea where Sri Lanka or Khatmandu or the Transvaal are—they probably don't care, either, but they'll feel good about being shown; it's like getting something for nothing."

"Transvaal?" asked a young man at the other end of the table.

"South Africa," Sybille said crisply. "Then there's the anchorman. Somebody should teach him not to drop his voice on the last word of every sentence; he needs bigger shoulder pads; his hair ought to be combed from the left instead of the right; and get rid of those glasses —hasn't anybody heard of contact lenses? Better yet, get rid of the anchorman."

Eyes swiveled to the head of the table, and it struck Sybille that the anchorman had been hired by Enderby. "He may have been good at one time," she said, "and he's nice-looking, sort of like everybody's neighbor, but that's one of the problems." Stubbornness crept into her voice. "He's stodgy and flat, like the husband every woman wants to leave, instead of a young, handsome guy every woman would like to take to bed, even though she and her dull husband know she never will."

"Nasty," said a tall red-haired woman admiringly. She sat at Enderby's left and gazed thoughtfully at Sybille through large horn-rimmed glasses. "Neat and nasty."

Sybille ignored her. "There are some other—"

"The script," Enderby snapped. His eyes were still closed; he had not stirred. "Sets and shoulder pads are fluff. Get to the script."

"It doesn't have any life," Sybille said. "There's nobody to hate. Every story in the world has a villain and we have to tell the audience who it is each time so they can hate him or her without feeling guilty or worrying about being right or wrong. Everybody believes the world is divided into good guys and bad guys; it's our job to help them sort out which is which."

"*Our* job?" echoed a pudgy man with thinning hair.

"Of course. Our anchors, our reporters; that's why they watch us. They want us to help them side with the good guys. Issues are confusing; we're here to make them simple."

"Not true." The woman at Enderby's left peered at Sybille through her glasses. "Our job is to report to people on what happened that week. They maybe don't have time to read a newspaper or watch a newscast every day, and they want to know what's been going on. That's all they want; it's not up to us to tell them what to think."

"You're wrong," Sybille said flatly. "And that's why nobody watches your newscast. You don't have a good anchor, you don't have jazzy graphics, you don't have heroes and villains. All you have is the news, and if that's all you've got to offer, you're dead. You have to tell people what to think because most of them are too lazy or too stupid to think for themselves. We've got to make them believe that when we tell them who to trust and who not to, only then can they deal with the mixed signals they're getting from politicians and newspapers. They're busy people out there, how can they know enough to make up their own minds? We can do it subtly—we don't have to hit them over the head with it—but the message has to be that unless they watch us they'll be helpless and frustrated in a very confusing world."

"God damn!" Enderby was laughing, huge guffaws making the table shake. "If that isn't pure gold! Tell the audience what they need, then tell 'em we're the only ones who can give it to 'em!"

"She has a pretty low opinion of people," said the pudgy man with thinning hair.

Enderby smiled beatifically. "Of course she does. That's why I hired her."

A silence fell over the table as the WEBN executives altered their thinking about Sybille Fielding and their attitude toward her. And then, with smiles and gentler voices, they got down to the business of the transformation of "World Watch."

Enderby shifted his weight in the small chair and took the drink Sybille offered him. "Not a decent chair in the place," he said, shifting again. He glared balefully at the doorway, where the door had long ago been removed. "Not even any privacy. And no men allowed upstairs. You didn't tell me you lived in a convent. Cramped and confined in a claustrophobic convent."

Sybille sat on a footstool near his feet, drinking sherry. "You can call it anything you like. It's for working women, it's safe, and I pay a hundred and fifty dollars a week for a decent room with maid service."

"And no men allowed in your decent room."

She shrugged.

"And no telephone in your decent room."

"It's in the hall; they buzz me if I have a call."

"And no private bath in your—"

"It's only for a while," she said evenly. She hated it. She wanted an apartment and a doorman. She wanted Fifth Avenue across from Central Park. "I'll move when I'm sure of my job and I get a raise."

He grinned broadly. "When do you think that will be?"

Confusion swept across her face and he knew she had been expecting him to say something else. "I don't know. I hope—not too long."

Enderby took a swig of his drink—good bourbon, he noted, and just the right amount of water—and swept his gaze up and down her figure. "Don't you ever dress? I asked you to an art opening and dinner, not an executive meeting."

She frowned. "This is all I have."

"Business suits," he said dismissively. "You ought to have frills."

Sybille shook her head. "I'd look silly."

"Not in the right kind of frills. Feminine frills and fanciful furbelows. We'll go shopping; I'll buy you what you need."

She tilted her head and gazed at him. "That would be interesting."

He snorted. "It better be. Well, let's go, I've had it with this chair. Next time have them find a bigger one."

"Next time you choose where we should go," Sybille said boldly.

His eyebrows rose. He worked himself out of the chair, using his cane, and held his hand out to her.

"My apartment. We'll go there tonight. After dinner."

He was crude, and not really sophisticated, Sybille thought as they rode in his limousine to the Laffont Gallery on Eightieth Street. Even Nick seemed smoother than Quentin Enderby. But there were other things about him: even when he was coarse, people listened to him; he was sloppy, with food stains on his ties and some of the buttons on his jackets hanging loose, but the ties and jackets were expensive; his eyes were cold, but they saw everything. At different times in the four weeks she had been working for him, Sybille had thought him cruel, sarcastic, lonely, self-centered, smart, foolish, interested, bored, and contemptuous.

She always felt tense and off balance with him, wondering how to behave. And all the time he was watching her, waiting to see how she would behave. I hate him, she thought.

The Laffont Gallery was blindingly bright: a crush of people, massed from wall to wall, screeching to be heard, cupping plastic wine glasses protectively to their chests and squinting at hotly illuminated ten-foot sculptures and wall-size phosphorescent paintings. Enderby recoiled. "Damned torture chamber," he muttered. "Don't know why my secretary gets me involved in these things."

"You told me you might buy something," Sybille said.

"I said that? Well, that doesn't mean anything; I always say that. But I never do."

"You never buy anything?"

"Of course not. I don't like art; never did."

"Then I don't know why you're here."

"Neither do I. That's just what I said."

Sybille looked up at him to see if he were mocking her, but he was scanning the room. "Do you want some wine?" she asked.

"No. We'll look around and then get out." He saw the question in her eyes and gave a short laugh. "All right, it's a torture chamber, but we might as well have a little fun as long as we're here. I like to watch fools go scurrying after the newest fad, whispering, wiggling, worrying, watching out of the corners of their eyes to make sure nobody gets there ahead of them. Angling for clues to what they should spend their money on. *Panting* for *possessions*." He dragged out the words contemptuously. "I thrive on gallery openings: they're like a Roman circus."

Sybille had no idea how he wanted her to respond. "It's like an opening shot on television; if you got an overhead shot—"

"Quentin!" someone cried through the din of voices, and a slender young woman with close-cropped hair and a beaded jacket came close. "Wonderful, isn't he? So earthy."

Enderby cast a glance at the eight-foot mass of marble beside him. "If you like entrails."

She pouted. "He's all the rage; he's rising."

"Sexually or artistically?" He guffawed, and a stocky bearded man with a monocle turned on him.

"If you don't understand him, you should shut up. Some of us like to appreciate art in an atmosphere of silent, almost mindless pleasure."

"Try the john," Enderby snorted.

"Shame on you," said a pencil-thin man, nostrils quivering in anger. "This is no place for scatology; this is a place where we *worship art*."

Enderby stared at him. Slowly, he knelt and made the sign of the cross.

Sybille laughed.

Someone groaned.

Enderby used his cane to push himself up, and lumbered off, shouldering his way through the crowd.

Voices followed them. "Ought to put the bastard away."

"Yes, but if he's right?"

"Don't be an ass. This stuff gets top prices. Fucking old fart..."

Enderby turned. "That's one I would have used," he said gleefully, then pushed farther into the cacophonous room. Sybille stayed close to him. She wanted to be identified with him; she saw his crudeness now as strength. "Idiot writes for some high-flying ass-dragging art magazine," Enderby said over his shoulder. "Doesn't know what he's talking about, but nobody who reads him knows anything, either. How about this?"

He had stopped before a massive painting whose phosphorescent reds jumped and shimmied before their eyes. "The life spirit," someone near Sybille said reverently.

"More like a windstorm in hell, don't you think?" countered an amused voice.

Sybille swung around. She knew that voice. "Valerie," she said tightly across the intervening crowd.

Valerie looked up, shading her eyes against the bright lights. "Sybille! I can't believe it!" She pushed through the crowd, drawing attention. She was more beautiful than Sybille had remembered, her tawny hair streaming in artful disarray, her hazel eyes bright with surprise. She wore a dress of burgundy silk with a long strand of pearls. "Isn't this amazing! I was just thinking about you the other day. You look wonderful! What are you doing in New York?"

"I live here now. What about you?"

"So do I. We'll get together, shall we? We're not in the book; let me give you our number—"

"I have your parents' number."

"No, Kent's and mine; I'm married, Sybille. Are you?"

"I was."

A hand reached past Sybille, to Valerie. "Quentin Enderby."

"I'm sorry," Sybille said, flushing with embarrassment. "Valerie Ashbrook...no, I guess that's wrong. I don't know your married name. It's been so long and I haven't heard a thing about you."

Valerie shook Enderby's hand. "Valerie Shoreham. I've seen you at other openings."

"And heard my pronouncements, no doubt." His eyes were fixed on her. New York had many beauties; Valerie Shoreham was a great one. Surprising to find her popping up in Sybille's life.

"Do come to see me," Valerie said to Sybille. "You must. I've been wanting to talk to you for a long time. Here's my card; come this week. Come tomorrow, for drinks."

Sybille was having trouble breathing. Bitch. *You must*. Who the hell does she think she is? "All right," she said. Her voice didn't sound like hers. She looked at the engraved card and read the address aloud. "Isn't that somewhere near the Metropolitan Museum?"

"Across the street. You can't miss it. Five-thirty?"

"Yes."

"Wonderful. I'm so glad. You don't know how much it means to me. This is really so amazing. Who ever would have guessed...but then you always planned to come to New York. Are you in television?" Sybille nodded. "I want to hear all about it. So nice to meet you," she said to Enderby. "I'm looking forward to tomorrow," she said to Sybille. And she melted back into the crowd.

The lights seemed to dim when she left; the air no longer sparkled. Sybille let out her breath.

"You don't like her," Enderby said.

"Of course I do. We're friends. We've been friends all our lives." She looked up at him with that piercing look that made him realize he could not tell when she was lying and when she told the truth. He found that very exciting.

"We're going," he said. He took her arm and steered her through the room and out the door. Sybille reeled a little as the cold air struck her after the heat of the gallery, but Enderby had a firm hold on her arm and in a moment she was again in the mahogany and leather enclosure of his limousine. Quiet music came from the speakers, and the chauffeur had hors d'oeuvres and their drinks—sherry for Sybille, bourbon for Enderby—on the silver and ebony table in front of them.

"So," Enderby said, lifting his glass. "To art. Or what passes for it. What did you think of the show?"

"I don't know," she said; she was still thinking of Valerie. "I don't understand art."

"You don't have to. Do you like it?"

"I don't know. Some of it, I suppose."

"That painting your friend called a windstorm in hell?"

"I don't know. I don't think so."

"Neither did your friend. Are you hungry?"

"No."

"Neither am I. We'll skip dinner." He spoke into a small handset hanging beside him, and the chauffeur turned at the next corner. "They're all piss-ass frauds," he said. "Fools and fossilized fakes fawning over farcical fads. My father was an art and antique dealer; we never got along. He sold everything we had—paintings, furniture, sculptures. Our house was the showroom. It was all for sale. I learned not to get attached to anything because I knew it wouldn't be there long. He thought it was clever. Crude bastard. The best thing he did was die young and leave me his money so I could buy myself a television station. How did you and Valerie Shoreham get to be friends?"

She was silent.

"Sybille?"

She looked at him. "Our mothers knew each other. Quentin, I haven't told you this, but I want to be on camera."

"You're a producer."

"Yes, but it isn't what I want."

"A damn good producer. It's what I hired you for."

"I'll do it until 'World Watch' gets the ratings you want. Then I want to be an anchor or a host for a talk show . . . something like that."

"You've been here four weeks. Only a fool talks about a new job after four weeks. Give it four years and then I might listen."

"Four years? You're not serious."

"Try me."

She took a sharp breath, hating him. "I'm sorry. I know it's too soon to talk about it. It just occurred to me that I'd tell you. We wouldn't do anything about it for a while, a long time, maybe, but I just thought . . . I'd tell you."

"Well, you have. What did all that have to do with Valerie Shoreham?"

"Nothing! Why would you— Never mind, I really don't want to talk about it. You were right; it's too soon even to bring it up."

"But it's up. And I'm curious. Mostly about the beauteous Valerie."

"There isn't anything to talk about," Sybille said. "We've known each other since we were babies, and we were at college together. We were very close for a few years—she's the kind who has to have someone to confide in and she liked to talk to me—but then we drifted apart. She went to Europe, and I was married and working. I haven't seen her for more than three years, and I'd forgotten about her until tonight. That's all there is to it. Why did you tell me about your father?"

"I always talk about my father to young women I plan to take to bed."

Sybille stared at him. She was very angry. She'd felt small and plain next to Valerie, and she'd been furious at the way Enderby had looked at her; she hated feeling tense and off balance with him; she despised him for brushing aside the idea of her being on camera. Her shoulders went back. "Nobody takes me to bed. I decide where I want to go and what I want to do. And I haven't made up my mind about you yet."

He laughed, a kind of *Ho Ho* that set Sybille's teeth on edge. "You made up your mind long ago and you know it."

"What about your mother?" Sybille asked, anger making her reckless. "Do you only talk about her to women you plan to marry?"

Enderby reached out a long arm and pulled her to him, knocking her against the silver and ebony table. A glass rolled off onto the carpet at their feet. Sybille was half lying across his lap, his hand was beneath her head, gripping it, and his mouth was on hers.

Instinctively, she fought to get free. His lips were soft, almost spongy, and she recoiled from them. But he held her head with a strength that surprised her and when his tongue forced her mouth open she stopped struggling. He slid his hand beneath her jacket and grasped her breast, and then Sybille put her arms around him, remembering that this was what she had intended all along.

Enderby's apartment was a few blocks north of Valerie's, its eighth-floor windows overlooking the reservoir, Central Park's wide and shining lake. When they arrived, Sybille went straight to the windows. This must be almost the view Valerie saw. She gazed out and felt Enderby come up behind her. "Pretty good," he said casually.

"More than that," she replied. The scene had a grandeur that took her breath away. Central Park was a swath of black, surrounded by the brilliant lights of the city. A crescent moon was reflected in the quiet lake, as were hundreds of shimmering lights from the buildings across the park, like fireflies trapped in a dark mirror. Below Enderby's windows, Fifth Avenue stretched brightly; automobile headlights and the yellow rooftop lights of taxis swooped down the street. No sounds penetrated the closed windows; the room was hushed and the city beyond it was like the picture on a television screen, with the sound muted. We're above everything, Sybille thought. Much better than pretty good; it's perfect.

Enderby turned her around, pulling her against him, and kissed her roughly. When he let her go, her mouth felt crushed. "Is there anything you want?" he asked.

To get out of here, she thought. "No," she said.

He turned and led the way, and she followed, studying the furnishings: dark, heavy, Teutonic. Elk and boar heads hung on the walls; a cheetah crouched on a huge boulder mounted on a wall in the bedroom; the draperies depicted hunting scenes.

"I used to hunt," Enderby said.

"Why did you stop?"

"Somebody talked me out of it."

Sybille was silent, looking at the huge bed, twice as big as any she had ever seen. It was as if Enderby wanted the option of not being within touching distance of whoever he took to it, in case his feelings changed during the night.

"A preacher," he went on. "I'm a sucker for preachers. They're my weakness. Fortunately, I don't meet many; I'd have damn few pleasures left if I did. Undress for me."

Slowly, standing a few inches from him, Sybille took off her jacket and let it fall to the floor behind her. Enderby's hands hung at his sides and he watched as she stepped out of her shoes and took off the rest of her clothes. "You're a pretty girl," he said. "Nicely made. I could use a little help, here..." Sybille's quick fingers helped him pull off his clothes, and they lay on the velvet down comforter, its puffiness billowing around them.

"I'm not as quick as I used to be," he said. "It takes a little while."

He lay back in the circle of light from an antler chandelier, and

Sybille curled up beside him, bending over to take him in her mouth. She moved her tongue along his babylike softness and sucked on him. He was silent. She began to feel desperate and raised her head.

"Go on," he said.

She slid her hands beneath him, taking him again into her mouth, and soon his breathing grew louder and Sybille felt him swell and grow hard. His hands were on her breasts and she took him deeper into her throat until, abruptly, he pulled away and swung over, on top of her. She was not ready and instinctively she tried to push him away, but his bulk pressed her down and then he was inside her. He hurt her, but she would never let him know that. She closed her eyes, giving herself up to what she knew she did well without thinking. She moved sensuously beneath him, her knees gripping his hips, her teeth taking small bites of the slack skin at his neck. She squeezed him tightly inside her and it was only a few minutes before Enderby gasped and groaned in the silent room, his body stiffened, and then he was still.

Sybille waited, wanting to push him off. "You're a pretty girl," he said again.

She opened her eyes. He had a half smile and it suddenly seemed to her that he looked like Chad right after a feeding. It made her feel better to think about that.

"And you're good," he added. "I knew you would be; I'm always right about that."

"I'm sure you are." Sybille lay beside him, staring at the ceiling. The only times it had ever been good, or almost good, was with Nick. He shouldn't have kicked her out; they'd been good together. But there was no sense even thinking about that; it was over. She had to look ahead. She had to think about marrying Quentin Enderby.

This time, when I get married I'll get something out of it.

Chapter
9

alerie's apartment took up the top floor, sprawling in all directions. A sunroom furnished in wicker and chintz, with ficus and orange trees, was off a long living room furnished in bright silks with a marble fireplace at each end. On the other side of the living room there was a library with its own fireplace and floor-to-ceiling shelves filled with matching leatherbound books. In the dining room, a crystal chandelier sent thousands of diamonds dancing on ivory silk-moiré walls hung with sconces and a group of Rousseau clowns. There were fifteen rooms in all and the view swept the park beyond the roof of the museum. It was grander than Enderby's view because it was higher, even more aloof from everyday life. Following Valerie, Sybille walked through the rooms, absorbing the atmosphere, memorizing décor and furnishings, planning her transformation of Enderby's apartment.

"It's very nice," she said, as they returned to the library, where a decanter and cheese and fruit were set out before the fire.

Valerie nodded carelessly. She was gazing at the flames. "The first fire of the year," she murmured. "It always makes me melancholy. The end of summer, everything turning inward, a closing of doors..."

Sybille frowned. "I never heard you talk like that."

"Oh—" Valerie looked up. Giving her head a small shake, she smiled brightly. "I only do it once or twice a year." She poured sherry into amber glasses and sat in a deep velvet wing chair, kicking off her shoes and curling up in its depths. She wore a cashmere sweater and matching flared wool skirt, comfortable and casual and elegant. Sybille, taking the chair opposite her, sat straight: constrained and severe in her tailored suit. But she wouldn't have curled up no matter what she wore; this was enemy territory.

"Before we talk, I want to say something," Valerie said. "I'm so glad we ran into each other last night; otherwise I'd have gone on stewing over this for years and not been able to tell you..." She got up restlessly, and stood by the fire. "Sybille, I felt terrible when I heard what happened at Stanford; I never would have thought they'd do something so drastic—I still can't believe it—and I owe you an apology. Larry Oldfield told me I said you'd made up parts of that ape story. I can't believe I did, but I don't remember what I told him; it must have been an awfully dull party and I suppose I was making conversation to get through the evening, and if Larry says that's what I said, I'm sure he's right. So it was my fault and I would have undone it if I could—I wanted to do something to help—but by then you were gone."

"How did you know?" Sybille asked coldly.

"I tried to call you. All I got was one of those death-warmed-over recordings saying your phone had been disconnected. No forwarding number; nothing. I asked at the tv station in Palo Alto, but nobody knew where you were. So I let it go. But I did feel terrible."

"You could have called my mother."

"Your mother?"

"Your seamstress."

"Oh, my God, of course. Mother still uses her, but I haven't for years. How could I forget? That would have been so simple."

Sybille said nothing.

"I'm so sorry," Valerie said. She came back to her chair and sat cross-legged in its depths. "For all of it. Such a mess...and so awful for you. Where did you go?"

"San Jose."

"Because of a job?"

"I found a job once I was there. I went because that's where my husband wanted to live."

"Yes, you said last night you'd been married. Someone from Stanford?"

"Nick Fielding."

"*Nick?*" Valerie's eyes were stunned. "You and Nick?"

"Why not?" Sybille demanded.

"Well...no reason, I suppose. I was just surprised. I haven't thought of him in such a long time, it was surprising to hear his name. I'd really forgotten about him..."

Liar, Sybille thought, and a surge of triumph swept through her. Valerie Shoreham, wearing cashmere in her fifteen rooms above Central Park, with her butler and her maids and her chef, and even a private secretary, still thought about Nick Fielding. And Sybille, with nothing, had married him. And left him. "What about you?" she asked. "How long have you been married?"

"A little over a year. I can't believe it: you and Nick married....And now you're divorced? What happened?"

"We decided to go our own ways. We wanted different things."

"Did you? I thought you wanted the same thing, and you were both so serious about it, to make it big and to do it in a hurry....That wasn't what Nick wanted?"

"Mostly he wanted things to go his way. What does your husband do?"

"Nothing very much." Valerie smiled faintly. "He's vice-president of his father's bank, so he goes to the office every day, and he reads *The Wall Street Journal* a few times, to make sure he doesn't miss anything. What did you mean, mostly he wanted—" She stopped. "You haven't told me about yourself. Where did you go to finish college?"

"I didn't bother. I worked in television in San Jose, and I'm at WEBN here. Executive producer of 'World Watch.'"

"How wonderful! You started at the top. I'm not really surprised, though; you were always so good."

Enemy territory, Sybille reminded herself. Don't forget. But it was hard to steel herself against Valerie's warmth when Valerie was admiring her. Enfolded by the book-lined room, the fire and Valerie's interest, Sybille felt a mellow relaxation spread through her. "It is the top; it's the biggest producing job there, and everybody knows it. There are other things I want to do, but for now this is the best job I could have. It's the most important thing that's happened to me since I left Stanford."

"The most important...?" Valerie paused, but Sybille was taking a crimson grape from a cluster and did not respond. "Well, it's wonderful that you're still so excited about television. I think it's a lot of fun, but I can't get very worked up about it."

"You don't know anything about it. You only did those few spots in college."

"Oh, I still do that sort of thing. Not a lot, just now and then, for friends."

Sybille's fingers tightened on her glass. "I haven't seen you."

Valerie laughed. "I'm not surprised. Mostly they're public-service announcements that get stuck between commercials, while people are raiding the refrigerator. I did one a few months ago for the MS fund drive—that got a fair bit of attention, but maybe you weren't here yet—and I've done pitches for money to sponsor hungry kids around the world, and I was one of the hosts for a public-television pledge week..." She gestured with her hand. "Nothing special, just helping people out. It's something to do, and I like to do different things. I remember you used to talk about being on camera; whatever happened to that?"

"I haven't thought about it for years," Sybille said flatly. *Nothing special . . . it's something to do.* Stupid, she thought. Shallow. As flighty as ever. She hasn't changed at all; she never was anything; she'll never be anything. But she gets what she wants, without even trying. How the hell does she do that? "It's not nearly as important as producing; I'd much rather make things happen behind the camera than sit at a desk and wait for everybody to tell me what to do and what to say and when to say it..."

"Goodness," Valerie said with another laugh. "I'd better stop doing it right away; you make me sound like a trained monkey."

"Not really; it's..."

Valerie jumped up again, her skirt swirling, and walked about the room. She stopped at a table near the door, fingering some of the small vases on it. "You've got so many opinions on everything," she murmured. "And you're so *busy.*"

What does that mean? Sybille wondered. Does she admire me for being busy or does she think I'm a fool?

"Do you ever talk to Nick anymore?" Valerie asked.

"Every couple of weeks."

"Do you? Then you're friends."

"We talk about money and about Chad." She watched Valerie closely. "Our son."

"Your *son?* You have a child?" Valerie whirled around and came back to her chair, sitting on the edge. "Sybille, you didn't say a word! How could you not talk about him? His name is Chad? Chad Fielding. I like that. How old is he?"

"Almost two."

"I can't believe it. Nick always said he wanted children, but it doesn't seem possible..."

"What? What doesn't seem possible?"

"Oh—" Valerie gave a small laugh. "I think of all of us as so young; it seems as if we just graduated and we're still looking around, wondering what to do with ourselves."

"I never wondered what to do with myself," Sybille said coldly.

"No, you were different. You always knew. And so did Nick. Did he start his own computer company?"

"Yes."

"And? Is he a great success?"

"No. It's a tiny company—there's just two of them, and they work in a garage."

"But they just got started; it must take awhile."

"It's been years."

"But it takes years, doesn't it? He'll probably have a breakthrough one of these days and get everything he wants."

"I doubt it. They're not designing anything; they're just consultants."

"That wasn't what he was planning." Valerie shook her head. "Poor Nick. He had such big dreams. And he never doubted..."

The butler stood in the doorway, glancing swiftly at the sherry decanter to make sure it was sufficiently full, and at the tray of cheese and fruit which had barely been touched. "Mr. Shoreham called, ma'am. He's working late and asks that you meet him at the Walmsleys' at eight-thirty."

Valerie nodded. "Thank you, Morton."

How civilized this is, Sybille thought as the butler vanished as noiselessly as he had arrived. She sipped from her glass while Valerie shifted in her chair and absentmindedly nibbled a slice of Gruyère. Sherry in the library, a nice fire, a butler to make sure we have plenty of everything, and the chitchat of old friends, catching up after a long separation. Old friends, good friends. Such good friends.

"This has been very nice," she said, putting down her glass. "I have no one to talk to in New York and this has been...nice."

"You're not going," Valerie said quickly. "Stay awhile. You do have someone to talk to: you have me. And I'll introduce you to people.

New York is a terrible place to be alone. What about Quentin Enderby? Do you spend much time with him?"

Sybille hesitated, then decided she had to confide something if Valerie was to believe they were friends. "Not yet."

"You don't really want him, do you? He's old enough to be your grandfather."

"He can take care of me," Sybille said.

"Well, but if that's what you want, there are men nearer your age who can do it."

Sybille shrugged. "I don't know any other men. And he's fun to be with."

"Is he? He didn't strike me as the fun type. Domineering is more like it. I know a lot of men like that, Sybille, and I'd be careful not to confuse it with strength. When you're alone in a place like New York it's too easy to latch onto the wrong kind of person. You're so young and independent, I think you'd go crazy with... well, I don't really know him. Let me introduce you to some men who really are strong, and fun too. You don't have to make compromises."

"Thank you," Sybille said, and looked down, to hide the contempt in her eyes. She didn't need condescending advice on Enderby; she'd been studying him for weeks. And of course she had to make compromises; that was the only way she'd get anywhere. How the hell did rich, spoiled Valerie Shoreham think most people got along in the world? "What did you do before you got married?" she asked.

"Traveled." Valerie drained her glass: her third, Sybille thought, or maybe her fourth. "Europe, of course, a few times a year; somebody was always having some kind of party. Then there were a couple of African safaris, the Far East for almost six months, and touring Alaska in a friend's plane—the only way to see it, by the way, you'd love it. And Rio; I have friends there and they gave a nonstop party that lasted all of Carnival."

"And then you got married?"

"About halfway through Carnival. Someone suggested that the party needed a little something to keep it going, so Kent and I provided it."

Sybille looked uncertain. "That's why you got married?"

Valerie gave a small smile. "No, I shouldn't have said that. We were good friends and I couldn't see any reason not to. I thought it couldn't do any harm."

"And did it?"

"No, of course not. Kent is very sweet and he doesn't bother me."

Sybille wondered if that would describe Enderby after they were married.

"The problem is, he doesn't do much for me either," Valerie added. "So I can't imagine what would keep us together."

She said it lightly, but Sybille heard something else, a darker note that made her think of loss and loneliness. So much for all that money, she thought, and her looks; they haven't made her immune.

"What will you do if you get a divorce?" she asked.

Valerie gazed at the fire and turned her wine glass around and around in her slender fingers. "I have no idea. I could always keep on doing the same things: there are a few countries I haven't seen yet. Burma and Australia, Greenland . . . and I haven't trekked in Nepal. Or I might just hang around here and do more television. What do you think? Maybe one of these days I'll come to you and ask for a job." She laughed. "You'd hire me, wouldn't you, Sybille? If I asked nicely?"

"Of course," Sybille said smoothly. "Can you type?"

Valerie smiled. "No. Maybe I'd better learn."

The butler appeared again in the doorway, and somehow Sybille knew it was the signal that her time was up. Instantly, she was on her feet. "I meant to leave long ago," she said, almost angrily.

"My fault," Valerie said gently. "I asked you to stay." She stood and took Sybille's hand between hers. "Will you come again? Often? Let's set a date. I know, I'll have a few people for dinner. I did promise you some introductions. Morton, where is my calendar?"

The butler walked across the room to the desk and brought a leather-bound book to her.

"Damn," she said, perusing it. "Damn and damn. Well, I'll cancel something. The zoo benefit. They'll never miss me; they've got all those animals. And they've already got my check." She looked up. "Two weeks from tonight. But we ought to have lunch before that; next week sometime."

"I don't go out for lunch," Sybille said.

"Oh, that's right. Work. Well, then, we'll have drinks again. Or tea, if you'd like. My chef is a wonder with tea and scones. Next Thursday? A week from tonight. But come a little earlier. Five o'clock." She saw Sybille hesitate. "Please," she said, the first time, Sybille noted, and held out her hand. "Let me do what I can to help you."

"All right," Sybille said after a moment. "Next week."

"And bring Chad with you," Valerie said. "I'd love to see him, and we'll find things for him to play with while we talk."

"He's not here; he's with Nick." She saw the surprise in Valerie's eyes and became angry. Valerie hadn't even bothered to *have* a son; who was she to judge? "I'm going to send for him when I'm settled. Nick thinks it's fine."

"Does he?" Valerie smiled, her eyes far away. "I'll bet he's a wonderful father."

"He likes being one."

"Well, since you can't bring Chad, show me some pictures."

"I don't have any. I mean, not with me. Nick sent some, but they're at home."

"Well, then, bring them next week. I'd really love to see them."

Sybille nodded and left the room, following the butler's erect back. She was torn between wanting to get out of there and wanting to stay forever. There was something powerfully seductive about Valerie and her warm apartment and her butler, as capable of keeping outsiders away, to protect the perfect privacy they had had for an hour and a half, as he was of shepherding Sybille out of there at exactly seven o'clock so his employer could bathe and dress in her feminine frills and fanciful furbelows for a festive feast with friends.

Sybille smiled as the mahogany-paneled elevator doors closed behind her and she descended to the lobby. Quentin would be proud of me, she thought. How quickly I learn.

Nick brought Chad to New York for Christmas. They stayed in a suite at the Algonquin, which made Sybille's eyebrows rise. "You didn't tell me you'd won the lottery."

"I did better than that," he said. "We were the stars of the trade show."

"Stars," she repeated. "Enough to get you out of the garage?"

"We moved out a month ago." He let her go ahead as they followed the maître d' to one of the Victorian velvet sofas in the lobby lounge. He was surprised at how much she had changed. Her hair was tied back at her neck, an old-fashioned style that looked modern and right on her. She was dressed with more assurance than Nick remembered, both in the suit she had worn that afternoon and in the black silk dress she wore now, with small rhinestone buttons down the front, the ones at the top left open, and dangling rhinestones at her ears. She seemed to be deliberately provocative and sexually attractive. A hunter, he thought involuntarily.

He walked around the sofa where she sat and took an armchair at her left. A small marble table stood between them. "Out of the garage and into a rented space, half a floor, in a renovated warehouse," he went on, though she had not asked, and then sat back, looking around. He had never been in the Algonquin; Pari Shandar had recommended it.

Most of the lobby, set off from the reception desk by a large folding screen, was a lounge crowded with Victorian furniture, famous for over fifty years as a literary and theatrical gathering place. Nick had reserved a table for ten-thirty, when Sybille had said she could meet him, but even so they had had to wait; the room was full and the lobby door regularly swung open as people came for late-night suppers or after-theater drinks. In a corner, a pianist played show tunes and Christmas carols; conversations and laughter rose and fell, punctuated by the genteel clatter of silver and china; and a cacophony of automobile horns and doormen's whistles sliced through the lobby each time the hotel doors were opened. Sybille seemed unaware of the noise, but raised her voice. "Warehouse? What does that mean?"

"It means we'll be going into production in a few months." Nick looked up as the waiter stood beside him, but still he saw the quick narrowing of Sybille's eyes. "Cognac," he said.

"The same," Sybille said.

Nick looked surprised. "You never liked it."

"I've learned to." Her eyes flicked away from him as her thoughts shifted; then she was back. "Production of what?"

"Computers," said Nick. "That's my specialty."

Missing his irony, she nodded absently. "Who's backing you?"

"We're talking to some people."

"Venture capitalists," she said, liking the sound of the words. "Did they come to you?"

"Yes." Their drinks arrived and Nick turned away from Sybille as the waiter set them down. He wasn't really surprised that she was more interested in his new company than in their son; if she were any different they might still be married. Chad, asleep now in their suite upstairs, with a sitter provided by the hotel, had greeted his mother that afternoon with outstretched arms and a cry of joy that almost broke Nick's heart. So much need, he had thought. No matter how much he and Chad did together, how much love they shared, how naturally and happily Chad came to him for comfort and approval, Chad wanted his mother.

And Sybille, hearing that cry of joy, had almost responded. In the same quiet sitting room of the Webster Apartments where she had entertained Quentin Enderby, she knelt down and put her arms around Chad and began to say something to him about what a big, handsome boy he was at twenty-one months. But he flung himself forward, his arms strangling her neck, his face crammed against hers, and beneath the projectile of his nearly thirty pounds of solid muscle she almost went over backward. Anger flooded her face; she pushed him away, and he sat down hard in front of her.

Chad's eyes widened, round and filled with tears, and then his howls echoed off the walls. Sybille was reaching for him, saying, "I'm sorry, Chad, I didn't mean it—" but Nick had scooped him up.

"It's okay, Chad, it's okay," he said. He held him tightly against his shoulder, Chad's arms gripping his neck, his face buried in his father's neck. His sobs filled the quiet room.

Sybille stood up, straightening her suit jacket. "I'm sorry, I didn't mean to do that; I was falling and I just—I said I was sorry!" Nick had turned away. "I never do anything right, do I! I miss Chad so much, I think of him all the time and wish I could see him growing up, but then I do one thing wrong, just one thing, and you take him away from me again. You're always so much better than I am, aren't you, you always know what to do . . ."

Furiously angry, Nick did not trust himself to speak to her. "Chad," he said quietly, "your mother is sorry; she feels awful about that. I think she isn't feeling well; a cold or the flu or something; we'll ask her later, at dinner. Right now maybe we should just let her get used to having us around. She'll be feeling better by the time we have dinner and then we'll talk about what we're going to do while we're in New York, all the places we'll go and all the times we'll have together. Will that be all right?" He waited. After a moment, through his sobs, Chad nodded his head once, then again, more vigorously. Nick tightened his arms around his son, so filled with love for him he could not think of anything else.

But then, feeling a long shudder run through Chad's body, his fury returned. "That's the last time you hurt my son," he told Sybille through tight lips. "You'll never get close enough—" He saw the hatred flash in her eyes and he bit off his words. "We'll talk about it later."

"You're not telling me how close I can—"

"We'll talk about it later!" He was shouting over Chad's sobs and he turned and strode out. He was trembling with rage.

"I said I was sorry!" Sybille cried, following him. "I don't know what you want from me; just because I'm not as good as you ... You can't take a baby from his mother just because she's not as good as some people ..."

Nick stood still, his back to her. Through the churning of his thoughts, he heard her words. *You can't take a baby from his mother....*

She's Chad's mother. And Chad loves her, and needs her love. Maybe, if she saw more of him and was more comfortable with him ... But she saw a lot of him in San Jose. She hadn't been comfortable with him from the day he was born.

Still, she was different now. New York had changed her. She was growing up; she was more sophisticated, proud of the work she was doing, probably meeting new people, making friends. If she was more at ease with herself, wouldn't she be more at ease with her son? And didn't he owe that to Chad? To help him have a mother?

He turned back to her. Chad had stopped sobbing, but his face was still hidden and he breathed in gulps. "Sybille, if we lived closer to you, would that make a difference?"

She looked confused. "Here? In New York? I hadn't thought about it. How could you live here?"

"I don't know. But if it's important for Chad, I'd try to find a way."

Slowly, she shook her head. "I don't know. I hadn't thought ..."

A clock struck the hour and she started. "I didn't realize it was so late. I have to leave; I have a dinner date—"

"Dinner? I thought we were eating together. I just told Chad ... Isn't that what you said on the phone?"

"I said I'd try. Nick, you can't come to town with two days' notice and expect me to erase everything on my calendar. This is a date I can't break. We'll have dinner together on Christmas, I promise. And we can talk tonight, if you want; if you'd like to meet somewhere, I'll be free about ten-thirty."

And at ten-thirty, Chad was asleep and Sybille and Nick were drinking cognac in the Algonquin lounge.

"You're not doing consulting anymore?" Sybille asked.

"No, that's finished; we're a different kind of company now. We've changed the name." She was listening intently and he began to talk, indifferently at first, then with more enthusiasm. "Remember when we moved into the garage, and had our big celebration because we thought we were on our way? That was when we began building microcomputers. You watched us do it, build every one by hand, all the circuit boards, all the ..." He saw her eyes begin to glaze and he steered away from technical terms. "By the time we'd made a dozen computers, we'd hired a couple of technicians and a secretary. Before we were—"

"Technicians? Secretary? I never saw them. I never saw anybody but the two of you. How did you pay all those people?"

"You never saw them because you were gone by then. We paid them the same way we paid ourselves: we used our own money and borrowed the rest." He smiled. "Scared the hell out of ourselves. But we kept climbing, a step at a time, not thinking about how far we could fall. And then we took one of our micros to the computer show."

"And you were a star, whatever that means."

He smiled again. "It means we got orders for seventy of the hundred we had. We'd prayed we'd sell twenty-five."

Sybille leaned forward. "And then what?"

"We got calls from investors." He put down his glass, pushing it away, as if he needed more room to talk. "You can't imagine the excitement, Sybille; you'd have to be in the middle of it to understand what it meant to those people, and the kind of success it meant to us. We had something new. The first computer small enough to have everything all in one package—computer, keyboard, monitor—and an operating system and programming language that goes with it and that isn't hard to learn. We jazzed it up with a design that made it look like something from outer space—somebody told us science fiction sells—and we called it the Omega 1000, because somebody else told us four digits sound sexier than three. Anyway, we probably made at least 999 that didn't work before we got one that did, so 1000 might be legitimate."

Sybille nodded, missing Nick's humor, hearing only the key words —*investors, success, sells*—and the enthusiasm in his voice. It was reflected in the vibrancy of his face, and she was amazed at how attractive he was. Had he always been this handsome? Had he always seemed so strong and self-assured, his body so vigorous, the set of his shoulders so powerful?

It didn't matter. She had other plans now. She didn't want his dreary world of microcomputers and production companies and eighteen-hour workdays; she wanted money and recognition and glamor, and the power to make things happen. And she'd found a direct way to get there.

"—Omega Computer Inc.," Nick said.

"Sorry, I didn't hear that," Sybille said. "I was thinking about how you've changed. You're so much more sure of yourself."

"I was thinking the same of you." Nick gestured to the waiter for more drinks. "You're more...slick. Is that a good word? You even walk differently. As if you're pretty sure you're going where you want to go."

"*'Pretty* sure'?"

He contemplated her. "I'd guess you still have doubts, about yourself and the things you do every day, where you're going and what you've left behind."

"No," she said flatly. "You might want to believe that, but it isn't true. I don't have any doubts at all. You haven't told me what Omega Computer is. Or anything about your venture capitalists."

"There's nothing to tell about the investors; not yet. They've said they want to come in, but we haven't worked out the details."

"How much are you trying to raise?"

Briefly, he debated not telling her, then heard himself answering. "Four hundred thousand. More would be great, but four hundred would give us enough for equipment and a larger staff and the rest of it."

Her eyes had narrowed. Once she would have been awestruck by such a figure. But no longer; not since she had been in two Fifth Avenue apartments. Still, it was a large enough sum for her to know that investors were taking him seriously. "How much of the company would you keep for yourself?"

"Ted and I would each keep twenty percent. That's the plan." He watched her digest the information, and wondered why he had given it to her. Maybe he still wanted to impress her and make her sorry she'd left. But he didn't miss her, and hadn't, from the time she moved away. Sitting with her now, he could not recapture any of the feelings of pity and admiration he had thought were love, or imagine taking her to bed. It was strange, he thought, that he had been blinded by Sybille, whom he had never loved, and clear-eyed about Valerie, whom he loved passionately in spite of the faults he had accused her of in their last quarrel.

He hadn't done too well with either of them. Maybe that was why he'd told Sybille about the money: to convince her, and himself, that he may have been a failure with women, but in his work he was going to be as successful as he had always dreamed.

"Tell me about yourself," he said. "Your job and how you like New York. Have you made friends here?"

"No, I don't know anyone. I've been too busy. Most of the time I'm at work, on 'World Watch,' and some new shows. Our ratings are up for 'World Watch,' but the station as a whole isn't doing well. Quentin wants me to think up something that will get lots of attention, especially from the press."

"Quentin?" Nick asked.

"Enderby. The president; he owns the station. 'World Watch' is on tomorrow night, by the way; would you like to watch it from the control room? Chad, too. He'd have to sit on your lap and be quiet, but as long as he's not in anyone's way we'd be glad to have him."

"Then we'll be there," Nick replied. "Thanks; I'd enjoy it." He watched her drink her cognac and thought it would be good for Chad to see his mother at work, and for Sybille to have Chad close by while she did something successfully. In some form or other, he told himself, they would have to come to terms with each other, for Chad's sake. He'd do what he could for the few days they were here, but he wouldn't stay too long, on this trip or future ones. Because as far as he could tell from the short time he'd been in New York, there was nothing and no one here for him.

Sybille seemed taller in the control room, even when she was sitting down. She wore a brown pinstripe suite with a white blouse that tied in a small bow at her throat; Nick thought she looked formidable. Often she stood as she talked on the telephone or bent over to make notes at the long narrow desk with telephones, notepads, and clusters of buttons that connected her to everyone in the studio and other parts of the building. When she sat in her upholstered executive chair on the upper level of the large room, she had the air, Nick reflected, of a ruler surveying her kingdom. Below her sat the director and assistant director and, beside them, in his own space, the technical director with his enormous panel of lights and buttons that looked as if it came from the cockpit of a jumbo jet. Looking past them, Sybille could scan the banks of TV screens filling the wall of the control room, some of them showing what each camera in the studio was focusing on at the moment, others showing reporters at remote locations, still others showing taped segments, and titles and graphics.

Nick and Chad sat on a bench behind Sybille, their eyes moving back and forth from her and her assistant producer at the long desk to the screens on the wall. When Sybille picked up one of her three telephones, pushed a button on the panel before her, and said, "Warren, pick up your telephone," they saw the anchorman in the studio, who had heard her on his earplug, reach out of camera range and bring a bright-red telephone to his ear. "We've got a new expert on the Exeter nuclear plant," she said, "so we're moving the story back; we'll run it as soon as he gets here. I'm writing a new lead; I'll let you know when he's here."

Nick saw the man on the screen talk protestingly into the telephone. Sybille was writing on the program schedule before her, the phone wedged between her shoulder and her chin, but as the man talked her fingers stilled. "It *was* the top story; it isn't anymore. Your lead was fine, but we need a new one for this guy, and I've written it. It's done." He spoke again; Nick heard his raised voice through the telephone, cut off by Sybille's icy words. "Warren, I'll say this once, so you'd better get it. No one else has this guy; he's always refused to go public. I found him, I'm using him, and you'll talk to him when I tell you to. If you can't handle that, you can come to my office after the show and tell me why not. And fix your handkerchief; it's crooked." She slammed down the telephone and went back to revising the hour-long program schedule. On one of the television screens in the wall before her, Warren's red face seemed to swell, then shrivel. He rotated his head as if his collar were too tight. Slowly, he raised a hand and straightened the handkerchief in his pocket.

Below Sybille, the director shook his head. "A killer," he murmured to the assistant director, and no one seemed to care that, of course, Sybille heard it.

Nick held Chad on his lap and remembered the tearful, hesitant girl who had told him about being expelled from college and fired from her job. And now, in this control room, she was a ruler surveying her kingdom. A killer.

The directors and Sybille's assistant producer went about their tasks under her watchful eye, while the huge clock in the midst of the wall of screens ticked the seconds away. Everyone was purposeful and serious; only the director cracked irreverent jokes and lolled in his chair, drinking root beer. As the time came closer to the hour, Sybille's assistant producer and the director in charge of remote cameras and crews were making final checks on their own telephones; the technical director, deceptively relaxed, chewed beef jerky from the supply he kept in a jar beside him, and read the revised schedule Sybille had just handed him; and the director finished his root beer while joking with his assistant director about the girls in the editing room. "One minute," he said, still telling jokes but bringing his chair closer to his desk, preparing for work. "Thirty seconds." Sybille stood, watching the screens. "Ten seconds," said the director. He tossed his empty paper cup into the wastebasket and sat straight. "Fasten your seat belts, ladies and gentlemen; make sure your seat backs and tray tables are in their upright and locked positions. . . . Five, four, three—"

Nick felt Chad's body tense with the countdown; his own was the same, and so was everyone's, in the quiet room.

"Two, *one*." At that, the technical director punched a button, and a bold graphic appeared on the screen, sliding past planets and nebulae to curve around planet earth with the words "WEBN World Watch."

"Five," said the director; the technical director pushed a button, and camera five brought Warren Barr, the new host of 'World Watch,' to the screen, filling it with his smiling face, maroon tie, white handkerchief and serious dark-gray suit. "Good evening," said Barr, and, as he introduced the program, the camerman pulled back to reveal the set, where five men and two women sat around a low coffee table on a raised carpeted platform. A huge, colorful map of the world was behind them; at the introduction to each story a beam of light pinpointed its location. A coffee mug stood on the table before each guest, but no one drank; why take the chance, on live television, of someone jostling an elbow and sending a plume of hot coffee down the front of an impeccable business suit?

"Three," said the director. The technical director pushed a button, and camera three focused on the first expert as Barr introduced her. The assistant director gave another command, and the technical director made the expert's name appear across the bottom of the screen. "Two," said the director, and camera two showed the next expert, and so it went, rapidly, cameras switching, names appearing and disappearing as each expert was introduced. Barr returned for a few words, followed by a film clip of a riot in India that had become the top story, described by one of the guest commentators. Two other stories followed, separated by six commercials. In the middle of the fifth story, one of Sybille's telephones rang; she listened for a moment, then picked up another one to tell the floor director the nuclear physicist had arrived. In a minute the physicist was in the studio in a chair vacated, off camera, by one of the other commentators. Barr, when the camera picked him up, happily introduced their guest, a physicist who opposed government policy on nuclear plants. A quick background film was shown, and then Barr began to make sparks fly by asking sharp, rapid-fire, hostile questions of the two experts on each side of the nuclear-plant issue.

Nick watched Sybille. Her hands were clenched, her face frozen. When the debate in the studio grew acrimonious she nodded. Nick glanced from her to the screen, where the government's expert was shaking a finger at the physicist. Barr had set them both up. In his hostility to both, he was oddly neutral. What Sybille had done on "World Watch," Nick saw, was to give viewers Warren Barr as their stand-in: someone who liked no one, admired no one, trusted no one and believed no one. The most sceptical audience, Nick thought, would cheer Barr on: he was their nasty surrogate, doing their finger-pointing and doubting and sneering for them. And then, at some point in the debate, he took sides. With a raised eyebrow or carefully timed pause, or a small chuckle, suddenly Barr was no longer neutral: he had shown the audience where he stood. Nick wondered if they decided in advance which side he would take. Probably not, he thought; Sybille had no politics; she only had ratings. If what she wanted was to give the audience a hero and a villain, she wouldn't care who played which part, only that they were identifiable to viewers. He thought of the Colosseum, and Christians thrown to the lions. And Sybille in the front row, giving thumbs up.

No wonder the ratings were up. People would watch out of curiosity, if not belief.

Within the control room there was constant movement. Sybille or her assistant talked on their telephones; the director called instructions; the technical director hummed a Sousa march as his fingers flew over the control board; the voices of "World Watch" came loudly from the studio; reporters in remote locations, shown on screens as they waited their turn to go on, stood and sat, combed their hair, picked their noses, rehearsed their scripts . . . and "World Watch" raced along. No story was given more than three minutes; most had two or less. There were no pauses between background films and live reports. Maps appeared and disappeared as if from outer space. The commercials seemed louder than usual to Nick, and faster. He shook his head in wonder as the images sped past. Not even time to go to the bathroom, he thought.

A few minutes before the end of the show, the door to the control room opened and Nick watched a large gray-haired man walk in, crossing behind Sybille. As he did so, his fingers touched the back of her neck in a small grasping motion. It was very quick; it was very possessive. Enderby, Nick thought; president, owner of the station, and obviously more than that to Sybille. He felt a sharp, perverse admiration for her. She'd found the main chance. Again. She got out of Palo Alto by marrying me, he thought; she got to New York by divorcing me; now it looks as if she might get a piece of the television industry by hooking up with Quentin Enderby. He's too old for her, but then, I was too young: not experienced enough or ruthless enough to get to the point without pausing for friendship or companionship. Or love.

He wondered, suddenly, how much Sybille really had known about the Ramona Jackson story. She might have thought that was a main chance, too, until it blew up in her face.

Enderby stopped and greeted him, his eyes sliding incuriously over Chad. "Enjoying yourself?" he asked.

Nick stood, holding Chad. "Very much. I've never seen a television production from the inside. It was good of you to—"

"Sybille did it; you can thank her. This is her turf when we're on the air. You're visiting from California, I hear."

"For a few days," Nick said, answering Enderby's unasked question. He saw Sybille glance at them before turning back to the screens, her fingers constantly moving over the buttons that were her connection to the world.

"Things are in flux around here," Enderby said. "We're revamping the station. There's a lot at stake, for Sybille and all of us. In case she didn't tell you."

In other words, Nick thought, don't bother her, don't distract her. Keep out of my territory.

"She did tell me," he said. "I wished her well. I know how good she is at building audiences."

Enderby turned to look at Sybille. Nick was stunned by the greed and possessiveness in his face. "She knows a lot," Enderby said. "Needs a strong hand to keep her in line, but she learns fast. Have a good trip back." He took a chair at the long desk, his back to Nick, who was left standing, with Chad weighing heavily on his arm.

Sybille was concentrating on the end of "World Watch," but Nick felt her awareness of Enderby, sitting a few feet away, watching her. She never looked at him, but every move she made was for him, every word was spoken so he could hear it. Her seductiveness, and Enderby's devouring gaze, made Nick feel like a voyeur, and he was glad to leave a few minutes after the program ended, thanking Sybille and telling her he would see her the next day for their Christmas dinner.

But the next morning, she telephoned him at the Algonquin to say she could not, after all, have dinner with them. She and Enderby were going to his country home in Connecticut, to be married.

Chapter
10

"Congratulations," Valerie said, raising her champagne glass. "You must be very happy."

Sybille touched her glass to Valerie's. "But you thought I shouldn't do it."

"I thought somebody younger... But it doesn't matter what I thought; you got what you want. Tell me where you're living now; I don't know how to reach you."

Sybille took a small case from her purse and handed her a card with "Sybille Enderby," and her address and telephone number, embossed in gold script.

"We're neighbors!" Valerie exclaimed. "It's wonderful up there, isn't it? About as private as you can get in town."

"It's too quiet, as if we're not really in New York. I want to move farther down, but Quentin won't do it."

Valerie smiled. "It's not bad, now and then, to feel as if you're away from New York; it can be positively restorative. Where did you go after your wedding?"

"Nowhere. We stayed overnight in Connecticut, at an inn, and then came back; Quentin doesn't like the country and I had my show to do."

"You didn't even take a few days? Sybille, what about a honey-moon?"

"Oh, I suppose sometime we'll go somewhere; I didn't want to leave the station..." She saw amusement and curiosity in Valerie's eyes. "What difference does it make? I'll do my traveling later. The most important thing right now is 'World Watch,' and the other shows I'm working on. It's not enough just to be married; I need a lot more than that, and until I train people to take care of what I'm doing I can't go anywhere. But I will. All those places you went after college: I wrote them down. I'll get to every one."

Valerie nodded. "I'm sure you will." There was a brief silence.

Sybille watched the waiter refill her champagne glass, bubbles breaking the surface in tiny sprays. Glancing up, she saw her image in a gilt-framed mirror across the narrow room, and Valerie beside her. Two polished women, both wearing soft wool dresses, Valerie with a necklace of gold links at her throat, Sybille with five gold and pearl chains of varying lengths, a gift from Quentin on their wedding night. They sat in a velvet booth, Valerie's beauty a little subdued beneath the soft lights, Sybille's darkness more dramatic, and Sybille hated Valerie with a force that made her breathless.

They were sitting in Valerie's private club; New York was Valerie's city; the wealth and freedom and power that drove the city like an engine belonged to Valerie and her friends; it was Valerie's Fifth Avenue neighborhood into which Sybille had moved, not on her own, or through her family, but because of Quentin Enderby.

"What about Chad?" Valerie asked. "Did he come to your wedding? And for Christmas?"

"No. He had the flu and they canceled their trip at the last minute."

"I'm sorry. I thought I might get to see him."

"Who?" Sybille's eyes challenged her.

"Chad." Valerie said, smiling faintly. "I told you I hoped I'd meet him."

"He won't be coming to New York. Quentin doesn't like children. I'll go to California to see him."

"Then I won't get to know him. I'm sorry. He looks charming in his pictures, smart and funny and lovable..." They were silent. "You'll go on working full time?" Valerie asked.

"Of course. What else would I do?"

"Play. You've always been so serious, Sybille, working, studying, writing in those notebooks you told me about...why don't you take off once in a while and just have a good time?"

"I am having a good time."

"Okay, you love your work, but you have to take time just for yourself too; think about yourself and nobody else. None of us can work all the time—"

"Work? You? At what?"

"Whatever I work at," Valerie said calmly. "I know you think I don't do anything, Sybille, but I do keep busy. And I play a lot because I'm good at it and it's the way I like to live. Look, I'll give you a list of places. You should use them now that you can afford it, and it's a good way to get to know New York." She took from her purse a small leather-bound notebook and began writing with a gold pen. "Sandra's," she murmured. "You have to meet Sandra. She keeps your dress form in her shop, and her own fabrics, and whatever she makes for you, you'll be the only one wearing it. And Bruno...a lovely man... Madison around Eighty-first, I think; he makes models of your feet; nobody makes shoes and boots the way he does. And Nellie at Les Dames; she knits the most wonderful sweaters. Let's see. Salvatore is the best masseur in town; he comes to you, and he'll fit you in at the last minute if you use my name. And Ormolu, it's a cosmetics shop that mixes up incredible creams; I don't suppose they really do a lot for your skin, but they're great for the soul; they make you feel polished and loved, and that has to be good." She wrote a few more names. "Alma's my shopper in New York, so you don't have to spend your life in stores, which would be very dull." She looked up and smiled at Sybille. "The best thing about New York is that it's filled with people whose entire job is to make you happy. And they're very good at it. You'll have a wonderful time with them." She added a few more names. "A lot of these people won't take you without a personal introduction. When you call for appointments, use my name."

The hell I will, Sybille thought. I've got my own name. If she thinks I'm going to go around this city like a beggar—please, sir, please, ma'am, let me into your shop, I'm really quite respectable, Valerie Shoreham will vouch for me—if she thinks I'd use her fucking name—

"Sybille?" Valerie was staring at her. "Are you all right? You're so flushed; maybe you have a fever."

"No, I'm fine." Sybille drank from her water glass. "It's a little warm in here. Or maybe it's the champagne."

"Do you want to go outside and get some air?"

"No. I'm fine. Really." She folded her hands in her lap. Don't be a fool, she thought. Use her.

Valerie signaled the waiter and ordered tea and another plate of finger sandwiches.

"I appreciate what you're doing," Sybille said. She put her hand on Valerie's arm. "It means so much to me to have you care about me, and it's such a help . . ."

"You don't sound too sure of that," Valerie said.

"I am; I'm just not sure I can do anything with it." Sybille's voice faltered. "I'm not good at going into strange places alone and asking for help; I'm always afraid people will laugh at me because I don't know how to choose the right clothes or makeup or shoes . . ."

"Laugh at you? Why would they? They want you to spend money, not run away with hurt feelings. Anyway, what do you care what they think? The only thing you should care about is whether they give you what you want. Sybille, I can't believe you're worried about this; you're absolutely sure of yourself when you talk about your work."

"That's different. It's when I get away from work that I feel lost." She shrugged slightly. "It's silly to talk about it; it's my problem, not yours. I'll just have to work on it. You're right about that: I've gotten as far as I have by doing things alone, and I'll do this too."

"Oh, for heaven's sake, you don't have to do everything alone. Why don't you just ask for help? If you're afraid of starting out by yourself, I'll go with you. All right?"

"No, I can't ask you to do that. I shouldn't need you to hold my hand; I'll work it out myself."

"You'll let me take you around, that's what you'll do. Four or five mornings will do it; you can arrange that, can't you? No arguments, Sybille, I'm glad to do it. Things have been dull lately; this will be fun."

"Well, if you're sure . . . I really would like it; it would be almost like a treasure hunt." She looked at Valerie with a kind of innocent eagerness. "I've had this feeling that most of New York is invisible, at least to me. Sometimes I walk part of the way home, after work, and I know there are hidden places on the upper floors of buildings or on little streets that I don't know anything about, and I don't know how to find them . . ."

"Well, now you've made sure you will." Sybille shot her a look. There was nothing on Valerie's face but her open smile, and warmth in her eyes, but Sybille knew that she understood exactly how she had been maneuvered into offering her help. I don't suppose she's always a fool, she thought.

The waiter was arranging their tea and sandwiches, and Valerie sat back. "I meant what I said: you shouldn't wait until I offer. If you want something, ask me. I know how hard you work, and you've had a rough time, and New York is a tough place to feel at home without somebody to show you around; there's too much of it and it hits you all at once. Quentin can't do it all for you; he doesn't know what you need. By the way, I have some good antique galleries, too—you'll be redecorating his apartment, won't you?"

"Not if he has his way. I'm working on it." They exchanged a smile. "He's very lovable and of course I'm crazy about him, but he's so stubborn.... He's been living alone too long—three years, since his last divorce—but I don't suppose he ever was much good at taking advice. Did you do your apartment?"

"With Sister," said Valerie. She saw Sybille's blank look. "Sister Parish. She's the perfect decorator; she uses lots of prints in combinations you'd never think of, and they always work. You saw my apartment; you know what she does. Let me call her for you. Quentin couldn't possibly object."

"No," Sybille said flatly. She was flushed again, and silently furious. *Bitch. Tripping her up so she'd show her ignorance. How was she supposed to know somebody named Sister? How was she supposed to know any decorator?* She bit her lip. *But how could she learn, without Valerie or someone to teach her?*

"I'm sorry," Valerie said. "Of course you don't know Sister; how could you? You've been living in California. Think about it, though; I'd be glad to introduce you to her. And we'll have our treasure hunt; let me know your schedule so we can arrange it." She smiled with faint mockery. "It'll give me something to do to fill my days." She gathered up the wrapped packages on the seat beside her. "I have to go; it's Kent's birthday and he's invited two hundred intimate friends to help celebrate. You and Quentin must come for dinner; just the four of us so we can get acquainted. I'll call; we'll set a date. I haven't bought you a wedding present; is there something you want, or shall I choose?"

"You choose." Sybille stood, arranging her new sable coat around her shoulders. It was a mild February day, not nearly cold enough for fur—Valerie wasn't wearing one—but she'd just bought the sable that week and she was going to wear it until she got tired of it, or until summer came.

Valerie's limousine was waiting at the front door. "Can I give you a lift?" she asked.

Sybille shook her head. "I'm meeting Quentin." They touched cheeks in a parting embrace and Sybille waited a few minutes before hailing a taxi. I need a limousine, she thought. Then, when Valerie spends her mornings leading me to her little boutiques, she'll be the one to ride behind my driver.

But even in a taxi she felt the thrill of going uptown to go home, the traffic thinning slightly as the street numbers got higher, the atmosphere more rarified, the shops tinier, the prices more stratospheric. I've got to get used to the prices, Sybille thought. I won't feel wealthy and happy until I stop thinking ridiculous prices are ridiculous and start thinking they're perfectly reasonable.

And I will, she told herself as the taxi drew to a stop at Quentin's— no, *her*—building and her doorman came to open her door. He called her Mrs. Enderby as if that had been her name for generations, and took her in her elevator upstairs to her private foyer and waited while she found her key, to see if she needed anything else. It's just a question of experience. And I'm learning to get that where I need it.

Quentin was not there, and she relished being alone in the large rooms. She walked to the front windows and gazed at the dark reservoir as if it were her private lake, then turned back to the brightly lit living room with its marble fireplace and heavy furniture sitting squarely on an Oriental rug, wondering how Sister would decorate it. She drifted into the library, turning on lights, and sat at Quentin's desk. She thought of Nick. She always thought of Nick after she'd been with Valerie. She hadn't talked to him in a while. On impulse, she picked up the telephone and called him.

He was at work, and impatient, but there was a note of alarm in his voice. "Is something wrong?"

"I just felt like calling," she said. "I forgot about—"

"That's all? You just felt like calling?"

"That's what I said; what are you snapping at me for? I forgot about the time difference. It's six o'clock here."

"And three o'clock here. Is there anything else you want to know?"

"You never used to be mean, Nick. You could tell me how Chad is."

"You could call him and find out. He'd love to hear from you. He's at home now if you want to call."

"I tried. There was no answer."

"No answer? He has a cold; Elena said they'd be in all afternoon.

Unless he was worse and she took him to the doctor—"

"How sick is he?" Sybille asked.

"I thought it was just a cold. Sybille, I'm going to call home; he must be worse. We'll talk some other time."

"Maybe I called the wrong number," she said quickly, and read off his home number, deliberately changing one digit.

"Four, not five," he said, his voice light with relief. "Try again; you'll find him there. Tell him I'm bringing him a new book; I haven't had a chance to call him today."

"You must be busy. It sounds noisy there."

"Sybille, I'm swamped. What is it you want?"

"Just to talk! To say hello! Why shouldn't we, now and then?"

"We should. It's probably a good idea. But not in the middle of the day. Call in the evening; you can talk to both of us."

"But you're out every night—aren't you?—with all your lady friends."

Nick frowned. She sounded jealous. What was wrong with her? And where was her husband? "I'll call you tonight, when I go home for dinner," he said. "Or later, when I'm back here. Call Chad, Sybille; he'd love it."

He hung up before she could say anything else, and immediately forgot her in the rush of work just beyond his door. Omega was growing so rapidly it seemed like a new place each day; sometimes Nick was not sure how many engineers and technicians and assemblers were working there. Once, at dinner, Pari had asked, "Do you feel you're losing control of it?" and he had nodded. "If we could go a little slower..." "Ah, but if you were the type to go slowly, then I would not have invested in you," she said, her hand on his. "And neither would the others."

He knew that was true. He and Ted had raised half a million dollars from three investors, including Pari, because their computer was ahead of every other except Apple, and their company was moving the fastest to grab the most customers. Nick had been courting customers for a year: small businesses and schools to whom he had sold the Omega because it was fast, versatile, dressed up with a high-tech design, small enough to fit their limited space and priced to fit their limited budgets.

So they had customers and they had a product and then they had the money. Ownership of the company was divided five ways, with each investor, and Ted and Nick, holding twenty percent. And then, with money flowing in, Omega seemed to explode, growing in the first month from twenty-five people to one hundred, and planning to move to a single-story building in an industrial park a few miles from San Jose.

Nothing was routine anymore; nothing was calm. They were successful before they had time to organize themselves with office procedures and filing cabinets, and so chaos seemed to reign everywhere. Each day, each hour, a crisis sprang up: in getting the right parts, in equipment breakdowns, in finding that they still didn't have enough people, or that their competitors had cut prices, or that there was a bug in the software.

Nick found himself dreaming about bugs in the software. Once, a long time before, there had been a real bug: a moth had flown into one of the original 1940s vacuum-tube computers, sizzling on the wires and causing a short circuit that brought the whole system to a crashing halt. That moth became immortal. After he was fried, every problem with software or hardware was called a bug, and bugs were what Omega and its competitors wrestled with every hour of every day.

Mostly, though, the engineers who daily created new designs and carved out new territory were having a wonderful time. Much of their work was like an elaborate game, a huge maze with prizes hidden around corners, and they worked day and night to discover them; in fact, it was hard to keep them away. The atmosphere was electric; nothing was slow or dull. And when the orders came in, first a few, and then an avalanche, production took off and everything speeded up. There was never enough time to ponder, there was only time to make quick decisions, give orders to employees who ran to execute them, then go on to other decisions. As the weeks and months passed, new people were hired, those with talent were rapidly promoted, the top employees were given stock in the company. The smell of triumph and riches was in the air.

Nick, as president, began to travel. He signed contracts, toured sites for computer installations in America and Europe, and appeared at meetings of computer users who were learning as fast as they could to use the tools that would completely change the way people worked. But most of the time he was in San Jose, working on the Omega 2000, an advanced hardware and software system that would become the standard of the industry. He had already talked about it to investors, using words and ideas that were barely imaginable for microcomputers: word processing, spread sheets, computer graphics. But to design and build such a computer, and write the programs for it, he needed more money, more engineers to help Ted, more programmers, more space—and he needed all that at the expense of the Omega 1000, now in production, which demanded all their energy and money if it was to be the huge success everyone predicted.

He worked on the 2000 mostly at night, after he had put Chad to bed, while other engineers came and went, working for a few hours, then leaving to be replaced by others who hadn't been able to sleep because of a problem they'd left at their desk and so came in, at two or three or four in the morning, to tackle it again.

Then the company, by now two hundred people, moved all their equipment to the single-story building that became known, two and a half years later, when they had grown to over a thousand employees in twelve buildings, as the first real home of Omega Computer.

They bought furniture from a factory going out of business and built a row of small, sparsely furnished offices along one side of the building. On the other side were a drafting room, programming room, testing rooms, machine shop and lunchroom. In the center was the huge production room with a high, unfinished ceiling from which rows of fluorescent light fixtures hung over long assembly benches. Carts piled with equipment filled the aisles between benches, constantly being rolled to where they were needed, unloaded, reloaded, and rolled somewhere else. "Someday we'll get conveyer belts," Nick promised every time one of the carts ran into someone. "As soon as we can afford them." Everywhere, circuit boards, video monitors, printers, keyboards and cases were in different stages of assembly with technicians and workers standing, sitting, moving about, soldering, bolting, fitting, chewing gum, and talking about surfing, sailing, baseball and sex.

And in July, when the rooftop air-conditioning unit was laboring against summer temperatures over 110 degrees, a new batch of orders came in and Nick and Ted found themselves working more frantically than ever. They had to deliver fifteen hundred computers by September first.

"We'll do it," Nick said to Chad at dinner. Elena had gone to an early movie with a friend, and the two of them were eating alone. "I wish I could put you to work, but there are laws about child labor."

"Labor?" asked Chad.

"Work."

"Chad can work," said Chad solemnly. "Chad hammered and hammered and maked table ring."

"Ring? You're sure you have that right?"

Chad picked up a spoon and struck it rhythmically on the table top of his high chair.

"I like the rhythm, but I don't hear a ring," said Nick. "Which table? Your worktable?"

"Daddy table," said Chad with a peal of laughter. "Chad hammered on Daddy table and fixed it like Daddy did when it broke and it ringed loud like a *bell* and it *shaked!*"

Nick pictured the steel legs of his drafting table in the study off his bedroom. "Listen, friend, you're not supposed to be in there."

Chad's eyes grew round and his lower lip quivered. "Not Daddy papers." Vigorously he shook his head. "Chad never touch Daddy papers, Daddy says no."

"He sure does," said Nick. He sighed. "I think I missed a bet; you need a xylophone, or better yet, a drum. Give me a day or two and I'll bring you one. Are you going to finish your chicken?"

"Yes."

"It's good, isn't it?"

Chad nodded. "Elena sweared."

"What?"

"She sweared. Damn shit oh sorry Chad."

Nick's mouth twitched. "Why did she say that?"

Chad pointed to the floor. "Chicken falled down. It bounced."

Nick looked at his plate. "That's what we've been eating?"

Chad shook his head. "We goed to the store. Elena buyed me popcorn and more chicken. We did a very busy day."

Nick laughed. "You and me both, my friend."

After dinner they read together, Chad snuggled deep in his father's lap, repeating words as Nick said them and pointing to pictures he recognized. "Okay," said Nick at last. "Time for bed."

"No," said Chad positively.

Nick laughed and lifted him onto his shoulder.

"Chad can go to work with Daddy and hammer and fix things. *Please.*"

"You will, one of these days. But not at eight o'clock at night when you belong in bed."

"*Chad* go to *work* with *Daddy. Chad* go to *work* —"

"I said no." Nick lowered him to his bed and sat beside him. "We've got fifteen hundred units to ship. When they're out of the shop, I'll take you there. I promise we'll do it, Chad. Is it a deal?"

"Deal," Chad said. He petted Nick's face as he did his terrier puppy. "Good Daddy. Good boy."

Nick burst out laughing, and put his arms around him, his cheek against his son's dark curls. "I love you, Chad." Chad's arms were around his neck, and the two of them sat warm and silent, holding each other in the shadowed room that was a jumble of toys and stuffed animals and books. "You're a great guy," Nick said, his voice low. "I don't know what I'd do without you." Chad slid down and Nick pulled the top sheet over him. "I wouldn't be a whole person," he said, to himself more than Chad. "I wouldn't have a whole life."

He turned out the light and stood for a moment, looking down at Chad's flushed face as he fought to keep his eyes from closing. "I love you, Daddy," Chad murmured, and Nick bent again and kissed him. "Lots of love around here," he said. "Sleep tight, my friend."

Quietly he left the room. Sybille had called again that morning, and as always he had been filled with alarm, expecting to hear her say she had changed her mind and was going to court to get Chad. She hadn't said it—in fact, she had let slip once that Enderby wouldn't have children around—but she kept Nick dangling by dropping small hints that one of these days she might decide to try to take him anyway. She won't get him, Nick thought; she'd never convince a judge to give him to her. It's been almost a year since the divorce; she's visited us twice, never for more than a couple of days, and we've been to New York once. No one would take Chad away from his home and give him to a mother who doesn't want him.

He said those words every night, more fervently on the days when Sybille called. And still he could not absolutely believe them.

He closed Chad's door partway, then read in the living room until Elena returned from the movie. And then, as he did every night, he went back to work.

"This is a hell of a life," Ted remarked as he walked into Nick's office. "It's ten o'clock at night; why are you here and not at a restaurant or theater with some lovely lady? Better yet, in her bed."

"I decided you needed company," Nick said with a smile. "Did I miss anything?"

"It's pretty quiet; the big push will come after the printer ICs come in from Sawyer. What's happened to you and Pari?"

Nick pulled a stack of reports toward him. "I haven't seen her in awhile. Since May."

"Was that mutual? You seemed pretty good together."

"I guess we both got too busy. You're as busy as I am; how many dates have you had in the last six months?"

"More than you. Has it occurred to you that you're not doing much but work these days?"

"Has it occurred to you that I have a son? When I have free time, I spend it with him. Or is that too complicated for you?"

"Hey, what's with you? I'm not telling you how to run your life. I just see you getting crabby and glum, and if you don't watch out you'll wake up one of these days grizzled and gaunt and flaccid—and then where will you be?"

Nick burst out laughing. "In deep trouble. Thanks, Ted; I like it that you worry about me. And I'll slow down at some point. As soon as we make this shipment and get some office routines written I'll take some time off. You should, too." He picked up one of the reports and glanced at it.

"I might do that." Ted fiddled with the pencils on Nick's drafting table. "There's something else besides the hours you're working."

Nick looked up. "What's that?"

"You're stepping on people's toes."

"What?"

Ted sat on the edge of his desk. "I'll tell you what I'm hearing, okay? And you listen. Don't talk; just listen. Everybody thinks you're terrific, they like working for you, they think you're the best, but they're pissed off because you don't let them do their jobs from start to finish; you butt in and take over something they're doing, including things you shouldn't be bothering with. Look: we all know you're good; you can do a decent employee interview, you can plan our advertising, you can talk to the lawyers, you can order equipment, but why should you do all that? You are the world's best programmer; why aren't you spending more time on the 2000 instead of sticking your fingers into things we hired other people to do? You even do the secretaries' work, for Christ's sake; I've seen you make calls they ought to be making—"

Nick slammed down the report. "A lot of times it's faster to do something than explain it to somebody else. We all wear different hats these days, you know that. I apologize for not running a nice orderly office—"

"I don't want your apologies; I'm trying to tell you what's going on around here!"

"I know what's going on around here; I run the place!"

"We both fucking run the place!"

"Sorry; we both run it. Okay, you told me what you heard. Thanks. Now I'm going to work."

Ted glared at him and stomped out, leaving the door open. Nick closed the door and went back to his desk, spreading the reports in front of him.

He read until two in the morning, then went home to sleep until six, when Chad came into his room, wanting to talk. By eight, he was striding up and down the aisles of the production room, checking the assemblies, talking to project leaders, answering engineers' questions and working with them on bugs that had cropped up overnight. At nine he made a second pot of coffee and opened the box of doughnuts he had bought on the way to work. Ten minutes later his production manager walked in, his face a dark scowl. Nick put down his coffee. "What's wrong?"

"Sawyer fucked up; they sent the wrong printer interface chips. I called them; that's all they had."

"Bullshit." Nick swept some papers aside on his desk. "I talked to them two weeks ago; they had more ICs than we needed."

"The stupid ass in the warehouse got his parts numbers mixed up. Nick, they don't have them. Period. We've gotta get 'em somewhere else."

"God damn son of a bitch..." Nick shoved back his chair, slamming it against the wall of his tiny office. "Who else is there close enough to get them to us today or tomorrow?"

"Nobody. Belster has one almost the same; they say you can't tell the difference."

"I know that part; I've used it. Is the cost the same?"

"A few cents cheaper, but—"

"How many do they have?"

"Enough for what we need. Trouble is, by the time we get 'em tested we're so far behind we'll never make the release date."

"Then we won't test first; we'll—"

"Nick, there's no way I'll let a goddam IC get past me without testing it."

"—we'll test while we're assembling. I'm sure enough it'll work. I've done it that way before." Nick was scribbling dates. "A couple of days late; that's not bad." He pulled the telephone to him, flipped through his Rolodex and made a brief call. "We'll have them tomorrow morning if we can send a truck for them. I'll take care of that; you get your people set up to do the assembly and I'll set up the testing."

"I can set up the whole thing, that's what I'm paid for. But I gotta tell you I don't like it."

"Neither do I, but we don't have a choice. Don't worry about the testing; I'll talk to Ed about it."

The production manager started to say something, then shrugged. "It's your baby."

The words nagged at Nick. In the early days, when the company was just beginning to grow, and he and Ted had hired a few other engineers, they all felt every project belonged to all of them. It got harder to keep that feeling as Omega grew larger, and maybe, Nick thought, it was impossible now that they were more than two hundred and still growing. Still, he liked to think that at least the top people had that sense of sharing. Those words, *It's your baby,* bothered him, but he put them aside to think about another time, because right now he had too much to do. They were completing production on one set of contracts, working on the fifteen hundred units, an engineer quit in the middle of the day after a quarrel with the chief engineer, two technicians went home sick, an experimental circuit board failed, a mathematics program being written for high schools developed a bug that made every equation equal zero, and the air-conditioning went out.

With a threatening phone call, Nick had the repair service there in half an hour, and by late afternoon cool air was circulating through the tropical heat that had built up in the large production room. That night he and Ted helped the engineer fix the bug in his mathematics program; the substitute IC chips arrived the next morning; and they swung into the final stage of production on the fifteen hundred computers. For the next two frenetic weeks, Nick saw less of Chad and nothing of anyone outside work; he ate erratically and barely slept. Everyone worked overtime, buoyed up and driven by the sense of mission that was like a spell cast over the whole company. And then the computers were shipped, only three days behind schedule, and everyone went into slow motion in the luxurious relaxation of exhausted triumph.

They barely had time to enjoy it. "Nick, there's a call from Emerson School," said his secretary when he came in after a weekend at Lake Tahoe with Chad. "There's something wrong with their new computer." That was when their triumph evaporated.

"We keep getting garbage on the screen," said Darrel Browne, the headmaster of Emerson School. "It does just fine, but as soon as we try to print, everything on the screen disappears and a lot of junk shows up. Letters, numbers, asterisks, periods, question marks... like aliens invaded the computer. Garbage."

"How many have you tried?" Nick asked.

"All five. They're all the same. Nick, we're supposed to demonstrate these things for our trustees in two weeks. I went out on a limb to get them—the expense, you know; we're always close to the line around here—and *they don't work!*"

"Hold on, Darrell." Nick stared at an oversize circuit diagram on the wall. His heart began to pound. The print command was controlled in part by the substitute printer interface chip. And he'd forgotten to tell Ed to test it while the units were being assembled.

You stupid son of a bitch; you forgot to tell him. There'd been a lot going on, he remembered: the bug in the mathematics program and the engineer quitting, and some other things. And the air conditioner had gone out; he remembered calling the repair company. *You do the secretaries' work, for Christ's sake; I've seen you make calls they ought to be making.*

"Nick?" asked Darrel Browne. "What's going on? We paid a fortune for these things. You sold us on how good they are, and how reliable you are.... So what are you going to do about it?"

"We're going to fix them," said Nick shortly. "Our word is good, you know that, Darrel. Whatever it takes, we'll get you a working system. We'll send someone out to pick up the computers and we'll have them back to you within a week. I guarantee it."

"A week. Well, if you really do that..."

"We'll do it. We'll have someone out this afternoon. Have them ready for us, will you?"

He hung up and sat still, his body tense. He could hear telephones ringing in the other offices.

"Don't worry about the testing; I'll talk to Ed about it."

"I can set up the whole thing, that's what I'm paid for."

"...you butt in and take over something they're doing, including things you shouldn't be bothering with."

"It's your baby."

He felt sick. *What have I done?*

Ted was standing in the doorway, his face ashen. Behind him, the production room was in an uproar. The telephones kept ringing.

"How many have called?" Nick asked.

"Fifty-three; I can't believe all of them will, but..."

The production manager was behind Ted. "I just checked the ones we kept here. It's the printer IC."

Nick nodded. "I thought so." He fought to keep his churning stomach steady. "What have you told them?" he asked Ted.

"That we'd pick them up and fix them."

"That's what I told Darrel. Emerson School. We need trucks. I'll call—" He stopped and met Ted's eyes. "Mary should line up trucks to go to the local customers. Everyone else who calls should be told to return the units collect."

"Right. And the ICs?"

"We'll find the right ones, have them shipped overnight. The likeliest places . . ." He scrawled a few names and handed the paper to Ted. "Whatever it costs. I blew the chance to save money. Time, too. Can you call them?"

Ted gave a grin and a small salute and left. And while the noise level rose higher in the production room and all the telephones rang, with customers calling to report the failure of their systems, the chief engineer, the testing supervisor, the technical supervisor and the foremen crowded in. "What the fuck's going on?"

Nick told them, not sparing himself. "Busy week ahead," said the chief engineer, and that was all he said; everyone knew that recriminations would have to wait until the crisis was past. Nick, almost numb, kept his voice level as they plotted a scenario of repairs and returns. And the telephones kept ringing.

Omega's major distributor called while they were still planning. "I heard you got a little problem, Nick. They don't work? We got a thousand units sitting in the warehouse and they don't work? What'm I supposed to do, Nick? Sell 'em to kids for Christmas?"

"We're working on it. I'll call you this afternoon or tomorrow. We're taking care of it."

"You better, Nick. This is a lot of space I got tied up here with your goodies; cost me money if I can't ship 'em to my customers, and I got no time to ship 'em *back* to you and get 'em *back* again and stack 'em *up* again and hope they work. You figure it out or I send 'em all back and cancel the order. Kapeesh?"

"Look, wait a minute." Nick paced behind his desk, dragging the telephone cord behind him. He put his hand over the receiver and told the technical supervisor to pick up the extension on his secretary's desk. "I've got our technical supervisor on the phone," he said to the distributor. "I want him to verify this. If this is a simple fix—I don't know if it is yet, but if it is—we'll send a crew to your warehouse and fix them there." He shot a questioning look at the technical supervisor, who made a small circle with his thumb and third finger. "You wouldn't have to do anything but let us in and stay out of our way," he said to the distributor. "Would that do it for you?"

"Fix 'em here?"

"Right."

"You can do that? We got no equipment."

"I don't know what we'll need. If we can do it with what we can carry, we will."

"Huh. Well. I don't see anything wrong with that. You'll know— when?"

"I hope this afternoon. I'll call you. You won't do anything until then, right?"

"Right. Okay. You call me."

As Nick hung up, Ted stuck his head in the door. "Two days on the chips, air-shipped from Boston. Don't ask the price; only one of us at a time should have a heart attack."

"I'll ask later. Can you talk to Wilt about setting up an extra testing station? And line up people to do it all night."

"Right." He left, then peered around the edge of the door again. "Nick, we'll get out of it. Worse could have happened. They could have self-destructed the first time somebody hit 'enter.' *That* would've been a problem."

A chuckle broke from Nick. "Thanks, Ted." He turned back to the group around his desk. "Where were we?"

"Defusing the distributor," said the technical supervisor. "You did good, boss."

"Thanks," Nick said, loving them all for their generosity. "What else do we have?"

"Who does what in assembly," said the foreman. "If it's a simple exchange of parts, we could get them out of here the same day. Logistically it's a nightmare, but everything else ought to be a piece of cake."

The others laughed. They went around the room, each one assigning himself a task, then reviewed the schedule once again until they felt they were ready to move as soon as the chips arrived. When they left, Nick, taking a quiet moment, sat down and stared again at the wall. *What did I do to this company?*

Almost destroyed it.

I built it—Ted and I built it, worked our asses off—and then I almost blew the best chance we've had.

He knew they would repair the damage, all of them, working together, knocking themselves out to do it; they'd fix fifteen hundred computers and get them back to the customers, and no one outside the company would know how damaging it had been. But Nick knew it would cost a fortune to make all those smooth, swift repairs and get out of the mess he'd made with their reputation intact. That meant money wouldn't be available to develop the 2000 as early as he'd hoped, and that could hurt them in the future, perhaps more than anything else.

Even more painful, at least to himself, he was learning things about Nick Fielding he didn't much like. For all his talk of the spirit they'd shared in building the company, he hadn't fully trusted anyone. *You're stepping on people's toes.* That was putting it mildly. He'd always tried to be in control.

Afraid of failure, he thought. *Afraid of losing, the way I lost Valerie. The way I might lose Chad. So damned afraid that I went haywire and put the whole company in jeopardy. And did damage in other ways too. I let Pari slip away in this crazy summer; I haven't talked to my other friends in months; I haven't spent as much time with Chad as I should. As I want to.*

We'll get out of this bind, he promised himself, *and then I'm taking off. Chad and I are going to take a vacation for at least a month. Well, maybe two weeks.* He laughed at himself, still afraid to let go. He'd have to work at that. Anyway, he could be working on the 2000 on his vacation, after Chad went to bed.

"Nick," his secretary said. "Sybille is on the phone. I told her you were busy, but she insisted."

He picked it up, alarm flicking through him. "Hi," he said casually.

"I'm going to have a show, Nick; I'm going to be on camera."

He tried to make sense of what she was saying. It seemed to have nothing to do with anything, especially in the midst of all that had happened that morning. "That's what you called to tell me?"

"What do you mean? This is important to me, Nick; I called because I want you here when I have my first show."

"Why?" he asked.

"Because I want you to watch me! Why are you being so insensitive? I've wanted this all my life, you know that. And I thought Chad would be excited to see his mother on television."

Nick threw down his pencil. "Fine. We'll try to be there. When will it be?"

"I'm not sure. I'll let you know. A couple of months, probably."

"A couple of—"

"I just heard about it today." Sybille heard her voice grow defensive and she became angry; why should she defend herself to him? "I wanted you to know about it. I'll call you as soon as I know the date. How have you been?"

"Fine. I have to go, Sybille; I'll talk to you—"

"You know I hate to bother you at work, Nick; I was just so excited... Are you very busy?"

"We're always busy. And we've got a small crisis this morning."

"Oh. I'm sorry. A serious one?"

"No worse than disastrous. I'll talk to you soon."

"Nick—!" But he was gone. Sybille stared at the receiver, then slammed it down, disgusted with herself. She shouldn't have called him. But she and Quentin had been at Valerie and Kent's apartment the night before for one of their big parties, and then today Quentin had told her she could be the host of "Financial Watch," the latest program she had created, and she couldn't wait to tell someone and of course it had to be Nick. She had no other friends, except for Valerie, and she didn't confide in her. Anyway, she had to tell Nick. She had to make sure he knew how happy and successful she was; that all it took was getting away from him for her to get exactly what she wanted. He had to understand how wonderful her life was in New York, and how small and dreary his was in San Jose.

Well, he knew. So, once again, she could forget him in the busy hours of her days. She was producing "World Watch," working on two new programs she had created, and going every day to her voice coach and body coach, to prepare for her debut on camera. In August she and Quentin had gone to Maine, and when he insisted on staying for the whole month to play golf, she came back alone to continue with her coaching. She had scheduled "Financial Watch" for mid-September, when all the new shows were premiering, but when Quentin came back from Maine at the end of August he said they weren't ready.

"Why not?" she demanded. They were in her gold and silver bedroom, redecorated from a guest room connected by a dressing room with Quentin's bedroom, and Sybille was fastening bracelets on her arm. "I've been working on this show since June; it's ready, and you know it."

"It may be; you're not," he said.

"How do you know? You have no idea what I can do."

"I watched your tape yesterday; your coach sent it over after you finished. You don't think I'd put you on the air without knowing what you look like, do you?" He gazed blandly at the anger and alarm in her eyes. "There's no rush with that show; our surveys say it'll be a hit and it'll be a hit whenever it gets on. But not if you can't carry it. And you've got a ways to go yet."

"Walter said—"

"Walter's a coach, a tepid toady of a teacher, not a tycoon of television." He grinned broadly, pleased with himself. "It'll come, it'll come; you just calm down. I'm right about this, and you probably know it. If you don't, don't tell me." He put his arm around her and pulled her close. "Let's come home early tonight."

"Fine," she said.

"Where are we going for dinner?"

"I told you three times: Côte Basque with the Giffords."

"Did you tell me? I don't remember." He bent his head, and Sybille lifted her face to his. "You look very pretty tonight," he said and kissed her with a hunger as great as the first time, more than a year earlier, when he had pulled her across his lap in his limousine. "Nuts about you," he murmured, his lips against her cheek. "Bitchy, sexy, ambitious dame. As good as a three-ring circus. I figured you'd be like that. We'll come home early tonight."

"Fine," she said again. "When can we schedule that show?"

He chuckled. "Can't let go, can you? I told you: when you're ready."

"That's not good enough, Quentin." She stayed in his arms, looking up at him. "We've been doing publicity on it; I have to know how to keep it going. I've got to have a date."

"January," he said after a pause.

"January! I don't need another four months!"

"You probably need more," he growled, suddenly peevish. "I'm tired of talking about it; aren't we supposed to be going out tonight? Where are we going, anyway?"

Sybille opened her mouth to snap at him, then closed it. He's seventy-eight, she thought. He'll die soon. I have to find some new ways to get around him, but it won't be for long. And then the station will be mine, the money will be mine; whatever show I want will be mine.

That's when Valerie and Nick and all of them will see what I can do. That's when my life will really begin.

Chapter

11

"Financial Watch" premiered the second week in January. For all her preparation, when she sat at the desk a few minutes before airtime, Sybille froze. Her heart was racing and she was sure it was missing beats. I'm going to have a heart attack, she thought; I'm going to die before Quentin. But I can't; that's not the way I planned it.

Someone came up with her microphone and she took it from him, threading the cord beneath her suit jacket and clipping the microphone to her lapel by herself; she couldn't stand it when people put their hands on her. Someone else gave her an earplug, which she fitted into her ear; he taped the wire to the back of her jacket, out of sight. "Three minutes," said her assistant producer through the speaker in her earplug, and Sybille nodded, clasping her clammy hands. Her teeth felt locked together and her mouth was dry.

Then the music came up and she saw on the monitor the logo she had designed for the show, with a fat, black, masculine Mont Blanc pen, held by an invisible hand, scrawling "Financial Watch" across the screen. The floor director held up five fingers so she could see them as he counted off the last seconds; the announcer introduced the show; the red light on her camera lit and Sybille Enderby was on the air.

She kneaded her hands in her lap, hidden beneath the desk, and looked straight at the camera, reading the scrolling script on the Tele-PrompTer and smiling at the lens, trying to think of it as a friend. Valerie said you had to make love to the camera. After more than six months of coaching, Sybille still had no idea what that meant.

It was the longest half hour of her life. Later she could remember none of it. She knew she had interviewed, by satellite, an embezzling financier who had fled the country for a sumptuous mountain chalet in Yugoslavia; she knew her panel of experts had given their opinions on which stocks and bonds to buy or sell; she knew the film clips of financial news from around the world had appeared and disappeared exactly on time as she read the text that accompanied them; but the minute the half hour ended all of it vanished from her mind.

"Wonderful, Sybille!" exclaimed the floor director as the screen went to black and a commercial came up. Sybille felt a wave of exhilaration surge through her. She'd done it; she'd proved herself. "Wonderful!" said the floor director again. He fussed over her, removing the wire taped to her back. "I never saw so much news crammed in one program; it never slowed down, never got dull; terrific idea to have what's-his-name in Yugoslavia; how you managed to do that..."

Sybille's exhilaration began to seep away. "Good show," said one of the cameramen as she unclipped her microphone. "Really zipped along," said another cameraman as she walked past him, feeling cold now, none of her exhilaration left. "Great format," said the film editor as she walked down the corridor. "You really put it together," said her assistant producer, meeting her outside the newsroom. "Not too bad for the first time," said Enderby as she entered her office.

"What was wrong with it?" she demanded.

"You tell me."

"I don't know; it's all a blur. But everybody's been telling me what a great show it was and nobody says one word about *me*."

"That so?" He crossed his legs. "Well, I guess they all saw something wrong."

"What? What did they see?"

"That you got a ways to go yet."

"Damn it, what does that mean?"

"What it says. Come off it, babe; you know what I'm talking about. You haven't got it, not yet anyway, and you'd be the first to say so, only louder, if somebody wanting an anchor job read like you."

"Like what? Read like *what*?"

"Like somebody reciting to a convention of cooling corpses. Like a teacher who got saddled with misfits and morons. You explain, you don't chat. You want it straight? You're getting it straight. You don't connect with an audience. You act like there *isn't* an audience. You smile, but it doesn't get to your eyes. You come across hard and cold, not sexy. Shit, Syb, all that coaching—"

"Don't call me Syb. I've told you not to."

He shrugged. "Sometimes you warm up an inch or two and then you're not bad. That's what you'll be working on, starting tomorrow. You might still get it. If not, we'll find somebody else."

"When?"

Again, he shrugged. "No time limits, babe. You work on it some more, we'll see what happens."

"When?"

"Six months. That's more than you'd give somebody you hired. I don't need a star in my bed, you know; I like you whether you're on camera or not. Seems a damn-fool thing anyway, a producer as good as you screwing around with an anchor job; damn-fool thing."

"Not to me." Her voice dropped. "I'll work on it. I'll fix it."

Enderby stood and enveloped her in his arms. "You make me feel all worn out—all that ambition and greed—but other times you make me feel damn good. Young and sexy, like you. Like I could live forever. Lucky for you you found me; not many men with the stuff to handle you."

"Not luck: skill." Sybille tossed it off, making it a joke. "I was looking for a strong man and I found him." She extricated herself, forcing herself to do it gently. It was Nick's fault, she thought. She'd practically begged him to come to New York for the premiere of the show, but he'd said he was too busy. If he'd been there to give her support, she might have done better; she needed friendly faces. He'd let her down. He and Valerie: they always let her down.

"Now what?" asked Enderby impatiently. "You get that faraway look on your face and I never know what you're thinking, but it's usually not good."

"I was thinking we'd better go home and change. We're meeting the Durhams at the Plaza at nine."

"Durhams? Who the hell are the Durhams?"

"I have no idea. You made the date; you said we'd sit with them. It's the Cancer Fund Ball."

"Oh, that thing. She's on the committee giving it; he owns a little

cable network in Washington. Damned deadly dull, but she's a devilish little dish. We'll come home early."

"Fine," Sybille said, as she always did. "Just as long as we stay late enough to get the early editions of the papers and see if there are any reviews of the show."

"Too soon; they'll be in the late editions. Forget the show. Time enough to read reviews tomorrow."

Sybille did not answer. It was better to let him have the last word than to argue with him when he was being stupid and not understanding her. They still talked more than most married people, she thought; they talked about the station, about the programs she produced and others being planned, about the apartment as it was being redecorated, all except Enderby's bedroom, which he insisted be left untouched, and they talked about people.

Enderby loved to gossip. With the same viperish tongue he had used in the art gallery on their first evening together, he dissected everyone. He wove together past histories, family feuds and alliances, bankruptcies, divorces, murders, suicides, lawsuits, even good marriages. But he never spent much time talking about the good ones; they provided no fertile ground for malice.

For Sybille, it was the malice that made marriage to him tolerable; she relished his unsparing eye and skewering adjectives. Soon, as she came to know his circle, and met people he did not know, she was matching him story for story. By the time they had been married a year, their early evenings, when they were briefly at home to dress before going out, were times to exchange tales about the people they had seen that day; and a few hours later, when they returned from a dinner party or benefit ball or gallery opening, they had more fodder for more stories. Often, if Sybille was clever, she could keep Enderby talking until he was so tired he wanted only to go to sleep. Like Scheherazade in reverse, she thought cynically: keep the husband spinning stories so he'll leave me alone.

If gossip was the seasoning that kept her marriage palatable, socializing was the food itself. Sybille passionately adored the social life of Manhattan, and everything connected with it, and would have stayed with Enderby for that alone. She could not buy enough clothes, and since she had learned to ignore price tags, and she was known at most shops and designers' studios, there were thousands from which to choose. She hired a consultant to tell her which colors she should wear, which clothes, which makeup and hairstyle, which jewelry. She joined a gym to work out in the early mornings, and took up tennis.

She found a club in Flushing where she could go back to skeet shooting, loving the feel of the shotgun in her hands, an extension of her
carefully controlled body. She began to feel taller and more slender in
her new clothes; for the first time she left home each day or evening
without the nagging feeling that what she wore, though it had seemed
fine in her bedroom, was all wrong. And she knew, from the glances
she got from other women, that she looked just fine.

Each night they came home too early for her because Enderby was
tired and wanted to be in her bed before going to his own room, but
still Sybille had her social life. They dined on exotic foods that she
commanded herself to enjoy; they mingled at fashion shows and theater parties with the men and women who owned much of the world's
wealth; they danced at benefit balls with couples who raised hundreds
of millions of dollars for each year's popular diseases.

Enderby danced enthusiastically, his right arm pumping his partner's
arm up and down, bending her backward beneath him, twirling her
around without warning, or grabbing both her hands so he and she
could revolve under the arch of their raised arms. His steps were long
and eccentric; no one, often not even he, knew where he would go
next. He navigated the dance floor with dazzling speed, and others
soon learned to get out of his way when he and a startled-eyed partner
came swooping in their direction.

Sybille hated the way he danced. She knew people were always
watching them, and she felt exposed and ridiculous, a party to her
husband's antics, a victim of his exhibitionism, and so she eagerly accepted offers from other men to dance, no matter who they were. She
danced with men she hated and men she scorned, she danced with
men whose paunches kept them at arm's length and with men who
could only shuffle in the middle of the room, talking about business.
Once in a while she got a man who could dance, and with him she
moved skillfully in the steps she had learned from a private teacher. It
was all right then that people were watching.

For some reason Sybille could not fathom, Valerie seemed to enjoy
dancing with Enderby. Several times a month, during the height of the
season, the four of them met at some affair, and between the appetizer
and the soup, or the soup and the sorbet, Enderby and Valerie would
go to the dance floor, leaving Sybille and Kent Shoreham behind.
Sybille wouldn't have minded, because Kent was easygoing and a
good dancer, but it annoyed her that Valerie seemed to be having a
better time with her husband than she ever had. She would watch
them, Valerie's head tipped back in laughter, Enderby grinning at her

and bending her backward as if making love to her. When he twirled her around, his hand holding hers high in the air, Valerie was like a ballet dancer, her feet barely touching the ground, her tawny hair flying outward as she whirled, and when they danced off across the floor, Valerie never looked surprised: she always seemed to know where they were going. There was nothing foolish about Enderby when Valerie was his partner.

"He's a challenge," said Valerie, laughing, when she returned to their table at the edge of the dance floor and Sybille asked if she had had a good time. It was June, one of the last balls of the season, and Valerie was wearing a sheath of white satin that outlined her slender curves and ended in a flare of black lace below her knees. At her throat and ears she wore jet and diamonds, and, as far as Sybille could tell, she had on no makeup at all. Sybille, wearing black silk, knew she was as perfectly dressed as Valerie, but she wished she had worn white. Waiters were serving passion-fruit sorbet in tall crystal flutes, and Valerie sipped her wine as she caught her breath from the dance. "He's unpredictable and exhausting, and absolutely one of a kind. I see you don't mind letting the rest of us monopolize him on the dance floor."

"Mind? I'm delighted," Sybille said. "It's not my kind of dancing."

"Nor anyone else's, thank God," laughed Valerie. "But he's irresistible, you know: like a little boy having the time of his life and not afraid to show it."

"Irresistible," Sybille echoed, leaving it unclear whether she was agreeing with Valerie or sweeping the word out of sight.

"I suppose he's able to show it because he doesn't care what the rest of us think," Valerie said shrewdly, "but he's fun to dance with, anyway. And it's nice to find a man who's willing to let us see the little boy inside him. Most men don't remember what it felt like to be one or they really are little boys who've never grown up."

Sybille followed her gaze and saw Kent, in the middle of the crowded dance floor, kissing the hand of a willowy black-haired beauty. Valerie turned suddenly. "No, it's not what it seems. He's absolutely faithful. Poor Kent; he hasn't grown up enough even to go through with an affair."

Sybille stared at her. "Is that what you want him to do?"

"I did once. It doesn't much matter now."

"Why did you?"

"Because then *something* would have been happening." She sat back in her chair, ignoring the plate a waiter set in front of her, and contemplating Sybille. The music had stopped so everyone could eat the next course, and in the sudden quiet, with only murmured conversations on all sides, it was easier for Sybille to hear Valerie's low voice. "You don't understand that, do you? You're always busy with your programs, and Quentin is busy running his station, and you have your visits with Chad...I admire you, Sybille. You're always doing things and making things happen. You're very lucky."

She's playing some kind of game, Sybille thought. Valerie Shoreham doesn't envy people; people envy her. "But you're always busy," she said. "Your board meetings and your horses, and shopping, and whatever you do on television..."

"You know perfectly well what I do on television," Valerie said, and it infuriated Sybille to see that she was amused. "But you're right; I'm so busy there's never enough time for everything. I've even taken up hunting, did I tell you? I haven't decided whether I like it or not, but at least it's something different." Her eyes grew thoughtful. "The trouble is, I can't always figure out at the end of the day what I've done with my time. It just seems to be gone, and nothing to show for it." In an instant, the thoughtfulness vanished and she was smiling gaily. "Isn't it dull to listen to people complain? Anyway, I don't let myself think about it very much; it doesn't lead anywhere."

"What does Kent do?" Sybille asked. "Besides the bank."

"He's getting very good at his crossword puzzles. Poor dear, he's frantically bored, but the world seems so overwhelming to him he's afraid to go out there and tackle anything."

"He married you," Sybille said bluntly.

"Oh, his father and I worked that out." Valerie smiled. "Goodness, you look so shocked. That sort of thing is done more often than you think. His father thought if Kent had a family he'd have enough confidence to take hold at the bank, and I was feeling at loose ends after all that traveling, and Kent and I were friends, and I wanted to make a home. So his father and I suggested it to Kent, and he was very relieved and very happy. It couldn't do any harm and it seemed like a good idea at the time."

"And?" Sybille asked.

"It wasn't a good idea and it's about over. And poor Kent thinks he's failed again, even though I keep telling him it's my fault."

"Is it?"

"Oh, who knows? I tell him it is, because he's miserable about not being good at anything and you can't let someone feel that way if you can help it. He wants to believe I'm right, and he's happier when he does, and what do I care? Life is full of things that go wrong. You can't wallow in them; you just pick yourself up and do something else. So we decided to finish the season, show our happy faces at the balls and parties and little dinners we'd accepted, and then go our own ways. Haven't you noticed Kent stalking attractive women these last few weeks? He doesn't want to be alone and he's getting nervous because it's June, and our last dinner party is next week, and he hasn't found anyone he wants."

"He should commission his father to do it for him," said Sybille.

Valerie's eyebrows went up. "That's very nasty."

"I'm sorry, I didn't mean to be. I couldn't ever be nasty to you; you've been so good to me. But it does seem odd . . ."

"Perhaps it does. It all seemed perfectly natural at the time."

"And then you've been dancing and looking as if you were having the most wonderful time . . . are you glad you're getting rid of him?"

Valerie shot her a look. "Were you glad you got rid of Nick?"

"I didn't get rid of him; we had a terrible time saying goodbye. We hated being apart, but we couldn't figure out any other way; we just had to be in different places to do what we wanted to do. Nick kept trying to find another way, he wanted to come to New York, but we both knew his business was in California and he had to be there."

Valerie was watching her keenly. Then she smiled, almost to herself. "That sounds like Nick. He's a very constant person."

Sybille said nothing.

The musicians began to play, and the dance floor filled with swaying figures. A revolving ball on the ceiling sent pinpoints of red and white light whirling about the ballroom. "When will you go to California again?" Valerie asked.

"I don't now. July, maybe. I was there in March, for Chad's birthday. We went to San Francisco."

"Just you and Chad?"

"No, Nick came along. Three-year-olds are totally unpredictable, you know, and absolutely exhausting. They want to run off everywhere and pick up everything and talk to everybody . . . one person couldn't possibly keep up. It was a nice weekend, but I can't go back for awhile; I can't leave New York. We'll be making some decisions about my show and I won't let them do that without me." She paused. "What do you think of it?"

"Of what? Your going to California?"

"No, of course not. 'Financial Watch.' You said you'd seen it."

"I've seen 'World Watch'; I like it. I don't watch money shows; I'm not interested in finance."

"Not interested?"

"Why should I be? Men in gray suits are always trying to make it more complicated than it is, probably so the rest of us will feel ignorant and they'll sound like experts, and I'm just not interested. I have advisers who take care of my money and we talk a couple of times a year, and that's enough for me. Why should I do more than that?"

"Because that's what's between you and disaster," Sybille said. *And if I could take it all away from you, you arrogant bitch, I would; you need a few lessons in what's really important.*

"I'm sorry," Valerie said gently. "I know it depends on where we're coming from. I've been lucky; I've never had to think about money. I know some people do and I understand it; it's just not the way I live. Tell me about 'Financial Watch'; you'll be back next fall, won't you? The ratings must be good; most people aren't like me, they're fascinated by money."

Enderby came up, saving Sybille from having to talk about ratings. He made a brusque excuse to Valerie, who was claimed by a dance partner, and he took her empty chair. "Remember Stan Durham? You met him a while back—"

"January," Sybille said. "The cancer benefit. He owns a nothing cable network in Washington, he has a mousy wife and he can't keep his hands to himself."

Enderby gave a bark of laughter. "You never told me that."

"Why would I? I took care of it."

"I'll bet you did. He's here tonight, somewhere over there"—he waved vaguely across the ballroom—"and I'm bringing the two of them back for drinks as soon as we can leave this shindig."

"To our place? Last time we had to pry them loose and that was only in a bar."

"Did we? I don't recall that. Well, that's your job, then; you're good at it. Flash one of your sincere sparkling smiles and get 'em the hell out after an hour. I may be doing some business with him, so I'm being a gentleman, but I don't have to overdo it."

"What business? We don't have anything to do with cable."

"We will if I buy his network."

She stared at him. "There's nothing there. He told us about it; he puts together packages of programs and almost nobody buys them."

"Then somebody's got a chance to build it up." He took her wine glass and drained it, and looked around for a waiter. "Staff used to be better here. What are you surprised about? You've been hocking at me to do something...be bigger, better, braver, bolder...WEBN isn't enough for you. I thought you'd be jumping up and down with joy. Doesn't your little heart go pitty-pat at the idea of owning a network? I may put you in charge of it. CEO of the Enderby Broadcasting Network; that sound good to you?"

Sybille looked at him through narrowed eyes. "I don't know anything about cable."

"Don't worry about it; I do." He glared at a waiter who approached to refill his glass. "Took you long enough." He turned back to Sybille. "I'll teach you everything you need to know."

She shook her head. Panic was welling up inside her. The slow music had given way to something harder and she was deafened by the pounding of the bass. The dancers were jumping and hopping like puppets gone wild; they made her dizzy. "Something's happened. This is a bone to keep me quiet. What have you done?" When he was silent, her voice rose. "What the hell are you up to?"

"Keep your voice down! You want us to be in the morning papers? I'll tell you about it tomorrow, in the office where this belongs."

"Not tomorrow! Now! It's my show, isn't it? You've done something with my show." Once again she waited. "Quentin? You didn't take me off my show!"

He puffed out his cheeks. "It was discussed."

"It was discussed," she mimicked. "Who discussed it?"

"Everything was discussed," he said and abruptly pushed back his chair and stood. "You know what the ratings are—so low you could walk over 'em in a dark room and not even trip—and you know we've gotta do something; that's not a secret or a surprise or a sellout. We'll talk about it at the meeting tomorrow. Nobody's trying to screw you, Syb, you know that."

"A lot of them would love to."

He shrugged. "You made that bed. Remember once you said something about not being in a popularity contest? You just wanted 'em to know you were there. Well, they know it. You turned us around with 'World Watch' and the other stuff you're producing; you got us terrific ratings, and everybody in town knows it was you who did it. Do you want to dance?"

"No."

"Well..." He stood indecisively, watching the dancers, one foot tapping the rhythm, heel and toe. "Let's go, then. Durham's waiting. You going to be okay with them?"

Sybille looked up at Enderby, her mouth tight to keep from screaming at him. *He'll die any day. Tomorrow maybe. And then I'll have it all.*

"Of course. They're easy to handle. Let me know when you want them gone and I'll take care of it."

"Good girl," he said, his voice rich with satisfaction, and when she stood he gave her rear a little pinch as they walked away.

That summer, the new host of "Financial Watch" prepared for his fall premiere. His name was Walt Goddard, he had hosted newscasts in St. Louis, Phoenix and Seattle, and he had broad shoulders and shrewd eyes and a handsome, rugged face that polls had shown was trusted by women and men alike. Sybille barely spoke to him. She turned him over to her assistant producer and then walked out of the station and rented a house in the Hamptons for two months. "You can come along if you want," she told Enderby, "but I'm going, whether you do or not."

"We're going to Maine," he declared. "The way we always do."

"I've left my address and phone number on your desk. If you want to come out, you don't have to let me know in advance; your bed will always be ready. And I'll be alone. I hope you have a pleasant summer."

She left him roaring at her and drove out to Long Island, fury and shame like a hard knot inside her. She'd tried so hard, harder than she'd ever tried in her life. She'd wanted it more than anything else. Every time she faced the camera, knowing she was appearing in thousands of people's homes, it didn't matter that nervousness clutched at her stomach; she still felt a rush of excitement and ecstasy, and for the thirty minutes she was on the air there was nothing else she wanted.

But they took it away from her. They kicked her out. Damn them, damn them, damn all of them who took things away from her. No one had defended her. No one had argued that she should be given another six months to learn how to talk to a camera as if it was a good friend, or a lover. No one was on her side.

The traffic had thinned and she speeded up. The farther out she drove, the more open the landscape became; now and then she caught a glimpse of sunlit water, a boat pulling a water skier, a stretch of beach. Nobody at the station was on her side. She'd been working with them for over two years, but not one of them came to her defense. It had nothing to do with friendship—she'd never cared about friendship—it had to do with professional respect and standing together when one of them was under attack. They were that way with each other, but not with her. They're all against me, she thought. No one wants me to succeed. They're jealous and hostile.

She reached Amagansett and drove slowly, looking for the address the rental agent had given her. They kicked her off her own show. And left her with nothing. Except a husband who danced as if he planned to live for another seventy-eight years, and a job as a television producer. *There has to be more. More, more, more. I'll think of something; that's why I came up here, to be alone and to think about what I'll do next.*

Her maid and houseman had gone ahead, and the house overlooking the ocean was ready when she arrived. She was there at the height of the social frenzy that grips the Hamptons every summer. There were lunches every day and three or four parties a night with people who invited her because she was Quentin's wife and the host of her own television show and no one yet knew that the show had been taken from her. There was no one to bother her in the cool privacy of her bed, and there were riding lessons and hours spent at perfecting her skeet shooting. "What I really want to do is hunt," she told her instructor. "I'm going to do that this fall."

"Anybody in particular you're aiming for?" he laughed.

"I don't know yet."

"Hey, that was a joke. You know, a joke? You were thinking of foxes, right? Dutchess County, right?"

"Of course," she said and went back to shooting the clay targets that were ejected like missiles in a high arc over the Sound. She seldom missed.

By September she was at the station again, producing "World Watch" and two other programs. "My cool, collected colleague who's clever enough to conquer her crabbiness," Enderby said, pleased with himself for leaving her alone all summer to get over her pouting. As far as anyone could tell, nothing had changed. As she had always been, Sybille was aloof, efficient and clever, intimate with no one, one of the best producers in New York.

She never produced "Financial Watch" again.

In October, Enderby bought Durham's cable network, and Sybille went with him to Washington to sign the final papers. It was the first time she had been away from New York since Walt Goddard began hosting her show and her humiliation began. It had been impossible to keep it a secret—how could anything played out on television be kept a secret?—and rumors were everywhere that the problem was her, not the show; that she'd been dumped because of abysmal ratings. Everyone asked her about it, usually with a small lift of the eyebrow or pretended sympathy, and it got so she didn't want go to anywhere. She didn't even have a social life anymore.

In Washington there were no rumors. She told anyone who asked that she had left the show because she and her husband had so much to do to build up their new cable network. She said it so often she began to believe it. After two days, Washington seemed to her a far more civilized city than New York, its people more intelligent, its atmosphere more interesting, its society more desirable. After a week, the knot of fury and shame inside her had shrunk almost to nothing. She felt free.

"Why don't we move here?" she asked Enderby. They were leaving the lawyer's office late in the afternoon after signing the last of the documents that made the sale complete.

"Move where?" he asked vaguely. He was tired and his back ached; he felt old.

"Here. Washington." She helped him with his coat. "Wouldn't you like that?"

"No. Where the hell's the limousine? It's supposed to be waiting."

"He'll be here; we said five o'clock and it's almost that. Are you tired?"

"Don't treat me like an invalid. He doesn't have to wait till the dot of five; he should be here early."

"We won't use him again. If we move here we'll have our own driver."

"Who said anything about moving here?"

"I want you to think about it. I'm tired of New York, and you know you've been saying it's too noisy and hard to get around. I think we need a change. There's not a lot more we can do with the station, you know; we should be doing something new. Isn't that why you bought the network? Why not move here and concentrate on it? We could look at apartments while we're here; shall we?"

He was scowling. "Are you out of your mind?"

"I don't think so. I think it's a very good idea."

"I never said New York was noisy."

"You said you'd like someplace quieter."

"I'm damned if I did. The grave is quiet; I don't need quiet until then."

"It isn't a question of quiet. I'm tired of New York. I'd like something different. Quentin, I want to live here. We don't have to stay if we don't like it, but I want to try it for awhile. A year. Let's try it for a year."

He shook his head. "I can't think about it now. That lawyer ran me ragged, and I'm tired."

"You'll rest at the hotel; we'll talk about it at dinner." The limousine pulled up to the curb and she slid in first. "It's just the two of us tonight, so we'll have a chance to talk." She tucked the lap robe around him. "Think about it, Quentin. It's what I want."

He gave her a sharp look. "You want out of New York, is that it?"

Startled, she looked away from him. He kept surprising her with his sudden swings from a vague fog to the shrewdness that had made him a millionaire. She started to deny it, then stopped. It was his fault she wanted to leave New York; let him know it. "Of course I do. For now, anyway. It's damned hard, facing everyone. They know you forced me out."

He grunted and fell silent. And there's something else he'll never know, Sybille thought. We're going to leave New York because he likes it there, because he's comfortable with familiar places and people, because he doesn't like change. We're going to leave New York because he's going to pay for what he did to me. They drove smoothly, in silence, along the broad streets to the Willard, where a doorman sprang forward to open the limousine door. "I'll give it some thought," Enderby said. "There's no rush."

"Yes there is," she insisted. "I don't want to live in New York anymore. I'm serious about this."

He peered at her as they walked into the lobby. "You never cared before what people think."

"I always cared," she said coldly. "I just don't whine about it. Quentin, I want a year, to see how we like it; if we don't, we'll go back. We won't sell the apartment; we'll always have a place to go back to."

He was silent, brooding as they walked past the Peacock Alley promenade to the elevators.

"This isn't a whim," Sybille said, her voice hard.

"Well." He shrugged and let his breath out in a long sigh. "It might not be a bad idea. I don't know what the hell I'm doing with this network; all it's got so far is a couple cooking shows, some news, and sports. . . . Well, we might do it. We'll talk about it at dinner. Did you make reservations?"

"Yes."

"Good. You're good, Syb." In the elevator, he put his arm around her and pulled her against him. "You warm a man's heart and hearth and happy home. Stubborn, though; a pain in the ass sometimes. But exciting—when you don't wear me out. I suppose you've already picked out a place to live."

"No, but I can, if you give me an hour."

"I'm going to take a nap. That's your hour." He straightened his sore back and grinned. "Some people'd say I'm too old to start again. They'd be wrong, wouldn't they, babe?"

"Of course they would." They walked to their suite, her hand beneath his elbow. Let him think what he wanted. She knew better. The truth was, he was at the end of his life. She was just beginning.

Chapter
12

he had closed the drapes when they went into her bedroom, and when Nick woke, with a start, he thought it was night and he had slept through dinner. "God damn it," he said furiously and threw off the sheet and flung himself out of the bed.

"Nick! Where are you going?" She reached for him, her arm a pale ribbon in the darkness. "What is it?"

He was at the window, throwing open the drapes. Sunlight poured into the room. "My God, it's still early."

"Of course it's early. You said you had to leave at five. I wouldn't let you oversleep. Are you angry at me?"

"No, of course not." He looked at his watch. Four-thirty. He had time to stop at the office on the way home. He walked to the trail of his clothes on the floor and bent to pick them up.

"Nick!" She slid out of bed and put her arms around him, pressing her body against his. "You promised we'd have the whole afternoon. Come back to bed; we have lots of time."

His arms came up to move her away from him but instead tightened around her. She was warm and extraordinarily soft, her skin as rosy and dimpled as a baby's, her blond hair tousled from the time they had already spent together, her body yielding before he made any demands on it. She pulled back her head, looking at him with a little smile and pulling at his hand so that he moved with her to the soft carpet. Roughly he pressed her backward, and lay with her, his hand between her legs.

"So nice," she whispered against his lips. "Nice, nice..." Her sharp nails left little indentations in his skin, the sun beat upon them, her murmuring voice filled his head. She opened her legs wide and rose to meet him as Nick raised himself above her. Then he pushed into her, pounding into her, feeling her movements match his, hearing her small cries, until there was only her pliancy and her softness and the white sun on his back.

But later, as he drove home, he was disgusted with himself. Because he could not remember her name.

There had been months when he had always slept alone: when he was working crazy hours and spending all his free time with Chad. But when there were fewer crises, and new routines established, and free time, he found as many women as he wanted, and there had been a lot of them after Pari: women for an afternoon or an evening or, rarely, a few weeks or months; women who were looking, as he was, for a place to settle, a life to build. He never took them to his home, and most of them Chad never knew about. Once or twice, with someone he had hopes for, he brought Chad and the three of them went to dinner, but nothing ever came of those. Nothing came of any of them. No one he met brought the magic of Valerie, and he would never again let himself confuse pity with love, as he had with Sybille.

Christie, he thought as he turned into his driveway and pressed the remote control that opened his garage door. That was her name; of course he hadn't forgotten it. Christie Littell, a nurse, a lovely woman, the most pliant he'd ever met. Not a woman with whom he wanted to spend his life.

Chad was waiting for him, as he was every night, listening for the sound of the garage door, then dashing to the front steps, scrunching down on his haunches, and looking bored. "I was waiting for *hours,*" he said.

Nick laughed and swung him to his shoulder. "I ran into a small dragon at the corner."

"Wrong." Chad shook his head. "Dragons are *enormous.*"

"This one was small and powerful; he's been doing a lot of bench presses to develop his muscles."

Chad giggled. "What does he do with them? Kill bad people?"

"No, he doesn't believe in taking the law into his own hands. His biggest muscle is his tongue—he's been eating broccoli and asparagus for years to get it strong—and he licks up bad people and takes them to jail."

"He does not!"

"Oh no? He licked up my car. Thought I was a robber and swung me up on his slithery tongue. Then he saw I was really a pretty nice guy with a terrific son waiting for me, so he let me down. But the car got a good washing; if you don't believe me you can see for yourself."

Giggling, Chad ran off to check the car Nick had had washed that day, and, with relief, Nick went to the kitchen. His coming-home game with Chad was getting out of hand; each night the story was supposed to be different and he was having trouble thinking up plots. Computers are easier, he thought; I'd hate to have to think up stories to make a living.

He pushed open the kitchen door and smiled at Elena. She had married two months earlier, and she and her husband Manuel had taken a month-long honeymoon Nick had given them in Mexico, to visit their families, while Elena's sister took care of Chad. Now Elena and Manuel lived in the apartment over the garage of Nick's new home in Portola Valley. He had bought it in January, while they were in Mexico—the same time Sybille had called to tell him she and Enderby were moving to Washington and she'd be too busy for awhile to come to California—and Chad had run through the twelve rooms, yelling that he was lost, that he'd never see his dad again, and that Elena would never find them when she got there. Then he got busy decorating his room, drawing on the walls Nick had had prepared with a special surface, choosing drapes and matching sheets and bedspread, and strewing his toys around the room. "They'll be lonesome in a strange house if they can't see me," he said solemnly, and Nick, with a laugh, dropped all talk of Chad's organizing his toys and games and stuffed animals on his new shelves or in his new toy chest at the foot of his new bunk bed.

The house was spacious and cool, skillfully decorated by a young woman who was living with Ted in another spacious house just a block away. Often, when the two men were working at night in Nick's study, after Chad had gone to sleep, they would look around and grin at each other, remembering a family room and garage in San Jose.

In the three years since they had celebrated their move into that garage, they had expanded to fill six buildings with eight hundred employees. They were shipping a thousand computers a week; their sales were close to a hundred million dollars a year; and the two of them had been interviewed for stories in California newspapers and magazines. With Nick's brilliance in software, which now included word processing, accounting, payroll and games, and Ted's genius for hardware—including printers, modems for hooking computers to telephones, monitors, disk memory and internal memory—Omega Computer had never lost its lead even though new competitors cropped up all the time.

By now Nick was no longer involved in the day-to-day operations of Omega. He had resigned himself to leaving that to a general manager and department heads while he concentrated on what he called, wryly, presidential things: being a leader and conciliator within his company, and marketing it to the rest of the world. At the same time, he was leading the technical development of the Omega 2000, which would be as revolutionary in its own way as the 1000 had been three years earlier.

He and Ted had decided to launch the 2000 this year, at the time they made Omega Computers a public company.

All through the previous fall and winter, Nick had been meeting with lawyers and underwriters, preparing for the Omega stock issue. He had taken brief trips around the country and to Europe, coming back to be with Chad before flying off again, and again and again, for six months. He traveled with the underwriters who were his coaches, advisers and, he said wryly, chaperones because they kept him too busy for anything else. In each city he spoke to major investment houses, pension-fund managers and other institutions, to get them interested in Omega Computer and to convince them to make commitments to buy large chunks of Omega stock when it came on the market in the spring. Because he was president of the company, he was the one who had to go.

At first he was stiff and self-conscious; he called himself a performer in a dog and pony show. He was reluctant to talk about himself, and he disliked the formality of overhead projectors and easels with full-color charts and graphs, and photocopies of company history and financial reports.

But all of a sudden, about the time he faced his fifth audience, he found himself having a good time, and being good at it. He liked talking about the company; he and Ted had nurtured it until it was almost like their child. For years he had talked about Chad at dinner parties with friends—showing his latest pictures and describing his exploits and vocabulary, his good temper and fantastic mind—and wondering, when he got home, how bored his friends had been, even the married, sympathetic ones. But he could talk about Omega without worrying: his audiences had come to listen. They wanted him to talk about himself too, and that was all right, as long as he talked about himself only as the president of Omega, and as long as he could be honest.

One morning, when he thought his standard pitch was getting stale, he rewrote part of his speech without telling the underwriters, and when he met with a group of investment executives for a breakfast meeting he included the story of the crisis at Omega over the fifteen hundred computers. It was a tricky moment: the underwriters turned pale, and the executives looked startled, but Nick turned it around.

"When the president reaches so far he stumbles and nearly cracks his skull," he said, "either he's mortally wounded and gets shoved aside or he figures out what he's done, which was to rob his top people of the chance to do what they do best and what they love to do. We've got a bunch of brilliant engineers at Omega, talented and eccentric and fiercely independent. They're on the cutting edge of this whole crazy industry we're inventing as we go along, and they'll work together like kids in a sandbox if you give them the sandbox and then leave them alone. But they won't give you the time of day if you make their decisions and do even a part of the job you told them was theirs. That's what I learned. Omega is the top company in Silicon Valley because it's made up of creative engineers who don't want anybody else to do their work. These days I have a job to do there and it's the only one I do, and if I forget it, there are a lot of people to remind me."

The laughter was warm and genuine, and that anecdote became part of Nick's standard speech. It was quoted in newspaper articles on him, in March, in *The Wall Street Journal* and *The New York Times*, and in cover stories in *Time* and *Newsweek* when Omega Computer was offered to the public, and one billion dollars' worth of stock was snapped up in the first few weeks.

Nick, his twenty percent of the company now worth two hundred million dollars, had become an instant celebrity.

Sybille called. "It's amazing. It's just...astonishing. Who would have guessed, when we were in that awful house...'The American dream'—which magazine said that? Both of them, probably. And 'new breed of entrepreneur'—do you feel like a new breed? And 'boy wonder of Silicon Valley'—I never thought of you as a boy...how old are you now?"

"Thirty-one."

"Definitely not a boy." There was a silence. "Congratulations," she said. "What will you do now?"

"Probably what I've been doing. If you read the stories you know the 2000 was released this week; there's a lot to do to market it—"

"But you don't have to do that anymore! You can do anything you want!"

"Right now this is what I want. I have to go, Sybille, we're in the middle of Chad's birthday party. I'm sorry you aren't here; he enjoyed talking to you last night. You'll be here in April?"

"Yes, unless something comes up at the office."

"I'll talk to you soon." He paused. There was no longer any pretense that she would try to take Chad from him; she had stopped hinting and they had never even talked about it. But the relationship between Sybille and her son was still vague and Nick was never sure whether he should suggest other ways they might get to know each other, or leave it alone. Today he left it alone. "Thanks for calling," he said. "We'll talk to you soon." And he hurried back to the din of twenty four-year-olds who had taken over the backyard.

The games were over, the fried chicken and lemonade had disappeared, and now Chad stood beside the birthday cake, baked by Elena in the shape of his favorite stuffed monkey. He carefully held the knife Elena had taught him to use. "Daddy, we're waiting!" he yelled over the jabbering of the children as Nick came from the kitchen. "I'm blowing out the candles and then Elena said I could cut the first piece."

"Hold on." Nick grabbed his camera from a redwood bench and focused it. "All set. Who's singing 'Happy Birthday'?"

Elena's husband Manuel began it, his baritone rolling like an aria as the children lustily picked up the words and followed along. Chad, deeply serious, bowed when they finished. He took a long breath and blew out all the candles arranged in the shape of a 4, bowed again when everyone applauded wildly, then very carefully cut a wedge of cake as Nick captured it all on film. While Elena and Manuel handed out the remaining pieces, Nick moved among the children, talking to them and taking more pictures as they stuffed cake and icing into small mouths that were never still.

"Could I have more cake?" one of them asked.

"Sure, there's plenty." Nick reached out to the table where Elena had left extra pieces on paper plates. "Do you still have your fork?"

"I don't need it."

"Of course not." He grinned. "Why would you need a fork?"

"How come Chad lives with you all the time and not with his mother?" asked the boy.

Taken by surprise, Nick said, "She lives in Washington."

"Yeh, Chad told us. So how come he doesn't live in Washington? My dad lives in Phoenix and we visit."

"There are lots of ways of doing things—"

"But you're doing it the wrong way!"

"Who said?"

"I said! And everybody at school."

Nick frowned. "Everybody?" Chad had never said a word about that. He loved school; he chattered about it with delight, he wouldn't even let his father call it nursery school. "It's pre-kindergarten," he would say indignantly. "It's a real school!" But how much trouble was he having? Nick wondered. How much did he have to defend the way he lived because it was different? "Does Chad say it's wrong?" he asked the boy.

The boy shook his head. "He says to shut up."

"Do you?"

"Sure. Chad knows how to hit."

"Chad knows how to hit," Nick repeated, bemused. He had never seen Chad strike out at anyone.

"So how come he lives with you?" the boy asked again.

"That's how we worked it out," Nick replied, knowing it was a poor answer for a curious four-year-old. "It isn't wrong, it's just different. Chad's mother has a job that keeps her very busy and she thought she couldn't spend enough time with him."

"My mom works and I live with her," the boy said doggedly. Nick felt a strong urge to help him stuff the rest of his cake into his mouth all at once.

Instead, he stood and raised his voice. "I think it's time for the magician."

Twenty small bodies shot up. "Magician?" "A real magician?" "Chad didn't tell us!" "I didn't know!" Chad yelled. "Daddy just said there'd be a surprise!"

Like the Pied Piper, Nick led them into the house, where they sat in a semicircle in the large den. In front of them a tall man in a white suit, with red shoes, a red tie, and a red wig beneath a red straw hat bustled about setting up a table with paraphernalia. He paid no attention to the children. Suddenly, without warning, things began disappearing, then reappearing in various parts of the room, sometimes in the children's hair or the fold of a sleeve. The magic show had begun.

Standing at the side, Nick watched Chad and the others. He listened to the chatter of their sweet, high voices and he ached with the beauty of them in their small perfection. They laughed in quick peals of pure delight; their faces were rapt as the magician whirled from wonder to wonder; nowhere was there a sign of boredom or smugness, or greed or hatred or arrogance. Great kids, Nick thought; I hope they figure things out the first time around better than a lot of their parents did.

Later, Chad could not stop talking about his party. "Remember the water in the pitcher? He filled it up and then he turned it over and nothing came out? And those three toy poodles? He stuck 'em in that doghouse and they were gone and then they were"—he started giggling—"in the refrigerator!" He took his bath, reliving every magic trick, and put on his pajamas, talking about the games they had played, and crawled into bed, talking about his birthday lunch.

"What's this?" Nick asked as he sat beside him. He held up a piece of birthday cake, wrapped in a napkin, that had been tucked behind Chad's pillow.

"It's, uh, I guess it's a piece of my cake."

"You had three pieces after dinner; I thought we agreed that was enough."

Chad frowned at the slice of cake. "Yeh. I don't know how it got here."

Nick's eyebrows went up.

"Well, see, Daddy, there's this hand"—he held it out—"and it does things I don't even know about."

Nick burst out laughing, and Chad laughed with him. "Do you really want it?" Nick asked.

"I guess I could wait till tomorrow."

"Then I'll take it back to the kitchen. Did you thank Elena for making it?"

"Uh-huh. She said it was my birthday present from her. I gave her a kiss. A hug too."

"Good."

"Can we read out of one of my new books?"

"Sure. But I'd like to talk a little bit first, okay?"

"What about?"

"Why your mother couldn't be at your party."

Chad's face closed up. Watching it, Nick realized that was what happened every time he began to talk about Sybille, and that he talked about her less because of it: it was so painful to see Chad struggle with the dilemma of how to feel about her that Nick simply avoided it. *But that doesn't solve anything: it just makes it tougher for Chad, because then he has no one to talk to and bottles it up inside.*

"I know it's hard to talk about," he said, "but I think we should."

"Why?"

"Well, for one thing, it seems your friends at school are talking about it."

"So what?"

"So I thought you might like to have some answers."

He shook his head angrily.

"Chad," Nick said gently, "we're doing something different here, you and I, and your mother too, and I should have known the little bits we talked about it weren't enough. I kept thinking we'd wait till you're older, but I was wrong."

"You weren't! Everything's okay! You're ruining my birthday!"

Nick hesitated. Four was awfully young; he could wait a while longer.

But that was what he had been saying for two years. "I'm sorry if I'm ruining your birthday, but this is important and it might not be as terrible as you think. The reason it's so important is that sometimes people, like your friends at school, for instance, get the idea there's something wrong with you"—Chad shot him a look of surprise—"and there isn't. Just because your mother lives somewhere else doesn't have a single thing to do with you. There is nothing wrong with you, Chad. You're the most terrific guy I know—"

"You're my daddy! You always say that!"

"I'm usually right, too, remember how often you've told me that? Anyway, lots of other people agree with me." Nick reeled off a list of his friends, especially the married couples who included him and Chad in Sunday brunches and backyard barbecues. He swung his feet up on the bed and leaned against the headboard with his arm around Chad.

"You didn't take off your shoes," said Chad.

"Right. I should." He put his shoes on the floor and once again held Chad, ignoring his son's clear unwillingness to be held. "Look, this isn't simple, but I'll try to make it as clear as I can. Some people like to be left alone; they aren't comfortable living with other people. Your mother is like that. It isn't that she—"

"She's living with Quentin."

"Yes, but I get the feeling they don't spend a lot of time together. We hardly saw him, did we, when we were in New York last time? I think they got married because they like each other, but they also like to do things by themselves and that's the way they live. It isn't that your mother doesn't love you, Chad; it's just that it's very important to her to make her own kind of life, with her own work and her own way of doing things, and there isn't a lot of room in it for anybody else."

There was a silence. Chad held his body stiffly within Nick's embrace. "She doesn't want me." Nick bent his head to hear. "She doesn't love me!" The tears welled up and ran down his cheeks. Chad was gulping through his sobs and then he gave up trying to hold himself straight and collapsed against Nick, clutching his shirt, his body heaving against his chest. "She doesn't love me!"

God damn you to hell, Nick raged silently to Sybille. He closed his eyes against the tears that stung them and pulled Chad to his lap, holding him tightly.

"Listen," he said firmly. "Are you listening? She loves you in her own way. She can't show it the way I do, but she thinks about you a lot. You know how many presents you get from her; who do you think buys them—the mayor of New York?" A strangled giggle came through Chad's sobs. "And she calls, or we call her, a lot, and she'll be here to visit in a few weeks...no, I'll tell you what. Why don't we surprise her and go to Washington?"

Chad jerked upright, eyes wide, cheeks glistening from his tears. "Could we?" Then he shook his head. "Uh-uh. She doesn't want us."

"Of course she does. She may not think so because she's pretty busy, but we'll call tomorrow and tell her we're coming. The two of you will go out to dinner, maybe you'll go to the zoo—you haven't been to the Washington Zoo—and you'll have a great time. It'll be like another part of your birthday. Chad, listen to me."

Chad's eyes were wary. "What?"

"Your mother isn't going to be like other mothers, no matter how much you want it. Whether we go to Washington or she comes here, she's not going to change. Sometimes she has trouble managing her life, but I guess she's doing the best she can, and we can't ask her to change or expect her to be different. We just have to take her as she is and love her if—"

"You don't love her!"

"Not the way I used to, but that has nothing to do with you. You should love her all you want, and not be ashamed of it or think there's anything wrong with it. You tell your friends at school that we have our own way of doing things and it's not wrong, it's right for us. You can tell them you have a big family—your mother and your dad and Elena and Manuel and Ted and lots of other people who care about you and think you're the greatest, even though they don't happen to live with you. I know it's hard, just having a father—"

Chad threw his arms around him and mashed his face against his. He was crying again, noisily. "I love you, it's not hard, I love you..."

Nick, unable to reach the handkerchief in his pocket, wiped Chad's face with a corner of the sheet. "I love you, my friend," he said softly, his voice husky with his own tears. He kissed Chad on his closed eyes and clasped him tightly, his arms wrapped around him like a cocoon, letting no dangers in. "Dearest Chad. My dearest son, my friend, my companion, my champion birthday-cake eater with a hand that does things he doesn't even know about..."

Another giggle burst from Chad in a little explosion of air. They sat quietly then, and Nick felt he was holding his whole life in his arms: the meaning and the purpose, the beauty and the joy. He loved his son with a passion he had thought only a woman could arouse; it stunned him and convinced him that Chad was all he needed. This passion, so different, so crucial to him, was enough, he thought, and he would do everything he could to make up for the pain Chad had already known, to bring back the delight that had illuminated his face during the magic show, and to keep it there. Chad would have no more pain if Nick could help it; he would always know he was loved and cherished and needed; he would have the best chance Nick could give him to become a man able to love, to give friendship, to share.

"Daddy," said Chad, his eyes suddenly widening, "would you ever marry somebody who doesn't like me?"

Nick's heart sank. *There is no end to the fears of childhood.* "No way," he said with absolute finality. "I don't marry anybody until the two of you are friends. But it doesn't look like it's going to happen for a long time, Chad; it looks like it's going to be just the two of us for quite awhile. That sounds okay to me. How about you?"

"It sounds okay to me too. Could we read out of one of my new books now?"

Nick laughed. "A short chapter; it's getting late. Did you choose one?"

Chad pulled a book from under his pillow and settled back against Nick's chest, snuggling against him like a puppy making a protective hollow in a field of tall grass. He held one side of the book while his father held the other, and he concentrated on the pictures and the wonderful deep sound of his father's voice, rising and falling with the descriptions and what the people were saying, and after awhile his father's voice was like the sea, a steady, rolling sound, farther and farther away, and then it was gone, and Chad was asleep.

Sybille's secretary took the message while she was out, and it was that evening, when she went through her messages at home, that she learned that Nick and Chad were coming to Washington. "No," she said aloud. Why did he always do this to her when she was busiest? She was trying to learn how to run a cable network. She was overseeing the remodeling of the two adjoining apartments they had bought into one. She was getting used to Washington. She had scheduled buying tickets to the Symphony Ball, the Opera Ball, the HOPE and the Corcoran balls; that would get her seen by the right people. She had made her contribution of a hundred thousand dollars to the Kennedy Center Endowment Committee, and ten thousand to the Senatorial Committee Trust. That would get noticed by the right people. She was learning where to shop, where to dine, where to have tea. She had had someone nominate her for the F Street Club. She had so much to do; she had no time for visitors. I'll call him, she thought; he'll have to change his plans. And then she read the next message: Valerie Shoreham had called, from Hawaii. What the hell, she thought; they must have called one right after the other. "What time is it in Hawaii?" she asked Enderby.

"Six hours earlier," he replied from behind his newspaper. "What was that 'no' about?"

"Nick wants to bring Chad to Washington." She looked at her watch. "Six o'clock. So it's noon there." She picked up the telephone and dialed the number. When Valerie answered, she sounded as close as if she were in the city.

"Sybille, I'm so glad you caught me; I was just going swimming. How are you? When I called, your secretary gave me your number in Washington; when did that happen?"

"January. We bought a television network, cable, and moved here to run it."

Valerie laughed. "So much for my advice about taking time to play. It sounds exciting, though. What did you do about your finance show?"

There was a pause. "I forgot you'd been out of the country all this time. We found a new host. They wanted me to stay on, and commute from Washington, but Quentin needed me here. If I have time I'll do another one, but I'd have to think about it; it got to be awfully dull. Once you've been on camera awhile there's no challenge anymore."

"Do you think so? I've gotten to like it more than I used to. Of course I don't do it very often; maybe that's the reason I feel that way."

"You were on television while you were traveling?"

"A little. It was great fun, working with people who do things so differently from us."

"But what did you do?"

"Interviews, mostly. A couple on Italian and French television—"

"In English?"

"No, I speak Italian and—"

"Why were you interviewed?"

"Oh, all of a sudden I was the visiting American expert on horses. I thought it was a joke, but they were serious, and when people take me seriously I never try to talk them out of it. Anyway, it was such fun. I was staying with friends in France and Italy who raise and train horses and they knew people in television and so there I was, talking about American training techniques. We even went out and filmed some in action. I did it on the BBC too; you'd think all I know is horses."

"What else would you have talked about?"

After a moment, Valerie laughed faintly. "Well, that's a good point, Sybille. What else could I possibly have to talk about?"

Sybille said nothing.

"But in Yugoslavia I talked about American fashion—in English; my Yugoslav consists of 'hello' and 'goodbye' and 'thank you'—and I used my own sketches. That was the best of all. Tell me about you. Where are you living in Washington?"

"The Watergate."

"Oh, one of my favorite buildings."

"What does that mean?"

"It's so curious, don't you think? All those sharks' teeth on the balconies."

"Shark's teeth?" Almost furtively, Sybille looked behind her, at the balcony facing the city. Rows of decorative concrete outlined its railing, as they did every railing in the four buildings of the complex: tall, tapering, pointed. Shark's teeth. That bitch, she fumed; she has to make fun of everything she doesn't have. But then she thought about it again. What was wrong with sharks? They were smart and fast and almost always won their fights. I could do worse, she thought.

"Do you like it?" Valerie was asking.

"It's fine."

"Did you sell the apartment in New York?"

"No, we'll use it if we go back to visit."

"And Chad? Has he visited you there yet?"

"Not yet." *That's why she called. She wants to hear about Nick. She has to come to me for that. But what does she care? No one could possibly be interested in someone after all this time . . .*

There was a long silence.

"Oh, Sybille," Valerie sighed, her voice amused but also faintly reproachful. "I thought you could tell me about Nick. I just saw *Newsweek* and *Time* and there he was on both covers, and you're the only one I know who knows him. He must be feeling wonderful."

"Of course, he's all excited. We had a long talk about it the other day. It was Chad's birthday party and I just couldn't be there so I called to talk to him and of course I talked to Nick too. He said he feels vindicated; so many people thought he couldn't do it."

"Vindicated? What an odd word for Nick. I'd never have thought he'd use it."

"Why not?" Sybille asked sharply.

"Because he never feels—felt, anyway—he has to prove himself to anyone but himself. That's a word an insecure person would use; someone who feels misunderstood or mistreated."

"I was married to him," Sybille said furiously, aware of Enderby's scowl. "I know what he's like."

"Of course," Valerie said. "And I suppose"—her voice grew doubtful—"people do change."

"No. Not much." Sybille's fingers were clenched around the telephone. *I just pulled that word out of nowhere,* she thought, *to have something to say; she couldn't know whether Nick would use it or not. She's faking to impress me. How would she know that much about him? She knew him for a few months six years ago.*

"Well, it's amazing," Valerie said lightly, "how many things happen when I'm out of the country. I always feel I've been gone for years instead of months. I hope you have a great success in Washington; call me when you're coming to New York and we'll see each other."

"Are you coming back to stay?"

"Probably not; I'm feeling so restless lately I don't know what I'll do. I'm really tired of traveling, but it's better than staying home and I haven't exhausted my list of places I haven't seen. I met some people last week who are going trekking in Nepal; remember I talked about that once? But call when you're in New York, Sybille; my secretary always knows where I am, and she knows my schedule, as long as I have one."

"And you call, when you're going to be in Washington."

"I can't imagine what would bring me there, but I'll remember. Good luck, Sybille; I hope everything works out the way you want."

The way you want. Sybille thought about it after she hung up. Enderby was behind his newspaper; the den where they sat was wood-paneled and solid. On one side of their apartment was the dark ribbon of the Potomac, with the lights of Virginia on its opposite bank; on the other side was Washington, with its broad boulevards and white marble buildings. To a New Yorker, it was an unbelievably clean city, with an air of timeless serenity that withstood modern traffic, the pace of government, and the rush of office seekers looking for whatever they could get. *The way you want.*

I don't know what that is anymore.

She was learning a new business, driving herself as she did every time she had something new to learn, but she hated it and she hated Enderby for dragging her to Washington and thrusting her into a kind of television that seemed to have nothing to do with the kind she had spent years in mastering. He had taught her the basic system, then named her assistant manager of the network, renamed EBN for Enderby Broadcasting Network. "And you'll be manager by the end of the year," he said. "So pay attention."

EBN was small and easily squeezed out by larger networks. "But we'll get bigger," Enderby said to Sybille at dinner as they sat near the fireplace at La Chaumière in Georgetown. They had just moved to Washington and already Sybille felt she might have made a mistake. At least in New York she knew what she was doing and they had a powerful, profitable station. Here they had an infant barely able to stay alive. "Cable's just about to burst," Enderby went on, waving away the waiter; he was in no hurry to order. "It's about to be one big beautiful babe of a booming bonanza. And the networks that make it the biggest will be the ones who put together programs that grab people — clever, funny, maybe pornographic—"

"You can't do that," Sybille said. "You know it's not allowed on the air."

"It's allowed on cable. Nobody tells anybody what can be on cable. One hundred percent unregulated. You like that? I like that." He looked around. "We need wine."

"You told the waiter to leave."

He thrust up an imperious arm and ordered a bottle of Montrachet.

"So this is what happens. A network like EBN can buy shows from independent producers or we can produce our own in our own studios. We'll buy most of it; lots of little companies putting out half-hour, hour shows, cheap. We'll produce our own news shows; can't buy those. So we buy shows or produce them; sell time to advertisers and cram as many commercials as we can get away with in each show; then string a bunch of shows together to make a whole day's programming—quiz shows, soaps, whatever. That's what we sell to cable operators. They pay us so much, a couple of bucks, for each subscriber they've got. You following this?"

Sybille watched the waiter fill her glass. She nodded.

"The operators are the ones who string wires—cables, to you—to homes and apartments everywhere in the country and send programs over the cables to subscribers. The subscribers pay a monthly fee to get the programs. Very simple."

"So all you have to do is put together some shows, and cable operators will be knocking down your door to buy them."

He gave her a sharp look. "Don't make fun of it, babe, it'll make you a hell of a lot richer than you are now."

"How?"

"Damn it, you're not listening. I told you: this is big business. You want to hear my prediction? Here it is. If you're as good as you were in New York, we might get twenty-five to thirty million homes buying our powerhouse package of prime programs from cable operators. Since the operators will pay us two to three bucks a subscriber, that's fifty to ninety million a year. Then there's advertising revenue—figure sixty to seventy-five, maybe more—minus a few expenses, and we could expect a tidy profit somewhere around ten to fifteen percent."

Sybille's eyes were narrowed; she sat very still. He was talking about a minimum profit of eleven million dollars a year. "How solid are those figures?"

"Solid enough for me to buy the kit and caboodle from Durham."

She toyed with her glass. "What did you mean: if I'm as good as I was in New York?"

"You know damn well what I mean. You'll be the manager. Or president, director, chief honcho; whatever you want to call yourself. I'll be looking over your shoulder and talking to people who need talking to, but at my age I'm not going to spend my days in the trenches."

She gazed past him at the flames in the open-sided fireplace. All that money; a huge national audience; her husband leaving her alone—

and, more often than not these days, leaving her alone at night too. Why didn't she feel happier?

Because the humiliation of New York hung over her like a cloud, darkening everything, and the passing months only made it worse, as if the farther back it was in time the more vivid it grew in her memory.

"Syb? Come back, babe, you're wandering off somewhere."

She sat straight. "Of course you wouldn't be in the trenches. I'll take care of that. What are the problems? Just getting the right programs?"

"That's the biggest. Then we have to get assigned the right channels. The cable operators—nasty, narrow-minded, nattering Napoleons—decide which channel goes to which network, and so far ours has always been stuck with Channel Thirty or above. Known in the trade as Siberia. Nobody wants to be there. Audiences sit in their comfy armchairs pushing buttons on their remote controls and you can bet they never start at ninety-nine; they start low and work up, and most every time they'll settle down with something before they get to fifteen. So if we're higher, who sees us?"

"So we buy a lower channel."

He chuckled. "Little Syb; she always cuts right to the heart. The official word is they're not for sale, but I'll be looking into it. If we can, we will. What number do you like?"

"Twelve."

"Why?"

"Because people don't like to quit searching too soon—they think they might miss something. But if they've searched from two to twelve and like what they find they'll probably stay put."

"Sounds about right. Let's order, for God's sake; I'm starved."

From that night, Sybille took over the network. Once again she kept notebooks filled with what she read and learned on the job, her impressions, her ideas. She worked from early morning until midnight or later, often in planning sessions with Enderby in her office or his. They ate dinner together at a restaurant and then he went home while Sybille went back to work. He was frequently asleep when she got home; if she saw his light as she came in, and knew he was waiting for her, she drooped in the doorway, too tired to do more than touch her lips to his forehead and disappear into her bedroom.

But, at work, they were getting along better than ever before. Enderby never saw the rage that had become part of her fiber; she hid it beneath cool efficiency and ambition, and the more they got done, the more content Enderby thought she was.

"We need a name for what we do," Sybille said when they were beginning to buy taped programs from independent producers. They were sitting in her office in the building that housed the EBN offices and studios in Fairfax, on the Virginia side of the Potomac. "A kind of slogan that makes us different from other networks."

He scowled. "Slogans are for advertising."

"Of course. We're advertising ourselves. *The New York Times* says, 'All the News That's Fit to Print.' The *Chicago Tribune* says, 'The Greatest Newspaper in the World.' One of the networks says, 'Home of the Stars.' What are we going to say about us? It has to be simple, so people can remember it."

His scowl deepened. "'Television for Everybody.' How's that?"

"No. No punch to it. 'Television for You.' That's better."

"That has punch? I don't like it. How about 'Television for Dogs, Debs and Doddering Dads'?"

"Quentin, I'm serious."

"Well, then, what about something to make 'em switch from the doom-and-gloom networks? 'Happy Television.'"

Sybille's look sharpened. "That's not a bad idea."

"What? It was a joke."

"I know. I'm thinking about the idea. Concentrate on one special kind of programming and be famous for it. Like MTV and the Weather Channel. People would know in advance what kind of shows they'll see. No tragedies or worries, no dire predictions about the ozone layer or nuclear plants; they can get that anywhere and they're probably sick and tired of always being told what they should be worrying about. We'd be upbeat, optimistic, heavy on entertainment—it would all be entertainment; even the news. There shouldn't be any noticeable difference between news and other shows; they'd all show the bright side, the good side. Lots of *moments*—stories about little people doing good things, celebrating a seventy-fifth anniversary, saving kids from drowning in swimming pools, helping old people get new furnaces, making Thanksgiving dinner for two hundred homeless people..."

They looked at each other. "Little Syb," said Enderby finally. "I knew I could count on you."

"We'll call it 'Television of Joy.' Or 'Hope.' Or 'Television on the Bright Side.' Something like that. And we'll need news anchors who can handle it; most of the old ones couldn't make the switch. I think I'll call Morton Case."

"Who's that?"

"He was one of the interrogators on my first show, in San Jose. You saw the tape before you hired me."

"Don't remember. Which show?"

"'The Hot Seat.'"

"That show? That guy? He's a rattlesnake. Damned good, but a rattlesnake. What the hell does he have to do with joy or hope or whatever?"

"You need a snake to make bad news sound happy. He's very smart, Quentin. Trust me."

He nodded, suddenly feeling exhausted. "Lots of work in my office; better get there. See you later."

"Do you need help getting there?"

"No! Getting where?"

"Your office. You said you had a lot of work to do."

"I know what I said, damn it!" He went to the door, leaning slightly to the side. "See you at . . . at . . ."

"Dinner," Sybille said. She had not moved from her chair. He never forgot things or fumbled for words when he was rested; it was only when he got tired. He needs to do more work, she decided calmly. He's the chairman; he has to hold up his end. She knew he had gone to his office to take a two-hour nap on his couch. She rang for her secretary. "Call Mr. Enderby in half an hour and remind him of the meeting at four-thirty. And when you've done that, take him the letters I dictated this morning; I want him to review them before they go out."

That became the pattern of their days: they worked all morning, had a quick lunch at Sybille's or Enderby's desk, or with others in the conference room, and then Enderby went to take his nap. Every day Sybille had him awakened half an hour later. To escape, he began going home after lunch, taking work with him. Sybille stayed at her desk.

Through the gray winter months, through March when Chad's birthday party came and went and Valerie called from Hawaii, through April and May when tourists arrived in Washington by busloads and Nick brought Chad for four days, she worked. In those months she created what they were already advertising in newspapers and magazines as EBN's "Television of Joy." And when the new format was ready to premiere, it was all hers, and everyone knew it.

That day, she sat in a control room and watched her staff put on live newscasts, sports segments ten minutes long, and national weather reports. Between the live programs were movies and taped shows: cooking shows, children's shows, a dance-contest hour, and dramatic features on people and animals around the world. All the programming, live and taped, was sent out via satellite to cable operators who had bought the package in response to the heavy promotion Sybille and Enderby had been doing. Only a small number had signed up, with a combined audience of a million and a half homes, but everyone was sure more would come. And only a small percentage of time for commercials had been sold, but everyone was sure that would change, too.

The first day, Sybille sat in the control room, almost unmoving, for the eleven hours they were on the air. From seven in the morning to six at night, she watched what she had created unfold before her. Afterward, there were congratulations in the control room and telegrams and telephone calls from around the country. There were criticisms that the programs were shallow, the whole effect unreal. But she was more interested in the praise.

That night, Enderby gave a dinner party at Le Pavillon for the twenty people who were the executive staff of EBN. Wearing black tie, feeling rested from his nap, he escorted Sybille from the Watergate to their limousine. "You deserve a party," he said as grandly as an emperor. "The best little producer in the—"

A spasm of pain pinched his face.

"In the—"

He crumpled, sprawling on the sidewalk. Someone screamed. Sybille took a step backward and stood frozen. The doorman rushed up and knelt beside him. "Mr. Enderby!" He lifted Enderby's head and looked wildly at the people gathering around.

"A doctor!" someone said. "Police!" "Ambulance!" "He alone or with somebody?"

Sybille knelt beside Enderby. His face was colorless and slack. He did not seem real to her; his prone figure seemed far away, and unfamiliar, as if she was watching a film about someone who had died. She looked up at the strange faces clustered above her. "Call an ambulance," she ordered. "And he can't stay here, on the sidewalk; get him inside."

"Somebody help me," said the doorman. "There's a couch in the lobby. I'll get an ambulance—"

"He must not be moved," said a deep voice. It rolled through the crowd like a rumble of thunder. Sybille looked up into a narrow face with hollow cheeks and deep-set eyes as gray and flat as the surface of a lake at dawn. The man towered above her. "May I offer my help," he said. "My name is Rudy Dominus. I am a preacher. And this is my assistant." He drew forward a young woman with white-blond hair, delicate features and a small, slender figure. She seemed quite ordinary, but Sybille could not take her eyes off her. The eyes, perhaps, or her sorrowfully curved mouth...Everyone else was looking at her, too, she saw. They couldn't take their eyes off her.

"My assistant," Dominus repeated. "Lilith Grace."

Chapter
13

he was small and thin, with gray eyes beneath pale brows and silky white-blond hair, and it was her fragile face Enderby first saw when he woke in the hospital. He had no idea who she was, but something about her made him feel almost happy in the midst of the confusion in his mind. "Welcome," she said softly, smiling at him. "We've been waiting for you. I'm so glad you've come back to us."

She seemed to be with him the whole time he was in the hospital. Sybille came occasionally, and Rudy Dominus was there most of the time, but Lilith Grace was always there: when Enderby woke and when he went to sleep and when he finally went home in an ambulance.

"We have nurses full time," Sybille said. "We don't need anyone else."

"But Mr. Enderby wants us near him," replied Rudy Dominus. "His doctor asked him, in the hospital, and he was very definite about wanting us. Perhaps you would let him decide."

"I make the decisions here." Sybille tried to stare him down. "What are you after?"

"To take care of a sick man; in all conscience, we can do no less. Lilith and I were traveling to New York and it is no problem for us to make a small detour. It is our mission." His protruding eyes met hers without expression, and Sybille was annoyed to find herself faintly intimidated by them. His face was gaunt, deeply shadowed, surrounded by tangled black hair. Probably dyed, she thought, and his eyebrows too. She didn't like him. Eccentricity annoyed her and made her nervous, and she was suspicious of the way he had suddenly appeared when Quentin had his stroke, as if he had been hovering, waiting for something to happen. But it did seem that Quentin was less agitated when he was around. He liked having the girl nearby, too, she thought, and there certainly was no harm in her, odd as her relationship with Dominus appeared. Sybille was never very curious about other people, and she was impervious to that strange quality that drew others to Lilith Grace; all she saw was that the girl was pale and very young, oddly passive, frequently fumbling for words, and often wary, even fearful. No harm in her; probably no harm in either of them.

"Do what you want," she said dismissively to Dominus. "Just don't bother anyone."

From then on, they were always there, one or both of them, sitting beside Enderby, reading or talking to him, praying with him, or, if it was Lily alone, singing to him as he fell asleep. They left the room whenever Sybille came in, but as soon as she was gone they returned, their footsteps silent on the thick carpet, their voices low. For a few hours each night they returned to their separate rooms in a motel on the outskirts of Washington; the rest of the time, as the humid days of June slid past, they stayed in the hushed, cool air of Enderby's shadowed bedroom. And then Lily was preparing to leave.

Dominus told him about it late in the afternoon, when a ray of sunlight had pierced the small space between the closed drapes and Enderby's closed eyes wrinkled in a frown. "If you are awake," Dominus said, "I would like you to say goodbye to Lilith."

"Where she going?" Enderby's eyes were still closed, and his words were slurred; one side of his mouth did not move.

"Back to school. I thought she had told you. I doubt you will see her again before Christmas."

Enderby's right eye opened; the other remained shut. "I take another nap?" Dominus nodded. "How long?"

"Three hours."

"*Three hours?* I told you always get me up after an hour! You promised!"

"You were deeply asleep, Quentin; you need your sleep."

"No, no, I need... Where's Syb?"

"Ah, I imagine at the office. She says very little to me, as you know."

"I know; damn silly. Asked her why, she clammed up. Don't let me sleep, Rudy. Old men sleep all day; not me. You get me up... counting on you. Promise! Counting on you!"

Dominus leaned over and wiped the dribble from Enderby's mouth. "You must count on me to do what is best for you; in all conscience I can do no less. Your body and your soul, together, will forge new bonds of wholeness, and gain the strength of redemption and rebirth, only as you follow my guidance. I am here for this: to lead you from the chasm of pride and pretense into which you had fallen. You had fallen, your stroke showed you how far you had fallen, you were doomed, but I bring you another chance; I am here for you. We will work together to wipe away all the sins that weighed you down and felled you with a stroke; your spirit will become trembling and fearful of the powers that keep you from the chasm. I have come to bring this to you, knowledge of these powers, a new birth, redemption. I will bring in Lilith now."

"She's a good girl," Enderby said dreamily. Rudy Dominus's deep chant always made him feel soothed and drowsy. He didn't really believe that he had any sins, and he scoffed at the idea of trembling fearfully before anything or anyone, but when Rudy spoke it didn't matter what he said as much as how protective he sounded: *I am here for you*... No one else was just for him, Enderby thought. He'd been trying to push old age away for a long time; now he'd found someone who would do it for him. That was worth everything he had.

Dominus opened the door and held it as Lilith Grace walked past him and stood beside the bed. Her long hair was pulled back in a ponytail that stretched her delicate skin; she wore a long-sleeved white cotton blouse and a shapeless blue cotton skirt, almost to her ankles. On her feet were white stockings and tennis shoes. She laid a cool hand across Enderby's forehead. "I'm so sorry to be leaving you; it made me happy to help take care of you and I wanted to see you up and getting about."

"Fat chance," Enderby snorted and tears filled his open eye. "Never again. Used to dance up a storm... should've seen me. Would've liked to dance with you, Lily. Light on your feet."

She leaned down and kissed his cheek. "But you have your wheel-chair and that's better than being in bed all day. And you still have one perfectly good side; how many people would envy that?"

"Nobody." But he gave her a wavering smile. "Sorry I cried; cry at every damn thing these days; like a baby."

"It's all right to cry." She frowned. "I wish I could find the words ...Rudy says they'll come when I'm older, but I have trouble... Crying is good; so is laughing. They're part of you. It's like your good side and your paralyzed side; you're still a whole person, it's just that one side can do more than the other. Do you believe that?"

"No." He peered at her. "Dinner with us tonight—Rudy and me—not Syb. She works."

"I'm going back to school, Quentin. Did you forget?"

He looked confused. "Isn't it summer?"

"Yes. July. But we have summer school."

"Where?"

"Renwyck Academy. In Massachusetts. And I must be going." She kissed him again. "I'll think about you, getting stronger, and I'll pray for you. I have faith in you, Quentin. I believe in you."

"Wait—" He struggled with his good arm to push himself up, then fell back. "Don't go. Schools in Washington ... lots of 'em. Why you have to go ... where is it?"

"Massachusetts. And I go there because that is what Rudy tells me to do. Goodbye, dear Quentin, I'll pray for you; I'll see you soon."

"When?" he asked. *"When?"*

"Christmas," Dominus replied. His voice was like deep velvet after Lilith's cool high one. He put his hand briefly on her head in what may have been a caress or a small push out of the room, and she left. He sat beside Enderby. "She is only fifteen, you know, and in my care, and I do what is best for her. In all conscience I can do no less."

"Up," grunted Enderby.

Dominus cranked the handle on the hospital bed Sybille had had delivered the day before Enderby came back to their Watergate apartment, and raised him to a sitting position. "We'll soon have dinner; can I get you anything until then?"

"Drink."

"Ah." He poured a shot of Scotch into a large glass of water and handed it to Enderby. "What would you like with it?"

"Less water, more Scotch. Please, Rudy, you trying to kill me?"

Dominus chuckled and helped Enderby hold the glass as he poured from the bottle. "Enough, Quentin; in all conscience—"

"Talk to me about Lily," Enderby said.

"Ah, yes, Lily. Someday she will be a fine preacher. She learns from me, but there is something special in her that I do not have. What she said about crying and laughing—that was good, you know; it needed refinement and polishing, but it had depth. Lily has depth. She does not know that yet, and of course I will not tell her until she is ready, but in time she will be superb."

"Fifteen," Enderby said. "No parents?"

Dominus spread his hands. "As far back as she can remember she has known only foster homes. She was a wild little creature shifted from one place to another when she became uncontrollable. By the time I met her—"

"Where?"

"Kentucky. I was preaching there, but my parishioners were too poor to support me and I took a job passing out leaflets in a shopping mall—a tragedy, of course, when I had greater work to do, but, still, I talked to people about their souls as I handed them the leaflets, and Lilith was one of them. So small and frightened; she had run away again. She was wearing shabby blue jeans and a work shirt, and her hair was every which way. She took my hand when I went to dinner; she said she was hungry and belonged nowhere. She said she was twenty-one and had heard me preach and wanted to study preaching with me. If I closed my eyes, she sounded somewhat older than she looked, and she was so pathetic, and of course she admired me...Ah, am I in the way?"

The nurse was there, carrying the tray prepared by the cook. "I'll just put it here," she said stiffly. She could not get used to Dominus's presence and was happy only when she had her restless, demanding patient to herself for a few hours. She leaned forward and wiped Enderby's mouth before Dominus could stop her, then marched out.

For the first time since he came home, Enderby did not grab for his food like a greedy child. His eye was fixed on Dominus. "Not twenty-one," he said.

"Alas, no. She was not quite fourteen. But she wept so bitterly when I said she must go back to her foster home that I decided I could be a better guardian than they, whoever they were, and so when I heard of a small pulpit in New Jersey, she came with me. I know, I know," he said, though Enderby had not interrupted. "It was wrong to take a child to another state, but you see no one cared about this child but me, and I cared a great deal. She was so grateful, she made me feel like a truly good man, though I am as weak as anyone. She kept to herself; she went to school like a good girl, calling me her father; she cleaned and cooked for us; and she has never been—"

"Concubine," said Enderby, a glint in his eye. "Mistress. Wife. Daughter. Chef. Maid. Lucky fella."

Dominus drew himself up. "She has never been in the slightest danger, from me or anyone else. She has placed herself in my care. In all conscience I could do no less than protect her. There can be no redemption if you nurture evil thoughts, Quentin. Do you doubt that she is a virgin?"

Enderby shrugged. "Can't tell. Never could. Got fooled a couple times when I was young." He burst into a high giggle. "Fooled a girl myself, when I was fourteen...how I learned it all. God she was something, wasn't anything she said no to, and I learned fast. Virgins. Hard to spot."

"She is a child," Dominus said flatly. "And I am a preacher."

"Sounds pretty combustible," Enderby said with another giggle.

Dominus stood, towering above the bed, turning away. "I will leave you to your dinner. Perhaps later, when you can speak of Lilith and me with sensitivity, we can—"

"Wait! Christ's sake, wait!" Enderby's voice rose in panic. "I didn't mean it! Just a joke...stupid joke...you wouldn't leave just 'cause I...Rudy, *don't leave me!*"

Dominus turned back. "It was a joke in the poorest possible taste."

"I know! Sorry! Won't do it again! Listen, Rudy, sit down, eat with me! Christ, you know I can't be alone, can't stand it—"

"You have your nurse."

"Not the same! I want you! Always liked preachers, always had a weakness for preachers. Find sin, sweep it away. Rudy, *I count on you!*"

Slowly, Dominus sat down. Very slowly, he took one of the linen napkins from the tray and tied it around Enderby's neck. Enderby sighed deeply and picked up his fork. His hand shook.

They ate in silence. Dominus stopped now and then to wipe Enderby's face and clean up the food he spilled, and Enderby made murmuring sounds when he wanted more, but they did not speak until their plates were empty. "Want to do something for you, Rudy," Enderby said then. He closed his eye."Tired. Hard work, eating. Never used to be. Do something for you."

"Later," Dominus said. He removed the tray and cranked down the bed. "Right now you must sleep."

"Television. God show." Enderby chuckled sleepily. "That's what we call 'em. You ever hear that? News, sports, weather, talk shows, sitcoms, movies, God shows. Do your preaching on television. You like that? Bigger audience than Kentucky or New Jersey. No more leaflets in... where was it?"

"A shopping center," Dominus said. His voice was husky.

"Right. No more of that. You like the idea? Do it for you. Have to clear it with Syb. You like it?"

"Yes," said Dominus with a long sigh. "I like it very much."

"Good. Clear it with Syb."

"You want me—?"

"No, no, Christ's sake, keep out of it! I'll do it. Tomorrow. Remind me...sometimes I forget..." His head lolled to the side. "Clear it... Syb..." He began to snore.

But he did not see Sybille the next day; she left early in the morning, before anyone was awake. It was a Sunday and the air was still fresh, and she put down the top of her sports car as she drove across the bridge to Virginia. She kept going past the turn to Fairfax, past the offices and studios of the Enderby Broadcasting Network, and on toward Leesburg, speeding on the empty highway. The sun spread a misty gold wash on the rolling fields that stretched beyond the city, and the wind was cool, whipping loose a few strands of hair from her braided chignon.

Past Leesburg, she slowed for the turn to Carraway Farms, and drove the half mile to the stables. It was exactly eight o'clock when she stepped out of her car. Sleek and trim in her riding habit, she nodded to Wink Carraway, her riding instructor, who was waiting for her, holding her horse. She was known everywhere for punctuality, but here especially she would never be late: she had too much to learn and she was in a hurry.

A step at a time, she was becoming the person she had determined she would be. She was an expert skeet shooter, a hunter who brought down birds, foxes and deer with unerring accuracy, and she was on her way to becoming a strong rider, as determined in the hunt as in the ring and the steeplechase. She was wealthy; she dressed impeccably and bought herself fine jewelry and furs; she could do what she wanted. And she had the power of the cable network to herself; Enderby was no longer a consideration. It would be better still when he was dead, and her life could really begin, but at least he was out of the way, and for the first time it was Sybille Enderby, not her husband, who was making a name in the world of television.

And she had discovered this countryside, Loudoun County, Virginia, where wealth lived privately behind unbroken miles of stone walls and weathered rail fences, and within the high-ceilinged rooms and broad porticoes of mansions from another age. The first time she drove through the county she knew it was what she wanted: this would be her country home. Someday one of these mansions would be hers, and stables of horses, and the hundreds of acres that would guarantee her the attention of the others in the county, especially in Middleburg, the town where she had decided she would live.

For the first part of her lesson, she and Wink rode in the Carraway Farms ring. It was the only time Sybille took criticism in silence, gritting her teeth as she tried to move with the horse, to guide it without force, to shift deliberately as she sat forward, then up, then back, tightened her thighs, moved her wrist. Impatience ate at her. She hated exercises; she wanted to gallop, to push her horse through the countryside with the same abandon with which she drove her car. But she said nothing; she did what Wink told her. Because she hadn't started as a child, the way some people did, born to a saddle, a rifle, tennis, travel around the world... She was starting late—twenty-six last January—and she had to catch up.

The second half of the lesson was jumping. And then she took another lesson, changing to a different horse for riding cross country. That was when she came to life. The faster she went, the closer she came to danger, the more perfect was her day. After awhile, she was barely aware of Wink or the passage of time; there was only speed and those perfect moments when she crossed the boundary between safe and hazardous, and she was terrified and excited and alive.

When Wink pulled up, having circled back to the barn, she was angry. "What are we doing here?"

"Ten o'clock," he said, dismounting. "You were good today."

"Was I? What did I do wrong?"

"The usual. You have to watch your hands; your movements get too large. Small wrist movements, right? You got a sensitive animal here, you don't want to tear him to pieces by jerking him all over the place."

In the barn, a groom took the horses, and Wink walked with Sybille to her car. "You'll get it; you're like a bull, no offense, fixed to get what you want. If you could sort of connect with the horse, you know, the way you connect with people. Kind of love him, right? You do that, you'd be great."

"Like a camera," Sybille muttered.

"What?"

"Nothing."

"Listen." He stopped walking. "You'll get it. You've got a real fix on things; nobody can stop you. You shouldn't get bent out of shape if I tell you what needs fixing; that's what you're paying me for, right?"

"I should have learned it by now; by now I should be perfect."

"Wow," Wink muttered under his breath and walked on.

Sybille reached the car ahead of him. "Next week," she said, sitting behind the wheel, but her thoughts were on her lesson. Soft hands on the reins, connect with the horse, *love* it, for God's sake. She'd figure it out. She'd be the best in Loudoun County.

She was forced to drive more slowly on the way back; traffic was heavier than in the early morning, and she drummed her fingers on the wheel, turned up her radio, and braked sharply each time she was almost upon the car in front of her. When she reached her apartment, the excitement of the morning was gone. All she remembered was Wink's criticism of her hands, and the traffic on the road. She walked through the foyer, dropping her jacket behind her.

"Mrs. Enderby." Sybille jumped. Rudy Dominus stood in the hallway, blocking the way to her bedroom. The shadows in his face were like small patches of his black suit and black vest, and she wondered how Quentin tolerated the gloom that clung to him. "Quentin would like to see you," Dominus said, and held his hand toward Enderby's bedroom, as if he were the envoy, ordering Sybille's appearance.

"I'll be in later," Sybille said coldly. "After I change."

Their eyes held and then Dominus nodded. "Please. As soon as you can. He is very anxious."

"Is he dying?" she asked sharply.

A small smile touched his thin lips. "No, you must not fear that. I should think he will live for quite awhile."

Sybille turned and went into her sitting room, slamming the door behind her. While her maid ran her bath and helped her take off her riding habit, she thought about Dominus. It was time for him to leave. Quentin could damn well do without him; they didn't need an intolerable bug-eyed preacher with dyed hair and dirty fingernails in their home, no matter how good he was at keeping Quentin quiet. Valerie wouldn't have tolerated it for a day, much less seven weeks.

Two hours later she went to Enderby's room, wearing a brightly striped silk caftan, her hair loose and held back with a gold band. The bed was raised halfway and he was holding a glass and scowling at Dominus. "Kept me awake," he said to Sybille. "Told me you were coming and I couldn't sleep."

"Of course you can sleep. I'll come back."

"Sit down," Dominus said, holding the chair he had vacated when she came in. "May I offer you tea? We've been keeping it warm."

"No. I'll talk to Quentin alone."

Dominus shot a look at Enderby, but Enderby did not see it; he was gazing at Sybille's caftan. "Pretty. Like a peacock—parrot—whatever. Rudy, get yourself a suit like that. Lots of colors. Too goddam much black in this room."

Dominus leaned over and wiped Enderby's mouth. "Mrs. Enderby wants me to leave," he said.

"Whatever she wants. Keeps me young, Rudy, like you. Two of you, working on me. Live forever."

"I'll wait in your sitting room," Dominus said reluctantly, and left, leaving the door slightly ajar.

Sybille closed it. "I want him out of here," she said, returning to the chair. "He makes me nervous, and he's acting like he owns the place. I don't like him, and we don't need him."

"I need him."

"You're doing fine with the nurses. Look how strong you are. I want him gone, Quentin."

"Promised him a God show."

"What?"

"God show. We don't have one. Do we? You get a God show while I was sick?"

"No. We don't need—"

"Hell we don't. Big audience if you get a good one. Rudy's good. Lots of people out there want a preacher in their living room. Don't have to go in the rain to go to church, don't have to shave or get dressed, watch him in bed if they want. Rudy's good, grabs people." He shut his eye. "Christ, I'm so tired. Syb, give him a show."

"What do we get out of it?"

"Audience..."

"That's not enough. We can't sell commercials on a God show."

"Donations. Different...daddy...drift...desperate..." Tears squeezed through his closed eyes. "Can't do it anymore. So much fun, putting words together, took people by surprise. Now I can't do it. Gone."

Sybille pushed back her chair. "Go to sleep. And tell your friend he's to be gone by tonight. If you can convince me we need a God show, I'll find someone who fits in better with our style."

Enderby opened his good eye and fixed it on her. "Donations. We take a piece of them."

She paused. "How much?"

"Rudy says fifty-fifty. Renegotiate it later."

"How much could he get?"

Enderby shrugged one shoulder. "Oral Roberts gets millions."

"How much has your friend ever gotten?"

"Never had a tv show."

"How much in a church?"

"Christ sake, leave it alone, Syb! I want him, give him a chance! Half hour a week, maybe an hour, what do you care? Hard to fill those hours, specially if we expand . . . you're doing that, right? More hours? You doing that? Remember I told you to—"

"I'm running the place," Sybille lashed out. "I do all the work! I make the decisions!"

"Shit—" Enderby struggled to speak; his chin was wet with spittle. "Who owns the fucking—"

"You do." She took a deep breath. He might live for a long time; that's what Rudy said; the doctors said it could go either way. "I'm sorry, Quentin. Of course we're going to expand, to fifteen, maybe sixteen hours. I didn't forget that was what you wanted. I wouldn't be anywhere without the plans you made, you know that. I'm just doing my best until you get back and then we'll expand even more. When you're strong enough I'll bring you everything I've done; just tell me when you want it."

"Not now." He sighed. "You're a good girl. You going to give Rudy his God show?"

"What about the girl? Lily. Is she part of it?"

"She's gone. Boarding school somewhere. Can't remember. *What about Rudy?* He get his show?"

She thought for a moment. It would keep him busy; less time to hover over Quentin. And she'd get rid of him when Quentin died.

"Syb? He gets it, right?"

"Yes," she said.

"What time?"

"Sunday, I suppose. I can give him eleven-thirty in the morning or six-thirty at night, right after the news."

He sighed again. "Don't ask me; talk to him." He closed his eye and moved his head from side to side, making small barks of laughter. "Little Syb. Getting religion. Not likely. Roll down the bed."

Sybille turned the handle until Enderby lay flat. She bent over and brushed her cheek against his forehead. "I'm going out tonight. I wish you could come; I'll miss you. I'll see you tomorrow."

"Tell Rudy to come in."

Once he wanted to know where she was going and what she would be doing every hour of the day. Now he wanted only Dominus. But that won't last; he won't be here long, Sybille thought as she came up to him in Enderby's sitting room. "Sunday morning or night," she said curtly. "Tell me which you want, and as soon as you get an audience—"

"Congregation," he said with a smile.

"—a bunch of people sitting in front of you, to make you look legitimate, we'll talk about a contract. Don't keep Quentin waiting."

She walked past him and crossed the hall to her own sitting room. *He won't be here long. The day Quentin dies, Rudy Dominus will be gone.*

Nick first heard of Rudy Dominus in March, eight months after the television premiere of his ministry, when Sybille came to California for Chad's fifth birthday. She sat on the sofa, Chad at her side, her arm loosely around his shoulders. He sat carefully, touching his mother but not pressing against her: he knew that would make her angry and he was careful to follow her rules because that meant she would come again. "Nick, have dinner with us," Sybille said. Chad knew she would say that; she always did. "Chad's birthday ought to be a family celebration."

Nick looked at Chad. "What would you like?"

"All of us would be okay," said Chad, knowing what Sybille wanted and she rewarded him by giving his shoulders a little squeeze.

"I have presents for you," she said. "Would you like them now or after dinner?"

"Now, please." Chad jumped down. "Can I get them?"

"They're in my large suitcase. You can open it; just don't take anything except the wrapped packages."

"I wouldn't," said Chad, offended, and ran off.

"He's so grown-up," Sybille said to Nick. "You always did know just what to do with him. And he looks exactly like you."

"He has your hair."

"But your eyes. And your mouth. And his fingers are long, like yours. He's so beautiful, I can't believe he's mine. Does he like your new house?"

"We've been here over a year. Yes, he likes it. And his school, and the friends he's made in the neighborhood."

"It's amazing, how incredibly well you've done. I can't get used to it." She surveyed the large, square living room with its suede and leather furniture, two large Bakhtiari rugs, and the Georgia O'Keeffe desert paintings and Giacometti sculptures Nick was collecting. The house was luxurious, with a simplicity that made its luxury more striking. "All this, and a housekeeper to help Elena, and a handyman, and landscapers . . . do you take it all for granted by now? Does anyone ever take two hundred million dollars for granted?"

"Tell me about your television network. You said, at Christmas, you were working on some new shows. And longer hours."

"This is a *lot*," Chad said, coming in with five brightly wrapped packages.

"One for each year," Sybille said.

"Can you handle them alone?" Nick asked, "or do you need some expert help?"

Chad grinned. "You just like to open presents."

Nick laughed. "You're right. Okay, it's your birthday, you do it all. We'll just watch."

"O-*kay*," he said happily, and bent to the first package. Sybille began to resume her conversation, but Nick held up a hand and they watched in silence as Chad ripped off the paper. A family at home, Nick thought wryly, and the words hurt. Chad swept aside the wrapping paper and opened a large box. Bewildered, he looked at the spheres and connectors, motors and strange parts in neat compartments. "Capsela," he read. "How does it work?"

"We'll do it together," Nick said. He had seen in an instant how the various parts could be used, and he joined Chad on the floor. "We're going to make some very special contraptions here. I think you'll be amazed." He looked up at Sybille. "A good choice."

"Thank you," Chad said quickly. He went to Sybille and reached out his arms and she leaned forward so he could kiss her. "Thank you very much. I'll have lots of fun with it."

"You may be a little young for it," she said, "but I thought, with Nick, you wouldn't have any trouble."

"We'll do fine," Nick said, already joining two spheres, one of them enclosing a miniature motor.

"*Daddy*," Chad said reproachfully.

With a laugh, Nick put it down. "Sorry, friend; I couldn't resist. I'll wait till you're ready." He sat back and watched Chad open the other gifts: a set of a hundred crayons, a wooden train with a dozen cars, three Dr. Seuss books, and a pair of pajamas and matching robe decorated with grinning dinosaurs.

"Fantastic!" cried Chad, looking at the hoard. "This is the most fantastic birthday!" Once again he went to Sybille and held out his arms, carefully, so she would not feel jumped on. "Thanks a lot. There's a lot here."

"They're really all right?" Sybille asked Nick. "I wasn't sure. I don't know much about this."

He sat again in his chair. "Who helped you?"

"One of the managers at F.A.O. Schwarz. I called and told them a five-year-old..." Her voice fell away. "What else could I do? I don't know what he's interested in; I don't know what five-year-olds can do. And he changes so much between visits I can't keep up."

"They're great," Chad said loudly, looking earnestly at Nick. "Sybille did great; she got everything I wanted. I really like them."

Nick was silent, unpleasantly struck, as always, when Chad called his mother by her first name, as she insisted.

"Daddy, they're great," Chad said again. His eyes were worried. "You think so, too, don't you? Don't you think Sybille did great?"

"Yes, she did," Nick said quietly. "It's a terrific bunch of presents."

"When does Chad get his present from you?" Sybille asked.

"Tomorrow. On his birthday. And for now," he said, standing up, "we should be getting ready for dinner. Chad wants Chinese food for his birthday, so that's what we're going for. Sybille, do you need anything in your room?"

"No, it's fine," she said. "You always have everything I need."

Nick made no response. He was never sure how calculated her comments were and so he let them drop. There seemed to be more of them lately, he thought, since Enderby's stroke, but he preferred not to think about that. In fact, he thought very little about her, and then only in connection with Chad. When they talked about her, Chad said he loved her and missed her and Nick never asked what there was to love and miss, because he had long since understood that, for Chad, a remote mother was better than no mother at all. And, because he understood his son, and knew how quick and creative was his mind, he thought it probable that, even at five, Chad had created a fairy tale in which, somewhere in the future, there would be a reformed Sybille, a loving Sybille, a Sybille who wanted to be his mother.

That night, after dinner, when Chad had gone to bed, Nick and Sybille sat in the library, a bottle of Armagnac and a plate of biscuits between them. "Tell me about Quentin," Nick said.

She looked down and slowly shook her head. "It's terrible, what's happened to him." She raised her head and Nick saw bewilderment in her pale-blue eyes. "He was so vibrant, Nick, so much fun to be with and so excited about what we were going to do in Washington, and now he just sits in a chair and stares out the window. He doesn't seem to care about anything anymore."

"Not even the network? You're running it by yourself?"

"Completely. I have no one to turn to for advice or help; Quentin used to be there whenever I needed him, but now it's as if"—her lip quivered and she took it between her small white teeth—"as if he's already dead. He never even asked if we were going to expand our hours, and that was one of the first things we planned to do as soon as we had a good base of cable operators buying our programs. I've got us up to fifteen hours a day, and our audience is big enough now for us to raise our advertising rates; I'm even starting a production company for our own shows and others that I'll sell. Everything Quentin wanted to do I'm doing. But he's too sick to care, even to pay attention." She blinked as if to hold back tears. "It takes so much of the fun out of it for me. I really need someone to share the things I do; otherwise I feel . . . lost."

Nick contemplated her. "Is there any hope that he'll get better?"

"No." She held out her glass. "May I have a little more? It's wonderful." She watched Nick pour. "There's a preacher of sorts who's attached himself to Quentin, and he talks about spontaneous cures, but I don't believe in miracles; I never did. He's mesmerized Quentin, though; he got him to give him a show on our network."

Her voice was bitter and Nick understood that Enderby was not indifferent to everything. "What kind of show?" he asked.

"A God show. That's what we call them. He switches back and forth between preaching and asking for money. One minute he's talking about sin and guilt and a lowly spirit, and then he slides into money. His voice doesn't change, the crazy chant he has, but all of a sudden he's saying how much money it costs to bring other sinners under the mantle of his benevolent forgiveness. Or something like that. I don't watch him. Quentin does."

"Does anyone else?"

"Not if you go by the money. There's not much coming in. We could put another program in that spot, and sell commercials in it, but Quentin refuses. He says he doesn't care about the money."

"But he's—what's his name?"

"Rudy Dominus."

"What?"

"That's what he says."

"Colorful. It sounds as if he has a good imagination. He's not costing you anything, is he? Other than not being able to sell that time?"

"He's cost us eleven million dollars so far." She smiled thinly at Nick's raised eyebrows. "Quentin wanted him to have his own studio. It's almost a goddam church, with seating for two hundred; of course we make it look like more with the right camera angles, but we could have done the same with half that many seats. As it is, we're feeding them sandwiches every Sunday, to make sure they come. It's better when the girl is there. He has a ward or a mistress—he told Quentin, very high and mighty, that she's a virgin, but I wouldn't believe anything he said—whatever she is, she's very young, mousy, malleable; he probably does whatever he wants with her. But for some reason, when she's on the show the audience seems to wake up. We get more money those times, too. Maybe I'll dump Rudy and make it Lily's hour."

"Why is she on the show?"

"She wants to be a minister. I suppose she's practicing."

"What's her last name?"

"Grace."

Nick smiled. "I think you should sign her up. What better name for a minister?"

Sybille gazed at him. "I hadn't thought of that."

"How old is she?"

"I don't know. Sixteen, seventeen; she's still in school. I suppose he must be her legal guardian or the welfare people would be on his back. Quentin probably knows, but he doesn't talk about either of them very much. Or he forgets; he forgets more than he remembers these days."

Nick refilled their glasses. "Tell me what else you're doing." To his surprise, he was enjoying the conversation. He had never been interested in television; now he found it intriguing. That had always been true of him: hearing a little of a subject, he became avidly curious, wanting more. When he was growing up, it had been model railroad trains and airplanes, followed by his father's vegetable garden and principles of planting, harvesting and pest control, followed by a home chemistry set and, finally, computers. In my next life, he thought, amused, I'll take up television. He was beginning to feel restless at Omega, missing the excitement of its early years, being a part of building, rather than managing. Why not television? he thought. I'd like to do something different. "What kind of shows are you producing?" he asked Sybille.

She went back to the beginning, when Enderby had bought the network, and described the first programs she had bought to make ten hours of programming they could sell to cable operators. "I expanded it in the last few months with old and new movies: mysteries, romances, pornography; there's more kinky stuff out there than you can imagine. And I bought a bunch of new programs on Hollywood and European royalty, skeletons in the closets of the rich and famous, odd people doing odd things, heroic medicine, sports, that sort of thing."

"Like a magazine," Nick said.

She looked pleased. "Exactly. The kind of things people really care about. Short pieces—nobody wants to spend a lot of time on anything these days—and lots of sharp graphics, very fast. You don't want anything on the screen for more than two seconds; people have a remote control in their lap and they'll change channels and then you're through. The only way you can keep their attention is to make sure they don't have time to think."

"That's the goal of your network?" Nick asked.

"Oh, Nick, the goal is to make money, and you know it. And to expand; you can't sit still in this business. So far it's cost me about seventy-five million: new studios and equipment, remodeled offices and bigger staffs in the office and studio, and reporters—I've got ten cities covered now and I want at least another ten in Europe and Asia, all looking for the happy side of the news—and then there are the new programs I'm buying and the ones I'll be producing. It's expensive, but it will all come back; the money is enormous, Nick, you can't imagine the potential. It's the most incredible feeling, manipulating all of it. I could never have it just by being on camera; I can't imagine why anyone would want that."

"What shows are you producing?" he asked again.

"Right now, just the news. I'm thinking about game shows, interviews, soaps, sitcoms, whatever it pays us to do. Sometimes it's cheaper just to buy them. We're trying different things with our new shows; would you like to see one? I brought a tape, in case you cared about what I was doing."

Nick smiled slightly. "How could I refuse?" He opened a door in a rosewood-paneled wall along one side of the library, revealing a stereo, television set and video cassette recorder. When the tape was running, he returned to his chair and watched the opening: a swift succession of pictures in a montage of world figures and events as background for a boldly designed title—"The Victors"—that looked like a newspaper headline.

"A strange name for a news show," Nick observed.

"You'll see," Sybille responded.

The round, cheerful face of Morton Case, whom Nick had last seen skewering a guest on "The Hot Seat," appeared on the screen, announcing the sinking of an excursion boat off the coast of Mexico. But nothing of the tragedy was seen by the viewers. Instead, a film appeared, narrated by Case, showing a lovely young girl swimming toward shore, struggling against high waves and approaching sharks. It could be seen when she rose out of the water that she was nude, having torn off her clothes, said Case, before jumping from the doomed ship. She was tired, slowing down, her eyes filled with fear, when a boat appeared behind her, racing at top speed to reach her before the sharks did. Just in time the young man at the helm cut his motor, reached down and lifted the girl into the safety of the boat. He wrapped her in a colorful blanket, poured brandy from a flask, and put one arm around her, holding her close. The two of them looked at each other in a way that made it clear that this was a beginning for these two, not just an isolated rescue. The young man restarted the motor and raced off toward shore, and a cheering, waving crowd awaiting them.

Nick marveled at it. He remembered the story: over two hundred people had drowned. But Sybille had transformed the tragedy into a banal romance. There was nothing to mourn; on the contrary, there was every reason to be joyful. Love had triumphed, death was invisible.

"You staged it," he said.

"Of course," Sybille replied. "We filmed it the next day. But there had been a girl who swam from the boat; she even took off her clothes before she jumped. Her skirt, anyway. And she was picked up by a boat. We were told it was a fishing boat, with some old man on board; somebody we couldn't use. We didn't change the story, only some of the details. The response to that segment was very good."

Nick thought of apes in the engineering building. He watched as a new segment began, this one on a flood in India, the scenes focusing on families who were reunited, and a baby boy, orphaned by the flood, taken in by neighbors who had always wanted a child of their own. It was followed by a similar mini-drama, and another and another, a relentless parade of joy snatched from disaster.

They watched in silence. At first Nick had found it amusing, but as the hour neared its end he found himself bored and repelled. It was not as bad as "The Hot Seat," though it showed the same contempt for viewers, and he was not as upset as he had been when they had watched that show together; he was not married to Sybille now, and so what she did was no longer a reflection on him and his judgment in marrying her. Still, when the tape ended and he was rewinding it, he could not think of anything to say.

"You don't like it," Sybille said accusingly.

"It's not my kind of news show," he replied. "You knew that before you showed it to me. I suppose some people would like it."

"A lot of people. The ratings are the highest of any we have."

"How long has it been on the air?"

"Three months. I know what people like, Nick."

"So it seems." He handed her the tape. "I wish you luck with it."

The words echoed in the room from an earlier time, when he had walked out after seeing part of "The Hot Seat." Everything he had now was different from that time: his work, his relationship with his son, his friends, the women he knew. The only thing that had not changed since he left Sybille was his memory of Valerie. He had never found anyone to take her place. *Valerie. That short, magic time. She made me believe in magic.*

"Have you seen Valerie since college?" he asked. The words were out, before he thought about them.

Sybille's face froze and then, almost immediately, became bland. "No, have you? I haven't thought of her for years; do you know where she is?"

"No." He was shaken by that brief, frozen look. "I'll say good night—"

"Of course she always did flit about so much it was hard to keep up with her. She was so childish; never settling down or being serious; I wonder if she ever managed to grow up. You haven't written to her or talked to her at all?"

"No. I'll say good night, Sybille."

"But it's early! What time is it? Midnight! Is it really? But that isn't late, Nick; stay and talk."

"I have an early meeting tomorrow. When is your plane? Maybe I can drive you to the airport."

"Ten o'clock. You'll be in your meeting. If you really have one."

"We start at seven. I'll call if I can't be back in time to pick you up."

"Oh, Nick." She sighed as she stood near him. "This has been wonderful. I have no one to talk to in Washington. Or anywhere. It's very lonely, with just the business to run, and nothing else. All I have is Quentin, and he's dying. I was too young when we were together, Nick, I was selfish and stupid; but I've learned so much, and what will I do with it when Quentin dies? He'll die, Nick, and then it will all be gone, all the love and companionship he and I had... and I have no one else to keep the loneliness away."

She had learned to look appealing, Nick thought; she was much more polished at it than she had been in college. "I'm sorry," he said, knowing it would be foolish to talk about the help she might get from friends. She had made no friends in San Jose.

"May I go upstairs and kiss Chad good night?" she asked. "I'd like to kiss his father good night, too, if he wouldn't mind."

"Chad will be enough," Nick said easily, holding in the dislike that rushed through him. "Of course you can go upstairs; I'll wait here."

Angry and frustrated, she met his eyes. There was nothing to do but go upstairs. She was back in a few minutes. "Sound asleep," she said. "Do you remember how nice it was to go to sleep at night without any problems?"

"Chad has his own problems," Nick replied. "Perhaps you've forgotten how important they are, at five."

She shot him a look. "I hate it when you're clever," she said, and Nick remembered that too from the years of their marriage.

"I'll see you tomorrow," he said, and watched her retrace her steps up the stairs, picturing her walking to her room at the other end of the hall from his. He stood in the library, thinking again how much he had changed in the years since they had lived together. He could not imagine, now, desiring Sybille, pitying her, living with her, thinking, even for a moment, that she could be to him what he dreamed of. He tried to remember the needs and false image of himself that had led him to marry her. It had to do with Valerie, he knew that; but it also had to do with his youth: he was so certain that he could change Sybille into the kind of woman he wanted her to be; he was so sure he could achieve whatever he wanted if he just concentrated and worked hard enough at it. He knew better now. He knew there were some goals he might never attain, some dreams he might never bring to reality.

He heard Sybille's bedroom door close, and he went through the downstairs rooms, turning off lights. He stood at the foot of the stairs filled with the longings that never left him: for love and laughter, a hand reaching out to his, an unquenchable joy and curiosity to match his own, a readiness to share whatever lay ahead. Once he thought he had found those things, and the promise of more, with Valerie. But not since then. He had tried—at least he believed he had tried—but sometimes it seemed to him that he held back with other woman, reluctant somehow to give up the memory of Valerie; as if he would lose something irreplaceable if he ever let her go enough to commit himself to someone else.

He had Chad, he had enormous success, wealth and prestige, he had friends who loved him. He had a good life. But the longings were there, and he knew they would never be satisfied until he accepted the past as a dream that had ended, and woke to embrace someone new.

And it was a dream, he knew that. He went for long stretches without thinking of Valerie; she was no part of the life he had built. But then something would bring back memories that made him ache with a loss as painful as the day they parted. Then he would begin to fantasize about her, about the two of them, about the chances of meeting, any day now, on a street corner or in a theater or at a dinner, seated together by a hostess who had no idea . . .

But then what? Why would he think they would do any better now than before? He might have changed in some ways, but he was still as serious, still as disciplined and involved in his work as ever, and those qualities were what she had most disliked in him. And Valerie— wealthy, fun-loving, lighthearted, ruled by her own pleasures—was surely no different now; why would she have changed any more than he had? What had come between them once, would again, and in Nick's controlled life there was no room for a second wrenching loss with the same woman.

He had to let her image go. He was thirty-two; it was past time to stop clinging to a dream that probably had become exaggerated and prettified through the years. *I'll have to change some more, enough to stop wanting what I remember. And I'll have to keep looking. Just possibly, I might find another Valerie.*

He climbed the stairs to go to bed. He didn't really imagine, after all this time, that he could stop wanting what he had loved so deeply and remembered so vividly. Or that he would find, and love, another Valerie. But still, he thought, looking in on Chad before going to his own room, *I owe it to both of us to try.* And he promised himself, once again, that he would.

Chapter
14

 uentin Enderby died three years after his first stroke, at the age of eighty-three. Lily Grace and Rudy Dominus were at his side. They had been talking about the low ratings of "The Dominus Hour" when he had another stroke, his fourth, and died within minutes. It was Dominus who called Sybille with the news.

For the past year, Enderby had seen almost no one but Dominus and the nurses, and Lily when she was home from school. Sybille stopped in once a day, but she would leave after a few minutes, as soon as they began to quarrel. She was impatient and irritated at his stubborn refusal to die, and her anger was ignited whenever he would suddenly have a spark of interest in the cable network and demand that she bring him up-to-date. Most of the time he seemed uninterested— in fact, he seemed almost to have forgotten it—but then, without warning, his head would come up; he would square his shoulders and become alert and forceful, sending for paper and pencil, gesturing broadly as he expounded ideas, loudly pressuring Sybille to do nothing until she cleared it with him. He would look at the books and make scathing comments about the amount of money she was spending, and challenge her to justify it; and when she grew defensive and said it took time to make a floundering network profitable, he would shout her down, saying she'd had a year, two years, three, and nothing to show for it but a steady outflow of money. Sybille refused to discuss it. "I'll make it the biggest there is," was all she would say. "I just need the right mix of new people and new programs, whatever it costs; then I'll—"

"It isn't more money you need; it's brains!" he would roar, and at that she would storm out of his room.

His fury of activity might last for as long as a week, and then vanish, and once again his days would blur into each other in a numbing routine of watching television with the glazed look of someone who really saw and heard none of it, or sitting in his chair beside the window overlooking the Potomac, or half reclining in bed, dozing as Dominus read the Bible to him or Lily sang folk songs. And Sybille would return to the routine she considered rightfully hers, of running the network without answering to anyone or being pestered by meddling comments and questions.

And then Enderby was dead. He died on a cold, gray December afternoon, and two days later Sybille dressed carefully in a black suit trimmed in black fox for the funeral. She had decided there would be only a graveside service, conducted by Rudy Dominus, who had begged for the honor and in any event was the only minister she knew. She had sent a notice to the press, and everyone at the network, announcing the date and time of the funeral, and coffee at her apartment afterward. It would be done properly; no one would be able to criticize her for not being a good wife, or widow.

It was cold at the cemetery, with leafless trees stark against a lowering sky. But there was a crowd at the gravesite and that was what Sybille cared about: they were all employees of EBN, but to the reporters it would look as if she and Quentin had dozens of friends. And then she saw, at the back of the crowd, Valerie, bundled in fur, arriving just as Dominus began to speak.

Sybille paid no attention to what he said. Scraps of phrases floated to her, but, as always, she was bored with anything she could not see or buy. Quentin's soul was between him and Dominus; it had never had anything to do with her. She half turned from him, bringing the crowd into view while seeming to gaze mournfully at the coffin suspended on a frame over the open grave. Beneath lowered lids, she scanned the faces. No one was paying attention to Dominus, she noted, which was why his ratings had been bad from the beginning: he had never been able to make anyone care about being saved by him. In fact, Sybille thought bitterly, he had the same problems Enderby had accused her of having when she was trying her damndest to prove herself on camera. He could not connect with an audience. But Enderby had not seen that in Rudy Dominus, or had turned a blind eye, and so Dominus had his show, while Sybille had been robbed of hers.

Her gaze reached Valerie. Of all of them, she was the only one really listening to Dominus, her face intent and curious. Faking it, Sybille thought; trying to act pious. Why does she bother? And why is she here at all? Because she danced with Quentin a few times?

"He has finally attained the peace we all long for in our sinful lives," Dominus intoned. "And thinking only of forgiveness in his last moments, he showed us the way to find our own." He fell silent, his head bowed. Behind Sybille, the others looked around for clues, then they too bowed their heads.

"Quentin was our friend," Lily Grace said into the silence, and her high, cool voice made everyone look up. "He loved us with the love of a good man who discovers that he has more to give than anyone ever asked of him, much more than he would have thought he *could* give. Quentin learned that very late in his life, when he was mortally ill, but he found it in time to treasure it with the joy of self-discovery. Quentin learned to trust himself, to believe in himself, to like himself. What more could any of us ask than that: to see, as if a curtain had been pulled away, the riches within ourselves? Quentin closed his eyes for the last time with the peace of a man reborn, who finally believed that he was truly good."

Her voice, small but true, rose in a French folk song. Looking again at the people behind her, Sybille was astonished to see some of them dab at their eyes and spontaneously bow their heads. And Valerie was watching Lily with admiration. Sybille's eyes narrowed and she turned back to Lily, studying her as she sang, wondering what she had missed about her. The girl was dressed in a black wool coat that came to her ankles; she wore heavy boots and black cotton gloves, her small features were pale in the cold air, and her hair fell straight, covering her shoulders like a white-blond veil. Ordinary, Sybille thought; very young, incredibly badly dressed; as simple as a farm girl.

But Valerie had seen something to admire. A familiar bubble of rage began to form inside Sybille. What had Valerie seen in Lily Grace that had been invisible to Sybille? Something, something, something. It hammered inside her: *She saw it; I missed it. She saw it; I missed it.*

So, for the first time, she began to think about Lily as a person separate from Rudy Dominus. Dominus, of course, was no longer with EBN; Sybille had canceled his program the day after Enderby died. That meant she no longer had a God show. At one time she would not have given that a second thought, but the climate in the country had changed since Enderby bought the network; God was big business now, and the people who had gotten in early, like Oral Roberts, Jimmy Swaggart, Billy Graham, Jerry Falwell, and Jim and Tammy Bakker, were cleaning up. Lily Grace was no competition for those big hitters, but maybe, as someone's assistant, she could add something different, if Sybille could figure out what it was.

I'll think about it later, she decided; there's no rush. She'll be tied to Rudy's apron strings until somebody cuts her loose. And I can do that anytime, if I want to.

The coffin was mechanically lowered into the grave, moving silently downward within the steel frame. Sybille watched it absently, thinking of the network and what she would do with it. She wasn't sure she wanted to keep it. It was a constant drain, and brought her no pleasure; it hadn't even brought her prestige, because it was small compared to others, especially a network like CNN. But there were those figures Quentin had held out tantalizingly that night at La Chaumière —all those dollars, all that influence and power—when he spread the whole glittering prospect of cable television before her and talked her into plunging into it with everything she had.

That was the exciting time, when her Television of Joy, backed up by an enormous advertising campaign, was being written about in newspapers and magazines. Her audience grew, and the ratings climbed, advertisers clamored to be part of what they thought was the new wave of television programming, and cable operators signed up by the dozens to carry the EBN package. Sybille was busier than she ever had been; her name was known; her picture, taken by a well-known photographer of models and society women, appeared in articles in the local and national press and in the glossy pages of *Town and Country, Washington Dossier* and *Vogue*. Often there was also a photo of Enderby, seated at a desk, although, when Sybille was asked about him, she could not force herself to lie, and so she told the truth: that he did nothing anymore; she was completely alone in carrying the burden of EBN and its Television of Joy. She was also alone in becoming part of the Washington social scene, but she managed that bravely, always enlisting someone at EBN to be her escort to the whirl of dinners and cocktail parties that included government officials, congressmen, lobbyists, bankers, lawyers and newspaper and television figures: a glittering array that made her feel, at last, part of the heights she had eyed for so long.

And then it ended. Her ratings began to sink, slowly, then more precipitously, as viewers deserted her for the ordinary programming they had watched before she came along. Bewildered, Sybille began to make changes: she rearranged the schedule, hired new anchors, bought a soap opera set in Palm Beach, a women's wrestling show, and a new set of X-rated films, and increased her advertising. Nothing helped. Movies, especially Westerns and pornography, held their ratings, but the rest of the schedule soon was a desert. Fewer articles were written about her, and the ones that did appear were critical. And with that, her social life dried up. There was nothing that the network brought her anymore.

Why keep it? she thought as she led the mourners from the cemetery and settled back in her limousine for the short ride to her apartment. She stared unseeing at the streets of Georgetown. What did she care about a network Enderby had bought? She'd have all his money; she didn't need to work; and, anyway, she could get a fortune for EBN. She'd find a buyer and get out of Washington—a horrible place; she'd always known it would be; all wrapped up in itself and its own sense of importance—and go somewhere and—

And what? What would she do?

The limousine stopped at the entrance to her building in the Watergate. *I'll think about it tomorrow. I'll think of something. I can afford to do anything I want.*

Everyone came to her apartment and drank coffee and Scotch and martinis, and devoured the feast catered by Ridgewell's. Clusters of people she saw at work every day stood about, crowding her rooms as they had not been in the entire time she and Enderby had lived there, talking about ratings, politics, sports, and the price of housing. No one talked about Enderby.

Valerie stood to one side, drinking sherry and watching Dominus move through the rooms as if building a constituency. When he reached her, she asked about Lily Grace. "I sent her home," he said. "She was chilled and emotionally drained by the funeral; I made her apologies to Sybille." His protruding eyes were fixed on her. "You are an extraordinarily beautiful woman; I hope you guard against letting that warp your life."

Valerie's eyebrows rose; then she broke into laughter. "Thank you. That's the most graceful compliment anyone has ever given me."

"It was not a compliment. It was a warning."

She was still smiling. "But half of it sounded like praise. Do you always have a knife handy when you say something kind?"

He frowned. "Meaning what?"

"Oh, the kind of things you said about Quentin at the cemetery. You said he was a superb entrepreneur who built a major independent station in the cruelest city in the world, and then you said his arrogance had driven him to overreach himself so that he knew only unhappiness and low ratings."

Dominus stared at her. "Those were my exact words."

Valerie nodded. "And you did it over and over again. Every time you praised him you'd stop and take a breath, and then stick in the knife. Is Lily the only one who says something kind without contradicting it in the next minute?"

"I do that? I stop and take a breath?"

"Every time. As if you're getting ready to lunge."

"That is a wicked thing to say. You have beauty and intelligence"—he took a breath—"but you are too proud; you will suffer loneliness and terrors because of it."

Valerie gazed at him in silence, a small smile on her lips, and in a moment he scowled deeply.

"The world is not a pretty place. You should be pleased that I find anything at all to praise in you. There are many people in whom I find nothing, though I wrestle with myself, attempting to find good in them. There are people even God could not find good in, though He almost never takes the time to look for it; He directs those of us on earth to do it for Him."

Valerie gave a small laugh again. "Even God gets mixed reviews. You must be very alone, judging a world where everyone is flawed, without God to turn to."

"I do not judge; I observe and comment, no more. And of course I turn to God; the two of us share the burden of a troubled world. He could not do it without me and I would have a much more difficult time without Him."

Valerie began to laugh, but there was no responsive smile in Dominus; he was absolutely serious. "Tell me about Lily," she said. "Is she your daughter?"

"In spirit only. I have cared for her for years, since she was a girl. Lily is absolutely pure and sees only purity in others."

"And she believed what she said about Quentin."

"Of course. Lily cannot lie."

"Was she right? Did he know he was a good person before he died?"

"No. But Lily believed he did. Lily always believes the best of everyone. Her charm—perhaps her genius—is that she convinces others that she's right about them and thus makes them feel good. And then, of course, they give more money, which allows us to continue our work." He saw Valerie's curious look. "How can we bring our message to the needy, if our own needs stand in the way? We satisfy ourselves so we can satisfy others. We will soon organize a church in New Jersey, in a house I have bought with Quentin's help. I will allow Lily to preach there occasionally; mostly she will visit the sick and comfort the bereaved. When we are ready, you will come and listen to us—yes?—and I am confident that you too will give us money, for you will want us to carry on. But you have not talked about yourself at all." He glanced at her wedding band and the diamond that flashed beside it. "Do you and your husband live in Washington?"

"No, in Middleburg."

"Ah, then you have horses. And children?"

She smiled. "Only horses."

"And your husband— You must forgive me, I don't recall your name. There were so many people when Sybille introduced us at the cemetery..."

"Valerie Sterling."

"Sterling?" Sybille came up to them, repeating the name. "I didn't know you'd married again."

"A few months ago. Why don't you come out for a few days, Sybille? It must be hard to be here alone."

"It's terrible. I keep looking for Quentin, to tell him about something at the office or to watch a program together..." Sybille's back was to Dominus as she edged him aside, only Valerie saw his scornful look. "Come out where?"

"Middleburg. Sterling Farms. It's a wonderful place that Carl's father built. We have plenty of room; you could stay as long as you like." She took Sybille's hand. "Sybille, I'm so sorry about Quentin. I remember when you were married, you said he was fun to be with and he took care of you, but I think you must have been just as good for him. Do visit Carl and me; let me know when you want to come." She put down her glass. "I have to get back; we're flying to the Adirondacks early tomorrow morning; Carl has a sudden urge for cross-country skiing."

"Flying? You have a plane?"

"Yes. We'll be—"

"And a house there? In the mountains?"

"Yes. We'll be back in a week; I'll call you. Maybe you'll come for Christmas; we'll have a houseful—some friends of Carl's, and my mother—and we'd love to have you join us." She looked past Sybille at Dominus, who hovered where Sybille had slowly pushed him, his back against an Oriental table. "Good luck with your church. Please tell Lily I thought she was very fine today."

"I'll help you find your coat," Sybille said, and walked with Valerie toward the foyer. The rooms were heavy with the scent of huge flower arrangements, most of them ordered by Sybille from Bill Dove. A smaller one of gracefully bowed sprays of pale orchids caught Valerie's eye. "Whoever sent that understands grief," she said.

"He understands *me*," Sybille replied, and stopped beside the flowers. Valerie had no choice but to look more closely at them, and so she saw the card: *Our sympathies; we hope to see you soon. Love, Chad and Nick.*

She stood still for a moment, one finger barely touching a delicate petal, then she turned and walked on, with Sybille just behind. Sybille waited, but Valerie said nothing. In the foyer, as the attendant found her fur coat, the two women looked at each other. Sybille thought she saw a shadow of contempt in Valerie's eyes, and inwardly she bristled. Who did she think she was, coming here to lord it over the widow, with her talk of a rich husband with his own plane, and a house in the Adirondacks, and horses, and a huge spread in Middleburg... Middleburg! The town Sybille had chosen for herself.

Wherever she turned, Valerie was there, a few steps ahead. Was there anyplace in the world where she could be first, where Valerie would be consumed by envy of her, where Valerie would suffer because of her, as she had suffered because of Valerie?

"Let me know if I can do anything," Valerie said.

Sybille nodded briefly. "Thank you for coming."

She closed the door and stood against it after Valerie left. I have to do something. Something new. I haven't gotten anywhere. Quentin didn't do anything for me; all he did was saddle me with a second-rate network and his stupid ideas about joy and upbeat programs that no one wants to watch. I'll get rid of it; sell it as fast as I can. Then I'll be free of everything and my life can really begin.

A waiter approached with a tray of drinks, and she took a cognac. *He did do one thing for me. He left me his millions.* She wondered how many, exactly. He had been secretive about that.

Her lawyer was in the living room and she went to find him. "How much did he have, Sam?" she asked as soon as she had led him to the library. "I don't know exactly."

Samuel Breeph gave her a quick look. "Why don't we wait till tomorrow, when we read the will?"

"Because I want to know now. My God, Sam, all you do is plod. I can't imagine why Quentin kept you around. I want to know how much he was worth and you'll tell me this minute or it's the last time you'll work for me or my network."

Breeph put down the plate he had been carrying when Sybille cornered him. "Quentin left you one million dollars," he said precisely, almost with pleasure. "Also your apartments here and in New York, and the Enderby Broadcast Network. Apparently you had drained much of his money and incurred heavy debts as president of the network, but he was confident you could manage; he said you had done very well without much money before you met him. He left five million dollars to Rudy Dominus."

"Five million—" She stared at him. "You're crazy. It's a lie."

He shook his head.

"He wouldn't do that to me." Dizzy with rage, she focused on his small, pursed mouth. "He'd never do that to me! He loved me!"

Breeph shrugged. "I don't know anything about that; he didn't mention it. I have his will, written four months ago, on his eighty-third birthday. Lily had baked him a cake. You were at a meeting, in New York, I believe."

Sybille's fingers curled like claws. *"You fucking—"* The loud sounds of conversation in the living room recalled her, and she clamped her mouth shut. She swayed; she was dizzy and thought she was going to throw up. "Get out," she said hoarsely. "Get out of here. *Get out.*"

He scurried from the room. As soon as the door closed behind him, Sybille crumpled to the floor, slamming her fist against the Oriental rug. "Bastard," she whispered. "After all I did for you, all the crap I took from you, letting you take credit for my successes, letting you have me, night after night, even though I hated it, *using* me... bastard, bastard, bastard..."

She lay there as the sky grew dark and, beyond the closed door, her guests, looking around for her in some confusion, finally left, followed by the caterer and his staff. Then, stiffly, she stood up in the dark room. She looked about until her glance reached the telephone. *Nick would never do anything like that to me. He'd want to help me. He always*

*was the only one who understood me. I shouldn't have married Quentin;
Nick and I would have been back together by now if I hadn't married
Quentin.*

She sat at Quentin's desk and turned on his lamp and, from memory, dialed Nick's number at home.

"Mother called," Chad said when Nick got home later that afternoon. They sat on a leather couch in the book-lined study where the day's mail was piled on Nick's desk. "She wants to talk to you. It sounded like she was crying."

"Quentin's funeral was today; she probably wants a friendly voice. I'll call after dinner. What else happened today?"

"She said he robbed her of everything."

"Who?"

"Quentin. She said he was a bastard and she shouldn't have married him and she—" He stopped.

"She what?"

"She should have stayed with you."

Nick shook his head. "It sounds like she dumped an awful lot on you, all at once." He looked closely at Chad. "What did you think of what she said?"

There was a pause. "Nothing."

"I think you probably thought something. But we won't talk about it if you don't want to."

Chad scuffed his foot on the carpet, looking intently at his shoe. "I thought it sounded okay. You know, then we would've been like other people and have a whole family."

Nick nodded. "And what else?"

"And I thought...well, you could still do it. If Mother wants it and...but I guess you don't."

"No," Nick said quietly. "I don't. And I don't think your mother wants it, either. I think she's feeling sad and alone, because Quentin died, but she knows we can't live together."

"But you did once and it was okay—you said you loved each other when you got married—and you could just pretend it was like it was then, and you could have another baby, and then I'd have a brother or sister, and a real mother too. And we'd all be together."

Nick put his arm along the back of the couch, behind Chad. "We might be able to do that, if we were other people." He kept his voice relaxed. Chad had never asked him about marrying Sybille again, perhaps because of Quentin, perhaps because he was afraid of a refusal that would crush a dream he had clutched for most of his seven years. It's time to crush it, Nick thought, then immediately thought, as he always did when he knew something would cause Chad pain, that it could wait. Why do it now? Let him have his dream. If it made his life easier, why destroy it?

Because, even at seven, my son will live with the truth, not a bunch of pretty lies. His mother lives with lies; he won't.

He put his feet up on the coffee table and settled back, his arm coming down naturally to embrace Chad's shoulders. "There are a lot of differences between your mother and me, in the way we think about love and family and work, and the way we think about you. We were always different, from the time we met, but we thought that wasn't important, or maybe each of us thought we could make the other one act the way we wanted. Which is pretty silly, when you think about it; why would somebody who'd been one way for twenty-one or twenty-five years, and probably thought that was an okay way to be, suddenly switch over and be different?" He paused to let Chad think about it. "That doesn't mean that one of us has a good way to be and the other a bad way; it just means we have different ways. When we were married, it was like trying to attach one of your Lego pieces to one of your toy cars; it wouldn't work, because they aren't made to go together. They're fine when they're apart, but not when they're together."

"You could use some wire," Chad said after a moment, "and tie the Lego piece to the car."

Nick ached for his son's tenacity, and the plea in his voice. "It might work," he replied, "until the car hit some rough spots. That's what happens to people. They try to tie things together and sometimes it works pretty well, but when something rough happens that makes them nervous or worried or afraid, then the ties they've used tend to pull apart. It's not—"

"They could make new ones."

"They try that. But usually they pull apart, too. It's not that they aren't trying, Chad, it's just that they have a lot of things to worry about at once, and the things that aren't good and solid from the beginning are the ones that can't weather the storms."

"What storms?"

"That's a way of saying bad times. Like arguing about things, or worrying about a job or money or whether people like your work."

"Or whether they'll buy your computers."

"You've got it. But it isn't only when there are problems, Chad; sometimes two people just can't live together, whatever happens. They can try and try to share a life, and be kind to each other, and be happy, but they just can't do it. Your mother and I are like that. And if we can't live together in a good, happy way, it's better for all three of us if we live apart."

Chad shifted within Nick's embrace, as if struggling beneath a weight. His head was down and one hand plucked rhythmically at his pants leg. "You did once," he said stubbornly.

"We tried once. We couldn't do it. We can't do everything we want, Chad, even if we try."

Chad's fingers kept plucking. "So you don't think you could do it."

"I'm sure we can't, Chad."

He looked up then, his face working, tears in his eyes. "Ever?"

"Ever."

Chad looked away, swallowing hard, and then there was a long silence. They sat together, close, touching, but separate: Nick could not enter Chad's thoughts. He let him deal with his own pain, hoping his son would come back to him if the pain grew too strong to bear alone.

"Then why don't you marry somebody else?" Chad blurted.

Caught by surprise, Nick was silent. His glance took in the room: the study he had made for himself, with leather furniture, a white Berber carpet and black walnut desk; the walls lined with oak shelves crammed with books upright and on their sides; small Giacometti sculptures on a table near the window; an early Jasper Johns painting on an easel across from his desk. It was a warm, deeply comfortable room with no trace of any presence but his own. His house, large, bright, handsome, was his and Chad's, two people in twelve rooms, leaving a lot of space for the presence of someone else. *My life has a lot of space for the presence of someone else.*

"I haven't found anyone I want to bring into our house and into our lives," he said at last. "When I do—"

"You go out a lot," said Chad. "Elena tells me."

"I tell you, too," Nick said a little defensively. "I don't keep secrets from you."

"You don't tell me about all of them," Chad said wisely. "I know. Sometimes you go out after I'm in bed and you come back real late. I hear you, sometimes. Is that when you fuck them?"

Nick's eyebrows shot up. "What does that mean?"

"I don't know," Chad said loudly. "The guys at school said that's what we have to do on a date when we grow up."

"What guys?"

"The eighth-grade guys. They were walking next to us in a fire drill and telling us things about being grown-up. They said it was fun."

"Growing up?"

"Fucking. Is it?"

"It can be." Nick floundered; he had no idea how to begin or how much to describe.

"Well, I won't do it till I want to," Chad said decisively. "Those guys said I had to, but they can't make me; I can do what I want."

Nick waited, but nothing more came. Not too interested, he thought. Not yet. I still have a while to think about what I'm going to tell him. "Chad, remember when I told you I wouldn't marry anyone until you knew her?" Chad nodded. "That hasn't changed. When I find somebody I want to live with, I'll bring her home and the two of you will get acquainted, and if everything seems fine that's when I'll get married again. You're right, I've gone out with a lot of women, and I'd like to be married again. But it doesn't seem to be something I can order, like a hamburger at a restaurant."

"Medium rare," said Chad. "No, rare," he added, grinning at his joke. "You could order a wife who's blond, and sort of greenish eyes, and kind of tall, but not as tall as you, and rich and beautiful and they'd serve her to you."

Nick let the words echo in his mind. With a few modifications, they described Valerie. He looked at Chad. "Why blond and greenish eyes and so forth?"

"I don't know. It sounded pretty. And different."

Different from Sybille, Nick thought. As different as one could get. "Chad," he said, "I've been thinking of making a big change, and I'd like to talk to you about it."

Chad scowled. "You just said you weren't going to get married."

"This isn't about marriage. It's about work. Can we talk about it?"

Chad sat straight, his face serious. "Okay."

"I'm thinking of selling Omega and finding something different to do. I've talked to Ted about it—"

"You can't sell Omega! You made it and it's the best in the world! Somebody else could mess it up!"

Nick smiled. "Somebody else might change parts of it, but I've been getting a lot of calls lately from people who want to buy it because it's terrific the way it is."

"Then why sell it? Don't you like it anymore?"

"I do like it. I like knowing it's something Ted and I built, and I like the people we work with. But in a lot of ways it's not the same company we built. We started with two of us; now we have more than twelve hundred, and I don't know most of them. We started in one room of a house; now we have thirteen buildings and I don't go into most of them for weeks at a time. I make decisions and never see the steps that go into carrying them out. I used to dream up an idea, and then make something, and figure out how it could be better, or maybe it wouldn't work at all and I'd have to come up with new ideas. I haven't done that for years. And I've been building Omega for a long time, Chad. Maybe there's something else I can do, something I haven't even thought of yet. This is all I've done, and I've been doing it for almost ten years, ever since I came to San Jose."

Chad shot his father a look. "Would we go away?"

"We might. I think I'd like to. How would you feel about that?"

"Leave my friends? And my school?"

"You'd find other friends in another school. You've never had any trouble making friends."

Chad shook his head firmly. "I don't like it."

"Well, we'll talk about it some more. It might be a good idea for me."

"Why? This is where we *live*."

Too much at once, Nick thought. We started with Sybille and ended with moving from San Jose. How did I think he could handle all that?

"We aren't going anywhere right now," he said. "I still work at Omega. We'll take it one step at a time."

Once again Chad shook his head. "You made up your mind, I can tell. You want to move. Well, not me. I'm staying here. I'll stay with Elena and Manuel. They know how to take care of me." He burst into tears. "I *live* here! I won't go away!"

Cursing himself, Nick held Chad close. The promise to stay trembled on his lips, but he held it back. He would not make that promise, not even for Chad. Because it was time for him to leave San Jose and find something else to do with his energies and growing restlessness. He was almost thirty-five years old; there were too many productive years ahead for him to mark time in a job that no longer challenged him, and to live in a town that no longer interested him. It was a big country, a big world, filled with adventures. He would take his time, and choose well, and Chad would think of it as an adventure, too, because they would be sharing it.

"You didn't call Mother back," Chad said, and Nick understood that all talk of change and uncertainty inevitably would lead Chad to think of Sybille.

"All right," he said. "Do you want to check with Elena and find out when dinner will be ready?"

"Are you going out afterwards?"

"Nope. You and I are spending the evening together. What would you like to do? Read, or watch a movie, or a play a game?"

"A movie and then Monopoly and then read a story in bed."

"That takes us to about three in the morning. We'll have to modify it a little bit. Hey, friend," he added as Chad went to the door.

"What?"

"I love you. You're the best son in the world and the best housemate and the most special friend I could have. And I won't force you to do anything that makes you unhappy. Okay?"

"But what if something makes you happy and I hate it?"

"Then we have a conflict and we work it out."

"But you're bigger," Chad said shrewdly, "and you buy everything and you run our family."

"You're talking about who has the power here. You're right; in lots of ways, I do. But it evens out because I love you and won't make you unhappy if I can help it, so that cuts down my power. Do you understand that?"

"Not really."

"Well, power is a complicated subject. We'll talk about it some more. I just want you to understand that you're the most important person in the world to me and whatever we do, we'll do it together. Okay?"

Chad nodded slowly. "I guess."

"You *guess?*"

Chad ran to his father and threw his arms around him. "Okay," he said, the words muffled against Nick's chest, and then he ran out of the room. And Nick was not sure what was okay. We'll have lots of these little chats, he thought, and for the first time he felt a twinge of weariness. *I wish I had someone to share this with me. It's not just that Chad needs a mother; I need a woman to help me do this whole complicated business . . . and to live my life.*

Order one at a restaurant, he thought wryly, and the image of Valerie once again flashed through his mind, and then disappeared, as he went to the desk to call Sybille.

The telephone rang a long time; he was about to hang up when she answered.

"Did I wake you?" Nick asked.

"Oh. Nick. I wondered if Chad would give you the message. I was going through papers in the other room. Something terrible has happened, Nick. I need a friend, I need someone to help me."

He had never heard her sound so distraught. "Do you mean Quentin? I knew he died, Sybille; you called three days ago to tell me."

"No, no, that's not—of course it's terrible that he died; I can hardly stand it; it's so awful here without him; I'm so alone. But it's something else, Nick—I just found out—something he did to me. I don't know how he could do it, I loved him so much, and did everything for him, and then he made a fool of me, a *fool*—"

"Sybille, what is it?"

"He cut me out and left his money to a fucking preacher—!"

Nick sat back, as if backing away from her screech.

"I'm sorry," she said hoarsely. "I'm not . . . I'm having trouble . . . He left most of his money to this Dominus—I told you about him, didn't I?—a crazy preacher who couldn't even get his ratings up. And I got the network, and I don't want it; I'm sick of it!"

"Wait a minute. Quentin left you the network?"

"And a million dollars. Peanuts."

Nick smiled to himself. Once that would have been a fortune to Sybille. It still would be, to most people. "How much to Dominus?"

"Five million."

"Five? I'd have thought there was more."

"There was. He put it all into the network. He was crazy, Nick, the way he spent money on it . . . he thought every problem could be solved by just spending and spending and spending . . ."

"But if the money is in the network, and you don't want to keep it, why don't you sell it?"

"I thought of that. But—" Sybille sat straighter in her chair, and stared out the window at the lights of Washington. "Quentin ran up some debts," she said slowly. "Not huge, but any debt makes it harder to sell a company."

"It depends on the kind and the size of the debt. And how much potential there is for someone to pay it off and begin to make a profit. Sybille, you should be talking to accountants and lawyers; they can do a lot more for you than I can."

"I will, as soon as I get myself together." She was still staring out the window, but what she saw was Nick's twelve-room house, the luxurious furnishings, the Mercedes and Porsche in the garage, Elena and Manuel, the maids, the landscapers...and the cover stories in *Time* and *Newsweek*. Two hundred million dollars.

"Nick," she said. "I know you're all involved with your company, and it's all you really care about, but do you think you might be interested in buying a television network—at a very good price?"

Chapter
15

he put a price tag of three hundred million dollars on the network. It was far more than the experts told her she could get, but after Nick said no she had raised the price. She had asked him and asked him, in a number of telephone calls: "Just think about it. Take a while and then let me know." And though at first he had insisted that he knew nothing about television and wasn't interested in owning any part of it, finally she thought she heard a change in his voice and she was sure he was beginning to think seriously about it. But he'd lost his chance to take advantage of their relationship and get the network at a ridiculously low price. To him and to everyone else, the price had gone up. She wanted her three hundred million and she would get it. The experts were wrong; she knew they were wrong. EBN was worth every penny she was asking: it had state-of-the-art studios and equipment that she'd spent a fortune on; its programs needed only a little fine tuning to get top ratings; and there was the whole western part of the country where she hadn't managed to break in, just waiting for EBN, and that would bring advertisers, spending huge sums to reach those audiences. In the end she'd get the money

she wanted; she was sure of it. She was always having to prove the experts wrong.

At the beginning of the new year she hired a manager. She did not tell him that EBN was for sale. "I don't have time to run the network myself, or make it as powerful as it can be," she said. "I've formed a production company and that's where I have to be, most of the time. Though you're to call me if you have any questions, and I'll stop in whenever I can, to make sure everything is all right."

"Somebody sure messed things up," he said contemptuously, studying the jagged line on a large chart that showed the high ratings Television of Joy had received at first, and then their precipitous decline.

Sybille looked at her clasped hands. "It was my fault; you can't blame anyone else. I was too busy taking care of my husband, all the time he was dying, to pay attention to my job, and then my husband was incredibly stubborn—but he was so sick; how could he understand?—he was really irrational; he didn't want me to take over without him and manage the network the way it should have been managed. He wouldn't even let me hire someone like you. It was his, you see, he bought it and he wanted to feel it was his until the day he died. And I couldn't ignore him as if he were already dead..."

The manager, who would have given everything he had for a wife like that, blushed when he recalled how contemptuous he had been. He put his hand on Sybille's. "I'll take care of it for you," he said solemnly. "And in honor of your husband's memory."

Sybille's fingers trembled beneath his like a helpless bird's. "Thank you," she breathed, and with that she left EBN in his fervent care.

Her production company was called Sybille Morgen Productions. She formed it alone, without anyone to criticize her or tell her what to do or how to do it. From now on, the power would be hers alone: power over the lives and fortunes of those who appeared in her shows, power that reached into millions of homes, forming opinions, fueling people's thoughts and conversations, lingering in their memories. As soon as I sell the network and get my money, she thought, then I'll have everything; then my life will really begin.

When she had formed her production company, she had bought a building two miles from EBN, and had it converted to ultramodern offices and studios. After Enderby died, Sybille had a sign announcing "Sybille Morgen Productions" erected in front of the building, and she settled into the office she had enlarged and decorated herself with angular Italian furniture and a dark plush carpet. She told herself she was not ignoring the network; she was still in charge, and would keep an eye on it, and its new manager, to make sure she had something to sell. But all she really cared about was molding her new company, the only one she had ever started on her own. The one that would give her everything she wanted.

All through the spring and summer following Enderby's death, while she waited for purchasers for EBN, she worked on producing two new game shows and a late-night pornographic soap opera. She was in her office every day, and until late at night, too busy to be part of the Washington social scene. She knew she could rejoin it at any time—she knew perfectly well that she had been ignored only because no one liked Quentin—but her work was more important, and certainly more interesting, than the stuffy, pompous, incredibly boring social set she'd once thought she wanted.

She never admitted that she was lonely, or that she became frantic when she was alone. Even a dying Quentin and an intrusive Dominus had been better than no one. The nurses were gone; the chef had been let go because she never ate at home, and the maid came during the day, when Sybille was not there. When she came home, all she had were empty rooms, and she could not bear them, even with all the television sets on. And so she worked. She slept at home; the rest of the time she stayed in her office and the studios where she was taping pilot episodes of the game shows and the pornographic soap. All three of them, she had decided, would be shown on EBN, and she would also sell them to stations in parts of the country where EBN did not appear. Eventually, Sybille Morgen Productions would be everywhere, even in Europe: bigger than the network ever could be.

But she needed more shows: she had to provide a variety that would eventually fill the air. She needed a morning exercise show and two or three children's shows, some kind of pet show, a couple of fashion shows, an afternoon cooking show and a daytime soap opera that titillated without stepping over the line to pornography. If she produced all those, and sold them through a hard-driving sales force, no one could ignore her: she would dominate the time on independent television. She would have everything she needed.

Except for a God show.

She couldn't get away from it: stations wanted them. God brought in money and ratings, and advertising too, because sponsors could run commercials before and after and know they were targeting a specific audience. It was easy to get a preacher, Sybille knew that; they were all over the place, trying to scrape up the money to buy time to get on the air. A few, like Jim and Tammy Bakker and Pat Robertson, had their own networks; they were the ones making real money. The others had contracts with stations to have their shows carried for a year, two years, sometimes more. What Sybille needed was a preacher, a big one, who didn't have his own network and who hadn't signed any contracts with other networks or stations. Offhand, she couldn't think of any who were available. And she didn't want one who was unknown unless she could control and manipulate him.

Or her.

And that was how Sybille came to visit New Jersey, to bring Lilith Grace home with her.

It was easier than she had thought. Rudy Dominus had sent her the name of their church, and she reached it on a cloudy Sunday morning in April: a nondescript building near Hackensack with barely two dozen people scattered about its chilly interior. Sybille slipped into a seat in the shadows at the back, and listened to Lily preach.

"Of course you must believe in yourselves every day of the week, but this day, Sunday, it is especially important, because we are together, helping each other, believing in each other, loving each other. Sometimes it may seem that you are alone in your struggle to find the best within you, and that you can never really find your own core of goodness, but you are never alone, and here is the proof: your friends are here. They are your true family, helping you, holding you up when you despair, witnessing your goodness, your kindness and strength, your *abilities*. Whatever you want to be is already inside you. Whoever you want to be is waiting within your hearts to be released. You need nothing more than that: to trust the goodness that is already you, to believe me when I tell you that because you are made in the image of God there can be no evil or smallness within you, but only undiscovered, untapped wisdom, goodness, greatness..."

Sybille watched the rapt faces of the audience. Two of them were crying; several nodded rhythmically. All of them seemed mesmerized.

A small shiver touched Sybille. It was not Lily's words; they did not touch her. What impressed her was the absolute silence of the church, the concentration of the audience, and Lily herself: small, prettier than Sybille remembered, her face scrubbed, without makeup, glowing with her belief in herself. She wore a baby-blue dress with puffed sleeves that was all wrong for her; like a ten-year-old trying to look experienced, Sybille told herself. What she needed was white: ethereal, virginal, incorruptible. I could manage her, Sybille thought. She stayed in her seat as everyone stood for some kind of hymn. I could make her the greatest of them all.

She waited while the audience filed out, moving slowly past Lily, touching her hand, pausing to tell her something, to which she listened gravely and nodded before turning to the next person in line. Then Sybille came up. "You were very good."

"Thank you," said Lily. She showed no surprise at Sybille's appearance. "How nice to see you again. I hope you are better now."

"Better?"

"You were so upset at Quentin's death, and then there was his will ... it was a trying time. Rudy and I felt helpless; you were very hostile —and we understood that—but it made it difficult for us to help you."

"Where is Rudy?"

"He has a slight cold. Otherwise you would have heard him preach this morning."

"Is that the only time you preach? When he's sick? You should be up there all the time; you're far better than he ever was."

Lily's eyes brightened, but, quickly, she lowered them. "Not better: different," she corrected gently.

"But you do want to preach. You do want your own church, your own audience—"

"Parishioners," Lily corrected gently.

"Of course. With no one standing over you, telling you what to say and how to say it."

"Rudy never tells me what to say; he trusts me. And I trust him. I do long for my own pulpit, and he knows that; he's said he'll tell me when I'm ready for it."

"Has he mentioned it lately?"

Lily frowned slightly. "I don't think ... not for awhile, but—"

"Shall we have lunch?" Sybille asked abruptly. "It's not easy to talk, standing out here, and you must be cold."

"Yes, it is cold. I'm hungry too; I didn't have breakfast."

They stood there for a moment. "Well, where's your coat?" Sybille asked impatiently.

"I didn't bring one. I thought, April, it would be warm. And the sun was shining when I left home."

"Come on." Sybille walked rapidly to her rented car, with Lily close behind. "Who takes care of you?" she asked as she drove away.

"I do! I'm eighteen, you know. Nineteen in a few months."

"But not old enough to keep warm."

Lily gave a small, embarrassed laugh. "You sound like a mother."

"I don't want to—" Sybille stopped. Don't mess it up, she thought; she's ripe for being rescued. "I don't want to be just a mother, though God knows you need one," she said. "I want to be your friend too."

Lily gave her a sideways look; then she sighed. "Could I have a hamburger for lunch?"

"Where?"

"Hamburger Heaven; if you turn right here . . ."

Sybille turned right. "How far?"

"About a mile. Rudy never lets me go there."

"Why not?"

"He doesn't like the people who go there and he hates hamburgers."

She sounded very young. In the space of a few minutes, the confident young preacher who had mesmerized an audience had given way to a cold, hungry girl who longed for a mother, or at least someone— definitely a woman—who would guide her and be close to her while she grew from a girl to a woman. She wasn't fully aware that that was what she wanted, but that didn't matter: Sybille knew it.

And here I am, she thought.

"What else does Rudy say you can't do? Do you date?"

Lily shook her head. "Not yet. We go out sometimes with people Rudy knows, to restaurants and movies; or I cook for his friends in his apartment."

"You don't live with him?"

"Oh, no, I never have. Rudy says it would give an appearance of impropriety that would be terribly damaging to me."

"Why do you cook for his parties, then? Doesn't he have any women?"

"I don't know."

"And you don't ask him? Do you wonder if he does?"

"No. Rudy does what he wants."

"But you don't."

There was a pause. "I'm too young," Lily said, but her voice was doubting. She leaned forward. "It's in the next block."

Sybille found a parking place near the low brick building. An enormous hamburger was painted on the window, surrounded by garish clouds and red-cheeked angels, and the doorknob was a plastic hamburger. Sybille followed Lily inside. A jukebox blared; teenage boys and girls in blue jeans and sweatshirts half perched, half stood at the stools at a long counter; others sat squashed, six or eight together, in the booths. "Here," said Lily, her light voice somehow piercing the din, and she led Sybille to a smaller booth at the back, waving to a girl who called her by name.

Not a stranger, Sybille thought; here or other places either, I'd bet. "It's a terrific place," she said to Lily as they sat down. She took one look at the pink Formica tabletop, then tried not to look again. "How many times have you been here?"

Lily was beaming. "You really like it? Only a couple; once Rudy brought me, for my birthday, but he hated it, and once I came alone, just to . . . sit here. Just to feel like I was part of it. I didn't think it was wrong."

"It wasn't," Sybille said briskly. "What doesn't Rudy like about it?"

Lily gave a small shrug. "He thinks if I make friends they'll take advantage of me. And he doesn't want me to be with boys. He wants me to stay pure."

"For anyone in particular?" Lily blushed and Sybille cursed herself. "I'm sorry; that wasn't very nice. But you've been here before; I guess Rudy doesn't know about that?"

"No." Lily blushed again. "I don't lie to him, but I don't tell him everything. I'd like to, because I'd like to ask him . . . things, but he'd forbid me to come again, so I can't ask him."

"He probably wouldn't have any answers. Would you like to ask me?"

Lily gave her a long look, surprising Sybille with its shrewdness. "I don't know. I don't know why you would want me to."

Sybille took a breath, but just then a teenager wearing an apron came up and Lily gave him her order. "The same," Sybille said, not caring what it was.

"Beer?" he asked.

"Coffee," she replied. "Are you drinking beer?" she asked Lily.

"Not really; it won't go down when I try to swallow it. I get it because everybody does, and Rudy—"

"—doesn't let you."

Lily giggled. Then she looked away, scanning the crowded room.

"Are you looking for someone?" Sybille asked softly.

"No!" Once again the color rose in Lily's pale cheeks. "Well . . . a friend."

"Have you gone out with him?"

"Oh, no, I can't; Rudy was so strict about that. We just sat here and talked."

"You can't date, but you can drink beer."

"I don't drink it; I only order it. Anyway it's not the same," she said

reproachfully. "Beer and hamburgers . . . those are little things. Dating
. . . could change my whole life."

"You mean you could lose your virginity."

Abruptly, Lily's eyes filled with tears. "I'm so scared . . ." she said,
her voice barely audible.

Sybille felt a rush of exultation. *Ripe for being rescued.* What luck,
that she had come at just this time. Never in her life had she had real
control over another person; sometimes she wasn't sure she had control of herself, especially when her rages ripped through her, blocking
her thoughts and making her feel she had no way of knowing what
was coming next. But now she couldn't understand why she had
waited so long. Why had she schemed to have power over distant
audiences, and the people who worked for her, when it might be even
more satisfying, at least for awhile, to totally dominate one person?

Her lunch was set before her: an oblong basket holding an obscene-
ly fat hamburger in a sesame bun, riding precariously on a mound of
thick french-fried potatoes and a glob of coleslaw in a pleated paper
cup. "Isn't it beautiful?" Lily sighed. She raised her hamburger in two
hands and bit into it, taking an astonishing amount into her small
mouth.

Sybille gazed at her hamburger. She wouldn't do it; it was no way
to eat. Even here, where no one knew her, she was not going to look
like a gluttonous teenager who'd never learned to use a knife and fork.
Valerie would do it. Her head came up, as if she were listening. *She'd
think it was fun, something different; she'd make it a game and laugh it off
if anyone made a crack about the way she looked.*

Damn it, Sybille thought with something like despair. Why can't I
ever do that?

She picked up her hamburger and nibbled at the edge of the bun.
She took a small bite, and then another, larger one, suddenly realizing
how hungry she was.

"Isn't it delicious?" Lily asked blissfully. Hers was almost gone.

"Wonderful," Sybille replied, and in fact, to her astonishment, it
was. "Do you want another one?"

"Oh, no, I mustn't; Rudy says I mustn't get fat."

"He's right, but that doesn't seem to be a problem for you. Could
you eat another one?"

Lily ducked her head and nodded. Sybille ordered another, then
watched in disbelief as she ate it.

"Thank you," Lily sighed at last. "I get awfully tired of fish and
chicken and healthy soups; that's all Rudy wants. This was heaven."

She nibbled french fries. Her beer was untouched.

"Do you want coffee?" Sybille asked.

"I don't drink it. Ginger ale would be wonderful."

When it arrived, Sybille pushed aside her empty basket. "Lily, I'd like you to come back to Washington with me."

There was a brief silence. Lily put down her glass. "I know," she said.

"What do you know?"

"That you want to take care of me. I don't know why; you didn't like me before, when I was with Quentin. Maybe you think you did me a wrong and you want to make up for it? Or you have no children and you want to pretend you have a daughter? Or you just like me and want to watch over me, and that would be so nice, but I don't know why you would, all of a sudden..."

Lily's words trailed away and Sybille let the silence drag out, making Lily wait. "I do like you," she said at last. "More than you can imagine. You're right, I don't have a daughter; I've always wanted one, but it just never happened. And now I'm thirty, and I can't imagine being married to anyone after Quentin, and that means I'll probably never have a daughter, or anyone to care for. My life is so empty, Lily. I never thought about it very much; I just took it for granted; and then one day I realized I missed seeing you in the apartment, and hearing your voice. I know I wasn't kind to you when you were there; I let my suffering dominate me and I didn't think about how I was behaving to other people. I apologize for that; I know it made you unhappy. But I'm not asking you to live with me because I feel guilty, Lily; I want you with me because even in those terrible months you made my apartment feel warm and full of love and I miss that so much..." There were tears in her eyes and a tremulous smile on her lips. "Isn't this ridiculous? A grown woman crying in a hamburger joint— heaven; isn't that what you called it? Wait a minute." She held a handkerchief to her eyes. "I thought I'd cried myself out over Quentin; I guess there's always more, isn't there? Let me be honest with you, Lily; I hope we'll always be that way, with no lies or secrets between us. I want more than to have you share my home. I've started a new television production company and I want to produce a program for you. You can do what you want: preach in a church—we'll find you a church—or speak to small groups in a studio, or anything else you can think of; anything you want. You don't know how amazing you are; you must give yourself this chance to reach millions and build the kind of following you deserve; you won't ever again have to pour out your heart to a handful of people. You need a little help with your voice and some of your phrasing, and talking to the camera almost as if you're making love to it, but I can give you that help. And I can give you the audience. It's waiting for you, Lily; you'd be famous. And you'd be adored by millions of people who need what you can give them. I want to do that for you. I want to give you a home, and my love and protection, but I also want to give you a way to use your gifts to reach those millions of people who are waiting for you."

She stopped. She thought she must have gone too far, but Lily was so young, it was possible she hadn't gone far enough.

Lily sat very still, eyes downcast, hands clasped on the table. Slowly, she looked up and gave Sybille a wavering smile. "It's too much; it doesn't seem real. I never dared pray for all of this; I never thought I could have it all...A pulpit of my own; a mother...Oh, Sybille, I can't even imagine what it will be like!" A delighted laugh burst from her. "It will be like a fairy tale!" She put out her hand and when Sybille laid hers on top of it Lily closed her fingers around Sybille's. "I can't ever do enough for you to match what you're giving me; I'll always be in your debt. I'll pray for you every day, but that isn't all...you'll have to give me things to do for you, chores and jobs and errands, whatever you need; will you? Let me do things for you, Sybille. I love you already; I love you so much."

"Well, let's get you to Washington, first. How long will it take you to pack?"

"Not long; I don't have much. But Rudy...I have to talk to Rudy."

"Call him up."

"Oh, no, you don't mean that. He's been so good to me, as good as he knew how. I'll go there now; I'll cook his dinner, and we'll talk. He wants the best for me; he'll be happy for me."

"He might be jealous."

Lily's eyes widened. "How could you think that? He'll be happy."

"Will you come with me even if he isn't happy?"

There was a long silence. Lily pulled back her hand. "We'll pray together and then he'll be happy."

"But if he isn't," Sybille insisted.

"Sybille," Lily said quietly, "Rudy will be happy for me and then I will come with you. You must believe that."

Her eyes held Sybille's, and for the first time Sybille had a moment of doubt. The little girl who had sighed over hamburgers, and ordered a beer she didn't want, was gone; in her place was the young woman who had so confidently preached, and held an audience, only an hour

before. The possibility occurred to Sybille that Lily Grace might not
be as malleable as she seemed. But then Lily's tremulous voice echoed
in her memory—*I'm so scared*—and she dismissed that flicker of
doubt. Lily was a child: an instinctive actress in the pulpit, a little girl
the rest of the time. And she was hungry for someone to manage her,
and let her be as young as she wanted. This time Sybille was the one to
put out her hand, and Lily put hers in it.

"I believe you," Sybille said. "You and I are going to do very well
together. Do you know something? This is the real beginning of our
lives."

Ted McIlvain hosted a party for Nick on his last day as president of
Omega, and Chad was there, wearing a new sports jacket and a tie. It
was June and school was out, so he had more time to think about what
his dad was doing and thinking, and he was pretty worried, because
his dad was making jokes about looking for a new garage to start a
new company in, and Chad was pretty sure he wasn't thinking about
starting anything new in San Jose. Ever again.

Chad didn't know how much more he could argue, either. His dad
was about the most stubborn man in the world, and he was kind of
like a magician too, because lots of times when Chad thought his dad
was giving in he was sort of getting his way. Like the time Chad
wanted to see some gory movie the guys were talking about at school,
and his dad didn't, and something happened between lunch and dinner that made Chad not want to see the gory movie after all. He
couldn't remember what made him change his mind; he just knew
they'd gone to see something else, and it was great, but still . . . the
gory one had really sounded neat and now it was gone forever and
he'd never see it.

And then there was the whole thing of his dad selling his stock in
Omega and not being president anymore, not being anything over
there after he was such a big wheel and everybody wrote stories about
him and he was even on tv a couple times and stuff. They'd talked
about it a lot, selling his stock and all that, and then, like overnight
almost, Chad thought it was okay for his dad to do it, in fact it was a
great idea, but just, like, yesterday he'd been sure the idea stunk. How
did his dad get him to think that? He didn't know. It was really weird.
Or magic.

There was something else that was weird, and that was all the tv
stuff his dad was reading: books and newspaper clippings and reports
he got in the mail from finance experts and lawyers and accountants.

When Chad asked what it was all about, he said he was just curious, in case someday he wanted to buy a tv station, maybe more than one, maybe even start his own, and what would Chad think about his doing that? Chad thought it would be great, then he could be on it whenever he wanted, and meet all the other people who were on it, but so far his dad hadn't bought anything at all; he just kept reading and watching a lot more than he used to, and, maybe, thinking about it.

Nobody knew what they were going to do; that was the problem. Elena and Manuel didn't know; Chad didn't know; his dad didn't know. It didn't sound good, Chad thought. They'd probably end up doing something weird in some stupid place with lots of inventors for his dad to talk to but no friends for Chad, and he'd never see his mother 'cause she wouldn't want to come to a place like that, and his dad would be busy making a new company and Chad would be all alone and no one would care.

"How about it, Chad?"

Chad sat up guiltily. They were doing this fancy dinner party for his dad and he wasn't even paying attention. "What?"

"Do you want to make a toast to Nick?" asked Ted. "You said, before dinner, you wanted to."

"Oh. Yeah. I do." His dad was next to him and he saw his look of surprise as he fumbled in his pocket for the small piece of paper on which he'd written his toast. They were sitting at a round table in a private room in a restaurant, with lots of other round tables where all the people who had gotten Omega going in its first couple of years had eaten dinner and had lots of wine and told long stories about how the company used to be, and when Chad stood up he recognized almost all of them from his visits to the company and from the meetings they'd had with his dad at home. They'd been sort of like a bunch of uncles, like they were a family, Chad thought sadly, and now he wasn't going to have them anymore.

He unfolded the piece of paper. Ted had told him what a toast was and he'd decided he ought to do it. Just about everybody else was, and his dad ought to have somebody in his family do it, too. If he had a wife she'd do it, but he didn't, and Chad's mother hadn't come for the party—he thought maybe somebody would have invited her, but he guessed nobody did, because she wasn't there—so there was just him. He didn't like the idea of getting up and talking in front of everybody, but he didn't want his dad to feel like Chad wasn't as proud of him as the rest of them, so okay, he thought, I'll do it, and he'd written it out the night before.

"My dad is great," Chad read loudly, to cover up the shaking in his voice. "He's good at everything, and he listens when you want to talk, and he doesn't yell when you do something stupid. He doesn't laugh at you, either, if you make a mistake, and we do things together and they're fun because we like all the same things. It'd be great if we could stay here where he's got all these friends and stuff, but we probably won't, but it was nice that everybody liked us and helped my dad make Omega 'cause that was his favorite thing for a long time, except for me. So I guess I should say good luck to us, like everybody else did, and tell my dad he's great, like everybody else did, only the difference is, he's mine, I mean he's my dad, and he's my friend, too, not the same as the guys at school but a different kind and maybe the best kind and that's . . . I guess that's the best of all."

There was a silence as Chad sat down, as if everyone was holding his breath. Then someone started clapping and in a minute everyone was standing and applauding and grinning at him. And his dad had stood up and pulled him up with him and was hugging him so tight he thought he'd crack in two. But it didn't hurt; it really felt good. It was the best feeling in the world, and whatever they did, wherever they went, as long as his dad kept that up, as long as he kept loving him a lot, they'd be okay, and he wouldn't ever have to worry about being alone. Not ever.

Sybille had invited them for Christmas, and since Chad was absolutely sure he did not want to go alone, the two of them flew to Washington as soon as Christmas vacation began. Before meeting Sybille for dinner, they went first, as they always did, to the Air and Space Museum, on the Mall, so Chad could walk through Skylab, peer inside the Apollo moon-landing module, stand beneath planes suspended from the ceiling, and point in amazement at the samples of rocks from the moon, even though he and Nick both knew they looked just like rocks anyone could find anywhere on earth. They spent the entire afternoon at the museum; it was Chad's day. The next day would be Nick's and they would go to the National Gallery of Art, but Chad was used to that; part of the time he spent with his father, and the rest of the time he wandered around on his own, admiring the huge Calder mobile and riding the people-mover ramps. And the next day they'd go to the Children's Museum. That was the deal they had made: they split their time so nobody would feel bad.

They had quiet dinners with Sybille for the four nights of their visit.

"I have to leave three days after Christmas," she had told Nick when they were planning the trip. "I've been invited to a house party in Virginia. I'd rather be with you and Chad for New Year's, but there's no way I can get out of this. We'll have Christmas; that's better, really."

They exchanged gifts in Sybille's living room and, as usual, Nick was uncomfortable and restless, pacing, leafing through magazines and newspapers, trying to sit still. He had not found a way to avoid these family occasions that Sybille created, and he knew Chad loved them, so he went along, feeling helpless, and angry at his helplessness, convinced it was really weakness. If he were stronger, he thought, he'd send Chad alone to visit his mother, or at least see Sybille only in restaurants and other neutral places, and put a stop to the whole farce that had gone on ever since they divorced. But he did not know how to do it. He even brought Sybille a Christmas present, because, a few years earlier, Chad had burst into tears when he realized Nick expected the only exchange of gifts to be between him and his mother. This year Nick gave Sybille a small lapel pin, a leaping gold cheetah with diamonds for eyes. Her gift was far more elaborate: an eelskin briefcase fitted with gold pens and pencils, and sterling-silver letter opener, stapler, tape dispenser, clipboard and stamp holder. The stationery had been printed with his name; his initials in gold were on the briefcase.

He was so angry he could barely thank her. But Chad was watching, his eyes round, and so once again he went through his pretenses, and then they went to dinner at the Olympian, where Sybille had reserved one of the black velvet booths at the back. By the time they were drinking coffee and Chad was sipping his third lemon seltzer through a straw, Nick was more relaxed. Sybille had done most of the talking. As if she knew how angry he had been, she was at her most pleasant and entertaining, talking about television, her production company, the actors and actresses with whom she worked. She found ways to bring Chad into her monologue, with questions or little jokes, and it seemed she was choosing anecdotes about entertainers who would most likely be familiar to him. Nick had never seen Chad so delighted with her.

"Dad knows all about all that," Chad said at last. "That's just about all he does lately, is read about television. Books and magazines and the works." His eyes widened as a huge wedge of chocolate mousse cake was placed before him. "Wow," he whispered, and he picked up his fork.

Sybille looked at Nick. "Really?"

"A small exaggeration," Nick replied. "I read about a lot of things; television is one of them."

"You watch too," said Chad through a mouthful of cake. "Lots more than you used to. You're an expert, too, as much as anybody."

"Maybe he should buy a television network," Sybille said to Chad.

Chad nodded vigorously. "He said we might. Or a tv station, or maybe start a station of our own. A big one, as big as NBC or ABC or whatever. We have lots of time now because Dad's not president of Omega anymore and he says he's looking for another garage, to start a new company in, but he's not; that's just a joke."

"Not president of Omega?" Sybille repeated.

"Not for a while," Nick said.

"You didn't tell me!"

He looked at her in silence until she colored and looked away. "Of course you're not required to tell me what you do, but you know I'm interested in you . . . and Chad . . ."

"It was in the newspapers," Nick said evenly.

"But I only read the news about television. Something as big as that, Nick . . . I would have thought you'd tell me yourself."

Chad was frowning, looking from one of them to the other.

"Next time," Nick said, keeping his voice light, "you'll be the first to know."

Sybille tightened her lips and Nick remembered her saying *I hate it when you're clever* so many times during their marriage, and after. He led the conversation away from television, to films he had seen, and books he had read, and events in California. Chad ate his cake, listening to the comforting sounds of his parents' voices in friendly conversation.

They were friendly for the next two days, sightseeing together around Washington, and then it was the last night of their visit and after dinner Sybille begged to come back to their suite at the Madison Hotel. She wanted to say good night to Chad in his bed, and goodbye, since she wouldn't see them in the morning; she was leaving early for her friend's house in Virginia. Nick, though not hiding his reluctance and annoyance, finally said she could. So Chad kissed his mother in bed, clinging to her and breathing in her perfume with his eyes shut. "Merry Christmas and Happy New Year," he said. He wanted to tell her he loved her, but every time he thought about saying it he tightened up inside. She didn't seem to like it when he did, and he felt funny about his dad; he wasn't sure how he would feel if he knew

Chad was saying it. So he settled for "Happy New Year," and in a minute Sybille moved away.

"Happy New Year, Chad. I hope you'll help your father decide what to do next..." She paused, looking at him thoughtfully. "I wish you could live in Washington; then we could see each other whenever we wanted."

Chad's eyes widened. She had never said that before. "I wish we could, too," he said.

"Well, we'll have to think of a way. Maybe your father will buy a television station here, or start his own. He might like that, and it would be a good place for you to go to school. But you probably wouldn't want to leave San Jose."

"Well, no, I mean, I didn't, but Dad wants to. He promised he wouldn't until I wanted to, too, and I said no, but... I don't know... maybe..."

Sybille leaned down and touched her lips to his forehead. "We'll have to think about it, won't we? You get to sleep; maybe your dad and I will talk about it for awhile."

Chad slid down in bed, his thoughts churning. "If you decide anything, wake me up and tell me."

But Sybille was already out of the room, and on her way to the sitting room that joined Chad's room and Nick's. "He's so grown-up," she said, settling into an armchair. "Could I have a drink, Nick? I'd like to talk for awhile; God knows when we'll see each other again."

"Whenever you want," he said. "It's an easy plane trip from Washington to San Jose. Cognac?"

"Yes. Are you relieved to be out of Omega?"

"It wasn't a burden. It was just time for me to look for something else to do." He handed her a drink and sat in a nearby chair with his own. "What about you? Have you sold the network?"

"No. I would have told you if I had." She paused to let it sink in. "It's very strange. I have some new programs; my ratings are going up; I've even gotten some columnists to write about me. And there's been a lot of interest: phone calls, accountants coming to look at the books; you know all about that. But no one's come up with the money. They're such frightened little boys; there isn't a man among them! My lawyer says they don't want to take risks with cable, but that's crazy; look what CNN has done; look at the possibilities! Of course there are risks in television; no one should go into it unless he's ready to put all his energy and creativity into it—and a hell of a lot of money—and even then he could fall on his face. It isn't a place for

timid men, or men who don't have absolute confidence in themselves."
She sipped her cognac, and sighed. "Well, I suppose I'll find someone.
The trouble is, there aren't many men who have confidence in them-
selves, and the money to back it up, and I'm so anxious to sell..."

Nick grinned. "That's very good. It's almost as if you had someone
in mind to buy it."

"Damn you, Nick, don't play games. You know I do. I want you to
buy it. Why shouldn't you? You want something new and you've never
cared whether something was hard or not; why don't you do it?" She
paused, looking at the deep-amber liquid in her glass. "Chad says he'd
love it."

"What does that mean?"

"He says he'd love living here because then we could see each other
whenever we wanted."

"Chad said that?"

"Just now, when we were saying good night."

"What the hell did you tell him?"

"Not much. When he said that, I felt so sorry for him—he looked
so unhappy because you're leaving tomorrow—and I said maybe
you'd buy a television station in Washington, or start one yourself. I
didn't say anything you hadn't already said yourself! And his face lit
up; it was amazing."

Nick frowned. "You shouldn't have said anything."

"Why not? He's my son! Why shouldn't I have him living near me if
that's what we both want?"

"Is it what you want?"

"I've always wanted it. There were just too many other things going
on; I couldn't put my life together and do what I really knew was best
for me...I always had to think of other people first. Nick..." She rose
and went to sit on the arm of his chair. "We could do so much together. I think of you all the time, you know; what an idiot I was to let
you send me away without a fight; what a fool I was to marry Quentin
when all the time I loved you, you were the only one, and I've never
stopped wanting you and needing you—"

Nick left the chair and strode across the room. "I thought we'd
gotten past that," he said, his voice hard and flat. "There is nothing
between us, Sybille, there hasn't been for years, and you know it as
well as I do. You don't love me any more than I love you. We aren't
even friends; we don't have enough in common for that, and since we
don't really like each other, there isn't the remotest chance that that
will ever change." He contemplated the rigid anger in her face. "For

God's sake, don't act as if I've insulted you; I only told you what we both already knew. Now we can go on to something else. You've made two pitches tonight; you failed with one, but we can talk about the other if you still want to."

Slowly, the words sank in, and Sybille sat up straight on the arm of the chair. "You mean the network."

"That's what I mean. Why don't you have another drink; I have some questions I'd like answered."

Sterling Farms covered nearly six hundred acres of Virginia pasture-land that ebbed and flowed in rolling hills of close-cropped grass. A dusting of snow covered the land and clung to the branches of trees; weathered, unpainted fences followed the contours of the hills, stretching to the horizon; stone walls topped with rails bordered gravel roads. A painted rail fence bounded six acres near the center of the spread, and in their center was Carlton Sterling's house, twenty-five rooms sprawling over two floors beneath a steeply pitched gray shingle roof with eight chimneys and gabled second-floor windows. Stands of trees shielded the house from anyone who might wander onto the main road half a mile from the front door; behind the house, where no road intruded, were nestled two guest houses, the terrace, tennis courts and swimming pool. Sybille's room overlooked the terrace and the fields beyond and, beyond them, in the distance, the purple haze of the Blue Ridge Mountains. She had studied the house as Valerie led her through it. It was furnished in a hodgepodge of country pine and oak, overstuffed couches, worn antique rugs on hardwood floors, and floor lamps with fringed shades. It might have been chaotic, but instead it was harmonious: warm, inviting, lived-in. And it had the look of very deep, very old money.

"Lunch in the small dining room at one," said Valerie as she checked on towels in the bathroom. "We'll only be five; everyone else should get here by dinnertime. I think you have everything, but if you get sudden urges, tell Sally. She's been here since Carl was a baby, and her mission is to make all of us happy. She's very good at it. Can I get you anything now?"

"No. Thank you; it's fine. How many will there be for dinner?"

"Twenty-five; Carl's off hunting with friends and won't be here for a couple of days. You'll like all of them, I think; they talk horses more than I like, but everybody should be passionate about something, and that's what they're passionate about. Shall we go for a walk before lunch? I'll show you our horses." She broke off in a laugh, her eyes dancing. "Look who's complaining about people talking horses too much. We do have other attractions; the greenhouses are wonderful, and I like the pond this time of year: frozen at the edges, with bare trees and a gardener's hut against a low hill—it's like a black-and-white photograph. And of course there are the horses. Did you bring your riding things?"

"Yes. I'd like to see your horses."

"Good. Let's go. And we'll ride after lunch, if you'd like. Whatever you want, Sybille, just speak up. It's going to be a very loose three days."

Sybille nodded. She could not imagine an unstructured hour, much less three days, but this was Middleburg, and Middleburg society, and she had a lot to learn before she became part of it. It was the second time Valerie Sterling was initiating her into a new way of life. The best way to learn, Sybille thought; make use of someone who owes me everything, and doesn't even know she's being used.

Valerie pulled on a royal purple down jacket and a pair of high boots. "It gets muddy," she said. "If you don't have any, we can find you some."

"Only riding boots," Sybille replied.

"Well . . ." Valerie rummaged through a wooden box with a hinged lid. "Try these. They may be a little big, but that's better than too tight."

"Are they yours?" Sybille asked, sitting on a bench and removing her shoes. "They look new."

"They are. I bought them in the fall and never wore them. Will they do?"

Sybille stood up. "They're fine." She gazed at the leather and rubber sorrels, and smiled to herself. She had always wanted to be in Valerie's shoes. "Where do we go first?"

"The riding ring, the barns, the pond, the greenhouse. Is that all right with you? I don't much care; I just want to be outside. It seems I've been inside all week."

"Doing what?" They were walking through a passageway that led to an open area of vegetable and flower gardens criss-crossed with brick paths. Along one side, attached to the kitchen wing of the house, were the greenhouses.

"Board meetings," Valerie replied. She led Sybille through a break in a low hedge to a broad field with an outdoor riding ring. "And I filmed a television spot for a new exhibit at the Children's Museum in Washington—I produced that one, in fact; the first time I've done anything like that. It's more your field than mine."

"Maybe you'll do more of it," said Sybille.

Valerie turned quickly, and Sybille thought her voice must have given her away, and shown her anger. "I mean," she said more smoothly, "maybe you'd rather do that than appear on camera."

"I don't know." Valerie turned back and they walked on, around the riding ring. "God knows I want something more, but I don't know what it is." She gave a rueful laugh. "It's hard to look as if you have everything; it seems so insatiable to ask for more."

"More what?" Sybille asked. "There's nothing you don't have."

"You mean I have money. Well, you have money; do you have everything?"

"Not enough. Anyway, I want more than money."

Valerie laughed again. "There you are. There's always something more. And lately I've been feeling I've missed out on something; I don't know what, but I feel on edge, as if I'm waiting for something to happen, for something to show up that forces me to act, to be different in some way from the way I've always been.... It's a little unnerving, waiting for something when I have no idea what it is, or if there really is anything to wait for. I've never felt this before; it has a kind of urgency: if I don't do it now I'll never have a chance..." She stopped and leaned her arms on the top rail of the fence surrounding the ring, as if she were watching a horse go through its jumps. "I think about children a lot. I don't think that's what I'm waiting for, but maybe it is. I have to make up my mind pretty soon, but I always stop short of deciding. What about you, Sybille? Do you want more children?"

"No." Sybille heard how abrupt she sounded, and tried to soften it, though she had not once thought of having more children. "I've thought about it, and I'd love to, but I don't see how I can. I'm not going to get married just so I can have a baby, and I have to earn a living, you know; that takes just about all the time I've got." She leaned against the fence next to Valerie and averted her face. "I messed up so badly, with Chad—letting Nick take him away from me, letting him talk me into not visiting very often because it upset Chad's schedule, letting him get all the fun of Chad's growing up—I shouldn't have allowed any of it; I should have insisted on having my own son and then I wouldn't be so alone now..."

Valerie tried to see her face, but Sybille kept it turned away. "I didn't know Nick made it hard for you to visit them," she said, puzzled. "It doesn't sound like the kind of thing he'd do."

"You don't know what Nick would do! You haven't seen him for eight years and you were never married—" Sybille bit off her words. "I'm sorry," she said miserably. "I get so upset about Chad, and then Quentin being gone, and there's so much to do at work and I don't have anyone to talk to or ask for advice . . . I'm sorry I was so rude."

"You weren't rude; it's not important." Valerie stared at the center of the ring, not seeing it. She was remembering the times Nick had talked about their having children.

"What about Carlton?" Sybille asked, her voice muffled as if she were forcing back tears. "He must want children."

"He wants to wait, but he isn't the one who has to worry about being almost thirty-one. He likes being an investment counselor and he's one of the best there is; he loves playing polo and he's one of the best at that. He's happiest working and playing; he doesn't seem happy at all about fatherhood."

"Or being a husband," Sybille said shrewdly.

"He doesn't know that." The two women looked at each other in a rare moment of understanding. "He thinks he loves being a husband, and sometimes he does. It depends on how easy I make it for him. If I'm like his polo team or his clients, and don't demand true intimacy—" She broke off, having said more, it seemed, than she allowed herself. "He's still a good friend, and I wouldn't ask more of him than that."

"You don't want any more than that?"

"I might, but I'll take what I've got. Weren't you and Quentin good friends?"

"Yes, and business partners. But I wouldn't have married him if I hadn't loved him." Valerie nodded and Sybille was not sure whether she believed her or not. "So you don't love Carl?" she asked.

There was a pause. "Yes," Valerie said quietly. "I love him. Well, now, you've seen the riding ring; the barns are next." She stood and strode off, leaving Sybille to follow on a tour of the bleached-wood barns in which were boarded twelve horses for friends and neighbors who spent most of their time traveling, and the eight owned by Valerie and Carlton, and the indoor winter riding arena with a glass wall that displayed the panorama of the snow-covered countryside and sunsets over the distant Blue Ridge. And for the rest of that day, and the three days that followed, Valerie never again talked about herself, or Carlton.

But Sybille did not care. She had learned a great deal that day, and while she was there she learned more. She watched and listened, she noted the clothes and jewelry of the guests who were, to her, Middleburg society, and she memorized the speech patterns and phrases of people whose comfortable lives were bounded by horses and wealth. She watched Valerie, who was the most perfect hostess she had ever seen: watchful, genuinely interested in her guests, helpful without being officious, gracefully bringing everyone into the life of Sterling Farms. She seemed to be everywhere at once, making sure no one was ignored, yet she never intruded on the authority of Sally, the head housekeeper, who really ran the house and kept the schedules moving smoothly. Reluctantly, Sybille admired her: as shallow and stupid as Valerie was, she did this one thing superbly.

And so Sybille watched and learned, and within two days she began to think of herself as one of them. All she needed was her own house and farms, and staff, and she would truly be part of Middleburg.

On the last morning of the year, Carlton Sterling came back from his hunting trip. In the confusion of greeting his twenty-four guests, he barely acknowledged Sybille, and she had only a quick impression of a long face with shadows at the temples, blond hair thinning on top, a sharp glance that seemed wary, and a boyish grin that made him look young and innocent, almost untested.

Sybille watched him that day as he talked with his friends, laughing at inside jokes she did not understand, tossing out names she could not identify, bantering with the intimacy of one who had shared a way of life for years, and whose parents had shared it before him. When he came to her, she had no idea what to say to him. "Sybille Enderby," he said. "You've known Val for years; since childhood. You lived in New York but now you're in Washington, at the Watergate; your husband was Quentin Enderby and he died last year—I was sorry to hear that —and you own EBN. What else should I know about you?"

"I can't imagine," said Sybille coolly.

"Oh, hell, I've offended you. Have I? My God, you have the most incredible eyes; like beacons. Look, I always do that when I meet someone—go through my inventory—otherwise I never remember a name and Val says that's what really gets people's backs up. It's like my portable Rolodex; it doesn't mean a thing. Am I forgiven? I want to know all about you; Val says you always do what you set out to do. I want to know how you do that, what you like and what you don't like, what you look for when you go shopping, what kind of horse you like. Books, movies, music. And so on. Can I have enough of your time to get all that?"

He was behaving like a teenager leading up to a first date, Sybille thought, and wondered what he was hiding behind that pose. "You can have all the time you want," she said, not as cool this time. "I'd like to know about you, too. Valerie's said enough to make me curious."

He shot her a look. "You said that so I'd trot off to Val and ask her what she's been saying about me."

Sybille shook her head. "I said it so you'd want to spend more time talking to me so you could find out what she said."

He laughed. "You're as honest as they come, aren't you? Well, I'm flattered. Why don't we settle down in the den? There's a fire there, and the place ought to be deserted for an hour at least, until everybody descends for drinks. Shall we sit and talk for a while? Or would you rather ride? You do ride?"

"Yes. Not as well as you, I'm sure."

"Never apologize before you do something. Plenty of time afterward. Well, what will it be? Riding or talking?"

"Talking, for now."

"Good." He led the way to the den, but in fact it was not empty, and before Carlton could choose another place he had been drawn into conversation with the group already sitting near the fire. He and Sybille had no time to talk all that day. Sybille did not mind. She was satisfied to stay near him, watching him, knowing he was aware of her, and intrigued. He'd admired her eyes; she knew he admired her looks: sleek and polished next to most of the country-casual guests. He was interested, he was intrigued. He was Valerie's husband. She watched him, and stayed close. Once, taking a step back, he bumped into her and put his arms around her to steady her. She said nothing, but she made it clear she was extricating herself with reluctance. And then, when the last of the guests arrived and drinks were poured, Valerie stood near the fireplace. "This is the first time you'll hear this tonight, but not by any means the last," she said, and raised her glass. "Happy New Year, my friends."

The phrase was repeated by others; the wood-paneled room echoed with warm voices and laughter. In the corner, silently, Sybille looked at Carlton and held his eyes. Their glasses touched, their fingers brushed against each other. "Happy New Year, Carl," Sybille murmured, and she smiled.

Chapter
16

ick and Chad moved to Washington in June, as soon as Chad's summer vacation began. The moving van came early and stayed late, emptying the rooms until the house looked to Chad like a skeleton, bare and cold, with nothing familiar about it. Then, while Elena and Manuel drove across the country on a month's vacation that was a present from Nick, Chad and Nick flew to Washington in one leap that changed everything in their lives, forever.

Nick had been there twice, alone, working with his lawyers on the purchase of EBN and, on his second trip, buying a house. It was on N Street in Georgetown, dating from 1819, four stories high, of red brick with black shutters, big square rooms with fireplaces, steep narrow stairways, and high ceilings with carved moldings. Tall trees made a leafy tunnel over the sloping street and the brick sidewalk in front of the house. A few blocks away, on Wisconsin and M Streets, were restaurants, little shops, and art galleries, and an enormous shopping mall built to look like a turn-of-the-century main street with gas lamps, paved streets, splashing fountains, and wrought-iron railings on the staircases.

Georgetown was like a small village, and Chad and Nick explored its narrow streets together. They rode their bicycles along the thin slip of the Chesapeake and Ohio Canal, sharing the path with other bikers and hikers, and watching the mule-drawn barges, thinking they were like pictures in Chad's history books. They rode past shops and restaurants made to look like buildings of the 1700s and 1800s, and then along the residential streets, past rows of Federal-style houses pressed against each other the length of each block and built right up to the sidewalk, with small front porches or stoops, their backyards hidden behind high walls. All the houses were at least a hundred years old, sometimes two hundred, their bricks mellowed to a dark lustre, their mullioned windows reflecting the old-fashioned streetlights in wavery images, their doors heavy, with carved wood and etched-glass inserts. Nothing could have been farther from their neighborhood in San Jose, where the houses were new, the yards big and open, with the hot sunlight reflecting off pastel colors and towering palms.

Chad had been absolutely sure he would hate living in Washington, but he never had time to hate anything. His room in the house in Georgetown took up most of the third floor, and he spent an ecstatic week with Nick buying furniture for it and finding perfect places for all his familiar possessions. He helped Nick organize the other rooms, getting used to the high ceilings and tall narrow windows that contrasted with the square shapes he had been used to in their house in San Jose.

The second week, he began going to a day camp in Virginia, learning archery, horseback riding, swimming, tennis, soccer and polo. He took the bus early in the morning and returned just before dinner. He barely had time to think of California, much less miss it, nor did he have more than a few minutes a day to wonder why his mother had arranged an evening with him only once since they arrived; hardly the regular visits she had predicted.

"We'll work out a schedule when we're all settled," Nick said at dinner the fourth week they were in Washington. They had taken a long walk to Vincenzo for Italian food. "You may not see her as often as you'd like, but you'll be able to visit without me hanging around and that's a whole different way you'll get to know each other."

"I like it when you're hanging around," said Chad. He concentrated on his fish. "Sometimes . . . I can't think of things to say. Like we don't have a lot to talk about. But she's my *mother.*"

"Well, that's not so terrible," Nick said casually. "It happens to everybody, not just you. Sometimes conversations just run out of steam. The trouble is, most people worry that there's something wrong with them if they can't think of something to say. But nothing's wrong; they just need a little rest, a chance to decide what's important enough to share with another person. Babbling just to fill a silence is worse than silence itself. My suggestion is, if you can't think of something to say, sit quietly and look thoughtful and wise. That impresses everybody. Pretty soon your mother will find something to say. Or you will. Just don't worry about those pauses; they definitely don't mean you and your mother have nothing to talk about."

"Okay," Chad said. "Thanks." He moved snow peas around his plate. "So you won't be coming with us when we go places?"

"It's better if I don't, Chad."

"Will you go out with other people when I'm with her?"

"I might. I'm just beginning to make friends, though. Like you."

"You've met a lot of people."

"Mostly business people. That's part of my job."

"But a lot of business people are women."

Nick grinned. "And a good thing, too."

"And you go out with them?"

"Sometimes."

"But you work, too, at night, after I go to bed, like at Omega. I mean, you don't always go out with people."

"I'm working lots of nights and it is like Omega. I've gotten myself into another job that takes a lot of time and concentration."

"Why?"

"Because I'm learning a new business, and I've hired two vice-presidents and we're learning to work together, and because we need new programs, new ideas, a whole new way of thinking about what we're doing."

"What's wrong with the way Mother did it?"

"I didn't agree with a lot of the things she did. I told you that."

"Yeh, but . . . Like what?"

"Like making everything seem happy. She called it 'television of joy' and it was full of something called 'moments'—little dramatic scenes that take people's minds off the big story by focusing on small human-interest ones. I think people are grown-up enough to know that the world is full of things that are sad or tragic or dangerous, as well as happy and funny and hopeful, and I think television's job is to show all parts of the world as accurately as possible, whether they're pretty or not. So I'm making a lot of changes."

Chad nodded soberly, though Nick knew, from past discussions, that he grew bored whenever the talk turned to television's responsibility. "Are you firing lots of people?" he asked.

"A few."

"Famous people?"

"Hardly. We don't have any. I hope we will, pretty soon."

"Who did you fire first?"

"A man named Morton Case. I've been thinking he should be fired for almost nine years."

"That's when I was born."

"I first saw him when you were a baby. He was on a show called 'The Hot Seat.' I've never liked him."

"Did Mother?"

"Yes; it's another thing we don't agree about."

"Does she know you fired him?"

"I'd guess that by now she does."

Chad was silent for a moment, watching the waiter put a plate of *zuccotto* before him. "I guess it'll be all right," he said, and Nick did not ask him what he meant. Whatever it was, Chad was making his own adjustments. If something was not going to be all right, he hoped Chad would come to him, but even then he would not push it. At nine, Chad had a quick, curious mind and a wide-ranging imagination; he read voraciously, watched the television Nick allowed, enjoyed sports, and made friends easily. He had a full life, as full as Nick could help him make it. He knew what it was to be deeply loved, and he was learning to deal with pain. There wasn't much more Nick could do for him, except be available when he wanted to share joy or be comforted.

One thing he would not do was work out the arrangements for Chad and Sybille to be together. They were barely fifteen minutes apart now, from Georgetown to the Watergate, and it would be up to them to work out their visiting schedules. Nick was going to concentrate on himself for a while. He had a demanding, challenging job, and he wanted to meet as many people as possible and find someone to love; he wanted to remarry. He had no idea why he thought it would be easier to find someone in Washington than in California; probably because everything was new, and expectations always rise with a change in scenery.

While Chad was in camp he explored Washington by himself, discovering parts of the city he had never seen, and looking at the familiar parts for the first time with the eye of a resident. The streets were broad and clean, the traffic circles dizzying, the buildings low, regular, evenly spaced, giving an impression of harmony that never became monotonous. Space and light were everywhere, an East coast light a little dimmer and denser than California's, not as ethereal; and as it illuminated grassy expanses and marble monuments, there was no sign of the murky business of government. For the visitor or the new resident, Washington offered a facade of cleanliness, openness, honesty, diligence, sobriety, and hope for a shining future. It symbolized, as few capitals do, its own myth, and the dream and prayer of every populace.

Nick, a part of the media now, felt keyed up as he walked through the city. For the first time, he had a share in it; in a very real way, he was one of its emissaries to the world. He was buoyed with anticipation: new things were going to happen; he was going to be different than in the past.

Even Sybille, who called him frequently at work, seemed different to him now that they were in the same city and the same business: she seemed smaller, somehow; and younger. At first, when negotiations for EBN started, she had been as hard as he had ever seen her, raging at him for offering only two hundred million dollars for the network.

"It's worth more!" she exclaimed as they sat in her lawyer's office. "Three hundred!"

"Two hundred," Nick said quietly. "That's a final offer. You don't have the audience or the programs or the people to make it worth a penny more. And you know it; you've researched it."

"I know what its potential is! It's a goldmine—!"

"Then mine it yourself." Nick stood. "I'll be at the Madison until tomorrow afternoon if you want to reach me."

"Nick, you can't do this! Stop; you can't go! What's the matter with you? It's not as if we're strangers; we *know* each other! It's funny, isn't it? Who would have thought, just a few years ago, when we could barely afford a movie..." She gripped her hands in her lap. "I'm sorry; I meant to keep this businesslike. It's just that it's hard, when we've been through so much and now I need..." She shook her head; her lips were trembling as she tried to smile. "I won't do it again, I promise. It's just that I feel so alone...Nick, it's worth three hundred, I know it is, but I really want you to be the one to buy it. I'd consider two hundred if you assume half the debts."

Nick saw her lawyer's lips tighten and he guessed the lawyer had told Sybille not to try that ploy. But she hadn't been able to help herself, and Nick knew why: her debts at EBN were at least a hundred and ninety million. When she paid them off, she would have, from Quentin and the sale of EBN, about ten million dollars. That would satisfy most people, Nick thought; but not Sybille. "When you're ready to talk about my offer as it stands—two hundred million for the network, clear of debt, exclusive of your production company and its assets, which you keep—I might still be interested. Though the more I think about it, the more curious I am about other networks that might be for sale. Chad and I have a whole country to choose from; it doesn't have to be Washington. My plane is at three tomorrow afternoon."

"God damn it—!" Sybille cried, but he had closed the door behind him. The next morning, her lawyer called with her acceptance. "I deserve better than you," she told him, tight-lipped, when they met again. "I always knew you were mean and stingy and self-centered, but I never realized you were vicious too."

"I'll buy you a drink," Nick said, thinking of Chad. He took Sybille to the Fairfax Piano Bar and they sat for two hours, talking about Washington, about Sybille's riding and hunting, and her production company. They avoided other subjects, letting the music fill the silences between them. And when he took her back to the Watergate, they seemed to be friends. "I'm glad you're in television," Sybille told him as they said good night. "It's something for us to share, besides Chad."

After that, though she called him regularly, he saw her only once, when she and Chad went to dinner early one evening, and that was when he thought she seemed oddly smaller, almost meek. When he canceled the game shows she produced that had been airing on EBN, she tried only briefly to convince him to change his mind. And when he canceled "The Hour of Grace," she said only that he was making a mistake: Lily Grace was a sensation and soon would be one of the biggest names in television.

"He's not important," Sybille told Lily the evening after Nick canceled her show. "He has nothing to offer us; he doesn't know the first thing about television. He'll be bankrupt in six months. I'll have you appearing all over the country before he figures out how to put a schedule together. Try on another dress."

Lily turned to the pile of white dresses on the bed. It was her bed, and they were in her room in Sybille's apartment, the prettiest, largest room she had ever had. Even though she had been there for quite a while, she hadn't gotten used to the silk sheets and the deep carpet that curled luxuriously around her bare toes, and the bathroom, with its huge tub and separate shower with sprays on all sides that made her feel shivery and almost embarrassed. The room was so wonderful she didn't mind when Sybille sometimes asked her to stay in it while she entertained, the way she had done at Christmas when her son and his father were there. "I like to pretend we're still a family," Sybille had said with a small, sad smile, and Lily had understood completely, and had stayed behind her closed door until they were gone.

But that almost never happened. Most of the time Sybille was so pleased to have company in the big apartment that she demanded Lily's presence whenever she was there. And then she would bring surprises home, like the pile of dresses that lay on Lily's bed. "Try them on," she said, spreading them out. "Whatever we both like, we'll keep."

Lily watched herself in the full-length mirror as she put on one after the other. "Not the cotton," Sybille said. "It's wrong for you. Try the silk."

Lily took off the cotton dress. "Rudy said I should wear bright colors to attract more attention."

"He was wrong." Sybille watched her slip a silk dress over her head. "Much better; the other one made you look like a nurse."

Lily smiled. "What does this one make me look like?"

"A virgin." And something else, Sybille thought; something elusive. A girl who was almost a woman, a fantasy that was remote but still somehow attainable. Impatiently, she shrugged it off: she didn't like to waste time trying to figure people out. "A virgin," she repeated. "You're perfect."

"Perfect for what?" Lily asked.

Sybille did not answer. "Now give me one of your sermons."

"Again? Sybille, we've done it over and over for two months, ever since I went on the air, and all the mail we get... people say they like me... don't you think I'm all right, the way I preach now?"

"Of course you're all right; you're a sensation and you know it. But getting people excited on Nick's second-rate network is one thing; doing it in the whole country is something else. I want to make a new tape tomorrow and send it to some people I know; I'm going to offer you the same way I offer the other shows I'm producing."

"No!" Lily cried instinctively.

"You're nothing like them, of course," Sybille said carefully. "You have a style and a message all your own. But we have to get television producers to understand that, and most of them aren't smart enough to do it on their own. It's not easy to get them to look at a tape, Lily, much less buy a program or schedule one. I don't expect them to spend their money to buy 'The Hour of Grace,' but I do want them to give us a regular time slot."

"But why wouldn't they? They must want people to watch their stations, and if we tell them how much mail I get, they'll give us the time."

"They can't run commercials during a religious broadcast, so they have to sell the time itself. Most television preachers buy time on one network or another. But it's a huge expense and it's not necessary. If I'm right about you, I can get stations to give me an hour a week, maybe two, if not now, a year from now. It's just a question of making them want you so much they'll give me the hour before I take you to their competition. But I've got to be sure you're perfect; otherwise they'll give a quick look at yor tape and toss it. Go ahead."

"If you think it's so important..." Self-consciously, Lily began to preach, standing amid the dresses and shoes. But in a minute her self-consciousness disappeared; she was lost in her words, in her belief in her message. "And there is another person within each of you," she said, "and you can reach—"

"Wait. Repeat that."

"Repeat what?" Lily said, blinking as if waking up.

"'Another person within each of you.' Say it twice, to emphasize it. Or better yet, can you find a couple of ways to say it? I don't want anyone to miss it. It's the main idea, isn't it?"

"Well...one of them."

"Try it again."

Lily closed her eyes. "...another person within each of you, a person you want to be—"

"How about 'dreamed of being'?"

"Oh. Yes. I like that. Another person within each of you, a person you want to be...no, a person you've always wanted to be, a person you've dreamed of being. You may have thought it was impossible to be that person: good and kind and loving, a person who can do anything, a person who has confidence in you, who admires and believes in you. We always want others to believe in us, but—"

"Not 'we,'" Sybille interrupted. "You're not one of them; you're above them—"

"Oh, no, Sybille, I'm not above anyone."

"Separate, then. You're the one who's doing the talking; you're bringing them new ways to think about themselves. You mustn't sound as if you're as confused and needy as they are. I've told you that before, Lily; I don't know why you can't understand it."

"Because I want to be one of them."

"No, you don't. If you were, you'd be sitting on a couch, turning on 'The Hour of Grace.' You can't tell me you wouldn't rather be Lily Grace, preaching to people."

Slowly, Lily nodded. "Yes, but that still doesn't make me above them, better than—"

"Separate," Sybille said again, holding in her impatience.

Lily thought about it, then took a breath and went on with her sermon. "You've always wanted others to admire you and believe in you, but, more important, you should—"

"'More important, most important, the most important of all,'" Sybille said. "Rhythm, Lily, cadence: that was one thing Rudy did well."

"Yes. I remember. Well... More important, most important, the most important of all is for you to believe in yourself. And you can, *you can*, because you are good, you are special, you can trust yourself to be whatever you have dreamed of being—"

"Love," said Sybille. "Push love. And you ought to get God in earlier."

"Do I really need to do all that?" Lily asked worriedly. "I have to say it the way I feel it, you know."

"Yes, of course. I'd never try to change what you say: I'm so moved by you, Lily. But I want to make sure everyone is as moved as I am; I want them to be excited, mesmerized, crying with joy, like those people in that church in Hackensack. Television is different, Lily—how many times have I told you that?—you have to punch your words to make them stand out; you have to be sharp and clear or you'll never seem real or important to all those people in their living rooms. They look at their screen and they see a flat little image, not a flesh-and-blood person. Millions of people want to believe in you, but they can't unless you help them."

"Millions," Lily breathed. She looked at her hands clasped loosely in front of her. "To do so much good, all at once..." Her eyes closed and her high, sweet voice took on a lilting rhythm. "Love is within you, *so* much love, the *love* you give to *God* and the *love* you give to those whose *lives* touch *yours*. You may be *afraid* that you can never *love* as much as you *want to love*, as you *dream* of loving, because the pain and hardship of life interferes, but you *can*, you *can* love, you can love *greatly*, because you are a person of *goodness* who has more *love* to *give* than you have ever *imagined*. And as you *give* love, you will *receive* it. Others are *waiting* to love you, to *help* you, to *lift* you up so you will not be alone ever again. Once you *unlock* the chains that *imprison* the good, *loving* person within you, others will gather around; they, *too*, will find the *goodness* within *themselves*; they, too, will *believe* in themselves, and *together* all of you will *discover* how much you are, how much you can *be,* how much you can *do,* now that—"

"Good," Sybille said.

Lily's eyes flew open. "I forgot you were here."

Sybille did not believe her, but it didn't matter; if Lily believed it, her preaching would be better. "Just one thing," she said. "Talk about yourself as often as you can. *Listen to me; I'm here to help you. Believe me when I tell you* ... That sort of thing. We don't want those millions of people to think they can do it alone, without you. And then there's the money." Lily frowned. "Now listen carefully. You know we can't do anything without support from your audience—"

"Congregation," Lily said gently. "I've asked you—"

"All right, your congregation is going to want to support you. They know you can't produce shows—"

"Religious hours."

"You can't produce religious hours without money; everyone knows that. They know you have to live on something besides love; and they'll want you to have the money to build your cathedral."

Lily's head came up. "Cathedral?"

"The Cathedral of Joy. You don't think I'd let you preach for very long in a television studio with folding chairs for your aud—congregation, do you? You can't stay in a place built for Rudy Dominus; you need much more. You need grandeur, Lily; you have a message and a delivery and an image that can sweep this country. I want to build you a cathedral where a thousand people at once can hear you, and millions more can see you on television."

Stunned, Lily sat on a hassock. *"A thousand* ... When did you ... how long have you been thinking about this?"

"Since we began 'The Hour of Grace.' You were right: the mail is fantastic. And most of it includes money. Small amounts, but you hadn't asked for anything. From now on, as part of each sermon, you'll tell your congregation about the Cathedral of Joy; about the—"

"Where would it be?"

"I've been looking at land near the mountains, around Culpeper."

"Culpeper?"

"Virginia. I wanted it near the horse farm I just bought, in Leesburg, but there's not enough land around there for the cathedral and some other ideas I have. Culpeper's less than fifty miles south, with much more land."

"What other ideas?" Lily asked. "We mustn't get too grand, Sybille;

I think maybe the cathedral is too much. All I need is a simple place, a small, plain church...."

"We're not going after anything small and plain," Sybille said flatly. "It doesn't interest me, and it shouldn't interest you."

"Why? What I have to say isn't very complicated."

"I thought you liked the idea of reaching millions of people."

"Yes," Lily said, as if embarrassed at her own ambition. "Yes, I do like it."

"Then we'll need a cathedral. And about ten million dollars to build it."

Lily stared at her. "That's impossible. We couldn't ever get that much."

"We'll get it. It's not a fortune; it's only a beginning. There's so much good you can do, Lily, so many people you can help. I've never felt this excitement before: we'll make people happy, and make a better world. But all that takes money."

"I just don't understand very much about money," said Lily sadly.

"It doesn't matter; I do," Sybille said easily. "That's one of the reasons we make a good team. Now, we'll keep these five dresses, and the one you've got on. These six we'll return. And, Lily, I'm giving you a key to the apartment; you don't have to depend on me so much anymore. After all, we have our own activities."

Lily looked confused. "You're going away? Or you don't want me bothering you? Did I do something wrong?"

"No, of course not, I'm not going anywhere, and you don't bother me. But if I'm working late or you want to go somewhere by yourself, you should be able to. We'll still be living together, and I expect you to tell me what you do with your free time and who you meet and want to see again, but I need—each of us needs a little space. And as a preacher you know better than anyone how important space is: your own time for solitude and reflection..."

Lily's face cleared. "Yes, I do." She knelt beside Sybille and laid her head on Sybille's knee. "How wonderful you are to know that. And how unselfish of you. Thank you for being so good to me; you make me so happy I can't imagine how I got along without you. Rudy was sweet and he was good to me and I loved him, but he didn't understand me very well, he didn't know anything at all about clothes, and I think he really didn't want me to preach. And you do, you know how important it is to me; you're working so hard to make it possible, and in a *cathedral;* it's all a dream..." She raised her head and looked at

Sybille with shining eyes. "I love you so much, Sybille. Thank you for loving me."

Sybille put her hand on Lily's smooth white-blond hair. "You've helped me find the goodness in myself."

Lily's face became radiant. "Have I? But you were always good; I knew that. But if I've helped you, oh, how wonderful..."

Gradually Sybille moved away and stood up. "We'll have dinner in twenty minutes; you'd better clean up."

"Yes," Lily said. She was still sitting on the floor, her eyes level with the white dresses, belts, sashes, lace cuffs and shoes on the bed beside her. She sighed, and then she too stood. She went to Sybille and kissed her lightly—she knew Sybille hated to be touched—and then, with a gentle smile, she left the room.

For months, from New Year's Eve to the first crisp weekend in October, Sybille did not see Carlton Sterling alone, even after she bought CrossHatch Farms near Leesburg. At forty acres it was ridiculously small, and much too far from Middleburg, but she was in a hurry to buy something and become part of Loudoun County, and she considered it a first step to the grander estate she deserved.

In August, she invited the people she had met at Valerie's New Year's party to a catered dinner in her two-story white frame house, but Carlton did not come; he was in Canada, Valerie said, on a fishing trip. And then, in October, there was a fox hunt in the fields near Purcellville, and, at the lavish breakfast that began the day, Sybille found Carlton at a table on the veranda, momentarily alone.

"May I—?" she asked, holding the plate she had filled at the buffet. "Or are you waiting for someone?"

"A cheerful smile," he said, pulling back the chair beside him. "That's what I need most, this early in the morning."

Sybille smiled. "How was your fishing trip?" she asked, sitting down and reaching for the coffeepot that stood in the center of the table.

"Fishing?"

"In Canada."

"Oh, last month. It was good. Walleyed pike and bass; do you fish?"

"No. Well, yes; sometimes for compliments, and always for audiences."

He looked startled, then began to laugh. "I remember: you're so honest. I like that. Val's the same way; took me a while to get used to it. What kind of audiences? For yourself?"

"For my programs. I've never cared about audiences for myself, being on camera, that sort of thing. It seems so . . . fake . . . talking to a camera as if you were about to take it to bed—"

Carlton gave a nervous laugh. "Sounds uncomfortable."

"Well, someone once told me a good television personality makes love to the camera. I don't know exactly what that means, but it sounds like something I'd be ashamed of."

"Val does it, you know," he said abruptly.

"She does? Still? Oh, I'm sorry; I had no idea she was still doing it, I thought she'd outgrown . . . oh, *damn,* why can't I keep my mouth shut? Carl, I'm so sorry; I'd never say anything against Valerie; I think she's wonderful. I've looked up to her all my life."

"Have you? She thinks you don't like her."

Sybille stared at him. *"She thinks I don't —"*

A couple came to their table, carrying heaping plates. "You two plotting something illicit?" one of them asked jovially.

"No such luck," Carlton said with an easy laugh. "Come on; sit with us. We were talking about fishing."

Sybille picked at her smoked pheasant and cheese soufflé, half listening to the talk around her, occasionally glancing at Carlton. Once she met his eyes and, flushing, looked quickly away. When, at last, the couple rose, saying they would stroll a bit before the hunt began, she kept her eyes lowered.

"Thank God," said Carlton cheerfully. "The dullest couple in Loudoun County. Pity we had to get them. You looked thoroughly bored."

"I was rude," Sybille said in a low voice. "I hope I didn't embarrass you; I just kept wishing they'd leave."

"Well, they did, and you didn't embarrass me. Why would you? I'm not the host."

"Because they're your friends."

"Not mine. And not Val's. Our hosts' friends, I assume, though God knows why?"

"Why does Valerie think I don't like her?"

"Have you been brooding about that? I shouldn't have said it; stupid of me. It was just something Val said a while back, New Year's, I guess; nothing major; I probably got it wrong."

"But what did she say? It's not true that I don't like her! She knows that! I love her; I always have. She's like my older sister; I think she's the most wonderful . . . *What did she say about me?"*

He sighed. "Something about you never getting over something at

Stanford. She didn't say what, but what difference does it make? It's ancient history, and pretty childish, if you ask me; and I don't believe it, anyway. In fact, I'm sure I heard it wrong and I apologize for babbling about it. Tell me I'm forgiven."

Sybille's pale-blue eyes held his. "Of course you're forgiven. I couldn't be angry at you. Ever since we met I've felt something—I feel foolish saying this, please don't laugh at me—I've felt as if I've known you before and trusted you not to hurt me."

"Good God." He sat straight, distancing himself from her. "What does that mean?"

"Nothing." She pushed back her chair. "I'm sorry I said that; I knew it would sound foolish. I'm not usually mystical; I'm very practical. But there was something about our meeting I couldn't be cold and rational about. I would have kept quiet, but you said you liked my honesty..."

"Wait, I do like your honesty. I like you. But what did you mean?"

She made a small, helpless gesture with her hand. "I meant that it's hard to find anyone to trust. Don't you think so? There are so many unknowns, pitfalls..."

"That doesn't tell me what you meant."

"Oh... I'm not very smart about men. I think there must be something wrong with me. I can't be tough and careful and calculating; I just rush in, all ready to love, wanting so much to be loved..." She turned away. "But it never works out; I always get hurt." She turned back to him and gave a short, hard laugh. "I'm getting pretty tired of it, to tell the truth. Most women find someone to share their lives; why shouldn't I? I don't think I give too much or ask too much; I think I'm pretty normal; I just don't seem to choose men who are right for me. Or I'm not right for them. Maybe it's my fault for not paying more attention and figuring out what they need and then giving it to them. I'm just in such a hurry to find someone to be with, and I can't always bury myself deep enough in work to forget I'm alone. A lot of the time I can, but then all of a sudden something will make me feel such a failure..." She touched the corner of her eye. "I'm sorry, Carl, I didn't mean to spoil your breakfast by whining about myself; of all the things you don't want to hear, that probably heads the list." She looked behind her. "They've all gone! What have I done? Carl, if I've made you miss the hunt, on top of everything else..." She shoved back her chair and stood up. "I've done a great job of ruining what could have been good friendship, haven't I? I'm so ashamed. I wish I could go back to the beginning and start this conversation again—"

"Sit down," said Carlton. He was frowning. "Val said you seemed happy with Enderby."

"I was; oh, I was so happy. But it was just at the beginning. After a while he wasn't home much. I didn't know it at the time, but he had another woman. I think it was important to Quentin, at his age, to keep proving how virile he was. I loved him the way he was, but he just couldn't be satisfied with himself, so he kept finding young women, one in particular, but I'm pretty sure there were others. I never even tried to find out; it made me feel so . . . inadequate. I found out about the one, just before he died. And then he left most of his money to her, and some of it to a preacher he'd met; I suppose he got worried about his soul or something, when he was sick."

"He didn't leave anything to you?"

Sybille shook her head.

"I thought you got the television network."

"Oh. Yes. But it had enormous debts. And even if it didn't, it seemed so cold and unfeeling—a lot of equipment—nothing personal, nothing to show that we'd loved each other."

Carlton thought briefly that there was something wrong with that: why would money seem more personal or loving than a business they'd owned together? Still, she had touched something deep inside him when she said she'd felt inadequate. He often felt that way with Val. She did everything so well—riding, steeplechase, giving parties, those little things she did on television, raising money for some cause or other, being a wife—and everyone praised her; he did, too. It was a good thing she never wanted to do anything really serious, he thought. If she did, she'd probably leave him behind in the dust.

"You shouldn't feel inadequate," he said to Sybille. "He probably didn't know how to appreciate you, and on top of that he had his own problems, with his illness. It must have been a rotten time for you."

Sybille said nothing. She ran her riding crop slowly through her fingers, as if lost in thought.

"Why did you think I wouldn't hurt you?" Carlton asked.

She looked up again. "I don't think you'd hurt anyone, if you could help it. That first time we talked, New Year's Eve, I felt something special. As if we'd known each other for a long time, and laughed together, maybe even loved each other. Not with passion, but with . . . oh, with affection. Closeness. Trust. You know so much more than I do; I had the feeling that I could come to you for advice and comfort when things were bad, that we could share some of the craziness of the world . . . that we'd had—or we could have—the kind of love that makes life bearable."

Carlton could not take his eyes from her. "You're an incredible woman."

Slowly, still holding his gaze, she shook her head. "I'm glad you think so. But I think it's just that silly honesty; I can't lie to you, Carl . . . I can only love . . . or wish . . ."

He stood and pulled her up to him, covering her mouth with his, forcing it open, his tongue crushing hers as if he would subdue her by force, though she was not struggling. With a little sob deep in her throat, Sybille put her arms around him and gave herself up to his kiss with the submission of a child, and the passion of a woman.

Carlton swept her into his arms and carried her across the veranda into the house. "No," Sybille whispered. "Your friends . . . the hunt . . ."

"They don't need me."

"But this house . . ."

". . . has lots of bedrooms and they're all empty." He laughed, buoyant and excited. "God, Sybille, we've got the whole day. You're very small, you know that? You fit right in my arms, like a little girl." He climbed the stairs, still holding her, and she snuggled against him, making herself smaller. He turned into the first bedroom off the landing, a guest room with flowered curtains and flowered armchairs. He laid her on the flowered comforter on the bed, then looked down at her, laughing again. "Damned riding clothes . . . wait a minute."

He disappeared into the hall and returned a moment later with a boot pull. Sybille had not moved; she lay wide-eyed, waiting for him. "Now," he said, and pulled off his boots and clothes, while Sybille lay still, watching. He felt her eyes on him, burning into him; he thought he had never been so excited about a woman. "God, you're a witch," he said, and leaned over her to tear off her boots and clothes, roughly, flinging them from the bed. Sybille felt his fingers rake her skin as he pulled away her brassiere and silk underpants, and then she gave a long moan and pulled him onto her. She spread her legs and felt him fit himself between them, felt the hairs on his chest as he lay on her breasts. She raised her hips, whispering his name, and he pushed into her. The only sound in the room was their breathing, sharp and quick. Sybille bit the side of Carlton's neck, sucking the skin between her teeth, running her tongue along his perspiration. She felt him shiver as she licked him. She moved her hips in ways she had practiced since college; her breathing grew more rapid, matching Carlton's, and then he thrust deeply into her, pulled up, and thrust again, and cried out. At just that moment, Sybille too cried out, and then they both lay still.

"Incredible," Carlton murmured. "Incredible little witch." He lay heavily, crushing her small body beneath his. She made him feel powerful. In a few minutes, very slowly, Sybille began to move her hips in circular motions beneath him, and he raised himself halfway and gazed down at her, at her piercing eyes. "My little witch," he said, and bent again to her mouth. And Sybille sighed, a long, deep sigh of passion. Or perhaps it was satisfaction. Carlton did not wonder which, because he did not think about it. He thought about her body, and the feeling of a little girl in his arms and beneath him, and her low voice saying she knew he would not hurt her.

Carlton had always been too lazy to expend the kind of energy that true intimacy required. He came closest, he thought, with Valerie. But now he was feeling something new. He was transfixed by Sybille Enderby. Something different, he thought, and heard her sigh again. Passion. Or satisfaction. Either way, he knew it was for him, and only for him. She trusted him; she'd hinted that she loved him. And that sigh, and the movements of her hips and hands, roused him as if he were a boy of sixteen. Sybille, he thought exultantly; you're mine.

Nick's days and nights were like the early times at Omega: there was only work and Chad, the exhilaration of creating something new, of learning and doing, of gathering a small staff that worked well together, and developing a list of customers who helped spread his growing reputation. His first act had been to hire two vice-presidents, for news and entertainment, and the three of them had spent the next three months planning a totally new schedule to replace Sybille's. They also had a new name: the E&N network.

"I get the N for Nick," said Les Braden, his vice-president for news, at their first meeting. "But who's E?"

"Entertainment and News," said Nick with a grin. "Straight and simple. I decided I don't need to splash my name in front of the public to feel good about myself."

Les chuckled. "I like that; a man who doesn't have to tell the world how important he is. Is that all? Entertainment and news?"

"What else is there?"

"Oh, the heavy stuff. Documentaries about athlete's foot and trench building in World War One; that sort of thing."

Nick laughed. "We'll have documentaries that are so well done they're entertaining. I don't think athlete's foot would qualify, unless you can think of a way to tie it in with swimming and diving competitions."

"Not my job; I do news. I'll talk to Monica about it; she's so good she'll probably work it out. What do you think of Tracy Moore as anchor of the six and ten news?"

"I like her. She's tough and warm; a good combination. But we need a man too. Or do we? They always seem to come in pairs, like make-believe marriages. It's as if someone decided viewers need to think the world is full of happy couples grinning at each other and making little jokes; otherwise the news won't be palatable."

"Sounds like the way television executives think," said Les. "Connie Chung does weekend newscasts alone, and she's damn good. I think we could get away with Tracy on her own; we'll have plenty of male reporters."

"It's fine with me. Sign her up."

The planning went on all through September, during the day at the offices of E&N, in the evenings at Nick's house. At the same time, Nick was reading everything he could find on each part of the business; he was calling on dozens of people for information and advice, and he was traveling, to meet with cable operators. "Another dog and pony show," he told Chad. "I'm still trotting out what I've got to offer, hoping somebody buys."

Most of them bought his ideas and agreed to stay with E&N, at least for a year after he began programming in October. As they agreed, one by one, the planning sessions with Les and Monica became more cheerful: they had a beginning.

"I have an idea," Nick said one morning early in October. It was three weeks before they would switch from Sybille's programming to their own.

Les sat back and stretched his legs. They were sitting in Nick's office, once Sybille's, almost bare since Sybille had removed her furniture. The two men sat on folding chairs beside unpacked boxes of books they were using as coffee tables; nearby were six more chairs, and across the room, in front of windows looking into other office windows, was Nick's desk and drafting table, shipped from California. That left him no desk for his office at home. One of these days he planned to go shopping; so far he had not taken the time.

"What idea?" Les asked. He poured two cups of coffee and handed one to Nick. The two men had become friends almost the moment they met. On the surface, they could not have been more different. Les was twenty years older, a self-proclaimed failure as a radio announcer who had lost two jobs when his stations were sold and a third when he quit after being ordered to report early election returns and projections in favor of certain candidates before the polls closed. He was happily married to his high-school sweetheart and struggling to send two children through college. Compared to Nick's brilliant success, he seemed to have little. But the two of them shared ideas about television, about news, and about the world they lived in; they were at ease with each other, and worked together in the same harmony Nick had known with Ted McIlvain at Omega.

"What would you think of a program called 'The Other Side of the News'?" Nick asked. "Subtitled: 'What Didn't They Say? What Didn't They Show?'"

Les considered it. "I like it. We show a speech, the President for example, a senator, somebody at the UN—"

"Or someone in business. Not just politics."

"And then we have somebody else give the speech, parts of it anyway, with what was left out."

"Or what was bent out of shape."

"Lies," Les said. "People lie and politicians lie better."

"We're going to think of every way of saying 'lie' without saying it." Nick grinned. "Or we don't say anything; we use a scene—some action that shows, without any words, or as few as possible, what was missing or false about the statement we just heard. We can do the same with television, and newspapers, by the way. If a reporter distorts a story, I'd want to show that too. No sacred cows."

"Good title," Les murmured. He was making notes. "So who's going to produce this show? Everyone is already overloaded."

"We'll have to hire someone. If you have any names, I'll follow them up."

"I might, in my office. I'll go look. Any other ideas?"

"Yes, but they're for Monica."

"Entertainment. Like what?"

"'The Bookstall.' Review of new books."

"Nobody'll watch it."

"Nobody?"

"A handful."

"Then we'll do it for a handful. There are two shows reviewing movies on the networks; I want one for books."

"Good," said Les promptly. "I don't mind a handful if you don't.

Monica can probably produce it herself. Anything else?"

"A few dozen; we'll talk about them later. Do you have anything new?"

"A notebookful; you'll get them all eventually. You and Chad want to come to dinner tonight?"

"Sure. If you don't mind listening to Chad talk about his new school."

"Still? He's been doing that since September."

"He hasn't stopped. I hope he doesn't; I've never seen him so happy."

"How about you?" Les asked. "Are you happy?"

Nick laughed. "Coming from a married man, that means, have I met someone. No; not yet. But I'm having a good time, and you know it, Les; this is as much fun as Omega ever was. I'll meet women—how couldn't I, in this town? I'm outnumbered about five to one. And I'll probably manage to get married one of these days. But I'm not going to be in a hurry; it's not important, as long as I'm having fun along the way." He stopped. The words echoed from a distant memory. Someone else had said that. *Why should I be in a hurry when I'm having so much fun along the way?*

Valerie, sitting on the grass at Stanford, sunlight glinting on her tawny hair, laughing at him for being so serious. The scene came back so vividly Nick could hear her laughter, feel the warmth of the sun, recall even the names of the books she had bought at the bookstore a few minutes earlier, when they had just met.

"Nick? You with me?"

"Sorry," Nick said. "I just remembered something."

"Must be quite a woman, whoever she is." Les clipped his pencil into his shirt pocket and went to the door. "I'll look for producers. And I'll write up my ideas for 'The Other Side of the News.'"

"Ask Monica to come in, will you? And the three of us will meet tomorrow."

"Right. Hell of a deal to see things moving, isn't it?"

The third week in October, the same week Sybille called Nick from her new home near Leesburg to tell him she'd been at a fox hunt and had met an interesting man, E&N signed off at midnight and came on the air six hours later with a completely new schedule. It had none of the excitement of that trade show in California, when Nick knew, the minute Omega's new computers began to sell, that they were on their way; with television, they had to wait for mail and telephone calls from viewers, and to see if the number of subscribers rose, or fell. Still, as they watched the first day unfold, the steady march of programs they had bought, and the news they were producing, there was an air of excitement in the E&N studios that Nick would not have exchanged for anything in the world.

After that, through the fall and winter, as Nick drove back and forth across the Key Bridge between Georgetown and Fairfax to be with Chad as much as possible, he and Les and Monica and the executive staff they had gathered worked the crazy hours of people who are absolutely convinced they can overcome any obstacle. They made plans and schedules, and projections of audiences and advertisers, and steadily expanded the programming and the reputation of E&N. Through heavy advertising, and then by word of mouth, the audience started to grow. By July, a little over a year after Nick and Chad had moved to Washington, the network was broadcasting eighteen hours a day to twenty million households. "Piddling," Les said, making light of his excitement. "But it's a hell of a deal to see things moving."

E&N produced some of its own programs, but bought most of them. Monica chose American and foreign films, but the greatest part of the programming was chosen by an Acquisitions Committee that Nick had formed. The committee screened the thousands of tapes sent by production companies, and selected the best, to fill over a thousand hours of programming a year.

Most of the programs were aired three times: once in the daytime, once during evening prime time on the East Coast, and again during prime time in the West. A program guide was printed, and a separate version of it, for schools, listed books and movies that could be used with some of the programs for classroom discussion. Reporters were hired and news bureaus opened, at first in just a few cities around the country; later, in major cities around the world. And, in August, one of the programs in "The Other Side of the News" series won an Emmy Award in the news category. "A hell of a deal," said Les jubilantly, and the next day Sybille called Nick to congratulate him.

"It's amazing, the way you grab hold," she said. "You didn't know the first thing about television when you bought EBN, and now you're winning awards."

"I read a few books," Nick said dryly.

"Well." Sybille took a breath, and Nick knew she was about to change the subject to herself. "You might be surprised at the things I'm doing; you haven't asked, but—"

"You haven't been around for quite a while."

There was a pause. "I know. I did call Chad; didn't he tell you?"

"Yes. Once in the last five weeks."

"And he called me. Did he tell you that?"

"No," Nick said, surprised. "But he doesn't tell me everything he does; I'm glad he called. I hope he does it more often."

Sybille waited for him to ask what she had been doing that kept her away. "Well," she said again, "what kept me away was the cathedral I'm building for Lily Grace."

"Cathedral?"

"Nick, you don't understand what Lily can do to an audience. You've always underestimated her. And *me;* you've underestimated me. You didn't give me credit for being able to mold her into a valuable property. I told you you were wrong; remember? You were so wrong, Nick. I've done incredible things with her; I've taught her what to say, how to speak, what phrases to use, what to wear...she's more polished now, more believable. I've got her to the point where she can make people in the audience cry; you wouldn't believe the look in their eyes. Haven't you seen her lately? Don't you watch your competition?"

"Not all of it and not all the time. Who carries her?"

"Channel Twenty in Baltimore at seven on Sunday nights, and Channel Eighteen in Philadelphia at seven-thirty on Tuesday nights. You can get both of those. I wish you'd watch her, Nick."

"I'll try. I've been working most nights."

"Still? What about your social life? Nick, would you come out and see the cathedral? It's not far; just outside Culpeper. I'm building it with money people are sending in—isn't that fantastic?—all those people wanting Lily to have a place of her own to preach. Come this weekend, Nick; I really want to show it to you. Chad too; he'd like it. We can go back to my farm afterward and he can do some riding; last time he was there he was getting very good."

"I'm sorry; I don't have the time. But I'll drive Chad to your farm; I'd like him to do some riding, and he could spend the day with you."

"Nick, I want you to see the cathedral. It's something I'm doing. I saw your show, the one that got the award; I watch most of the series. The least you can do is take a few hours and see what I'm doing. You're not the only one who's being successful, you know."

Nick heard the defensive anger in her voice. "All right," he said after a moment. "And Chad will get a couple of hours of riding."

"Of course. Saturday morning, ten-thirty, at my farm. We'll drive together from there."

She was waiting for them when they arrived on Saturday, and she sat in the front seat of Nick's car, with Chad in back, for the drive to

Culpeper. The brilliant fall foliage spread golden and russet swaths across the rolling fields; the weathered fences were dark silhouettes against the pale grass of the pastureland; a few clouds trailed long fingers across the dense blue sky. Driving in silence as Sybille pointed out the farms they passed, naming their owners and their pedigrees, Nick felt a deep sense of melancholy. The landscape was so beautiful he longed to share it with someone he loved: a woman whose heart would be touched, as his was, by the timeless serenity of these fields and woods, the embrace of the golden sun in the arching blue sky. I've missed so much, he thought as he drove on the almost-empty road. All these years—good ones, with work and Chad and friends—and once I thought that was enough. Or told myself that it was enough, I needed no more, in fact, I should be grateful for what I had. He smiled slightly. The lies we tell ourselves, he thought.

"What?" Sybille asked, seeing his smile.

"Just a passing thought," he replied. "Tell us about your church."

"Cathedral. We'll be there in a few minutes. It will seat a thousand people and it's on two acres—room for lots of parking—and the money comes from everywhere—wherever Lily is on the air."

"How many stations do you have?"

"Twenty-two, but I'm getting more all the time. It snowballs, you know; the more viewers I have, the more other stations want to be in on it. And of course everyone likes the idea of the cathedral: if Lily can pull the audience she does now, from my studio, with an audience of a couple of hundred, imagine what she can do in a cathedral that seats a thousand!"

"How much money comes in?" Nick asked curiously.

"Enough to build the Cathedral of Joy, and fund 'The Hour of Grace.' And a little more."

Her evasiveness was the first clue that the numbers must be very big.

"Here," Sybille said. "Take the next right; the road is about a quarter of a mile farther."

"Look!" Chad exclaimed. "It's gigantic!"

In fact the church was not as big as Nick had imagined, but, sitting by itself in the midst of the fields, near the edge of dense woods, it seemed to tower above them. Nick parked near a dozen workers' cars and vans in a churned-up dirt area near a side entrance. "Parking lot," Sybille said. "I'll have two more, one in back and one at the other side."

"Can we go inside?" Chad asked.

"That's what we're here for," Sybille said. "I wanted you to see it."

Nick glanced at her as they walked around the building to the high carved double doors at the front, looking for the kind of excitement he had seen in her face the evening they watched the first airing of "The Hot Seat," and again when he and Chad sat in the control room during one of her newscasts. But what he saw, instead of excitement, was cool calculation: the keen, encompassing survey of a woman who was thinking not only of this moment, but beyond it, to bigger moments to come. Bigger what? Nick wondered. She had always clawed so feverishly for attention, yet she had always been behind the scenes... what was she after now? He could not believe it was attention for Lily Grace.

It could be the money, if in fact there was as much of it as her coy answer had hinted.

Or it could be power. But it was not clear where her power would lie.

"What the hell—!" Sybille exclaimed, and Nick looked toward the altar, following her gaze. They were in the nave of the church, the light a faint blue from the dark-blue vaulted ceiling painted with stars. The windows were of dark-blue stained glass set with abstract shapes of brightly colored glass like small explosions of light. There were as yet no pews, but the altar was finished: an expanse of warm pink marble with built-in planters for flowers and a pink marble pulpit with marble candlesticks on either side. Near the pulpit stood a tall man, his head back, inspecting the arched ceiling. He had a thin face, and his blond hair was a little long in back.

"What's the matter?" Chad asked. He had run up the nave and had just returned to Sybille and Nick.

"We've seen enough," Sybille said. "It's stifling in here."

"But there's some stairs," Chad said. "Couldn't we see where they go? It'd be great if there was a dungeon, like in the old days."

"No!" Sybille said sharply, but Chad had turned and was running up the nave again toward the altar. "Chad!" she shouted, and at that the man on the altar swung about.

"Sybille?" he called. He came down the broad marble steps and strode to them. As he came closer, he saw Nick, and slowed. "I didn't know you were bringing someone." He held out his hand. "Carl Sterling."

"Nick Fielding." They shook hands.

"We were just leaving," Sybille said. "I promised Chad he could go riding this afternoon."

Carlton looked behind him, back toward the altar. "Chad. Your son?" he asked Nick. "I didn't make that connection. I don't think Val told me Chad's last name when she said Sybille had a son."

"Carl, we're leaving," Sybille said, an edge of desperation in her voice. "Call me tomorrow if you want to talk about the cathedral."

"Your wife's name is Valerie?" Nick asked. "And she's a friend of Sybille's?"

"Yes, do you know her? Oh, of course, you probably do; you met Sybille at Stanford, didn't you? You'll have to get together one of these days; talk about old times—"

"Why not now?" Nick asked. His heart was pounding; he was filled with a crazy anticipation. He had not even thought of their meeting like this, accidentally, after so many years; he had never thought of the possibility that she and Sybille had kept in touch.

"What?" Carlton asked.

"Why don't we have lunch together?" Nick asked, his voice steady. "Do you live near here? We could pick up Valerie"—his voice caught on the unfamiliar sound of her name spoken aloud—"and go someplace nearby."

"That's not a good—"

"No," said Sybille flatly. "I have plans for later. Nick, if you want Chad to ride, you'll come now. I didn't plan to spend my Saturday wandering around the county—"

"Sybille's right, you know," Carlton said quickly. "Our weekends are busy and we don't do much socializing during the day. You and Chad could come down sometime if you want—you don't need to bring Sybille. You don't even need me there; just call Val and say you're coming. I'm sure she'd be pleased to see you."

"Then let's do it now," Nick said. His rudeness and stubbornness amazed him, but he suddenly felt he did not want to wait another day. He did not want to come down at some vague time in the future at Carlton's invitation; he did not want to show up alone on Valerie's doorstep. He wanted to see her; he wanted to see her now; he wanted to see her with other people around so they could call it a normal social occasion and he could banish this adolescent excitement he was feeling over a woman he had not seen for twelve years and had parted from in a quarrel.

"I'm buying lunch," he said firmly. "For old times' sake. I'd like to see Valerie again; I haven't seen her for a long time. We won't be more than a couple of hours, Sybille; I think that leaves plenty of time for Chad's ride."

Sybille stared at him, her light-blue eyes as flat as frozen ponds. She swung her look to Carlton, waiting for him to refuse once more; he had plenty of reason to. But he was silent, looking helplessly from her to Nick. A gentleman, Sybille thought contemptuously. Weak. Useless.

"If you want," she said, and walked up the nave and out of the church. Nick and Carlton looked at each other as Chad ran up. "Just a basement," he said sadly. "No dungeons, not even a place to bury any princes. Only I guess in this church it would be a princess, wouldn't it?" He looked expectantly at Carlton, and Nick introduced them.

"We're going to lunch with Carl and his wife; it turns out she's an old friend of mine, from college."

Chad's face fell. "Can't I go riding?"

"Yes; after lunch. That was a promise. I hope you won't be too bored at lunch; we'll try to keep it short."

"Thanks," said Chad gravely. "Do you own horses, too?" he asked Carlton.

"Several," Carlton said. "I'll show them to you, if you like."

"That would be great. Is it far?"

"Not too far. Sterling Farms in Middleburg." He took a business card from his pocket. "I'll draw you a map," he said to Nick, and quickly sketched a few roads. "Half an hour at most. I'll see you there."

Sybille was standing beside Nick's car, staring into the distance. As they drove away, she spoke without looking at him. "I'd hoped we could have the whole day, the three of us."

"We'll have a good part of it," said Nick. He was feeling elated and a little lightheaded, and he drove at high speed over the quiet roads. When he turned in at the stone gates with STERLING FARMS embedded in bronze plates, he had a strange feeling of watching himself do something that would change his life. And then he was pulling up beside Carlton's car in the circular driveway. He had a quick impression of a wonderful house, old and settled, before the front door opened and Valerie stood there, shading her eyes with her hand.

Nick leaped from the car and went to her. "It's good to see you," he said, and found her hand in his.

Chapter
17

hey drove to the restaurant in separate cars, and, during the short trip, Nick still heard Valerie's low voice, as if she sat beside him. "So strange," she had murmured as he held her hand at her front door. "I never pictured you anywhere but California. Are you here for long?"

"We came out for the day. I'm living in Washington now."

Her eyes widened. "Your whole life must have changed."

"Several times," he said, and they exchanged a long, steady look. She was far lovelier, Nick thought, than the college girl he remembered. Her figure was as slender, her bearing as regal, but her tawny hair was more golden and less wild than in his memory. Twelve years had enhanced her beauty; it seemed to Nick that she was smoother, more finished, as if she were the center of a painting.

"Val, Nick wants to go to lunch," Carlton said. "Do we have time to go into town?"

"Yes." She was still looking at Nick. "I'd like that." She looked away, and saw Chad.

"My son," Nick said. "Chad Fielding, Valerie Sterling."

"I've wanted to meet you for a long time," Valerie said with a smile, and they shook hands.

"If we're going..." Sybille said brusquely, and then they all moved apart at once. Nick took Sybille and Chad in his car, and Valerie drove with Carlton, and in a few minutes they met again at the Windsor Inn, where they were led to a large round table in a room at the back, overlooking a garden.

The room was small and homey, paneled with dark woods, its tall draped windows set behind deep sills. A chandelier hung from the high ceiling, bookshelves extended above the doorways, and soft wing chairs surrounded the well-worn wood tables. A place for lovers, Nick thought. The Windsor Inn, perched on Middleburg's main street in the midst of the modern world, preserved the atmosphere and leisurely pace of an earlier time. It was a place for lovers to linger over dinner, talking in low tones and watching the dancing flames in the fireplace before ascending the stairs to the suites on the upper floor.

Instead, Nick sat at a round table near the fire with Sybille and Carlton Sterling on his right, Chad on his left, and, beside Chad, Valerie. When Nick glanced at her, their eyes met over Chad's head. More beautiful, Nick thought again, but one thing was the same: she still shifted her position frequently, and gestured as she spoke. He wondered if that was the restlessness he remembered or a new nervousness.

He wondered if she was happy.

"Sybille told me about her church at the hunt breakfast," Carlton was saying. "The day I wasn't feeling well and never got to the hunt. I've been meaning to look at it for months, and never had a chance until today. It's incredible, Val, especially the way it's all by itself, as if someone just set it down in the middle of the fields."

"It sounds incredible." Valerie put aside her menu. "What else will you have there, Sybille?"

"What else?" Sybille repeated sharply.

"You must have something in mind. I can't imagine you'd build a church in the middle of the fields and leave it there without building anything else. It sounds to me like the beginning of a town. Isn't that how it was done in Colonial times? First the church, then the school, then the town hall."

Sybille shook her head. "I built a church because I believe in Lily; I haven't thought beyond that."

There was a small silence. It made Carlton uncomfortable. "How was it built?" he asked. "Was it all donations? If your Lily did that, in such a short time, she must be remarkable. I'll have to watch her some-time."

"It was all donations," Sybille said. "Seven million dollars so far, and we'll have the rest soon. Of course she's remarkable, even though Nick doesn't think so. He canceled her show."

"Not your style?" Carlton asked Nick.

"It isn't what I have in mind for our network," Nick replied briefly.

"What did you have in mind?" Valerie asked.

"Something tougher and more interesting. At least that's what we're trying to do. We won't appeal to everybody, but we'd rather do what we think we can do best, and what we don't do best are programs full of easy explanations. We'll have a lot of entertainment, a lot of history, a fair bit of science, book reviews, and some different kinds of news programs that, I hope, have more integrity than our competition."

"But not religion," Valerie said.

"Our own." He smiled. "We'll pray we make it against all the competition. But that's all. There are plenty of stations offering preachers for just about any belief you can think of, and that's fine with me. Sybille does what she does very well; it's just not for us."

"Even if they bring in big audiences?"

"The world is full of audiences. All we can do is try to find the right one for us."

"I thought stations wanted to be right for the largest audience."

He smiled again. "We're trying to turn that around. We're putting ourselves and our ideas out there, and if there are any takers we'll do all right. If not, I may have to find another job."

"You mean you won't change your ideas or pretend to be something you're not," Valerie said.

Their eyes held. "I think we've had this discussion before," he said.

"We should order," Sybille cut in. She had been watching them as they spoke to each other. It was not possible that they would take up again after so long; she would not tolerate it. "If Chad wants to ride this afternoon, we'll have to hurry."

"Fine with me," Carlton said, gesturing to the waitress. "I don't want to stay long, either."

Nick turned to Chad. "Have you decided what you want for lunch?"

Chad nodded and looked up at the waitress. "Roasted peppers with goat cheese in oil, please, and chicken chausseur."

Carlton stared at him. Valerie's eyes danced. "I'll have the same. I like your taste."

"My dad taught me," Chad said. "We eat out a lot." He had been watching Valerie with fascination since the moment they met; she was so beautiful he wanted to look at her forever, and her voice was wonderful, low and soft—like a kiss, Chad thought, trying to find words to describe it; or like she was putting her arms around you and holding you tight.

"But doesn't your dad cook?" Valerie asked while the others were ordering. "He used to, when we were in college. He was the best cook I knew."

"Sometimes he does, but he's awful busy. Were you friends in college?"

"Yes. Good friends. We had a lot of fun together."

"So how come you aren't now?"

"We went different directions; your dad stayed in California and I moved to New York."

"But you could write letters."

She nodded. "We could. I'm sorry we didn't."

"Me too," Chad said boldly. He tried to think of something else to say, to keep her from talking to anybody else. She'd knelt and kissed him when they met, and given him a hug, saying she'd wanted to meet him for a long time, and how handsome he was and how much he looked like his dad, and Chad thought she was just the kind of person he wished his dad would marry: somebody with a nice laugh who didn't hate to be touched. She was already married, though. But she could get divorced; lots of people did. And Valerie's husband didn't talk much; he was probably boring to live with. "Did Dad cook for you in college?" he asked.

"Sure," said Valerie, smiling. "I didn't know how—I still don't, in fact—so he had to do it all."

"You must know how. All mothers do."

"But I'm not a mother."

"You're not?" He shot another look at Carlton.

"Not yet. Tell me about going to restaurants. Which kind do you like best?"

"Chinese and Italian and French and seafood and hamburgers and pizza. We'll try anything."

Valerie laughed. "A pair of iron stomachs. What else do you do together?"

"Oh, stuff. Frisbee and hitting a soft ball, and hiking, and we read together, and we go to movies and plays, and concerts sometimes at the—you know that place, the Kennedy Center, with this huge black head, like a hundred feet high, of President Kennedy?"

"A bronze head, and not quite a hundred feet, but who's counting?"

"Right. We go there; I like the bronze head. And all the lights."

"You do a lot together," Valerie said, and there was a wistful note in her voice.

"Yeh, Dad makes all these plans. He goes out a lot, though; he has all these women he takes places, and then I stay with Elena and Manuel. They're okay, they're just not as good as Dad."

Valerie nodded, her eyes thoughtful.

"I ride horses, too," Chad said, trying to keep Valerie's attention. "There's no room for any where we live, but Mother asks me, sometimes. How many horses do you have?"

"Eight. And we board twelve more for our neighbors. Do you like to ride?"

"Yeh, lots. Do you ride all eight of them?"

"One at a time," said Valerie with a grin.

Chad grinned back. "Are they all different?"

"Every one."

"Who's your favorite?"

"Oh, a sassy one named Kate. I named her for a character in a Shakespeare play. She's very stubborn, but she's proud and smart and trustworthy, and I really love her best of all."

Valerie saw Nick watching her and knew he had heard her. "Perhaps you'd like to ride at Sterling Farms someday," she said, both to Chad and to him.

"Oh, yeh!" Chad cried.

"I don't ride much," Nick said. "But if we could find a way, of course Chad could."

"My dad works a lot," Chad said to Valerie, thinking his dad hadn't been very nice about the invitation. "You know, he owns this television network and he's the most important person there, and he's got to be there a lot. At night too, sometimes."

Valerie nodded gravely. "It's hard work, running a television network."

"He comes home for dinner, though, and we read and talk and stuff, and then lots of times he goes back to work. He did that at Omega too. There's always something going on around our house."

Valerie smiled. "But don't you like that? There's never enough going on around mine. I'm always looking for something new and different and exciting."

"Try moving across the country. That's different and exciting."

"Different and good?"

"Yeh. I thought it wouldn't be—like, I didn't want to go, from San Jose?—but it's okay. It's great. School's great. And our house is great; you should see it. And Georgetown is great."

"You live in Georgetown?"

He nodded again. "N Street. You could come and visit sometime."

Valerie met Nick's eyes. "I don't get to Washington as often as I'd like."

"It would be something new and different," Chad said boldly. "Like you're always looking for."

"The trouble with new and different," said Nick, "is that nothing stays new or different very long. As soon as they become old and familiar, they have to be replaced."

"That's a little judgmental, don't you think?" said Valerie. Her voice was light, but Nick saw the quick scorn in her eyes and knew she was thinking he had not changed: still narrow-minded and stuffy and bound to his work as she had thought him before. But why should I have changed? he asked himself. She hasn't; she's still looking for something to happen, something to keep her from being bored and restless.

We should never try to recapture the past, he reflected. We might find it was exactly as we remembered it.

He wondered why he had been so insistent on meeting Valerie again. The surprise, he thought. The unexpectedness of discovering that their lives had overlapped, against all odds; that they could meet once more and part once more, this time in uncomplicated fashion, as casual acquaintances; no more.

Bullshit, he told himself. I wanted to see her because I've never been able to forget her.

But now that was finally over: this meeting had finished off the tag ends of his adolescent fantasies. As soon as they could get out of here, Chad would have his ride, and then they'd go home. They'd read the Sunday papers and sit together while Chad ate dinner, and then Nick would go out with a pretty, quick-witted, hardworking magazine editor who had a busy life and didn't worry about being bored.

A deep sadness filled him. It could have been different, he thought involuntarily. And he knew that his dreams were far more than adolescent fantasies, and that, whatever happened in the life he was making, he would not so easily wipe them out. He looked at Valerie. She was listening to Chad talk about school, and her attention was completely on him, absorbed in tales of fifth grade and soccer and computer programs. It could have been different, he thought again. Then he pulled his thoughts back, and turned to Sybille. She could get them to the end of the meal with talk about herself. "Tell us more about your church," he said.

At five o'clock, after Chad and Nick had left her farm, Sybille sat in the living room of her house, furnished by the previous owner in checks and plaids she hated but had not yet replaced because she thought she would be buying a bigger place any day. She had tried to get the two of them to stay, so she would not be alone for the evening. Lily was in bed with a cold, and Sybille would have no one to talk to, but Nick had insisted on leaving. A date, probably, Sybille fumed. That's all he cares about. Women.

She thought again about their lunch. Nothing would come of it. Valerie was married, and, in any event, Nick had outgrown her. But the signals had been mixed, and she couldn't be sure. I should be, she thought; after all, I understand the two of them perfectly.

But after ten minutes of thinking about it and imagining the two of them together, leaving her out, she was so tense and angry, and frantic at the silence, that she telephoned Floyd Bassington and told him he had to come over.

He arrived half an hour later and accepted the weak drink she offered him. "You always remember," he said, sitting beside her on the sofa. "So many people prefer not to think of someone's weak heart; they don't like to think of illness at all."

"You're not ill, not to me," Sybille murmured. "You're one of the strongest, most dedicated men I know."

He smiled and raised his glass to her. He was short and square and sat upright in a corner of the sofa, as if to make himself taller. With his bent nose, broken in high-school wrestling, his full lips beneath a heavy mustache as gray as his hair, and his thick, black-rimmed glasses, he had the look of someone who enjoyed attention, an actor, perhaps, or a politician. In fact he had been a minister in a prominent church in Chicago until, at fifty-seven, he had been discovered in the bed of Evaline Massy, his choir director, by Olaf Massy, her husband and the president of the board of directors of Floyd's church. Olaf Massy, energized by fury, investigated Floyd with dogged persistence, and found evidence of many women, and of embezzling: a bank account with close to two hundred thousand dollars, patiently, methodically added to over thirty respectable years.

Floyd Bassington retired from his pulpit. His wife divorced him, and he bought a small house in Alexandria, Virginia, where his son's family lived. He told his new neighbors an elaborate tale of a massive heart attack and orders from his doctor to retire and live quietly, with no stress, and he began to garden. He gardened for a year until he thought he would go mad from boredom and insects and his grand-children, who had seemed so charming from a distance. Finally, des-perate, he took up volunteer work in shelters for the homeless. In the next year he became known for his good works, and was widely ad-mired for coming out of retirement and risking another heart attack to help others. He had met Sybille at a party in Leesburg. Lily Grace had been there, too, and Floyd had been attracted to both of them: the one so strong and sophisticated; the other all goodness and innocence.

"You said you were troubled," Floyd said. He sipped his weak drink, wondering if he could trust Sybille with the truth about his healthy heart so he might have a decent Scotch and water, and sat back in the air-conditioned chill that kept the July heat at bay. He admired the checks and plaids of the living room. Elegant and sharp, he thought; like Sybille. He had been there twice before, a guest at her dinner parties, but this was quite different: just the two of them, quiet, friendly, one needing help, the other poised to give it. "How are you troubled, and how may I help?"

"I have a great many plans," Sybille said. She leaned toward him intently. "I'm afraid they may be too grand. I'm afraid I might seem ambitious when what I really want is to bring happiness and peace to large numbers of people."

Floyd contemplated her. "Large numbers. Are you talking about your church at Culpeper?"

"Cathedral. The Cathedral of Joy. Yes, but more; so much more. No one has any idea"—her voice faltered, then went on—"no one knows what I'm thinking of—I have no one close enough—it involves so much money, you see, it terrifies me; I can barely talk about it, even to you." She paused, as if marshaling her courage. "Floyd, I want to build a town around the cathedral. A real town; a place for thousands, hundreds of thousands, to visit. They could come for an hour, a day, a week, for as long as they need—with their families—to listen to Lily preach, to meditate, to relax with sports and games, to buy whatever they want in dozens of shops, to spend their time close to nature, away from the pressures and temptations of their everyday lives."

There was a silence. "My dear," said Floyd at last. He put down his drink, and Sybille refilled it from a decanter on the coffee table; it was stronger than before. "My dear. Ambitious indeed."

"Too ambitious," Sybille breathed. Her eyes were filled with apprehension. "Too much money, too much effort...does it show ambition more than goodness?"

"No, no, that was not what I meant. How could I mean that, when you've told me your only reason for building this town is to bring happiness and peace...?"

Sybille nodded. "You do understand. But you're so good, Floyd; you don't know how many people are jealous of me and want to stop me. And they may succeed. I can't do this alone. I'm a very good businesswoman, you know: I usually get what I want, even if I have to be hard and cruel, sometimes underhanded—"

"Nonsense; why do you speak of yourself this way? I believe that you're a good businesswoman, I believe that you're strong when you need to be. Certainly I believe that. But nothing else."

Tears filled Sybille's eyes; two of them spilled over and lay like glistening jewels on her olive skin. She touched her handkerchief to them. "I never cry," she said with an apologetic smile. "Strong businesswomen aren't allowed to, you know. But it isn't often that someone is as generous as you. Thank you, Floyd. I need to talk to someone like you now and then, to keep my perspective."

"Whenever you wish. We don't stop being ministers, my dear, just because we retire from a pulpit; we always are here for those who need us."

"I need you," Sybille whispered, but it came out barely a breath.

"What was that?" Floyd bent closer.

She shook her head. "Nothing. I shouldn't say...I don't allow myself weaknesses. I've learned over the years to do what I have to do; you only see the good in people, Floyd, but there's no way I could get anywhere without doing some things that aren't really me. People have said I'm tough, even ruthless, and I think they may be right. Not inside, but on the surface, you know; I can compete with anyone. I'm always sick, later, if I've hurt someone in a business deal or any other time; I can't bear it when I succeed at someone else's expense. I don't set out to do it, but sometimes things happen—"

"Sybille." Floyd put down his drink and slid along the couch until he could hold her hand. His blunt fingers were cold from holding his glass. "We can talk about this town you want to build, we can talk about the great sums of money you seem to be worrying about, we can talk of many things; but you must stop castigating yourself. I have an instinctive understanding of people, and I know you would never be ruthless. Things happen, as you say, and we may be forced to behave in ways we might not have planned from the beginning, but it is not our fault. Intention is what matters, and your intentions are noble. Don't shake your head at me, you foolish girl. I know you better than you know yourself. Now, tell me the name of this town you want to build."

"Oh." She laughed slightly. "I'd almost forgotten it. I want to call it Graceville."

"Ah. Well named. Lily must be pleased."

"Yes, but overwhelmed too. And afraid. And so am I, every time I think of it. It's too big for one person, Floyd. You're right; I'm worried about the money; all that we'd spend and the huge amounts that would come in. There's just too much to think about. I can't do it alone. I need someone to help me with it, to advise me, to stand by me when I'm accused of..." She began to tremble. "...of competing... with...God..."

"Good Lord! Who dared to say that to you?"

"Some ministers—I won't give you their names, you mustn't ask me—and some financial consultants, when I mentioned the idea of a town. Nothing specific, I didn't even give a location, I just said how wonderful it would be to provide people with peace and quiet and time for contemplation, and the chance to meet others with the same needs."

"And you were mocked."

She nodded, her head lowered.

Floyd put his hand beneath her chin and raised her head until she was looking at him. Her pale-blue eyes were unwavering and he thought he had never seen such pure honesty and longing for understanding. A strong, successful businesswoman making her way in a man's world, yet starved for love and a helping hand. And so innocent she had no idea how much money might be raked in through this town of hers. It was proof, Floyd thought, if he ever had needed it, that women might act tough, but, beneath their striped suits and cool facades, they would always be more fearful and vulnerable and naive than men.

Floyd felt a surge of power. With Sybille's small, sharp chin trembling slightly in his fingers, he exulted in his superiority, his strength, his brilliance. "I'll help you, Sybille," he said, his voice resonant and deep. "If that was what you called me for tonight, to ask me that, my answer is yes. I would be privileged to help you, and no one will accuse us of overweening pride or ambition, because what we do will be for the good of others, not for our own satisfaction or to line our pockets."

"Oh, no. Not that. Never." She let out her breath in a long sigh. "I don't know what I would have done if you had refused to come tonight or refused to help me."

Potency coursed through Floyd; he could not contain it. "I'll never refuse you," he boomed. "I'm here; I'll always be here." His arms went around her, engulfing her, smothering her against his tweed jacket.

"No," Sybille gasped, pushing against him to come up for air. "No, I can't, Floyd."

"Can't? There's nothing we can't do, Sybille, as long as we're together. Trust me; I understand you."

"No, you don't know...oh, damn..." She put her face in her hands.

"What? What? What the hell...?"

"Floyd." Her face came up, streaked with tears. "I don't enjoy sex. I never have. I've tried, I want to. I know there's something wrong with me, but—"

"Not you!" he burst out. "Nothing wrong with you! It's the men you've known! You poor little girl, you must've hooked up with the damndest bunch of wimps this side of the Himalayas. You need a man who knows what he's doing, and knows women, and knows you." He pulled her to him again and began unbuttoning her blouse. "I'll take care of you, baby. Sweet baby, poor little baby, you've been waiting for Floyd for a long, long time."

Sybille shuddered and lay back against his arm as his short fingers laid open her blouse and slid beneath the wisp of silk that covered her breasts to grasp her nipple. A faint smile trembled on her lips.

She lay passively as Floyd pulled off her clothes, and his own, and then brought her with him to the thick rug before the sofa. She lay quietly as his hands rubbed over her and his fingers slid into her, and then, slowly, she began to move her hips. "Floyd," she whispered. She pulled his head to hers. Her lips were closed; she let him force them open with his mouth, and then, as if suddenly discovering passion, she thrust her tongue sharply against his. He reared up. "See?" he cried hoarsely. "See what you can do?" He swung a leg over her. "Sybille!" he cried jubilantly. "You're mine!"

Lily's white dress glowed like a beacon on the altar of the Cathedral of Joy. Her small face was pale, her hands fluttered like tiny birds when she gestured to emphasize a point. She stood on a box behind the marble pulpit. Sybille had told her to do that so everyone could see more of her. "They must feel your power," she said, and showed Lily how to lean forward toward the audience: shining in her white dress like a brilliant sun above them.

"What we are searching for," Lily proclaimed, her voice high and youthful in the cavernous, still-unfinished church, "is ourselves, the hidden selves buried inside us—buried, invisible, inaccessible *for the moment*—waiting to be discovered."

The church was full: a thousand men, women and children who came from as far away as Maryland, Pennsylvania and West Virginia to hear Lily preach. Those who could not come watched the service on television; still others saw it on tape, during the week. Lily knew they were watching: they sent letters, postcards, small gifts, and money.

Cameramen trained their television cameras on Lily, and on her parishioners, from four strategic unobtrusive spots. In the studio in Fairfax, the director chose which of the four should be broadcast at each moment of "The Hour of Grace." Most of the time, Lily was on the screen, devout and virginal, her makeup giving her a scrubbed, sweetly pretty look. But when the director saw a parishioner touch a handkerchief to tearful eyes, or a face openmouthed in admiration, or a man nodding agreement, he would issue a command to the technical director, who punched a button which brought that picture to the screens of millions of viewers, making them feel they too were in those pews, listening, absorbing, nodding, worshiping, weeping.

"What can you do?" Lily asked her congregation. "In this confusing world of contradictory signals—contradictory and often dangerous if you misunderstand them—from your employers, your friends, and those who govern, even from your relatives...what can you do to make sense of the world?

"*To make sense of the world.* It sounds so simple, but it's so difficult, when you are already burdened with finding enough time for home and family and job, for a night out with friends, for reading a newspaper or watching a television newscast to give you clues about the world you live in. You are so busy...there are so many demands on you...how can you make sense of the world?

"You begin to think you can't; you think you must leave it to the experts. You think they have more time than you to look around, to learn. You think they know more than you. And after a while you just let them run things. You think you're not as good as they are; they run the world; you just live in it.

"*That is not true!* You are every bit as good as they are! God has made you every bit as smart; every bit as wise as any other person in the world! Listen to me! I know you! I've met you and talked with you in your homes; I've held your children in my lap; I've eaten at your tables. You are strong and good; there is so much in you to love; there is so much wisdom and thoughtfulness in you that you could do any job, fill any position in the world! But you do not know this.

"*You are afraid to know it.*

"Why are you afraid? What keeps you from going inside yourself and discovering *and unlocking* that other, hidden self *that I know is there because I have seen it?*

"You are afraid of the unknown. You are afraid that what you discover may change your life, and it seems more comfortable to stay with what you know. Or you are afraid that the person hidden within you is not the wise person you long for, but an ignorant person; perhaps even an evil one. You do not trust yourself, the self you have not yet met."

Lily held out her hands to her parishioners. They were absolutely silent, holding their breath, waiting.

"Trust yourselves! Believe in yourselves, in the wisdom and goodness within you that God puts in all His creatures! And if you cannot yet believe, if you cannot yet trust yourself, trust me! Believe in me! I *know* what you are capable of! I know what lies ahead for you—self-discovery, joy, wisdom, love! I know there is nothing you cannot do or understand or share with another! Trust me, believe in me, help me to help you!"

A young man in the audience rose to his feet and stumbled down the aisle. "Reverend!" he sobbed. "Reverend Lily, I trust you, I believe in you, I love you!" He fell on his knees at the base of the marble steps, holding out his hands to Lily, as hers were held out to him, and all one thousand parishioners.

In the Fairfax studios, the director snapped out camera numbers and the screen flickered with images: Lily stretching out her arms, smiling, tears in her eyes; the young man reaching up to her, tears streaking his cheeks; others standing in their pews, making their way to the aisles, and down the aisles, to kneel on the marble steps. Some were crying, others were excited, a few were ecstatic.

"I'll help you!" cried an elderly woman. She began to climb the marble steps, but in that instant two dark-suited young men, clean-cut and handsome, stepped forward and firmly took her by the arms, moving her back with the others. "Oh, I'm sorry!" she cried. "I got carried away..." She opened her purse. "I wanted to give Reverend Lily money, to help her finish the cathedral and visit people and do good! It's all right, isn't it, Reverend Lily? You won't say no! I want to help!"

Lily's color rose; this was the part she hated. "You are blessed," she said, her voice reverberating almost sadly through the church. She gestured with her hand to a carved column about three feet high and open at the top. "For those who wish to help . . ." she whispered.

"Thank you!" exclaimed the woman. "God bless you!" She dropped her money into the column. Others followed. Lily turned to speak directly into one of the cameras; her voice was a little higher than usual, and a little mechanical. "It is good to help; it is the first step in unlocking the self within you. And it is good to receive. I cannot refuse your help, not the youngest one who would help, or the oldest, not the smallest contribution or the largest. Each is precious; each is to me like a hand held out from you to take my hand, to become my partner, to become my beloved friend. It doesn't matter how little or how much you send; you send what you can spare; you must not take from your families. Everything you send touches my heart and helps me bring to everyone the joy of finding that self you long for, and pray for, and dream of, and love . . . as I love you. Good night, my beloved friends; I send you my blessings, God's blessings, for the days until we touch each other again."

An organ chord sounded and Lily began to sing; her voice was small and quavering, and a chorus behind her stood and sang with her. The camera pulled back to show her above the crowd at the foot of the marble steps. Enormous arrangements of flowers were everywhere on the altar, and glittering lights seemed to shed sparkles of gold throughout the Cathedral of Joy. Another camera turned to the crowds standing in the pews, singing with the chorus. Still singing, they slowly filed out of the church. An address appeared on the screen, and a sonorous male voice read it aloud, telling the audience to send money, or write to the Reverend Lilith Grace, saying or asking anything they wished. Then a short list of towns appeared, and the voice read it aloud, saying that was where Reverend Grace would be in the next two weeks, and anyone who wished to have her visit their home should write to the same address. One person in each town would be chosen by lot to receive Reverend Grace, and would be notified the day before she arrived.

Lily walked to the back of the altar and disappeared through a small door, where Sybille waited. She put her head on Sybille's shoulder. "I'm so tired," she murmured.

"You were inspired," Sybille said. "You might have mentioned God a few more times, but everything else was the best you've ever been."

"Did you see them?" Lily asked, raising her head, her eyes shining. "They were *happy!* They loved me, they loved what I told them; Sybille, they do need me!"

"Of course they do," Sybille said caressingly. "Their lives would be miserable without you. And there are millions of others, Lily, waiting for you. You mustn't stop now; wait until we have Graceville. All our dreams for it will come true. I promise you."

Lily nodded. "I believe you. I just wish I didn't have to—"

"But you do. And you've got to do it in a stronger voice. We can't build without money; we can't do good without money. You know that."

"Yes. Thank you, Sybille. I'm not very practical; if it weren't for you I'd only be able to help a few people at a time. I'll do whatever you say. And I'll try not to complain."

They left the church through the back door and slipped into Sybille's limousine. Sybille kept her arm around Lily and let her drowse against her shoulder while she sipped a martini and the chauffeur drove them back to Washington. So simple; when had anything been so simple? She gazed absently at the small towns and horse farms they passed. She had just that afternoon received from the accountant the total for what Lily had brought in in the first three quarters of the year. If the fourth quarter was the same—it should be better, but figure the same—the take for the year would be a nice round twenty-five million dollars.

Enough to do a lot of good for the people who most deserve it, she thought. In the darkness of the car, she curved her hand around Lily's shoulder. "You're a treasure," she said, and Lily, drowsing, snuggled closer, with love.

Tuesdays and most Fridays belonged to Carlton. He had rented the guest cottage on a friend's horse farm, and it was there that he and Sybille spent their time, from midafternoon to late at night. Once in a while, they flew in his plane to his house in the Adirondacks for a whole weekend, but only during those months when Carlton and Valerie never went to the mountains. That way he kept his two lives completely separate.

Valerie thought he was in New York on those weekends, and on Tuesdays and Fridays, meeting with friends, other investment counselors, and clients whose portfolios he managed. In fact Carlton had given up most of his clients; it was enough to manage Valerie's money, her mother's and his own. He wanted the rest of the time for his horses, and for Sybille. He knew he was obsessed with her, but he didn't know what to do about it, and he didn't spend time looking for a way out. When they were apart his hunger for her was so powerful it made him feel ill. He longed for her helplessness that contrasted so oddly with her business acumen, her soft adoration of him that made more fascinating her biting anecdotes about people in the television industry, her uninhibited sexuality that had grown over the months as she became confident he would not cause her pain.

Valerie was stunningly beautiful, the perfect hostess, the perfect wife. He loved her as much as he could love any woman, he told himself; after all, he knew he was a fairly selfish fellow, and it was difficult for him to care deeply about anyone—women had been telling him that all his life. But he was enthralled by Sybille.

It was going so well that Sybille was beginning to take it for granted. But then, on a Tuesday morning in the last week of September, in the eleventh month of their affair, he was not at the guest cottage when she arrived, nor did he call or come at all that day. She still had not heard from him by Friday, and as she drove to the cottage that afternoon she was gripped by anger and fear. When she saw his car parked discreetly at the back, in its usual place, she was so relieved she almost ran into the cottage. "I thought you'd gone away without telling me," she said. "And I'd be alone again."

He was sitting in a wicker armchair, slumped in its depths. "You know I wouldn't do that," he muttered.

Sybille stopped short, in the center of the room. "What happened?" Usually, within thirty seconds of arriving, they would be on their way to bed. This time he did not even look at her. "Well?" she demanded. "Are you going to tell me?"

He looked up at her. "You don't like to hear people's problems," he said shrewdly.

"Not everybody's, but I want to hear yours. Maybe I can help. Carl, what happened?"

After a moment, he shrugged and forced out the words. "I lost... some money. In the market. Got careless, didn't pay attention; thinking of you—" He saw her stiffen, and said quickly, "Not your fault;

I'm not blaming you. There isn't anybody to blame; just me. That's the worst, you know: nobody to dump on; it was all me. I made some stupid half-ass moves, my timing was off. I thought I had a sure thing, but it was bad information . . . and then the stock took a dive . . ."

"When?"

"Monday afternoon. That's where I was Tuesday: in New York, watching my money go down the fucking drain."

"How much?"

"Not only mine. Christ, that would have been bad enough. But it was Valerie's and her mother's too; their whole goddam motherfucking portfolios blown to hell and gone."

Sybille felt a high-pitched thrill of excitement. "Valerie's? All Valerie's money? Gone?"

"Don't overdo it," he snapped.

"How much was it?"

"All together, hers, her mother's and mine, almost fifteen million."

A long silence fell in the cottage. Sybille began to walk back and forth in the small room. *All her money. It's gone. She doesn't have any money. It's gone. She's got nothing.*

"Can't you sit down?" demanded Carlton.

She shook her head, pacing and pacing, so excited she could not stop. Glee bubbled in her throat. "I'm thinking about what we can do."

"For Christ's sake, *we* can find *me* fifteen million to replace what I lost." His voice rose; his eyes were burning. "There's nothing you can do, and all I can do is start selling everything I own. And tell Val. How the hell do I tell Val?" He slumped deeper in the chair. "Her father trusted me; I managed his money. Did a damn good job, too. Everybody trusted me. Everybody thought I was the cat's fat ass when it came to money; never let anything by me. Christ. How the fuck— how the *fuck?*—could I do that? Lost my touch, lost the money; shit, I'll have to sell the horses, the farm, my plane . . . and tell Val. The apartment in New York, the paintings, Christ, a goddam fortune in paintings . . . I had everything—you know? *everything!*—and now most of it'll be gone. And I have to tell Val."

Sybille paced. She was hot and cold, intoxicated, rapturous. Her gaze darted everywhere, as if she were seeing the world for the first time. At the windows, she paused. *Don't go too fast. Think about this. She's in my power; I can decide her future.* She gazed through the windows. There were the pastures and fields of Virginia, green-gold in the morning light. Acres of land, stretching to the horizon. Stretching to Culpeper, where, beside the Cathedral of Joy, there would be a town called Graceville.

"Carl," said Sybille softly. An idea was growing in her mind, growing, spreading like a great tree. There was no limit to how far it could grow.

She pulled a wicker chair close to Carlton and sat down, her knees almost touching his. "Carl, you haven't lost me. I'm here. I'm going to help you."

He shook his head.

"Carl, listen to me. Look at me. I have an idea."

He looked at her from beneath reddened lids. He was unshaven, and it occurred to her that he had probably been up all night.

"Are you listening?" she asked.

He nodded.

"You know my cathedral; you've been there." She waited. "Yes?"

"For Christ's sake, of course I know it. You were there."

"I haven't told you about Graceville."

He looked at her. "Never heard of it."

"It doesn't exist yet. Now listen. Do you know how the cathedral was built?"

"Donations. You said seven million—three more to come."

"Good; you remember. The money was given to the Hour of Grace Foundation. Tax-deductible contributions to a nonprofit religious institution run by a board of directors headed by a retired minister, a very respectable man named Floyd Bassington."

"For Christ's sake, Sybille, I haven't got time—"

"Damn it, listen to me; when have I ever wasted your time? The treasurer of the board is Monte James, president of James Trust and Savings; the vice-president and secretary is Arch Warman, president of Warman Developers and Contractors. The board pays me to produce 'The Hour of Grace.' The board takes in all contributions to 'The Hour of Grace,' and expends them. The board is planning to build a town called Graceville on land it will buy adjoining the two acres it bought for the Cathedral of Joy."

Carlton was frowning. "They spend the money any way they want? No strings? No oversight committee?"

Sybille nodded approvingly. Sometimes Carl was very quick. "Yes," she said.

"And you've got a bank president and a developer."

"He's also a contractor."

Their eyes met. "What do you have in mind?" Carl asked.

"I think the board will ask you to be a shareholder in a development company that will buy the land we need for Graceville. The market price for that land is about ten thousand dollars an acre. If you buy it for that—thirteen hundred acres for thirteen million dollars—I think the board will buy the land from you for the price you quote them as a package. Say, thirty million."

Carlton was staring at her. A profit of seventeen million... "Where do I get the thirteen million to buy the land?"

"Can you raise it? Sell the rest of your portfolio, borrow on those assets you were talking about—your New York apartment, Sterling Farms, your paintings...?"

Slowly, he said, "Just about." He nodded twice, "And I'd get thirty million when I sell the land to the board."

Sybille smiled faintly. "Only twenty-six, and it will take about three months. Floyd and Monte and Arch each get one, and I get one, for our devoted efforts on your behalf. That leaves you thirteen for Valerie's portfolio, and her mother's, and yours, and another thirteen to pay off the notes or mortgages you signed to raise the money."

"Back where I started."

"With no one knowing."

His face closed in. "I'm not sure... I don't much like it."

"Neither do I," she said quickly. "I'd rather do everything openly, honestly; I don't like some of the things I have to do; they keep me awake at night, because I know this isn't really me. But, Carl, I can do so much good with Graceville; what difference does it make how we get the money, when good will come of it? It's good for you too."

"Where do you get thirty million to buy the land from me?"

"Donations. We're raising a hundred and fifty million to cover the start-up cost for Graceville. Last year Lily brought in over twenty-five million; this year it will be close to thirty, and next year we should hit seventy-five. But we'll need every penny of it."

He was staring at her. "You're doing this with one show?"

"She's on twice a week."

"And people send in..."

"We've just begun; we're not even close to Swaggart and Jim and Tammy Bakker. But we'll leave them behind, they can't compare with Lily."

"How much..." He cleared his throat. "You said one hundred and fifty million for the town."

"Yes, but we'll take in far more before it's finished. The rest we need for producing 'The Hour of Grace,' which includes my salary as producer, and my expenses; paying the board its salaries, office space, cars, a corporate plane . . . it's expensive to keep an expanding organization going, Carl."

He fell silent. "The board," he said at last. "You trust them?"

"They're deeply committed to building Graceville and bringing peace and joy to Lily's followers. Floyd, the president of the board, is a religious man who says he has a weak heart. I checked on him and he was fired for a few other weaknesses, but he's perfect for the Hour of Grace Foundation; devoted and energetic. Monte James will make the construction loans to the Foundation so the board can pay Arch Warman to build the town; both of them are as deeply committed as Floyd."

"And you?"

"Of course."

"No, I meant, what position do you have on the board?"

"None," Sybille said promptly. "I work behind the scenes. I've done it for so long it's where I'm happiest."

"I don't believe you."

"Oh, Carl, what difference does it make? I have no position on the board, my name isn't connected with the board or the Foundation. Are we going to discuss the development company you're going to invest in?"

"I haven't said I'll do it."

"What are you waiting for? Where else will you make a quick thirteen million, Carl, with no one knowing?" She jumped up and went to the door. "I'm going home. If you want to call me . . ."

"Wait! Damn it, Sybille, I didn't say . . ." He stood and began to pace the same path around the room Sybille had taken earlier. "When would you need the money?"

"Early December. Two months from now. It will probably take you most of that time to raise it. Three months, if absolutely necessary. Monte is talking to the owners of the land; he could drag it out, but I don't want to go past the first of the year."

"Three months. I could manage that." He took a few more steps, then looked at her across the room. "Why would you do this for me?"

"Oh, Carl, for so many reasons. I love you; you know that. I'd do anything within my power to get you out of this."

"And?"

"It's a good match. You get a quick thirteen million profit and we can always use the extra four for spending money."

He focused on her. "And?"

After a moment, she sighed. "You'd never leave Valerie destitute. If she gets her money back, she can be on her own; she's good at that. And you can come to me with a clear conscience."

"Come to you. With a clear conscience."

"Why not?" She held her voice steady while beneath it excitement rippled through her. *Sybille Sterling. Mrs. Carlton Sterling. Sybille Sterling of Sterling Farms.* "A straight business deal," she said, and then her voice dropped further, to a husky passion. "Your mistakes covered up without a trace, Lily and Graceville bringing in a nice income, and the two of us together. Oh, Carl, what could be more perfect? To be together after all these months of waiting. Wonderful months," she added quickly. "The most wonderful months of my life, when I knew that I could really love, and be loved, and not be afraid. When you helped me grow up. When you brought me to life." She paused and let the silence draw out. "I know I shouldn't be greedy; I know I should be satisfied with whatever joy I can get. But we've talked about being together, Carl, we've talked about it, and waited . . . so long . . ."

He was silent. Her voice etched itself into his thoughts like sweet acid. Yes, they'd talked about it. He dreamed about it. He fantasized about it while stocks were being analyzed, while he rode his horse, while he drove around his farm. He thought about her when he was eating, when he was dressing and undressing, when he was making love to Valerie.

"Carl," she said very softly. "Let me give you the kind of joy you've given me . . . a new life . . ." Her voice wrapped itself about him as if it were her legs twined around his hips. Everything else fell away and he gazed at her as if they had just arrived at the cottage after being separated for several days. "Sybille; Christ it's been a week." He strode across the room and swept her up in his arms. "God, I've missed you," he said.

By Christmas, in the midst of parties and house guests, Carlton and Valerie were barely speaking to each other. Carlton was tense and withdrawn, sleeping badly, eating sporadically, and convincing himself that their frenzied schedule would keep Valerie from noticing any of it. But Valerie noticed, enough to challenge his moodiness more than once before pulling away from him. She was too busy running Sterling Farms and their entertaining to probe too deeply. She was sure he was having an affair with someone—he had been careless a few times in talking about his trips to Manhattan, and there had been other clues—

but she didn't know who it was, and didn't want to know. They had too many other things to talk about, starting with their marriage. If they ever found time, she thought: these days, the most they talked about was what time the next party would begin.

Carlton watched her lost in her own thoughts, and went into a panic. If she was angry at him for some reason she might kick him out, or demand a divorce, which would require opening up all their finances. Even if she didn't want a divorce, if she no longer felt close to him she might decide to manage her own money. He felt immobilized with fear as the days slipped through his fingers, and he and Valerie drifted farther apart. And then her mother came to visit, and he envisioned the two of them plotting together, watching him with suspicion. One of these days, they'd sit him down and demand an accounting of their finances; he could imagine the whole conversation.

His frenzy grew, so that when Valerie told him, the day before Christmas, that she wanted the two of them to get away for a while, he had no idea what she was talking about. "You don't want to be here for the holidays? Why not? What's the matter with being here?"

"Nothing, if we were alone. I'm tired of fighting the crowds for a little time with you, Carl. I think we need a vacation from the farm and everyone on it."

"We can't leave; we can't tell everyone—"

"I know; we're stuck for now. But I want to go somewhere after the first of the year. Just the two of us."

He thought about it. "I might be able to do it then; if not right after the first, at least by the middle of January."

"No," she said firmly. "That's not good enough. I don't want to wait. We need this, Carl, and you know it."

He shrugged. He couldn't leave. He had to keep an eye on Sybille; he had to know what was happening. "We could go to New York, if you want. I could check with the office once in a while, and the rest of the time we'll do dinner and the theater with the Stevensons and the Gramsons and the—"

"Carl, I said alone. We'll never get anywhere if you keep making parties wherever you go. Either we have a marriage worth talking about or we don't. And I'm not going to wait to find out."

Those were the words he had dreaded most. "For God's sake, of course we have a marriage. What is it you want, Val? I'll do anything you want; just don't threaten me."

Her eyebrows rose. "I wasn't threatening; I was saying I can't wait months to talk. I told you what I want: to go somewhere quiet where we don't have a mob at every meal, and get reacquainted, and make love, and ignore the rest of the world. I don't think that's a lot to ask; you can call it a New Year's present."

Carlton put his arms around her so she could not see his face. "It sounds wonderful. Where would you like to go?"

"To the mountains. Wouldn't you like that?"

"Yes," he replied after the tiniest hesitation. "Especially if it makes you happy. We'll leave right after the first of the year." His arms tightened around her. "A week in the Adirondacks, away from the rest of the world."

Chapter
18

he house was on its own small lake a few miles from Lake Placid, its back against the pine forest, its broad front porch facing a narrow stretch of beach. Built of huge logs, with a high, pitched roof and wide stone fireplace, the house had three bedrooms, and Carlton managed to fill two of them with the group he put together for the trip.

"Alex and Betsy Tarrant; they asked to come along and I couldn't turn them down," he told Valerie as they were leaving for the airport. "They won't get in our way, and you've always liked them."

Valerie had never liked Betsy, but she let it pass. "This was going to be just the two of us," she said quietly.

"I know, Val, and I'm sorry. It just happened. We won't pay attention to them. They can go off by themselves."

Valerie did not respond. On the flight to Lake Placid she told Alex to sit up front with Carlton, and she sat behind them with Betsy, letting her talk about herself. She should have known this would happen. Carlton never took quiet trips if he could help it; he always surrounded himself with a group, even for a weekend in Washington or New York. There was no reason to think he had invited the Tarrants because he was nervous, though he seemed more distracted and jumpy than she could ever remember; this was just his way. And after all, she told herself, this was a pretty small group for Carlton. They'd still have plenty of time to talk.

They landed at the Lake Placid airport, and drove to the house in the Wagoneer they kept garaged there. Valerie discussed meals with the housekeeper, who lived in Lake Placid; Carlton and the mainte- nance man walked through the house, talking about a small leak in the roof and a broken pipe that had been repaired the week before. The Tarrants took the large back bedroom upstairs; Valerie and Carlton unpacked in the master bedroom on the main floor. And Carlton dis- appeared into his office, a small room off their bedroom.

That day and the next, he worked there, with the door closed. He urged Valerie and the others to go snowshoeing or skiing, or to take the snowmobiles for rides around the lake. "I'll join you as soon as I can," he said on Friday morning. He was sitting at his desk, his head resting on his hand. "I'm sorry, Val; as soon as I can we'll go off to our own corner. Maybe later this afternoon."

"You'll be there alone," she said coldly. "I'm taking the Tarrants into town for the day and we won't be back until dinnertime. You make it awfully hard to patch up a marriage, Carl; if you—"

"Patch? We don't need patching; we're doing fine. I've been busy, I haven't paid much attention to you, I know that; but that doesn't mean anything; Christ, Valerie, do you have to build up a case every time I've got a lot on my mind? If every couple who doesn't spend a lot of time together—"

"Oh, stop it," she said impatiently. He shrugged, still leaning his head on his hand, and in a moment Valerie bent down and kissed his cheek. "I'm sorry; I'm as nervous as you these days. If you'd tell me what's bothering you, I might be able to help, or at least we could share it. Unless it's this woman you've got; I don't imagine I'd be much help there."

"Woman? What woman? What are you talking about?"

"Your regular trips to Manhattan. Carl, do you think everyone in the world is blind but you?" She picked up her shearling coat and went to the door. "I'll be in town until about six. If you're willing to talk after dinner, we might make a start at being married."

"We are married, for Christ's sake. I can't talk to you if you're obsessed with these crazy ideas. There isn't any other woman!"

"Good," said Valerie lightly. "Then that's one less thing we have to discuss, isn't it? I'll see you tonight."

He heard her close the door, but he did not move; he was exhausted, even though it was only the morning. He wondered how he had slipped up and made her suspicious. He wondered why she felt they weren't married. He was home most nights, they went to parties together, they took quick flights to New York and Washington, they entertained, they rode together on their farm. What more did she need to feel married?

He shook his head, and turned to the papers on his desk. It was all done. For three months, handling a few transactions at a time, he had mortgaged their properties, borrowed on their horses, their collection of antique furnishings and their twentieth-century art, and converted the remaining stocks and bonds in the three portfolios to cash. Then he had bought thirteen million dollars in bearer bonds from his broker—bonds that were completely negotiable and safely unregistered—and sent the bonds to a bank in Panama. The bank had cashed the bonds and opened an account held by a company which Monte James had set up, with a local president. From there, the money would be transfered to another account in the name of a development company in which Carlton Sterling was the major shareholder. That whole trail was invisible, since the bearer bonds were unregistered, and therefore, once he bought them, untraceable.

Eventually—Carlton had never asked Sybille for all the details of the trail it would take from there—the thirteen million dollars would be used to purchase thirteen hundred contiguous acres of land near Culpeper, Virginia. And then the land would be resold to the Hour of Grace Foundation for thirty million dollars.

Massive fraud. The phrase had sprung at him the moment he sent the bearer bonds out of the country. Since then it had growled through his thoughts day and night, never leaving him alone. And there was something else. *Sybille.* Besides committing himself to fraud, he was committing himself to Sybille. Tying himself to her, irrevocably and forever.

Thoughts like that never occurred to him when he was with her. But as he and Valerie and the others took off for Lake Placid, he had been startled to feel a lightness and a sense of freedom, and the higher he climbed, the more certainly he had known that the freedom was from Sybille.

With a grunt of exasperation, he shoved back his desk chair and went outside, pulling on a down jacket. The sun and the sparkling snow were blinding, and he put on dark glasses as he began to walk along the lakeshore. He took deep breaths of the biting air, walking faster until he was almost trotting, leaving deep footprints in the snow. And by the time he came back to the house, breathing heavily, sweating, he knew he could not do it.

What it came down to, he finally admitted, was that he knew damn little of Sybille's machinations, with Graceville or anything else. He wasn't even sure he knew very much about Sybille. What he did know was that he wanted out.

Back in his office, he called her, and told her he had changed his mind. "You haven't bought the land," he said when she remained silent. "The money is still in the development company's account. I'll arrange to withdraw it next Thursday, when we get back." She still was silent. "I'm sorry, Sybille; I know you wanted to help me, and that means a lot to me, it's not that I'm not grateful; I just... changed my mind."

"And what about you?" she asked at last.

"I don't know. I don't know what I'm going to do. I'll just have to figure something else out. I have to talk to Val. I should have known I couldn't keep it from her; it's her money, too."

"Carl, you know you can't—"

"Damn it, I don't want to talk about it! Sorry; I didn't mean to yell. You'll just have to go along this time, Sybille; I'm doing what I have to do, and I've made up my mind. I know you'll understand; you've always understood me, and been there when I needed you. I want to see you next week—okay?—as soon as I get back."

There was a silence. "Of course," she said softly. "You know I want that, too, Carl."

But Sybille had no intention of waiting. That night she called Valerie and invited herself to the Adirondacks. "Just for overnight," she said. "I've been so busy and stressed out I just have to get away and breathe some different air. Your housekeeper told me you'd gone to the mountains and it sounded like just what I need. Would you mind? Or don't you have room for me?"

"There's an empty bedroom, and of course you can come," said Valerie, thinking it made no difference how many guests filled the house; she and Carl could talk anywhere, if that was what they both wanted. "We haven't seen much of you lately; we'd be glad to have you. You should be able to get a flight first thing in the morning."

"I have the Foundation jet; don't worry about me. This is so good of you, Valerie. I'll see you tomorrow morning."

The Hour of Grace Citation, bringing both Sybille and Lily, landed in Lake Placid on Saturday morning. Half an hour later the two of them had taken possession of the last empty bedroom, with its twin beds and private bath, and had joined everyone for lunch at the round dining table near the fireplace. Sybille praised the house, admiring its views, the size of the rooms, the comfort of the furnishings. "I've never been in the Adirondacks before," she told Valerie and the others at the table. "It's a treat to be here. And thank you for letting me bring Lily. She needs a rest even more than I do; I couldn't leave her behind."

"We're glad you're here," Valerie said to Lily, and began to ask questions about her television program and the new church, still unfinished, though she had been preaching in it for five months. Carlton, stunned by Sybille's presence, torn by his desire for her which reared up with monstrous force as soon as he saw her, pushed his spoon through the chili in his soup bowl, and took huge bites of cornbread. He had to stay away from her; not only because of Val, though that was bad enough—what possessed her to come up here when they'd been so careful for over a year?—but because all his logical thinking of the past few days could collapse if he got close to her. Stay away, he told himself, taut and quivering with wanting her. Stay in the office; go there now. The housekeeper was serving coffee. Go there now; don't wait for dessert; no one will care. Go now!

"Carl," Sybille said, "May I ask your advice about a business deal I'm trying to work out?"

"Not now," he said wildly. "I've got a lot to do. Later, maybe, tomorrow or the next day..."

"Please," she said. "I'm leaving tomorrow and I do need your advice." She put out her hands, pleading. "There aren't many people I can really trust, Carl. Won't you give me just a little of your time? I brought something to show you."

Carlton's look sharpened. The money, he thought. She'd withdrawn the money herself; she didn't want him to wait, or worry. Damn it, he'd underrated her. "I'll be glad to help," he said and led the way to the bedroom, and through it to his office.

He closed the door. "Carl," Sybille murmured, and she was in his arms, her tongue twisting around his, her arms clasping him to her. Carlton's hands were on her breasts, between her legs, pulling her against him; he wanted to crush her, to throw her to the floor, to enter her and devour her. But she was the one who led the way: she slid down his body until she was kneeling in front of him. Her quick, clever hands opened his pants and took him inside the clinging, powerful grip of her mouth, and Carlton, moaning silently at the back of his throat, found the explosive release that sent him plummeting from the taut craze of the lunch table.

Breathing heavily, he pulled away and leaned against the wall, his worry returning as his passion ebbed. "You brought the money?"

"Oh, Carl," said Sybille mournfully. "How can you talk about money? I missed you; I had to be with you. And I thought we might talk a little bit, about the future."

The next afternoon, Sunday, Sybille returned to Washington. Lily stayed behind. "If you have any questions about Graceville, ask her," Sybille told Carlton as he drove her to the Lake Placid airport. "You only began to worry because you had no one to talk to."

"Is that why she's staying with us?" he asked harshly. "To keep me in line?"

Sybille sighed deeply. "She's exhausted, and Valerie very kindly offered to let her stay on and fly back with you." Her voice trembled. "You make me sound very devious, Carl."

"Calculating," he said flatly. "Always prepared. The perfect Girl Scout."

Alarmed, she gazed at him for a long moment. Her eyes were hooded. "I'll return your money," she said icily. "I don't want to have anything to do with someone who thinks I'm *calculating*. All I wanted was to make thirteen million dollars for you, clean up your mess, give you my heart and soul for the rest of my life and do my best to be everything you've ever wanted. I'm sorry that's not good enough for you." She stared straight ahead. "As soon as you get back to Washington, you can have your money. We don't have to see each other; my assistant will give it to you. We won't see each other at all; there's no reason to."

Carlton jerked the wheel and brought the car to a stop at the side of the road. He pulled her to him, fingers digging into her arms, his mouth against hers. "Don't play games with me; I've got too much on my mind. I told you I'd go ahead with it; we'll do it and when it's over I'll tell Val I'm leaving. She won't mind; there isn't much between us anymore—she said that herself—and she's getting impatient; I know she'd rather be free and find someone else. I don't want any more crap from you about not seeing me anymore; is that clear? You'll see me all the time; we're doing this together and we'll *be* together."

Sybille nodded. "Forever," she breathed, and locked her mouth to his.

They did not speak for the rest of the drive to the airport. When they pulled up, Carlton said, "I'll have a cup of coffee with you before you leave."

"No." She opened her door and slid out. "My pilot's been here for an hour; I want to leave right away." She gazed about her. "Where's your plane, Carl? I don't see it."

"At the end of the field, near the hangar."

She strained to see it in the fading light. "At the very end? Oh, there it is. We've had some good trips in it, haven't we? Especially up here, when we had the house to ourselves."

He took her overnight bag from the car. "I'll call you tonight."

She kissed him, her lips clinging, reluctant to pull away. "I'll wait for that. And I'll see you soon."

"Next Thursday."

He watched her walk to the Base Operations office, to meet her pilot, and then he drove away, back to his house, back to Valerie, back to Lily who was waiting to reassure him about Graceville, back to the worries that began again as soon as Sybille was out of sight.

He could still feel her mouth locked to his. *Forever.* He and Sybille. Guilty of fraud. *We're doing this together. We'll be together. Forever.*

He avoided Lily, whose troubled gaze followed him as he paced the great room, from the fireplace at one end to the open kitchen at the other. He spent the evening in his office; when he called Sybille, the sound of her voice drove him into a frenzy of desire and revulsion and he cut the call short. He stayed there all night, angry at himself for his indecision, angry at Sybille for putting him through this agony, angry at Valerie for not caring about him enough to insist he tell her the truth so he could share the mess he'd made and let her find a way out for both of them.

At dawn, he glanced at the calendar on his desk. Monday. The day they were to close on the purchase of the land.

"No we won't," he muttered in the chilly room. He swept the papers off his desk; memos, mortgage documents, stock and bond transactions, financial projections, and stuffed them into a cardboard folder. I'll be damned if I'll let myself be sucked into this. Sucked into her. Val said we'd share it. I trust Val.

As he said that, he knew he did not trust Sybille and never had. He only wanted her. But this time he was through. "I'm going back," he said, his determination stiffening as he heard the sound of his words. "She won't close on that land; I won't let her."

"I'm going back," he said to Valerie, finding her lying wakeful in bed. "Right away. I have things to do; I can't put them off any longer."

She sat up. "We'll all go."

"No. You stay; I don't want you to—"

"We'll all go." She flung aside the bedclothes and went to the closet, pulling out pants and a shirt and sweater.

Carlton's eyes passed over her slender nude body as if she were not there. "I don't want you to go. I don't want to ruin your vacation."

"It isn't a vacation; you couldn't ruin it, because it was a farce from the beginning; and I have no desire to stay here." She was pulling on her clothes. "Wake the others, Carl. We can be ready in an hour."

"I can't wait that long."

She looked at her watch. "In an hour it will be eight o'clock. We'll be home by ten-thirty. That should be time for a full day's work. Carl, we're going with you."

"Look, I promised Betsy and Alex nine days—"

"I don't give a damn about Betsy and Alex. I still give a damn about you, and I'm going with you."

Carlton's breath came out in a long sigh. She was taking care of everything. Thank God. He wanted her with him. He hated going home to an empty house. He hated worrying about problems alone. And he didn't want to be with Sybille; he wanted to be with Val. She was clean and straight and that was what he needed. I love her, he thought, and felt a cold sinking within him when he thought of the harm he had done her. I have so much to make up to her for; it'll take all the years we have ahead of us to tell her how sorry I am, and to get back what was hers. It'll take all those years just to make her believe how much I love her.

"Carl, I'm ready," Valerie said. She touched his arm. "We'll work it out, whatever trouble you're in, and then we'll do something about us."

Her voice was soothing, as if she knew everything and had already forgiven him, and Carlton felt a wave of relief. He didn't have to worry about Val; she'd stick with him; she'd help him; she'd be fine. "You get the others," he said. "I'll close up the house."

A little over an hour later, they were at the airport, shivering in the bitter morning air while Carlton opened the door of his plane and stowed their luggage. "Lily, Betsy, Alex," he said, barking orders, and they took three of the seats behind the two in front, fastening their seat belts. Lily seemed in a daze; she had not said a word on the drive from the house to the airport. Betsy had complained bitterly—she'd turned down four parties to come to the Adirondacks—until Alex told her to be quiet; Carl wouldn't leave in a hurry unless he had a good reason.

Carlton gave a cursory glance at his preflight checklist, then put it aside. He didn't have time for the whole thing, and they'd been here only a few days, not long enough for anything to change. In the pilot's seat he started the engines and checked his instruments while Valerie locked the door and climbed into the seat beside him.

"Everybody strapped in?" he asked happily. He was feeling better: he was on his way, he was taking action, he was in charge of his life again. "Okay, then, we're off. Home in a couple of hours."

And the small plane lifted off, into the gray January sky.

Part Two

Chapter 19

Everyone said she should marry again, someone wealthy, right away. They came to visit her in her mother's Park Avenue apartment, where she had gone when she left the hospital, to begin the long recovery from the crash. And her friends sat with her, discussing her future. "You have to marry," they repeated. "All your money gone ... how else will you manage? What would you do?"

"Clean stables," Valerie said with biting humor. "I've been on the other side so long, it's probably time I learned."

"Be serious, Val," they said. "Think about the future."

"I will," she said gravely, as if she were not already thinking about it every hour, every day, and dreaming about it at night. Her bruises were fading, her feet were healing, but her thoughts were still in turmoil. She could not mourn Carl without being furious and bewildered. "It makes no sense," she said to Dee Wyly, who visited almost every day. "If he was in trouble, why didn't he tell me?"

"He didn't gamble," Dee said thoughtfully. "Not much, anyway; he didn't like it, did he?"

"He said he didn't. I can't even be sure of that anymore." Valerie nibbled on one of the chocolates Dee had brought. The two of them had been close friends for a long time, and Dee was one of the few women Valerie could talk to comfortably. Blond, warmly attractive and without affectation, Dee was the only one who had wondered aloud if it was a good idea for Valerie to marry Carlton. She had not mentioned that to Valerie since the crash, but both of them remembered it.

"He could have been fleeced by someone," she said, looking past Valerie at a photograph of Carlton on a side table. "He was like a little boy sometimes, don't you think? Every now and then I thought he looked downright lost." She studied the photograph. "Don't you think somebody could have taken advantage of him?"

"He was a grown man and a successful investment counselor," Valerie replied dryly. "How naive can we pretend he was? Anyway, why wouldn't he tell me? We could have seen it through together." She paused. "Of course, there's the other woman. He might have wanted to disappear with her."

"I don't believe there was anybody. I never saw him with anyone, or heard anything. Those things get around, you know."

"All he had to do was ask me for a divorce," Valerie went on. "But he never said a word, not even that he was thinking about it." She spread her hands. "He cared for me—I'm pretty sure—so how could he have wiped me out?"

"He did care for you; I could tell." Slowly, Dee shook her head. "Poor Valerie, you can't even get good and mad at him; you're mourning him at the same time. He died so young, and you did have good times together...What a mess. I wish there was something I could do."

"You're doing it," Valerie said with a smile. "You're wonderful, Dee; you've listened to me try to figure this out for a month."

"Probably a few more months to go," Dee said cheerfully. She stood. "I have to go; I'm taking Emily shopping. I wish you could come along; Emily likes to shop with both of us. 'My two elegant mothers,' she calls us."

"I will as soon as I can trust my feet to get through Bergdorf's." Valerie's face changed. "No, as a matter of fact. I guess I won't."

Their eyes met as they thought of the difference, now, between their finances. "You'll give Emily advice," Dee said easily. "Your taste has nothing to do with your checkbook." She kissed Valerie. "Till tomorrow."

As soon as she was gone, Valerie's logical thinking collapsed into a maelstrom of anger and mourning, fear of the future, and feeling sorry for herself. I don't deserve this, she thought, and then panic filled her. How could I think about Bergdorf's? I don't even know if I can afford groceries.

All her other friends, less intimate than Dee, told her in the nicest possible way that she didn't have the training, skills or temperament to earn a living. "Can you even keep a budget?" they asked. She didn't know; she'd never done it. And then, besides those visitors there were investigators probing the plane crash and the loss of her money, plunging her, with every question, back into the confusion and resentment that engulfed her whenever she thought about Carlton.

"I just can't believe he did that to you!" Sybille exclaimed. It was the third time she had come to New York since the plane crash, and the two of them were in Valerie's sitting room in her mother's apartment. "He always seemed so responsible and stable: not at all the kind to—"

"Sybille, we've been through this," Valerie said. She had a piece of needlepoint in her lap, something she had started in the past month. She took pleasure in using her hands in this new way; it soothed her anger and gave her a feeling of accomplishment as an intricate Persian design emerged from the mesh. But for some reason Sybille always made her so nervous she could not make a stitch, and so she put it aside. "I don't want to talk about how responsible Carl was; obviously he wasn't."

"But you should talk about it; otherwise you'll brood. He must have said something, given you some hint about what he was doing, or thinking... you lived with him; you must have seen some clues."

"Not about money," Valerie replied briefly.

Sybille pounced on it. "What about, then? He did leave clues? About something?"

"No," Valerie said after a barely perceptible pause. "Nothing."

"Valerie, tell me about it. You can talk to me; it's good for you to talk, and I want to help you."

Valerie contemplated her. She was wearing a cashmere suit trimmed in fur; a large diamond flashed on one finger, an emerald on another; her gold earrings, instantly recognizable to anyone who shopped, were from Bulgari; her perfume was Scheherezade; and when she arrived she had been wearing her sable coat. Overdressed for an afternoon visit, Valerie thought; she's a walking bank balance. Panic flashed through her again. I have no bank balance. Everything I took for granted... it's gone, it's gone. Sybille is the one who has everything now. I used to feel sorry for her. Laughter rose in her throat, but it was wild and afraid, and she pushed it down.

"Tell me," Sybille urged. "Tell me about Carlton, anything he said or hinted... we might be able to figure out what happened."

Valerie shook her head. Why was Sybille so interested in Carlton? They'd met only two or three times. *But I know the answer to that; it's always been the same: Sybille following me around asking questions, mimicking the things I do. Skeet shooting, riding, hunting, even a farm in Virginia...*

She's probably harmless, Valerie thought, but I don't like her prying. I've never liked her prying. Five more minutes, and then she's out of here. "I have to think about these things myself," she said, "before I can talk to anyone else. Tell me about your work. How many shows are you producing now?"

Sybille hesitated. She drained her glass of wine and set it on the table for Valerie to refill. "I've sold four and I'm working on three others: a soap opera and two sitcoms. I sold two game shows last summer. And of course I'm selling 'The Hour of Grace'; that's going to be the biggest of all, but I have to fight for Lily's attention; she's all wound up with Graceville these days."

"Graceville?"

"You haven't heard of it?"

"No, should I have? Has it been in the papers?"

"Not yet. But Carl was at the cathedral."

"Yes, I remember. You talked about it that day at lunch. And I asked if there would be a town around it."

"I hadn't even thought about a town until you mentioned it," Sybille said. "But then I knew it was the right thing to do. And Lily was ecstatic at the idea."

"You're building a town, then. Graceville. A real town?"

"Of course. Shops, theaters, houses, town houses, apartments, hotels, a hospital... everything."

"And churches?"

"The cathedral."

Valerie smiled faintly. "It's a real town, but it has only one religion."

"Anyone who comes to Graceville wants to be close to Lily Grace. People who don't believe in her won't come. I don't want them."

Rosemary Ashbrook knocked lightly on the open door. "You've been talking to visitors all day," she said to Valerie, and turned a social smile on Sybille. "I'm so sorry, but I really must protect my daughter; she never thinks of herself at all."

Sybille's face showed disbelief, but she stood up quickly, reaching for her purse. Valerie followed, wincing as the pain shot through her feet, still hurting after two months. "It was good of you to come," she said, hobbling beside Sybille. "And thank you for all the flowers."

They came every week, with a card that said "Love, Sybille"—huge, lavish bouquets that reminded Valerie of the towering arrangements that accompanied funeral processions of dictators and Mafia dons. She always threw out the protea that looked as if they would devour her at any minute, and made five or six small arrangements from what was left.

"And thank you again for coming to Carl's funeral; it was very thoughtful of you."

"I couldn't miss it," Sybille said. "I'll be back to see you as soon as I can; it's hard to get away; we're so busy . . . But if you want to talk, call me; call anytime. You know I want to help."

In the foyer, the women touched cheeks and Valerie's mother closed the door. "She's so devoted," Rosemary said. "It's amazing that she comes so often, living in Washington. Valerie, Dan Lithigate is in the library, with that detective, what's his name. I told him you were busy, but they said they'd wait. Do you want to talk to them? I can say you're not feeling well."

"No, I have to see them, Mother; I have to know what they've found." Valerie had already turned and was walking as rapidly as she could toward the library.

The men stood as she came in, and Lithigate held a chair for her. Valerie cut off the casual chatter with which he ritually began every meeting. "Dan, I'm a little anxious about this. Could you tell me what you've found?"

"Ah. Of course. Of course, you're anxious. And I can tell you right up front, Valerie, it's not a pretty story. Not a good one for you and your mother either, I might add. I have to tell you again, I am absolutely astonished at Carlton's behavior; I cannot fathom what went through his mind—"

"Can we begin?" Valerie asked edgily.

"Yes. Well, let me review the overall picture first. Last September, Carlton made some bad investments. Very bad. He lost about fifteen million dollars. In the next three months, before the end of the year, he raised approximately thirteen million dollars. In December, he bought thirteen million dollars' worth of bearer bonds from his broker. And that's as far as we can go. Bearer bonds are unregistered and as negotiable as cash. There's no trace of them and most likely there never will be. We do know, of course, that Carlton seemed desperately anxious to fly back from the Adirondacks early in January, and it seems probable that that had something to do with those bearer bonds, but we cannot even be sure of that."

Valerie was watching him intently, giving no sign that she was hearing a tale of personal disaster.

Lithigate gestured to the man beside him. "Fred can tell you what he's found."

Fred Burstin was the detective Lithigate had hired after Carlton's death. His investigation went on simultaneously with the one being conducted by the National Transportation Safety Board. The NTSB investigates every crash in which there is a fatality, taking up to a year or more to release its findings. Valerie had heard nothing from them after their initial questioning of her. She knew they had sent a team to investigate the crash site and to remove what was left of the plane for study; she knew other investigators had examined the maintenance records of Carlton's plane, and interviewed the Tarrants, Lily, and the maintenance men at the Lake Placid airport. And she knew that the medical report would become part of their findings: that the autopsy had shown that Carlton had not been impaired by drugs or alcohol; that he had died of a massive head injury.

Valerie had gotten the medical results the day she was flown in an ambulance plane to Virginia, for Carlton's burial in his family plot. She had returned to New York to face more questions from insurance investigators, Fred Burstin, and the New York State Police about the possibility that Carlton had been the victim of foul play, and perhaps had been involved in illegal activities. All those investigators shared some information, and held back some. From everything he had gleaned, and found on his own, Burstin had compiled his report.

"I'll run through all of it," he said, as Lithigate had done. "Just to get the whole picture. Where I am is, it's pretty clear your husband didn't go through his preflight check. You told us you were helping the other passengers get settled, and didn't pay attention, but it seems someone would have noticed if he'd been going through all the steps; there are a lot of them. And none of you noticed him using his gauge to check for water in the fuel tanks."

When he paused, Valerie said, "I suppose not. I didn't."

"You said you trusted him."

"Yes. That's what I told you. I had no reason not to."

Burstin sighed. "He lost twenty-eight million dollars, a lot of it yours and your mother's, and you trusted him. Okay, I'll go on. He didn't gamble much, you said, and I haven't been able to place him in the Las Vegas or Atlantic City casinos in the past couple of years. He might have gone out of the country, but you said you usually traveled together. Okay, next. You said he didn't own any overseas companies and, as far as you know, wasn't a partner in any, and I've been through his office and personal files, his bank and brokerage records, and his appointment calendar, and haven't found any evidence that he was. I've interviewed his secretary, his business associates, his friends and the others on the plane with you, and they couldn't help, either. No evidence of foreign companies, foreign partnerships, or illegal dealings here or overseas. No evidence of other women either. I checked hotels, talked to the doorman of your building in New York, and your house-keeper in the Adirondacks; the usual stuff. I've searched his safe de-posit box, his club locker, and the crash site—the NTSB's helped me in a lot of this—your apartment, the house in the Adirondacks, and Sterling Farms, and didn't find anything, including the bearer bonds; I thought he might have died before he had a chance to use them, and they'd still be around. But no such luck.

"So, where I am is, I'm assuming he was trying to recoup his losses in the market by gambling. We couldn't place him at casinos in this country, but all those other places—England, Spain, Africa—have their own gambling setups and he might've preferred them; a long way from home. So he lost even more, and then had gambling debts to pay. Those guys don't fool around, you know; he had to come home and raise the money in a hurry: thirteen million in under three months is pretty quick work. Since we never found the bearer bonds, and you haven't heard from anybody looking for money, I assume he paid off those debts before he died. I haven't found any evidence that he was planning to disappear, and he doesn't seem like the type who'd do that. The police haven't found anything that points to foul play; of course that won't be final till the NTSB report comes in."

He stopped. Valerie had not moved during his long recital. "He told me it wasn't an accident," she said at last.

"I took that into consideration. So did the NTSB. Right now, where I am is, you were the only one who heard that, and you were in a state of shock. And he had fatal injuries and was probably delirious. I can't rely too strongly on a statement made in those circumstances."

"He knew what he was saying," Valerie insisted, "And I know what I heard."

"Okay, then, who did it? Who wanted him dead? Who had a chance to fool around with his plane and make sure he'd crash? Who hated him so much he didn't care whether he killed four people while he got your husband?"

There was another silence. "I don't know," Valerie said. Her voice was barely audible. Then she looked at Burstin. "You haven't found anything," she said bitingly. "All I've heard so far is what you haven't found."

"Those are findings, too, Mrs. Sterling. We have to rule out wherever we can. We've ruled out a lot with your husband. And I gave you my conclusions. I think any further investigation is pointless; there's nothing left to uncover. The money is gone and it's a good bet it won't ever show up. And your husband's death was a tragic accident, no more."

"No more," repeated Valerie coldly. "That was quite a bit."

"Valerie," said Lithigate, "there are some things we must discuss. Fred will leave us his written report."

Valerie took the large envelope Burstin handed her as he left. "He didn't find anything. He just made some guesses."

"Sound ones," Lithigate said. "You should not dismiss them out of hand. Sometimes the obvious answer is the correct one."

She contemplated him. "I don't think there's anything obvious about what's happened in the past few months. What did you want to talk about?"

"Your situation. It's very bad, Valerie, and I can't help you by keeping it from you. We have all the information, now, and we'll face it together."

Valerie gave a brief, wintry smile. "Mother and I are the ones who have to face it, Dan. Go ahead."

"When Carlton raised the thirteen million dollars, he realized four million by selling the rest of your portfolios, seven million by mortgaging your various properties, and two million in personal loans. The payments due on the mortgages and loans come to just over a million dollars a year. As you know, he carried five hundred thousand dollars in life insurance, with you as the sole beneficiary. His will leaves two million dollars to a number of relatives and charities, and everything else to you."

Rosemary, who had so far not said a word, held out a bewildered hand. "Can we handle a million dollars a year in payments?"

'No," said Valerie. "That's right isn't it, Dan?"

"I'm afraid so. Your portfolios are gone and all your property is mortgaged or sold. What you must do, as trustee of Carlton's estate..." His voice faded away. "I'm sorry, this is very difficult for me. If you sell Sterling Farms and the New York apartment, you'll have about a million dollars after you pay off the mortgages. Once you sell the horses, and the art and sculpture, and pay off the money Carlton borrowed on them, you'll have close to another million. That would leave you a total of two million dollars."

"Well, then," said Rosemary, her face brightening.

Valerie shook her head. "Carl left two million dollars to some charities and all his relatives. I can't imagine why; he almost never saw them."

"But that's not right!" her mother cried. "Valerie, the circumstances have changed! No one would take that money when they find out you don't have anything! They'd understand...!"

"I don't have a choice. That's right, isn't it, Dan? If the money is available, the conditions of the will must be met?"

He nodded.

Valerie spread the fingers of her hands and contemplated them. "Which leaves me nothing."

The room was silent. *Damn Carl, damn him, damn him for putting me through this.*

Why did he do this? Why did he leave me this way?

What am I going to do?

Lithigate left, and Rosemary sat beside Valerie. Her hands fluttered in her lap, her breath came in long, trembling sighs, and she watched Valerie, waiting for solutions to all their problems.

"I don't know," Valerie said at last, to herself as well as to Rosemary. "I don't know."

Her friends knew. They had been telling her since word got out that Carlton's finances were not in good shape. "You have to get married," they said. "To someone wealthy. And right away."

They all said it even though they knew she had been much admired on television, and with her horses, and as a... Well, Valerie admitted to herself, that was the problem; she had no other credits. She was an excellent shopper, a knowledgeable traveler, a good friend, a noted hostess, and a delightful companion at a dinner party. But no one is willing to pay for that, she thought, except a husband.

Thirty-three years old and decorative. And not much else.

And that was the most depressing of all.

That was depressing, but her finances were terrifying. And yet, the more she repeated the facts Dan Lithigate had reeled off, the more unreal they seemed. They were terrifying, they were the stuff of nightmares, but she could not believe they had anything to do with her.

But she knew they did when, bit by bit, her possessions were sold. Sterling Farms was listed with a realtor, but everything else was gone: the Adirondacks house and the New York apartment had sold quickly because she was not in a position to price them high and wait for the right buyer; the horses and the art collection were sold; and all the bequests had been made. And Valerie was living in her mother's rented Park Avenue apartment, which was the sole survivor of the debacle. She had nothing of her own.

She kept repeating it, and she and Rosemary talked about it endlessly, trying to understand that it really was happening to them. Neither of them had ever worried about money; how could they start now? "It won't last," Valerie said one day in April, as she did every day. She and Rosemary were sitting at the breakfast table overlooking Park Avenue. It was cool and sunny, with new leaves on the trees below them and a fresh look to the air, as if everything were just beginning. A policeman directing traffic at the gridlocked corner looked like a ballet dancer pirouetting, stretching one arm to the front, the other to the back, occasionally leaping to a new position in the street. Valerie watched him with a smile. "Of course it won't last. Dan could be wrong—the bearer bonds could still show up—or the money will turn up, or I'll meet someone I can care about...Something will happen, and we'll get back to the way we were. Nobody's life changes like this, totally, all at once; people go through little traumas, but then they settle back to normal."

"Of course," Rosemary said. She stirred her orange juice and sipped it pensively.

"After all," Valerie went on, still watching the policeman, "no one could get rid of that much money that quickly and that invisibly. That business about Carl gambling is ridiculous. He told me he didn't have the stomach for it; he hated all the unknowns. Whatever he did, it was something else. We just haven't been looking in the right places. It will turn up; it has to."

"Of course," Rosemary repeated. They had been through this conversation before.

"But all that may take a while," Valerie said at last. "And while we're waiting, it looks like I'll have to get some kind of a job."

"Well, I suppose I should, too," replied Rosemary. Another silence fell. Both of them felt a great weariness whenever they talked about jobs; the subject was so foreign to them. They had discussed calling their friends—the bankers, the chairmen of great corporations, the directors of hospitals, the owners of newspapers—but they had not been able to do it. Each time they reached for the telephone they drew back, hating to ask for favors when they were in no position to recip- rocate, and faintly ashamed, as if Carl's disaster was their fault. But their friends were uncomfortable, too. They were sorry for Valerie and Rosemary, but they were a little embarrassed by their own continued good fortune, as if they ought to apologize for having no tragedy to share. It would almost be easier, Valerie thought, to look at want ads.

But when they did open the newspapers and scan them, and thought of making appointments, interviewing, talking about them- selves to strangers, it all sounded impossible and demeaning. And even if they managed to do it, what could they say about themselves? They could not type or take shorthand; they had no training as nurses or nurses' aides or teachers or teachers' aides; they had never written ad- vertising copy or newspaper stories or memorized those funny marks proofreaders make on manuscripts; they knew nothing about book- keeping; they had no idea how to run a switchboard or work a com- puter; they had never cooked or waited on tables or cleaned house.

"Information desk in a museum," Valerie said. "Or tour guide. I know the collections."

Rosemary brightened. "You'd be perfect. I could do that, too." Her face clouded. "But there don't seem to be many of those jobs around."

"Not many." Valerie yawned. "Well, if it's not that it will be some- thing else, something to fill in. It's not as if I'm looking for a career, you know." She toyed with her pencil. "The odd thing is, except for a museum job, I can't think of anything at all, even as a fill-in. I may have been right about cleaning stables after all."

"Absolutely not," Rosemary declared. "You shouldn't even joke about it!" Her mouth trembled. "Shame on Carlton! What possessed him to do this to us? He did love us, you know; after Daddy died he said he'd take care of us! Not leave us in the cold...at my age... thinking of jobs..."

Valerie was silent. There was nothing to say.

And it was that week, when they had reached that weary point, that Edgar Wymper called.

He was the wealthy son of wealthy parents whose sprawling farm on Maryland's Eastern Shore had bordered Ashbrook Farms. Valerie had known him all her life, and had found him amusing, especially when they were sophomores in high school and he told her he planned to marry her when they graduated. He had never wavered from that goal, though they had not seen each other since her father sold Ashbrook Farms. He had never married. He squired numerous women to social events in the great capitals of the world, sent Valerie flowers on her birthday, and waited.

When he called, it took her a moment to picture him; a round face, she remembered; small hooked nose, small chin, close-set soft brown eyes, a happy smile, a pudgy body clothed in the world's most expensive suits. He had just returned from Europe. "I want to see you and do what I can to help," he said in his soft voice. "When would be a good time?"

"I don't go out much these days," Valerie said. "Come this afternoon, if you'd like."

He arrived at four and stayed until six in a proper first visit, entertained by Valerie and Rosemary for part of the time, alone with Valerie the rest. Once Valerie got used to his beard, which hid his small chin and gave him an almost rakish look, she found him just as she remembered: cheerful, kindly, interested in everything about her, but with the unconscious arrogance of those who never have to count the cost of anything. *That never would have occurred to me before*, she thought. *I suppose I was the same as Edgar, all these years.*

She wore a long silk robe with broad stripes in many colors, and her hair fell in waves to her shoulders. "You're wonderfully beautiful; lovelier than ever," Edgar said, his brown eyes shining at her. "I wouldn't have thought that was possible. I'm so sorry about Carl; I liked him. But I condemn what he did. To treat any woman that way! Especially a wife one had vowed to protect! He's put you in a dreadful position. A dastardly thing to do."

Oh, Edgar, Valerie thought. She remembered, in high school, accusing him of expressing the obvious with the portentous air of someone discovering gravity for the first time. *Still the same*, she thought. *Amusing and impossible to take seriously.*

"It certainly is dreadful," she said with a solemnity that matched his. "Mother and I are trying to figure out what to do."

"You have no money at all?"

"A few thousand dollars in a checking account. And Mother has her jewels. If she sells them, and we're careful, we might get along for a year."

"My God, that the day would come that you would have to talk like this! A woman of the most perfect refinement and beauty, the most exquisite taste, the most elegant understanding of the world; it is impossible that you should have to tarnish your thoughts with anything as crude as money and *getting along*."

Valerie broke into laughter, but seeing the sudden narrowing of his eyes, she stifled it. She had forgotten how much Edgar loved drama. Once they had been in a high-school play together, and from then on he inserted dramatic phrases into his daily speech, made broad, dramatic gestures, and strutted like an actor, even in the required after-school sports. No one made fun of him because, in spite of soft eyes and soft smiles, everyone knew Edgar could be vindictive and had a long memory.

"Of course I don't like to think about money," she said, her lids lowered. "But Mother can't seem to concentrate on it, so I'm the one who has to do it. And I'm learning, Edgar; it's amazing how quickly one learns."

"But that's wrong; you must not clutter your mind. You already know how to live well. You need nothing more."

Valerie smiled. "What I need has gone through some changes." She looked up as Rosemary came into the study. "I asked Mother to have tea with us."

"Wonderful," Edgar said, and he meant it. Everything about him declared that he wanted to be an intimate part of her small, tragically victimized family. He was not a subtle man: he expected Valerie to understand, from the moment he walked into the apartment, that he was there to rescue her and protect her for the rest of her life, and her mother too.

From that day, Valerie was always aware of him. He sent fresh flowers every morning, delicate sprays of orchids, tasteful arrangements of plumeria, roses, camellias, iris and tulips, or baskets of azaleas heavy with blooms. He telephoned two or three times a day, and took her out at night to restaurants, theaters, concert halls, nightclubs, and to balls and dinner parties given by people both of them had known all their lives.

It was a way of life as familiar to Valerie as the wallpaper in her bedroom, and so it began to seem that nothing had changed very much. Of course Carl was dead, and all her money was gone, but when she was with Edgar none of that had any reality. What was real was a social schedule she moved through instinctively, with never a false step.

Once again, she was transported through the cacophony of New York streets in the hushed silence of a limousine; she whirled through the same ballrooms, planned her days around the same parties and dinners and benefits, dined on caviar and *marquis au chocolat* on the same gold and vermeil place settings in the same dining rooms hung

with tasseled silk she had known since she was a child, made the same
kinds of conversation, and saw the same people. She never once said to
herself, I am poor, because she never once felt as if she were. With
Edgar's solid figure at her side, in the lulling atmosphere of a world
where money could make almost everything right, Valerie sank back,
as if into a featherbed. I knew everything would be all right, she
thought.

Her mourning became a sadness for all that had gone wrong for
Carl and for their marriage; her anger and fear sank beneath the surface of the social schedule Edgar was making for her. And she and
Edgar became a familiar couple in New York: Edgar sleek and rosy in
black tie and neat beard; Valerie six inches taller, dressed in last year's
silks, her tawny hair gleaming, her gaze often turned inward as she
grew quiet during a dance, or fell into a pensive mood at a dinner
party. Her friends remarked on that strange, new thoughtfulness, but
it was not unusual, they said to each other, after all she'd been
through. Once she married Edgar she'd once again be the lively, careless, laughing social butterfly they'd always been able to count on to
keep a party going.

Everyone was waiting for the announcement of Valerie Sterling's
engagement to Edgar Wymper. At every party, their friends peered at
the two of them, looking for a clue: a ring on Valerie's finger to fill the
space left when she'd removed the rings Carlton had put there; a new
kind of excitement in Edgar's round face; a speech by Edgar toasting
his bride-to-be. But the weeks went by, and soon it was the middle of
June. Everyone was preparing to leave New York for cooler climates,
and Rosemary worried.

"What will you do if he doesn't ask you?" she asked as she and
Valerie dressed for the last party of the season. It was being given by
Edgar's mother and father in the Plaza ballroom.

"He'll ask me," Valerie replied, slipping on her dress. "He expects to
marry me."

"And of course you'll say yes."

"I suppose so." Sitting at her dressing table, Valerie looked at her
mother's reflection beside her own. Rosemary, dressed and arranging
her bracelets, was stately and elegant in black and white lace. "It's
Edgar or someone else; I can't think of any alternative. Can you?"

"Well, but, my dear, you do like him. You're fond of him; he's pleasant to be with; you have a good time...don't you?"

Valerie smiled ruefully. "Those are the words I used with Kent and

Carl. I liked them, I was fond of them, they were pleasant to be with; I usually had a good time with them."

"And you loved them."

Valerie ran a comb through her hair, debated pinning back one side with a gold clasp, then decided to leave it loose.

"Valerie, you did love Carl!"

Their eyes met in the mirror. Valerie's were somber. "Sometimes I thought I did. Sometimes I thought I could love him much more, if we gave ourselves a chance. But mostly, I felt sorry for him, and I'm not sure how much I was confusing love and pity. He always seemed to be a little bit lost. One minute he'd make me feel I ought to be mothering him, and the next he'd be forceful and sure of himself, and I'd relax and we'd have a good time. No, I don't suppose I really loved him. I liked him. Most of the time I thought we were good friends. I think—I'm a little afraid—I don't know how to love anyone. I haven't—"

"Don't say such a thing! It's not true!"

"I hope not," Valerie said quietly. "But it's been a long time since I felt I loved someone in that lovely, deep, magical way the poets write about." She ran a comb through her hair.

"And Edgar?" Rosemary asked.

"I like Edgar. I'm fond of him, he's pleasant to be with, we have a good time. He keeps me entertained and he likes to do things for me." She stood up and surveyed her image. "Edgar lives in a wonderful world, Mother, where no one worries about survival. And he loves me and he'll take care of us. Doesn't that sound like the perfect man?"

Rosemary ignored the irony in Valerie's voice. "You'll learn to love him," she said firmly, certain in her own mind that it was a good thing, as well as a necessary one, for Valerie to marry him. "He may not be perfect, but he sounds just right for you."

Three hundred people came to the Wympers' party at the Plaza, for dinner and dancing and to say their farewells before scattering about the world on their summer jaunts. Valerie wore red, a strapless, sinuous silk sheath that set off her creamy shoulders and gave her face a glow that looked like happiness. Edgar's mother had lent her jewelry for the evening, since she knew Valerie had sold most of her own, and so she wore diamonds and rubies at her throat and ears. Everyone told her she was stunning: the real Valerie, back with them at last. And at eleven at night, as the guests sat at round tables finishing their coffee and *crème brulée*, Edgar stood at his parents' table, and the orchestra gave a small fanfare to bring quiet to the room.

"I have an announcement," he said.

In quick protest, Valerie put her hand on his arm. They had not talked about this. It had to be a decision the two of them made together.

Edgar paid no attention; the first time in six months he had ignored her. "Not really an announcement," he said. His voice carried to all thirty tables; there was a quiver in it, but still it had the slightly pompous drama he had cultivated so successfully. "It's really a request. I decided to make it here, because our friends and our families are here, and it's the end of the season when we make plans for the future." He looked down into Valerie's eyes. "My darling Valerie, I made the decision to speak to you here without asking you, and that may trouble you, but I promise you now that it is the last decision I will ever make without you, if that is your desire. I've been thinking about these words since I was sixteen years old; a long time, a faithful time, as you know, and they are so momentous they require a grand and proper setting. I could have spoken them at any time in the past six months— I know, and so do you, that everyone has been waiting for me to do so—but it seemed clear to me, and I hope it will to you, that the only way to emphasize the significance of this moment is to do it before witnesses, for all time, for eternity."

He stood straight and scanned the faces of the guests. Murmurs of amusement and approval ran through the ballroom. Valerie, exasperated, wanting to laugh, but also angry, saw Rosemary watching her. I have to stop this; it's a circus, she thought. Once again she put her hand on Edgar's arm. But then she pulled it back. She could not do it; she could not shame him before his family and his friends. And what difference did it make? One way or another, she was going to marry him; if he wanted to propose in the Plaza ballroom before three hundred witnesses, why should that affect her one way or the other?

Edgar's voice, loud and well modulated, rose again, still with that slight quiver, as his eyes met hers once again. "Valerie, I love you. I've loved you, I've adored you, for more than half my life. From the moment I first saw you, I've wanted to take care of you. I intend to devote myself to making you happy; your desires will be mine, your pleasures will be mine, your world will be mine. And my heart will always be yours. Valerie, my love, my dearest most exquisite Valerie, I am asking you to marry me."

The echo of Edgar's dramatic voice rolled across the dance floor and through the swinging doors to the kitchen where the serving staff stood still to listen. In the ballroom, someone began to applaud. Others took it up, the guests stood, and soon the ballroom was filled with applause and congratulations, happy cries and good wishes, and predictions of joy.

Edgar held out his hand and Valerie took it and stood beside him. She looked at the sleek smiling faces all about them. This was her world, familiar, comfortable, predictable, accepting. This was where she was safe.

And decorative.

Well, so what? she thought. If that's what I've been perfecting for thirty-three years, it's what I ought to keep doing. It's what I do best.

The sound of applause was like a rising wind, and for a brief second she recalled the whoosh of the snow and wind on the lake as Carlton landed the plane and they slid through that powdery whiteness to the forest on the far shore.

I was more than decorative then. I saved people's lives; I saved my own.

In one burst, like a shock wave, all the feelings of that long night returned to her: the cold, her fear, her exhaustion—but also being needed, being depended on, doing something painful and frightening, triumphing over danger, knowing she was involved in something bigger than the fleeting desires of the moment.

I want it again. As soon as the thought came to her she knew it had been there since she began to recover. The thought that she might never again know those feelings of triumph and being needed was terrible.

But maybe once was all I'm good for. Maybe at the next crisis I'll fall apart. That's what everyone expects of me.

Or I'm a lot better than they give me credit for. Maybe there's a lot more to me than anyone ever thought. Including me.

The guests were crowding around now, and Edgar put his arm around her, holding her close against the crush. She knew he would always do that for her: protect her from whatever approached. He would never do what Carl had done; he would make sure she was never alone against the world.

She leaned against his solid body, feeling the warmth and strength that came not from workouts in his health club, but from his net worth. Edgar would never allow the slightest danger into her life.

But if there's no danger, how can there be any triumph?

Well, there won't be, she thought; at least not the spectacular kind I had that night. Who needs it, anyway? What people really need is security and pleasure.

"You're so perfect together!" someone was saying.

"Wasn't it nervy, proposing that way!" a young girl exclaimed. "Such a brave man, your Edgar! A real hero!"

Valerie looked at her contemptuously. A hero. For proposing in a ballroom.

"Happily ever after," said a woman nearby. "Such a mess, but you landed on your feet, Val. You're a gutsy lady."

Valerie stared at the speaker. A gutsy lady for landing on my feet. Landing a rich husband, you mean.

The crowd of grinning faces pressed around her; mouths stretched until they looked huge and voracious, roaring with laughter, gossiping, already anticipating the fall social season, with Edgar and Valerie Wymper in the center of it. Valerie forced herself to stand still. Security, she reminded herself. Pleasure.

But what about doing things I never thought I could do? What about being better than everyone thinks I am?

She looked at the grinning faces. They were so sure they knew her. What did they know? Had they ever saved anyone's life?

Her thoughts had taken only a few seconds. *They think I'm only good enough to be Edgar's wife. Who are they, to decide what I'm good enough for? I'll show them what I can do on my own . . .*

Fear clutched her. She had no idea what she could do on her own. Maybe nothing. But she couldn't believe that: that was what everyone else thought. There was a lot she could do. How hard could it be, really? She was young and smart and she knew the top people in the top companies in the world. She'd find something really tough, and then she'd know once again that feeling of triumph, of proving there was more to her than the prize social catch of any season.

She ignored her fear. I'll get over it, she thought; it goes with finding out what I really can do.

She took Edgar's arm from her waist and stepped away from him, one step back, and then another. He turned a look of surprise on her, and she saw it mirrored in the faces of those closest to them. She stood alone, and her low, clear voice rose above the chatter of the guests.

"No," she said.

Chapter
20

"I have the perfect job for you," Sybille said smoothly. She was in New York for the day, on business, she said, and had invited Valerie to tea at the Carlyle. "You can start right away. You'll have to move back to Virginia, but you do like it there, and my company is the best place for you right now."

"You have a job just waiting for me?" Valerie asked.

"As a matter of fact, I do, but if I didn't I'd make one; I worry about you, Valerie. I even feel a little bit responsible for what happened."

Valerie's eyebrows rose. "Responsible?"

"Well, in a way. I ran into Carlton a few times in New York, last fall, and the people he was with seemed awfully peculiar; shady, I thought, not like the men you'd expect to see him with; almost crooked...oh, I shouldn't say that now; what good does it do? But I'm truly sorry I didn't say anything then; you and I might have been able to stop him before he got in so deep he couldn't get out."

"Deep in what?" Valerie asked sharply.

Sybille shrugged. "How would I know? But if I'd warned you—"

"You're not responsible." Valerie's voice was cool. "You don't have to adopt my problems, Sybille; I can handle them by myself."

Sybille's face froze.

Valerie sighed. "Forgive me; that was rude. I know you want to help, and I do appreciate it. Tell me about the job you want me to take. It's amazing it worked out this way: that you have a production company and I've done all those spots on television."

Sybille sat back, revolving her cup in its saucer. "It is amazing. Remember once, a long time ago, you asked me if I'd give you a job? Who would have thought...Well, I can't tell you too much about the job now; I have to work it out with my directors. But you'll definitely have a place, and it will be where you belong. Trust me, Valerie, I know what's best for you. Come to my office in a couple of days, and we'll talk about the details."

Valerie contemplated her cup of tea. She was in a quandary. In the four days since she had refused Edgar, she had overcome her earlier reluctance and called a number of friends, each of whom said he had no job for her at the moment but would call her if anything came up. She had tried to read the help-wanted advertisements, but it was no easier than before. Already, before she had even begun to apply anywhere, she felt helpless and discouraged. Her brief flare of confidence at the party sputtered out like a flame; she couldn't fathom her next step. The words in the advertisements all ran together, like a foreign language, and everything about them was dreary: the word "job" was harsh and gray; when she said it aloud, it groaned. Even if she was anxious to work she didn't have the skills or experience everyone wanted. It was almost enough to send her back to Edgar. But here was Sybille, holding out a job. She took a notebook and a gold pencil from her purse. "Your office is in Fairfax?" she asked.

And so, the following week, on a brilliant Monday at the end of June when boats skimmed the Potomac and riders galloped in freedom through the hunt country of Virginia, Valerie walked into the offices of Sybille Morgen Productions, wearing a pale-gray suit and crisp white blouse, and reported for work.

She was given a desk, introduced to Gus Emery and Al Slavin, two directors whose desks were near hers, and handed a large basket of mail. She stood beside the desk, reluctant to sit down, and contemplated the stacks of envelopes. All of them were addressed to the Reverend Lilith Grace. "What am I supposed to do with this?" she asked Gus Emery.

He was her height, handsome in a soft, almost pretty way, with long eyelashes, pale skin and a startlingly rough voice. "Sort it. Love and adoration in one stack; questions in the other."

Valerie frowned. "Am I supposed to know what that means?"

"Just do it; you'll catch on. It won't stretch your pretty brain more than it can handle." He turned to go.

"Just a minute," Valerie said coldly. "Take this to someone else; I'm not here to do this kind of work."

"No?" His gaze moved in leisurely fashion from her feet to her face. "Could have fooled me. Ms. Morgen said you're the new assistant."

"She couldn't have said that. She brought me here to work on camera; I expect to write my own scripts, too. That's what I've done and she knows it. I'll talk to her about it; there's been some mistake."

"Wrong. Ms. Morgen doesn't make mistakes. Okay, Val, we got work to—"

"Mrs. Sterling."

"Wrong again. I call you what I want, *Val;* it helps my digestion. Okay, enough of this crap. You were hired for me and Al; you belong to us; you're our assistant. This is our assistant's desk; this is our assistant's chair; this is our assistant's basket of mail to sort for the Reverend Lily every morning, rain or shine. There's a big turnover around here—people come and go; lots of 'em can't get along with the queen bee—Ms. Morgen to you—but me and Al been here from the beginning and we're staying. That means we do our job and nobody interferes, and we do it with an assistant. That's you. I have to be any more specific than that?"

Valerie turned on her heel and strode the length of the room to Sybille's office. "I have to see her," she said to the secretary and kept walking, opening the inner door.

Sybille looked up sharply. When she saw Valerie her face smoothed out. "I can't talk, Valerie, I have a meeting—"

"I just want to clarify something. Gus Emery says you hired me as his assistant."

"His and Al's. I told you that."

"No. You did not. You told me I'd have an anchor job—or interviewing—and write my own scripts."

"I told you, if you recall—really, Valerie, I'm sure I said this clearly —that I'd use you as much as possible on camera, but that you'd be working in production first, until I found a way to use your skills. Isn't that what I said?"

"Yes. You didn't say I'd be anyone's assistant."

"I may have neglected to say that. Are you really so worried about titles? I want you to learn as much as possible—you're very special to me, Valerie; I want you to be an important part of this company—and Gus and Al are very good at what they do; they can teach you more than anyone. Is that so unreasonable?"

"Who do you think you—"

"I beg your pardon?"

Valerie stood very still. The echo of Sybille's amused, tolerant voice, and the slightly childish tone of her own complaints, hung in the air. She could feel the shift in power, as if an earthquake had tilted the floor. A coldness settled within her. *I work for this woman; my salary depends on her. Once she followed me around like a puppy. But she's learned a lot in all the years since college, all the years I was playing.* "No," she said evenly. "It's not unreasonable. I'll be at my desk if you need me."

Finally, slowly, she sat at her desk, thus admitting, by taking possession of it, that it was hers. I'll have a place for you, Sybille had said; it will be where you belong. Valerie swallowed the bitterness of that and sat with her back straight, her head high, looking about the room, trying to believe she was really part of it.

It was a large room, low-ceilinged, blue-white with fluorescent lights, divided by low partitions into cubicles for producers and directors. Secretaries and assistants sat in the open. The room was carpeted, the desks were only a few years old, the equipment in the office, the studios and the control room was the best that could be bought, but still it all seemed dull, no different from any other television studio Valerie had seen; in fact, this one struck her as more confining than all the others.

Because I work here. I'm not dashing in like a visiting star to tape a brilliant ninety-second spot and then dash out, back to my horses and my freedom and my most beautiful Sterling Farms.

She closed her eyes against the tears that stung them. Too many changes in too short a time, she thought; she hadn't had a chance to get used to any of them.

The day after she refused Edgar's proposal, when she had to stop pretending her life was the same money-lined cocoon she had always known, she had felt the full weight of what Carlton had done. Then Sybille had appeared, with a job, and two days later Valerie moved back to Virginia, not to her spacious farm in Middleburg, but to a small apartment in Fairfax, with two small rooms and a tiny kitchen, sparely furnished with straight-legged furniture, a bed that sloped to one side, and a few aluminum pots and pans. It's only temporary, she told herself every morning and every evening. It's like a bad hotel. I don't really live here; I'm just staying for a while, until I have the money to get a decent place of my own.

But she had no idea when that would be.

Her mother was all right for a while. As soon as she found a smaller apartment and moved from Park Avenue, she could live on the money in the account Carlton had missed, and the sale of her jewelry, at least until Valerie found a way to help her.

Which meant, she had to earn more at Sybille's company, or find a different job, or . . . There was nothing else. And she could not face the thought of looking for another job; she hadn't handled that part very well the first time. She had a kind of security: a job, a salary. It was so tiny no one should have to try to live on it—she was sure she couldn't, for very long—but at least it came regularly, and she had not had to hunt for it: Sybille had dropped it into her lap.

But she hated it. She hated everything about work. She hated having to wake up at a set time, dressing and eating breakfast in a rush, driving to the studio in a stream of cars that made her feel she was just one of a crowd, and walking into the offices of Sybille Morgen Productions where she was still nobody: one small part of a machine controlled by someone who didn't care what she was thinking or feeling or worrying about, who cared only about getting a full day's work out of her. She felt she didn't have a life of her own; even in the evenings and on weekends, she couldn't forget that she really wasn't free: in a few hours she would have to go back and be answerable to someone else.

Where was the triumphant exhilaration she had felt in the Adirondacks? Where was the excitement and satisfaction of knowing that people were depending on her? Where was the feeling that she was better than people gave her credit for?

Not in this job. Sybille's company wasn't a place for heroism. Probably most places weren't, when it came right down to it. But there had to be something she could do. Something that would make her feel in charge of her life once again.

One thing she would not do was go back to Edgar. She had thought about it, more than once, but she knew what would happen if she did: he would magnanimously forgive her and marry her with a triumphant generosity that would set her teeth on edge and doom their marriage from the start. No, not Edgar. Another man, perhaps, someone who would have faith in what she could do. Or her money, or part of it, would be returned to her. Or . . . something else. Something she hadn't even thought of yet.

It could all change overnight, Valerie told herself. But the only thing that changed in the two weeks after she moved back to Virginia was that Sterling Farms was sold.

Dan Lithigate had told her, the day before she began working for Sybille, that someone had made a good offer; he did not know who, since negotiations were handled through the buyer's attorney—but the price was excellent, and the buyer's financial statement looked solid. Valerie would soon have a large chunk of money from the sale, to help pay off Carl's debts. A week later, the sale was confirmed.

It's all gone. Someone else will have it now; I'll never walk through those rooms again, or ride through those fields, or cut flowers for the dinner table in the gardens and greenhouses . . .

"All sorted?" Gus Emery stood beside Valerie's desk and reached for the basket of mail.

"No," she said. "I'll do it now."

He looked at the clock on the wall behind her. "Reverend Lily expects them by eleven A.M."

"You didn't tell me that."

"I gave you an order. That meant now, not when you get around to it."

Valerie shot him a cold look. "Do you need to be rude to feel important around here?"

A long whistle snaked from his pursed lips. "My, my, we're very brave this morning, considering we're brand-new on the job and could be fired in a minute. You let me take care of my importance, and you take care of your job. Okay?"

"No. If we have to work together, why can't you be a gentleman, and make it more pleasant for both of us?"

"A gentleman," he repeated. "There ain't no gentlemen in business, Valerie; if you'd done a day's work in your life you'd know that. Bring me the mail when you're done; I have a bunch of other stuff waiting for you."

"How do you know I haven't worked all my life?"

"Oh, come on. Newspapers, tv, your attitude, and the queen bee. See you later."

"And that bothers you? That I've never had to work?"

He looked at her over his shoulder. "I don't get bothered, except by people not taking orders. People like you don't take orders real well; you have to learn. So this is a lesson I'm teaching you: I give orders, you jump. You have to learn that, just like you have to learn everything else. Every goddam son-of-a-bitch thing else we got to teach you. That includes doing something *when I tell you* and not sitting around with this fucking chitchat when you got work to do." He strode to his cubicle, fifteen feet away.

Valerie's gaze followed him. You mean, envious, slimy little worm, she thought. You hate people with money. You hate me because I had money and you never did, and probably never will. And Sybille foisted me on you and you don't like it. Well, isn't that too damn bad. This is my job and no one's taking it away from me.

She dumped the basket of mail onto her desk and began to pull letters from envelopes, skimming them and separating them into piles. "Dearest Reverend Grace, my life is glorious now, because of you..." went on one side of the desk; "Dear Reverend Lily, I don't know what to do about my son, he's on some kind of drugs—" went on the other side.

But soon her hands slowed as she began to read the letters from beginning to end. They were intimate, passionate, even worshipful; they were written to Lily Grace as if she were mother, sister, idolized teacher, lifelong friend, and beloved; they ached with genuine feelings. Valerie read them with astonishment. The young woman who had been a passenger in Carlton's plane on that last, terrible journey had been quite ordinary. Even the brief talk she had given earlier, at Quentin Enderby's funeral, though moving, had been unmemorable. What had happened to her? Maybe someday, if I have time, she thought, I'll go to her church.

"Looks like you need some help," said a light, pleasant voice at her shoulder, and a long arm reached around her to grab a stack of letters.

"No, I do not," Valerie said angrily, and then, turning, saw the arched eyebrows and open smile of Al Slavin, the other director for whom she worked.

"Let's finish these," he said, pulling up a chair. His beard and hair were flame-colored and as he bent over the letters Valerie saw a small bald spot at the top of his head. He gave each letter a cursory glance, put it in the proper pile, and took up the next. "Can't take too long on these; anyway, they all sound alike after a while."

"Are there always this many?" Valerie asked, skimming the letters almost as fast as he did.

"Every day. We get eight, nine hundred a week, sometimes more, and we divvy them up, a hundred or more a day. The adoring fans get an effusive thank-you; the worried ones get a written answer or they get one on television."

Valerie looked up. "How?"

He wagged a reproving finger. "You're giving yourself away. Never admit in public that you don't watch every episode of every show produced by Sybille Morgen Productions. It means death at dawn. Just between us, Lily has a show every Wednesday night at ten, called 'At Home with Reverend Grace,' when she sits by a cozy fireplace with lilies and candles on the table, and answers some of her mail. Reads the letters aloud, no names of course, gives advice, dispenses wisdom and encouragement, smiles at the camera with love and tenderness—"

"You don't like her."

"On the contrary. I love her. No one can't love Lily. I just don't want her managing my life or my country, and I get worried when people fall in love with an image on the screen and think it can translate to political or moral leadership."

Valerie nodded, not really paying attention. She wasn't that interested. At another time she would have been intrigued enough to learn more about Lily Grace, but now, with so much to think about, she didn't have enough energy to try to understand a young preacher who had no part in her life. "Done," she said. "Shall we get some coffee?"

"I'll get it; you ask Gus what he wants done next."

"I meant we could go to the coffee shop downstairs."

"I know what you meant. We don't take breaks. The coffee machine is in the kitchen; I'll show you later."

Valerie contemplated him. "Is this an act you two put on? He's the bad guy and you're the good? He makes people unhappy and you go around smoothing ruffled feathers?"

He grinned at her from the thicket of his red beard. "You are one smart lady. It's not an act; it's an accommodation. He gets more work out of people, but I keep them from quitting. For a while at least."

"Do you like him?"

He shrugged, "We're a team; we're used to each other. Go on, now, find out what he wants next; I'll get some coffee."

They were like two halves of a whole person, Valerie thought, and it was Al Slavin who kept her from despair a dozen times in the next three weeks. There was a streak of cruelty in Gus Emery that puzzled her; he was so good at his job that she would have thought he could afford to relax. But he never did. He drove himself and those around him; he seemed bitter toward everyone; and with his whiplash tongue and cold cynicism, he seemed indifferent to anyone's opinion.

Except Sybille and Lily. With Sybille he was smooth, smart, cool and admiring, never deferential but never harsh. With Lily he was cautious; it was as if he tiptoed around her, careful with his vocabulary, soft with his voice, fatherly with his directions and smiles when they were taping a sermon or "At Home with Reverend Grace." He had made himself indelibly a part of Sybille Morgen Productions; but almost no one but Sybille and Lily liked him.

It was Al Slavin whom everyone liked, and soon he was Valerie's closest friend in the company. In every spare moment, he taught her the details of production: how a rough script was transformed into a final, taped program. He taught her tape editing and the workings of the control room; he explained satellite pickups and transmissions, camera and lighting techniques. And he often called on her to help him in the studio.

The soap opera, "The Art of Love," was taped every day, following a rehearsal in the morning. A weekly game show, "The Winner's Circle," was taped before an audience every Monday. Another game show, "Top This," was taped with an audience every Thursday. "At Home with Reverend Grace" was taped on Wednesday morning for airing Wednesday night; and Lily's sermon was broadcast live, and simultaneously taped for reruns, on Sunday morning at eleven.

Al was in the control room; Valerie was in the studio. She stood to the side, wearing headphones and holding her clipboard and pencil, ready to do what she was told. They were in the final rehearsal of an episode of "The Art of Love" before taping that afternoon.

"Lola's scarf is crooked," Al said to Valerie through the headphones, and she walked onto the set to straighten Lola Montalda's scarf.

"And tell her to fasten the third button on her blouse; what is it with her? Ask her how much she had to drink at lunch."

Valerie smiled at Lola. "Al would like you to button your blouse. And he says you're looking very lovely today."

"Of course," Lola said. "I always do. My button?" She looked down. "How strange. It must have done that by itself."

"Valerie," said Al, "we're all waiting."

"Lola," she said, "everyone is waiting."

"Of course," Lola said. "They always wait for me." She buttoned her blouse and took her place beside the sofa, holding a painted ceramic vase.

"Okay," said Al. "We're going to try it from 'You treat me like a slave.'"

"Lola," said the floor director as Valerie withdrew to the sidelines, "we're taking it from 'You treat me like a slave.' And this time, aim for the middle of the fireplace."

"His head is higher than that," Lola said haughtily.

"Your aim is bad; if you aim at the fireplace, you'll get close to his head."

"My aim is perfecto!"

"Let's go," said the floor director.

"You treat me like a slave!' screamed Lola, and threw the vase with wild passion in the general direction of Tom Halprin's head. The vase sailed three feet above him and crashed against the top of a window in a freestanding wall, causing it to tremble and sway.

"Damn it," Al breathed. "Valerie, another vase. And see if she dented the window frame. And make sure the crew sweeps up all the pieces; we don't want it to look like a tornado went through there; only a lover's quarrel."

"Pete," said Valerie to another assistant as she crossed the set to check on the window frame, "get another vase."

"Not me," he replied. "I only take orders from Gus."

She swung on him. "Do what I tell you! Now!"

He backed away from her sharp voice. "Right," he said, surprising himself. "In the prop room?"

"On the bottom shelf. Bring two."

"Right," he said and was gone.

Valerie examined the window frame and found it undented. She paused to watch the crew sweeping up broken glass, and then she returned to the sidelines. She felt better than she had in a long time; she'd given an order and it had been obeyed. Briefly, wonderfully, it had brought back the past, when staffs of servants had stood ready to carry out her orders. It's a lot better to give than receive, she thought wryly. She wondered if she had sounded like Gus Emery giving orders to her. Maybe she had; and maybe Gus felt just as good when she jumped to obey him as she had just now, when Pete went off to the prop room. We all want somebody below us, she reflected, watching Lola pout because the floor director was telling her yet again that she always aimed high. Even if we only have a chance to have power over one other person, we grab it. She wondered if that was why people had children. Then she wondered if she would ever have children. And that reminded her that she was single and without money, and working for someone else, and that made her aware of Al's voice in her headphones, speaking to the floor director.

"I want Tom to duck whether she gets close or not. If we use camera three we can probably fake it. She's trashed eleven vases so far; she isn't going to get a lot better."

"Got it," said the floor director, and set up the scene again.

"You treat me like a slave!" screamed Lola and hurled the vase. Tom Halprin ducked as it flew two feet above his head and crashed against the wall over the mantle. Lola went on in full stride. "I hate you! I gave myself to you; I moved into your house like you asked me—"

"'*As* you asked me,'" Al said in the headphones.

The floor director put up his hand. "Lola, it's '*as* you asked me.' That's the right way to say it; it's what the script says."

"I know what the script says; I changed it. Nobody talks like that." She pursed her lips and tilted her head left and right. "'*As* you hoity-toity la-di-da-di asked me.' Who talks like that anyhow? Not me. I know how people talk; they talk like me and I talk the way I feel good."

The floor director looked up, in the direction of the control room.

"What do you think, Valerie?" asked Al.

Surprised, Valerie thought about it. "If she said 'when you asked me' there wouldn't be a problem."

Al's chuckle came through the headphones, making her feel warm and useful. "I like that. Let's try it."

The floor director conferred with Lola and she picked up where she had left off. "I moved into your house when you asked me, so I could be around when you wanted me! Doing what you wanted! Anything you wanted! And now you think you can tell me you found somebody better? And you won't always be here? 'Cause you're gonna see her, too? Well I won't be here! If you think I'll just be hanging around, you're crazy! You're—" She looked around for something else to throw, and at that Tom Halprin strode across the set, grabbed her by the shoulders and forced her down to the sofa.

He held her down with one hand and ripped open her blouse with the other. She wore nothing underneath, but Tom's bulk and the angle of the camera allowed nothing more than teasing glimpses of her full breasts.

"No!" Lola cried. "I don't want—you can't—!" She struggled as Tom pinned her hands above her head. "Stop!" she screamed, but the scream became a whimper. Tom's mouth was on her breasts; his hand was beneath her skirt. The camera's eye slid to the floor, lingering on the shards of the broken vase before the fireplace, moving slowly back along the floor to the sofa, where Lola's hand now hung limply, the fingers just brushing the rug. "Tom," she whispered. "Anything you want..."

Valerie stood at the side, rigid with anger. She had never watched "The Art of Love"; no one had told her that it was soft-core pornography. The worst kind, she raged inwardly: a woman adoring the man who rapes her. Why would Sybille do it?

Because there was an audience for it. Valerie knew "The Art of Love" had been bought by stations in thirty-five markets so far, and it was beating the network soap operas in its afternoon slot. When Sybille found an audience, she would cater to it, no matter with what kind of program. She would provide what people wanted, or she would create a demand by offering what no one else did; that was how she made her money.

I wonder what she wouldn't do for money, Valerie thought.

But then she wondered about the rest of them: Al Slavin, Lola and Tom and the entire cast, the floor director, the camera crew . . . and Valerie Sterling. All of us working on Sybille's porn. We're all just as bad as she is.

No, she thought; that's not quite true. It's our job, and probably every job has something we'd rather not do. Who am I to think people ought to quit rather than work on one piece of porn? It's Sybille who has the real choice; for the rest of us, it's more complicated.

The next scene was being set up, and Al's voice came through the headphones. "Valerie, could you get that telephone table closer to the bed? And make sure that rug is out of the way so the camera can move in on the bathroom; God forbid we shouldn't see Tom's buns in the shower."

She did everything she was told, but her thoughts were elsewhere. Never before had she given any thought to people who had to work, whether they liked it or not, whether they had to compromise their beliefs to keep a job they couldn't do without. But now she was part of that world, and she was stunned by how many adjustments had to be made. Why didn't anyone complain? Al seemed happy in his job; so did Gus Emery. Lola and Tom did what they were told—whether it was fighting, raping, being raped, or eating breakfast—with a casual air that made it seem not much different from being a salesclerk or an accountant. Everyone did the work that had to be done, and none of them seemed unhappy.

Maybe because they were earning good salaries. I should be paid more, Valerie thought at the end of that day, when the studio was quiet and a crew was setting up scenery for the next day's rehearsal. If Sybille won't let me do what I want, at least I ought to get paid enough to live on.

But this time she would not storm into Sybille's office. She had to pick the right time. In the meantime she did the jobs for which she had been hired, annoyed and bored because they were so simple-minded: running errands, telephoning for prizes to be given on the two game shows, checking props for "The Art of Love," making coffee, bringing in sandwiches for lunch, making notes for script changes, telephoning to get permission letters for the use of copyrighted songs and articles, and making endless Xerox copies of prop lists, lighting schedules, scripts, and production schedules. She was the only assistant who did all those jobs; secretaries did them for other directors. And it was always more than she had time for.

"He wants me to fail," Valerie said to Al at the end of her third week. "Just because I had money once."

Al shook his head. He was sitting at his desk nearby, jotting down suggested lighting changes for "The Hour of Grace." "There's more to it than that. It has something to do with Ms. Morgen. I think he's jealous."

"Jealous?"

"She pays a lot of attention to you, walks over here a lot, just walking through, you know, but you're the one she's watching. In fact it's like she's always watching you, whatever you're doing, even when she's in her office. You must have seen it; everybody else has. I think Gus may be worrying about you taking his place; not directing, but you being the one she talks to, instead of him."

Valerie gave a small laugh. "Tell Gus he's safe. Sybille and I aren't close."

"But you knew her before she hired you?"

"Yes." She didn't want to talk about it, even to Al. She threw down the pages of a script she was collating. "I'm so sick of this; any eighth grader could do it. I've got to get a different job, Al, something I feel good about, something I like to do."

"Most of the world wants that," Al said gently. "Give us a chance, Val; you haven't even been here a month. We'll find something interesting for you. Tell me what you'd like; I'll try to fix it."

Valerie smiled at the earnestness of his brown eyes. He was a good friend, happily married, with a large family, which made it easy for her to think of him as someone she relied on, and loved. "Thank you, Al. I think Sybille doesn't want me to do anything very complicated right now, but if something occurs to me I'll take you up on that."

Gus Emery walked by and gestured to Al. "I need you on Sunday to do the Lily."

"No problem," Al said easily. "Anything special?"

Gus shook his head. "The usual. The crew can get the equipment trucked up to the church, and tape the show; they know it by heart. All you have to do is run the control room and get the sanctimonious shit out to the faithful. Piece of cake."

"What about you? On vacation this week?"

"I've been drafted to help the queen bee. She bought a horse farm in Middleburg; wants me to carry stuff out."

"She's already got a horse farm. In Leesburg, is it?"

"She bought a bigger one. Sterling Farms." Gus turned to Valerie. "Any relation?"

She was sitting as if frozen. "No." They were both looking at her. "I have work to do," she said numbly and stood up. She looked around, as if wondering where she was, then moved away, toward her desk.

Someone else will have it now; I'll never walk through those rooms again, or ride the horses through those fields, or cut flowers for the dinner table in the gardens and greenhouses . . .

She kept walking, past her desk, past all the other desks, and down the corridor to the large studio. It was chilly and dark, empty until a taping would bring it to life the next morning. *She can't have it; no one can. It's mine.*

But it wasn't simply that someone had bought Sterling Farms. What staggered her was that it was Sybille.

Still, what difference did it make who bought it? Yesterday she didn't know who it was; today she did. What difference did it make when the most important thing was that she had lost it and could never live there again?

It made a difference. She had the eerie feeling that Sybille had been stalking her for years, trailing her into boutiques, cosmetics shops, skeet shooting, horseback riding, hunting—even Nick, she thought with icy clarity—and now Sterling Farms. At first Valerie had thought Sybille wanted to mimic her way of life; now it seemed she wanted to take over everything she ever had.

As if she wants to punish me. But what did I do to her? I thought I helped her; she came to me in New York and I . . .

No, she thought suddenly. Not New York. Before that. A memory tugged at her.

Stanford.

She'd done something . . . no, said something that made trouble for Sybille. It had been such a little thing, but the result was that Sybille had been expelled. That was why she had befriended her in New York; she'd felt guilty. And she'd apologized.

She stood still in the center of the studio, her thoughts spinning upon themselves.

That was thirteen years ago.

She began to pace near the sofa where Tom Halprin had raped Lola Montalda and a steady stream of sex scenes was played out day after day except when the sofa was used as a part of the set for "At Home with Reverend Grace." *I did something stupid, and thirteen years later she still remembers, and she wants to punish me. My God, if she's been waiting all this time for a chance . . .*

She had almost forgotten the pain of losing Sterling Farms. *What else does she want? If I had a husband I suppose she'd want him. But I have none; I haven't anything else she could possibly want. I wonder if that means she's satisfied.*

She shivered. In her mind she saw an implacable Sybille, always unsatisfied, tracking her forever.

But that was insane. Even though Sybille was no longer her friend —probably she never had been—and might even think of herself as Valerie's enemy, she wasn't a monster; she could be reasoned with.

Well, let's not overdo it, Valerie thought, a smile breaking through. I won't try to reason with her; I won't bring up the past at all. But there are some things I want from her, and by God she's going to give them to me.

I want a lot more money for all the work I do around here.

And I want the kind of job she promised me. She doesn't have a show for me yet, but when the new interview show goes into production, she's going to give it to me.

A feeling of virtue pulsed through her. I've shown her I'm a good worker. I don't complain; I get everything done. Now I want a couple of things in return.

Propelled by righteousness, she walked back through the corridor and into Sybille's outer office. "I have to see her," she said as she had three weeks earlier, and opened the inner door.

Sybille was on the telephone. "I told you to schedule a board meeting for the day after tomorrow. Call Arch and Monte right now; we have to—" She looked up. "I'll talk to you later." She slammed down the telephone. "My secretary is supposed to ring when someone wants to see me."

"I'm sorry; I should have waited," Valerie said, walking into the office, "I have to talk to you."

"Well?"

"I need a higher salary, Sybille."

Sybille seemed to settle into her chair. "Why?"

"Because I'm getting the bare minimum, and I'm worth more."

A small muscle quivered at the corner of Sybille's mouth.

"I'm secretary and assistant for Gus and Al; that's two full-time jobs. I ought to be getting two salaries."

"Two salaries," Sybille repeated.

"I'm not asking for that, but I expect to be paid fairly for the work I do. And there's something else. Al was working on the new interview show yesterday; I want to be the host. I've been here three weeks and this is what I've been waiting for; you know I'd be right for it. And the sooner you say I can do it, the sooner I can start working with Al on developing it; that's really what I should be doing."

Sybille gazed at her for a moment. "It sounds as if you think you should be sitting in this chair."

Valerie smiled, forgetting that Sybille never joked. "Not today."

Sybille's face darkened. "I could have refused to see you; no one else barges in here the way you do. I'm getting tired of the way you take advantage of an old friendship." She stood. "We have performance reviews after six months for new employees and every year after that. You know that."

"Gus told me I wouldn't get a raise for a year. I'm not taking advantage of anything—I don't stoop to that—I do what I think—"

"You do what you want. You always have. It hasn't gotten you very far, has it? I'd think by now you would have learned how to behave."

"You mean, how to grovel," Valerie said icily. "I don't grovel, Sybille; not to you, not to anyone." She stopped. *I work for her; I work for her; I work for her.* She took a breath. "I'm willing to discuss my work, my salary, the interview show—"

"Willing! Who do you think you are to tell me what you're willing to do! You work for me; this is *my* company; you take *my* money for the piddling work you do. You always thought you were better than I was, but now you know—"

"That's not true. I never thought I was better than you. I had more—"

"The hell you—"

"Listen to me! I had more money than you, but that didn't take talent; I was born to it. It's not the sort of thing that would make me feel I was better than anyone. In fact, I envied you! You always knew where you were going and how you'd get there . . . in fact, I told you I envied you for that! You remember so much about the past, you must remember that too!"

"*Don't tell me what I remember!* You've always looked down on me, treated me like a stupid country cousin, and I hated every minute of it. It's taken me a long time—"

"The only part of that that's true is that you hated it. And you hated me."

"I never hated—" Sybille bit off the disclaimer that came automatically to her lips whenever anyone accused her of anything. She sat rigidly in her chair, gazing at a painting just to the right of Valerie's head; for some reason she couldn't meet her eyes. "Why not?" she said, and years of hate poured out through her hoarse voice. "Why should I like you? You never gave a damn about me; you did everything you could to make me feel inferior. You flaunted Nick at me, and then when he began to like me you got me kicked out of school so you could have him to yourself. A lot of good that did, didn't it? I was the one he married; not you. And then you dragged me all over New York, to all your precious little shops, so you could show off how generous you were, taking the time to introduce poor little Sybille to those simpering idiots who made your shoes and your sweaters and your makeup.... You invited me to your house for New Year's Eve so I'd feel out of place because I was the only single person there.... What have you ever done for me that I should like you?"

Stunned by Sybille's onslaught, Valerie had taken a step back, but as it went on, her eyes narrowed and she looked at Sybille with contempt. "I offered you friendship; I thought that was what you wanted. But you don't have the faintest idea of what friendship is all about. If you really want to know what I thought of you, I'll tell you. I thought you were a fraud. You were always so sweet and innocent and grateful, so naive and full of nice feelings about everyone ... good God, Sybille, did you think we'd believe that? You used to—"

"Shut up!" Sybille cried.

"You used to tell me how much you loved Quentin, and Nick, and Chad, even me, and how you needed help because you were helpless and lost in the big cruel world."

"Shut up! You can't—"

"For awhile I thought you really believed all that, or you'd convinced yourself it was true, but then I changed my mind, especially about Chad, because you never told little stories about him. Parents usually have wonderful little anecdotes to tell about their kids, but you never—"

"You don't know anything about kids; you don't have any! You don't have anything! I have it all! You think you can make me feel I'm no good, but I'm better than you; I have everything!"

"Do you? I wonder how much you really have. There's something wrong with you, Sybille, something warped, as if you see everything reflected in one of those crazy mirrors at a carnival. I think you got me here—"

"You bitch, you can't talk to me that way!" Sybille was on her feet, leaning over the desk. "Get out! Get out! Get out!"

"Let me finish! You got me here to humiliate me, didn't you? To lord it over me because I'm down now. That's just like you; it's what I thought you were like: you're mean-spirited and vengeful and you know how to hate but not how to love—"

"You fucking bitch!" Sybille stabbed at a button on her desk, her finger stiff and furious. "Get in here!" she screamed when her secretary answered. And when the secretary appeared in the doorway, she said, in a strangled voice, "This woman is leaving. Write her a check, whatever we owe her, and make sure she doesn't walk off with any supplies when she goes."

"Walk off!" Valerie exclaimed. "You're crazy; I wouldn't take anything from you. I don't want anything from you."

"You wanted a job. You wanted somebody to take care of you." Sybille's eyes slid over Valerie's. "All those nice security blankets disappeared, didn't they? Husband, bank accounts, all that cushiony life... whoosh. Gone. So you came begging. And I scrounged around and found you a job, but that wasn't enough for you. Who said you don't want anything from me? I took care of you, gave you more than you deserve, and *three weeks later* you barge in here and tell me I broke a promise, you don't like what you've got, and *you expect* me to give you everything you want..."

"Sybille, stop it! You can't make things up and pretend they're real!"

"Don't call me a liar! You're the liar; you can't stand it that you had to come to me and beg! You're a liar, you're disloyal, you're too spoiled to do a decent job, and you're a cheap tart—making up to Al Slavin, who's got a wife and four kids, so he'll work on me to give you your precious interview show. But nobody wants to see you on television; nobody wants to see you anywhere! You're a failure; you haven't got a goddam thing in the world, and nobody wants to have a fucking thing to do with you!"

Valerie backed up, away from Sybille's venom. Her stomach was churning; she thought she would be sick.

"Get out of here," Sybille rasped. She sat down and picked up a piece of paper at random, swiveling her chair away from Valerie. "Get the hell out. I have work to do."

Valerie left, stumbling in her haste, She had to get away, as far as possible. Whatever waited for her out there, she would rather face it today than stay another moment in Sybille's orbit. She grasped the doorknob to shut the door behind her. But just before the door closed, she heard Sybille's voice, low and intense, reverberating in the room. "That's everything. Everything. Finally, this is the real beginning of my life."

Chapter
21

need a job," Valerie said. She sat in a leather chair across the desk from Nick, her head high, her white linen suit slightly wrinkled from the drive to his office in the July heat and humidity. "I have no money. I found out, after Carl died, that it was all gone, and there were debts... It's a very long story, but the point is, I need a job, and I thought you could help me."

She was facing the wall of windows behind his desk, her features illuminated by the morning sun. It had been a year since Nick had seen her, at their lunch in Middleburg, and he was struck again by the perfection of her oval face: the steady gaze of her large hazel eyes beneath level brows, her translucent skin, and her tawny hair falling in loose, heavy curls to her shoulders, the lively play of emotions in her eyes and on her full mouth. She had the kind of beauty that made others want to draw close and coax a smile from her; the kind of looks that led most people to the happy belief that great beauty is accompanied by a greatness of soul, since they cannot believe that perfect beauty could mask a warped or evil nature. And so they drew close, thinking that anyone as lovely as Valerie Sterling had to be a person of such goodness, loving kindness and generosity that she would bring some of her perfections to their lives, warm them, embrace them with her virtues and thus, by some kind of osmosis, impart virtue, even perfection, to them.

Nick, who knew she was not perfect—or at least had not been thirteen years earlier—still found himself believing in the possibility of it as he gazed at her. He found it harder to believe that she was there at all: suddenly a part of his life when, for so long, she had been only a memory that would not fade. He reminded himself of that lunch in Middleburg, when he had been sure she had not changed at all, but, even with that reminder, he felt a sense of excitement and anticipation. He felt, in an odd way, very happy, and that was when he knew that he could love her again.

Or perhaps I've loved her all along, he thought. He did not think that could be true—he did not believe any love could be sustained for thirteen years without contact or hope—but the possibility intrigued him: he liked to think of himself as a constant lover. And why else would he be filled with this happiness?

Valerie's eyes were shadowed, and suddenly he realized she was worried at his silence. "Carlton died last January," he said. "What have you been doing since then?"

"Nothing. Nothing important." She met his eyes, and a small exasperated breath escaped her. "I was working."

"Where?"

Her head moved higher. "At Sybille's production company. She offered me a job working with two directors, and I took it, but she and I had different ideas about what I could do, so I . . . left."

He nodded calmly. It sounded as if Sybille had fired her. What a crazy situation, he thought. Sybille's always envied her, and then to get a chance to humiliate her . . . "How long did you work for her?" he asked.

There was a pause. "Three weeks."

He nodded again, as calmly as before. "And before that?"

"I was living with my mother in New York. We were trying to find a smaller apartment for her; she can't afford to stay where she is. I . . . thought about marrying again, but that wasn't what I wanted." She leaned forward. "I want to do something interesting, Nick; something important. I have to work, but I can't spend my time at silly jobs that a child could do; I have to do something I like, something I'm good at. I want to do an interview show, or an investigative one, or a newscast, and write my own scripts. You know how long I've been doing it; I've kept it up. I could have done much more if I'd had the time." She paused, thinking of all the time she had had: hours, days, years, to do exactly as she wished. So much leisure time, all her own. It had been as much a form of wealth as her considerable fortune, and she had never realized it. "I know you produce some of your own programs; I want you to build one around me."

Nick sat back, amused at her audacity. For a moment he thought she might be disguising uncertainty, perhaps even fear, but a long look convinced him otherwise: she was absolutely serious, and as arrogant as ever. Adrift, almost alone, victimized by her husband, left with no fortune to buoy her up, she was more than brave: she was foolhardy.

"I am good at it, Nick; I can do it," she said. And then, unexpectedly, she added, "It's about the only thing I can do," with a small, rueful smile that tore at his heart.

He thought about it. She would be wonderful on camera; he knew that. He did not know whether she could sustain her wonderful presence on camera for half an hour or longer; he did not know if she could write. And he had no reason to think she took the world any more seriously now than in the past, even though her fortune was gone. She's not looking for a career, he thought: more likely she's waiting for a man to rescue her, or for someone to find her money, or for some other miracle to happen, and then she'll take off.

But even though he was sure of that, he could not send her away. Not with this odd happiness inside him, and her hazel eyes watching him steadily, waiting for his answer.

"Are you still living in Middleburg?" he asked.

"No. I had to sell the farm." She steadied her voice. "I have an apartment in Fairfax. I plan to move soon, to something better, but I won't go far. I don't want to leave Virginia."

"Good." He picked up his telephone. "Susan, what do we have open now?" Rolling a pencil between his fingers, not looking at Valerie's quick frown, he waited. "With Earl," he said. "That sounds fine. I have a friend here, Valerie Sterling; she may want to talk to you about it. I think she'd be very good."

He turned back to Valerie. "We do have an opening." His voice sounded formal, almost brusque. "We're expanding the staff for a new program called 'Blow-Up,' and we need another person in the research department."

Valerie's frown had deepened; she looked at him in bewilderment. "Research?"

Nick nodded. "We have nothing else right now." It sounded like an apology, and he became even more brusque. "It's a good place for you to start. You'll get to know everyone and you'll learn how we operate. A lot of the time we're learning ourselves; everything still seems new around here, and all of us do half a dozen jobs when we have to, to get through whatever the latest crises are. But we do get through them; we don't repeat our mistakes." His voice had grown warm, picking up enthusiasm as he spoke. "We're growing so fast it's hard to keep track of where we were last week and who was doing what. It was like that at Omega, you know...well, no, you don't, but it was pretty much the same. I guess I haven't found a way to start a company without trying to do everything all at once, and I bring in people who are the same, so we charge ahead and then slow down to see where we are, and then start up again, faster than before. It's the most exciting time in a company; nothing comes near it when things get settled and a lot of it gets predictable and routine. So it may be chaotic around here, but it's never dull. And our people don't leave; the five top people I brought in two years ago are still here, and so is everybody we've hired since then. Two years ago this month, in fact, that we started; you can help us celebrate."

Valerie gave a flicker of a smile. "I don't know anything about research."

"You'll learn in no time." Nick's voice was still warm and buoyant with energy. "Earl DeShan runs the department; he'll give you all the help you need."

"But that's not what I—" She stopped.

There was silence in Nick's office. Valerie stood up, propelled by panic, and walked across the large room. She couldn't believe what was happening: it had never occurred to her that he would not help her. She stood beside an Eskimo sculpture of a bear standing on his hind legs, dancing. It was a superb piece: she had seen similar ones in private collections, and knew how rare and valuable it was. She didn't know Nick liked Eskimo sculpture. She really didn't know anything about him. Once she had been sure he was uncomplicated, so easy to understand. But that was when he had two loves—his work and her —and spent his time at a battered desk in the engineering building or in an apartment furnished with castoffs, with juice glasses for wine.

Now he had an office that seemed so simple she knew how very much it had cost, paneled in mahogany, furnished in leather and rosewood and a fine Navaho rug. It was the office of a successful, ambitious man who had excellent taste and the money to satisfy it. Once that was all she would have thought it was. But now it seemed to her to be the office of a man who had grown hard; who might sound boyish in his enthusiasm but was really as unimaginative as she had always thought him, especially when he was asked to do something different, like give her a chance. *He is giving me a chance.* In her panic, she brushed aside the thought. It wasn't the right kind of chance. After working for Sybille, she needed something she knew she could do; she needed to feel some confidence in herself.

She moved to the fireplace, and nervously picked up and put down a group of small soapstone sculptures of seals and puffins and a fisherman reeling in his line. The office was very quiet. When she turned, she found Nick watching her, waiting for her to settle down. He was one of the most attractive men she had ever known, more so now than in college. His face had new lines that made him look more interesting; his hair was graying at the temples; his smile, though less ready than before, lightened his face more than she remembered, and his deep-set eyes seemed more shadowed. His shirt collar was open and casual, but his lightweight wool jacket hung perfectly on his broad shoulders, and Valerie was certain, without looking, that his socks matched.

In the years since they had been together, when his clothes had been shabby, he owned only one tie, his hair was unruly, and his socks did not match, he had been married to Sybille—how could he? how could he have loved her, desired her, needed her?—divorced from Sybille, fathered a son, built two companies, moved across the country and, according to Chad, had lots of women. *I don't know him at all,* Valerie thought again. Everything about him brought back memories, but still she might as well be talking to a stranger.

But he's not a stranger, and I counted on him. How can he do this to me?

"You've done a good job of showing me how wrong I can be about someone," she said with something like despair. "I was so sure you'd help me."

Nick's eyebrows lifted. "You mean, offer you what you want."

"I mean, offer me something I'm good at. Anyone could offer me a job doing research."

"Anyone could, but I doubt that anyone would. You said it yourself, Valerie: you don't know anything about research."

"Anyone could offer me anything," she said edgily, "if they didn't know what I've done, and what I'm good at. But you do. I was sure you did; I was sure you understood me."

"Let me rephrase that," said Nick, his voice very cool. "You came to me because I know you, and therefore I couldn't resist giving you anything you want."

Valerie's color rose. "That's a crude way of putting it."

"Give me another way."

"We call on friends when we need them. I thought that was what friendship meant. It would be a pretty dreary world, otherwise: everyone alone, cut off from everyone else..."

He nodded. "You're right. But you did call on me and I offered you a job and told you I wanted you to become part of what we're creating here. That means you wouldn't be alone. How much more than that do you need to make the world less dreary?"

Involuntarily, Valerie smiled. It had been a long time since she sparred with a quick-witted man. Her eyes met Nick's; he was smiling at her, relaxed and confident, and her own smile faded. She wondered how long it would take her to get used to losing the status she had taken for granted all her life.

"I think you'd like it here," Nick said casually. "You might even like research, though I imagine we'll find something else for you after you've been here awhile."

Valerie's head tilted slightly as if she had heard a small warning bell. "You mean after I've settled down. This is a test, isn't it? To see if I can fit in and take orders. That's what Sybille did—"

"No, it's not," said Nick instantly. "And you don't really believe that." Once again his voice was almost brusque. "I want to help you find your own place, something you can always rely on, if that's what you really want. If it is, I'll do everything I can to help you. But as long as you want to do it on my network you'll have to trust me to do it the way I think best."

Valerie was silent. She was ashamed of herself for accusing him of behaving like Sybille. But she had said it out of frustration. He was like the rest of them; he didn't believe she could do anything. He'd always thought she was frivolous, and now he thought the way to help her was to tuck her away in a corner where she couldn't do any harm or get in anyone's way. I'll go somewhere else, she thought; I have lots of friends.

But she didn't want to go anywhere else. Of course she believed friends were there to help, but she hated to beg. The few friends she had called before she went to work for Sybille had not offered her anything, and even Dee Wyly had not been able to help, though she called regularly: the only one, after a while, who kept in touch even after Valerie moved to Virginia. It had been hard enough to call Nick and ask to see him, much less plead for a job. And then his formal, businesslike attitude had shaken her. She couldn't imagine doing this again, and perhaps again and again, with no assurance that she would get what she wanted.

Well, then, I'll do it here. No more favors asked. Standing beside the fireplace, her head high, she looked at Nick and smiled. *You stuffy, rigid, tight-ass businessman—how in God's name could I ever have thought I loved you?—I'll show you what I can do; I'll show you how wrong you are about me. You don't know anything about me.*

"Fine," she said lightly. "Research." He tongue almost tripped on the word. "As I recall, I was pretty good at it in college; I'm sure it will all come back to me." She smiled again and walked to his desk. "If I'd known what was ahead, I'd have worked a lot harder at it." She held out her hand. "Thank you."

He stood with her, looking at her searchingly. "I'm very glad you'll be with us."

Their hands met, and Valerie felt a shock of recognition at the clasp of his long, thin fingers. Quickly she looked away. Her glance fell on Chad's picture on his desk. "I didn't ask about Chad," she said as she pulled her hand back. "How is he?"

"Wonderful." Nick's eyes brightened. "This is his latest masterpiece." He picked up a painting that had been standing against the credenza behind his desk. "I'm looking for a place to hang it."

Valerie studied the painting as Nick held it upright on the desk. A young boy and a man rode their bicycles along a canal—she recognized it as the C&O Canal in Georgetown—while a dog frolicked alongside. In the distance, a woman watched from the upstairs window of a house. The canal and the sidewalk were dappled with sun and shade, but the man and the boy were in an open space between the trees, brilliant with golden light. The woman in the window was a dark silhouette.

It was a quiet scene, resembling the paintings of Pisarro, but with its own sureness of touch that made Valerie shake her head in wonder. "He *is* wonderful. It's amazing that a young boy...how old is he?"

"Eleven."

She shook her head again, this time with a feeling of melancholy. *Eleven years. And Nick has done so much, lived so much, while I let the years get away from me...*

"I liked him, when we met at lunch last year," she said. "And now it seems he's going to be an artist."

"I think so," said Nick. "I hope you—" The intercom on his desk rang and his secretary announced his next appointment. He put the painting back on the floor and walked Valerie to the door of his office.

"I hope you and Earl get along," he said, changing whatever he had begun to say before they were interrupted. "I'm sure you will. Go to personnel, the last door on the left when you leave here, and ask for Susan; she'll walk you through the paperwork and introduce you to Earl. You can start right away, can't you?"

"Yes. Thank you again."

Once more, they shook hands, quickly, and then she left, walking down the corridor to personnel.

Starting over, she thought, surprising herself. With Nick.

E&N, the entertainment and news cable network that Nick had created out of the old Enderby Broadcasting Network, had just expanded to twenty-four hours a day. Its audience had grown to over twenty million households. "Still a long way to go." said Les Braden. "CNN is over thirty-five million." But he was grinning as he said it, and everyone at E&N had the same air of jubilation: they had almost doubled the households they reached in only two years, and they'd done it with off-beat programming that many of the experts had said would never get them off the ground.

"The Other Side of the News" not only had won their first Emmy; it had been their first show to register two million viewers, and the first to make the heads of the national networks sit up and take notice.

The award-winning program had begun with Jed Bayliss, running for Congress, pontificating in outraged tones, "My opponent wants to cut your Social Security benefits by forty-six and a half percent!"

"Does he?" asked the anchorman. "This is what his opponent said five days ago."

Bayliss's opponent appeared on the screen, the date of his speech below his name. "Social Security must not be cut," he said flatly. "Forty-six and a half percent of the people cannot survive without it."

The anchorman returned, his face bland. "Now, why did Jed Bayliss use that percentage in the wrong way? Did he misunderstand it when he heard it the first time? If he'd like to respond, we'll be glad to have him appear on next week's show."

Next, the president of a Colorado mining company declaimed, "We have a perfect record of land reclamation in our mining operations." But before his words faded, the picture of a dead lake was on the screen, gleaming dully in the sun, surrounded by a moonscape of barren land punctuated by a few skeletal trees. The date was in the upper left-hand corner as the camera panned silently across the ghostly scene. On the periphery was the green and virgin land that had filled the entire valley before the company arrived. Not a word was spoken.

The mining-company president returned to the screen with more of his speech. Other scenes appeared, contradicting what he said, and a number of experts gave figures and anecdotes that showed how parts of the speech were skewed or missing some vital fact.

Back and forth it went, a rapid-fire fifty minutes of revelations that spared no one. Politicians, educators, business executives, foreign leaders, reporters and community activists were all fair game.

Within a year, speakers, especially political candidates, were being challenged more often when they made their charges, and advertising reminded people that "The Other Side of the News" would appear on Sunday at 7 P.M. Eastern Time with the actual figures, the hidden facts, the complete story.

Newspapers wrote about "The Other Side," as it came to be called; viewers began to look forward eagerly to Sunday night, to see who would be exposed this time. They talked about it on buses and com-muter trains on Monday mornings, and in their offices. High-school and college students saw it in class, if they had not already seen it at home, because their schools bought the tapes for use in government and communications courses. Preachers talked about it in sermons about lying. Audiences became restless when speeches were being given, as if they couldn't wait to hear the other side.

"A winner," Les declared. "Hell of a deal to have a real genuine winner the first year we're on the air. But it's only the first; wait and see."

"The Other Side of the News" was produced in the E&N studios. The second winning program with over a million viewers was one they bought: a series on circuses from every country in the world, perform-ing for three hours with only three breaks for commercials.

"Our prize duo: news and circuses," Earl DeShan told Valerie as they walked to the research department on her first day at E&N. "Be-sides them, we have a nifty lineup of shows that don't break any records, but we get sponsors; we make a profit. We got foreign films and U.S. of A. oldies and goodies, a couple of newscasts a night with debates afterward—real debates, no holds barred; we had to break up a fistfight once. Now, that was an awesome sight: two grown men putting up their dukes over toxic waste; can you believe it?" He paused. "Where was I?"

"A nifty lineup," said Valerie.

He shot a glance at her. "Right. We have a doozy called 'Backstage' that shows how movies, plays, Broadway musicals, whatever, are made. Rehearsals, costume fittings, building the sets, getting the actors made up . . . good stuff. Nick and Monica love it—she's v-p for entertainment; Les is v-p for news—they love it, all of us love it, and so do a few hundred thousand intelligent people; it oughta be a million; we can't figure out why it's not."

"I like it," Valerie said. She had often watched it when Carl was traveling and she was alone at Sterling Farms. "I didn't see it the last few months, when I was living in New York."

"That's a tough apple to crack." He grinned at her so she would not miss his joke. "We've only sold 'The Other Side' in New York; we haven't found a cable operator to buy our whole package yet." He stopped at an open door and stood aside for her to enter. "Home sweet home. Any kind of info, dirt, scandal, or plain boring facts anybody asks for we give with a cheery smile. Nick said you'd be working mostly on 'Blow-Up'; he tell you what it's about?"

Valerie shook her head. She was looking at the bright, windowless room, lined with shelves overflowing with books and newspapers, with more books and papers stacked on the red-carpeted floor. Rows of track lights hung from the ceiling, aimed at the shelves and four desks in the center of the room, three of them cluttered, one clean, each with its own word processer. I haven't typed since college, Valerie thought; I don't know if I remember how. I don't know anything about computers. I don't know much about research techniques. Or info, dirt, or scandal. I might be okay with plain boring facts.

"Your desk," Earl said, and pulled its chair back for her.

Valerie sat in it, her hands in her lap.

He peered at her, head cocked. "Something bothering you?"

"I don't know how to use a computer," she said bluntly. "I haven't typed in years. I don't know much about research; I did some in college, that's all. I suppose I could have lied to you and tried to fake it, but that's not my style. I have to learn everything from scratch; it's going to be awhile before I'm much help around here."

"Not to worry. Nick says you'll be good, and he's right more often than he's wrong. How about trying out your desk?"

Valerie hesitated, then turned the chair and pulled it forward. In the center of the clean desktop was a memo pad with a note scrawled in a large, angular handwriting she had never forgotten. *Welcome from all of us. I hope you find us a good crowd to hang out with.*

Valerie smiled and touched the note with her finger.

"Chair seems to fit," said Earl casually. "That's the first requirement: you'll probably do okay. Here's the rest of happy crew; I'll make the intros."

Still smiling, Valerie folded the note and tucked it into her pocket as Earl made his introductions. "Sophie Lazar and Barney Abt: Valerie Sterling. I'm going to brew some java; you all get acquainted. And then Valerie and I start with some ABCs and everybody gets to work. I run a tight ship around here and nobody should forget it."

"We couldn't," said Sophie. "You tell us so often, I'm getting sea-sick. Hi," she said to Valerie. "I'm glad you're here; we're overworked and understimulated; we need a new face. Let me show you around what we laughingly call our library."

"I'll talk to you later," said Barney Abt. "When you're ready to use the microfiche, if you need any help, ask." He looked at Valerie's blank face. "Uh-huh, you'll need help. I'll be around."

"You didn't come from a research department?" Sophie asked.

Valerie shook her head. "No."

Sophie waited. "Well. Where did you come from?"

"I was working with horses."

There was a silence; then Sophie burst out laughing. "Sounds like a great way to prepare for television. Let's have lunch together, shall we? Then we can talk."

"Yes," Valerie said, liking her. She was tall and slender, with broad hips, close-cropped black hair, brilliant black eyes, and a wide mouth that was always moving: chewing gum, talking, muttering to herself as she worked, laughing, or pursed in a silent whistle. She wore—every day, Valerie would discover—a tailored suit with a silk blouse tied in a bow at the neck and one strand of beads, either amethyst or lapis lazuli.

"Twelve-thirty? There's a place down the street where they know me; they'll give us a booth and we can gossip. Now, about our library; because we don't really have what you'd call a system..."

Sophie, Barney and Earl DeShan took up Valerie's first day at E&N, and all of her first week there. And Sophie and Valerie went to lunch every day at the little place down the street, where they ate soup and salad and talked about themselves. "Married at eighteen; divorced at twenty," Sophie said at their first lunch. "Not too traumatic; we didn't have kids. I'd like some, though, and thirty is a time to do a lot of thinking about that. How about you? Divorced? Kids? How old are you?"

"My husband died. I'm thirty-three and no children, and I'd like some, too. How did you learn to do your job?"

"Library work after school in high school and after. I'd always wanted to go to college, but then I decided it wasn't important and got married instead. Wrong decision, but I was only eighteen, and by the time I was divorced I didn't have any money, so I kept working. I got good at it, too. There's nothing hard about research, you know, if you're naturally nosy and don't give up in a hurry. You just have to keep digging and get the whole story. You're going to be on 'Blow-Up,' right?"

"Yes, but I don't know what it is. Automobile tires? Sun spots? The end of the world? Lovers' quarrels?"

Sophie was laughing. "Nothing like that. It's blow-up as in photography. We're going to have a picture of something—a ship launching, maybe, with very important people all around—then enlarge part of the picture to show a small number of very important people, then enlarge it again to zero in on somebody, a man, say, who's standing innocently in the background, and enlarge his picture so it gets bigger and bigger until it fills the screen and he's what we do the story on."

"Who is he?"

Sophie spread her hands. "Guess. Maybe the engineer who blew the whistle on the Navy for fudging specs on an earlier ship. Or the Washington lobbyist who got Congress to give the contract for the ship to one company over another. Or the guy who's been accused of pocketing the money from cost overruns in the design and construction of the ship."

"Creative, but what if he's none of the above?"

"We find somebody who is. Or we don't do that ship; we do another one. There's no shortage of hanky-panky out there, you know. But that isn't all we're looking for. This show is about people: who did what, and when and how and why, and what happened to him or her because of it. Every week we'll pick out three people—sixteen minutes to a person—and tell his or her story, good or bad but never, please God, dull."

"Everybody has a story," Valerie said reflectively.

"Right. But we have to find the dramatic ones audiences want to hear about. Are you the Sterling who saved a bunch of people when their plane went down? New York State? Sometime last winter?"

"January."

"That was you?"

"Yes."

"Good story. We could do it on 'Blow-Up.'"

"No."

"Well, I can't say I blame you. It's surprising, though: when you start doing research—and that includes interviewing people who might be on the show—you'll find most of them are dying to have their story on the screen. Unless they're crooks; that's when we really have to dig to get the facts. I always wonder, when I read a story like yours, how I'd act if it was me. I hope I'd be able to do what you did, but how do I know? Did you ever do anything like that before?"

"No."

"Isn't that amazing? We don't even know what kind of people we are, inside. How come you're working? I didn't think people who had their own planes had to grub for a living."

Valerie looked at her in surprise. No one in her circle would ever ask questions about someone's income.

"I mean, that's the kind of thing we dream about," Sophie went on. "A private plane and everything that goes with it: big house, an apartment in Paris and maybe somewhere else, travel, designer clothes, a yacht . . . the whole thing. Did you have all that?"

Valerie smiled. "No wonder you're good at research."

Sophie flushed. "You mean I'm nosy. I'm sorry."

"No, *I'm* sorry," Valerie said quickly. "I didn't mean that. I meant you're good at asking questions." She smiled again, warmly this time. It was hard to resist Sophie's guileless charm. But why should she resist? Sophie Lazar was offering her friendship at a time when she needed it. She had called a few friends in Middleburg, but they had seemed as uncomfortable as those she had gone to for a job. And, in a way, she understood their embarrassment: they did not know how to talk to her without stumbling over the wall that divided their security from her fragile status. Valerie had been so irritated at their fumbled attempts at conversation she had been almost rude in cutting them off. But she had felt bereft afterward. More losses, she thought; what a shame I can't blame Carl for them. It's so much easier to have only one villain than a bunch of them.

But Sophie accepted her as she was; Sophie was curious about her income but not judgmental or embarrassed; Sophie was not looking for anything but friendship. To keep the world from being a dreary place, Valerie thought with a smile. "I did have money once," she said. "I don't anymore. I'll tell you about it sometime."

"I'd like that," Sophie replied. "I love to read about rich people, but I don't get much of a chance to talk to them. Is there anything you do want to talk about? Like your husband?"

"Not now. Do you want to tell me about yours?"

"Oh, that was so long ago. I'd rather tell you about my current friend, who wants to marry me. But you'd rather wait—right?—until we know each other better."

Valerie smiled. "Usually it's as hard to listen to intimacies before we're ready as it is to reveal them."

Sophie looked startled. "I like that. Where do you live?"

"In Fairfax."

"Nice and close: I'm in Falls Church." She finished her soup and sat back with a broad smile. "Tell you what. I'll teach you all I know about research, and we'll make lunch a regular habit, and before you know it we'll be old friends, and talking about everything. At least, that's what I'd like. How about you?"

"Yes," Valerie said. "I'd like that, too. I'd like it very much."

When she had been at E&N for almost three weeks, Valerie came home to find her mother waiting for her. "I know I should have called first," Rosemary said as Valerie unlocked the door and they went inside. "But I couldn't wait. I took the train. Did you know there's a wonderful train from New York to Washington? So fast—seventy-five miles an hour, the conductor told me—and extremely clean, though the food is not what one would hope for...snacks, you know, sandwiches, not full meals, and they make you carry it yourself. But still, for the most part I was impressed. Except that one has to go through Penn Station; it was terrible...terrifying. Have you any idea what it looks like? Of course we've read about it, but that's not the same as seeing those people, all those people sleeping there, you have to walk around them...I couldn't believe..."

"Sit down, Mother," said Valerie, cutting off the overwrought stream of words. "I'll make you some tea. Tell me what happened."

"This is where you live?" Rosemary asked. She looked about the tiny room. "This is where you *live?*"

Valerie was filling the teakettle. "I can't hear you."

"I *said*—" Rosemary stopped. She sat back, her hands over her face.

Valerie sat beside her. "You thought you'd stay with me for a while, didn't you?"

Rosemary nodded.

"I thought you were looking for a smaller apartment in New York."

"I was. It's been the most dreadful experience. I've gone from one dreadful apartment to another; you can't imagine what people have the gall to charge rent for. Tiny, dark places with barely room to turn around, nowhere to put my furniture—" She gave a swift glance at Valerie's living room, and the bedroom beyond, and fell silent.

They sat together for a moment, until the teakettle screeched and Valerie returned to the kitchen. "Where is your luggage?" she asked.

"At the train station," Rosemary said; her voice was subdued.

"How much do you have?"

Rosemary did not answer.

"How much, Mother?"

"Nine..."

"Nine suitcases? You're ready for all four seasons."

"Don't be sarcastic, Valerie; I wasn't thinking about it. Everything was so awful, and I was so frightened...I couldn't afford that apartment and I couldn't find another one and I didn't know what I was going to do, where I could go; I thought I'd end up on the street like those people you read about; I had nightmares about it. So I had to come here. I had to. I'm sixty-one years old and I couldn't imagine...I didn't know what else to do."

Valerie put her arm around her mother. "I'm sorry." She hesitated. She was having trouble saying the obvious words: that her mother could live with her for as long as she liked. "The tea is ready," she said at last, and poured from her white-and-gold English teapot.

"This is from Sterling Farms," Rosemary said, running her finger over the gold scrollwork on the lid. "It's a very fine piece. Where is the rest of the set?"

"In storage. I couldn't bear to sell it."

"What did you sell?"

"Most of the china; two sets of silver—I kept one; all the silver serving pieces; all the Royal Doulton and Waterford and Lladro; most of the crystal."

"And the Russian candelabra?"

"It didn't fit with the décor here."

Rosemary cast another quick glance at the room, and shuddered. "How can you live here? How could you stay one night, much less— how long has it been?"

"A little over six weeks. It's not permanent, Mother. It's just a place to stay for a while, like a hotel room."

"A terrible hotel; we don't stay in terrible hotels."

Valerie felt a flash of exasperation. "I remember when I used to say that. I'd rather not be reminded." She added more tea to Rosemary's cup. "Are you hungry? I have fish and salad for dinner."

Rosemary's head shot up. "You're cooking dinner? You don't know how!"

"I do now. And I stay in a terrible hotel room. And I have a job, and a salary that's a lot better than my last one but hardly enough to pay for a cook. How long are you going to talk as if things are the same, Mother? Nothing is the same: not one thing is the same as it was before the plane crash. I'm trying to get used to that, and I'm having enough trouble without you coming here and talking as if—"

"Don't talk like that to me!" Rosemary cried. "You don't want me here! That's what you're really saying, isn't it? You want me to go back to New York and leave you alone!"

"Yes, but I won't let you do it."

"Yes? You really said yes?"

"Would you rather I lied? I'm telling you how I feel, Mother; I think we owe each other that much. In one way I'd much rather be alone. I have to figure out how to live, and how to think about myself; I don't feel like the same person I've been all my life. I have to think about Carl, try to understand—"

"What good does it do to think about him? You married him and he ruined us!"

"You mean I should have asked for a few references before I said yes. Well, but I didn't, and now I'm trying to understand what happened, and get used to living here, and working, and not having many friends, and no man... Mother, can't you understand that this isn't easy for me?"

Rosemary shook her head. "You're hard and flip, you make jokes about getting references, you say you want me to go back to New York... I don't know what's happened to you."

"Yes you do, a lot's happened, almost overnight, it seems, but you're too busy feeling sorry for yourself to pay attention."

"I told you, I can't stand it when you talk to me that way! Why shouldn't I feel sorry for myself? Who's going to, if I don't? I'm sixty-one years old and I don't know what's going to happen to me! People my age, especially widows, have a right to expect that their children will take care of them!"

"I intend to," Valerie said quietly. She felt trapped by her own bad temper as well as by Rosemary's demands. All her life she had done what she wanted without being responsible for anyone else, and now, when she had to concentrate on building some kind of life out of the ruins Carl had left her, she had to take care of her mother. *It's not fair; daughters ought to be able to think their mothers will take care of them.*

Rosemary was crying. Tears squeezed from her closed eyes and ran down her face, making it glisten as if she were standing in a rainstorm. Well, that's what's happening, Valerie thought. She's standing in a storm, watching her world blow away. Valerie was caught between pity and anger; her muscles were tense and her head hurt. Every day she seemed to have fewer choices; with every step she took, she moved farther away from the life she had led, and still thought—though not very often anymore—she might return to. And how much farther could she be, she thought, than earning a living and organizing a life for two people?

It didn't matter; there was nothing else she could do. She put a handkerchief into her mother's hand and put her arms around her. "I don't want you to go back to New York. You'll stay here, with me. We'll work it out."

Rosemary's tears slowed and stopped. "Here?" she asked.

"Wherever I decide to live," Valerie said shortly, then gave a quick sigh. She had to watch her tone of voice; why make her mother feel worse? "Right now we're going to cook dinner," she said lightly. "Together. The Ashbrook women in the kitchen; who would have believed it? I'll tell you the truth: I'm not really a cook; I'm more like a junior technician. I read the instructions and put a bunch of things together and hope I end up with something familiar."

A small laugh broke from Rosemary. "It sounds chancy."

"It is, but it's got its good points. There wouldn't be any fun in it if we knew exactly how it would end up."

Rosemary shook her head. "I like knowing how things end. I won't go to a movie if I know it ends in tragedy, and I always read the last chapter of a book first, to make sure it has a happy ending."

"Do you really? I never knew that. But that ruins it, doesn't it? If the writer planned it from beginning to end..."

"I don't care. I don't want to spend my time on anything but happy endings."

Valerie nodded. "I'll do my best," she murmured.

The next day they began to look for a larger apartment. Rosemary made a list of addresses while Valerie was at work, and telephoned for appointments, and in the evening they drove to one after the other, swiftly appraising them with the critical gaze of women who had always had the best. Then Valerie would reappraise them in terms of their incomes: her own salary and her mother's small bank account, swelled now from selling her jewelry.

It took two weeks to find a place they could agree on: not an apartment but a coach house left over from an estate that was being divided into small lots for tract houses. The coach house too would be torn down when its lot was sold, but meanwhile it was theirs for a rent so low it was worth it, to Valerie, to move in even though they had no idea how long they could stay. Rosemary was unhappy because, even though it had two floors, it was not nearly large enough for her furniture. But to Valerie the five rooms felt grand and spacious after sharing her tiny apartment with her mother and, because they were across the street from a park, the rooms were always sunny and looked out on trees and bushes instead of other buildings. The house was in Falls Church, a few blocks from Sophie, who had told Valerie about it, and they moved in a few days after renting it. Rosemary had her furniture shipped from New York and they fit what they could into the five rooms; what was left over Valerie insisted on selling.

"It's too good to sell!" Rosemary protested. "Someday you'll want it. When you get your money back, or find someone to marry; you can furnish a whole house with what's here!"

"Or we can use the money now, when we need it," Valerie said firmly, and Rosemary, as she did all the time now, subsided, letting Valerie make the decisions. She would not help with the sale, however. That weekend she sat in her room with the door closed, trembling as she heard the footsteps of strangers and their murmured comments as they fingered her prize possessions. She sat there until the rooms were silent, and when she emerged almost everything had been sold.

"How much did you get?" she asked Valerie.

The money was in small piles on the mahogany coffee table. "Almost five thousand dollars."

Rosemary gasped. "It was worth thirty! Forty!"

Valerie nodded. She was looking at the money, fanned out before her. *I used to spend five thousand dollars on one dress. Now it seems like a fortune.*

"You gave it away!" Rosemary cried accusingly.

Valerie swept the money into one pile. "I don't think so. I went to a couple of house sales and saw what people were charging. I didn't want anything left. And it isn't as if I sold it all, Mother; for heaven's sake, look around you."

Stubbornly, Rosemary looked steadfastly out the window, at the people strolling in the park. Watching her, Valerie felt a stab of tenderness, as she would for an unhappy child. The coach house was crowded: oversized Oriental rugs covered the floors, the extra length rolled under along the walls; groups of tufted, braided, overstuffed furniture were jammed together to accommodate the pieces Rosemary could not bear to give up; lamps, silver-framed photographs and vases were crammed on tabletops. It all looked wrong: furnishings that had looked elegant on Park Avenue now looked heavy and dark, too formal for the small, plain rooms of a suburban coach house. But the pieces were familiar, and so, in spite of everything, the house was more like home, and much more comfortable, than the one Valerie had just left. For the first time since moving back to Virginia, she felt she had a place where she belonged.

But that meant this was permanent. She felt as if the last door had closed on her other life. She looked down, at the money on the table, then once again at her new living room, the solid furniture lit by the golden late-afternoon sun, and her body tensed with the urge to run away. But she had nowhere to run. Nowhere but forward, wherever that went.

She stuffed the money into her Coach bag, to be deposited the next morning on her way to work. Then she reached in and took some of it out. "We're going out to dinner," she told Rosemary. "We'll celebrate our new house, and our brilliance in squeezing all these possessions into it, and our new life in Falls Church." She put her arm around Rosemary's shoulders. "This is where we live now." She knew she was talking to herself as much as to her mother. "We'll get to know Falls Church as well as we know New York; we'll go to Washington for excitement; we'll make lots of friends. We're going to be very happy here."

Rosemary sighed. Valerie ignored that drawn-out expression of doubt, but later that night as she lay in bed, it echoed in her thoughts. For the first time in years, she was in the fourposter she had slept in from the time she was a child, and, gazing upward at the lace canopy, she could almost imagine she was a teenager again, living at home with her parents, everything made smooth for her, no matter what she wanted to do. She remembered the boys who had pursued her in high school, the ones she had ignored and the ones she had dreamed about; she remembered the parties she and her friends had given, where they learned about kissing, about how it felt to have a boy's hand under their skirt and inside their sweater, about dancing in erotic rhythms while rubbing against each other, scrupulously vertical since they could not imagine being horizontal with a boy, at least not then.

She moved restlessly in bed, her body heavy and longing. She missed Carl. He had been a skillful lover and they'd had good times together; far better than she'd had with Edgar, who was all drama and no sensuality. She closed her eyes and imagined Carl's hands on her breasts, holding them while his tongue moved slowly over the nipples. She sighed, her legs moving apart as she felt him bending over her, one hand still on her breast, his lips moving lingeringly over her warm skin, at her waist, on her stomach . . . "Nick," Valerie sighed.

Her eyes flew open. Her legs snapped together, and she stared at the lace canopy curving above her. Whose hands and lips had she been imagining? Not Nick's, it couldn't be Nick's, not after all this time. It was a slip of the tongue, no more. She had not even seen him, except at a distance, since their interview five weeks earlier. Part of the time he had been out of town, and the rest he had been exceptionally busy —Sophie had told her this—expanding E&N through agreements with cable operators in all fifty states and in Europe. E&N went through spurts of activity, and this was one of them, Sophie said; it might go on for weeks or months. In the meantime, Valerie was becoming a researcher: a rather lowly position that gave her no reason to have anything to do with the president of the company. And the way things were going, it could be six months before she saw him again.

It was a slip of the tongue. She'd probably been thinking of work, and so it was his name, not Carl's, that she said aloud.

I need something to do, she thought. It wasn't enough to shove furniture around, and shelve books and put away china: she needed more. "Like a teenager bursting with sexual energy," she murmured wryly. "I've got to find a way to work it off."

She slipped out of bed and went to the French-provincial desk in the corner: the same desk she had used for homework and love letters and poetry writing when she was young. Snapping on the porcelain lamp, she looked at the piles of clothes still to be hung in her closet and armoire and organized in bureau drawers. That's good for a couple of hours, she thought, and, naked in the warm night, she set to work.

"One of those investigators was here," Rosemary said when Valerie returned from work a few days after they moved in. "I can't imagine what they still have to ask you; it's been nine months since the accident. I told him you'd be home at five-thirty."

Valerie went to the kitchen to put on the teakettle. She was back in a moment. "You didn't do the breakfast dishes."

Rosemary was looking at a magazine. "I didn't have time."

"You had nothing but time. You were here all day."

"There wasn't time! I thought about doing them, but the day just got away from me. I'll do them tomorrow."

"You said that yesterday, and the day before."

Rosemary flung the magazine down. "I just have to get used to the idea! You ought to be able to understand, Valerie, it's not easy to change, at my age. I'm sixty-one and I've never done dishes; I never even thought about doing them."

"You never talked about your age, either, until it became an excuse." Valerie heard the bitterness in her voice and, angry at herself, retreated to the kitchen. She was so tired. She'd been sitting in front of a computer and a microfiche machine all day, reading the tiny print of newspaper stories about a series of unsolved murders over the past five years, and her back and neck hurt, her eyes hurt, and she was bored. At first the stories had been fascinating, but she had had to read dozens of them, most repeating the same information, in all the major newspapers and magazines. Then she culled the most important points from all of them and typed them up on her computer—a slow two-finger process, though she was teaching herself to type from a book—in a memo for Les Braden, who might use them in planning a story for "Blow-Up." Of course, he might decide he didn't want the story after all, and her whole day's work would be for nothing. She poured a cup of tea, feeling discouraged and irritated. She gazed at the teapot, then poured a cup for her mother. She was carrying it into the living room when the doorbell rang and Rosemary opened the door.

"Bob Hayes of the National Transportation Safety Board," the investigator said, shaking hands with Valerie. "We have our final report and I wanted to bring it to you, instead of mailing it."

"Final?" Valerie sat down, shifting her thoughts from her job to Carl. "You've found something new?"

Hayes shook his head. "I wish we had. We've put together everything we've got"—he took an envelope from his briefcase and handed it to her—"and this is what we've come up with. If you want to know basically what's in it . . ."

"Yes," Valerie said.

"The crash was caused by water in both auxiliary fuel tanks, and the failure of the pilot to do a complete preflight check. If he'd done it, he would have found the water; there's no way he would have missed it. But it seems he skipped some of it. Also, the pilot didn't follow standard flight procedures: he apparently switched to both auxiliary tanks at the same time."

Valerie waited. "Is that all?"

"That's it."

"In this whole report?"

"There's a lot of background: interviews, tests, analyses, the whole investigation. But that's our conclusion."

"But that doesn't solve anything! Carl said it wasn't possible to have water in both tanks; he said it hadn't ever happened before."

"We understand that's what he said. It's not often that water would be in both tanks, but that's what we found; probably from condensation."

"Carl said it was done on purpose. I told the police that, and I told your investigator."

"It's in the report. But we can't make that claim without some evidence. And we have none. All we have for sure is that there was water in both tanks and the pilot didn't do a thorough check before taking off."

Valerie stood and gave him a level look. "That's how it's worded in the report?"

He nodded.

"That it was Carlton's fault, and no one else was involved?"

"On the basis of the evidence we have, that's the only conclusion we can draw."

"But he talked about a woman. He said he would have thought she might do ... something."

"We included that in the report, but people do call planes and boats 'she,' and we've found no evidence of a woman. The mechanics at the Placid airport didn't see one; neither did anyone in the terminal. These accusations, you know ... they were made at a time when you were probably in shock; you may not have heard too clearly. And your husband did admit he lost control. He apologized to you for it. And all the passengers said he was delirious. You did, too."

"I said he was feverish and excited. I hope this report doesn't misquote me."

"I don't think it does. I'm sorry, Mrs. Sterling. We would have liked to answer all your questions, but we aren't always able to do that."

"I'm sorry, too," Valerie said stiffly, and stood where she was while he left.

Rosemary took one look at her face and went into the kitchen. In a moment, Valerie heard the sound of running water, and dishes banging against each other. I wonder how many she'll break, she thought.

Not many, she decided. Mother cares about china. She'll discover, to her great disappointment, that she's very good at doing dishes.

She looked at the report in her hand. I don't know any more now than I did nine months ago. I assumed all those investigators would take care of it for me, but all they did was blame Carlton. How easy to do that; he's dead.

But why shouldn't I do that, too? He wiped me out; why should I defend him?

Because I believed him when he said someone had done something to the plane. And if that was true—if there's the slightest possibility that it's true—that person murdered Carl and almost murdered the rest of us, and I want to know who it was. That isn't idle curiosity; that's a desire for justice.

She glanced at the report again. What could she do that teams of government investigators could not do? She had no idea. But if a woman had been involved, she wanted to know it. Until now, for some reason she hadn't wanted to pursue it; it opened too many awful possibilities. But now she had to know. Carl had been having an affair; she was sure of that. Why not assume that was the woman he'd been accusing? And there was the money. No one had found it, but maybe they hadn't looked in the right places. There were those shady characters Sybille said she saw Carl with in New York; maybe they knew something about the money, and maybe that had something to do with the plane crash. I'll have to talk to Sybille, she thought. I should be able to manage that. Now that I don't work for her anymore, we can be civil to each other, as long as we keep it short.

"Valerie?" Rosemary called. "Where does the cream pitcher go?"

"I'll show you," Valerie said. Suddenly she was filled with energy. There was so much to do. As soon as she could take some time off work, or organize her weekends so she had some hours to herself, she would do her own investigating. She wouldn't rely on other people anymore; she'd do it herself. And this time she would get the answers she wanted. She wasn't going to stop until she did.

Chapter
22

ybille stood in the side doorway of the Cathedral of Joy, watching the congregation stream into the warmth and brightness from the drizzling November day. The organ music mingled with the voices of a thousand people, and Sybille looked at her watch, picturing, to the minute, what Lily was doing in her small suite behind the altar. First she would stand quietly while her maid slipped over her head one of her ankle-length white silk and lace dresses she bought with the help of Sybille's personal shopper at Saks Fifth Avenue, buttoned it up the back, then knelt to put on her white flat-heeled shoes. Then she would sit at her dressing table while the cosmetics expert Sybille had hired fastened a huge bib around her and made up her face. Lily still thought it wrong, but when she saw how sickly she looked on television without it, she reluctantly agreed that it had to be done. Her maid would brush her long hair until it flowed over her shoulders like a silken veil that would reflect the television lights, while Lily reread her notes from the morning sermon, repeating phrases to make sure they were what Sybille wanted, spoken in the way her voice coach had taught her. At one minute to ten she would leave the suite and walk down the corridor to a heavy door at the side of the altar, and wait there until she received word that everyone was seated. The taping had begun five minutes earlier, to record "The Hour of Grace" for repeat broadcasts around the country.

At precisely 10 A.M., as the organ rose to a crescendo, the heavy door swung open and Lily appeared, small and fragile against the background of solid oak. The worshipers who sat in front saw her first; they craned for a better view, and that alerted those behind them, so that they were ready, some of them even standing on their toes for a clearer look, when Lily walked slowly, pensively, up the marble steps to the marble altar and then to the marble pulpit etched with tall graceful lilies reaching up as if to embrace her as she stood there, head lowered, eyes closed in prayer, waiting for everyone to be seated again and the music to die away.

Unseen by the audience and the camera, Sybille nodded as everything was done to the minute. It was her best production: pure, unsubtle drama with nothing to distract the audience from its concentration on Lily Grace. It was the kind that played best anywhere, and especially on a small screen. It was one of the reasons that "The Hour of Grace" was a goldmine.

"Such a dear girl," Floyd Bassington said, coming up beside Sybille. "I never saw anyone do God's work more sublimely."

My work, Sybille thought. She looked up at the vast height of her cathedral, its stained glass lit from behind, making it seem that the sun always shone on Lily Grace. She looked at Lily, gesturing carefully for the cameras and the congregation as all one thousand of them leaned forward, toward her high, sweet voice. She looked behind her, at the town of Graceville, rising from the rich Virginia soil. Mine, she exulted. Mine.

For a fleeting moment, she felt satisfied. It was all because of her. She did it all, from behind the scenes. Once she had wanted everyone to know she was there. Now she wanted them to be unaware of her, to have no idea who had power over them, or how it was being used, or how they were being manipulated. No one knew. But everything here —and much that was not visible—was here because of her, and no one else. It was all hers.

"Arch and Monte are here," Bassington said. His hand was kneading her arm above her elbow, and Sybille moved away.

"Let's not keep them waiting," she said, and walked ahead of him across the trampled grass behind the church to a two-story white house with a broad front porch. It had been there when the board bought the land with Carlton's thirteen million dollars, and, rather than tear it down, they had made it the headquarters of the Hour of Grace Foundation. Bassington had converted the living room to a luxurious office in black puka wood and nail-studded suede; the other rooms were used by secretaries, clerks and bookkeepers, twelve in all. The renovation had been completed in September, and the operations that had been spread between Fairfax and Culpeper were now centralized in Graceville.

Sybille found the others waiting in Bassington's office. Monte James, treasurer of the Hour of Grace Foundation, and president of James Trust and Savings, was tall and slouching, with pouches beneath his eyes, flaring nostrils above full lips, and a protruding stomach bisected by a cowboy belt. He wore embossed cowboy boots with high heels, whether he was in a tuxedo or bluejeans. He was taller than Arch Warman, vice president and secretary of the Hour of Grace Foundation and president of Warman Developers and Contractors, but Arch was wider: egg-shaped from his sloping shoulders to his ample hips, with small feet and hands, twinkling eyes behind square, black-rimmed glasses, and dyed black hair left gray at the temples, because he thought it was dignified. The two of them sat on a suede sofa, a bottle of Scotch, a pitcher of water, a plate of doughnuts and a thermos of coffee on the black coffee table before them.

"Ah, breakfast," Bassington said with satisfaction. "Sybille?"

"Coffee." She put her briefcase on the table, beside the doughnuts, but did not open it. "Begin," she said to Bassington.

He handed her a cup of coffee. "Jim and Tammy Bakker. The newscasts are having a field day with them. Why doesn't that damn story die out? Most stories do; this one just gets bigger."

"Greed, sex and money," said Arch Warman. "Why should it go away? It's what everybody wants to hear about."

"Well, they don't want to hear about us," Monte James said. "I've been thinking about it; we're too dull for the press. No greed and no sex; just straight business."

"Straight," said Warman with a laugh.

Bassington studied his fingernails.

"You've been careful," Sybille said. "I don't see a trail leading to you, even if the networks send out their dogs."

"Might get rid of a few perks, though," Warman said thoughtfully. "I mean, one of those smart-ass lady tv reporters checks into us and finds we're flying a Citation, and driving pretty cars like Monte's

Porsche and my BMW and Floyd's Mercedes, shit, she might get to wondering about what a religious board needs with all that high living and where we get the moola for it."

"You don't get rid of anything," Sybille said. "Those are legitimate expenses. *Are* they looking at all the tv ministries?"

"I imagine they'll get to all of 'em sooner or later," Warman said. "Most of 'em are red meat to a hungry lion. But we're okay, you know. You're right, Syb: we've been very good. Very careful, very clever, almost invisible. We don't leave a trail like the Bakkers."

"Don't get smug," she said. "Lily hates smugness."

There was heavy silence. There was always a heavy silence when Sybille let drop Lily's name in that way, a casual reminder that there would be nothing without Lily, and there would be no Lily without Sybille.

"Monte," said Sybille, and felt the brief flush of pleasure it gave her every time she snapped out their names and watched them leap to respond.

"Donations this year will top seventy-five mill," Monte said promptly. He sat back, speaking without notes, reviewing the finances for the year that was drawing to a close. From the seventy-five million dollars, Monte and Warman and Bassington would pay for the Foundation jet, their cars and their travels. They would skim ten percent of the cash that came in the mail and divide it among the three of them and Sybille, with Sybille taking the largest share. They would pay the highly inflated charges from Sybille Morgen Productions for producing Lily Grace's Sunday-morning service and Wednesday night's "At Home with Reverend Grace." And they would pay the legitimate administrative costs of the Hour of Grace Foundation: postage, equipment, supplies, office maintenance, the salaries of secretaries, clerks and bookkeepers.

"Graceville," Monte said pleasantly, and reviewed those figures. The initial phase for building the town would take one hundred and fifty million dollars. By borrowing the money they could complete construction in two years. That was made possible by the fact that James Trust and Savings made regular construction loans to the Foundation as they were needed. The loans were made at thirteen percent interest at a time when most construction loans were at eleven percent. The extra two percent was distributed to Monte, Warman, Bassington, and Sybille, who took the largest share.

There was a brief silence when Monte finished. "Arch," said Sybille.

Arch Warman's black eyes twinkled. "Marrach Construction is right on schedule. The retail stores, restaurants, what have you, will be finished as scheduled, in early June; they'll open when the first wing of the hotel does, at the end of July. Recreation facilities moving right along; they'll open between July and the end of the year. The town homes will be last; we're scheduling them after the hotel is finished, which won't be until a year from now, but we'll sell them early at pre-construction prices from plans, drawings and a model home. So far I don't foresee any cost overruns; everything is coming in on budget." He beamed at them. There was no need to mention the prices charged to the Foundation by Marrach Construction, Inc., wholly owned by Arch Warman and created solely for the purpose of building Graceville. All prices, for materials and labor, were twenty percent above the prices that other construction companies would have charged, and the extra money was returned to Monte, Warman, Bassington, and Sybille, who took the largest share.

"Floyd," Sybille said.

Bassington put down his doughnut and read from his notes. "The full board of directors of the Foundation will meet on Thursday of this week; I'll be proposing Lars Olssen as a new director. He's a minister, teaches religion at Fletcher School for Girls; married, four kids, a good, solid reputation. Exactly what we need."

"That gives us seven," Warman said. "Four besides the three of us. Sounds like too many to me."

"It's the upper limit," Bassington responded. "But I'd hate to lose Olssen; he's so damn respectable . . ."

Monte frowned. "It's too heavy on the other side. Syb, if you'd be a director, I'd feel better about it."

"No," she said. Her muscles had tightened; she did not like surprises. "I don't intend to be up front."

"I think maybe you should," Monte insisted. "I'd feel a whole lot better if we were all the same level, right up front."

"Up front," Warman said and laughed.

"Is that your full report?" Sybille asked Bassington.

"I raised a question," Monte snapped. "I want you on the board. This whole Foundation is your baby, you had it all on paper before we came on board, and you did a nice job, we like what you did, but that was a while ago and we're overdue for a few changes."

Sybille looked at Bassington.

"Why?" Bassington asked Monte. "Everything's going fine; why change it? Sybille is a modest person; she likes to stay behind the scenes. I admire that in her; I wouldn't ask her to be any other way. And I certainly wouldn't vote to force her to."

"Well, I'm not sure about modest," Arch Warman said. "But that's not the real problem. The real problem is money. Sybille takes a bigger piece out of every dollar than we do, and I'm feeling uncomfortable about that."

Bassington shot a glance in Sybille's direction, then wagged his head at Warman. "You're making more money now with Marrach Construction than you ever made before. You ought to be grateful. *I'm* grateful, God knows: I never thought I'd be a millionaire. Men of God usually aren't. Why do you have to start being greedy?"

"Arch isn't the one I'd call greedy," Monte said flatly.

"Oh, for shame," Bassington cried. "Shame on you both. Sybille brings Lily to us, she nurtures and teaches her, she gains her trust so that she performs on schedule and brings in *seventy-five million dollars this year.* And you sneer at Sybille. This is not Christian of you. Or smart. Lily appreciates Sybille; did you forget that?"

There was a silence while they remembered that Sybille held all the power as long as she held Lily. "We'll talk about it another time," Warman muttered. "I didn't say it had to be decided today."

"At the next meeting," said Monte. He was flushed with anger. "Or the one after that."

There was another silence. Sybille took a breath, so furious she could not yet speak. She'd taken two half-assed piddling businessmen and a failed preacher, and made them millionaires, and they thought they could dictate to her. She could get rid of them at any time; she didn't need them.

But she knew she did need them, at least for now. She needed Marrach, which Warman had set up specifically to build Graceville so they could get a piece of every dollar spent in building it; she needed Monte for his steady supply of money, and the extra interest they skimmed off that; and she needed Bassington. It galled her to admit it, especially when she thought of his body pumping on top of hers, his hands kneading her breasts and buttocks as if he were making bread, but he was useful as an amiable liaison with the public, and to help keep Arch and Monte in line.

He stays for a while, she thought; they all stay for a while. But then they'll go. Graceville is mine. If they think they can take any part of it away from me, they'll find out how wrong they are.

She turned to Bassington. "Do you have anything else?"

"Well." He riffled through the papers in his hands. "I did have a thought about Jim and Tammy Bakker, and all those accusations Jerry Falwell and some of the others are making. What a dark day, all these men of God pointing fingers, besmirching our calling; it keeps me awake at night with sadness and despair..."

"Get to the point," Monte growled.

"I am. The point is, I'm afraid that if the whole thing doesn't die away pretty soon people are going to get worried about all tv ministers—not Lily specifically, just in general, just the *idea* of shenanigans going on—and they might hold on to their money, at least for a while. It occurred to me—"

"Fucking greedy little bastards," Monte burst out, his anger turned on the Bakkers. "Couldn't be satisfied with preaching; had to go after every last fucking dollar...They're putting us at risk!"

"Greedy," said Warman, and laughed.

"It occurred to me," Bassington went on, "that Lily might put some pressure on when she asks for money: talk about maybe not being able to open Graceville on schedule because of extra costs, inflation, whatever, unless people send a few extra bucks a week."

"Not a bad idea," Warman said grudgingly. "Keep the faithful feeling guilty if they let Lily down."

Monte nodded. "Okay with me, but I want her to do it on Wednesday nights too. I've asked that before."

"Lily refuses," Bassington said. "She doesn't like to ask for money at all, but she does it because Sybille convinced her how important it was. On Wednesday, when she's answering her mail and sort of acting like a counselor, she won't do it."

"Talk at her," Monte said to Sybille. "It could bring in another twenty percent."

"I know that," Sybille said coolly. "Lily knows I want her to do it. And she will; at some point she'll agree. There are some things," she added pointedly, "you cannot force."

"Well," Bassington said into the silence, "is there anything else?"

Sybille handed each of them a sheet of paper. "This is a plan I intend to present to the full board on Thursday."

"Memberships," said Warman, skimming the page. "Lifetime memberships in Graceville? Interesting..."

"Oh, very interesting," Bassington chimed in as he read. "A membership for five thousand dollars, entitling members to an annual five-day stay in the Hotel Grace for as long as they live. What a lovely idea; such a gesture of love and caring; such a boon for people who can't afford fine vacations!"

Monte smiled thinly. "A boon," he repeated. "That's what we're here for: to pass out boons. I like the numbers," he said to Sybille, "Although you're probably too optimistic in figuring fifty thousand memberships."

"I don't think it's optimistic and neither do you," she replied coldly.

"Well, we'll have to think about it. Fifty thousand at five thousand apiece . . . two hundred and fifty million . . . a nice round number. Have you figured out how it would work with families?"

"No. That's for the board and your finance committee."

He nodded. "I'll try to have something for the meeting on Thursday."

"You make sure you have something for Thursday."

His face changed; he gave her a sharp, malevolent look. "Yes, Mama; I make sure I do."

"Well, now," said Bassington brightly, "why don't we help ourselves to more coffee and doughnuts and then talk about Lars Olssen. I would certainly like to propose him as a new board member next Thursday."

Arch and Monte exchanged a swift glance, agreeing to keep quiet for today. They knew they would have to meet privately. Sybille's greed was getting out of hand—even Bassington had shown signs of worrying about it—but they'd have to live with it until they could figure out a way to get Lily away from her. They didn't think that was likely in the near future, but they'd do what they could until then.

Lily's sermon had ended when they walked back to the church across the wet field of trampled grass; they heard the chorus singing the final hymn, and the worshipers joining in as they filed to the large double doors where Lily waited to shake the hand of every one and have a brief private word with as many as she could. It was a ceremony that took an hour every Sunday, and Lily never wavered in doing it properly: she held her smile and her warm handshake until the last congregant had gone, and she never forgot to face the camera, even after she knew it had been turned off and the technicians were packing up their equipment. It was good practice, Sybille frequently reminded her, to remember the camera at all times, even to pretend it was there when it was not. That way, playing to it would become automatic even when her mind was on other things.

At first Lily had demurred. "I don't want to 'play' to it, Sybille. I'm interested in people, not cameras."

"Of course you're interested in people; that's why our ratings are so high. But you must always be *aware* of the camera. You need it, Lily:

how else can you reach millions of people who need you but can't get to the cathedral to hear you?"

"Oh." Lily nodded. Often, when she was alone, she could not remember why Sybille's advice had seemed so sensible and inarguable, but at the time she could never think of an answer.

Sybille stopped at the corner of the church and watched Lily greeting the last of the worshipers. The drizzle had stopped and no one was in a hurry. Arch and Monte had gone to their cars; Bassington hovered nearby, waiting for Sybille to come with him to lunch. She knew that what he really wanted was to go home with her to Morgen Farms—the former Sterling Farms, renamed and redecorated—and an afternoon in bed, but she would put him off; she had enough to do without faking orgasms for Floyd Bassington. He was becoming an intolerable nuisance, she thought, and then reminded herself that she had just decided she still needed him. Well, then, a few more months of careful handling; it wasn't difficult, just time-consuming and irritating.

She walked toward Lily, to tell her she would meet her at the car for the drive into Culpeper, where she lived in a small house Sybille had bought her a few months earlier. The last of the worshipers were talking to Lily, two women, their backs to Sybille. One was tall with cropped black hair; the other had heavy tawny hair that reached below her shoulders. Lily's face was bright and eager as she talked to them; her fatigue from the past hour seemed to have dropped away. As if she knows them, Sybille thought, and then one of the women turned slightly and she saw it was Valerie.

She froze where she stood. She didn't believe it. She'd erased Valerie. She'd taken everything from her, then pushed her to the back of her mind and hadn't even thought of her since firing her in July, four months before. Well, she did think about her now and then, she couldn't very well not, since she was living in the house that had been hers and Carlton's, keeping her horses in the stables that had been theirs, repainting and refurnishing rooms that had been theirs, looking out on gardens that had been Valerie's. Everything that had been Valerie's was now hers; Valerie had sunk to nothing. So of course Sybille thought of her now and then, especially since she was still waiting for the satisfaction and contentment that she had expected would come when she vanquished Valerie. It had not come; she was still driven by dissatisfaction and gnawing angers, almost as if she had not won, but each day she told herself she had what she wanted and soon she would feel completely satisfied.

But now, here she was: Valerie Sterling, standing quite relaxed in front of Sybille's cathedral, dressed in a turtleneck sweater and a country tweed pants suit that made her look perfectly at home in this part of Virginia, talking to Lily as if they were old friends. Sybille strode up to them.

"Sybille," Lily cried. "Valerie came to hear me preach! Isn't that wonderful?"

"Yes." Sybille looked at the other woman.

"Sophie Lazar," the woman said and held out her hand. "I work with Valerie, and when she told me she knew Reverend Lily I said I had to meet her."

"Why?" Sybille asked.

"I've been watching her on television. She says things I like. I'm just now beginning to study preachers, so I don't know too much about them, but I'd bet everything that Reverend Grace is different from all of them."

"She's different from everyone," Sybille said coolly. "Why are you studying preachers?"

"To see what they're like, and whether I ought to listen to them. I'm always looking for all the help I can get."

"We could talk sometime, if you'd like," Lily said. "I'm in Fairfax on Wednesdays, to tape my evening program. We could meet then, just the two of us."

"I'd like that," Sophie said.

"Where do you work?" Sybille asked.

"E&N. It's a cable net—"

"I know what it is." Her face a mask, Sybille turned to Valerie. "You work there, too."

"Yes. Lily said she'd give us a tour of Graceville, Sybille. Would you join us? I'd like to talk to you about something."

"Oh, yes, Sybille, please come," said Lily. "You know much more about the town than I do."

"Are you in charge of it?" Sophie asked.

"No. I have absolutely nothing to do with it. It's run by a board of directors that hires me to produce Lily's shows. I don't know as much about it as Lily thinks, but I can tell you what I know." She turned her back on the church where Bassington waited. "I have a few minutes."

"Oh, I'm so glad; it's much nicer with you here," Lily said happily as the four of them walked down the wide front path. "All of this will be gardens," she said, pointing to left and right. "Gardens, trees, a small lake; you should see the drawings, they're so beautiful." The path branched, leading in one direction to the parking lot, in the other toward the town. "And straight ahead is Main Street."

They paused for a moment. Before them, skeletal buildings rose from foundations streaked dark gray from the morning's drizzle. Wet mounds of earth stood beside gaping excavations and piles of brick, lumber, steel beams, window frames, and belts of nails, like machine gun bullets, ready for automatic hammers. Concrete curbing outlined Main Street and the side streets crossing it. Tractors and construction equipment had been left wherever they had been shut down, helter-skelter, making the building site look like an abandoned children's sandbox.

They walked down the center of the dirt road that would be Main Street. On both sides were the steel and wood frames of long, low buildings. Ahead was a tall structure that, when finished, would be the tallest building in town, taller even than the church. "That's the hotel," Lily said, enjoying the role of guide. "Main Street goes straight to it, except it divides halfway there to go around the village square. On both sides of Main Street, and all around the square, will be shops and restaurants, two movie theaters, some places of recreation, plazas with benches and fountains and, of course, gardens—"

"What kind of places of recreation?" Sophie asked.

"Oh . . . bowling and bingo and video-game parlors, only two . . ."

"Video games?" Sophie asked. "Isn't this supposed to be a religious town? Sort of a retreat?"

Lily flushed. "Reverend Bassington said it was important that we respond to people's secular desires as well as their spiritual ones, because we have to compete with the attractions of the outside world. And I just don't know. I mean, I'm not happy about it; it does seem wrong to me, when people have serious problems and troubling questions, and we ought to be concentrating on those instead of encouraging them to spend their hard-earned money on those silly games, but . . . I just don't know. Reverend Bassington knows much more about the world than I do, and he's a very good man, and he's always so logical . . ."

"Who is he?"

"The president of the Foundation. His office is in that house." Lily gestured, and Sophie looked at the neat white house with its broad front porch. "The golf course will be beyond it," Lily said. "A miniature golf course too, and a huge lake, for boating and swimming and water slides. Horseshoes there, next to the picnic area; stables there; and, on the other side of the golf course, all along it, will be town houses for people to buy."

"Ambitious," Sophie said. "I'm really impressed. How many town houses?"

"I don't know yet. I don't think it's been decided."

"How many rooms in the hotel?"

"I don't know."

"Five hundred," said Sybille.

"God, it's a real town," Sophie said. "What does something like this cost?"

Lily shook her head. "I don't know. It depends on what people are willing to send us. We can't build if we don't have the money. Sybille knows about the plans."

Sophie turned to Sybille, her eyebrows raised.

"Two hundred fifty million for the initial phase," Sybille replied. "I've told you that, Lily; you just don't like to think about money."

"That's true: I'd rather think about people."

Sophie's lips were shaping "two hundred fifty million." "You don't get that kind of money in church collections."

"Oh, yes, you'd be surprised," Lily said. "I always am. But mostly it comes from people who write to me. There's so much goodness in people's hearts. I always knew it was there, but still, to see the evidence of it every day...it makes me feel strange. Glad, but a little scared sometimes." She saw Sybille's warning look—she was being too personal about herself—and fell silent.

"I gave money today," Sophie said abruptly, a little embarrassed. "After your sermon, when you talked about your dreams for Graceville...I never give, you know. I mean, I'm basically immune to pitches for money."

Lily smiled. "It was the right time for you to give, and the right cause. Thank you." She and Sophie walked down Main Street, talking together. Valerie and Sybille hung back, keeping distance between them.

"You wanted to talk to me?" Sybille asked.

"Yes, about something you said a few months ago, after Carl was killed. You told me you'd seen him in New York with some men who looked shady; not the kind you'd expect to see him with. I'd like to find them; I was hoping you could tell me more about them."

"I don't remember saying that."

Valerie stopped walking. "You don't remember?"

"I did run into Carl a couple of times in New York, but . . . shady characters? Really, Valerie, it sounds as if you've been reading cheap thrillers."

"Or you've been writing them," Valerie said evenly.

Sybille's head snapped around. "What does that mean?"

"That you make up stories as you go along. Either you made up the first one or you're making it up now. You did tell me—"

"Don't call me a liar! You've done that before, and *I've told you*—" Sybille turned on her heel, as if to walk away, but then turned back. "I never talked to you about seeing Carl with any characters, shady or not, in New York or anywhere. Why did you come here today?"

Surprised, Valerie said. "I came with Sophie. She wanted to meet Lily."

Sybille shook her head. "I don't believe it. You came because you had something in mind."

"Sybille, not everyone plots the way you do. I came because my friend invited me." *I didn't want to come at all, but I won't talk about that.* In fact, she had dreaded coming; she had not wanted to return to the forests and fenced fields she loved, and know she was only visiting. And it was not any easier being there than she had thought it would be. Everything reminded her of what she had lost: the space and serenity of the rolling countryside, large houses blurred and dreamlike in the misty air, horses grazing on farms whose names and owners she knew well, the sharp fresh scent of rain-soaked grass, the roads disappearing into the distance, reminding her of privacy and comfort: a world she had lost. *I didn't want to come and now I don't want to leave, but I won't talk about that.*

"And I do have something in mind," she said, a little mischievously, since Sybille was obviously concerned about something. "I've been wanting to talk to you ever since—for a couple of months."

"Since—what? What's happened?" Sybille looked at her. "Tell me; you know I'm interested."

They were walking again, drawing near Lily and Sophie, who had reached the end of the street and were standing before the hotel. "Since the NTSB brought me their report," Valerie said. She didn't really want to talk about it now, but, having begun, she thought she might as well finish it and then get Sophie away from Lily and leave. "There was water in the plane's gas tanks, and Carl didn't do his full preflight check. That was all they found. I'm trying to find more."

"That was all they found? Nothing more?" When Valerie nodded, Sybille said, "Then why are you playing detective?"

"Because I don't believe their explanations; there are still too many questions. That's why I wanted to talk to you."

"I can't believe you're doing this. Why not drop it? You have an explanation; why isn't it good enough?"

"Because Carl thought someone tampered with the plane."

"*Tampered?* How could... How do you know?"

"He told me before he died."

"You mean he thought someone put water in the tanks to make him crash? Did the NTSB know he said that?"

"I told them. They didn't seem to take it seriously."

"If they didn't, you shouldn't, either."

"That's my decision, Sybille. And I've decided to take it seriously."

"I can't imagine why. You have so many other things to think about, don't you, now that you're working *under* Nick?"

Venom had crept into her voice. Forget it, Valerie thought. I can't talk to her. She looked past Sybille, at the raw, bulldozed earth and uprooted trees piled to the side, ready to be hauled away. "What a shame you had to tear up so many trees."

Sybille shot her a look of fury. How dared she criticize? She took a long breath and when she spoke her voice was very smooth. "I suppose you miss the trees, living in Fairfax, and everything about the country; it's such a common suburb, where you live. Why don't you come out to Morgen Farms sometime; I'd be glad to let you borrow a horse. I'm sure we can find one you like, and you could ride as long as you—"

She stopped at the sight of Valerie's blazing eyes.

"Whatever Fairfax is, it's not as common as your mind," Valerie said contemptuously, "and it leaves a much better taste in my mouth." She strode off, leaving Sybille standing in the middle of the road.

"Valerie, I'm telling Sophie about the hotel," said Lily as she came up to them. "It's going to be fabulous; there's even going to be a ballroom—"

"And four conference rooms," said Sybille, joining them. She smiled at Valerie, triumphant at having struck a nerve. "And fifty cottages behind the main building, with two bedrooms each."

"I hadn't gotten to the cottages," Lily said. "And we'll have gardens and another small lake, and lots of new trees. It's so sad that they took out so many trees, but the new ones will grow; it will just take a while. I like the way the hotel and the cathedral face each other, don't you? Reverend Bassington says we'll give our guests a comfortable mattress at one end of Main Street and a comfortable religion at the other."

Sophie laughed, but then she saw that Lily was very serious. She glanced at Valerie, looking again more closely when she saw her face. "Do you want to go?"

"Yes," Valerie replied. "If you've seen enough."

"But we could have lunch!" Lily cried. "I could make something in my house. I have a wonderful new house in Culpeper," she said eagerly. "Sybille wanted me to stay with her—she's incredibly generous about sharing her home—but I said I really should be on my own, and when she knew how serious I was, she helped me buy it. Please come for lunch. I want you to see it; I'd love to have you there."

"Not today," Sybille said. "You're speaking to two groups this week; you need to prepare."

"Oh, Sybille, just this once . . ."

"I'm afraid not. You know how hard you work on each talk."

"Yes." Lily's voice was low.

"We'll do it another time," said Valerie with an effort; she was so anxious to be gone she could barely stand still. "We'll call you and make a date for lunch."

"Oh, yes, please," Lily replied, her face brightening. "I've had such a lovely time. I don't talk to many people except Sybille; I'm so busy, you know . . ."

They had all turned to walk back the way they came, up Main Street. Valerie had gone on ahead; Sybille lagged behind. "No friends?" Sophie asked Lily. "No dates?"

"Well . . . of course I have friends. Everyone has friends. But I don't go out on dates."

"Don't? Not at all?"

"No. I can't. Rudy told me—a man I worked with once, another minister—he told me I had to be a virgin, to set an example of purity and perfection. And to preach with a kind of spirituality I couldn't have if I were"—her voice dropped—". . . sexual. He told me if I was a virgin people couldn't ever think of me as a rival, they would just love me. And you know, one time I was chosen by God to survive, when I could have been killed, and it's all the same, don't you think? God's hand saved me, and God's hand is the only one that should touch me."

Sophie listened to the rhythmic chant that had crept into Lily's voice as she's talked, and she shivered slightly. "Probably," she murmured, thinking she should say something, and then they walked in silence to the church, where they separated.

Sophie shook her head as she and Valerie walked toward the parking lot. "That is the strangest thing." She looked at Valerie. "You okay?"

"Yes. Did I look angry?"

Sophie snorted. "Wrong word. Ready to crush somebody underfoot. Sybille, I suppose. What happened?"

"She invited me to come riding, to borrow one of her horses."

"At your own farm?"

"It isn't mine."

"I know, but it was, and it hasn't been that long... How could she—"

"Let's not talk about her, Sophie. What is it you were starting to say? What's the strangest thing?"

"Oh. Well, Lily. When she's in her church, up there on that marble mausoleum they call an altar, she makes me feel like I'm needy and troubled—which God knows sometimes I am—and she can help me because she seems to understand a lot and she has good ideas. And then a minute later she'll say something that makes me feel *she's* needy and I'm the mother, or at least the big sister, who ought to be taking care of her because she's so young and sort of ethereal. And then it's like she's lost, or in some kind of trance. She doesn't have friends or family, so she's talked herself into this whole thing because it's all she's got. She seems so innocent. Vulnerable. Whatever. Do you know what I mean?"

"Yes," Valerie said. "I think that may be why she's got such a big following. I used to think the most successful preachers were men, because they were like a stand-in for Jesus, and that's what people were looking for. But Lily somehow makes people want to help her at the same time they believe *she's* helping *them*. It's very personal; it's almost"—her eyes widened as a new idea came to her— "it's like a marriage. A two-way relationship; nobody being passive; everyone giving and taking at the same time. That's incredibly powerful. I wonder if she really understands that. It's a shame she's so dependent on Sybille. Did you get what you wanted?"

"I got a little. You'd need to dig into the finances to know what's really going on. Sybille's a witch, isn't she?"

Valerie nodded thoughtfully. "Probably."

"She sure wanted to know what I was after. I wonder what she would have done if I'd told her I was researching a special on tv ministers."

"Grabbed Lily and vanished, I imagine. She doesn't like questions about anything she does. Do you think Les really wants to do that special?"

"Who knows? We research forty for every one they decide to do. Why? You want to work on it?"

"I might. But I'd like to write it and report it after we research it together. Don't you think we'd make a good team?"

"Sensational. Has Les invited you to step up to writer and reporter?"

"Not yet."

"Lots of luck," Sophie said as they got into her car. She pulled out of the parking lot. "I didn't know we needed another writer and reporter."

"Neither does Les."

Sophie laughed. "But you'll let him know. Well, good for you. Let me know what I can do to help."

"It's a little too soon to talk to him," Valerie replied. "After the first of the year, when I've been there six months, then I might do it. And maybe ask for your help."

She was learning to be patient. She was learning a lot of things, but that was the first: to think about her next step and to lay the groundwork for it, instead of drifting, as she once did, into whatever new diversions attracted her attention. In fact, she was beginning to get interested in the new life she was building for herself. Sophie's friendship helped, and so did the coach house, which had begun to seem charming and cozy instead of tiny and cramped, but what helped more than anything else was her job. And that was because of the most wondrous discovery of all: the excitement of using her mind.

By now she was using research tools and the research library as easily and skillfully as she had once arranged the flowers she cut in her own greenhouse. Most of the time she worked at a computer with a modem, which allowed her to call up on her screen entries from encyclopedias, newspapers, magazines and hundreds of reference books without ever leaving her desk. She gathered material and wrote reports that went far beyond the summaries she had been told to write. When she thought a subject would not work on "Blow-Up," her report was brief and dismissive. But when she found one that interested her, she wrote a report that was a complete outline of the program she thought should be produced, with lists of people to be interviewed, locales that should be visited, which E&N news bureaus should be used, and what was the central issue in the story.

She wrote dozens of reports, and sent them to Earl, who sent them to Les, who discussed many of them with Nick, but Valerie was not part of their discussions and so she did not know the fate of her suggestions. "They could at least tell you if they throw them away or not," Sophie said. "It's not like Les and Nick to be rude."

"Maybe they're afraid I'll write longer ones if they thank me, and none at all if they criticize," Valerie said with a smile.

"But you must care what happens to something when you spend a lot of time on it," Sophie insisted.

Valerie nodded. She did care. But it was more important to her that she was writing the reports at all, because she was so excited to discover what she could do. She had never known how many ideas she could think up, how swiftly she could link them with other ideas, how well she could identify and solve problems, how vividly she could envision a piece of dialogue, a scene, an entire program, and the script that would bring it to life. And the more excited she became, the longer her reports grew, the more elaborate, the more ambitious. She could not believe how much pleasure it gave her to do a job and do it well.

Her mind stretched, like a cat, and woke up. And soon, in spite of the constraints of a full-time job, which she never got used to, she discovered she was having a very good time.

She could not talk about it to Rosemary, who had made friends in the neighborhood and spent her days with them recalling past glories. She could not talk about it to the men she went out with, introduced by Sophie or others at E&N; even with the ones she liked well enough to see a second or third time she did not feel close enough to talk about her feelings.

I wish I could tell Nick, she thought one day in December. He'd understand; he's always felt this way. I didn't realize that until now.

But there was no opportunity to tell him, since they never exchanged more than casual greetings when they met in the corridors of E&N. Everyone knew that Nick was traveling more than ever, and when he came home he spent most of his time in his office with his business staff.

Those who had been there in the early months, when he had just bought the network and renamed it E&N, told Valerie how different things had been then, when Nick spent most of his time in their offices, getting acquainted, learning the business from those who had been in it for years, asking for programming ideas and suggestions for running the office, making everyone feel part of something that he was determined would succeed.

"He was terrific," Earl told Valerie. It was two days before Christmas, and the four members of the E&N research department were at dinner at a large round table set for five at La Bergerie, in Alexandria's Old Town. It was Earl's way of having an office Christmas party, and he was being nostalgic, as he was every Christmas. "He had us working our buns off, harder than we'd ever worked before, and we'd thank him for giving us the chance to do it. Weekends, Chad would come down and be our gofer—run errands, Xerox stuff, file, whatever—and we'd be like one jolly family. My wife finally came down one Sunday; said she couldn't fight Nick, so she'd join him. God, two, two and a half years ago; seems a lot longer."

"Or shorter," said Barney Abt. "Fastest two and a half years of my life."

"And fun," said Sophie. "Merry Christmas," she added, looking up as Nick arrived and took the extra chair. "We're talking about early times at E&N."

"It wouldn't be Christmas if you weren't," Nick said, smiling. He raised his wine glass, already poured at his place. "Happy holidays and a peaceful, healthy, prosperous new year."

They began reminiscing about an early incident at E&N, and Valerie watched them. They were relaxed and bantering, affectionate and comfortable together. It would not have been obvious to a stranger who owned the network, who ran the research department, and who worked for one or the other. It was not that Nick tried to talk the language of those who worked for him; it was that working came naturally to him. Valerie, accustomed to the distance her father and his friends had diligently maintained between themselves and their employees, found that attractive in Nick.

With their appetizers and soup, they talked about television. "Seventy percent of the market," Earl said. "That's my guess; cable will be in that many homes—about sixty-five million, right?—in another five years. But it ain't enough, folks. We ought to be able to reach out and touch ninety, ninety-five percent."

"If we get the young people, we will," said Nick. "If they order cable for their new house or apartment as automatically as they order water and gas and telephone, then we could get to ninety percent or better."

"Just give 'em what they want," said Barney. "It's an old principle of show biz."

Sophie looked at Nick. "We give them what men want," she said.

Nick chuckled. "Sophie and I don't agree on that," he said to Valerie. "We changed some of our programming last year to attract more male viewers, because advertisers prefer them; we added three historical documentaries and a special on weaponry, and one on hunting." He grinned. "All those male hobbies."

"Sexism," Sophie declared. "I'd feel the same way if you went heavy on fashion shows and documentaries on knitting and hair curlers."

"I understand that," Nick said. "But we didn't violate any moral principles; if women wanted to watch documentaries on the history of naval warfare they could. They did watch the one on four centuries of slavery; almost as many women as men watched it. You don't really believe we downgraded our programming, do you?"

"No. I just don't like the assumptions."

"The trouble is, they're not assumptions; they're reality. There's a different audience for different shows. The real trick is to attract the different audiences without pandering to the lowest level in each of them. I don't think we did that. We increased our male audience, we added another forty advertisers, and we did it with programs we're proud of."

"I know it," Sophie said. "I just wanted to make a point."

"Is it really male and female that brings advertisers in?" Valerie asked. She had been silent so long that the others looked surprised when she spoke. "I thought it would be age and income and education."

"It is," Nick replied. "But advertisers also like men."

"Big ticket buyers," said Earl wisely. "Women buy detergent and floor wax and aspirin; you don't see many of them buying cars and lawn mowers and insurance policies."

Valerie met Sophie's eyes. They began to laugh. "Oh, well, *single* women might..." Earl said, and was saved by the arrival of the waiter with their entrées.

Through the rest of dinner, the talk ranged from Virginia politics to the presidential election that would be held in the new year, violence in the Middle East, airline fares, and the Jim and Tammy Bakker scandal and a possible special on tv ministers if research could come up with a different angle for it. Sophie looked at Valerie, waiting for her to say something about Lily and Graceville, but Valerie was silent. She was silent through the rest of the meal, enjoying the friendship around her, and feeling part of it.

"Anybody need a ride home?" Earl asked, pushing back his chair as he finished his third cup of coffee.

They all followed his lead and began to stand up. "Valerie," Nick said. "Could you stay for a minute?"

"Of course," she said, and sat back.

Nick said goodbye to the others, then once more took his seat. They sat across from each other, glasses and coffee cups and crumpled napkins on the large round table between them. Nick signaled to the waiter and ordered another cognac. "Valerie?"

"Yes, thank you."

There was a silence. Nick leaned back in his chair, away from the table, his long legs crossed. He ran his napkin through his fingers. Valerie sat straight, her red wool dress, long-sleeved and high-necked, giving her face a rosy glow in the flickering candlelight. Her earrings, cut glass that had replaced the diamonds she had sold, caught the light and sent it in small sparks to Nick, who thought how remarkable it was that each time he saw her she was lovelier than the time before. Scientifically speaking, that was not possible, unless one believed in the principle of infinitely expanding beauty, so it had to be his flawed memory. And yet he could have sworn that his memories of her had never dimmed: the joys and the disappointments, in equal measure, as well as her extraordinary beauty, as clear through all the years as if he had been looking directly at her.

And now he sat opposite her and it was as if they were alone. And more, Nick realized. It was as if they had been apart for only a short time. He found himself leaning forward, with questions to ask, with stories to tell, with an eagerness to share.

But it was complicated by her working for him. He wished briefly that she did not... but if that were the case, they would not be here, together. And then he knew that it was too soon to think of sharing as they had so long ago, or to try to recapture it. Too many years, too many separate experiences, lay between them, and somehow those had to be understood and shared before they could discover, or rediscover, anything else.

Valerie was watching him with a slight lift of her eyebrows. Nick picked up the cognac that had appeared before him and sipped it. "Les wanted to tell you this," he said, "but he had to go out of town this afternoon and won't be back until after the first of the year, so I told him I would. We wanted you to know as soon as possible."

She held the balloon glass in the palm of her hand, and waited, her eyes on his.

"We haven't ignored those reports you've been writing; Les has

them all, and a few of them are being worked on for possible programs. We should have told you sooner; I'm sorry we didn't. We're all
too busy, but I imagine you've noticed that. The point is, I like—Les
and I like what you do, we like your ideas and the way you put them
together. Everything you've sent us has been thoughtful and intelligent
and imaginative. Sometimes you fly a little too high; there are things
we can't do, for legal or financial reasons; we'll talk about those specifically when we all sit down together, so you'll understand some of the
limitations we face."

He sat up straighter and recrossed his legs, as if his formal speech
made him uncomfortable. It did make him uncomfortable, but he was
not sure how else to talk; the weight of the past and the changed
relationship of the present held him back and made him sound, to his
own ears, unnatural. He thought it absurd that they were separated by
the white linen expanse of that round table instead of sitting next to
each other; he felt foolish, raising his voice slightly to reach her over
the murmur of the diners all around them, instead of speaking quietly,
as he always preferred. Her steady gaze seemed to draw him to her, as
did her perfect stillness, so different from the restlessness he remembered. So changed, he thought, as he had while reading her reports
over the past few months with growing astonishment. So greatly, un-
predictably changed.

"We want to make a change in 'Blow-Up,'" he said. "The ratings are
good, but we want them to be a lot better. In this case," he added with
a grin, "we want to increase the number of women viewers. We want
to add a personality profile, the kind of thing *People* magazine does so
well. Anyone from politics, entertainment, business, sports... all we
care about is that he or she is fascinating for one reason or another. We
haven't got a title yet, or a finished format; that will all be worked out
with you, we hope. We want you to do it."

Valerie leaned forward. "You mean, report it?"

"I mean all of it. Plan it, research it, write it, report it. You'll have to
clear your subjects with the screening committee—I sit in on it once in
a while—and our lawyers will have to read your scripts, but otherwise,
the show is yours. You can use the research staff, but you probably
won't need them. At least in the beginning you should be able to
handle it yourself."

She frowned. "You're not giving me a staff?"

"You'll have a director from the 'Blow-Up' staff."

"That's not enough. Sixteen minutes every week—"

"I'm sorry, I didn't make that clear. It's four minutes. That's all we can take out of the hour right—"

"*Four minutes*? Out of that whole hour, you're giving me four minutes?"

"We tried to make it more; we couldn't. If you make something of your report, we'll weigh it against the other three and then decide if we want to change the balance."

"You could change it now. Make it ten minutes; it still wouldn't be enough, but at least I could get some depth."

"Valerie, this decision is made. In the first place, Les and I don't assign a sixteen-minute segment to someone who has no experience in writing and reporting a show. And this is the way we want the hour to be structured. We'll talk about it again in a few months, after you've shown what you can do with the time you have."

"You made the decision without me," she said coldly.

Just as coldly, Nick replied, "We're scheduling a personality segment on 'Blow-Up,' not the debut of a Hollywood star. And we're going to run it, all four minutes of it, whether you do it or someone else does."

There was a silence. Valerie gazed around the dining room, at all the people having amicable discussions. No one seemed angry or impatient; they all seemed to have what they wanted. *Oh, stop it; you're feeling sorry for yourself. It's his company; he makes the rules; how come you haven't learned that by now? Why don't you take his measly four minutes, and show what you can do with them, and then force him to admit he was wrong, that you deserve a whole segment of your own?*

"Is it really four?" she asked.

"Not quite, I wish it were." He noted the change in her voice. No temper tantrum, he thought; thank God. She was obviously as arrogant as ever, but he'd still like to see what she could do on "Blow-Up," as long as she could keep her temper while she did it. "You'll have to write an opening and a close, and they'll cut into your four minutes. It's up to you how long they are."

"Five seconds each," she said promptly, and suddenly they were laughing together.

"If you can do an intro in five seconds, you can teach the rest of us," Nick said. "I take it the answer is yes."

"Yes." She was feeling better, and beginning to realize she might have lost the chance entirely. They did offer it to me after only four months, she thought. It's a chance most people would give anything for. Why do I always assume people owe me more than they're giving?

"Thank you, Nick," she said. "I'm sorry it took me so long to say that. I was going to ask you to give me a show; it's much better to have it offered."

He smiled. "You didn't have to ask. Everything you've been writing told us you could do this. You've earned it."

"Thank you," she said again. Earned it, she thought. The mundane words were as sweet as poetry. Earned it. No favors, no special attention. She had earned it.

Nick walked around the table and sat beside her. He raised his glass of cognac. "Welcome to 'Blow-Up,'" he said, his voice low, just for her. "I'm looking forward to working with you."

Chapter
23

uddenly, she could not wait to get to work each day. Rosemary watched her rush to shower and dress, eat a quick breakfast and leave as early as possible, and she grew fretful. "I can't understand you; it's as if you enjoy working." She looked closely at her daughter. "It's unnatural. You shouldn't look this happy over a job. If it were a man, of course, that would be different, but a job... I worry about you."

Valerie laughed and kissed her. "I told you all about this. I've got something new, something that's mine, and I have a chance to show what I can do, and I'm having a wonderful time. Maybe you ought to look for something like it."

"A job? Valerie, you're not serious. What could I do? Are you saying I'm a burden to you? I know I am; I worry about that, too, but I didn't know it was so bad that you'd tell me to... Didn't you get a raise when they gave you this show?"

"Yes. And you're not a burden. And I'm not telling you to do anything." She pulled on her suit jacket, picked up her briefcase and made her way through the crowded living room, impatiently pushing aside a small tiered table Rosemary insisted on putting in one of the few open spaces in the room. "But I think there are things you could do, and you might enjoy them. Wouldn't you like to find out? Wouldn't you like to know what you can do?"

"No," said Rosemary flatly. "I'm sixty-one years old, and I already know what I can do, and what I like to do, and I'm not going to start over, like a teenager getting a job at McDonald's."

"Oh, Mother," Valerie said with another laugh. "I don't think you'd do well at McDonald's. I was thinking of an art gallery or a museum —remember when we talked about my doing that? You know as much about art as I do."

"No, I don't."

"Well, almost as much. And you have taste and elegance and charm, and you're wonderful with people. You'd be perfect in a gallery."

"You mean be a salesclerk."

Valerie closed her eyes briefly. "I guess that's what I mean. There's nothing wrong with being a salesclerk, you know, but if it really bothers you, call it an art consultant. That sounds prestigious enough to me." She opened the front door. "I'll see you later."

"Valerie, don't be angry, you don't understand how hard this is for me. I'll think about it, if you insist."

"I don't insist. It was a suggestion." She turned to go.

"Will you be home for dinner?" Rosemary asked.

"Yes."

"You don't have a date tonight?"

"No."

"Valerie, it's not good to live like a hermit. You should be out having a good time; you're young and you need someone to take care of you. God knows I can't do it."

"I don't need anyone to take care of me," Valerie said. "I'm taking care of myself. And I have a new job, with a terrific future."

"*Working,*" Rosemary blurted.

"I'll see you for dinner," Valerie said, and closed the front door firmly behind her.

On three sides of the coach house, lots were marked off by stakes with orange ribbons tied to them; the developer was building houses on the lots, beginning at the other end of the block. Those still unsold were overgrown with grass and dandelions. In front of the coach house a lawn remained, planted by a former tenant, and clusters of tulips and hyacinths bordered the small front stoop. Across the street, the dogwood trees and lilac bushes in the park were covered with the pale buds of early March; the thick clumps of sumacs were still bare. Valerie walked around the house to her car and drove down the short driveway to the wide road between the house and the park. Rosemary's plaintive voice came back to her, lost and unhappy, her whole world gone. I don't know what to do, Valerie thought; I can't give her back what she's lost. She turned on the car radio and spun the dial until she found a Beethoven sonata called "Spring," and thought of spring, of new beginnings, of her program ... and then she felt better. Rosemary would find her way, she would have to; Valerie had four minutes to think about, four minutes to do with as she wanted.

She had named the segment "Keep Your Eye On ..." and she had been working on it for two months, since the first of January. Since she had more ideas than she could ever produce, she winnowed her list and submitted ten suggestions, as a start, to the screening committee. Those that were approved, she researched, and then began to write scripts. In the past, she had written ninety-second or two-minute public-service announcements; now she had to learn how to write an interview and background material within the constraints of a four-minute slot. She wrote and threw away and wrote again, asking for help from scriptwriters at the network, reading books on scriptwriting, studying short segments on television. And at last, in the first week of March, she was ready to tape her first segment for the show's premiere on Sunday night's "Blow-Up."

She had never been nervous under the glaring lights of television, but this afternoon she was. Les's words echoed in her mind. *There's an audience out there using remote controls like automatic attack rifles, and they'll shoot you down in three seconds if you're dull.* That had never before been a concern of hers. But now, for the first time, the responsibility was hers. She tried to hide her nervousness as she automatically crossed her legs, sat at the angle she knew from past experience was best for her, and spoke warmly into the black maw of the camera lens, but it crept into her voice and she heard the waver in her first few words.

"Do you want to do the opening again?" her director asked.

"Yes," she said. "Thanks." It had always been a matter of pride to her that she never had to repeat any part of a taping. That's the last time, she vowed, and then they began again.

Valerie's segment appeared after the third "Blow-Up" report, introduced by one of the "Blow-Up" reporters. At the taping, the floor director read the reporter's lead-in, so Valerie could follow it. "Those are our reports for the week," he said. "And now, Valerie Sterling, telling us to keep an eye on someone who may be grabbing headlines in the future."

"Keep Your Eye On ... Salvatore Scutigera," Valerie said. She stood beside a window, half turned from it to look at the camera. Through the window could be seen the skyscrapers of Manhattan with the Hudson River and George Washington Bridge in the background. "He may be a part of your government you didn't elect."

She wore a sky-blue dress with a silver necklace and silver earrings. Makeup made her hazel eyes even larger, her lips fuller, the lower one more moist. Her tawny hair was combed into long, heavy waves that allowed glimpses of her earrings when she moved, and her fingernails were pale coral. She leaned forward slightly as she spoke, giving an air of intimacy to her words.

"He's short and wiry," she went on, "close to eighty, or maybe past it and—"

"Hold it." The director's voice came from the control room. "Valerie, take off the necklace."

She knew what he meant the moment she heard the word. Damn it, she thought furiously. I know better; I *know* better. She reached up and took off the necklace, dropping it to the floor behind her chair.

"Let's start again," said the director.

After that, the taping went without interruption, and by the time it was done Valerie's nervousness had disappeared. But it returned an hour later when Nick walked in. She and the tape editor had finished splicing her lines, spoken in the studio, and the excerpted parts of her interview with Scutigera, and they were viewing the completed four-minute tape. Nick nodded to them and sat quietly in a corner of the room.

Aware of him, just behind her, Valerie watched herself on the screen. "Keep Your Eye On ... Salvatore Scutigera. He may be a part of your government you didn't elect.

"He's short and wiry, close to eighty, or maybe past it and rocketing toward his next birthday; a dynamo who uses the world as his office. He has an official office here in New York, and another in Rome, but he's seldom in them. The signs on the doors say 'Partnership Travel,' and that's his business—arranging group tours to every country in the world—but recently our Middle East news bureau reported that he may have another life, behind the scenes, as an agent for various governments, arranging political and economic meetings that someone, or many someones, want kept secret.

"His name is Salvatore Scutigera."

"No, no," said Scutigera, appearing on the screen, as small and wizened as a Mediterranean olive. He sat in an armchair across from Valerie in his New York office, holding out his hands as if to show they were empty. "I'm a simple man; I like to travel; I like to help others be happy. Now and then I do a favor for a friend. But—agent for governments? No such thing."

Once again Valerie was on the screen, this time sitting in a dark-blue armchair near the window. "Sal Scutigera was born in Rome in 1912. His parents emigrated to America just before World War One, and he grew up in New York City. From the time he was eight, he earned money by selling castoff clothing and furniture."

"Well, usually it wasn't exactly castoffs," said Scutigera to Valerie. "It was you could say borrowed. Lifted. Stolen. But we was young and impatient and we took shortcuts. Different days, different ways."

In her armchair beside the window, Valerie said, "In his last year of high school, he discovered a talent for organizing, and he began making arrangements for his neighbors when they were planning trips. And soon he was noticed by men who were in that business."

"You could call them travel agents," Scutigera told Valerie in his office. "They sent people different places, you know; this was in the twenties and thirties. Sometimes they sent them to other cities, sometimes they sent people to the bottom of the river packed in their own cement suitcase. I never did that. I told them it wasn't my thing; I was queasy. I just sent people out of town when they weren't welcome no more. But we was young and eager. Different years, different careers."

In her armchair, Valerie said, "Partnership Travel was born in 1952, created by three friends from those early travel-agent days. Sal Scutigera bought out his partners in 1970 and became sole owner of the agency: master of its many branch offices and multilingual staffs, friend or acquaintance of government and business leaders in at least the fifty-one countries where his agency arranges tours, expert in the art of arranging: that delicate task which brings together the far-flung, the far-fetched, and the unlikely. Our Middle East bureau reports that one of those unlikely combinations may have resulted when Sal Scutigera arranged a recent meeting in Morocco of leading government figures from the United States and four Middle Eastern countries."

"No," Scutigera said. He shook his finger at Valerie. "I like you, missy, you're sincere and good to look at and you try hard, but you jump to conclusions and you think I'll jump with you."

"You had nothing to do with that meeting?" Valerie asked softly.

"A small part. They needed hotel rooms and a room to meet in and they wanted it kept quiet. That's my business; I'm in the travel business and I don't gossip. And I like to make people happy. That's my real business: I make people happy."

From her armchair beside the window, Valerie asked her audience, "Is Salvatore Scutigera a simple travel agent? Or is he a roving ambassador whose expertise is for sale, maneuvering in the shadows to carry out the wishes of governments that don't want their people to know what they're doing? Keep your eye on him."

She turned to look at another camera. "I'm Valerie Sterling. I'll be back next week, keeping an eye on . . . Stanley Jewell. Until then, for all of us at 'Blow-Up,' thank you, and good night."

The small editing room was quiet. Nick and Valerie stood at the same time. "Well done," he said. "I like your writing and editing. And you're wonderful on camera. That hasn't changed. How many hours did you interview him to get those lines?"

"Six." She was glowing, still high from the excitement of performing and, for the first time ever, bringing her own work to life. And adding to it was Nick's praise. "Almost seven, in fact. He tended to ramble."

"But you got him to trust you."

"I liked him," Valerie said slowly, "but there's something wrong there. I believe what he told me, but I think the whole thing was a lie . . . or a distortion, because it wasn't the main story."

"Is that instinct? Or did you pick up something while you were in his office?"

"Instinct. There was nothing to pick up, that I could see. Everything was so clean I think the maid finished just before I walked in. I doubt there was even a fingerprint."

He glanced at her. "You think he's worth some more of our time, for 'Blow-Up.'"

"I think he might be."

"I'll talk to Les. Is there anything else I should tell him?"

"Tell him 'Scutigera' is Italian for 'Centipede.' And sometimes 'Spider.'"

Nick grinned. "I'll tell him. Thanks."

They walked from the dimly lit editing room to the bright corridor, poised to walk in opposite directions, Nick to his office, Valerie to hers. Nick did not want to move. He liked the swift, easy understanding of their talk, and he wanted more of it. He remembered it had been the same when they were in college; it was one of the things he most missed when they separated. And even now, though he had that kind of understanding with some close friends, with Les and with Chad, he had not found it with another woman.

Beneath the bright lights of the corridor, Valerie smiled at him. "I liked the way you picked up on what I said about fingerprints. It's nice to be understood without a diagram."

He remembered that, too: her openness in sharing her feelings. He had not thought of it in a long time. "It is nice," he said. "We might talk about that sometime."

"We might," she said easily. "Thank you for being here today." She turned and walked toward the dressing room.

"Valerie," Nick said. She turned back to him. "Who's Stanley Jewell?"

She smiled again. "A Barnum and Bailey lion tamer. You'll have to watch my program next week to find out the rest."

"I'll try to come earlier; I'd like to be there for the taping," he said, and he was, every Thursday from then on. In that first week, after Valerie's program on Scutigera, they did not see each other at all. Nick took a short business trip and Valerie was immersed in researching the life of Stanley Jewell, who had recently left lion taming to become chief fund raiser for the Republican Party.

But first, the day after her show on Scutigera, Les came to her desk. She had moved from the research department to the enormous room that served as office for thirty producers, directors, writers and reporters, and she was sitting there, her back to the room, making telephone calls, when he came to her and sat in the chair beside her desk. "Good show on Scutigera," he said. "Just a few problems."

She hung up the telephone. "Nick said it was good."

"He was right. It also had a few problems. First, the necklace."

"I know," Valerie said. "I'm sorry about that. I know silver reflects too much light; I can't imagine why I forgot it. I'm sorry."

He handed her the necklace. "You left it on the floor. Second, you let us see your disbelief once. Some reporters do a lot of that, especially on 'Sixty Minutes'; around here, we don't. Third, you let yourself talk too fast; not always, just now and then. Fourth, you didn't follow up on his last statement. When he admitted getting them hotel rooms, maybe you should have moved that up and made it the focus. Fifth, I would have liked a couple shots of him as a kid, and maybe his neighborhood. Sixth—"

"Will this take long?" Valerie asked icily.

Les sat back and crossed his legs. "I guess it'll take as long as you want. I can be finished in five minutes...or an hour, if I have to explain why I'm doing my job."

There was a silence at her desk, amid the hum of speech around them. Valerie thought of saying that she hadn't had enough time, that no program could be done properly in four minutes. But she did not say it, because she knew it could not be her excuse. Four minutes was more time than was allotted to most news items on the network news shows; it was as long as most interviews on "The Today Show" and "Good Morning, America," and "The CBS Morning News." Of course those weren't in-depth reports, but neither was hers: it was intended only as an introduction to people who might be newsmakers in the future. Within those limits, she knew she could do a lot with four minutes if she really knew her job. "I'm sorry," she said stiffly. "I knew I'd made mistakes; I even knew what most of them were. I'm still learning how to do this job."

"Okay, we know that," Les said with a grin. "We even expected it. So what happens now?"

Valerie saw in her mind Nick and Les sitting in an office, feet up, drinking coffee and discussing her mistakes. *How dare they pass judgment on me?* But then she remembered that she had demanded sixteen minutes, not four; she'd let herself in for this.

"You tell me the rest of my mistakes and I correct them," she said lightly. "Next time Nick tells me I'm good, I'd like to think he means it."

"He did mean it. You were good. You'll be better. There's only one more problem: you didn't give us a reason to think this guy might get bigger or more important. We've got this little fact about him and it's interesting, but what might he be doing that we should be thinking about, other than more of the same? Maybe that's enough, but if so, why? Why should we be interested in him other than the fact that he's got great connections and does some favors? Does that make sense to you?"

"Yes. It's probably the most important thing you've said. Thank you."

"You're welcome." He paused. "You don't have to prove you can do it yourself, you know. We're here to help."

She nodded absently. She was making notes, Les saw: listing her mistakes.

She kept the list in front of her for the rest of the week, while she prepared her next show. First she made dozens of telephone calls, to Jewell himself to set up an interview, then to people whose names she found in magazine and newspaper stories about him, asking them for information and opinions. When she knew what she wanted to ask, she went to New York, where Jewell was staying for the week, and spent a day with him in his hotel room, along with her director and two cameramen. The next day, she had slides made from the photographs he had loaned her, of himself, the circus, his new office, and some location shots she had requested. At the same time, she was writing her script, and when the first draft was finished she spent a day with a tape editor in one of E&N's editing rooms, splicing together quotes she thought would give her viewers the best and most complete picture of Jewell in his old life and the beginnings of his new one.

That was the pattern for all the weeks. And at the end of each week, Nick would appear in the studio or the control room as Valerie was clipping on her microphone and testing the sound level, and stand quietly in a corner, watching the taping. Afterward they would talk briefly in the bright corridor outside the darkened studio. As the weeks passed, their brief talks became longer. They always were about "Blow-Up" or Valerie's program, but now and then they drifted naturally into something personal: a play Nick and Chad had seen, a book Valerie was reading, a newspaper story Nick had admired, a statement by a congressman they both found amusing. There would be moments when the corridor was empty, and their voices would weave together in the silence, until someone walked past and greeted them. And it was then, when they were interrupted, that the moment became intimate. But neither of them acknowledged that; they would talk and laugh together for another minute or two; their hands might accidentally touch; and then they would go off in opposite directions.

It was as if they were getting acquainted all over again, much more cautiously than the first time. Valerie found herself thinking about Nick during the day, and much more often in the evening, when she sat at home with Rosemary, reading or flipping through television channels to see what the competition was doing. She thought of him most at night when she lay in bed in her small room crowded with furniture from her childhood, and fought the longings of her body that swept through her only then, only in bed, when she was not absorbed with work and the conversation of friends and co-workers.

She wondered if she was finding Nick attractive because he was wealthy, or because she was trying to recapture her youth, or because she was lonely for the closeness of a man, or because she genuinely was drawn to him all over again, for the same reasons she had been the first time.

I won't know until I spend some time with him, she thought. And it doesn't look like that's going to happen unless I make it happen.

Well, why shouldn't I? I sent him away, a long time ago. Maybe it's up to me to ask him to come back.

If that's really what I want. It wouldn't be fair to go after him and then decide I don't want him after all.

Besides, if I did that, I'd be out of a job.

Oh, the hell with it, she thought in exasperation, and sat up, turning on her light and picking up her book. Maybe reading about other people's dilemmas would put her to sleep. Thinking about her own certainly wasn't doing it.

It was a time when she made dozen of decisions a week about her program, and could not make one about her personal life. She no longer tried to push Rosemary into finding something to do, because it created tension between them and made Valerie feel guilty. She could not get interested in the men she met and so did not go out at night, unless it was with Rosemary to a concert or a movie. She bought a few new dresses and suits to wear on her program, but shopping was not the pleasure it once was and so she continued to wear the wardrobe she had brought from New York and Middleburg, now over two years old. It was a good thing she had her work, she thought; that was where she got all her satisfaction these days.

And then, suddenly, she went to Italy, and everything in her life changed.

Of course she had been to Italy many times, in a life that was now gone. But this was different. This time she was with Nick.

It did not begin that way. She knew he was going to Italy in June; he told her at the end of May, as he walked with her from the studio, where she had finished taping a program. It was the first time he had told her he was going away, though he took two or three short trips a month that she knew about, and perhaps more. "I'll miss a couple of your programs," he said. "I'm sorry about that."

"So am I," Valerie replied. "I've gotten used to knowing you're there, beyond the lights. I wonder what I'll do differently with you gone."

"Are you sure you will?"

She nodded. "I think everything we do is affected by whoever is watching."

His eyebrows rose. "You think people are always acting for the benefit of an audience?"

Valerie thought of Sybille. "Some people are always acting," she said thoughtfully, "no matter who's around. But what I meant was, we change the way we behave, depending on who's watching and what we think that person expects. The way we talk, whether or not we use complicated words and ideas, when we smile, how much we gesture . . . and probably a lot more. We're all chameleons of one sort or another."

"But you don't know for sure that I'm watching; you can't see me off in my corner, or in the control room. What if I walked out halfway through your program?"

"I'd think there was a crisis somewhere, because you're too polite to walk out for any other reason."

He chuckled. "That doesn't answer my question."

"It wouldn't matter whether you left or not. What matters is that I believe you're watching. That's why some people can't bear to be alone; they don't know how to behave without thinking that someone is watching."

Nick contemplated her. He thought of Sybille. "An interesting idea," he said. "I look forward to seeing the tapes of your program when I get back."

"I look forward to seeing them as soon as I've made them," she said, and they parted in laughter.

Nick left for Italy the first week in June. He had never been there, and on the flight over the Atlantic he looked up from his book frequently, at the dimly lit cabin, his fellow passengers reading or sleeping or playing cards, and wished he were traveling with someone who could share his discoveries. He had planned on taking Chad, but just the week before, as the school year was ending, a classmate had invited him to his family's summer home in Vermont where they could swim and ride horses and hike in the woods. "I want to do both," Chad had said in frustration as they sat at dinner. "How come things always come at the same time? Life isn't fair."

"Probably not," Nick said seriously. "It's just as hard for me, you know, because I'd like you to do both, too."

"So why can't we go to Italy in July?"

"Because I have meetings in three cities and I can't put off any of them. I wish I could. I do have some others later this year; what would you think of London in September?"

"School," said Chad gloomily. "The way things are going, I won't live long enough to do *a hundredth* of the things I want."

Nick chuckled. "Since you just turned twelve, I think you have time to do considerably more than that. How do you think I feel, at my advanced age?"

Chad studied him. "Old, I guess. You don't go out as much as you used to, and you never talk about getting married anymore. I'm going to grow all the way up without a mother." They were silent, both of them thinking about the mother that Chad did have. "I mean, a mother who's *here*. Telling me to clean my room and what time to be home, and things I can't do."

"I tell you those," said Nick quietly. "So does Elena. And Manuel."

"Sure." Chad concentrated on making a pyramid of peas in the center of his plate. "It's okay, Dad," he said at last, looking up with a mischievous grin. "I don't want you to rush into anything; you'd probably make an awful mistake. Give yourself another eleven years, just to make sure."

Nick burst out laughing. "Thanks a lot; I just might do that."

"That's what I was afraid of."

"Or I might not." Nick gazed at his son. "Do you remember Valerie Sterling? We had lunch with her—"

"In Middleburg. That day we went to the church. Sure I remember; she was terrific."

"She's working at E&N," Nick said.

"She is? Yeh, but she's married."

"Her husband died."

Chad's face brightened. "Good deal! Well, I mean, it's too bad, but ... I can't even remember him, you know, I mean, he didn't seem, like, special... Not that that makes it *good*..." He stopped to untangle his thoughts. "So is that why she's working for you? 'Cause he died?"

"That's one of the reasons."

"So are you taking her out, or what?"

"Not yet. I've thought about it."

"Well, you could wait another eleven years."

"I don't think I'd wait that long." Elena brought their dessert, and Nick changed the subject, relieved because he found he liked talking about Valerie but was uncomfortable with the directness and speed of his devastatingly logical son.

Still, sitting on the plane, he wished Chad were with him. The times they had traveled together had been journeys of delight for Nick, seeing cities and their people through Chad's innocent, unsparing eyes. Even familiar places had seemed new with Chad beside him. I won't leave him behind again, Nick thought. I'll find a way to reschedule meetings. If I don't he might never do a hundredth of the things he wants to do.

At dawn they were over the Italian Alps. Frothy clouds, tinged pink and coral from the rising sun, nestled in the valleys between the snow-covered peaks; the sky was a burst of light. And when they landed in Rome and the Italian passengers gave an ovation of ecstatic applause, the sun was up, already hot, turning the city's umber brick buildings to deep red-gold.

Nick's room in the Hotel Hassler, at the top of the Spanish Steps, looked out over red tile rooftops and the domes of dozens of churches interspersed with the dark green of cyprus, pine and plane trees. The cobblestone Piazza de Spagna, at the foot of the Spanish Steps, was a kaleidoscope of families, business people, tourists, and children climbing over the dolphins in the fountain of Barcacia. The steps themselves, broad and steep, with carts of bright flowers beneath picnic umbrellas, were densely populated with people of all ages who lounged in the sun, read, gossiped, held passionate discussions, climbed up and down, and photographed the panorama of Rome in the distance. The steps, Nick would discover, were never empty. They thinned out at dawn, but by late afternoon they were carpeted with people, shifting, wriggling, gesticulating, being part of the scene.

He took photographs for Chad, and then turned and photographed the other three sides of the piazza, bordered by ancient, peeling brick and plaster buildings separated by narrow streets that led into and out of the square like mysterious dark passageways drawing Nick to the heart of the city.

I want to see it all, he thought, standing beside a flower vendor in the square. And he smiled. Just like my son.

But he spent that afternoon in meetings, and the next day as well, working out the last of the details that led, finally, to signed agreements that allowed E&N to set up an Italian news bureau, including satellite uplinks and studio and office space for a reporter, a cameraman, a technician and a bookkeeper/secretary.

When the agreements were signed, it was four o'clock in the afternoon. He was in Rome, elated with what he had accomplished, wanting to celebrate, and his only plans were to have dinner in a few hours with his Italian business associates. Something of a letdown, he thought ruefully and, back in his hotel room, he picked up the telephone and called Chad. But it was morning in Vermont, and Chad and his friend were horseback riding. So Nick called his office.

"*Buon giorno,*" said Les. "Did it fly?"

"On schedule; everything we wanted," Nick replied. "That's a pretty good accent; you'd do fine here."

"You just heard my entire Italian vocabulary. Have you had any time to play?"

"This is a business trip, remember? What's happening there that I should know about?"

"How much can happen in two days? Let's see. Monica has an idea for a series of original dramas; it sounds chancy to me, but I have a feeling you'll like it. She's writing it up. Oh, one thing you might think about while you're there. You know Valerie's little guy? The one we're researching?"

"Scutigera. Did you find something on him?"

"Nothing much. Remember the newspapers picked it up after her show, but didn't find a lot more than Valerie had. Good publicity for her, though. Anyway, we found a yacht he chartered for a party off the Canaries, but who knows? It was billed as a cocktail party and it might have been. The son of a bitch is as tight as a tin can. Or he's clean. We'd like to ask him about the yacht, though, and a few other things; trouble is, he may not be around. We called for a follow-up interview and whoever answered said he was ill and going home to die."

"How ill? He was fine three months ago when Valerie talked to him."

"They didn't confide in me."

Nick thought about it. "Lousy timing. But if we get anything, we could do the piece without him."

"Sure, but who wants to? Listen, this is what I'm getting at. He went home to die. Where do you think home is for a guy named Salvatore Scutigera?"

Nick grinned. "I'd say somewhere around here. Where is he?"

"Siena. Small town not too far from—"

"Florence."

"Which I think is not too far from Rome."

"Four hours. There's a high-speed train. I could go up tomorrow morning—No, damn it, I'm leaving tomorrow afternoon for Paris."

"Can you put it off?"

"No. How close is he to dying?"

"Nobody gave me a timetable. Could you get to him after Paris?"

"No, but I could after Munich. Five days from now. I'll get an interviewer and . . ." He stopped, remembering past lessons at Omega. "You set it up, Les. We've got a Rome office now; they'll work with you. If you can have an interviewer and cameraman waiting for me in Florence in five days, we'll drive to Siena together and try to get something out of him; it may be our last chance. And send me the questions you've got for him."

He was beginning to feel excited. How did he always end up behind a desk, he wondered, when it was always more fun to be in the middle of things, doing the work?

"What else can we do for you?" asked Les.

"We need his address," Nick replied.

"Good idea. I'll ask Valerie to get it. She met his staff when she was at his house here; they'll give it to her. She could get his phone number too. In fact, she could call him, to set up the interview. He liked her."

"Fine. Unless it would be better to take him by surprise. Ask her what she thinks; she knows him, and we don't."

"I'll talk to her right away," Les said, and the minute he hung up the telephone he went to the main office and found Valerie at her desk, writing a new script. "Can I interrupt? I just talked to Nick."

She looked up. "Did they sign the agreement?"

"It's all wrapped up; Nick usually gets what he goes after. Listen, we need your help. We want to get an interview with Scutigera while he's still alive and kicking. I'm getting an interviewer and a cameraman from Rome, and Nick will go with them to Siena when he finishes up in Paris and Munich. What do you think, should we take him by surprise or call ahead? And if we call ahead, can you set it up? He trusts you, right?"

"Just a minute." Valerie gazed past him, at the windows on the far wall. Dark clouds moved sluggishly across the sky; it had been raining all day. And she had been missing Nick. It astonished her to discover how much she missed him. She had been seeing him once a week for a conversation that took place in a bright, public corridor and lasted less than ten minutes. Not what most people would call a haunting memory. But that was only a part of what she missed. Just as much, she missed knowing he was in the studio or the control room when she taped her program, and knowing he was in the same building while she did her work. She had not realized how important his presence had become, just the knowledge that he was nearby, while she tried to make up her mind whether to pursue him or not.

She made up her mind. "I should be there," she said to Les. "It doesn't make sense to use an Italian interviewer who's never met Sal, when I have. He's hard to get close to; why start from scratch? He knows me, he trusts me, he probably wouldn't be surprised to see me come back." Her voice grew more urgent. "Les, I want to do this. There's no reason for me to pave the way for somebody with a phone call. If I can pave the way, I should be doing the interview."

Les was grinning. "A true journalist; totally possessive about her story. I understand that; I admire it. But Nick's set it up, Val; I can't tell him I'm sending you to do it."

"Then I will." She had suddenly realized how much she did want to do it. She'd want it whether Nick was there or not. And with stunning clarity she saw how far she had come from the days when she and her mother had discussed her marrying Edgar because there was no alternative. She would fly across the ocean to be with Nick for awhile, away from the office, but she was driven just as much by journalistic fervor, and that made her feel very good. "I'll call him and tell him I'll meet him in Siena on"—she reached for her calendar—"Thursday. No, I can't. I tape my show on Thursday. It will have to be Friday. He'll understand." She looked at Les. "I'm sorry; I'm going too fast, aren't I? Is it all right, Les? Can I do it?"

He hesitated, but not for long. He knew she was right. "Yes. But I want you to take your own camera crew and director. We might as well do it right. And I'll be the one to call Nick; it's a change in plans that has to come from me."

"It did come from you," Valerie said.

"It's a phone call that ought to come from me," he said firmly.

Reluctantly, she nodded. "I'd like to talk to him about arrangements, when you're through."

"Good enough," he said. "I'll call you when we're ready."

He went to his office. Valerie sat still, looking at the heavy clouds through the rain-streaked window. It would be sunny in Italy, she thought. It would be warm and beautiful and wonderful in Italy.

She sat still, thinking about Italy, waiting for Les to finish talking to Nick. And then it would be her turn.

<h1 style="text-align:center">Chapter
24</h1>

he sun was shining in Florence; the air was warm and still. Valerie opened wide the tall windows and shutters of her room in the Hotel Monna Lisa overlooking the courtyard garden, and unpacked, hanging her clothes in the antique armoire. She had not asked where Nick was staying. Knowing that E&N would pay the bill, she made her own reservation, choosing a hotel she had never been in before: lower-priced than anything she would have chosen in her other life, but more expensive than she could afford on her own.

Five centuries earlier, the Monna Lisa had been a palace for a Medici prince, and it still felt like one, with soaring ceilings, high leaded windows, polished stone floors and a winding stone staircase to the second floor where niches held ancient statues and urns. The courtyard was lush with roses, pomegranates, and lemon and olive trees; and the enormous leaded-glass doors of the dining room, where breakfast was served every day, opened onto it. It was a small, very private hotel, neither luxurious nor grand, but to Valerie, taking her first vacation since Carlton's death a year and a half earlier, it was one of the most beautiful places in the world.

As soon as she unpacked, she telephoned Salvatore Scutigera.

"No, no; he is very ill," said his daughter, Rosanna. She was not friendly. "He refuses to talk to anyone, only me, and not even me, very much. He just reads and looks at his garden."

"It's very important that I talk to him again," Valerie said. "I came to Italy just for this reason."

"About what?"

"Parts of his story we didn't have time for; there's so much we didn't talk about."

"Well, you won't now either. You don't understand; he doesn't talk. And when he does, he talks only in Italian. It's like he's forgotten he was an American for most of his life."

"He might talk to me; we became friends," said Valerie in Italian.

"Ah!" cried Rosanna. "But, still . . . No, I'm sorry, I can't do it."

"Rosanna," said Valerie urgently. She tried to think of the right words. This was her story, and she couldn't let it slip away. "I think your father might like to record for history what he's done with his life. If he doesn't want to, of course I won't intrude on him, but what if he does? We ought to give him that chance. He's done so much with world leaders who will be immortal on film and television tape, why shouldn't Sal be able to do the same? Would you ask him that?"

There was a silence. "He always thought he was smarter than all those so-called leaders," Rosanna said at last.

Valerie was silent; it was not a time to push.

"I would be there, too?" Rosanna asked. "To protect him from the wrong questions," she added hastily.

Valerie smiled. It had nothing to do with protecting her father; Rosanna wanted to be on television, too. "Of course you'd be there," she said.

"Well, then. I think I could ask him. I don't know what he'll say, of course, but . . . in case he says yes, could you come at, say, ten o'clock the day after tomorrow?"

"Yes, that would be fine."

"But what shall I do if he refuses to have a camera there?" asked Rosanna, suddenly worried. "He doesn't like cameras."

"Tell him we'll cancel the interview," Valerie said firmly, knowing she was safe: Rosanna was on her side. "Tell him I haven't figured out how to do a television interview without a camera."

Rosanna laughed. "I'll tell him; he'll like that. Day after tomorrow, then . . ."

Valerie put down the telephone and whirled around her small room.

She was going to get her story. And if she was right, and she did find another side to Scutigera, she was going to put together a sixteen-minute report on him that no one could resist, and use it to move up from reporting four-minute segments to being a full reporter on "Blow-Up."

But that wasn't what she told Nick that evening, when he called from his room at the Excelsior Hotel. She told him only that she had an appointment, and her cameraman and director would arrive the next day.

"That was quick," he said. "You were right; no one else should be doing this. Have you had dinner?"

"No. But I made reservations, in case you got here in time."

"So did I. Shall we toss a coin?"

"You said you hadn't been here before."

"I haven't. I hope you'll show me some of the sights. I called from Munich; a friend there recommended Sabatini."

Valerie banished Enoteca Pinchiorri from her plans; they would go there another night. "It's very good," she said. "What time?"

"Eight. Is that all right? It gives you less than an hour."

"It's fine. I'll see you there. Do you know where it is? The Via Panzini."

"I'll find it. How long will it take me to walk there?"

"Fifteen minutes."

"I'll be waiting for you."

It was only when they had hung up that Valerie wondered at the casual ease of their exchange. It had not even struck her that it was strange to make dinner plans with Nick for the first time in fourteen years, and to visualize him, a couple of miles away, in a hotel where she had stayed a dozen times.

The Excelsior, she thought, lying back in the long bathtub. She lifted the hand-held shower from its stand and turned it on to wash her hair. Who would have predicted, all those years ago, that Nick would one day stay in the Excelsior?

Or that Valerie Sterling would feel so much pleasure at the thought of dinner with him, after being the one to send him away because there were other things she wanted to do with her life?

She wore a silk suit, and low-heeled shoes, the only kind that kept her feet and ankles from being mangled by Italian cobblestones, and walked through the crowded streets to Sabatini. Nick was waiting in the foyer. He was wearing a dark suit and a dark-red tie, and Valerie was briefly taken aback by his formality. At work he wore open-necked shirts, occasionally a sports jacket, and she wondered if tonight he were hiding behind formality, as he had seemed to do a few times before with her. But as their hands met, and held, she changed her mind, and thought how pleasant it was that he had dressed carefully for her.

Without warning, desire swept through her. She felt dizzy, and then she worried that desire was in her eyes, or Nick could sense it from the clasp of her hand. She pulled back, turning with relief to the maître d', who led them to a table in the far corner of the large room. Valerie sat on the banquette, her back to a floor-to-ceiling garden that ran the length of the restaurant, with espaliered trees, bushes and hanging plants behind a wall of glass. Nick took the chair opposite her.

"That's well done," he said approvingly, looking at the garden.

She nodded. "I used to come to Italy at least once a year. It gets in your blood, and then it's hard to stay away."

Nick studied her face, looking for regret. "You must miss it."

She knew he did not mean just Italy. "Yes, I suppose I always will. But it's beginning to seem like a dream. I'm not sure anymore how much I'm exaggerating the good parts or conveniently forgetting the ones that really weren't much fun." She smiled. "We edit our memories the way I edit television scripts."

"And cling to them," Nick said. He turned to the captain, to order wine, leaving Valerie to wonder what memories he had clung to through the years.

"I never understood your marrying Sybille," she said when he turned back to her.

He nodded slowly. "I'm sure you didn't."

She bit back a retort. She had not expected Nick to put her in her place. "Or why you moved to Washington after all those years," she said, keeping her voice level.

"It was time; I was ready to leave California." He was relaxed now; this was a subject he was willing to talk about. He was picking his way, trying to avoid reminiscing about the past. He would not do that until he was ready to try to recapture it, and he was not sure, even now, that he was prepared to plunge into the past before he knew what they were to each other in the present. "I'd done what I'd dreamed of doing, and for awhile I had everything I wanted—or almost everything—and then it began to change. I suppose that's the nature of dreams; they probably start to change the minute we get near them, because that means they're attainable and therefore different."

"Goals," Valerie murmured. "Not dreams anymore."

He smiled. "Yes. That's very good. And goals have schedules and routines and dollar signs, and other people with their own dreams or goals—" He watched the captain pour their wine, then lifted his glass and waited for Valerie to lift hers. "To dreams," he said.

Their glasses touched. "But you never dreamed about owning a television network," Valerie said.

"No; that was curiosity. And then the opportunity came at a good time. I was looking for something new."

"You wanted something to happen," she said with a faint smile, and they both remembered when he had criticized her for that, a long time ago.

There was a silence. Valerie turned slightly in her seat to look at the garden behind her. She was feeling uncomfortable: not used to silence with a dinner companion, not sure how to break it. The truth was, she couldn't define their relationship. How should she behave with a former lover whom she had once broken off with, who was now her employer and far wealthier than she, and highly successful in a field where she was just a beginner...and whom she once again found powerfully attractive? One thing she certainly would not do, she thought, was begin reminiscing about the past; it would seem as if she were grabbing for romance before they had taken the trouble to build a foundation for...whatever they might build together now.

Nick was perusing the menu, seeming not at all uncomfortable at their silence. "Have you some favorites?" he asked.

"I like to start with prosciutto and melon," she said, picking up her own menu. "And if it's the same chef, he's very good with veal."

The waiter arrived, and Valerie ordered in Italian. She had not planned it—she knew perfectly well the waiters at Sabatini were fluent in English—but suddenly she was asking questions about certain dishes and requesting changes in others in her excellent Italian. And as soon as she began, she knew why she was doing it: to help define her relationship with Nick. He might be her employer, but in Italy he was the tourist and she was the one who knew her way around.

"I ordered for both of us," she said when the waiter left. "I hope you don't mind."

He was watching her with amusement. "I don't mind; thank you. Are you planning to interview Scutigera in Italian?"

"If I have to. I hope he'll consent to English. Otherwise, I'll do a voice-over translation on the tape; we don't want subtitles."

"No, we don't. You seem sure we'll have a story."

"I'm sure there's a story there, if we can just get it."

He nodded, and another silence fell. Valerie repeated to herself the word "we" as they had used it; each time, it had given her a small jolt of excitement. He was talking to her as if she were already part of the "Blow-Up" team.

Nick was looking at her thoughtfully. "Did you work when you were married?" he asked.

"No," she replied. She was surprised; he had never asked her anything about her marriages. "Volunteer work," she added, "and the spots on television I'd always done."

He smiled. "At one time you would have said that was real work."

"It is," she said with asperity. "There are plenty of places—hospitals and museums and dozens of others—that couldn't function at all without volunteers. They do hard work, sometimes forty or more hours a week, and they don't get a lot of recognition or even, sometimes, gratitude."

"I wasn't making light of it," he said mildly.

"Weren't you? Then why talk about it as if it isn't real work?"

"Because you did. You said you hadn't worked when you were married, and then you said you'd done volunteer work."

A laugh broke from her. "You're right. I shouldn't have." She gazed at him reflectively. "The difference is the salary: the power behind it. Someone has the power to pay it, and the worker has the weakness to need it. Where wealth isn't involved in a relationship, there's no difference in power, and then it isn't thought of as work."

"You mean it's a cooperative effort. Or friendship."

"Or marriage."

He smiled. "That's always the hope, isn't it? But wealth isn't all there is; what about authority? Teachers have power over students; generals over corporals..."

"You're right, but the principle is the same: it's the power to give and take away from one who is needy and therefore weak. When I do volunteer work, I'm everyone's equal because they have nothing to take away from me. I certainly wouldn't be afraid of losing a volunteer job if I happened to displease someone."

"Could you lose it if you were incompetent?"

She paused. "I suppose so. But most likely I wouldn't be fired; I'd be shifted to a different job."

"Because of who you are?"

"Because nonprofit organizations are always desperate for help."

They laughed. Their appetizers were before them, and Nick tasted the prosciutto. He looked surprised, and took another bite. "Wonderful. Like nothing in America."

"No, what they call prosciutto in America isn't good. I always wait until I'm in Italy to eat it."

"But if you don't get to Italy often..."

"Then I eat other foods. Isn't it worth waiting for the best?"

"There are people who never get to Italy."

"Then they won't eat prosciutto. They can eat American ham; we do that pretty well. There's no reason to compromise."

"You've made no compromises since your husband's death?"

"Of course I have, but only when there was no other choice."

"For example."

"My first apartment. The house I'm in now. I can take the same number of dollars and buy a kind of ham that's approximately as good as prosciutto, but I can't take the money I've budgeted for rent and find another kind of housing even close to my farm in Middleburg."

He nodded. "What else did you compromise on, besides housing?"

"Nothing. I don't buy clothes, because I can't afford the ones I'm used to, and I have enough to last for a long time. They're not in style—I suppose that's my compromise—but they're still what I expect clothes to be."

Again, he nodded, his eyes somber. "This conversation would be incomprehensible to anyone who had always been poor."

She looked at him with a slight frown. "You think I'm being insensitive."

"I think you don't understand what it means not to have money. I'd guess that you think whatever has happened to you isn't quite real. You may feel that the past is like a dream, but, dream or not, you somehow expect to get back to it, even if you don't know how it will happen. If you had to put a date on it, I imagine you'd say before your clothes wear out."

Valerie's color was high. "I don't remember you being crude. Is that because I was so naive in those days that even you struck me as admirable?"

"I deserved that," Nick said abruptly. "I apologize." Seeing the flash of her eyes, the proud lift of her head, he suddenly wanted her, and admitted to himself that he had wanted her since they sat down together. It had added to the tension of the dinner, he thought, and wondered if it had added to Valerie's too. He looked at her, remembering her body in his arms, her mouth beneath his. The room blurred and receded; all he could see was Valerie's mouth; all he could feel was her body, as familiar as if it had been yesterday that she moved beneath him, drawing him in.

Then, forcibly, he locked it away; once again, he denied it. It was too soon. He wasn't ready to say he wanted her again, not to her, not to himself. "I apologize," he said again, and there was only the slightest tremor in his voice. "My manners are usually better, even if my judgment isn't. I think I'm having trouble because I don't feel we're alone."

Valerie raised her eyebrows.

Nick gestured toward the empty table beside them. "Nick and Valerie, fourteen years younger, eating dinner and trying to bridge the differences between them."

"They're not at that table," Valerie said. "They're inside us; we're the same people."

"I don't think so. I know how much I've changed and I can see—"

"You haven't changed at all."

"—that you have, too. I think I've changed, and we can talk about that sometime, if you'd like. What bothered me a minute ago was that I thought you hadn't changed. But I was wrong; I've seen you at work and I know how different you are."

She shook her head. "I don't think people change very much. I suppose we always wish they would, so the world would be orderly and predictable, but I don't believe any of us really becomes something else." Her look turned inward for a moment. "What might happen, especially if there's some kind of shock, is that we'd discover parts of ourselves we didn't know about. Whatever I am now was always there; people just didn't see it."

"Or you didn't use it."

"Or I didn't use it," she repeated evenly. "Thank you for reminding me."

Their eyes challenged each other as the waiter brought their dinners, refilled their wine glasses, and discreetly vanished. Nick let himself say it silently: he wanted her, perhaps more than ever. "Will you believe me," he asked, "when I say that I'm very glad to be here with you?"

"Yes," said Valerie. "I'm having a very good time."

They burst out laughing, and at that moment something relaxed between them, and they talked easily for the rest of the meal.

"I have two days in Florence," Nick said as they sat over coffee. It was late; the two of them were alone in the restaurant. For the first time Nick realized that the room, though sleek and handsome, was far too bright. It had not been designed for lingering. "I'd like to plan them with you, but not here. Is there someplace more relaxing we can go?"

"Why don't we just walk? Florence doesn't have much night life, but it's wonderful for walking."

Nick dropped his idea of an intimate corner with soft lights, quiet conversation and a late-night drink. "I'd like that," he said.

He had no idea, when he finally returned to the Excelsior, how far they had walked, but he knew he had never seen so many churches, piazzas or shuttered shops, and thought he would never see as many again. The streets were not as crowded as during the day, but still they found themselves veering to left and right to avoid the Florentine pedestrians who give way to no one, but mysteriously recognize other Florentines and weave safely past at the last moment. "I have the wrong genes," Valerie laughed when once again she failed to stare down an oncoming couple and had to sidestep nimbly to keep from being mowed down. "Maybe if I lived here I'd figure it out."

"If I didn't know better, I'd think you lived here now," Nick said, admiring her sureness in the city. He followed as she turned corners without hesitation and crossed piazzas to find just the street she wanted of all those that led into and out of it. He enjoyed striding beside her, their hands brushing now and then, their steps matched. He knew he had never been so attracted to her as now, when he was not sure, in fact, what they would find together. But he gave himself up to the warmth of her voice, the pleasure he took in her quick mind, and the sexual current that ran between them in the matched rhythm of their steps, their murmured words, the way their heads tilted toward each other, the quick awareness of each other whenever their hands touched. And he knew she felt it, too.

They emerged from a narrow street into the Piazza della Signoria, a quarter of it excavated to expose newly discovered foundations from the time of the Roman Empire. A roof had been built above it, and spotlights illuminated it. Nick and Valerie gazed through the wire fence at the stone stairways and interconnecting rooms that made a complex of apartments, some still filled with rubble, others neatly swept, their contents catalogued. "I wonder what we'll leave behind," Nick murmured. "Not television, I hope; at least not the television that's around now." He looked at Valerie and smiled. "That's a dream and a goal: to do something with television that we'd be proud to have other generations dig up."

She nodded. "You will. You've already begun."

"*We* will," he amended. "We've already begun."

She smiled to herself. *We've already begun*. They turned from the excavation and looked across the piazza toward the Uffizi Palace. "We'll come back tomorrow," Valerie said. "It's too beautiful to miss. Santa Croce too, and Piazza della Repubblica—and of course the Uffizi and the Pitti Palace and the Academy...Two days doesn't even begin it; you need at least a week, and you'd still be cheating yourself."

"Two days," Nick said firmly. "You give me a preview, and I'll come back when I can do it justice."

They walked along the Arno and crossed it on the Ponte Vecchio, the covered bridge lined with shops that, locked up for the night, looked like antique wooden jewel boxes. Nick thought the city was like a fabulous setting for an ancient tale. After the unrelenting newness of California's pastel houses and sprawling shopping centers, the ambiguous juxtaposition of Washington's marble and slums, and eastern Virginia's modern, urban bustle, Florence seemed to be a stage set that looked backward to a past of grandeur and violence, its buildings mellowed with age, its streets darkened by centuries of wagon wheels, marching troops, crowds of people, and automobiles. It was hard to believe people lived ordinary lives there.

"We'll have to come back," Nick murmured. "I want much more than a week."

They crossed back to the other side of the Arno on the Vespucci Bridge, and eventually reached the Excelsior. Both of them thought about Valerie's coming to Nick's room, and neither of them mentioned it. "I'll walk you back to...what is it?" he asked.

"Monna Lisa."

At the locked iron gates, Valerie rang the bell and the night receptionist let her in. "Good night," she said, holding out her hand. "Thank you. It's been a wonderful evening."

Nick held her hand, and then his arms were around her, and their bodies were together, solid, yielding, close. They stood silently in the large foyer with the fireplace and sofas on the left and the receptionist at his desk on the right. He was conscientiously writing, his head lowered. Probably wondering why we don't go upstairs, Valerie thought, and a laugh trembled on her lips. She put up her hand and touched Nick's face. "Good night," she said. She was trembling with wanting him, and quickly walked past the receptionist to the stone staircase, and ran upstairs.

Nick avoided the receptionist's eyes. *He thinks I'm a fool. An Ameri-*

can who knows nothing of love. But outside, walking back through the narrow Borgo Pinto, by now empty of cars and people, he knew it was all right. They had time. They had a lot to sort out, but whatever they finally found together, this time they would know what they wanted, and they'd stick with it.

He was happy. He could not remember when he had last felt like this. His stride lengthened; he felt powerful and immortal. Like a kid in love, he thought, smiling to himself, and he knew that was something else he had to think about. But not that night. By the time he was back in his room, it was almost three in the morning, and he did not think about anything: he went to sleep.

What he did think about, when he awoke, was calling Valerie. He reached for the telephone before his eyes were open.

She answered immediately. "I was planning our day; are you ready for more walking?"

"Anything you say, if I can start with breakfast."

"Why don't we do that here? It's served in the dining room, and I'm sure they'd welcome my guest. I'll see you downstairs in an hour."

That was the beginning of a day Nick never forgot: intense, exhilarating, stimulating, exhausting. At lunch, eating pasta with cream sauce in a small trattoria near the Pitti Palace, he wondered if that was what life with Valerie would be like. But of course it would, he thought; he had known that even at Stanford; what he had loved most in her then was her infectious excitement at everything life had to offer, and her determination to reach out for it. *To make things happen* . . .

Nick knew he had been like that himself, all his life, though too often it had been submerged beneath the fierce drive to succeed at work, and he knew Valerie had loved it in him as he had loved it in her. Now, as they toured Florence all that long day, they shared their excitement: the feeling that everything was a source of wonder and delight, and they were the most fortunate of people to be able to partake of it.

The center of Florence is small, easily traversed on foot, but most of the miles Nick and Valerie walked were on the marble floors of palaces that housed some of the world's greatest art, and the stone and marble floors of churches where they stood with heads back until their necks were stiff, admiring brilliant frescoes four and five hundred years old, trying to see those hidden from them behind the scaffolds and protective mesh of restorers, and contemplating the magnificent sculpted tombs of popes, artists and scientists. They walked through Michelangelo's house, the walls covered with frescoes he had painted while living there, and the science museum where, for some reason, a preserved finger of Galileo was displayed behind glass.

Much of the time they did not talk. The heart of Florence is memories, and Valerie and Nick, who were finding the way from their own memories to the present, let themselves fall under the enchantment of the city's past. And as they did, they became more aware of each other. For all the glories of the Renaissance, the best part of that day was the contentment they felt seeing them together.

But they were not always silent. When they were between palaces and churches, walking through the city beneath the hot, hazy sun and cloudless sky, they talked and laughed with the freedom of two friends on a holiday. They both wore slacks and open-necked shirts, both tucked their wallets into pockets so their hands were free, and both walked with the same easy stride through the cobblestone streets, navigating in the tumultuous scene that is daytime Florence.

They walked with jostling crowds of pedestrians down the middle of each narrow, shaded street until they heard a car or, worse, a bus approaching. Then, with everyone else, they moved to the thin strip of sidewalk on one side or the other, flattening themselves against a building until the car or bus had passed. They dodged motor scooters driven by men in business suits with ties flying like kite tails, or young women in the tightest of miniskirts, feet planted firmly together on the center floorboard. They emerged from the dark streets into the brilliant sunshine of the piazzas where flocks of pigeons wheeled above artists and cartoonists at their easels. They sat in outdoor cafés, watching the parade of people that never stopped. At two in the afternoon, when the museums and shops closed, the whole city clanged with the sound of iron shutters being slammed down over shop fronts. Then Valerie and Nick went to the Boboli Gardens, and the churches, which never closed. At four, when the shutters were flung up and the shops sprang to life, they window-shopped as they walked to their next destination.

Dinner was at nine. By then even Valerie could not walk another step. "You're very impressive," she said as they sat in the courtyard at Enoteca Pinchiorri. "Most people couldn't take that pace."

"Most people don't have you for a guide. It was a very special day. Did we leave anything out for me to see if I do come back?"

"Today was an appetizer. There's a feast waiting for you."

"Then I'll find a way to come back. If you'll come with me."

"I'd like that very much."

He smiled, realizing how much he was beginning to count on her openness and lack of pretense. "Tell me about your other visits here," he said, and all through dinner she talked easily about her trips to Europe that had begun when she was eight. She ended with the last trip she and Carlton had taken, to Switzerland, to visit friends.

"That was only a couple of months before he died," she said, and frowned slightly. "I never thought of that; I wonder if he had a bank account there. I wonder if that's where the money is."

"You've never told me that story," said Nick. "I only know parts of it from the newspapers. I'd like to hear it."

"I'll tell you sometime. Not now, if you don't mind. I feel so wonderfully far from it. Foreign countries always do that, at least for me; sometimes I can't even visualize home and the everyday things I do, and that makes the place I'm visiting, wherever it is, seem romantic. It's much more fun to think about romance than home and all those ordinary things."

"It's like the past," Nick said with a smile.

Valerie looked at him thoughtfully. "I'll have to think about that. You mean, we think about the past the same way we think about a foreign country: a long way off, a place we remember magically, something we'd like to find again."

"You said it far better than I."

"It's something to think about." She sat back with a sigh. Their coffee cups and small *grappa* glasses were empty; the remnants of the dessert they had shared had been removed by the waiter. A light breeze made the flowers in the courtyard sway, and the candles flicker. "I'd like to walk after that dinner, but it's not possible."

He chuckled. "We should have thought of that."

They were silent. At the same moment, they looked up and their eyes met. "I'd like you to come back with me tonight," Nick said quietly. "I'd come to you, but I don't think I can face that receptionist again."

Valerie laughed. "I think he felt sorry for us, more than anything." After a moment, she said, "Yes. I was hoping we could."

They stood at the same time and came together there, in the flickering lights of the courtyard, as they had in her hotel the night before. Everything in that long, shared day came to this moment, when they held each other and their lips met, lightly at first, then with a growing intensity that made them catch their breath. "No more," Valerie said. "I'm going to have enough trouble walking to the Excelsior as it is."

"A taxi," Nick said firmly. "There must be some around."

"Of course there are."

"You'd never know it, with you as a guide. Do we call for one?"

"The maître d' will."

"Right away. It's going to be too short a night as it is."

They smiled, and the joy in their smiles stayed with them as they took the taxi to the Excelsior. Nick's room overlooked the Arno; it was large and spacious, but Valerie did not notice. They were in each other's arms as the door closed behind them. "I thought about this today," she murmured, her lips against Nick's, "between paintings."

"Which paintings?"

"All of them."

His hands moved along her body as they kissed, holding her to him, rediscovering the long line of her back, the narrow curve of her hips, the fullness of her breasts straining beneath her silk blouse. A small spark crackled between the fabric and Nick's fingertips, and a laugh burst from him, breaking their kiss. "Electrifying..."

"I hope so," said Valerie. "But I'd rather..." Swiftly, she unbuttoned the blouse and Nick slid it off her shoulders. His hands were warm and hard on her skin, the hands of a man who worked with tools, in the garden, around the house, and as she felt them removing her clothes until she stood naked beneath their hard sureness, his touch lingered, like a long memory. She felt his palms and fingertips wherever they had touched her: she was enveloped by the feel of him.

At the same time, swiftly, as surely as he, she had removed his clothes, and then they stood in a silent embrace in the shadowy room. A single lamp cast a circle of pale-gold light on the patterned carpet and the edge of the bed. Nick turned Valerie with him, and they went toward the light, and lay on the silken spread. She brought him on top of her, arching slightly as his weight pressed her into the bed. "Oh, I like that," she murmured. "Meeting you halfway..."

And then, as naturally as they had shared the wonders of that day, he was inside her, matching the rhythm of her body. Lifting himself, he balanced on his long arms, and looked down at her, smiling. "I remember this; I remember your eyes looking up at me, and how it felt to be inside you."

"I remember you had to get used to talking when we made love," Valerie laughed. "I remember," she said softly. "Oh, yes, I remember, yes, yes..." She pulled Nick down to lie with his full weight on her once again, and she moved beneath him, trying to bring him deeper, trying to get more of him, all of him, so hungry for him she thought she could never get enough. They moved together, their mouths together, warm and sweet, their tongues together, their bodies learning again what they had known so long ago: to curve and lock together, to part and come together, until they were one.

Lying in the curve of Nick's arm, Valerie felt herself begin to drowse and sat up. "I don't want to go to sleep," she said and bent to touch the tip of her tongue to the hollow at the base of his throat. Slowly, she moved her lips down the dark curls on his chest. "So wonderful," she said, her words whispering against the hard smoothness of his waist. "Better than with anyone else."

"Probably not true," he murmured. One arm was crooked under his head and he watched Valerie's tawny hair, spread like a cloud over him, hiding her face and her mouth that moved like a flame along his flesh.

She raised her face. *"Probably not true?"* She was mocking him. "How many women have been as good? How many would you remember for fourteen years?"

"I can't remember," he said with a grin. "It happens with age; we forget."

"Not the special things. It's never been as good for me with anyone else."

"That's not necessary," Nick said quietly. "I don't need to hear that."

"I'm not saying it to make you feel good. I like saying it; I like knowing it's true. I don't lie, Nick; you know that."

"Yes. I love that in you."

In the pale-gold light, their eyes held, shadowed, almost somber. Then Valerie bent her head again, touching her lips to Nick's warm skin, feeling the tremor in his muscles as her mouth glided down the taut smoothness of his stomach. She tilted her head to look at him and watched the absorption on his face as her tongue stroked and caressed him. She bent again to take him into her mouth. She pulled him deep into her throat, drinking him in, loving the smooth, hard, hot wetness of him and all the ways he could fill her. Her breasts were crushed against his thighs, her hands were beneath him, and she felt as if she were melting into him, warm and open, as diffuse as sunlight yet filled with his solid strength, and as strongly clasping him.

"Valerie," he said.

She let him go and looked at him. "I wanted . . ."

"I know. But we have time. Come here."

"Yes." She lay on him, her mouth on his. "It's never been this good with anyone else because my mind doesn't wander when I'm with you. All I think of is you, all I see is you..."

Nick's fingers were in her burnished hair; he held her, and their tongues met and embraced. He started to tell her he loved her, but something held him back, and instead, because the joy within him had to find words, he said, against her lips, "You're right. No one else. You're magnificent—"

"You don't have to say that." Laughter rippled in her voice, and he knew it came from a joy as deep as his own. "I'm having a wonderful time without that."

"—because I always know it's you. Because the feel of you couldn't be anyone else, the way we fit together, the way your voice is like a kiss...I'd never wonder who you are, or forget your name."

Shocked, Valerie pulled away from him. "Have you really done that? How depressing that would be; it could make me give up sex. Why did you? Do you know?"

"I do now; I didn't then." He held her face between his hands. "I didn't realize you were in my blood. I didn't know that the harder I looked for love, the more you filled my head and heart, and I couldn't even pretend I was content with anyone else. I thought I'd brushed off the past, but it was so stubborn, it always got the best of me."

Valerie gave a small laugh. "How clever of it. It's not easy to get the best of you..." She bent over him, her mouth opening his. "I don't ever want to forget the past; I want to make it part of us again."

"Tonight. And all nights," Nick said, and lifted her off him and laid her back on the bed. He took her breast in his mouth, his tongue caressing the nipple, and Valerie lay still, her blood singing. The room was filled with a rushing sound, swelling and receding, like the ocean heard inside a shell. And the golden light from the lamp spread over them, and through the room, like sunrise.

Nick's lips moved down the silken ivory softness of her skin, and he parted her legs as his tongue found her sweet, warm, musky darkness and thrust inside. Valerie said his name; her fingers were in his dark hair. Nick put his hands beneath her, holding her, consuming her, until she cried out, arching against his mouth. Swiftly, then, he lay on her, taking her in his arms, sliding into her. Joined together, they lay still for a moment, waiting for their bodies to awaken together. And that was what they discovered and rediscovered that night, just as they had discovered it in their matched steps during the day. Valerie said it much later, when a real sunrise began to brighten the room. They were lying on their sides, kissing, both of them sleepy and slow but moving with a beat as steady as their hearts. "We don't even have to think about it," she murmured, "we just move perfectly together."

Salvatore Scutigera had come home to an apartment in a Gothic palace in Siena. The palace showed a blank face to the dark, narrow street lined solidly with other stone buildings that seemed to be leaning inward, pinching the slice of blue sky above. But within the stone walls of Scutigera's palace was a courtyard where a cluster of olive trees grew, and a riot of tangled rosebushes, their stems thick and woody with age. Scutigera sat among them in a wheelchair in the hot morning sun, wrapped in a bathrobe, a blanket over his knees. Rosanna stood beside him, her hand on his shoulder, her face stern.

"They must stay there, no closer," she said as the cameraman and the director walked in behind Valerie and Nick. "And you'll sit here; I had a chair brought out. I wasn't expecting two of you." She had glanced at them briefly as she gave instructions; now she took a sharper look through narrowed eyes, and Valerie knew that Rosanna had recognized the sexual glow that lingers after a night such as she and Nick had shared, and that cannot be wiped away just because it is time to go to work.

"This is Nicholas Fielding, the president of E&N," she said to both Rosanna and Scutigera. "He was in Rome on business and asked to watch the interview."

"I hope you'll allow it," said Nick, shaking hands with Rosanna. He bent to Scutigera and held out his hand. "I was impressed with your first interview; I'm glad you're giving us another."

"It was a show," chuckled Scutigera. "I told some cute stories."

"But they were true," Valerie said, startled.

"True. Sure they were true. They just weren't everything." He coughed, ending in a long wheeze. "I used some I knew you'd like."

"Which ones will you use today?" Valerie asked lightly.

A manservant brought another chair, and, when Valerie was seated, Nick sat a little behind her. The cameraman had begun filming as soon as he was told where to stand; the director, having clipped microphones to Scutigera's bathrobe and Valerie's suit collar, stood beside the camera; the technician squatted unobtrusively in a corner, running his equipment. Bees flew lazily among the roses; a cat stretched on a stone bench in the sun. Scutigera held out his hand and Rosanna placed a glass in it. And then he began to talk.

For thirty minutes he talked about almost everything and said almost nothing. Nick watched as Valerie kept after him with new questions, probing, circling, suggesting, letting silences stretch out, then abruptly taking a different tack. She even switched without warning to high-speed Italian, which brought a gleam to Scutigera's eyes. She was intelligent, quick-witted, knowledgeable: a superb interviewer. Nick was filled with admiration, but he also felt her frustration, because Scutigera was wilier than she, and he gave nothing away.

At the end of the thirty minutes, Rosanna put up her hand. "That's all the time I promised you. Turn off the camera."

Valerie knew when she was beaten. Without hesitation, she leaned forward and shook Scutigera's hand. "I hope you feel better soon."

"I'll be in the grave soon." He lifted his wizened face to her as she stood up. "I like you, missy. If I talked to anybody, I'd choose you." He peered across the courtyard, saw the cameraman putting away his camera, and turned back to her. "You thought I'd babble to you because I'm dying. But I've got family all over the world, running the business, taking care of *their* families. I wouldn't mess that up by blabbing to you. We don't work that way."

Valerie stood very still. "What would you mess up?"

"Come on, missy, you're too smart for dumb questions. Why are you here if you don't know the answer to that?"

"I don't know anything," Valerie said coldly. "I have some guesses."

Scutigera grinned. "Guesses we can live with. It's when you people get facts that we get nervous. Goodbye, missy; I hope you feel better soon."

At that last jab, Valerie turned without another word, and left the courtyard. "I shouldn't have let him see how angry I was," she said to Nick when he caught up with her at the front door of the palace. "But damn it, he really got to me. Hoping I'd feel better soon!" She stepped into the cool, shaded street. The two cars she had hired were parked half on the sidewalk, to leave room in the street for traffic, and she walked to the one in front. Standing at the door, she turned to Nick. "Would you mind if I drove?"

"Of course not," he said. "I'd enjoy it; I can look at the scenery."

The cameraman, director and technician came out behind them. "Val," said the technician. "The tape was running."

She spun around. "After the camera was turned off?"

He nodded.

"I'm glad to know that," she said. "May I have a copy when we get home?"

"Sure thing."

"Thanks." She looked at Nick. "Shall we go?"

"Yes. We have a plane to catch."

She drove off the sidewalk and down the street, and, once beyond the walls of Siena, on the open highway, she put down the gas pedal. Nick had forgotten how fast she drove and for a moment it unnerved him. Her hands were loose on the wheel, her body relaxed; and he knew she'd slept no more than an hour during the night. But after awhile he sat back. She drove surely and well. She was not reckless; she looked away from the road only for brief glances at the farmhouses and castles on the crests of verdant hills; and she seemed to be wide awake. He began to enjoy the drive, free to study the play of light on olive trees and towering dark-green cypresses. He and Valerie were comfortably silent, close together but absorbed in their own thoughts.

"Nick," Valerie said when they were approaching Florence, "I want to follow this story."

"What story?" he asked.

"Scutigera, of course."

"But what story is it that you'll follow?"

"The one he hinted at. There is a story there, something he doesn't want known. You heard him say it."

"I heard him drop some hints. But I'd also watched him play with you for half an hour. That may have been his last joke."

"I don't believe that," she said slowly. "I'm sure he intended me to know I wasn't wrong. I want to know what he was talking about, what he's hiding; I want the rest of the story."

"You have nothing to go on."

"Not yet. I haven't worked on it."

"Research has."

"I want it more than research does." There was a silence. "Nick, it's my story; I want to finish it."

He looked at her profile. "You want to use it for 'Blow-Up.'"

"Of course."

"And become a full-time reporter."

"Of course."

"But there are other stories. We wouldn't stop you from moving up if you didn't have this one."

"I've got a start on this one."

"You have nothing on this one. We don't waste time on stories that don't look promising."

"This one does."

"Since when? You've been tinkering with it for four months, and you have nothing new."

"I haven't been able to put a lot of time on it."

"You've given it enough time and thought to know it isn't worth any more. We have more story ideas than we know what to do with; we're not in the wild-goose business."

"Are you telling me I can't work on it?"

"I wouldn't do that; those decisions are up to Les."

"But you'll tell him I shouldn't do it."

"I don't tell him what to say," Nick said coldly. "But you might give some thought to how he makes his decisions. He has to allocate the time and talents of the people who work for him."

"I don't care what he has to do; I want to finish the story!"

"*You want,*" Nick said contemptuously. "That's all that matters, isn't it? Don't you get tired of saying that? I should have believed you when you said you hadn't changed. I can't imagine how I could have been so wrong."

"As I recall," Valerie said icily, "one of those absolute judgments you used to make about me was that I had no ambition. Now that I want to do something that could be important, you treat me like a child crying for a toy. There's no way I can please you, is there? You're so convinced I can't do anything worthwhile."

"That's ridiculous, and you know it."

Valerie did not answer. Her face set, she concentrated on driving. The traffic on the outskirts of the city was heavy and chaotic, with drivers cutting each other off in their tiny cars as if they were in an amusement park, and she was as good as the rest of them, sliding the Fiat into impossibly small spaces, speeding ahead, pulling around a motor scooter to pass buses and vans, then hitting the brakes to avoid serenely oblivious pedestrians. It was the last time, Nick thought ruefully, he would quarrel with her when she was driving.

Their silence lasted through the afternoon. They packed in their separate hotels and met again when the limousine Nick had hired drove them to the Pisa airport. Still silent, they boarded their plane and took the seats Nick's secretary had reserved, next to each other.

Valerie looked at a magazine. She was as conscious of Nick as she had been all the previous day and night, but she could not speak. Disappointment and frustration gnawed at her. For the first time in years, she knew exactly what she wanted, and she'd been so sure it was within reach. But then, in Scutigera's courtyard, she had felt it receding, and, without thinking, she'd grabbed for it. And Nick hadn't understood at all; he'd acted like an employer, as rigid and narrow-minded and judgmental as she'd always thought he'd been. Damn it, she fumed, feeling hollow inside; how did we let this happen to us?

"*Buonasera,*" said the steward. "Madame would like a cocktail?"

Valerie ordered wine, then gazed out the window. Nick ordered a drink and opened his book. The words blurred together. It was astonishing, he thought, how many kinds of silences there were, and how badly two adults could behave. After the perfect closeness of the day before, and last night, that they could have failed each other so completely was unbelievable to him. Valerie had been childish, and he'd been harsh. So what had they learned in the last thirty-six hours?

We don't even have to think about it; we just move perfectly together.

He felt hollow with the loss of the moment when she had said that. That perfect moment; that perfect night. What we learned was that we don't move perfectly together. And maybe we never will. Maybe there's something about us that can't . . .

For God's sake, it was only one quarrel.

But there seem to be a lot of quarrels, he reflected. What is it that makes some people smooth and easy together, while others start snapping, the way we did at dinner at Sabatini, and on the drive from Siena?

We don't seem to be able to accept each other as we are; we keep trying to remake each other. But I loved what she was yesterday and last night; I wouldn't have asked her to change a thing.

It was only one quarrel. We could get past it if we wanted to.

The steward placed their drinks on the tray inset in the armrest between them. Nick sipped his and found himself meeting Valerie's eyes as she turned away from the window and picked up her glass of wine. "You should sit in on this week's 'Blow-Up' planning session," he said casually, as if they were continuing a conversation, "so you can choose which projects you want for yourself. Each reporter works on two or three at once."

"I'm not a reporter for 'Blow-Up.'"

"Les thinks you could be; we've been talking about adding another one. It's up to him, of course, and the producer, but if you want it, you should go after it."

Valerie gazed pensively at her wine glass. "Thank you," she said quietly. "What kind of projects are they thinking about?"

"More than we'll have time for." Nick felt himself relax. Probably she wanted a truce as much as he; if so, they'd share it, as they had shared so much in Florence. They would carefully avoid the subject of Scutigera—she would have to resolve that one with Les—and talk instead about the other work she could do as part of E&N: something else they shared. He felt a sudden surge of happiness. It might be all right after all.

"Which ones?" she asked again, and he realized he had lapsed into thought.

He began to talk about the ideas the "Blow-Up" staff, the producer and Les fed into a thick file each week for the research department to evaluate. Through dinner and a bottle of wine they discussed them: politicians, entertainers, contractors, corporate executives, political fund-raisers, art collectors, officers of multinational companies, arms dealers and publishers, all of whom, it appeared, might have more to them than their public image indicated.

"I'd like to do a few of those," Valerie said as the steward refilled their coffee cups. "And I have another that I'm especially interested in. I'd like to do a program on Lily Grace."

"Lily," Nick repeated thoughtfully. "Could we find something to say about her that every producer in America isn't saying about tv evangelists?"

"I think she may be different. She fascinates me because she doesn't seem to fit into any category. I don't really know anything about her, but I don't believe she'd knowingly be part of a deception, or anything criminal. There's something more to Lily, and I'd like to find out what it is."

"Have you ever met her?"

"A couple of times. She's extraordinarily young and sincere and... pure. It could be that we'd learn something about television ministries through her that we haven't learned through the others because everyone's been concentrating on corruption."

"But what would be the story?" Nick waited for her to become defensive, as she had before, when he challenged her on Scutigera.

"I don't know," said Valerie, and this time there was no defensiveness; only a rueful laugh. "I'm just learning to think about a whole story, not just a terrific idea for one. But I was at Graceville a while ago, and it's very big business. In fact, it doesn't seem to have any limits, as long as people keep sending in money, huge amounts of it, obviously. I'd like to know more about it, especially how the money is used, and I can't imagine that Lily is anything like the Bakkers; it ought to be a different story."

"You said you didn't think she'd knowingly be a part of what's been going on. Do you think she's being used?"

Valerie thought about it. "I don't know. She seems very much her own person. But if she is . . ."

"It would be Sybille who's doing it," he said when she hesitated. "In which case, Sybille would be involved in Graceville."

"She says she's not."

"I know. There's often a chasm between the truth and what Sybille says. If she's part of Graceville, then this could be a story that goes far beyond religion. Sybille never cared much about the condition of people's souls."

"But Lily does."

"Probably. Are you sure you really want to do this story? You'd get no cooperation from Sybille; she'd think you were the enemy."

"Only if she's using Graceville for her own purposes, and I have no evidence of that, or any reason to think she is. I'm far more interested in Lily; it seems to me she's almost a symbol of what television is, or maybe the best that it could be." She smiled. "I don't know what to think of her, not yet. But I do think it could make a terrific program."

"And what if it turned out that Lily would suffer because of it?"

Valerie shook her head. "You're making assumptions. I told you, I don't think she's corrupt."

"That doesn't answer my question."

Valerie hesitated. "If I had enough to think it was an important program, I'd go ahead with it."

"And if you found Sybille was corrupt? Using Graceville, as you put it, for her own purposes?"

She looked at him steadily. "If it was important, I'd go ahead with it. Not to hurt Sybille—that would be a disgraceful thing to do—but because I'd be doing something important. Anyway, I think Sybille's real interest is in Lily; I think she likes having someone dependent on her who's young and impressionable." She hesitated again. "I don't know where this story would lead, Nick, but I'd like to follow it. It fits in with every headline these days, and Lily is incredible; I'm not the only one who's fascinated by her; everyone is, who meets her."

"It sounds all right to me. We'll talk to Les about it." Nick took her hand, easily, naturally, feeling at ease from the companionship of their talk, forgetting that he had decided to tread warily until their stormy drive from Siena receded to the past. For a moment Valerie's hand was unresponsive, then her fingers twined with his, and he felt a surge of buoyancy. There was still too much tension between them, too much readiness to leap to battle stations over relatively minor disputes, and he didn't know how they would resolve that, or even if they could, but for now the air was clear. And if they could find a way to share the important things of their lives . . .

"Something else," he said. "If Les approves, and you do a full-scale study of Lily Grace, and Graceville, I'd like to work on it with you."

Part Three

Chapter
25

he grand opening of the Hotel Grace was scheduled for July, and workers were scrambling to finish it when Sophie and Valerie visited Graceville for the second time. The shops along Main Street were almost finished; their glass fronts reflected the summer sun and gave glimpses of the workers inside, painting and installing shelves and carpeting and computerized cash registers. The streets were lined with antique lampposts and old-fashioned hitching posts; landscapers were laying squares of grass and planting flowers and shrubs; workers were installing street signs. Some distance away, rows of town houses were in various stages of construction; one row was almost complete.

"Marrach Construction," Sophie read on the first trailer they passed. "I wonder who owns it." She looked down Main Street, at other trailers with the same name. "It's a goldmine, building a whole town. Mr. Marrach, whoever he is, really lucked out."

Valerie wrote the name in her notebook; then they walked on, down Main Street and into the hotel. The workers paid no attention to them as they wandered through the lobby, into the dining room and then up a stairway to the mezzanine, where meeting rooms and offices were being painted. "What is it I'm supposed to be looking for?" Sophie asked.

"I don't know." Valerie contemplated the workers, and the view beyond the windows of groves of trees, and green, somnolent fields. Everything looked peaceful and ordinary, and she felt a little foolish for imagining scullduggery. "I just thought I ought to see it again before we start digging into how it works."

They turned to walk back the way they had come. "I thought I heard Nick say he wanted to work on this one," Sophie said.

"I suppose he will, if he can find the time."

Sophie shook her head. "I give up. For a whole week, ever since you got back, I've been hoping for a tale of pasta and passion, and all I get is a travelogue of churches and museums and the palaces of Siena."

Valerie glanced at her. "Why did you think there would be any more?"

"Because you've been working up to it for months. All those intimate moments in the corridors, leaning toward each other like trees about to topple over... The intelligent staff of E&N tends to notice things like that."

Valerie gave a small laugh. "We didn't look like trees about to topple over."

"How about two people having trouble staying apart? Anyway, when you flew off to Italy, we thought good things were about to happen."

"Good things did," Valerie said, her voice low. "We had a wonderful time. We had one perfect day and night."

"And then?"

They reached Valerie's car and she was silent until she pulled onto the main road. "We don't see things the same way. We quarrel about something, and then we laugh and feel wonderful about each other, and then we're snapping at each other again. We were together forty-eight hours and it was like a roller coaster. Half the time I didn't like him at all and the other half I thought I might be in love with him. I never knew how I'd be feeling from one minute to the next."

"Why, do you think? Nick's a terrific guy; I used to have fantasies about him. If we'd gotten together, I would have worked pretty hard to ignore anything I didn't like."

"Oh, you don't know what you would have done," Valerie said a little crossly. She drove at a sedate pace, slowing for more impatient drivers to pass. "It was as if we were trying to score points, to prove to each other that our way is the right way, and it always has been. I knew Nick a long time ago, in college, and we didn't see things the same way then either, and it's as if we're still stuck there, having the same arguments we had then. I wish we could wipe out our memories and just think about now. Though I'm not sure anything would be very different. We're both so stubborn..."

"Stubborn, but never bored."

Valerie smiled. "A little boredom might be a relief right now."

"You don't mean that, not for a minute. Boredom kills everything: friendships, marriages, jobs, vacations, hobbies... even wars: when the generals get bored they sign treaties. If you and Nick strike sparks, you ought to give thanks. God, I could use some sparks with Joe; we're so predictable you'd think we were married. I can't imagine why you're fussing; you're not bored and you keep making an impression on each other."

"Are those the only alternatives?" Valerie asked with another smile.

"I don't know, but what if they are and you have to choose one? How could you not choose sparks? Can you imagine never giving a damn, one way or the other, and if one of you left, the other one would hardly notice any change in the way you live?"

Valerie thought of Carlton. When he died, her life changed because her money was gone, not because he was no longer there. It had been one of the discoveries that saddened her the most: that she could not miss him; she could only feel sorrow for an untimely death.

She nodded, more to herself than to Sophie. "I'll have to think about that."

Sophie's thoughts had already moved on. "You two are gorgeous together, you know that? You're both beautiful and you move together like you're dancing. Things have to be awfully good between two people when they look like that; it's your inner selves speaking. If you ignore that, you risk ruining your life."

Valerie laughed. "You're a true romantic, Sophie. It sounds so simple there's probably a hook somewhere, but I'll give it some thought. Let's talk about Graceville, and Lily. Can we use any of the research you've done on the Bakkers and others?"

"I don't know yet. It all comes down to money, and either they play games with money at Graceville or they don't. I'd start at the beginning, with the land for the church and the town—who bought it, how much did they pay, where'd the money come from—and I'd dig into

Lily's background and how she's living now, and the same for the board members of the Hour of Grace Foundation. I got their names yesterday, from one of my foundation listings."

They talked about the newspapers, magazines and television tapes they would use to get information on the members of the board, and whichever of its dealings had been public. Not many had to be; Valerie was always amazed at how much could legally be secret in what she had thought was an open society.

When they returned to the E&N building, they went to the research department and Valerie pulled a chair to Sophie's desk. They were there for the next two days, Sophie searching board members' backgrounds while Valerie made telephone calls to realtors in the Culpeper area and the county clerk's office to see if the sale of the land had been recorded.

"Well, now, how about this," said Sophie at last. They were eating sandwiches at her desk, and she was skimming a newspaper story on her computer screen. "Floyd Bassington, president of the board of the Hour of Grace. He was a minister in Chicago—big church, big congregation—until some guy named Olaf Massy found him in bed with Massy's wife, Evaline. She sang in the choir. No, better than that: she was choir director. Olaf went on a crusade to expose the saintly minister and found out that Bassington not only slipped in and out of a lot of beds—did I say he was married, with lots of kids?—he'd also been embezzling over the years, a little here, a little there; he had about two hundred thousand bucks in his bank account. How's that for a resumé for Lily's president?"

"Was he in jail?" Valerie asked.

Sophie read further, and shook her head. "Paid back the money, resigned from the church. His wife divorced him. He moved to Virginia, and found grace."

Their eyes met, and they smiled. "I'd like a copy of that story," Valerie said.

"Sure," said Sophie. "Now for the others. Nothing crooked, I'm afraid. Vice-president: Arch Warman, president of Warman Developers and Contractors. Treasurer: Monte James, president of James Trust and Savings. They're all over the Eastern seaboard, headquartered in Baltimore."

"James," Valerie repeated, and wrote it down beside Warman's name. "Sophie, can we find out who holds the mortgage on the land under Graceville?"

"Maybe. Usually you can't. I'll check. Did you find out who bought it?"

"Yes, it's odd. It was sold twice. The first time, when it was all small farms, the farmers sold to a Panamanian corporation called the Beauregard Development Company."

"The what?"

"I know, it's a strange name. Beauregard bought it for thirteen million dollars—I got that from the realtor who handled the sale—but only held it for about three months. Then it was sold again, this time without a realtor, to the Hour of Grace Foundation. And, according to the realtor, there were rumors that the Foundation paid thirty million dollars for it."

"Thirty million?"

"It's only a rumor, and it has to be wrong. No one would pay that for land that was worth thirteen only three months earlier."

"Oh, I don't know. What do religious boards know about business?"

"This religious board has the president of a bank as its treasurer, and the president of a construction company as its vice-president, and an embezzling minister as its president."

Sophie nodded. "Not your typical religious group. Well, if they weren't stupid or naive, what were they?"

"I don't know." Valerie scribbled absentmindedly on the pad in front of her. "What's the number of James Trust and Savings in Baltimore?" she asked suddenly.

Sophie found it and gave it to her. "What are you looking for?"

"It occurred to me they might hold the mortgage; we could get the real purchase price that way."

"Not necessarily. And even if they do hold it, they won't tell you."

"Mortgage department, please," Valerie said into the telephone, and, when a loan officer answered, said, "Good afternoon, this is Valerie Sterling; I'm researching a television report on the relationship of savings-and-loan institutions to nonprofit organizations, especially in rural America." She met Sophie's wide eyes with a mischievous smile. "I understand you provided financing to the Hour of Grace Foundation to buy land near Culpeper, Virginia; could you tell me something about that?"

"It was a standard mortgage," said the loan officer. "It didn't come under the category of good works, or anything like that. The land was their collateral; it's prime land; we took no unusual risk at all."

"And the price of the land?" Valerie asked.

"We don't give out that information."

Valerie cut the call short and went back to her absentminded scribbling. "The treasurer of the board gave the mortgage," she murmured. "But so what? That's not illegal." She looked at her scribbling. "Sophie. Look at this."

Sophie craned her neck to read what Valerie had written. "Arch. The vice-president. Warman. So?"

"Marrach. The last four letters are an anagram of Arch."

Sophie grabbed the pad. "And the first three are in Warman." They looked at each other. "That's no coincidence," Sophie said.

"But why do it?" Valerie asked. "Unless he wanted a separate company just to build Graceville. I don't know why he would, but that's what it looks like. So the treasurer funds it, and the vice-president builds it, and Bassington does...something. One big happy family. Interesting, but not illegal."

Sophie gathered together the papers on her desk. "Well, let's put Arch and Monte away for now and think about—"

"Wait a minute." Valerie looked at her, frowning. "What did you say?"

"I said let's put Arch and Monte away—"

"Who's Monte?"

"James. Didn't I say that?"

"Maybe you did; I guess I didn't hear it. Arch and Monte. Sophie, I've heard that before. Somewhere. I remember thinking it sounded like a vaudeville act."

"It does. But you didn't hear it from me."

Valerie gazed unseeing at the wall of shelves piled chaotically with newspapers and magazines and annual reports. "It was in an office," she murmured. "I was standing and someone was sitting at a desk and saying something—on the telephone; she was on the telephone—saying something about a meeting." She struggled with the memory, and then she had it, all of it: part of a day she would never forget—the day Sybille fired her. She had stormed into her office to demand a different job, and Sybille had been on the telephone. *I told you to schedule a board meeting for the day after tomorrow. Call Arch and Monte right now; we have to*—She had hung up when Valerie came in.

Sybille demanding a board meeting with Arch and Monte? But last November, at Graceville, she had said she only worked for the Foundation, producing Lily's show.

There's often a chasm, Nick had said, between the truth and what Sybille says. He also said, if there was corruption in the Hour of Grace ministry, Sybille might be involved.

"What is it?" Sophie asked.

Valerie told her. "There's nothing illegal about it," she said. "Though it's peculiar that she was demanding a board meeting and she's not a board member. I don't know what it means, but I think I'd better tell Nick."

He was in New York, but as soon as he returned Valerie went to his office and told him what she and Sophie had learned. It was the first time they had seen each other since their trip to Italy, so they had had no time to discover how they would now behave together. The office made them feel formal, more self-conscious than before their trip, and Nick listened to Valerie carefully, nodding, agreeing that there seemed to be much more for them to consider than they had thought, while all the time he was waiting for a chance to say what he had been thinking about the whole time in New York. He found his chance as soon as she finished telling him all she had learned. He asked her to come to dinner the next day.

"Chad will be there," he said with the brusqueness that came into his voice when he was tense or nervous. "Not for dinner, but before, so if you could come early, say about five, we'd both be very pleased."

"Who does the cooking?" Valerie asked. "You or Chad?"

"Elena," he said. "I haven't cooked much lately. But I'll cook for you, if you'll come."

"Thank you," she replied easily. "I'd like to very much."

Georgetown was cooler than most of Washington the next afternoon, a hot, humid Saturday, when Valerie arrived at Nick's house. It was larger than she had imagined, beautifully proportioned and cared for, its heavy front door and wooden shutters newly painted in a glossy black that contrasted with its mellow red brick exterior. The leafy arcade above the sloping street, the long row of graceful houses and old-fashioned streetlamps, the air of serene confidence that came with antiquity and wealth gave Valerie a stab of pain: all of it a reminder of what she had lost, and not so long ago that she could not recall every luxury, every small pleasure, every invisible comfort of that cushioned life. She had not visualized Nick in such surroundings.

Chad opened the door before she rang the bell, and Valerie, about to greet him, stopped short. She had been thinking of Nick as a student and it was as if he stood before her. Of course Chad was much younger—twelve? thirteen?—but still it was as if her memories had come to life: he was almost as tall as Nick, with the same eyes, the same shock of hair, the same wonderful mouth. His skin was darker than Nick's, and his cheekbones were sharper, but the rest was the

young, handsome, raw, eager Nick she had loved for six magic
months.

"Hi," said Chad, holding out his hand. "Nice to see you again."

His grip was strong and his gaze direct, but Valerie felt she was
being scrutinized with more intensity than was called for.

"It's good to be here," she said, and followed Chad into the air-conditioned coolness of the house. It was everything she had imagined:
the nobility of another age when ceilings soared, moldings were intricately carved, and rooms were harmoniously proportioned, with space
for a grand piano and groupings of furniture on lustrous Oriental
rugs.

"Dad's in the kitchen," said Chad, adding confidingly, "which is
really weird, 'cause he hasn't cooked since we moved here. I thought
he'd forgotten how, but it smells okay so I guess we're safe."

Valerie smiled at the love in his voice, mixed with the attempt to
seem critical and worldly wise, and she was still smiling as Chad led
her into the kitchen. Nick watched her walk toward him, smiling, her
beauty glowing in the sunlit room, and he went to meet her. He felt as
if his body was leaning forward, ready to embrace her.

"Hello, Nick," Valerie said. She wore a peasant skirt and a white
blouse with a low neck; her hair was tied back with a ribbon, leaving
the beauty of her face unadorned, as if in a Renaissance painting.

"Welcome." His hands on her shoulders, he kissed her lightly on the
cheek. Valerie felt herself lean toward him, and then she thought of
Sophie—...*like two trees about to topple over*—and consciously stood
very straight. She looked around, trying to think of something to say.
"What an amazing kitchen," she said. Nick had had it remodeled as a
wonder of modern technology, and she focused on a Cuisinart and a
KitchenAid mixer, neither of which she had ever used, admiring their
mysterious, sleek design.

"I once dreamed of a kitchen like this," Nick said, "but this is really
Elena's; she helped design it. I'm just about done here; I've delegated
Chad to entertain you while I finish up. There are drinks in the gar-
den, unless it's too warm. You choose."

"I'd like to see the garden."

"Come on," said Chad. "I'll tell you what's there; I help Manuel do
it."

"Who's Manuel?" Valerie asked.

"Elena's husband."

"And Elena is the cook."

"She's sort of everything. She cooks and cleans house and grocery-shops and sews on buttons . . . like a mother, you know, only she isn't. Not mine, anyway. She is a mother, though; she has Angelina, that's her daughter; she's eight. Here's the garden."

He opened the door and Valerie stepped into a burst of color. A high brick wall surrounded a shaded stone terrace with padded outdoor furniture and a built-in grill, and, framing it, terraced rock gardens, a waterfall running sinuously down a slope of small boulders into a clear pool, miniature cherry and apple trees, and bonzai pines. Chad rattled off the names of flowers and bushes. "Not too shabby," he said, surveying it. "What do you think?"

"It's fantastic," Valerie said. "It's the most perfect garden I've ever seen." She knelt beside a stepped section of rosebushes heavy with blooms, and touched one of the flowers with a gentle finger. "I love roses. I used to have a lot of them; I miss them more than anything else in the garden." She stood again. "You and Manuel are experts."

"He does the planning," Chad said honestly. "I mostly dig around. It's good exercise for my wrists, for my drums, you know. I guess you've seen a lot of gardens."

"Yes, I have, and this is the best. Do you play drums in a band?"

"Band and orchestra."

"Do you practice at home?"

"Sure, in my room. Dad doesn't mind; I just can't do it when he brings work home. Sometimes we play them together, though. He's pretty good at jazz."

Valerie paused, diverted by the idea of Nick as a drummer. "Is that what you want to do when you finish school?"

He shook his head. "I'll probably be a scientist. But it's fun to do now, and the more things I do the easier it'll be to get into college."

Valerie looked startled. "How old are you?"

"Twelve last March."

"You're not even in high school, and you're already worrying about getting into college?"

"Not really *worrying*, just, you know, thinking about it. Not a lot, it's just that like a lot of my friends have older brothers and sisters and they're thinking about it, so we do, too, and we kind of talk about it like they do. Dad always gets on my case about it and says I shouldn't pay attention to it yet; it's like a job, he says; I wouldn't think about jobs now, they're too far away, and so is college. He says college is like a job and it's okay to prepare for it but there's a time to do it and seventh grade isn't it."

"That sounds pretty smart to me," Valerie said. He was so serious, she thought; too serious for his age. But quick and delightful to talk to. "Last time we talked, at lunch that day, you said you liked school. Do you still?"

"Yeh, a lot. They really pile on the homework, but it's still great. This summer's great, too; I go to these art classes at the Corcoran; they have sculpture and photography and painting and everything."

"I saw one of your paintings. The bicyclists on the C&O Canal path; I thought it was wonderful."

"You did? Really? Dad did, too, but he's not objective; you know, *fathers...*"

Valerie laughed. "Well, I'm objective and I think it's wonderful. Do you take painting at school?"

"Not now; I've got a lot of other stuff to do. I like everything, you know, my teacher says I have to be, uh, selective, but Dad says I should do what I like and find out what I'm best at, so that's what I'm doing. And if I keep my grades up I can do all this other stuff too."

"I'll bet your grades are terrific."

"Yeh, they're like mostly A's."

"I didn't have good grades in high school," Valerie said, reflectively. "I fooled around too much."

"*Fooled around?* You mean, screwed around?"

"I mean a little of everything."

"No way," Chad said admiringly. "So how'd you get into college?"

"I don't know. To tell you the truth, I was pretty surprised. Maybe because I'd done a lot of that extra stuff you're doing, and I wrote a major essay with my application and maybe that counted most of all. I got really good grades in college; I guess I'd grown up a little by then."

"The essay? That counts the most?"

"I don't know. It sure helps, though."

"Would you read mine when I get ready to write it? And tell me what you think?"

"I'd be glad to. But I think your dad would like to do that."

"I'd ask him too. I just thought, you know, having two people read it, and maybe you'd think of things he wouldn't, like a woman might look at it in a different way; think of different things..."

Valerie nodded seriously. "You're probably right. But this is pretty far in the future, isn't it?"

"A few years," Chad said, and added casually, "by then you'll probably be here a lot."

Valerie's eyebrows rose, and that was when Nick came through the back door to join them. "Didn't you want anything to drink?" he asked Valerie.

"Oh, I forgot," Chad said. "Sorry. Would you like a drink? There's wine and iced tea and soft drinks and the other stuff—gin, bourbon, vodka, Scotch, campari—we've got like a whole tavern here."

"Iced tea," Valerie said. "It sounds wonderful."

"If you're too warm, we can go in," said Nick.

"No, I'm fine. All I need is some iced tea."

Chad went to the bar built on the terrace, against the brick wall of the house, and Valerie and Nick sat in the cushioned chairs. "Has Chad been telling you about the garden?"

"Yes. It's quite wonderful. I have a tiny one where I live, but this is magnificent."

"Where do you live?" Chad asked.

"In a coach house in Falls Church."

"A coach house? That's like a garage, right?"

"Just about." She took the drink he handed her, and the three of them sat quietly at the round glass table. It was shaded by an arching red-maple tree, and as the sun moved lower in the sky a light breeze came up. Valerie felt warm and comfortable, and very happy. "It was built for horse-drawn coaches—the horses were in the stables—and there was an apartment upstairs, for servants. Now it's a two-story house, very tiny, but nice too."

"So do you live there alone?"

"I live with my mother."

Chad stared at her, and Valerie knew he was thinking she was a little old for that sort of thing. "Is she sick or old or something?"

Valerie smiled. "No, she's fine. She had some trouble and lost her money, so she came to live with me."

"So what does she do?"

"Chad," said Nick.

"Sorry." Chad's face was red. "I didn't mean to be nosy."

"It's all right; I'd tell you if I didn't want to answer," Valerie said gently. "My mother doesn't do much of anything. I think she might look for something pretty soon, though; she seems awfully bored lately. About a month ago she started cleaning out file cabinets that go back years." She smiled to herself. "I told her a job in an art gallery would be less work and more fun."

"What did she say?"

"She said I was probably right, but it's hard to go looking for a job when you've never done it."

"It must have been very hard," Nick said, looking at Valerie. "And even harder to make a success of a first job. Not everyone could do it."

"A second job," Valerie said with a faint smile. "I was fired from my first one." And then she remembered she had never told him that.

"Fired?" Chad asked. "What did you do?"

"Forgot that I worked for someone else and didn't make all the rules. Could I have some more iced tea?"

Chad jumped up and refilled all three glasses. "Did you lose your money, too, like your mother?" he asked over his shoulder.

"Chad," Nick said again.

"I'm *sorry*," Chad said loudly.

"Yes," Valerie said. "I lost all my money, and that's why I'm living in a coach house and working for your dad. And I'll tell you something, Chad. I hated losing my money—I still hate it because I can't do most of the things I used to love doing and I lost my farm, where you saw me that day, remember?—but right now, with all the things I'm doing, and the job I've got, and the friends I've made, I'm having a wonderful time."

"Oh." He set her glass and Nick's before them. "So do you—"

"Now that's not fair," Valerie said lightly. "There's lots more I want to know about you. Tell me what you do besides garden and paint and play drums."

Chad launched into a description of his school, his friends, his weight lifting, the books he read, and his bicycling. "Dad lets me go all over Georgetown; I really know my way around. It'll be better when I drive, though."

"Why?"

"Oh, you know, it rains, sometimes it snows; it's a real pain sometimes. I really wish I could drive now. Dad's going to teach me."

"Doesn't the school do that?"

"Yeh, but they're stupid. They mostly do the simulator; you hardly get in a car at all. There's this one thing they do, though, that's not too shabby; my friend's brother did it—"

"Chad," Nick said suddenly, "what time are you supposed to be ready to go out?"

"Oh, *no*," Chad groaned. "I forgot. Couldn't I call and say I can't come?"

"No, you know you can't. It's been almost two months since the last time, and you have to go. You should be in front of the house at—what time?"

"Six-thirty. It's not nearly that."

"It's six o'clock, and you have to get dressed."

"It only takes five minutes. Can't I at least finish this thing about driver's ed?"

Nick looked at his son's bright face, and thought about the past hour, when he had talked more openly with Valerie than, as far as Nick knew, he had ever talked to his mother. "Sure," he said. "Just don't drag it out."

Chad finished his story, but his enthusiasm was gone, and his face had lost its eagerness. "I guess I've gotta get dressed," he said reluctantly. "Or, wait, first I want to give Valerie a present. I mean," he said to her, "you might not be here when I get back. Well, you probably will, I won't be gone very long, but anyway I want to do this now, okay? Don't worry, Dad, it'll just take a minute." He went to a toolshed almost hidden behind a shrub, and took out a pruning shears. "You said you love roses and you wished you still had them."

"Yes," Valerie said. For some reason she felt like crying.

Chad knelt beside the group of rosebushes Valerie had admired earlier, and examined each flower, looking for the finest. Valerie and Nick looked at each other, and he covered her hand with his. "Thank you," he said very quietly. "You talked to him as if he's an adult. He loved that. So did I."

"He's a lovely boy," Valerie replied softly. "You must be so proud." Faintly, a sound caught her attention. "Is that a—?"

"Immensely proud," said Nick. He too had heard the doorbell, but it barely registered with him; he was thinking of Valerie's hand beneath his, he was breathing in her fragrance, he wanted to kiss her.

Elena also heard the doorbell, from the laundry room, and went to answer it. "Good evening, Mrs. Enderby," she said. "Chad is in the backyard."

"He's supposed to be waiting in front," Sybille said. She and Chad had agreed to that; she hated coming into this house, knowing Nick usually managed to be somewhere else when she arrived.

"You're ten minutes early," said Elena. "And they have a guest; Chad must have let the time get away from him."

"You mean he forgot." Sybille walked through the entry foyer to the kitchen and then to the breakfast room. At the back door she glanced through the window, and stopped short. On the terrace, dappled with sun and shade from the maple tree, Nick sat at the glass table, his back to her. And Valerie—Valerie!—sat beside him.

Standing in the shadowed room, Sybille watched Nick remove his hand from Valerie's as Chad turned toward them from the rose bed. She saw Nick sitting close to Valerie, and she saw her son walk toward them and place in Valerie's hands five perfect ivory-colored roses. She saw Nick smile and Valerie lean forward and kiss Chad on the cheek, brushing her hand lightly over his hair. She saw Nick put his hand on Valerie's again, as Chad threw his arms around her and kissed her cheek.

Sybille stood in the shadows and watched the three of them together, and then she turned, shoving roughly past Elena. Almost running, she reached the front door, and then was outside, where her limousine waited. She sat in the back seat, her breathing raspy and shallow. And as the driver pulled into N Street, and drove out of Georgetown, deep inside Sybille, so deep she was not yet aware of it, something snapped.

Sitting in the living room, beside three file cabinets crammed into a corner, Rosemary caught the scent of the five perfect roses from across the room. When Valerie had returned home, very late, she had put them into one of her mother's Baccarat vases before going to bed. The next morning, they were the first thing Rosemary talked about.

"They're very lovely," she said when Valerie came down to breakfast. "What time did you get in?"

"About three." Valerie skipped coffee; it was already too hot. Barefoot, wearing shorts and a tee-shirt, she put ice cubes in a glass of orange juice and joined Rosemary in the living room. There was no air-conditioning in the coach house.

"You haven't told me anything about him," Rosemary said.

"I know." She paused. "Do you remember Nick Fielding?"

"No. Who is he?"

"Someone I knew in college. I told you about him, and you met him when you and Daddy came to Stanford."

"I don't remember. That was fourteen years ago; how should I remember?"

Valerie smiled, a private smile. "It doesn't matter; I remembered."

"He's doing well if he lives in Georgetown," said Rosemary. She was sitting on a low stool next to the file cabinets, surrounded by stacks of paper, waiting for Valerie to tell her which she should keep and which to throw out. She had been doing it for almost a week, as if it were suddenly urgent that the files be organized. And it was urgent; Valerie knew that. It filled Rosemary's hours; it gave her something to do that could be seen and measured. It came close to a job. "How wealthy is he?" Rosemary asked.

Standing beside her, Valerie dreamily leafed through some of the papers on an end table. "Very," she said. "He made it all himself; he started with nothing."

"How impressive. And not married, I assume."

"Divorced," Valerie said. "He has a wonderful twelve-year-old son he's brought up by himself. They're so close, such good friends, I love watching them and being with them, being part of the little family they make when they're together."

"You're in love with him," said Rosemary.

Valerie's hands stilled on the stack of papers and she looked through the open window at the park across the street. "Sometimes," she said at last.

"What does that mean?"

"I guess it means I'm just not sure. Every time I think about Nick I start to worry about tomorrow or next week or next month...how much different we'd be from our first time around. I enjoy being with him—I had the most wonderful time with him and Chad—but there's always that fear that I'll make a mistake, or he will, and we won't be able to deal with it. I get the feeling we're so...fragile. As if we ought to tiptoe and speak in whispers to keep from breaking apart."

"I don't understand that," Rosemary said. "If you love him and he loves you...Does he?"

"Yes. I think so. But he's being careful, too. He's been married once; I have, twice; I think we ought to go slow and maybe tiptoe a little bit, don't you?" She smiled faintly. "I didn't use to do that, I know; I used to rush in, and figure I could take care of any problems that came up. I never used to be afraid of anything."

"You're not afraid; you have enormous courage. You know that, after what you did when Carlton's plane crashed."

"That was one time," Valerie said slowly, "one incredible time in my life when I was more than I ever thought I could be. I haven't seen much evidence that I could do anything like it again."

"But you've done so much since then! You work, you take care of me...Really, Valerie, you ought to believe in yourself. You and Nick too. I should think you'd both have learned enough by now to be pretty sure of what you want, and to recognize it when it's in front of you, and then to go after it."

Valerie smiled. "It sounds so simple. Maybe, one of these days, we'll get past what we're afraid of—"

"But that's what I just said: you shouldn't be afraid of anything! The worst has already happened to you: you lost all your money. After that, what could you be afraid of?"

A small laugh broke from Valerie. Bending down, she kissed Rosemary on the cheek. "Failure," she said quietly. "And being hurt. I guess I'm more afraid of that than anything else."

Rosemary hesitated. "So you want to love him. And have him love you."

Valerie sighed. "Yes," she said. She turned, wanting to change the subject, and sat in a chair beside her mother. She picked up a pile of papers. "Where did these come from?"

"The oak file cabinet."

"Carl's," Valerie said. "It was in his office at the farm. We probably ought to keep everything, at least for awhile. If anything ever turns up..." She picked up one pile and then another. "It looks as if he never threw anything away. These receipts go back ten years; I hadn't even met him then." She leafed through them. "Here's last year... repairs on the farm... heating bills for the Adirondacks house... maintenance on his plane... fuel... all those trips we took up there, I didn't realize there were so many." She put the stack of papers down, her face pensive. Then she frowned. "That's odd."

"What?" Rosemary asked.

"I thought I saw..." She leafed through the pile again, stopping halfway through. "Fuel bills from the Lake Placid airport for April, May, June, the spring before the crash, and then later that year, in October and November. That can't be right; we never went in those months." She went through them again. "April," she murmured. "May, June... Even if I'd forgotten one time, I wouldn't have forgotten all of them. We didn't take those trips."

"He probably went alone," Rosemary said.

"No; the only place he went alone was New York; he had a lot of business trips that year—" She looked at the papers in her hand, then at Rosemary. "My God, I can't have been that blind."

"You mean he lied when he told you he was going to New York?"

"He didn't lie. He said he was going to New York. And I assumed he meant New York City."

"But why would he go to Placid? That's no place to be alone. Oh." She looked at Valerie. "He wasn't alone."

Valerie nodded. "I'd bet on that."

"Do you know who she was?"

"No. I was sure there was someone, but he denied it and I didn't push. I thought we'd work things out, or we wouldn't, and another woman wouldn't be the cause of anything; she was only a sign that things weren't that wonderful between us. But now I'd like to know."

"Why? It's been a year and a half; why fret over it? Put it behind you."

Valerie slipped the fuel bills into an envelope. "I can't. I think about it a lot. I haven't been able to do much about it, but it's always there, at the back of my mind. There's too much I don't know."

"About what?"

"About anything. Carl's affair—or affairs; I don't know how many he had—what he did with our money, what he meant by the things he said before he died. They probably don't have anything to do with each other, but that bothers me, too. There are too many mysteries. If I can't find all the answers, that's no reason not to try to find some of them." She went to the telephone. "I'm going to Placid. If Carl was there with someone, Mae would know."

"Mae? Oh, the housekeeper. But the detective already talked to her."

"Of course. Obviously she didn't tell him Carl was up there in the spring and fall, without me. I'll have to ask her about that, too."

She called the airline to make reservations; she called Sophie to tell her she would not be in the next day; she called Nick at home and left a message with Elena. "I'll be back Tuesday. I have some business to take care of." And early Monday morning, she flew to the Lake Placid airport.

Mae Williamson still lived in town, in the house she had lived in all her life. After calling to make sure she was home, Valerie rented a car and drove to the house. "Oh, but it's good to see you!" Mae cried, hugging Valerie. She was tall and spare, with a narrow, long-nosed face, sharp eyes, and a warm smile for the few who won her approval. "You don't know how I've missed you, I cried for you when Mr. Sterling was killed, poor Mrs. Sterling, I said, she'll be alone now." She sat in the swing on the front porch and patted the seat beside her. "We'll have lunch in a few minutes, I fixed something when you called, but first tell me how you are and what you're doing."

"I'd love some lunch," Valerie lied, knowing she could not refuse Mae one more chance to feed her. "But then I'll have to leave; I have a job now."

"You? Oh, Lord, Lord, we heard about your money being gone, we didn't know how, but we heard it, and I said to myself, things'll be bad for Mrs. Sterling, I knew they would."

"Not too bad," Valerie said. "I'm getting along. Mae, I'm trying to find out some things about Mr. Sterling. I know it's been a long time, but you always had an amazing memory and if you could help me I'd appreciate it."

Mae fixed her with a melancholy look. "My memory ain't what it used to be, it skips around like a goat, there's whole patches it just misses, but I'll tell you what I remember if you're sure you want to know."

Valerie smiled. "That sounds like a warning. Mae, he had women up here, didn't he?"

"One woman. That he did."

"You didn't tell the detective."

"Why would I tell him, and make Mr. Sterling look like a bastard and you like a fool? It didn't make any difference to the detective, he was just poking around for whatever he could dig up, and he wouldn't care if you heard it from him or the town crier, but I cared, I thought if you ever needed to know I'd tell you, and it wouldn't be so hard, coming from me. I don't have secrets from you, you know."

"Who was she, Mae?"

"That I don't know; I never did get her name. At first, I thought it was you. I mean, Mr. Sterling told me not to come the days he was there—he always said 'he,' never 'we'—so I didn't, I'd come in when he'd left and all I knew was somebody'd been there, and why not think it was you, since your robe was out—" Valerie winced and Mae put her hand to her mouth. "Oh, damn me, I'm hurting you."

"No, it's all right. I want to know it all; there's no sense in just knowing part of it."

"Well, that's so; nobody ever pulled a tooth halfway out and called it a day. She used your robes, both of them, and there was a little of your face powder spilled on the dressing table, and one of your lipsticks not put away, that sort of thing. I never thought too much about it at first, but later that spring I started thinking something was fishy, you never calling me like you usually do, so the next time he called and said he was coming up, I was in the house when they got there, like I hadn't finished cleaning, and I looked all surprised when they walked in, not as surprised as he was, let me tell you, but then I really was surprised, no pretending about it, because it wasn't you. I made sure I saw her a few other times after that, but I didn't know who she was. But, hold on, what's wrong with me, I'm forgetting the important part. You know her. That was another reason I didn't tell the detective, I didn't want you to know your husband was playing around with one of your friends. I don't know how good a friend, but good enough to be a guest, because you had her staying here, her and that little blond preacher, that last weekend, just before Mr. Sterling was killed."

Chapter 26

t first, Lily was the only one who noticed a change in Sybille. She seemed distracted, unable to focus on anything for very long, and always very angry. Lily would have talked to her about it, asked her if she couldn't take some time off, maybe even go away for a vacation, but she did not. Because, just then, Lily had her own distractions. She had fallen in love.

Three months earlier, on her twenty-third birthday, Gus Emery had taken her to lunch. She was so surprised when he invited her that she went straight to Sybille to ask her what she thought. "He's probably looking for a raise," Sybille said. "Go ahead, find out what he wants; Gus never does anything without a reason."

After that, whenever Gus asked her anywhere, Lily kept it a secret. She had always liked him for his soft voice and careful manners, the way he seemed to be watching himself to make sure he was nice to her. Sometimes he reminded her of Rudy Dominus, trying to be fatherly. And she liked his looks: handsome, almost pretty, with pale skin, long eyelashes, and a mouth that shaped each word he spoke. His voice was rough, but he kept it low with her.

Lily knew no one liked Gus as well as she did; even Valerie hadn't gotten along with him when she worked there, and that puzzled her. But Lily often was not sure what made other people behave the way they did. Sometimes she lay awake in bed, worrying about that; she really didn't know a lot about people, so how could she be giving them advice? And if she didn't know much about others, probably she didn't know very much about herself either, and then she certainly had no business telling anyone what to do.

Those were the most awful times, when she doubted herself. But they passed. Sybille always told her how important she was to others; Reverend Bassington put his arm around her—which she didn't like, but he meant it lovingly—and praised her miraculous understanding of the human heart; and after every sermon her congregation touched her hand and told her they loved her. Then Lily forgot those black hours and believed she was unique.

And so she did not worry about Gus's unpopularity. She liked him; she saw the good in him. It bothered her that Valerie hadn't, but Valerie had been gone for a long time, and Gus was always there. At first they'd just worked together and it had been pleasant because he was so helpful and admiring, but later he sought her out. It was uncanny how he seemed to know where she would be, and he would be there first, or he would appear within a few minutes, at her elbow, monopolizing her, being helpful with whatever she was doing, telling her how wonderful she was. Often he gave her little bits of advice, like suggesting she use people's names more often as she answered their letters on "At Home with Reverend Grace," to make them feel she was talking right to them.

Gus knew a great deal about the world, and he seemed totally self-sufficient. Lily was intrigued by that: how could one person not need anyone else? She asked him that the first time they went to dinner in a small town near Culpeper. "You can teach yourself not to need anybody," he said. "It's hard, but once you've learned it, nobody can hurt you, ever."

"Who hurt you so badly that you feel that way?" Lily asked. "What happened to you?"

He shook his head. "You don't want to hear about me."

"Of course I do! I like you and I want to know all about you."

That pleased him, Lily saw . . . or was it satisfaction that had crossed his face so fleetingly? She could not be sure. She knew so little about him. Or about any man. Of course he was pleased, she told herself. He's pleased that I'm interested in him.

"Someday maybe I'll tell you about my past," he said. "It'll be short, though; I've forgotten most of it."

"That's not true," Lily said softly.

"It sure is. Well, for tonight it's true."

Sybille had asked about their lunch and Lily had told her exactly what had happened: they had talked about Graceville and "At Home with Reverend Grace" and the weather. "I think he just wanted someone to eat with," Lily said. "He wasn't after anything at all."

Later, when Sybille asked Lily if Gus had suggested lunch again, Lily said no, which was the truth, because by then Gus was asking her to dinner. They went out once a week, always on Wednesday when Sybille was at a meeting; she was having so many meetings lately she was paying much less attention to Lily. Gus thought it might have to do with the spreading scandal of Jim and Tammy Bakker. Everyone involved with television evangelism was absorbed in the story, trying to be prepared for any new revelations; everyone but Lily, that is, who was serenely confident that she had nothing to do with any of it, or anything like it, and felt only pity and sorrow for those who did. But since the scandal had broken, which happened about the time Graceville was becoming a real town, Sybille had been very busy, and Lily, in her small house in Culpeper, was on her own more than ever before.

And there was Gus, taking her to dinner every Wednesday night at tiny out-of-the-way restaurants where they sat for three or four hours, talking about themselves, their hands almost touching on the tablecloth. Gus told her about his past, a few small stories at a time. Most were sad, a few were tragic. Occasionally Lily had the terrible thought that he was making them up, but she was never sure why she thought it. It might have been the calm way he told them, or the fact that he never once had tears in his eyes, or the way he would pause and look at her to see her reactions. But all that could be explained by his pretended toughness, too. Lily was convinced he was far more sensitive than he said he was; she was convinced he was acting when he seemed so self-sufficient. And so she refused to listen to her doubts: she wanted to believe that he was completely honest with her, and she did. She believed she knew him better than he knew himself.

It was the first time she had made friends with a man who was not old enough to be her father or grandfather, and it gave her a warm, shivery feeling. She never asked herself what that meant; she only knew she looked forward to her Wednesday nights with a slight shortness of breath that made her feel a little odd, until Gus arrived at her door and then she began to feel wonderful.

She hugged her feelings to herself: she had a friend. Sybille had kept people away, women and men both; Sybille had said she had to conserve her strength and hoard her energy for her congregation; Sybille had said she couldn't take chances with strangers who would take advantage of her goodness and generosity. But it had been years since they even talked about that; Lily seemed so settled, and bound to Sybille, that the subject never came up anymore. Lily hadn't even thought about it very much until Valerie's friend Sophie asked her about friends and dates. It was a few months after that that Gus had asked her to lunch, and they became friends.

But even Lily knew it was more than a friendship. One Sunday night, Gus sent her a gardenia, with a note that said her sermon that morning had been the best he had ever heard anywhere. She had inhaled the heavy, dizzying scent of the waxy flower, and not one thought of religion had come to her. Instead, she thought of Gus's hand, close to hers on the tablecloth a few nights before, and the way his soft lips shaped her name. The following week, he sent two gardenias, and Lily had to put them outside, because the scent made her slightly ill, but all night long she visualized those pure white, glossy flowers nestled in their bed of green tissue paper, and she thought of Gus pinning them on her dress before her next sermon, his hands touching her, and she felt faint and very hot.

She remembered, years before, the girls in boarding school talking about getting hot and excited, but she had never dated, and had never experienced any of that herself. Still, she recognized it now, and thought she knew what was happening: her body had taken over and was having its own feelings about Gus, completely separate from her mind. Her mind said he was only a friend. Her body seemed to think he might be something else too. As soon as she let herself think that, guilt washed over her, and even in the privacy of her bedroom, she blushed.

For a week she avoided Gus and would not answer her telephone. She missed him and was miserably unhappy; she burst into tears without warning, and lost interest in food. I have to talk to Sybille, she thought; this is terrible. I mustn't be like this; it's all wrong. But Sybille did not come to church on Sunday morning, and it was the next day that Lily went to her office and found her changed. No one else seemed to notice, but Lily was so close to her that she felt her anger the minute she walked into her office. She seemed so angry, in fact, that Lily thought she must have found out about her dinners with Gus, but after a few minutes she knew it was not that: something else had happened that made Sybille hardly even aware of Lily. On the surface, she behaved quite normally, but Lily saw she was really turned inward, thinking, planning, plotting how to deal with something that enraged her so much it was consuming her.

There was no one to whom Lily could talk. She stood in the hallway outside Sybille's office, feeling uncertain and alone, almost afraid. She knew she ought to go to her own office and read her mail, and prepare for Wednesday's taping of "At Home with Reverend Grace," and next Sunday's sermon, and next week's talk to the Rotary Club of Arlington, but she couldn't concentrate on any of that. She wanted someone to tell her what to do.

She stood in the hallway. She was there only a minute before Gus walked by. And then she knew that was what she had been waiting for.

He shot a glance at Sybille's closed door. "Were you two talking about me?"

"No," she said, startled. "Why do you think we were?"

His face smoothed out. "I thought she might not like you and me being friends." He peered at her. "You okay? You want somebody to talk to?"

"Yes," said Lily, "that's what I need more than anything."

He took her hand, holding it tightly against her instinctive pulling away until he felt her relax. "We'll go somewhere; shall I take you for a drive somewhere? The mountains?"

"Oh, yes, perfect." Lily felt the warmth of his hand clasping hers. I love you, she thought involuntarily. She wished he would put his arms around her and hold her close and make her feel safe, the way Sybille used to do, when they lived together in the Watergate. I love you, she thought again, and shivered. She was twenty-three years old and in her whole life she had said that to only three people: Rudy Dominus, Quentin Enderby and Sybille.

Gus talked about himself as he drove to the mountains, but Lily was not as attentive as usual and he fell silent as they ascended the Skyline Drive along the crest. Now and then he turned off to an overlook that gave expansive views of the misty Shenandoah Valley on one side, or the Virginia hunt country on the other. At one point he stopped and they got out to walk. The forest smelled fresh and cool, and sumacs and maples and other trees Lily could not identify made a roof over the hiking trail and the two of them as they walked. Lily felt free. "Isn't it wonderful!" she cried

Gus created a smile for her. He hated forests and walking; he hated the mountains. He liked restaurants, motel rooms, television studios and the interiors of luxury automobiles. If he hadn't been convinced she was ripe, he wouldn't have come near the fucking Blue Ridge Mountains. "It's great," he said. "You talked about the mountains in one of your sermons."

"Oh, you remembered! Thank you for telling me, Gus; I love it when people remember what I say."

They walked on. Gus looked with distaste at the dust on his shoes. Lily plucked a small flower and held it tenderly, so as not to bruise the petals. A breeze lifted tendrils of her hair, and she turned up her face, breathing the scent of leaves and damp soil. "So much beauty in the world," she said, and looked at Gus with a shy smile. "You feel it, too; I know it. That means so much to me; sometimes I think it means everything. There's too much that I don't know—I'm scared by how much I don't know, and maybe that I'm wrong about things because of it—but if I can be with someone who cares about me and feels the way I do, it's not so scary. I need that so much; it hurts sometimes, needing to be with someone who understands how I feel, and feels the same way."

Gus took a deep breath. "Lily!" he cried. He grabbed her hands and fell to his knees before her on the dirt path. He was wearing good pants, but what the hell; this was the kind of thing that would get to her. "You're what's beautiful in the world; that's what I need. I need the same things you do. I need you to make the world beautiful and a place I can live in."

Dimly, Lily knew that was not poetry, but it did not matter. She'd been right: he was sincere and sensitive, he understood her, he was not afraid to tell her he needed her. Not so self-sufficient after all, Lily thought with a surge of pleasure.

"You have my friendship," she said, and her voice trembled. "You're my only friend. When you need me, I'm here for you."

That odd look of satisfaction flashed across Gus's face again, but it was hidden when he leaned forward, resting his forehead on Lily's breasts. She barely had time to realize what he was doing when, suddenly, he was even closer, his body pressing against hers, his arms around her waist. She felt his breath through her linen blouse, warm and moist on her nipples. "I love you," he said, the words muffled but clear enough for Lily to be sure of them. "Darling Lily..." He put back his head for a quick look at her face, then he went back to her breasts. "Sweet little girl...love..."

Her nipples were hard and her breasts heavy; she ached between her legs. She was terrified someone would see them; she was terrified of her body. Her heart pounded, and she squeezed her eyes shut. Tangled threads of bright color swam and surged in the darkness.

And Lily ran.

She ran frantically, trying to outrun her body, but she was not used to exercise and soon she slowed and stopped, leaning against a tree, panting. She began to cry. Gus found her that way, her head back against the tree trunk, tears covering her face.

"Don't do that," he said. "I didn't mean it. I mean, of course I meant I love you—you've got to believe I love you—but I didn't mean to make you cry. I forgot, you know, that I haven't any right to say those things to you. It was the forest, I guess, and the mountains —I love them, you saw that right away, and they make me say things I shouldn't—and then there's all this beauty; you know what that does to me, too. So I forgot I shouldn't even be talking to you, much less touching you; you're so far above me, I haven't any right—"

"You do!" Lily cried, gulping through her tears. "You have every right to say anything you want; I'm not above you, what are you talking about? We're two people who...care about...each other..." She began to make small whimpering sounds. "Can we go back to the car?"

"Sure. It's a little ways off; do you want...?" He held out his hand. Lily hesitated, then took it, and they walked hand in hand through the forest. Like Hansel and Gretel, she thought. She giggled a little wildly and forced herself to stop, and then walked quietly beside Gus, back to the turnoff where he had left the car.

"Shall I take you home?" he asked.

"Yes. Please."

He drove back the way they had come, to Thornton Gap and down from the mountains to the highway to Culpeper. His face was set; he was frowning and silent. Lily was sure he was angry, and she was as afraid of his anger as she was of herself. What had she wanted, up there on the mountain? His arms around her, yes, but also his mouth on hers, his body crushing hers. She had wanted him to make love to her.

Virginal Lilith Grace, chosen by God to survive, to be special and to do good, had wanted a man to make love to her.

She must not be very special if she wanted sex like everyone else. If God had known she was like that, he never would have helped her walk away unscathed from that terrible plane crash.

Rudy had told her to stay a virgin. Sybille had told her she was chosen to do great things: to preach, to lead a huge congregation, to bring Graceville to fruition.

Sitting in Gus's car, Lily began to cry again. If she was ordinary, what would she do with her life? She didn't know how to do anything but preach.

"It's all right," he said angrily. "We'll forget it."

And then she was terrified all over again. *Darling Lily... sweet little girl... love...* She thought she would die if she never heard Gus say that again. She huddled in the corner of the seat, confused and lost, wishing Sybille were there. But she couldn't talk to Sybille; how could she? She couldn't talk to anyone.

"Lily," Gus said hoarsely as he stopped the car in front of her house. He was frowning deeply. "I won't call you for a little while, okay? We'll think about things. I love you and I really respect you and I want you to be happy and do your preaching because people need you." He put his hand under her chin and brought her tear-stained face up so she was looking at him through wide, helpless eyes. "We'll figure out something so we can be happy. Remember the mountain and all that beauty. And I'll talk to you on Wednesday. Okay?"

After a moment, Lily nodded. "Thank you," she whispered, and fled from his car.

But she did not go to the studio on Wednesday. For the first time since she had begun preaching, she telephoned from home and told the receptionist that she was sick and could not tape "At Home with Reverend Grace." Gus showed a rerun, with an announcement that Reverend Grace had been called away to help a church in trouble, and would be back the following week. That alerted Sybille, forcing her out of the grip of rage that had held her since Saturday, when she had gone to pick up Chad for dinner. On Thursday morning she phoned Lily at home. "What's wrong with you? Have you seen a doctor?"

"No." Lily's voice was thin. "I just don't feel well. Sort of sick all over. I'm sorry, Sybille, I know I should have come in, but I couldn't face it. I'm sorry I disappointed you."

"You disappointed a few million people. You have a responsibility to them, Lily."

"I know. It's just... I feel so sick and I've got a headache and I feel like I'd throw up if I tried to talk. I just want to sleep all the time."

"I'm sending you a doctor. His name is—"

"No! I don't want a doctor! Sybille, just leave me alone!"

Sybille's head snapped around as if she had been slapped. *"Who do you think you're talking to?"*

"Oh, I'm sorry, I'm sorry." Lily was sniffling. "I didn't mean . . . I just want to be left alone. I'll be fine; I just need to sleep. I don't want anybody poking me. I mean . . ." She burst into sobs.

Sybille gripped the telephone. There was too much going on; she had too much to worry about. The Bakker scandal was growing, not fading; the media were like wolves, baying at the door of every evangelist; Floyd Bassington grated on her nerves, but she couldn't get rid of him yet. But all that faded before the enormity of the scene on Nick's terrace, burned into her memory. It was like a wound that made everything she did hurt. And now Lily. What the hell was wrong with her, that she had to choose this week to mess up Sybille's life even more? The silence dragged out. "Have you written your sermon for Sunday?" she asked at last.

"No. I don't . . . I don't know if I'll be there."

"You'll be there!" Sybille screamed. She leaped to her feet. "You'll be there if I have to drag you by your hair! You've got a job to do, and you'll fucking do it, is that clear or do I have to repeat it?"

Lily hung up.

Sybille held the receiver away from her, staring at it, then flung it to the floor. It dragged the telephone with it, and the crash reverberated in the office. No one came, not her assistant, not her secretary. They were used to sounds of breakage from her office.

She dragged the telephone to her desk, made sure it was still working, and called Gus to her office. When he walked in, she was standing behind the desk. "What's wrong with Lily?"

He looked surprised. "I thought you'd know. She called yesterday, said she was sick and couldn't tape the show."

She sat down, pointing to a chair, and Gus took it. "She didn't call me. How was her sermon last Sunday?"

"Terrific. Same as always. I wondered where you were."

"Something came up; I knew you could handle the show. Have you talked to her since then?"

Gus looked even more surprised. "I thought you would have."

"I didn't ask for comments; just answer my question."

"Right. Sure. Uh, no, I haven't, uh, talked to her."

Sybille looked at him with narrowed eyes. "What does that mean?"

"Uh, nothing."

Anger boiled through her. "God damn it, you're dancing around, dying to tell me something. Well, what the hell is it?" She watched him nibble on a fingernail. "I'm waiting!" she said.

He shrugged. "If you want to know . . . I've seen her a few times. Dinner, walks in the woods, you know, romantic things. She likes me. So much she got sick."

"You son of a bitch."

He shrugged again. "She was lonely, you know that? She's just a baby, Syb; she doesn't know a fucking thing."

"You son of a bitch."

"For Christ's sake, I was just keeping her company. Somebody had to."

"Did you screw her?"

"Are you kidding? The reason she's all cut up is she wants it but she thinks it'd be wrong or sinful or dangerous or whatever. We didn't do anything. I held her hand."

"Did you talk about me?"

"Some. Sure. We talked about lots of things."

Sybille thought of them talking about her, laughing at her, plotting against her. No wonder Lily had talked back to her—and hung up on her! She thought she didn't need Sybille; she had a man.

And Valerie had Nick. And Valerie had Chad. And Valerie had everything.

She felt she was about to explode. Too much was happening. Why wouldn't they all go away and leave her alone so she could get things organized her own way again?

Lily will. She'll go away, she'll leave you if you don't do something. She'll be taken away by this stupid bastard who thinks he can get her with his prick after all the years I've worked on making her what she is.

She poured a glass of water from the decanter on her desk, spilling some of it until she managed to get her hand still, and sipped it, letting Gus wait while she tried to concentrate on what to do. He was probably right: Lily had made herself sick because she wanted sex and was scared to death of it. But there was something else that Gus didn't know, because he was too taken up with himself. The real reason Lily got sick was because she loved Sybille more than anyone and she couldn't stand having secrets from her. Gus had talked her into having a secret, and it had made her sick.

Well, then, Gus would have to make her sicker. Because the more sick Gus made her, the more quickly she'd come back to Sybille. Who else did she have to come to? It might seem to some people that Lily was taking the first step toward shifting her allegiance, but Sybille knew better. Lily was waiting for a reason to come home. And that was what Sybille had to arrange. Lily had to be driven back to her arms.

"I think you should see her again," she said smoothly to Gus. "You're absolutely right; she's been lonely and I haven't paid enough attention to her. Anyway, it's time she had a man; she's too innocent to handle half the questions that come in her mail."

Gus stared at her. "You're not serious."

"I'm always serious when I talk about Lily. Go to her house. Make her let you in. She may seem upset, but that won't last, not if you're any good. I know Lily better than she knows herself: she loves to give in to someone stronger. You should have a fine time. And then you come back to me and, if you've earned it, I'll have something for you."

His gaze was fixed on her. "Like what?"

"I was thinking of station manager of KQYO-TV in Los Angeles."

"How would that work?" he asked, scowling. "Why would they hire me?"

"I'd hire you. I bought it a few months ago."

A slow smile spread over Gus's face. He stood and rotated his shoulders, loosening them up. "If you give me the day off, I might drive out to the country. It's kind of romantic out there, around Culpeper; lots of beauty around, you know."

Lily was lying on a chaise on the patio behind her house when Gus arrived. It was midafternoon, and shimmering waves of heat lapped at her; she felt she was dissolving into the sun. When he stood over her, casting a shadow across her face, she opened her eyes in confusion, thinking a cloud had come up. She could not see his face, only his silhouette, but she knew who it was. "You said you wouldn't call," she said, knowing how foolish that sounded.

"I didn't." He knelt beside her. "Don't be angry with me. I had to talk to you to say I'm sorry. It drove me crazy, you crying in my car; I kept thinking about it and couldn't sleep."

Lily closed her eyes and said nothing. Her breathing was shallow and quick and she was so hot in the sun she thought she would faint.

"Lily, talk to me," Gus begged. "Don't ignore me. You'll make me feel you don't like me. I want your friendship." He paused. "I thought, you know, I didn't need anybody, but you made me feel different about that. I need you, Lily, you caring about me and me caring about you. I want to be good to you, you know, because I don't think people really care about you the way I do. I mean, they love you in their letters and in church, but they don't *care* about you, like do you have nice clothes or good food or do you have somebody to keep you warm at night—"

"No!" Lily opened her eyes and found herself looking into his, a few inches away. "Please stop! I can't talk to you!"

"It's okay, don't talk, I'll talk."

"No, I get so confused..." She tried to sit up, but Gus leaned forward suddenly and kissed her. His lips were soft on hers, like the touch of a flower, and she was so surprised she lay still, and even when he pressed harder she did not move, because there was still a gentleness in his closed lips that was exactly what she imagined when she lay hot and twisting in bed, trying not to think about him. They stayed that way for a long time, lips touching, her eyes closed, and then Gus raised his head, and Lily felt cold, even in the hot sun.

"You're so beautiful," Gus said. "Beautiful and wonderful and lovable...like an angel..."

Lily put up her arms. She had not planned to do that, but they came up and Gus leaned forward again and her arms went around him. He slipped one hand under her head and kissed her, and this time he opened her lips with his and, very slowly, his tongue invaded her mouth.

Lily tensed, but Gus was holding her head still, and his tongue was sweet, not disgusting as she'd always thought tongues would be; it moved gently in her mouth, stroking her tongue in a different kind of kiss, not demanding, not forceful, just soft and safe. And as she relaxed under its hypnotic rhythm, Gus's hand accidentally brushed her breast, hesitantly came back to it, and rested on it. He cupped his fingers around it and held it more tightly, and then he was caressing it, rubbing the nipple as it grew hard and upright, teasing it between his fingers. And then his hand moved to her other breast.

Lily was wearing a cotton blouse, but she felt naked. His hand burned into her, turning her to fire; the fire burned between her legs and she pressed her thighs together, trying to hold it in, but she was so open, everything was running out of her; she was open, and waiting.

Gus's hand tightened beneath her head, and his other hand moved away from her breast, down her body, not so slowly now, along her skirt and then under it. He lifted her skirt, baring her legs to the hot sun, while his fingers slid upward, between her tight-pressed thighs, until they reached her heavy, aching center, and without a pause plunged inside.

Lily's eyes flew open. "No!" she cried against Gus's mouth. She felt as if an iron rod was inside her, moving around, hurting her. "No, stop, I don't—" She twisted her head, to break free of his mouth, but he pressed harder, holding her head. She arched her back, and flung her body wildly from side to side, like a horse trying to throw a rider. "Stop!" The word was a strangled cry beneath the clamp of his mouth. "Let me go!"

That was the moment when he might have stopped, if he had not remembered what Sybille had said. *She's always ready to give in to someone stronger.* So he shook his head. Any minute, he thought, she'll give in. She really wanted it; that's what Sybille had meant. "It's all right," he muttered against her mouth. "...all right...all right...all right..." He tore open his pants and shoved them down while holding Lily's head and keeping his mouth fastened on hers. She was still fighting him and he worked his finger harder inside her; how come she didn't know that he was stronger than her?

Lily bit his lip, and tasted his blood. *"Let me go!"*

"Damn bitch—!" he burst out and gripped the back of her neck so she could not move. She was dizzy; circles of blinding color whirled behind her closed eyes; and silently, fiercely, she fought. Just as silently, Gus held her down. And in that brief time that he waited for her to give in, he lost the moment when he might have stopped. Crazed with the twisting and arching of her slender body, her wet smoothness sucking against his finger, and the sun pounding down on him, on his perspiration-soaked shirt and his bare buttocks, he climbed on top of her, shoving her legs apart, and rammed his swollen, throbbing prick all the way into her.

In the summer stillness of the afternoon, Lily screamed.

ybille was asleep when her doorbell rang, and it rang several times before she heard it. The butler and housekeeper were on vacation, leaving her alone in the house, and she lay in bed for another minute, thinking she'd ignore it. It was probably Bassington; he'd pulled this once before: arrived at midnight for a quick toss in bed because he hadn't been able to sleep. She shook her head. Let him ring; she couldn't stand the thought of him.

But the bell kept ringing, a desperate peal that grated on Sybille's nerves, and finally she pulled on a robe and went downstairs. She looked through the library curtains, to glimpse whoever was standing there.

Lily. Wrapped in a long raincoat. On a clear, hot night in July.

"Come in," Sybille said, pushing wide the door. Lily walked stiffly into the entrance hall, as if she were in a trance. Her eyes were red and swollen; her mouth was raw. "My God, what's happened?" Sybille cried. "Lily! What happened?"

"Gus," Lily whispered. And she burst into tears.

"Gus? Gus Emery? He raped you?"

503

Lily nodded, once. And then she crumpled to the floor.

"Oh, for Christ's sake," Sybille burst out. Why couldn't people do things the way they were supposed to? Lily was supposed to have given in, hot and eager. Gus was supposed to arouse her to passion, not beat her up and rape her. It was supposed to be a simple seduction that would send Lily to Sybille for comfort and advice, especially after Gus left town for Los Angeles, deserting her. It was not supposed to be a messy rape with emotions Sybille wasn't prepared to deal with, beginning with tears and fainting. You'd think they were in a silent film from the twenties.

"Lily," Sybille said, kneeling beside her. "I can't carry you; you'll have to walk."

In a moment, Lily stirred. She opened her eyes. "What?" she asked.

Sybille helped her stand, and guided her, passive and stumbling, into the darkened living room. "Give me your coat," she said. Lily shook her head. Sybille shrugged and sat her on one of the sofas. Then she went around the room, turning on all the lamps.

"Too bright," Lily whispered.

Sybille turned off half the lamps and sat on the arm of the sofa. "What happened?"

"He..." She could not say the word. "He forced me. I fought with him, I really did, Sybille...I just wasn't strong enough. But the worst thing..." She turned her head away. "The worst thing is, just before that...and the other day too...I wanted him to make love to me. I didn't want to when he started...when he put his hand...when I knew..." Her teeth were chattering, and she clenched them shut for a minute and clasped her hands tightly in her lap. "But that doesn't matter, it doesn't matter, and what matters is that, earlier, *I wanted him to make love to me.*"

"But you didn't," Sybille said.

Lily shook her head. "He didn't even kiss me. Not then."

"Then why are you worrying about it now?"

Lily's mouth opened and closed. She looked at Sybille as if she were a stranger. "You don't understand."

"I'm trying—" Sybille bit off her sharp words. "I want to," she said soothingly. "Lily, I want to help you. You were right to come here; this is where you belong. You'll stay here tonight. You'll stay here as long as you want. You don't have to worry anymore. I'll take care of you."

Lily's shaking eased under the murmur of Sybille's voice. "Could I have a cup of tea?" she asked.

"Oh. Of course. Come to the kitchen, we'll sit there. And you'll tell me what you're thinking. You can tell me, Lily; you can tell me anything. I'll understand. I'll give you everything you need; you don't need anyone else. You never did. I'm the one you need."

"Yes," Lily said. She was so sleepy. She hurt all over, and though she had washed and washed, and taken a bath so hot it turned her skin bright red, and spread ointment on her torn flesh, there was still a terrible burning between her legs, like a scream, and she thought she could still feel the oozing he had left behind, and the trickling of her blood. She felt dirty and anonymous, as if she were a piece of merchandise that a store clerk had torn from its wrappings and then tossed on a shelf, for everyone to see.

"Tell me what happened," Sybille said. They sat at a long table in the kitchen, across from each other, waiting for the water to boil. "He came to your house?"

Lily closed her eyes. "I can't... not yet."

"Tell me," Sybille said urgently. She leaned forward tensely. "I want to hear everything."

"No! I'm sorry, Sybille, I can't. Not tonight. I just want to go to sleep."

"You don't want your tea?"

"Oh. I guess so. And then can I go to sleep?"

"Of course. You can do anything you want. You don't have to do anything at all until Sunday morning. We'll find an old sermon for you to give; no one will notice—"

"Sunday? Sybille, I can't preach Sunday. You wouldn't ask me to."

Sybille's mouth tightened; her eyes were flat. She had enough to worry about without Lily having a tantrum. The teakettle screeched, and she jumped up and went to the stove. "We won't talk about it tonight." She brought Lily a cup of tea. "How long was he there?"

Lily stared at the tendrils of steam rising from the cup. "He left right after..."

"What time was that?"

"I don't know. The sun was shining."

"This afternoon? And you waited until midnight to come to me? Are you sure he left right away? Or did he stay until you got used to him, maybe got to like it, and then you came to me because he left you?"

Lily dropped the cup. It broke into shards, and the steaming tea flowed over the table in a red pool, and onto her lap, darkening her raincoat. She did not notice. She was shaking. She began to strike the table with her fist, helplessly banging it harder and harder, her hand slipping in the spilled tea, the shards of china bouncing as she struck the wood. "You can't say that, you can't, you can't, you can't. You promised to take care of me, you said you'd understand, you said you were all I need." She struck the table, again and again, unable to stop. "You lied to me!"

"*I never lie!*" Sybille took long steps to the end of the kitchen. Her body felt ungainly, as if she could not completely control it. "Stop acting like an infant! Behave yourself! I can't deal with you if you're hysterical!"

"You think I liked it! How could you think that? You don't know anything about me!"

"I know everything about you! Maybe you didn't like it; what difference does it make? When you calm down you'll forget it—it's amazing how much you can forget if you put your mind to it—and then you can concentrate on your preaching. If you'd done that all along, this wouldn't have happened." She came up behind Lily and put her hands on Lily's shoulders. "Listen to me," she said carefully. "I said I'd take care of you; you know that wasn't a lie. Look how many years I've done it, and you've been happy and making other people happy. It's all worked out the way I planned it; you don't want to ruin that, do you? It's been fine for you, Lily; you know that. And it will be again, I promise, but only if you stay close to me. You've got to forget this idea that you can experiment with sex, play around on the side, and then come back to me for—"

"*Don't say that!*" Lily leaped from her chair and ran around the table, keeping it between them. She was still wearing her raincoat, tied tightly around her narrow waist, and she looked small and lost in it, her fragile neck and white pinched face rising from its wide collar, her eyes wide and fearful. "I don't experiment, I don't play around, I'm not even sure what that means. I wanted someone to love me. I thought you did, but you don't... Do you know who you sound like? Him! When he was on his knees, holding my hands and talking... oh, God, oh God..." She gasped as if she were strangling. "I hate it! I hate it and I hate you!"

"Shut up! You don't hate me, you couldn't hate me, I'm all you have in the world. You've had a shock, a bad one, but you don't have to overdo it; you'll forget in no time. These things don't even leave scars. You think you'll never be the same, but you will be; nothing is so important that it leaves scars, you know, Lily; we're too tough for that, you and I. We'll go back the way we were; you'll do exactly what I say, you won't go sneaking around anymore like a teenager instead of a preacher who has millions of—"

With a loud wail, Lily turned and opened the door behind her and flung herself through it.

"God damn it!" Sybille exploded, and ran after her. "Lily, come back here!" She stood in the rectangle of light from the kitchen, looking into the darkness. "Come back, I said! You can't leave; where will you go? You haven't anyone but me!" She stood still, listening. There was no sound but the rustling of leaves in a light breeze. "Lily, I order you to come in here!" She stood there, breathing hard, her shadow stretching before her like a long, thin finger, pointing at Lily.

Standing behind a lilac bush, Lily shrank from it. *You haven't anyone but me.* It was true. There was nowhere she could go. She could get into the small car that Sybille had bought for her birthday, and drive and drive and not find one person who cared about her. Millions of people watched her every week; thousands came to the Cathedral of Joy to hear her, but to them she was a preacher, distant, pure, all in white, with answers to their questions. They wouldn't want to know what a sad, soiled creature Lilith Grace had turned out to be. They wouldn't want to comfort her and love her; they expected her to do that for them.

She blinked back the tears that kept coming; there seemed to be no end to them. She wondered why she wasn't a dry husk by now, all the tears squeezed out, nothing left.

Nothing left. *You haven't anyone but me.* Sybille's shadow pointed at her.

"God damn it, I gave you an order!" The voice shrieked across the darkness. "You get back in this house!" There was a pause; then the voice, sounding strained, was lower. "You need a good night's sleep, then you'll feel better. Get in here; I'll put you to bed." There was another pause. *"Get in here!"*

Lily shivered. *I can't go back; I'll die.* Very slowly, one careful step at a time, she walked away from the house, making a wide circle to the driveway in front. She inched open her car door and sat inside. Instantly, her eyes closed. If she could just sleep awhile . . .

"Answer me! Where are you?"

Her eyes jerked open. She had left the key in the ignition; she felt it with her fingers in the darkness, and turned it at the same time as she slammed the door. The car leaped forward, skidding as she turned the wheel hard to follow the bend in the driveway. *I'll find a place to go. Somewhere . . .*

Tears blurred her vision and she slowed until she was barely moving. She stared at the two beams from her headlights, converging in the pitch blackness, leading her on. But they don't lead to anyone, or anything, she thought. I have no future. I'm just an ordinary person. I'm not a virgin, I'm not pure, I'm not special, and I have nowhere to go.

But I *am* special. Sybille always said I was. She said I was chosen. I walked away from that plane crash without even a scratch. Carlton was killed, everyone else was injured; I was the only one who walked away, untouched, in God's embrace.

But... Sybille. I can't be sure of anything Sybille told me. Not anymore. And I can't remember how I got out of the plane. I don't remember anything but walking away. And if I'm really not special, not different... what if I'm wrong about the crash too?

And then she knew what she had to do. She put her foot on the accelerator, speeding up, following her lights. She had to find out what happened in the crash. She had to talk to Valerie.

"I'll tell you anything I can," Valerie said, "but not tonight. You're more asleep than awake and I *was* asleep, so we're going to wait until morning."

"I don't need to sleep," Lily said doggedly. She was sitting on the edge of a chair. "I just have to know—"

"Come on," Valerie said gently. "It's two o'clock in the morning and you and I are going to sleep."

Lily let herself be pulled up. "Where?"

"In my bed. There's plenty of room for both of us."

"Oh," Lily said. She followed Valerie up the narrow stairs and into her bedroom, and let Valerie help her take off her raincoat and the slacks and loose shirt she wore underneath. And then she crawled into the still-warm bed and curled up as tight as she could, so she would not take up too much room. She felt Valerie slip into the other side, and she began to shiver. She didn't know why; she wasn't cold; but her whole body was shaking. "Lily," Valerie said softly, and moved closer, sliding her arm beneath Lily's shoulders. She pulled Lily to her, and cradled her. "It's all right, Lily, it's all right." Her voice was soothing, like a warm caress. "Don't be afraid, Lily, you're safe here, we'll take care of you." Lily pressed her body to Valerie's, snuggling against her within the tight embrace of Valerie's arms and the warmth of their bodies so close together, like a mother and child. In a few moments

Lily's shivering stopped. "I love you, Valerie," she murmured. And then she was asleep.

When she woke the room was bright with sunlight, and the bed was empty. "Valerie?" Lily said. In a minute she raised her voice. "Valerie?"

"Downstairs," Valerie called. "Breakfast whenever you're ready. There's a clean set of towels in the bathroom."

Lily showered and dressed in her pants and oversize shirt, and went downstairs. "Good morning," Valerie said. "This is my mother, Rosemary Ashbrook. Lily Grace."

They were sitting at the dining-room table. "Good morning," Rosemary said. "Will you have toast? Coffee?"

"Yes, thank you," said Lily. She avoided looking at Valerie, embarrassed by the memory of behaving like a baby in bed.

"I'm going to the office late," Valerie said, as casual as if nothing unusual had happened. "So if you want to talk, now's the time to do it."

Lily took a bite of toast, then another. Suddenly she was ravenous. "I'm sorry I woke you last night." Her mouth was full, and she waited until she had swallowed the last bite. "I didn't know where else to go." She began to spread jam on another slice. "Something happened, something awful, and I went to someone for help and that was awful, too, and I had to go somewhere, so I came here."

Valerie nodded, as if it were perfectly clear. "Why don't you tell us what happened?"

Lily did. She had thought she could never talk about it, but in that crowded, sunny room, with the memory of Valerie holding her through what was left of the night, and with Valerie sitting beside her now, so beautiful and interested, Lily felt as if she had come home. Her embarrassment was gone; she felt comfortable and trusting, and so she began to talk. And then she could not stop. She kept eating toast and drinking coffee as the words came, all of them, all the way to Sybille's last shriek across the yard as Lily fled in the dark, and the long ride through the empty countryside and all the small towns, searching for a pharmacy or gasoline station with a telephone directory, to look up Valerie's address, and then another search, through the streets of Falls Church, until she found the coach house and leaned against the door, her finger on the bell.

When she finished, Rosemary had tears in her eyes. "You poor child. But why didn't you report him to the police? You should have called them right away; it's harder, the longer you wait."

"No!" Lily cried. Vehemently, she shook her head. "I can't talk about it to anybody else. Not to *strangers!* I'm so ashamed... I'm so *dirty,* and they'll *look* at me and..." She started to shiver again.

"But how can they punish—"

"Mother, it's up to Lily," Valerie said quietly. She put her hand on Lily's. "It's a nightmare. It's terrible that you had to go through it, and that you have to learn how to deal with it now. We'll do what we can to help you, but in the end no one can do it for you; you'll have to confront it yourself."

Lily looked at her, her eyes wide. Sybille had always told her she'd take care of everything. But I'm twenty-three years old, Lily thought. I can't curl up in someone's house, or someone's bed, forever.

"One thing," Valerie went on. "I wish you'd try not to be ashamed, Lily. A terrible thing was done to you, but that hasn't changed you from the person you were. You're not dirty, Lily. He is. You're as good and decent and loving as you've always been. We can talk about that any time you want. Or anything else. You just let me know."

Lily was still gazing at her, her eyes wide and a little startled. Valerie saw the beginning of worship in them. "You wanted to ask me something last night," she said. "What was it?"

"Oh. Yes. It was about the crash, when Carlton was killed. I have to know what happened to me. I mean, I know I walked away from the plane and wasn't hurt, I didn't have a scratch or a bruise or anything, but I can't remember it. How did I walk out of the plane?"

"You didn't," said Valerie. "Alex and I got you out."

"You couldn't have." Lily shook her head. "I walked away from the plane and then I must have fainted, because I woke up a little way from it, and it was burning, and I ran away from the fire. I looked for all of you but I didn't see you, and I walked around the plane, not close, I was in the trees because the fire was so hot—I remember it was so strange, my feet were freezing but my face was hot; the air around the plane was so hot it was all wavery from the heat, and the snow was melting—and then I saw Carlton, lying down, and I was with him when you came back. But I was walking the whole time; I walked out of the plane and I walked until I found you and there was nothing wrong with me; I wasn't hurt at all."

Valerie gazed out the window, remembering the scene as Lily described it. "You must have been walking around the plane when Alex and I were looking for you. But you didn't walk away when we crashed, Lily. You were unconscious, and Alex and I got you out first because you were next to the door and we couldn't drag the others out over you."

Lily stared at her. "I was unconscious?"

"Lily, you said you didn't remember walking away from the plane."

"No, but I know I did. Not alone; God was protecting me. He kept me untouched when everyone else was hurt and Carlton died; and he gave me the power to walk away. Sybille said that was what happened. She always talked about it before I gave a sermon, especially when I used to be so nervous; she said I should never doubt that I'd been chosen for something special and she'd help me do it..." Her voice trailed away. "But I don't know what to believe about Sybille, anymore." She bent her head, then looked up at Valerie. "I was unconscious in the plane? You're sure of that?"

"I'm sure," Valerie said gently. "Alex and I got you out, and took you a little distance away, and went back for the others."

There was a silence. Lily bit her lip. "Then I'm not different, I'm not special, I'm not chosen. Everything I believed...I was wrong about everything. All those people, believing in me, *trusting* me...I haven't any right to tell them anything; everything about me is a lie."

"It's not a lie that you care about people," Valerie said quietly.

Lily looked up. "No, but..."

"Give yourself a little credit. You may be right that you're not different or special, but I doubt it. Everyone has some kind of specialness and yours may be very different from anyone else's; you may find you're quite extraordinary. You may not, but take a while to make a judgment about it. Don't damn yourself right away, Lily; it's hard to make a comeback from that and feel good about yourself again."

Lily was frowning. She was used to Sybille telling her she was special and wonderful. Rudy had done the same, and Quentin too. None of them had told her to do her own thinking about herself...and maybe discover she wasn't extraordinary at all. "I just don't know," she said helplessly. "If you're right about the crash...well, you have to be, you know what you did that day. You saved my life. And all this time I thought...Did Sybille know you did that?" she asked suddenly.

"I don't know," Valerie replied. "I may have told her when she came to see me in the hospital, but I don't remember."

"I'll bet she did." Lily's voice was very young and very hard. "I think she finds out everything and then does what she wants with it."

There was another silence. Rosemary began to clear the table. Valerie sat quietly, wondering how much Lily knew about the finances of

Graceville and about Sybille and Carl. She had held the information about the two of them to herself, trying to decide what to do with it. There was no reason to confront Sybille; they had nothing to say to each other. Unless Sybille knew what Carl had done with the money; it was possible he had talked to her about it. That was probably a good reason to talk to her, but the prospect was so unpleasant she kept putting it off.

Carl and Sybille; it was still so hard for her to comprehend it. She really did want to know more about them. Lily, she thought. She could ask Lily, in some kind of roundabout way. And of course she'd ask her about Graceville. Two completely separate stories, but the chances were that Lily might know something about Carl; she would surely know a great deal about Graceville. But she couldn't ask her yet. Lily had too much of her own to deal with right now.

"Valerie," Lily said suddenly. "Would you mind... Would it be all right..." She looked at her clasped hands, then raised her eyes and looked at Valerie with something like desperation. "Could I come to live with you, just for awhile, until I figure out what's going to happen to me?"

That afternoon, leaving Lily with Rosemary, Valerie went to work, and went straight to Nick's office. She had barely seen him since Saturday night, almost a week ago. He had called several times, late, after Chad was in bed, and they had talked for awhile, but they were awkward. Nick felt like a college student calling his girl, not necessarily a bad way to feel, just an unfamiliar one. And Valerie felt almost as if she had no experience at all. She thought she'd pursued him about as much as she could without being ridiculous, and she was getting tired of the peaks and valleys of their times together. She wished they had met for the first time this year; they probably would have been terrific together with no images or expectations to overcome.

But we're terrific now, she thought. At least sometimes. But she had no idea how often they could repeat the miracle of last Saturday night, with no quarrels, no tensions, no reminders of their memories: a long evening of what easily could have passed for love.

On Friday afternoon, pushing aside the conflicts she felt with him, she went to Nick's office to tell him about Lily. "She's very vulnerable, she's been hurt in so many ways, but she'll be living with me for awhile, and at some point I'm going to ask her about Graceville. I thought you'd like to be part of that."

"I would; thank you," he said. "I'd like to get to know her anyway.

I've watched her a couple of times; she has a remarkable quality of belief, in herself and others."

"She's lost the belief in herself, at least for now. But you should meet her. Come to dinner tonight. And bring Chad. It will be very casual; I don't want Lily to think I'm setting her up. I feel uncomfortable about this, anyway: questioning her while she's my guest, and in trouble."

"The mark of a true journalist," Nick said, amused. "Never pass up an opportunity."

"You mean I'm using her."

"I mean you're taking advantage of her living in your house. But if she wants to talk about Graceville, I don't see a problem. Except that it may hurt her. I asked you that before, you know; what you'd do if we find things about Graceville that will hurt her."

"I don't know. I'd have to find out how she feels about it. She's pulling away from Sybille; it may be that she's pulling away from the church and the town too. She says she won't preach this Sunday."

"That isn't what I asked," Nick said. "What we learn may hurt her whether she's still involved in it or not."

Valerie nodded. "It sounds like the kind of story that doesn't have a happy ending, no matter which way we go. And I have to ask you the same question, about Chad."

Nick picked up a pencil and rolled it between his fingers. "Yes, I've thought of that. If everything points to Sybille, it could be very bad." He flicked the pencil to his desk. "We don't know where any of this is going yet. Why don't we confront the moral issues when we know what's real and what isn't?" He stood. "I'm late for a meeting. I'd like very much to come to dinner, and if I can speak for Chad, he'd love it. What time?"

"Seven-thirty."

"We'll be there. What kind of wine would you like?"

Their eyes met and the memories came with a rush. *Wine seems to be your weak point. The only one I've found. So far.* She had bought wine and they had gone to his apartment, and cooked together, though she had barely been able to put together a salad. And then they had made love. *We'll talk about what we're going to do tomorrow. And every day after that.*

"I read some books," Nick said with a smile. He wanted to prolong the moment when memories bound them together, instead of keeping them apart. "And so did you, evidently, if you're cooking dinner."

Valerie laughed. "You won't know for sure until you've tasted it.

But I think we can trust each other. White wine, please. I'm looking forward to tonight."

She was still producing her four-minute segments for "Blow-Up," researching Graceville for a full-length feature, and beginning to work with the research department on another subject, this one a prominent political aide who had a criminal past. Scutigera had been pushed to the bottom of her list of possible subjects. No one talked about it; they all were willing to let the story die without causing her embarrassment. But Valerie still felt frustrated and bereft at her failure: her idea, her interviews, her script . . . and nothing to show for it. Graceville will be different, she thought. I'm going to make something of Graceville. And Lily.

Lily. Graceville. Sybille. What a combination. Working in her office after talking to Nick, she wondered again what Sybille had to do with the board of the Hour of Grace Foundation: how she could demand a meeting when, according to her, her only relationship with the board was to produce Lily's two programs.

But she didn't even do that, not really, Valerie thought. She picked up a pencil and began to roll it between her fingers. Sybille herself didn't work on any of the shows that her company produced. Al Slavin and Gus Emery did the work.

She reached for the telephone and called Sybille Morgen Productions. She had never forgotten the phone number. But when she asked for Al Slavin, the operator told her he no longer worked there. "He's at CNN in Atlanta," she said.

Valerie called him there. "Hey, Valerie," he said, "great to hear from you. Everything okay? What can I do for you?"

"I thought you might tell me something about producing Lily's shows."

"Whatever I can. How's she getting on? We see her down here; she looks good."

"Yes," Valerie said. "Al, does Sybille have anything to do with Graceville?"

"Not that I know of. I can't believe they'd want her, the way she screws them on production costs."

"What does that mean?"

"She bills them three times what they cost. We didn't say anything —none of our business—but it annoyed the hell out of me; dirty thing to do to a religious board."

"What was the usual profit?" Valerie asked.

"It didn't work that way. The Hour of Grace Foundation was the only customer we had that hired us to produce their programs. The rest of the time we made our own pilots and then went out and sold them for a thirteen-week series or whatever. The Foundation was the only one we produced for."

At the end of the conversation, Valerie made a note of it, to tell Nick. Nothing illegal, she thought, as she did so often in researching the Foundation. Sybille can charge whatever she wants, and if they're dumb enough to pay it... She went back to work, but she had trouble concentrating, and finally, an hour early, she went home. She had to plan her dinner.

She had learned to cook simple dishes and Nick had learned to buy complex wines, and, over dessert, sitting at Rosemary's Hepplewhite table in the overcrowded combination living and dining room, they raised their glasses to each other. "To progress," said Nick. "It was a wonderful dinner."

"With a perfect wine." Valerie's glass touched his.

Lily saw the way their eyes held, the way they leaned toward each other without realizing it, and she turned her head away. She would never have that. No one would ever love her the way Nick obviously loved Valerie.

Chad saw the sad curve of her mouth and tried to think of something to say to cheer her up. She was very pretty, he thought, not nearly as spectacular as Valerie, and she didn't have Valerie's smile or the way Valerie had of making you think you were the most important person in the world, but Lily was pretty, and nice, except she was awfully quiet. Her clothes looked too big, maybe that was why she was so sad. He cast about for something to say, and decided on food. "Did you like the trout?" he asked.

Lily turned to him. He was such a handsome boy, and so nice, almost as nice as his father. It was like a family dinner, she thought: Rosemary was the grandmother, Nick and Valerie were the parents, and she and Chad were the children. They were all so nice to her. Valerie had given her clothes to wear, and Rosemary had given her a comb and brush for her hair, and Nick had brought a book by Jamaica Kincaid about growing up that he thought she'd enjoy. A family, she thought again. It was such a comforting thought it made her sad that it wasn't true.

"The trout," Chad repeated.

"Yes," she said. "I loved it. I loved the almonds on it."

"It's called trout amandine," said Chad wisely. "It's one of my favorites."

"Trout amandine," Lily repeated. "I didn't know that. How many other favorites do you have?"

"A couple hundred. I like food a lot. I've seen you on television; you work for my mother."

"Your mother? I don't know who that is, but I couldn't work for her; I don't work for anyone. Only God." She bit her lip. "But I'm not sure about that anymore, either."

"Sure you work for her. She told me so. Sybille Enderby."

Lily stared at him. She turned to look at Nick, talking to Rosemary and Valerie. It couldn't be true. Dimly, she began to get a sense of complex relationships she could not begin to fathom. I have no experience of the world, she thought. She had thought it before, but it had always been a worry, not a truth. Now she knew how ignorant she was. She had kept to herself in boarding school; she had kept to herself with Rudy, and then with Sybille. None of them had taught her what she needed. She could only get that on her own.

"Sybille used to produce my programs," she said to Chad. "I always thought we were working together for a higher purpose."

"What do you mean, used to produce?" Chad asked. "Doesn't she do it anymore?"

"I guess not." Lily tried to smile. "I know that sounds silly; it's just that so much has happened I'm a little confused. I'm pretty sure I don't want Sybille to do it anymore, but I have a lot of decisions to make."

"About what?"

"About..." Lily looked around, hoping to be rescued from Chad's curiosity, and Valerie saw her. She brought her into the conversation, and the five of them talked casually for a long time, sitting at the table while the summer evening faded. In the gathering darkness, Rosemary lit candles. Lily found her gaze fixed on them hypnotically. Her head drooped. "I'm sorry," she said at last. "I'm falling asleep."

"Oh, dear," Rosemary said, "we haven't made up the sofa. And, anyway, you couldn't sleep here, with all of us talking."

"Sleep in my bed," Valerie said. "I'll wake you later, when it's quiet here and the sofa is ready. It's no trouble," she added when Lily hesitated. "Go on, Lily; go to sleep."

Lily nodded drowsily and climbed the stairs to the bedroom. Rosemary gathered the water glasses together. "I'll help," said Chad, jumping up. He stacked dessert plates and followed her into the kitchen.

Valerie looked at Nick. "Does he always do that?"

"As little as he can get away with. We discussed it on the way here."

She smiled. "Thank you. Mother's been cleaning up for the two of us, but I think she was feeling daunted by a dinner party. She'll be glad to have help. And company."

They sat in silence, close but not touching. They were working together, they were sharing, they were thinking of something other than themselves. The best part, Valerie thought with amusement, watching Nick divide the last of the wine between their two glasses: we're learning to be comfortable together by not thinking of ourselves.

"I found something this afternoon," she said. She kept her voice low so it could not be heard in the kitchen. "Sybille triples her costs when she bills the Foundation for producing Lily's programs."

"That's steep, even for Sybille," Nick said. "And it's hard to believe the board pays it. They must have gotten bids from other producers."

"Maybe not. If Sybille really is involved with them, they might want to do her a favor."

"In return for what? There isn't much creativity in producing Lily's two shows; what else could she be doing for them?"

"I don't know."

"They can't be that crazy," Nick said stubbornly. "Thirty million for the land; three times the cost of production...The only way that would make sense is—"

"—if part of the money goes back to them." Valerie said quietly. "The board members, not the Foundation."

They looked at each other. "That's supposedly what the Bakkers did," Nick said. "Took contributions from the faithful, and siphoned off a steady flow for themselves."

"But we don't know that about the Foundation. So far all we have is that they tend to overpay. Sophie thought they just seemed incredibly stupid."

"I'm not sure what we have. Would you bring me some paper?"

Valerie brought him a pad of paper, and he unclipped a pencil from the inside pocket of his jacket. "You heard Sybille setting up a meeting of the Foundation board; she mentioned two members by name. One of them owns the bank that seems to be financing Graceville. The other owns a construction company that's probably building the town. The construction company seems to have been set up to build the town; we found the date it was incorporated, and it fits, and that seems to be all they're working on. Which means, of course, all the money for construction gets funneled through one corporation. We probably won't ever know what Marrach bills the Foundation, but if Sybille's bills for production are any indication, the construction bills are probably inflated like a dirigible. Graceville is going to be a very expensive town."

"I can't sleep," Lily said. She stood at the foot of the stairs, blinking at them, her face flushed. She wore a robe of Valerie's that was too long; her hands were almost hidden in the sleeves. "Is it all right if I sit with you?"

Valerie and Nick exchanged a quick glance.

"Oh," Lily said blankly. "I'm sorry. I should have thought...of course you'd rather be alone...of course you don't want me. I'm sorry." She turned to walk upstairs.

"Of course you can sit with us," Valerie said quickly. She went to Lily and put her arm around her. "It wasn't that we didn't want you. We were afraid you might be upset if you knew we were talking about Graceville."

Lily sighed. "I knew you were. I heard you say it would be expensive. You think something is wrong with it."

"Something might be," said Nick. "But we don't know very much."

"But you must," Lily said. She looked at Valerie. "You must know a lot. You were in on the beginning. I thought that was why you and Sophie came out that day, to see what the town looked like, because you were part of it."

"Part of it? Lily, I've never had anything to do with it."

"Of course you did," Lily insisted. "Well, maybe not directly, but it was your money, too, wasn't it? Graceville wouldn't even be built—there wouldn't be anything there at all—if it wasn't for Carlton. He gave us the money to buy the land."

A silence fell over the table. Valerie stared at Lily.

"You knew that," Lily said uncertainly.

Nick grasped Valerie's hand, to give her something solid to hold, and twined her fingers in his. She sighed, a long, trembling sigh. Thirteen million dollars for the land. And thirteen million dollars that Carlton had raised by mortgaging everything they owned, and then ...spent. And now she knew on what.

"I don't understand," Lily said. "Why wouldn't Carlton have told you? It was such a wonderful thing to do; the kind of thing people do together."

Valerie looked at Nick. "I didn't tell you before. Carl and Sybille were having an affair."

"Oh, no!" Lily cried.

Nick put his finger to his lips. "We don't want Chad to hear any of this."

"Oh, yes, of course. But how could they—?"

"She got him to invest in Graceville," Nick said to Valerie. "But he didn't have the money, is that right? He'd lost a pile in the stock market."

Valerie nodded. "Close to fifteen million dollars. We didn't know anything about it until after he died. Carl never told me when things weren't good. Sometimes he told me later, when he'd pulled himself out—recouped what he'd lost, or whatever he did—but mostly he acted as if everything was fine, and I just assumed everything was. I never had any idea how bad things could be."

"Recouped what he'd lost," Nick repeated slowly.

Watching him, Valerie heard her own words. *When he'd pulled himself out—recouped what he'd lost . . .* "Sybille," she said.

Nick gripped her hand more tightly. "If she told him he could recoup the money he lost in the market by investing—"

"—in land," Valerie said, picking up the thought. By now it was a puzzle: less personal, and so easier to think about. "They'd buy it with his thirteen million and sell it for thirty—"

"—and he could make . . . well, we don't know how much he could make because we don't know how many people got a piece of the thirty million. But suppose he got twenty-five or so—double what he'd put up—enough to replace most of what he lost in the market and pay off his mortgages and loans. You wouldn't know anything about it, and he'd try to make back the rest—a million, two million, whatever it was—in the market."

"But Carl didn't buy it," Valerie said. "Neither did Sybille. Beauregard Development bought it."

"Right. A Panamanian corporation, which means it doesn't have to reveal the names of its stockholders, and there's no way of checking. But if you had to guess who they are, who would it be?"

"How about Sybille?"

"Or the Foundation," Nick said. "Run by those board members who keep cropping up. Either one would be a pretty good guess."

"That doesn't make sense," Lily said. She had been listening with a deep frown, her chin propped in both hands. "You're saying the board bought the land, and then bought it again, from itself. That just doesn't make sense. If Sybille or the Foundation already owned it, why would they take thirty million dollars from the Foundation—that's

money that people sent in, a few dollars at a time, because they believed in what we were doing!—why would they use that to buy land
they already owned?"

"To make a profit," Valerie said patiently. "That seems to be the
whole reason for building Graceville."

"That's not true!" Lily cried in anguish. "That's a terrible thing to
say!"

"I know," Valerie said swiftly. "And we don't know it for sure; we're
guessing about a lot of this, and maybe I went too far. We aren't sure
of anything," she said, looking at Nick. "We have no proof. All we
have are a lot of theories."

Nick was writing a sequence of events. "Right," he said absently.
"We won't have anything until someone talks, or lets us see the Foundation books. We can talk to the board members, though; interview
them for 'Blow-Up.' One of them might give us some answers. We
should start that as soon as possible. This week."

Valerie nodded. "Although . . ." She hesitated. "That will alert all of
them."

"We can't help that. At some point they're going to know. We'll just
keep it vague when they ask what we're looking for. You know something we don't have? Dates. When did Beauregard Development buy
the land, and when was it sold to the Foundation?"

"I don't know when Beauregard bought it. The Foundation bought
it three months later."

"I know that, but when did all this happen? Do you know?"

"No. Sophie might."

"Could you call her? As long as we're putting this together, let's try
to get it all."

"Eleven o'clock," Valerie murmured. "But she never goes to bed
before midnight."

Sophie answered on the first ring. "Of course I'm still up," she told
Valerie. "I brought work home; I'm at my desk. What do you need?"
Valerie told her. "I don't know offhand, but I brought home that file;
let me check." In a minute she was back. "Found it. Sold to Beauregard Development on December second; they closed the deal on January fifth."

A coldness clutched Valerie's heart. January fifth. The day Carlton
was killed.

She thought back, remembering. Everything about the crash was as
vivid now as the day after it happened. Carl had spent the night in his
office; she had heard him opening and closing desk drawers. He had

come into the bedroom at seven, carrying a folder of papers. *I'm going back. Right away. I have things to do; I can't put them off any longer.*

That was three days before they had been scheduled to return.

"—still with me?" Sophie asked.

"Yes," Valerie said. "What did you say?"

"I gave you the other date you wanted. The Foundation bought the land from Beauregard Development on April eighth. Was that all you wanted?"

"Yes. Thank you." When Valerie hung up, she looked at Nick. "Beauregard bought the land on December second. The closing was January fifth."

"That's the day the plane crashed!" Lily cried.

"Carl was in a hurry to come back," Valerie told Nick. "He said he had business to take care of."

"Either he decided he had to be there, or he wanted to stop it."

"I think he wanted to stop it," Valerie said. "He was terribly anxious, and in such a rush he didn't even do his whole checklist before we took off."

"Second thoughts," mused Nick. "Worried about losing the money and never getting it back..."

"Or it wasn't a straight deal and he decided not to go along..."

"Or he didn't want to be tied forever to Sybille."

Once again their eyes met and held. In the midst of the excitement of building from one thought to another was a different kind of excitement: working together, thinking together, making leaps from fragmentary information, perhaps too high, perhaps too fast, but together, in a rhythm that was almost sexual. "I suppose we'll never know," Nick said. "But it probably was one of those reasons. Maybe all of them."

Valerie was still remembering. That whole day rushed through her memory like a speeded-up film. *Sorry, Val... Tried to keep it. Now you'll know. Shit, lost control...lost it! Thought I'd fix it...get started again. Too late. Sorry, Val, sorry...Acted like water in the tanks...But—both tanks? Never had any before. Didn't check. Too much hurry to take off. Not my fault! No accident! Listen! Water in both tanks! Fuck it, should have thought she might...*

Valerie closed her eyes. She felt sick. "Nick, listen." She repeated what Carl had said.

"*'She'?*" Nick echoed.

"The investigators thought he meant his plane. Calling it 'she.' But if he meant a woman..."

"Don't say it," Lily whimpered. She held her hands over her ears and squeezed shut her eyes.

"She was there," Valerie said to Nick. "She and Lily were at the house with us, the day before we left to fly back."

They looked at each other for a long time, past Lily's huddled form. The day before the closing. The day before Sybille spent Carl's thirteen million dollars to buy land for Graceville. The day before Carl decided to rush back, maybe to stop the closing, maybe to change something involved in it, maybe simply to be more active in the deal. The day before the plane crashed.

"Nobody would do anything like that!" Lily said, her voice high and wavering. It was a question, and a plea, more than a certainty. "Nobody would make a plane crash! Five people . . . five people could have been killed! You can't think anybody would do that! Not . . . not Sybille . . . not anybody!"

"We don't know what happened," Nick said somberly, "but we have to find out."

Valerie had picked up Nick's pencil and was drawing dark lines with it on the pad of paper. "Even if she had something to do with it, she wouldn't have done it herself, would she?"

"Probably not. But that would mean hiring someone; she wouldn't take that chance."

"Her pilot," Valerie said. "She flew up there in the Foundation plane."

Nick put his hand on hers, stopping her from making any more jagged, anguished pencil marks. "We have to talk to him. There's nothing else we can do. We have to find out what happened that night."

Chapter
28

ray for Reverend Lily!" Floyd Bassington boomed, his voice rolling through the Cathedral of Joy and into the television cameras, where it traveled thousands of miles to the faithful throughout the land. "She is ill and lies in a narrow bed, desolate at not being here with you. She will return as soon as she can; she knows how you need her; she knows how you long to have her with you again. *She will be back very soon!* She is watching us now: hear us, Reverend Lily! We are longing for your return! We send you our prayers; we send you our love!"

Floyd Bassington was having the time of his life. Never had he preached in a setting of such magnificence, to so many bowed heads arrayed before him like a field of drooping flowers, and to all those invisible millions in the land of television, hanging on his words. He had never been televised. This was a first. His chest billowed out, he stood on his toes and looked up. I lift up mine eyes to the cameras, he thought happily.

"But we have an enemy!" he cried, ending his pause before his television audience could get restless and switch to another channel. Faces swam up to him; the field of flowers became a heaven of pale moons with startled eyes fastened on Floyd Bassington. "An enemy who wants to destroy our beloved Reverend Lily! An enemy who plots to throw her to the wolves of rapacious atheists and gossipmongers! An enemy who schemes to tear her frail body to pieces with bayonets of lies and innuendo!"

"Shit, he's off his rocker," muttered Arch Warman to Monte James and Sybille. They were in Lily's apartment behind the pulpit, watching Bassington on television. "Get him to tone it down. Signal him, or something. Nobody's gonna take this crap seriously."

"Of course they will," Sybille said absently. She was standing, about to leave the room. "He's like a cheerleader; the words aren't important, it's rhythm and volume that count. I'll be back in a minute."

"You leaving again?" Monte James demanded. "What the fuck's going on? This is important, damn it, you ought to know what he's saying out there."

Sybille slipped through the door without answering. She could not let them know, but she was going mad with worry about Lily. She had disappeared. Sybille had called every hotel and motel, every hospital, everyone at her production company, the members of the Foundation board; no one knew anything about Lily. Gone, gone, gone. The word hammered in Sybille's head. She did not sleep. She did not eat. She telephoned other ministers, other television evangelists, she even tracked down Rudy Dominus, altering her story so no one knew how frantic she was. "She's taking a trip and thought she might stop by to see you; I wanted to catch her if she was there. Not yet? Well, I'll find her somewhere else. Thanks so much . . ."

Gone, gone, gone. I have nothing without her, Sybille thought, and then wiped out the thought. She went to the pay telephone at the other end of the corridor and called the answering machine at her home. "Sybille, I'm staying with a friend." Lily's voice, high and tremulous, came through the tape. "I'll be here awhile. I don't want to talk to you. I can't preach. Don't worry about me. I'm fine." Sybille heard the sound of the telephone being hung up.

She stood still with the receiver in her hand. Her knees were weak. *Staying with a friend.* Lily had no friends. Whom had she latched onto? Who was working on her, poisoning her against Sybille, stealing her away?

"Sybille," Arch Warman said urgently. "We want you to hear this."

For the first time, she did not put him in his place. In silence, she followed him back to Lily's suite.

"Television! The blessed technology that brings Reverend Lily to millions of souls who hunger for her voice, this blessed technology is being perverted for evil, to cut her into shreds *and eliminate this church!*" Bassington took a long breath and sent a long groan into the microphone. "E-and-N. A cable television network called E-and-N has decided to hound Reverend Lily to her death. It's not enough for these media maniacs that they attacked Jim and Tammy Bakker—poor sinners who deserve compassion!—and have swept them from sight with their sanctimonious brooms. Flushed with victory, they search out new victims! They turn to the purest of them all, the apotheosis of virginal, loving womanhood, and *have sent their hired thugs to pry into the affairs of the Hour of Grace Foundation!* Like rats with quivering nostrils, they have invaded the offices, camped on the doorsteps and the very desks of the dedicated men who make this holy cathedral, and all of Graceville, possible."

"He shouldn't spend so much time on that," said Monte James. "Why give those bastards free publicity? He shouldn't even give the name of the network."

"Then how would anyone attack them?" Sybille asked angrily. She was angry at everything and everyone now—*staying with a friend, staying with a friend*. She was angry at all of them, and these two were the worst. Stupid fools, letting Lily go; how did she get saddled with such asses? "You haven't forgotten that we planned the attack; even you can remember what we did yesterday."

"You did it; we went along," he growled. "Right. But Floyd shouldn't talk about them asking us questions. He should just get on with it!"

"And so we will make them feel the heat!" Bassington intoned. "We will march shoulder to shoulder on *their* doorstep! We will invade *their* offices! We will camp on *their* desks, with millions of letters and telegrams! We will warn their advertisers with our protests! *We will shut that damnable E-and-N network down!*

"March!" he roared. "March shoulder to shoulder! The ushers are passing around the address of the E-and-N offices and studios, and it is appearing now on your television screens. Go there! March on them! Picket them! Lie on their doorsteps so no one can go inside and join them in their evil doings! Write to them! Telegraph them! *Tell them to leave our Reverend Lily alone or we will shut them down forever!* Tell their advertisers we will never buy their products until they withdraw their support from that devil's network. Tell them—"

He had to catch his breath. His excitement was a whirlwind inside him; he was dizzy and could not remember what he had been about to say. Tell them— Tell them what? The lights were hellishly hot. His shirt was drenched. Even his feet were perspiring; his toes slipped against each other. Behind his back he made an urgent gesture to the organist and the choir. Instantly the music rose, covering Bassington's confusion like the incoming tide, lifting the congregation on waves of glory.

The next day, the campaign against E&N began.

Pickets arrived early Monday morning, marching around the E&N building in three groups of ten. Every hour they were replaced by three new groups. "Too organized, and not enough passion," Nick said, standing at the window of his office with Les and Valerie. "They're probably hired. It has the staged look of something Sybille would do. She must feel this is a real crisis."

"Or it's the board that's doing it," said Les. "What did you say to those guys?" he asked Valerie. "You must have scared the shit out of them."

She shook her head. "I only talked to the three board members who aren't on the executive committee, and we were very low-key. I just asked questions, no accusations, and as far as I know Earl was the same. He talked to James and Warman and Bassington. And got nowhere."

"But something scared them," said Nick. "Or it was just the fact that you were asking questions. I suppose up to now they felt immune from all the scandals around them, because of Lily. Who could believe she'd be mixed up in anything illegal?"

"Not me," said Les. "Did you get anything, Val, from the ones you talked to?"

"Nothing; I'm sure they don't know what's going on. If anything is. One of them, a religion professor named Lars Olssen, is so good I thought Sybille might have invented him for the part."

"You mean a good actor?"

"I mean a good man. He believes absolutely in goodness. He doesn't pretend there isn't a lot of bad around, but he has no doubt that it can be isolated and turned to good if good men care enough and take action. If anything peculiar is going on at Graceville, he doesn't know about it."

"But you know some of them have got to be raking in millions."

"I'd put money on it," said Nick, "but not if I had to have proof. We've nibbled around the edges and made a lot of smart guesses. What can we do with that? We can't go on the air with innuendoes."

"So you haven't got a program."

"Not right now. And I don't see it happening."

"Shit." Les shot a glance at Valerie. "Lousy deal."

She was gazing at the pickets below. A crowd was watching from across the street. We should film it, she thought, in case we do have a program on Graceville. They already had a lot of background film, ready to be spliced together: clips of Lily preaching, footage of Graceville, the church, building permits for everything in the town issued to Marrach Construction, shots of Arch Warman's construction foreman making regular visits to Warman Developers and Contractors, Floyd Bassington's vacation houses in the Cayman Islands and northern Minnesota, Monte James's Hour of Grace Foundation Porsche, and his homes in Aspen and Beverly Hills, and the Hour of Grace Foundation jet.

But all that was only the tip of what was probably a very large iceberg. It was not enough for a feature on "Blow-Up." Valerie couldn't pretend it was; she and Nick had gone over and over it. It had been eating at her all weekend: her idea, her show ... and she couldn't do it. "Two in a row," she said to Les. "Is that a record: losing two stories before I've even officially begun?"

"Lousy deal," he said again. "I wish I could do something."

"So do I. Of course, if we could get a look at the Foundation books, or the construction company's, or find out who were the shareholders in Beauregard Development..." The pickets had started a chant; through the closed window, she could hear the rhythm, but not the words. "But that probably won't happen, so we're stuck. Graceville is still a mystery, and so is my first program on 'Blow-Up.' I may have to rely on superstition."

"Meaning?"

"The third time has to be a charm."

Les chuckled. "Sounds fine to me. First things first, though." He turned back to the window. "Why don't we get rid of that army down there? They don't exactly improve our image. If we tell them there's no program, they'll disappear."

"No," said Nick. "Why give it away that we haven't got anything? I don't mind a few pickets, and the publicity may jog somebody's memory, maybe even a conscience here or there; something could break that would give us a program after all."

"That makes two wishful thinkers," Valerie said, and she and Nick smiled together.

Les eyed them approvingly, feeling middle-aged and well married, and suddenly driven to nudge romance forward. "Why don't you two come to dinner this weekend?" he asked casually. "I kind of like the idea of the four of us spending some time together."

"I like it, too," Valerie said, still smiling.

"Friday," Nick suggested to Les. "Valerie and I have something to do on Saturday."

"I'll check at home," Les said, and returned to his office.

"Saturday?" Valerie asked.

"If you're free. By then Sybille's pilot will be back from vacation. Is that all right?"

"Yes. Thank you. I'd like to have this behind us."

"We may not learn anything," Nick said.

"Then we'll have to look somewhere else," Valerie said, trying to keep it light. "Do you know, Carl hated mystery novels and movies. I never would have thought he'd leave me a mess of them." She cast another look at the pickets. Someone was photographing them, and also the crowd across the street. Reporters, Valerie thought. And soon there will be television cameras. "I'd better get to work," she said. "I haven't started my segment for this week."

"Friday night," Nick said as she turned, "after we go to Les's for dinner, will you come home with me?"

"Yes. I'd love to. For a few hours."

He gave her a long look, then put his arms around her. "Listen. You know this, but I'll tell you again. Chad thinks you're terrific. He talks about you all the time, he can't wait to see you, he saves up things to tell you. Just like his father. He'd like nothing better than to find you at our breakfast table. Just like his father."

"He might, for a few minutes. But then he might start worrying, in case nothing comes next with us. Then he'd be worse off, not knowing and afraid to ask."

"Chad is never afraid to ask. His curiosity is insatiable and bigger than all of us. He'll ask."

"And what will we say?"

Nick paused. "I'd say, for two people who are rediscovering each other, with almost everything in their lives different from the first time around, we're moving very fast and having a wonderful time, and that's all we know right now. And then he'll ask you."

Valerie smiled. "I like your answer. But I still think I'd better not greet Chad at the breakfast table, at least until I have an answer of my own." She laid her hand along Nick's cheek and kissed him with a lingering softness. "And now I'm going back to work."

The next day, Tuesday, the first trickle of what would be a deluge of hundreds of thousands of letters and telegrams arrived at E&N, and the orderly pickets were joined by less orderly and far more emotional demonstrators. By noon they numbered three or four hundred, chanting and singing and parading with signs that said SAVE OUR ANGEL! and PROTECT OUR REVEREND LILY!

"What is it they think she ought to be protected from?" Les asked, reading the signs from Nick's office.

"Bassington was a little vague on that," said Nick. "In fact, I taped his sermon and watched it a couple of times and still couldn't think of anything he'd really said, except that Lily was in danger. From us."

"Look at this," Les said, and Nick joined him at the window. There were new signs: E AND N = EVIL AND NOXIOUS, and SHUT DOWN SATAN'S NETWORK, and CUT THEIR CABLES, and WHY DOES FAIRFAX HARBOR THE DEVIL?

"What the hell," Les expostulated. "They want the town to kick us out."

"It may happen to them first," Nick said. The police had arrived.

At first the police simply contained the marchers so traffic was not disrupted. But by midafternoon the demonstrators were lying across the sidewalk leading to the front and side doors of Nick's building. Owners of other companies in the building grew testy. At that, the police began to carry the protesters away. There were screams and sobs; men and women knelt in prayer in the middle of the street, bringing traffic to a gridlocked halt. Someone climbed a nearby tree and led the milling demonstrators in a hymn. Babies cried. Dogs barked. Drivers honked their horns An ice-cream wagon appeared, playing a tinkling tune, and mothers, still singing, bought their children Popsicles and cones.

"I've got two cameramen filming it," Les told Nick. "One on the roof, one through the window of my office. Any problem with that?"

"Absolutely not. Even if we never use it, we should have it on record. I'm glad you thought of it." Nick went back to his computer, where he was typing a statement.

"You're not going to be the one to read it, are you?" Les asked.

"Sure, why not?"

"They think you're the devil."

"I'm not reading it to them; this is for the six-o'clock news. I'll have copies to hand out tomorrow, when they come back."

"Which of course they will. What would they say, do you think, if they knew there was no program?"

"They'd probably try to shut us down for deception." Nick printed out the statement and in a moment handed Les two sheets of paper. "What do you think?"

Les read it. "I like it. Don't change a word."

The statement was taped for the six-o'clock news. Nick sat in the chair used by Valerie on her segment on "Blow-Up." Through the window behind the chair a tape of the demonstration could be seen.

"I'm Nicholas Fielding, president of E&N," Nick began, looking at the camera and reading from the TelePrompTer. He was self-conscious and stiff, and wished he could have delegated this job to someone else. But he knew he could not. He owned the network; he was the one to speak for it.

"Today, passionate demonstrators threatened to shut down this network if we continue our investigation into a church and its minister, who has a national following on television. I'm not here to criticize the demonstrators, or those who are sending us letters and telegrams saying the same thing. As far as I'm concerned, it would be far worse if there were no demonstrators, if America fell silent because no one cared enough to march and try to change things.

"But it's no good, either, just to give in automatically to a crowd of demonstrators. I'll listen; I'll think about what they're demanding; but on a practical level, I can't give in unless my convictions match theirs. Because if I issued orders just to please them, there's no obvious reason why tomorrow I wouldn't issue new, possibly contradictory orders because a different group of demonstrators, with a new agenda, had turned up. And the third day I might change my orders yet again, to please a third crowd. If I had no firm beliefs of my own, I'd be blown every which way by whoever shouted the loudest, and nothing would get done and no one would be pleased.

"But that's not the main reason why I can't give in. The real reason is passion. The demonstrators have theirs; I have my own. In fact, I have several.

"There is the passion for seeking out truth, because lies and evasions and hidden agendas are poisonous to a democracy. And the only people, whether you like them or not, whose job is to expose lies and evasions and hidden agendas are the journalists.

"There is the passion for collecting information and listening to all sides and then choosing a place to stand.

"There is the passion that says trust your judgment, be prepared to defend the place you've chosen, and invite others to share it with you not through force, but through reason.

"Those are the passions that guide E&N. If we work at it, we'll be able to live by them. If we falter, we hope you let us know, not with demands that we do what you want, but with suggestions for improvement. We're counting on you for that. Thank you." He held his position, looking somberly into the camera, until the tape was shut off.

"Bravo," Valerie said quietly.

He turned, shielding his eyes, and saw her standing to the side. "I didn't know you were here."

"I thought it might make you nervous if you knew."

"I was nervous anyway. Was I all right?"

"You were wonderful."

He was grateful for that; at this moment, she was the professional and he was the newcomer. "I'd better watch the tape before I let it go on," he said. "Come with me. I'd like you there."

They watched it in silence, trying to gauge its impact. "I don't suppose it will sway many demonstrators," Nick said when it ended. "But some of the audience may think about it and approve."

"I'm more interested in the Foundation board," said Valerie. "I wonder if they'll think you're talking to them, and what they might do about it. Especially Olssen," she added thoughtfully. "I have a feeling he's the unpredictable one."

Nick smiled. "You're assuming he watches our newscasts."

"Oh. You're right; he may not. Well, I'm going to make sure he watches this one. I'm going to make sure they all watch this one. If you'll excuse me, Nick, I have a few telephone calls to make."

At six-thirty that evening, half an hour after he watched Nick's statement on television, Lars Olssen telephoned him at his office. Nick was still there; he and Valerie had watched the news together and were planning to go to dinner. "I admired your statement," Olssen said. His words were measured, his voice resonant. It was a voice that always got attention. "I knew nothing about the demonstration until I saw it on your newscast. Of course I know how it arose: it was fomented by Floyd Bassington in his sermon on Sunday. I doubt that Floyd thought of it by himself. His imagination is quite limited, and he is close to two other board members who are more aggressive then he."

"James and Warman," Nick said. "There seems to be a split in your board."

Olssen was silent.

"Of course that may not affect your decisions," Nick said deliberately. "If you all agree on how to run the Foundation and manage Graceville, there's no problem."

Olssen sighed. "Two people from your network have been asking us questions. Valerie Sterling and Earl DeShan. I assume they did this with your permission."

"Yes," said Nick.

"I spoke to Valerie Sterling. Her questions were well chosen, and discomfiting. They made me look more closely at an organization to which I have, perhaps, paid too little attention. Lily Grace, a charming and talented young woman, lulled all of us, I think. We trust her, and so we trusted everything. But Miss Sterling's questions, and then this demonstration . . . Why would anyone unleash such an action unless he were afraid? In short, I no longer trust. I am very worried, though I have no concrete reason to be so."

Nick had turned on the speakerphone so Valerie could listen with him. Now she scribbled on a sheet of paper: *finances.*

"There is a way to settle most of our questions," Nick said to Olssen. "We could look at the Foundation books."

Olssen sighed again. "To find out where the money goes. I cannot get you the books, if that is what you are suggesting."

"But you might help an accountant who wanted to look at them."

There was a silence. "I might," Olssen said slowly. "I believe they are in the offices at Graceville."

"I have the name of an accountant," Nick said, his voice level to keep hidden his growing excitement. "He's familiar with religious foundations; he's been involved in the examination of the Bakkers' books at PTL. You might want to call him and arrange something."

Olssen felt a strong distaste. He liked Nick's voice, and his careful words, and he had been filled with admiration when he watched him on television. His statement was not inflammatory; he attacked no one; he named no one; he even paid a compliment to those who were trying to bring harm to his network. It was the kind of intelligent, measured response Olssen most appreciated in a world where people too often said whatever came into their heads, without thinking of shades of meaning or possible repercussions.

But to sneak into the offices of the Hour of Grace Foundation and to turn loose an accountant who would sniff around for damaging material made him feel sick. He had come to the Foundation to bring love and comfort and help to millions who needed it, a far greater number than he could ever have reached when he was in the pulpit;

infinitely greater than he could reach through his teaching. He had come to do good; not to be a spy.

But the demonstration also had made him sick. And then there were Valerie's questions. And, most important, Nick's statement. Its civilized tone had subtly eroded Olssen's unthinking loyalty to the Foundation. "Give me the accountant's name," he said.

The next evening, when the office staff had left for the day, the Reverend Lars Olssen and Alvin Speer, CPA, greeted the guard at the door of the small house on the Graceville grounds. "Evening, Reverend," the guard said. "Let me know if you need anything."

Olssen nodded thoughtfully. It was clear that the guard was used to seeing board members come in at night. To do what? he wondered.

He led Speer into the offices. "I know nothing about computers or account books. I'm of little help to you."

"No problem," said Speer. "I'll just be looking around."

Olssen sat in a corner; he had brought a book to read. He had considered bringing a Bible, but that seemed to be overdoing it; he had no reason yet to start praying. So he brought a novel, and tried to concentrate on it.

For three evenings in a row, until far past midnight, he read his book while Alvin Speer unfurled computer printouts, scanned columns of numbers, flipped through files of invoices, pored over bank statements and canceled checks, and sent his fingers dancing over his calculator. On Friday night, just before midnight, Olssen finished his book. Hands folded in his lap, he contemplated Speer's bent head.

"Okey-doke," said Speer, raising his head two hours later and squinting at Olssen. "For a preliminary, this does fine. Lots of stuff here. I can write it up or I can make it verbal."

"Verbal now, if you please," said Olssen. "And I'd like it written as soon as possible."

"Okey-doke. Straight from the top—I did a little research during the days, by the way, in case you wonder where some of this info comes from. So, straight from the top. Checks come in from all over, big and little. The names, addresses and amounts are logged into the computer, and the checks are sent to the bank."

"James Trust and Savings," said Olssen.

"No, a bank in Culpeper. All the names and check amounts are on these printouts. Problem is, the totals at the end of each day's printouts don't jibe with the numbers." He looked at Olssen's blank expression. "Somebody's programmed the computer to change the totals at the end of each printout. You add up the individual checks that were received each day and your total is higher than the one that's shown."

"Higher," Olssen repeated.

"My guess is they're depositing the checks in two accounts, one in the name of the Foundation, one private. The money in the private account goes to whoever's running the show. It's an old trick, you know; lots of folks do it, not just the religious ones. So when they skim money from what comes in, they gotta make sure the total on the printout equals the amount on the deposit slips to the Foundation account. In case the IRS or somebody's looking. You got that? Remember, the Foundation takes in close to a million and a half every week. That's five to ten thousand donations every day. Who's gonna add it up by hand? Most people just look at the totals. But I come along and add each and every number. You following me?"

"How much?" Olssen asked.

"How much they taking? I figure about ten percent."

Olssen closed his eyes. In the past year, the Foundation had received seventy-five million dollars in donations and memberships. Someone pocketed seven and a half million of that. Who? How many of them?

"'Course, that's only the beginning," said Speer. "You want the rest of it?"

Olssen opened his eyes. "I want it all."

"Well, straight from the top. Construction costs for Graceville. I did a little calling around, fella I know in construction in Rockville and a couple others, and it turns out you're paying Marrach Construction roughly twenty percent over what you oughta be, all down the line: labor and materials. Then there's your construction loan. You're paying two percent over other loans at other banks. And your production costs for the tv shows. They're close to triple what my friend Nick Fielding pays when he has simple shows like that produced. That's about it. Oh, salaries are okay, high but not out of the ball park. But you've got some expenses for board members that would raise some eyebrows: cars, travel, houses, stuff like that. I see there was a corporate jet sold a couple weeks ago . . . you know why it was sold?"

"I didn't know it was sold."

"Well, maybe they're starting to clean up their act. A little late, looks like."

There was a silence.

"You want to wait on my conclusions?" Speer asked. "They'll be in my written report."

"Please. All of it now."

"Well, then. You skim ten percent off donations, pay inflated constructions costs, an expensive construction loan, tripled production costs, and perks for your board members, and what you've got left for legitimate expenses for building Graceville and paying operating costs for the tv ministry is about fifty-six percent of what comes in."

"*Fifty-six percent!*"

"The other side of that, what it looks like from here, is that, over the two years it's supposed to take to build Graceville, roughly sixty-five million dollars would be diverted to Marrach Construction, James Trust and Savings, Sybille Morgen Productions, and who knows where else."

Speechless, Olssen stared at him.

"Now, I don't have any proof that any of this is illegal," Speer said, "except the skimming of the ten percent. Somebody could maybe give an interesting explanation for that, but I have my doubts. There's so much of this tv ministry stuff coming out now—it's kind of in the air, isn't it?—my own personal feeling is there's nothing good about anything I've dug up. It smells of kickbacks from the word go. So you've got a few things here. The IRS has to be told. First off, this outfit won't keep its tax-exempt status for a minute if all this comes out the way I think it will, but that's small potatoes. The big question is whether there's fraud involved: defrauding the Foundation and the government. That's a criminal matter."

Olssen was staring fixedly at him. A lifetime of helping people in need, he thought, my whole life. And now to find I've been a front man for crooks, thieves, defrauders, and *all in the name of the Lord!*

Speer was frowning. "You wouldn't ask me to keep this quiet, Reverend. I couldn't do that, you know. I mean, when I find evidence—"

Olssen was shaking his head. "I would not ask it. It would go against everything..." His voice trailed away. Graceville itself went against everything he believed in and taught and worked for. And he had let himself be used. He had turned a blind eye, he'd been lazy, complacent, inattentive...

"I guess I'll go, then," said Speer. "You should, too, Reverend. It's getting awful late."

"Yes." Olssen lifted himself from his chair. He was tired, but he knew he would not sleep tonight. He had to think about what he had learned. He had to think about the future. He had to make up for his sins of sloth and complacency. Lily must be told. The other board members—for how could he be sure who was a conspirator and who was innocent?—must be told that Speer's report would soon be public. Nick Fielding must be told. His was the voice of reason that had led to this night of revelation. Without Nick's statement, Olssen was not sure he ever would have lifted the stone of Graceville to see the dark life crawling beneath it.

Nick Fielding, Olssen recalled, was preparing a television program on Graceville. Certainly, he must be told.

Early Saturday morning, while the air still had a trace of the night's coolness, and only the joggers were out on the quiet streets, Nick received a telephone call, and then made one of his own. He called Valerie, who was just waking up, and told her she would have a program on Graceville after all.

An hour later, Floyd Bassington resigned from the board of directors of the Hour of Grace Foundation.

Chapter 29

ily heard the telephone ring when Nick called. She had been lying awake since dawn. The breeze that cooled Georgetown overnight did not reach Falls Church, and Lily had tossed on the living-room sofa or paced around the room, trying to ignore the heat that weighed her down like a heavy blanket. But at four-thirty, as she stood at the window, gazing at the motionless sumacs in the first pale light that washed the sky, she knew it was not just the heat that kept her awake. It was what lay ahead of her. This was the day she would betray Sybille.

In a way, she already had betrayed her. She had called the Foundation office and gotten from the secretary the home address of Bob Targus, the Hour of Grace pilot who had worked for the Foundation until two weeks ago, when the jet was sold. She had been prepared to lie—her first lie ever—if the secretary had asked why she needed the address. The secretary hadn't asked, but that only meant Lily was lucky, not that she was a good person who didn't tell lies.

Something is happening to me, Lily thought. She stood at the window, her thoughts slow and bewildered. She didn't know who she was anymore, or what she could do with her life. All she knew for sure was that she loved Valerie more than anyone in the world. She'd always had so much love inside her, but she'd never found anyone to give it to in a way that made her happy. Rudy Dominus had faded from her life, Quentin Enderby had died, and Sybille...well, nothing about Sybille seemed right anymore. And then there was....But she couldn't say his name. She would never say it. He was evil, he had made sex ugly and hateful, and she couldn't even think of him without shaking with revulsion.

But still she spent much of her time thinking about what had happened to her with him. Somehow he had known how worried she was becoming at being a symbol to people, but not a person to herself. She hadn't known she was worried about that, though she was beginning to think about it, but why else would she have leaped at the first man who treated her like a real woman? I wanted to be real, and I didn't know how, Lily thought. I wonder how I'll learn that.

Valerie could teach her. It was Valerie whom Lily loved, Valerie who made her happy. And now Valerie needed her help. That was why Lily had gotten Bob Targus's address, and that was why she was going along this afternoon: because Bob knew her and had always liked her, and would more likely be open with her than with Valerie or Nick.

She was sure she was doing the right thing, because of her love for Valerie, and because Valerie and Nick would never do anything evil, but, still, when she greeted Bob Targus that afternoon, she felt a stab of guilt at the broad smile on his face, because she could not be honest with him. "Reverend Lily!" he said, taking her hands in his. "I thought I'd have to come to your church to see you again!" Then he saw Valerie and Nick. "I didn't know you were bringing people."

"These are my friends," Lily said. "Valerie Sterling and Nick Fielding."

Targus shook Nick's hand and then Valerie's. "I'd ask you in but, you know, the place's a mess; we just got back from vacation and we're moving. I'm working for Nabisco now, would you believe it? From God to crackers. That's what the wife said; made me laugh. So if you don't mind, we can sit here..."

Lily saw how nervous he was and felt guilty again. "This is very nice," she said as he pulled garden chairs close together in the shade of a horsechestnut tree. She asked him about his new job, and the town where he and his wife would be living, and the house they had bought. She knew she was purposely making him relax so she could draw him out, and the dishonesty of that made her even more uncomfortable, but she had to do it. The better she was at it, the sooner they would find out what they needed to know, and then they could go home.

"You just drive Lily out here to see me?" Targus asked Nick abruptly, "or's there something else?"

"We have something to ask you," Nick replied. "Lily offered to come along and introduce us, since you're friends."

"So it's something I don't want to talk about." Targus's eyes narrowed as he looked from Nick to Valerie and then to Lily. "You know what this is about?" he asked Lily.

"Yes, but really it's just a question. We don't know anything; we just want to find out..." She faltered. "It's not a nice thing to think about, but we need to know..." She looked at Valerie, who looked steadily back, encouraging her, but not forcing her. If Lily could not do it, Valerie or Nick would.

But I owe this, Lily thought. If bad things happened, I was part of them. I always thought I could keep away from bad things; others would take care of them while I preached from my pulpit, way above everything. Oh, I feel so awful! she wailed silently. It's so much better not to be part of things!

But if Valerie had felt that way when Lily rang her doorbell at midnight, she wouldn't have asked Lily in, and given her a bed, and listened to her and let her stay.

Lily brushed her hand across her forehead. Even in the shade, the air was heavy, and though she wore one of Valerie's tie-back sundresses she felt weak with the heat. Just a while longer, she thought, and then we'll all go home. When she looked at Targus, her eyes were steady. "We want to ask you about a flight you took to Lake Placid. You flew Sybille and me there a year and a half ago, in January. Sybille went back the next day; I stayed behind and flew home a day later."

"That was the plane that crashed," Targus said. His face was like stone.

"Yes, and Carlton Sterling, the pilot, was killed. He was Valerie's husband."

Targus's head swung around. "I'm real sorry to hear it." He swallowed; the muscles in his jaw and neck were taut.

"The investigators found water in the gas tanks," Lily went on. "Both tanks. We wondered—you were there, at least part of the time, waiting to fly us back—we wondered if you might have seen anyone at the airport who might have been tampering with the plane."

"Why?" The word burst from him like an explosion. "Why'd anybody do that? Did he have, you know, people wanting to kill him?"

Lily flinched and closed her eyes.

"Shit, I'm sorry, Reverend . . . oh, Christ, I didn't mean to swear . . . damn it, shouldn't have said . . . oh, shit . . ." Tangled in words he used every day but not in front of Lily, he burst out, "Sorry! Can't even talk straight! I mean, I'm sorry, Reverend Lily, I don't mean to swear around you, I'm, you know, nervous with moving and, you know, starting a new job, and it's so damned *hot!* I'm sorry!"

Quietly, Nick said, "We don't know whether someone wanted to kill him or not. But after the crash, when he was injured, he said flat out it was no accident. He was sure someone did it. And he was sure it was a woman."

"Who?"

"We thought you might know."

"No. No, sir. I wouldn't know anything about that. I mean, I do my job, I fly people where they, you know, want to go. That's all I do."

"You pay attention," Lily said softly. Her eyes were open and determined. "You're an excellent pilot; you always know what's happening around you whether you're in the air or on the ground. You don't miss anything, Bob."

He shook his head. "Sorry."

"It's very important to me to know," Valerie said. Her voice was low; Targus had to lean closer to hear her. "In all this time, I've never known why our plane crashed. If I knew my husband was wrong and it really was an accident, I'd be satisfied. It isn't that I want to know anything particular; I want to *know.*"

"There's always mysteries in flying," Targus said.

"How many?" Valerie asked.

"Not a whole lot, but there's some things we never know. I don't know about your husband's flight."

"Oh, Bob," Lily sighed, "you're not telling the truth."

"I'm sorry, Reverend Lily."

"For lying to me?"

He did not answer.

"I don't think I've ever asked more from people than they could give," Lily said. Her voice was quiet, but it had taken on the rhythm and richness of the voice she used in the pulpit. She seemed older, and somehow taller, sitting upright in the lawn chair. "I only ask people to fulfill what is within them. I'm asking that of you, my dear Bob. You're a man with a wonderful talent for flying a great plane around the world, but that's only a small part of what you are. You're a good man, a loving family man, an intelligent, observant man. You have integrity. You don't countenance wrongdoing. You would not let evil triumph if you saw it; you would challenge it and try to defeat it. You care about people. You love them."

Targus was shaking his head, mournfully but persistently. "I'm not as good as all that. Most people aren't, Reverend Lily. You always think the best of people, you know, you think they're like saints, but they're not, they're little and selfish and all they care about, you know, is saving their own skins—"

"What happened at the airport at Lake Placid?" Lily asked. "Tell us. What did you see?"

"It's awful hard, you know, Reverend Lily, when somebody thinks you're good. I mean, it's heavy, it, like, sort of presses down on you..."

"I believe in you," Lily said simply. "Will you tell us what you saw?"

He looked at her for a long moment, his mournful face perspiring in the heat. "She told me to do something to keep him there," he said, and there was relief in his voice at finally getting out what he had kept bottled up for so long. "You know, so he couldn't fly back right away. There was a meeting, and she thought he might try to stop something she wanted to do, whatever, so she said, you know, fix his plane so he can't take off when he wants to. It wasn't to kill him, you gotta believe that, Reverend; my God, I couldn't do that, not in a million years. She wouldn't, either. She just wanted, you know, to keep him stuck there awhile. So, I figured the easiest thing was to, uh, put, you know, water in the tanks."

In the tree above them, a cardinal sang a long trill. Valerie's nails dug into her palms; she felt faint. *She murdered Carl. She murdered Carl. She murdered...*

Nick's hand was on hers and automatically she turned her palm to meet his. His fingers gripped hers so tightly they hurt, and that brought her out of her faintness. A deep anger coursed through her. She sat straight, watching Targus.

Lily, so pale she looked like a wraith, watched him too. "Yes," she said; it was almost a whisper.

"So he'd think there was a, you know, a leak, something serious," Targus went on, his voice a monotone. "Ordinarily it'd be real serious, to get that much water. You'd have to drain the tanks, have a, you know, mechanic check everything out, take on fuel again—that'd take most of the day. That was all she wanted."

No one spoke. "Well, I mean, how the hell could I know the stupid son of a bitch wouldn't do his preflight check? Sorry, Reverend...

sorry, Mrs. Sterling . . . it's just that, I mean, he shouldn't have crashed! No reason in the world! When I heard about it, first thing I thought was there was something else wrong with the plane. Hell of a coincidence, but it had to be, because there wasn't any reason for the water to do it; he would've found it. Well, anyhow, that's what I figured, until I heard the whole report, and then, you know, shit, just because he was stupid, I've got to feel like a *murderer?*" He put his head in his hands. "Sorry," he said again, his voice muffled. He looked up at Valerie. "I mean it; I'm real sorry. It about drove me crazy when it happened. I mean, I couldn't talk about it to anybody—what was I supposed to say? This guy died because of something I did, sort of accidentally?—but it drove me up the wall thinking about it. Couldn't talk to a living soul. Couldn't talk to *her;* she acted like we'd never even flown up there. There's not a lot you can talk to her about; she does her own thing and kinda lives in her own world where she can, you know, act like everything's the way she wants it. She paid me a lot of money for that little job, but she could have kept it, you know; there's no way I was gonna talk and she knew it. And anyway, you know, it wasn't so bad . . . I mean, I didn't kill him. You think about it, he killed himself by not doing his preflight check."

A hot gust of wind swirled dirt across his shoes and he scuffled his feet like a schoolboy. "So what happens now?" he asked.

Sybille was in her office at Morgen Farms when Valerie and Nick arrived. They had left Lily at Valerie's house in Falls Church, then driven to Middleburg. "She's probably in the house," Nick said as they drove toward the farm. "I'll understand if you'd rather not see her there."

Valerie was looking at the landscape. Once it had been a serene haven from the clamor of the world. Now there was something ominous about its beauty, because it harbored Sybille and her plots. "I'd rather not go in, but I don't see how I can stay away . . ." Her voice still trembled; she was so angry, and shaken by the enormity of what Sybille had done, what she had tried to do, what she had been willing to do, that she could not settle down.

"You don't have to," Nick said. His own thoughts were in turmoil, but he knew how much worse it was for Valerie. He pulled onto the grass at the side of the road, and stopped the car. "It's probably too soon—"

She shook her head. "She murdered Carl. Murder. I keep saying that, I keep trying to understand it, but it's so incredible, so awful . . .

Nick, it doesn't make sense! People don't turn to killing to solve a problem!"

"Not your friends; not mine. Not most people, thank God. But for far too many it's an option. I never thought of Sybille as one of them. It's terrifying, you know; we both knew her—I was as close to her, I suppose, as anyone could get—and neither of us suspected..." He took a long breath. "Valerie, I think, after all, you'd be better off if you come in with me."

"Yes, I know. That's what I meant. I don't see how I can avoid it. If I'm ever going to come to terms with it...Oh, my God, how does someone come to terms with something like that? *She murdered Carl.*" She closed her eyes for a moment. "Yes, of course I'll go with you. This isn't a good time to play the sensitive maiden."

Nick turned to her. They were alone on a straight stretch of road. It was almost evening, a time when most people were home, and the only signs of life were the grazing horses in the distance, moving slowly in the heat like flowing shadows. Nick took Valerie's hands. "This doesn't seem to be a good time for a lot of things. There's too much ugliness. But I want to tell you before we go any farther how much I love you. I've been too cautious, these last few weeks; I should have told you right away, though I don't suppose I've really hidden it. My darling, I love you; I've loved you since I first met you. You've been a part of me for all these years, whatever else I've done or tried to do with my life, and when I found you again I knew how deeply I'd missed you, and how much I wanted to bring it all back. I think we've done more than that—I think we've found something much better— and all I want now is the chance to enjoy it. There are so many things I want us to share—a lifetime, to start with—and it seems obscene to begin with what we heard from Targus, but we're in the middle of it and I was afraid it might get worse and then we'd have to wait inter- minably for a perfect time. Damn it, I'm being clumsy; I'm sorry. But there's so much that's wonderful when we're together, I couldn't let us get any deeper into this muck without telling you."

Valerie leaned toward him and kissed him. For a moment she was able to force aside her anger and disgust at Sybille; this was a tiny space of peace and beauty for her and Nick. We'll get back to it, she thought, after today. Or after tomorrow. Or whenever this is over. "It is the perfect time. Whatever happens around us, all our own bad times are past." It was true. They had grown so close. They'd left behind all the childish squabbling and irritation that had made her think they would never be content. She wondered if everyone had to go through a kind of childhood with another person before they could create an adult relationship. What a waste of time, she though ruefully. But maybe not; maybe it meant she and Nick had grown up together and were ready now to create something richer than either of them had known before.

"I love you, Nick," she said, her lips against his. "I love Chad and I love you and I love thinking about all the things we can do together, the three of us, the two of us, playing and working together... Oh. Oh, my God."

"What?" He held her away from him. "What is it?"

"Nick, we can't do a report on Graceville. I can't do it; your network can't do it. We can't be the ones to expose Sybille."

"Because of Chad," Nick said.

"Of course. Why didn't we think of it? We were so busy researching it, and trying to find a way to do it, but there is no way. Other people will, we can't help that; but it can't be us."

"No, it can't," he said quietly.

Valerie looked at him closely. "You're relieved. Nick, why didn't you say something? You've been thinking about it and you didn't tell me."

"It's your story; I didn't know how to kill it."

They exchanged a long look, and at last Valerie smiled. "Maybe that's my real job at E&N: to *almost* do reports on 'Blow-Up.' It's different, isn't it? Lots of people produce and report television features; how many of them make a living by *almost* doing it?"

"Thank you," Nick said. "I hated the thought of telling you."

"But I couldn't have done it. How could I live with Chad if I started out that way?" Nick pulled her close again, but she held back. "How long have you been thinking about it?"

"Only since this afternoon. Until then, I thought we could do a good feature and leave her out. She's not even a board member, you know; we could report on the board, the building of Graceville, Al Speer's findings, and keep the main focus on Lily, who's been used by all of them. We could do all that and never talk about Sybille."

"But you changed your mind when we saw Bob Targus. Because it was too much to dump on Chad all at once."

"That's it. He'll find out about Graceville—you're right, of course, we can't stop that—and he'll know about the tampering with the plane, because the police have to be told. But he doesn't have to know that his father and the woman who's going to be the first real mother he's ever known were the ones who broke the story on Graceville. Whether we mentioned Sybille or not, she's so deep in it that every television reporter would get to her within a day, and it would look as if we were the ones who pointed the way. I'm sorry, Valerie; I wish we could do it. I've said that before, haven't I?"

"I hope you don't have to say it again," she replied with a small smile. "It's all right, Nick; it's over; it's gone. I'll find something else. I'd have to anyway, once I finished this one."

He held her close, so grateful for her he wondered how he had done without her for all the past years. Holding each other, they kissed again, leaning across the gearshift and storage compartment between their seats, until they broke into laughter. "We're too old for cars," Valerie said. "We need a couch, a deep carpet, a bed . . ."

"Waiting for us," Nick said. "A house waiting for us, a life waiting for us . . ." They kissed again, but only briefly, because he had reminded them that something else waited for them first. "Let's get this over with." Valerie sat back, and he started the car, and drove to Morgen Farms.

"Mrs. Enderby is working," the butler said. "You could wait in the garden room, but it might be hours. I suggest you make an appointment for another time."

Nick wrote a few words on a business card. "I think she should see this. We'll wait here."

The butler hesitated, then took the card and left.

Less than a minute later, Sybille appeared in the entrance hall. "How astonishing," she said, her voice flat. Her pale-blue eyes took in both of them with no expression. "Now, where shall we go to talk? Valerie, you choose. You know your way around."

"It's your house," Valerie said clearly. "We'll go wherever you like."

Checked, Sybille turned and walked away without looking back. Nick and Valerie followed, down the hallway to the library, shadowed behind drawn drapes, air-conditioned to frigidity. Sybille sat in a dark wing-backed chair beside a Chinese screen. She wore dark linen pants and a white blouse and looked to Valerie like a black-and-white photograph, frozen in time.

Nick sat on a velvet loveseat. Valerie had been about to join him, but thought better of it, and sat across from him, on a matching sofa. A low coffee table was between them, and Sybille's chair was at the end of it. It struck Valerie that they had been in this position before, a long time ago, at a Chinese restaurant in Palo Alto. They had toasted each other; something about where they would be in ten years. But we never could have imagined this, Valerie thought. The three of us—strangers, lovers, friends, enemies. And from it, Nick and I will build a life.

The butler appeared in the doorway. "Would Madam care for refreshments?"

"No." Sybille kept her eyes on Nick, as if the two of them were alone, and waited.

"We went to see Bob Targus this afternoon," Nick said, "to ask him—"

"That's a lie," Sybille snapped. "He's moved."

"Not yet. He was packing. We went to ask him if he knew anything about the crash of Carlton Sterling's plane."

There was a brief pause. "Of course he doesn't. Why would he?"

"Because he was there. And he told us what he did to the plane before flying you back to Washington."

"Is this a game?" Sybille demanded. "I have no idea what you're talking about. Targus was an unreliable employee, dishonest and untrustworthy. He made up stories that no one believed. If he told you he did something up there, you'd be a fool to believe him. Anyway, that crash was a year and a half ago; it was investigated and it's done with. If that's all you came to tell me, I have work to do."

"Targus was your pilot for a long time; I'd think you would have gotten rid of him if he was unreliable. We came to tell you that he confessed to putting water in the tanks of Carlton's plane. He said you wanted to delay Carlton; not kill him, but prevent him from returning to Washington right away. Targus said you ordered him to make sure the plane would require maintenance that would take at least a few hours. It was Targus who thought of putting water in the tanks. And of course Carlton was killed."

"You son of a bitch, you're saying I killed him." Sybille's voice was so cold and flat it was almost mechanical. "You're saying I ordered Targus to—whatever he did—so I'm the one who's guilty. Is that what you're saying? You're accusing me of killing a stupid ass who didn't know enough to check his plane before he took off. You're crazy. Whatever that liar said, I had nothing to do with Carl's plane. Why would I? I didn't give a damn what he did."

"You were having an affair with him," Valerie said quietly.

"Not much of one," Sybille said with contempt, looking around the room without meeting Valerie's eyes. "He was stupid and dull and lousy in bed. You have low standards, Valerie; you'll settle"—she shot a quick glance at Nick—"for anything."

Nick and Valerie gazed at her in silence. She stared back at Nick.

"It was a long time ago, and I barely knew him. I didn't care what he did or when he did it; I just wanted him out of my way."

Nick nodded. "That's what Bob Targus said."

Her mouth drew tight. "You can't intimidate me, Nick; I know you too well." She was sitting stiffly, her face a mask. "You want to destroy me. You can't stand it that Chad likes me better than you; you've been trying to keep us apart ever since he was born. And now you want to ruin me, just because I'm successful. You're trying to ruin Graceville. You sent this woman to ask my board members questions she had no right to ask, trying to make them turn their backs on me. But you're crazy if you think they would; they admire me and respect me, and they need me. You won't get anywhere with this; I'm stronger than you. Whatever you try to do to me, you'll fail because I'm too strong, I've been through too much. I'm invulnerable."

Nick leaned forward. "Sybille, listen to me. We should have gone to the police with Targus's statement, but we couldn't do it, not yet. We have to think of Chad; we want to protect him as much as possible and we have to think of how to tell him about everything that's happened. And maybe we've got it wrong; maybe Targus wasn't telling the truth. If you've got another explanation, we want to hear it. And about the money Carlton gave you. We found out about that—"

"Who's this *we?*" Sybille demanded, looking straight at Nick. "I'm talking to *you,* I'll listen to *you,* but I'm not talking to any *we.* If you keep talking about *we,* you'll have to get out."

"You'll have to listen, whatever words I use. I'm not doing this alone. Valerie and I have been researching Graceville together, you know about that, and I'm helping her find what she can about her husband's death. We thought we had two separate questions to answer—about Carlton's plane, and about the finances of the Hour of Grace Foundation—but the two of them came together, and now it looks like one question. We came here to give you a chance to tell us our answers are wrong. We have information about the sums of money that are being taken from the Foundation; we have—"

"You have nothing!" she snapped mechanically. "You talk about police—to *me!* to your wife! You talk about going to the police! With what, for Christ's sake? A few rumors and innuendoes you scraped up that sound like those asses, the Bakkers, and you think you'll get a free ride—oh, you'd be a big man, wouldn't you, by screwing me. I was your wife! I'm the mother of your son! But you'd sacrifice me to get an audience that always wants more dirt! You bastard, you'd do anything—"

"We're not doing it, Sybille," Valerie said evenly. She was trying not to shiver in the icy room. Her bare arms and legs were covered with tiny bumps, but she would not rub them, she would not give any sign to Sybille that she was freezing. "The information will get out—it can't be a secret anymore—but we won't be the ones to put it on television. You must know, though, that someone else will."

Sybille was looking fixedly at Nick. The planes of her face were sharp beneath her taut skin, dark with anger. "No one will." She clipped her words to keep her voice under control. "Who does she think she is, acting noble, *not being the one* to tell lies about me on television? She isn't noble; she doesn't have anything! You don't know anything about me. Carl drove me crazy, begging me to take his money, begging me to marry him and get him loose from that scatterbrained bitch he was married to, but I couldn't stand him. He bored the hell out of me. You're a fool, Nick, getting mixed up with her; she ruins every man she touches."

Valerie stood up, angry, ice cold, wanting only to be away from there, outside, in the hot sun. For awhile Nick's presence had kept her quiet, but now even that was not enough. "You killed him. You took his money, our money, and killed him so you could keep it. There's never enough for you, Sybille, there's never been enough, and you'll do anything to get more. It wasn't enough that you killed Carl; you're robbing the people who send money to Lily. You've manipulated her, you've used her goodness and her innocence, because you could count on them. You knew she loved you; you knew she wouldn't listen to anyone who said anything against you. Even now she can't bring herself to believe what Bob Targus said—"

"*What are you talking about?* She doesn't know anything about it! She called me; she always calls me and tells me where she is. She's sick; she's staying with a friend—"

"She's staying with me. She was with us this afternoon when we talked to—"

"*That's a lie!*" Sybille leaped out of the chair and darted to the other end of the room, away from Valerie. "She'd never go to you; I know damn well she wouldn't! You're trying to hurt me. That's all you've ever done, tried to make me feel I was *nothing* compared to you. You think you can be like me and take everything I have! I saw you, at Nick's house, sucking up to Chad; you want my son, you want my husband, you want Lily! You can't stand it that I'm better than you; you want me poor and helpless, the way I was when we met . . . *goddam it, come back here! You're not walking out on me!*"

Valerie was at the door. She was shaking from the horrors of Sybille's sick rage, the venom stored up and nurtured all these years. She felt the grip of Sybille's poison like a thick-stemmed deadly plant wrapping itself around her, blotting out the beauty of life: Nick and Chad and work and friends. *I won't let her. She's not going to destroy what is wonderful in the world, and drag us down with her legacy of anger and death.*

"I'll tell you this now because I hope I never see you again," she said, her voice tight with the effort to keep from trembling. "A long time ago, I thought we might be friends. That was all I ever wanted from you. You've never believed that, but it's true. Nick and Chad and Lily are part of my life because we love each other, not because of some conspiracy to hurt you; we don't even think of you when we're together, though I know that's hard for you to believe. I'm sure you'd rather think we're always conscious of you, whatever we're doing. If you'd ever learned to care about one other human being, Sybille, you wouldn't be living here alone in this damned refrigerator, and Graceville wouldn't be collapsing around you. You don't know the meaning of love or friendship or even affection; you don't know what honesty is, or decency; you're incapable of telling the truth; you use people and then throw them away; you murdered my husband, and for all I care you can go to hell."

She opened the door. "I'll wait for you outside," she said to Nick, and was gone.

Sybille opened her mouth, but no sound came. She leaned against a chair, gasping. She was dizzy and something was wrong with her eyes; the room looked blurred and wavering, as if seen through water. She gripped the edge of the chair to keep from falling. *I can't stand it. Everyone's against me. I need protection!*

Nick was standing, and she squinted, trying to bring him into focus. "You're running away, too? These insane accusations... you said you'd listen to my side... and then you run away."

"You haven't told me your side," he said.

"Why should I? I don't owe you anything. I gave you the best I had and it wasn't good enough; you left me for her, anyway. I don't have to talk to you; you'll just use it against me. You're desperate, I can tell; you dug and dug and still don't have your precious show. You don't know what our finances are, and you never will! You have some bull-shit from a pilot we fired for lying, but that doesn't have a thing to do with Graceville. 'Water in the tanks!'" she cried in mincing tones. "Who the hell knows what that is, and who cares? People care about sex and money, and that's what you dug for in Graceville. But you didn't find any, did you? You didn't find anything that connects to anything else. *You're nowhere.* Why don't you just drop it? And drop that bitch, too. You and I could still get together, you know. This time we'd be working together, too. I'd make you a board member of the Foundation, and we could run Lily's sermons on your network, two or three a week if you want; you have no idea how lucrative they are. And you could—we could take care of each other. Chad would like it, you know he would. It's so simple; it's always been simple; we just took a few detours, that's all. Nick, listen to me!"

"Valerie told you we're not going to do the story." Nick's voice was slow and heavy with sadness, for Chad, and also for Sybille. "But that doesn't mean we haven't learned a lot that we have to pass on to others. And it does connect; it all connects through Carlton. He invested thirteen million dollars in Graceville while he was having an affair with you. I suppose that qualifies as the sex part; the whole story reeks of money. You've been skimming huge amounts from all the funds involved with Graceville—money for the land purchase, construction costs, donations, memberships—"

"You don't know that!"

"—over forty percent of it goes to you and your partners. Carlton was rushing back to be at the closing on the land purchase—perhaps to stop it; we can't know for sure—when his plane crashed, after it had been tampered with on your orders. Those are the connections we've made."

"Rumors! Lies! You've got no proof!"

"We've had an accountant go over your books. I imagine—"

"You're lying. There's *no way*—"

"We did it, Sybille. I imagine you'll be hearing from the IRS one of these days. And Bob Targus is coming to Valerie's tonight to tape his statement for us. If you have anything to say—if people have lied to us and we don't know it—tell me. Don't just accuse Bob of being a liar; tell me how all these things happened. You've got to defend yourself, or help with the investigation; otherwise, no one can help you."

"You son of a bitch. You want to force me to crawl. I'd rather lose everything I have."

Nick gazed at her. She was like a dark statue, the only sign of life her pale-blue eyes blazing in the shadows. "You may," he said. He suddenly was aware of how cold he was. He had turned down his shirtsleeves sometime back, but it was not enough. "If you change your mind, you can call me. I'll be at Valerie's, or at home."

"Get out of here!" She watched him leave, closing the door behind him. She stood where she was, leaning against the chair, breathing harshly.

I'll be at Valerie's, or at home.

She picked up a marble bookend and hurled it the length of the room. It crashed into the glass doors of her gun cabinet, flinging shards of glass over the dark carpet. They gleamed dully in the dim light that filtered through the closed drapes. When the sound died away, the room was silent except for the faint hissing of cold air, and Sybille's rasping breath.

No one came. They had been told too often to leave her alone. It had always been enough for her to know there were others in the house; she did not want them too close. She stood still until her breathing slowed. Sometime later the butler asked if she would be dining at home. "No," Sybille said. He cast a quick glance at the gun cabinet, adjusted one of the draperies that was letting in a sliver of sunlight, and left the room. Still, she did not move.

Nick was lying when he said there'd be no story on television. She knew he was. He was lying about the accountant too; no stranger could get past the security guard. She hadn't known Nick was such a liar. But no matter how flimsy or wrong his information was, he'd make some kind of show with it. That's what Sybille had always done; that's what anybody would do. She couldn't stop that; she'd just have to wait it out, and fight whatever they put on.

Lies and guesswork. The Foundation could survive those. They'd have to make some changes, though. Lars Olssen would have to become president; they needed his absolute purity to get through this. Floyd would go quietly; he always did what she told him. The butler said he'd called that morning, while she was working; she'd call him back tomorrow and tell him he'd have to resign as president.

But the Foundation isn't the real danger.

Slowly, she slid down until she was sitting on the floor, leaning forward, her arms folded tight against her breasts. She knew what the real danger was.

Bob Targus. She'd kept him on her payroll for years, given him bonuses, trusted him with some sensitive jobs . . . and now that weak-willed, disloyal son of a bitch was the real danger. All this time he'd kept his mouth shut, and then, out of the blue, to tell someone . . .

She had to stop him, prevent him from taping it. If there was no proof, if it was only his word against hers—a nothing pilot versus Sybille Enderby—who'd believe him? He'd be dead in the water.

Dead.

Of course. What else could she do? How else could she be sure he wouldn't find someone else to blab to? She couldn't stop Nick from doing whatever he wanted about Graceville, but she could stop Targus from talking.

She stood stiffly and went to the gun cabinet, stepping between the shards of glass. She opened the shattered door, and took out a rifle. She had not done any skeet shooting or hunting in some time, but she was not worried: she never missed. *I've missed hunting, though,* she thought, enjoying her own joke. *It's about time I got back to it.*

Bob Targus is coming to Valerie's tonight to tape his statement for us. How stupid of Nick to tell her that; you'd think he would have known her better. They'd been married, after all; lived together, raised a son together... Didn't he ever learn?

I learn, Sybille thought. *That's how I survive.*

She took a handful of bullets, and left the house through the door to the garage. She chose the nearest car: sleek and fast, a Testarossa, one of her first purchases with her new wealth from the Foundation. But as she backed out of the garage, she realized she had no idea where Valerie lived. *That son of a bitch,* she fumed; *why didn't he give me her address, while he was at it?* Leaving the gun in the car, she went back to the library and looked for Valerie's name in the telephone directory.

She found the name and address. *Falls Church,* she thought; *fancy place for somebody who'd supposedly lost all her money.* She probably had some hidden and never told Carl about it; *God, what a dishonest bitch.* Then she went back to the car, and drove to Falls Church.

The traffic was heavy as she came closer to the Washington orbit, and she dodged cars and pedestrians, feeling a sudden urgency. *Targus is coming tonight.* What did *tonight* mean? It was eight-thirty; the sun was down, but the heat clung, rising in waves from the pavement and blown by a hot steady wind. When did it stop being evening and start to be night? Eight o'clock? Nine? Ten? Midnight? She raced to the address, and then slowed as she saw it ahead: a small house sur-rounded by empty lots. Across the street was a park thick with sumac and horsechestnut trees. Sybille felt a thrill of satisfaction when she saw it. *Made to order.*

Nick's car was parked near the house, at the edge of a circle of light cast by a bulb over the front door. Not too bright, but enough, Sybille exulted. *Just fine.* And no other car was near Nick's. Targus wasn't there. She was in time.

She parked as far as she could from the nearest streetlamp and, holding the rifle against her body, walked to a nearby clump of sumac trees. It was not as fine as she had thought: the wind was high, tossing the thin sumac branches and blocking her vision. It won't last, she thought; it will die down. She rested the rifle beside a tree trunk, and stood perfectly still, waiting.

Once she saw movement through a window of the house; someone walking across the room. Otherwise the windows were blank, secretive, making her an outsider. She visualized Nick moving about inside, perched on the arm of a chair, biting into an apple, opening a newspaper. Before she could stop herself, she imagined him in bed with Valerie. *Damn it!* She smashed their image in her mind. *Maybe I'll kill him too. And her. They deserve it.*

A car pulled up and she tensed, but it belonged to someone in another house. He took a bag of charcoal from the trunk and went inside. In a few minutes, the acrid smell of kerosene wafted to her in her hiding place, and then the smell of burning coals. She visualized a family, having a barbecue. She was not at all hungry.

A woman walked by with a dog on a leash; a child rode a tricycle, with her father walking behind. Teenagers crossed the street, giggling. They'd better stay out of my way, Sybille thought angrily. And then another car drove up, and parked beside Nick's, and she watched Targus get out.

She raised her rifle, aiming at his broad back as he slammed the car door and walked up the front walk. But the wind was still high, whipping the branches in front of her. Angered, she shoved them away with the gun. He was ringing the doorbell; she was almost out of time. The door opened. She aimed again at his back. The branches tossed in front of her, but there was nothing she could do about them. She fired.

She heard a scream as Targus fell, and she saw him try to raise himself. Enraged because her aim had been off—the damned wind!— she fired again. But in that second, no longer than a heartbeat, Lily had rushed forward to help Targus, and she was the one whom Sybille's second bullet struck.

"*Lily!*" Sybille screamed. Nick and Valerie pulled the two bodies into the house and slammed the door. Sybille stood for a moment, frozen. And then she fled.

Chapter
30

t was dawn when Nick reached home, bringing
Valerie and Rosemary with him. He took Rosemary to the third-floor suite, carrying the small
bag she had packed before they left. She had been
trembling uncontrollably after the shooting, saying
she could not sleep in that house that night, she had to go somewhere
else, and Nick said it was very simple: she and Valerie would come
home with him, for as long as they wanted.

He settled her on the third floor, made sure she was comfortable,
and went to his own room. Valerie was in bed when he got there, and
when he joined her they clung together in silence, wanting comfort
and the closeness of knowing they were together, and would be, from
then on. They slept that way, in each other's arms, until, an hour later,
they woke at the same moment.

"We should call the hospital," Valerie said.

Nick was already reaching for the telephone. He dialed the inten-
sive-care unit. "Lily Grace," he said. "She had surgery a couple of
hours ago; we'd like to know how she is. This is Nick Fielding." He

held Valerie close with one arm. "Not a relative, no; she has none. But she lives with us; we're responsible for her."

"Yes, I remember now," said the nurse. "She's stable, Mr. Fielding. We won't know more than that for some time. If you want to call back in two or three hours..."

"Thanks," Nick said. "We'll be there by then." He lay on his side, bringing Valerie with him, her legs between his, her breasts crushed against his chest, her lips soft and open below his. "I love you," he said, kissing her with slow kisses. "I've dreamed of waking up with you. This isn't the kind of morning I dreamed of, but it's infinitely better because you're here. I want us to be married; did I tell you that yesterday?"

She smiled. "I took it for granted. Probably because it's what I want, too." They moved together, desire briefly holding at bay the memory of the night before. Slowly, Valerie moved her legs so they were no longer between Nick's, but encircling them, and very simply, as if continuing their talk, he came into her, smoothly, deeply, filling her as she opened to him. Lying on their sides, embracing, they smiled at each other with a look that was both somber and joyous, a promise that this was what they would always bring to each other: love and gladness to buoy them even in the midst of tragedy, warmth and closeness to sustain them in bleak or fearful times.

They lay almost still, yet their bodies moved in an imperceptible rhythm that brought them to a climax all the more explosive for being so quiet. They kissed again, and lay still in the quiet house. Home, Valerie thought. Wherever we're together. She smiled to herself, thinking of the passion for pleasure that had once ruled her life, and how it had expanded and changed. It was not that she loved pleasure any less, it was that her passion now was for living well and fully. She had lived only partially, she thought drowsily, never discovering all the things she could do: that she could work, and work well; that she could love, and love well; that she could give of herself, and do it well. *I should tell Lily; she'd understand. All her sermons have been about believing in ourselves, and what we can be, that we can be better than we think we are, better than others think we are...*

She stirred, thinking of Lily, and of all the loose ends she and Nick had to take care of. "I love you," she murmured, her lips on Nick's heart, "and I wish we could stay here all day, but we really have to get up."

He smiled. "One of these days we'll stay here as long as we want, and have trains of servants bring us food and drink, and play soft music in the next room."

"And take all our telephone calls." Valerie laughed. "I like your fantasies."

"I have more. But right now we have to think about Chad, and then Lily. And Bob."

"We should bring him something," Valerie said, reluctantly sitting up. "Books? Food? Magazines? What do you think?"

"Probably all of the above. I can't think of anything that will make him happy right now, can you?"

"No. He doesn't have a lot to look forward to." She shook her head slowly. "It's so terrible. So hard to comprehend, and so awful..." She stood for a moment, the memories coming back, then shook her head again. "I'll just be a few minutes." And she went to take a shower, leaving Nick sitting up in bed with his own memories of the night before.

The police had been all over the neighborhood. By the time they arrived, three minutes after Nick's call, it was too late to cordon off the park, or any streets, but they searched everywhere while three of them went to Valerie's house. Nick fended them off. "We'll be at the hospital; we have to know about Lily. You can talk to us there." Then he and Rosemary and Valerie followed the ambulance carrying Lily and Targus to the hospital.

Two other emergencies had been brought in ahead of them, and the emergency room looked to Nick like unmanageable chaos, but somehow the doctors and nurses sorted it out. Targus, who was not critical, with a bullet wound in his shoulder, was taken to a room. Lily was taken immediately to surgery.

Valerie and Nick and Rosemary waited in an alcove off the main corridor, furnished with foam-padded furniture, steel floor lamps, and magazine racks. The magazines were ragged, with the covers falling off and advertisements and recipes torn out; the crossword puzzles were half finished. Rosemary deliberated, then took two and sat in an armchair. "I have to," she said almost apologetically. "I can't bear to think about Lily, or what happened. It's impossible. Nothing like that ever..." Her voice trailed away, and for the next few hours she alternately read and dozed.

Nick and Valerie sat on a narrow couch and held hands. "The police will be here," Valerie said. "We have to tell them we recognized Sybille's voice, don't we?"

He nodded. "There's no way we can avoid it. We'll talk to Chad before any reporters get the story. Good God, what can we tell him? There's too much..."

"You're sure it was her voice, Nick? I thought so, but ..."

"I've heard her scream a few times," he said dryly. "And she had a reason to try to stop Bob from seeing us. I should have thought of that." He stirred restlessly, and stood up. "I'm going to call her again."

At the pay telephone in a corner of the room, he dialed Sybille's number and listened to it ring. "No answer." He sat beside Valerie and took her hand again. "Still driving back from a shooting spree in Falls Church."

They sat quietly, absorbed in their thoughts. "I wonder what will happen to Lily," Valerie said. "She'll have to find a way to live on her own. I don't think she ever has."

Nick nodded. "She has more growing up to do than Chad."

Valerie thought about it. "I'm not sure. Lily knows a lot more then she lets on. Or she doesn't even know how much she knows. Sophie said once that Lily sounded like someone in a trance. I think she's lived that way. And now she has to wake up. Can you imagine what she'll be then? She has such power to move people; I wonder how she'll use it."

"You'll probably be a part of it, whatever it is. She adores you; do you really think she won't come to you for help? My poor darling, you'll have Chad and Lily to think about before we ever have children of our own."

Valerie smiled. "We'll figure that out."

"We'd better do it soon. I don't want to wait; do you?"

"No, how can we? I'm thirty-four, and I've been wanting children for a long time."

"Once you weren't sure."

"Once I was very young, and didn't know what a family with you would mean to me."

They kissed gently; passion was out of place there. And then the police arrived.

They had one question: who had a reason to shoot Bob Targus and Reverend Grace? From what Valerie and Nick had told them, the sniper had gone after Targus first; he was alone when he was hit. But as soon as Reverend Grace was there, she was shot, too. So, who had it in for both of them?

"We got some eyewitnesses," said one of the policemen. "There was a scream in the park, some teenage kids heard it. You probably did, too. Sounded like 'Lee,' they said; close enough to 'Lily' to make no difference. They looked over there, and they saw a woman carrying what could have been a rifle get into a car. A Testarossa. Italian. There probably aren't a half dozen of them in the D.C. area, but you can bet every teenage boy knows what they look like. So we oughta be able to track that down, no trouble. You know anybody who drives a Testarossa?"

"Yes." Nick felt Valerie grip his hand more tightly. "Her name is Sybille Enderby."

"Enderby. You hear her scream?"

"Yes. We recognized her voice."

"Who is she?"

Nick felt a wave of helplessness wash over him. Who is she? A television producer. A former wife. A mother of sorts. Possibly the power behind Graceville. A woman whose ruling passion was envy. An angry woman. "She produces 'The Hour of Grace' for television. Bob Targus was the pilot for the Hour of Grace corporate plane, until the plane was sold a few weeks ago. He was coming to Mrs. Sterling's house to talk about Sybille's—Mrs. Enderby's—possible involvement in a plane crash a year and a half ago."

The policeman frowned deeply. "I don't get the connection. Reverend Grace and a plane crash?"

"We're still figuring it out," Nick said. "There's a lot we don't know yet. We can't tell you anything about Sybille Enderby we're not sure of."

"Why not? Everybody else does. Give us guesses."

"No. Ask her."

"We will, don't worry about that. You know where she lives?"

"At Morgen Farms, in Middleburg."

When they left, Valerie and Nick sat close together while Rosemary skimmed magazines and murmured about Sybille, remembering when she employed Sybille's mother as her dressmaker. Sybille, just a child, always sat nearby, silent and watchful, playing with scraps of fabric and listening to everything that was said, intent, observant and unsmiling, as if storing everything in her memory. When Rosemary gave her clothes Valerie was tired of, she took them without a word of thanks, just a look from those strange pale eyes, until her mother reminded her, and then she would say her thanks in a short, breathless kind of way. "She gave me the shivers," Rosemary murmured. "Or am I only thinking that because of what I know about her now?"

After three hours, the doctor came. Lily had been taken to the recovery room. Her vital signs were good; she had come through the operation well. She was young and strong. And lucky. "You should go home," the doctor said. "There's nothing more I can tell you, and you can't see her now. Tomorrow, maybe. Give us a call in the morning."

And so Nick drove through the pale, ghostly streets of Georgetown. Home, Valerie thought.

The whole night seemed clearer to Nick now, sitting in bed while Valerie showered, than it had in the hospital. Then he had been too overwhelmed by events to think about details. Her car, he mused. A Testerossa. She had always reveled in visible signs of wealth. It probably never occurred to her that it was like carrying a red flag.

"Dad? You awake?" Chad's voice, charged with early-morning energy, came through the closed door.

"Just about." Nick pulled on a robe and opened the door.

Chad looked past him at the tumbled bed, and Valerie's slacks and striped shirt on the chair. He looked at Nick. "I didn't hear you come in."

"We were very late. Something happened last night; we want to talk to you about it. We'll be down for breakfast in fifteen minutes. I'd like you to wait for us."

"Sure. It sounds like it's something bad."

"We'll talk about it in a few minutes."

"It's not about you and Valerie, is it? I mean, you're okay?"

"We're fine. We're wonderful. We'll tell you about that too."

Chad shot another glance at the bed. "I guess I already know." He grinned. "That's pretty great. See you downstairs."

Nick watched him leap down the stairs, so full of life and anticipation of a new day stretching before him that even the prospect of something bad could not slow him down. Nick's heart sank. What am I going to tell him?

"You can help," he said to Valerie when she came from the shower, a towel twisted into a turban around her head. "My God, you are so beautiful; how can I think of anything but you?"

"You're thinking of your son," she said smiling. "Keeping your priorities straight. I can help with what?"

"Talking to Chad." He watched her take clothes from her suitcase. "I'd like us to do it together."

Valerie paused. Slowly she shook her head. "I don't think you mean that. I think you'd like to talk to him alone. There's nothing I can do to help, Nick; I can't tell Chad how to feel about his mother, and I can't tell you how to talk to him about her. Anything I say would be irrelevant."

"You're never irrelevant. But you're right; this has to be between us.

You're a wise lady." He held her briefly, her cool body against his warm one, her slender strength molding itself to him. Then he let her go. "I'll take a quick shower and get down there. Do you want to wait here?"

"I'll go upstairs and see how Mother is. We'll be down later."

So Nick was alone when he walked into the kitchen ten minutes later. Chad's face fell. "Where's Valerie?"

"She'll be here soon. Good morning, Elena," Nick said as Elena finished squeezing oranges and handed him a glass of juice. He sat beside Chad on a cushioned banquette at the maple table in the break-fast room. "Her mother stayed here last night, on the third floor, and Valerie wanted to spend some time with her and bring her down to breakfast so she wouldn't feel strange."

"Her mother? What's she here for?"

"Something happened at their house last night. I was with them." He watched absently as Elena put a plate of pancakes and a thermos of coffee in front of him, and refilled Chad's plate.

"I'll be in the pantry," she said. "Call me if you want me."

"So what's this all about?" Chad demanded through a mouthful of pancakes.

"It's about Graceville," Nick began slowly. He saw Chad stiffen, pause in his eating, then go on, chewing steadily. But Nick knew he was listening. "You've been watching all the news reports about televi-sion ministries; you know what's going on. There's evidence that the Foundation that runs Graceville may be guilty of the same kind of fraud, and maybe a few other kinds as well. We don't know—"

"So is this about Mother too?"

"We don't know for sure. We think it is."

"She doesn't do things like Tammy Bakker does, like they showed on tv . . . you know, she had this air-conditioned doghouse and her closet was as big as my bedroom, bigger maybe, and it had this huge chandelier thing . . . Mother doesn't have any stuff like that."

"I'm sure she doesn't. I don't know how she spends her money, Chad, but there does seem to be evidence that she and some others are involved in a scheme to take money from Graceville, and the Founda-tion that runs it, for their own use. That's all anybody knows right now. But a lot of people are going to be investigating it, and the more they learn, the more attention television and the newspapers will give it. You know how that works. Nobody can hide when that happens. Sybille can't, and you can't. You have to figure it's going to be a tough time."

Chad speared the last piece of pancake with his fork and carefully swirled it around his plate, making a pattern in the syrup. "That's what happened last night? You heard about all this stuff?"

"No. That was something else."

"Are you going to eat your pancakes?"

Nick smiled, and slid his plate to Chad. "I'm not too hungry. It's better if they help fill your bottomless pit. Chad, this story goes back a long way. There was a time, about a year and a half ago, when Sybille wanted to stop somebody from being at a meeting in Washington. He was going to fly there, and she had someone put water in the fuel tanks of his plane, not to hurt him, just to delay him. He'd have to have a mechanic look at the plane, to find out if something serious was wrong with it, and then drain and refill the tanks. All that would take a while. The tragic thing was, he didn't do a proper check of his plane before he took off, so he didn't find the water. A little while after he was airborne, his plane crashed, and he was killed."

Chad was shoveling pancakes into his mouth. "Yeh," he said.

Nick watched his son as he resolutely kept eating. He watched Chad and felt the pain beneath that singleminded eating, and fought back tears. "The man who was killed was Valerie's husband, Carlton Sterling. Just yesterday, Bob Targus, the man who put the water in the tanks, finally decided to tell people what he'd done, and he was on his way to Valerie's house, to tell her. Sybille found out about it. And she wanted to stop him, just as she'd wanted to stop Carlton."

Chad had finished his pancakes. He sat still, his head down, staring at his empty plate. "Yeh," he said.

"This is terrible to talk about, Chad, but you have to hear it. If I don't tell you, some stranger will, and that would be the worst thing of all. I'd like to make you understand it all, but a lot of it I don't understand myself. We're going to have to work at that together. Are you following me?"

Chad's head was down. "Yeh."

"Something happened to Sybille in the past year. She was never a particularly gentle person, you know that, but she had good control of herself and could get along in all kind of situations, with all kinds of people. But in the past year she seemed to change, as if she was going on a downward path, as if she had an illness that she couldn't control. Before, when she wanted to stop Carlton, she only tried to delay him. When she wanted to stop Bob Targus, she tried to kill him with a rifle."

"She did not!" Chad glared at his father. "She wouldn't...she wouldn't try to...*she wouldn't!* And you know it, too! I bet she didn't do any of that stuff! People tell lies about her; she told me that. She said people are jealous of her and they tell lies; she told me all about it."

"I didn't want to believe it, either," Nick said. "And I'd rather have kept it from you. But nothing that's happened with Sybille is the kind of news that can be kept quiet. She always wanted to make big stories, and now she's created a story that stretches so far, and touches so many people, I'm afraid it's going to be broadcast everywhere. I can't stop that. All I can do is help you deal with it."

Chad shook his head stubbornly. "I don't have to. It's all lies, anyway."

"No. Chad, listen to me." Nick put his arm around him, but Chad angrily shrugged it off. "Look, this is going to be hard enough for us to get through, without pretending. Sybille has spent a lifetime pretending, and we're not going to do that; it never works. She tried to live as if the world was a big painting she kept changing as she went along, covering up some things, adding others, moving people and scenes from one place to another, and then painting over everything to make it look as if it was always that way. That's not how we're going to live. It's the way children live, and adults who never grow up, and it leads to anger, and sometimes tragedy, because the time always comes when you can't paint over something and make your life look the way you want it to look, and when that happens you try to find someone to blame, and you want to punish and hurt that person because you're not happy and somebody has to pay for it. You and I are going to live in the world as we find it, Chad. Some things we can change and some we can ignore, but most things we have to live with, in the best way we know how. Sybille never seemed to learn that."

"Well, if she's so terrible why did you marry her in the first place?" Chad yelled.

Nick hesitated. He and Chad had talked about this before. But he knew that children forget stories if they hear them when they are too young to absorb them and incorporate them into their experience. Each time they went over this, Chad would remember more, until one day he would remember the whole of it, and perhaps be satisfied.

"I was young, and she was different then," he said at last, and wondered how many millions of men and women said those same weary words, trying to explain a bad marriage. "She had a fierce drive to succeed, to get past the poverty she'd known and to make herself famous and influential. I admired that because I was pretty much the same and I thought we could understand each other. I thought she was courageous and strong and affectionate, and also lonely and needing protection. She needed someone to care about her—no one did, you see—and to keep her from feeling alone in the world. She said I did that for her, and since I wanted to believe it, I did. I needed to be needed and I mistook pity and admiration for love. Then you were born, and I found everything I'd hoped for: you needed me and I loved you so much I thought my life could be happy just because you were there."

Chad looked at his father. "Did she do bad things then? Is that why you didn't stay with her?"

Nick refilled his cup from the thermos Elena had left. "We really didn't have very much to share; a lot less than I thought when we were married. And there were too many things we disagreed about."

"Bad things!" It was almost a wail. Chad's eyes filled with tears that slid down his cheeks. "She's a bad person!"

Nick put his arm around his son, and this time Chad let it stay there, moving closer on the banquette. "Remember I told you it's like an illness? Sybille is an angry person, Chad; most things and people seem to make her angry. It doesn't matter how successful she is or how many possessions she collects, she can't be satisfied or serene. I thought the passion that ruled her was a drive to succeed, and then I thought it was envy, but I was wrong; it's anger. We all get angry at times—there are things that should make us angry, like injustice and cruelty and prejudice, and we get angry when we're hurt or disappointed—but most of us control our anger so that it doesn't control us. We fit it into a proper perspective in a whole life. Sybille can't do that. She is so deeply angry all the time that it's like a chemical, eating her up inside, and when the pain of her anger gets too much to hold in, she explodes. That's probably what happened last night. I don't think she could stop herself from doing what she did."

"And she doesn't love me; she never has," Chad said through his tears, as if he had heard nothing Nick said. But Nick knew he had, and would remember at least some of it, and think about it in quieter times. And perhaps he would have another way of thinking about his mother because of it.

Chad gulped and took a shaking breath and hiccupped. "When we go to dinner, I save up these stories from school or tv or a book, you know, and I tell her . . . and *she doesn't like them!* She listens and everything, but she doesn't laugh or tell another story right back, the way the guys do at school. And you too. She's just . . . *there,* you know?

Only, she's not really...*there*. I mean...oh, you know. I hate it, and then I...hate...her...Not really, you know, only it feels like I do... and then I get home and it doesn't seem so bad, like I figure it won't be the same next time...and I wish I could see her again..." He was sobbing now, rubbing his eyes and nose with the back of his hand. Nick handed him a napkin, and held him close while he cried. There was only so much he could do. Most of it Chad would have to do himself.

"I hate her!" Chad yelled. "I'm not ever going to see her again! She's mean and bad and she can go to jail, and be alone forever and ever, and I don't care! I hate her!"

Tears stung Nick's eyes. His son's pain stabbed through him; he hurt all over. "That's pretty strong," he said. "Why don't you wait before deciding that? You may change your mind. If she really does have an illness, you wouldn't hate her, would you?"

"Uh. I don't know...What does that mean, anyway? She's not sick."

"I wouldn't be too sure of that. When someone stands in the dark and shoots a person in the back, it sounds pretty sick to me."

"In the *back*?"

"She was across the street and he was ringing the doorbell, so his back was to her."

There was a long silence as Chad struggled with his thoughts. "I don't know."

"Think about what I said earlier, about being angry."

"Yeh, but, even if you're mad at somebody you don't go out and shoot him!"

"You don't, and I don't, and fortunately most people don't. That's why it looks to me like a sickness when someone does it. Most of us grow up and get our angers under control and stop pretending we can paint a new world whenever things go wrong. You've learned that, Chad. You're beginning to live in the world like a grownup."

"But I'm not, yet!"

"No, but you're on your way. You're learning a lot of grown-up things, and dealing with a lot of awfully hard facts. I'm very proud of you, my friend. And I love you very much."

There was a silence. "Yeh," Chad said, nodding. Silent tears ran down his face. "Yeh. I love you, too, Dad. More than anything." Abruptly, he slid down and lay full length on the banquette with his head in Nick's lap. Nick put his hand on his son's hair, stroking it. I have to tell him about Lily too, he thought, but not now. Soon, but not yet. They sat that way for several minutes, until Valerie appeared in the doorway.

She looked at Nick, and then around the room. "Isn't Chad here? I thought you'd be talking."

Chad shot up. "I'm here!"

Nick met Valerie's eyes past Chad's tear-streaked face. For all their sakes, he was very glad, at that moment, that Sybille could not see the joy that leaped to his son's face when Valerie appeared.

Lily had a private room on the top floor of the hospital, and she liked to sit beside the window looking out over the town. The nurses had identified buildings and sights for her, especially Falls Church, where George Washington had been a vestryman, and the Fountain of Faith, dedicated to four clergymen who sacrificed their lives early in the Second World War to save four soldiers. I don't deserve to be a vestryman, Lily thought. I've never sacrificed anything. I've never even known what it's like to be alone, without someone taking care of everything for me.

Sybille had been arrested, and was free on bond. So was Bob Targus, home now from the hospital, taking physical therapy for his shoulder, but facing conviction and a prison sentence. He'd told Lily he thought he probably wouldn't go to prison, or anyway not for very long, because he was going to testify against Sybille for the prosecution. But he'd lost his new job and it didn't look as if anyone else would hire him after what he'd done. He was so depressed about not flying again that Lily thought he'd already been severely punished.

She would be going home, too, she knew; she was recovering rapidly. "Young and resilient," the doctor had said that morning, as he did every morning. "And very lucky. If that bullet had been an inch higher, it would have hit your heart."

So I was lucky again, Lily thought. Not special, not saved for higher purposes. Just lucky.

But what am I going to do now? I have to have something to believe in, something to build my life around. Something I have a passion for. And I don't know . . . I don't know what it will be. What am I going to do? Where will I go when they send me home?

"You'll stay with me," Rosemary said that evening, when she came to visit. "It's been wonderful for me, having you there. I like feeling useful, and Valerie has become so independent, ever since the crash, I've felt quite superfluous. I'm thinking of getting a job, can you believe it? I've talked to some art galleries, and one of them may actually want me. But in the meantime, you'll stay with me."

"It's too crowded," Lily said. "You're very good, but I never expected to stay long."

"It won't be crowded at all; I can't imagine Valerie spending much time there anymore. I really do want you, Lily; that little place is going to seem enormous with just me in it."

Each night, the television newscasts had a report on the widening investigation into Graceville and the Hour of Grace Foundation. At the beginning of the week there had been long reports on the shooting of Lilith Grace, with reporters positioning themselves in front of the sumacs in the park, or next to Valerie's front door, finding various ways to repeat the little they knew, asking neighbors how they felt about all this, and showing pictures of Sybille's Italian luxury car, the Testarossa, which they had photographed by bribing a gardener at her farm. By the end of the week, the news of Lily had shrunk to a mention during the reports on Graceville and the Foundation: she was recovering, the newscasters said, but refused all interviews, and no one knew when she would resume her preaching.

Then, on Sunday, eight days after the shooting, when she had spent the silent hours thinking and praying, Lily made a decision. And because she was a child of mass communication, she knew exactly what to do: she called reporters from radio and television and the newspapers, and told them she had a statement to make.

She told no one except the nurses, who let her use their lounge for her press conference. And that evening, when Nick and Valerie came to visit, bringing Chad, she told them she wanted them to watch the seven o'clock network news with her.

"We'd rather just talk to you," Valerie said. "We brought some new books, and fruit"—she was emptying a shopping bag—"and a word game you can play by yourself or with someone—"

Lily shook her head. "Please, Valerie, I really want to watch the news."

"They don't want to because of me," said Chad. "It's hard, you know, people talking about your mother every night, so they don't turn it on. I watch at eleven o'clock, upstairs."

Nick's eyebrows rose. "You watch it alone."

"Yeh. I'd rather be with you or Valerie, but you're always too worried about me."

Nick chuckled. "From now on we'll watch together. I think you ought to be asleep by eleven, anyway."

Lily picked up the remote control. "It's all right if I turn it on?"

"Sure," said Chad grandly, but Valerie saw that his fists were clenched, and she went to sit on the arm of his chair, her arm around him.

Lily began with NBC, where the opening story was on the Soviet Union. Nervously, she switched to CBS, but it was reporting the same story, and so was ABC. She went back and forth, from one to the other, until she heard an anchorman say "—continues into the finances of the Hour of Grace Foundation. Two more members of the board, Arch Warman and Monte James, resigned yesterday, three days after the Reverend Lars Olssen demanded their resignation. But the main story tonight belongs to Reverend Lilith Grace. Reverend Lily, as she is known, was shot last week in a bizarre set of circumstances dealing with money invested in the town of Graceville. She held a hospital press conference today and it's such an extraordinary statement we're going to let you see it in its entirety."

Valerie and Nick exchanged a glance.

Lily was on the screen, pale and fragile, in a large wicker armchair, wearing a blue silk robe Valerie had bought her. "To all of you, strangers and friends and my congregation," she began in the high voice that was familiar to millions, "I came to tell you that I am leaving the ministry. I can't be the kind of minister I always dreamed of being until I understand more about myself and the world, and right now I don't understand very much at all.

"The people who trusted me for help and answers, all the people who trust their ministers and priests and rabbis, deserve honesty and seriousness and love. It is a truly terrible thing to take advantage of them.

"I know there are manipulators and exploiters in all fields, but I didn't think there were any in Graceville. Well, it seems there were, and I'm told they used the money you sent me, a lot of it anyway, for their own pleasures, instead of helping people. I didn't know it, but that's not an excuse, because I should have known. I knew the people involved in the Hour of Grace Foundation and the production of 'The Hour of Grace' and 'At Home with Reverend Grace' on television. I knew them very well. One of them I thought I loved; I trusted her and admired her. But I didn't look at her, or anything else, very carefully; I didn't demand information. I was naive and inexperienced and foolish; not the kind of person who should be giving advice and comfort.

"In my sermons, I always asked people to look within themselves to find the core of goodness that is there. I always said they could be better than they thought they were, or than others thought they were. But I should have been talking to myself!

"Please forgive me for not being a better person. Please remember that there are many good ministers, and good religious organizations, to help those in need. They shouldn't be swept away in the storm that a few selfish, cynical people have created.

"I think the biggest problem with ministries, especially in television, is that they're good places for bad people to hide. Too many of them tell you they'll make you happy and bring you peace. In other words, they're saying they'll take care of you. That makes you feel dependent, and when people feel dependent and helpless, it's easy for others to take advantage of them.

"You must not feel helpless! Don't let anyone tell you you are! Find the goodness and strength in yourself, build on them, take control of your lives! And if you do need help, find those who help you believe that you can be wise and good and *great*.

"I'm going to say goodbye now. I'll miss all of you: your letters and your love. I'll think of you and pray for you and maybe...maybe someday I'll...be able to come back to you."

On the screen, tears glistened in Lily's eyes, and a small smile was on her lips as her picture disappeared and the anchorman returned. "Reverend Lilith Grace, withdrawing from the ministry earlier today, while the investigation of the Hour of Grace Foundation continues. She'll be questioned by investigators as soon as she's released from the hospital, probably next week."

Lily switched off the television set and her head dropped back on the pillow. "Was I all right?" she asked.

"Yes," Nick said. "You were very moving."

Lily looked at Valerie. "You're so quiet. What was wrong with what I said?"

"Nothing. You said some things that needed to be said."

"But there was something you didn't like," Lily insisted.

"There was something that bothered me a little. You were smoother than I would have expected, more...professional. Especially since I imagine you're really upset by this."

Lily's mouth quivered. "I know. I can't help it. Sybille hired all those coaches and I took all those lessons about when to breathe and when to pause and when to smile and when to lower my voice and how to sound *soulful*...and I got so good at it, it's like I push a button, or Sybille does, and the words come out and I hardly hear them. You're so smart, Valerie, you saw it, do you think everybody did? I want to forget everything Sybille taught me; I want to be just me again... if I can figure out what that is. I want to go to college and catch up on being with people my own age and learn about the world and just think about things. But I don't want people to think I'm a...fake. Was I awful, just now? I wanted people to believe me!"

"They'll believe you because they want to," said Nick. "You were very good, and most people aren't as smart as Valerie. Anyway, it was the words that counted, and we both admired them. I think you shouldn't worry."

"Dad, could I talk to you a minute?" Chad asked. He was near the door, standing on one foot and then the other. When Nick went to him, he lowered his voice. "Do you think Mother saw that?"

"Probably. Didn't you tell me she watches all three network news shows at once?"

"Yeh, but maybe not now."

"Now more than ever, I'd guess. What are you thinking about, my friend?"

"I thought maybe I...well, I felt kind of bad, you know, thinking about her watching Lily say all those things. She's probably alone; she doesn't have any friends, and I thought maybe she'd feel lousy about what Lily said, how she'd loved her once, and trusted her. You know. So I thought, maybe, you know, 'cause she doesn't have anybody..."

"You want to talk to her."

"Well, yeh. I mean, she doesn't have anybody to tell her they'll, you know, just... *be around.*"

Nick held his son close, then ruffled his hair. "You don't mean a telephone call. You want a ride to Middleburg, right?"

"Yeh." Chad looked up at him. "Thanks, Dad."

"You know I won't go in with you."

"No, she'd be mad if you did. Could you just wait for me in the car? I mean, I won't be very long. We never have a whole lot to talk about, you know."

"I know." Nick went to Valerie, sitting in an armchair beside Lily's bed. "Chad wants a ride to Middleburg. It will take at least a couple of hours."

"I'll stay with Lily," Valerie said immediately. "You two go ahead; I'll be here when you get back."

He leaned down and kissed her. "Thank you, my love." And he and Chad left, to drive to Morgen Farms.

All the lights blazed. The house looked festive, each window a bright, welcoming sun, and lanterns illuminating the long driveway. "She's having a party," said Chad uncertainly.

"I don't think so," Nick said. "There aren't any cars."

"But..."

"I think she didn't want to be in the dark."

"Oh."

Nick parked a little distance from the house. "Go ahead, now. And take your time. You don't have to rush."

"Okay." Chad opened the door, but did not move. "Do you think she'll be glad to see me?"

"I don't know," Nick replied. "She may be glad and not know how to show it. She may be ashamed because of what she's done, and it will be hard for her to know that you know all about it. I don't think you should expect her to be more friendly than she's been in the past."

"Yeh. That's kind of what I figured. Okay." Chad propelled himself out of the car before he could think about it anymore, and dashed up the driveway, past the festive lanterns, to the front door. The bell sounded very loud when he rang it.

"Come in," the butler said. "Your mother is in the television room."

"Thanks." Chad ran past him, up the stairs to the room adjoining Sybille's bedroom. Once it had been Valerie's dressing room; now it held four television sets, two oversize leather chairs, and a round coffee table piled with books. A bottle of cognac and a balloon glass were on a small table at Sybille's elbow.

"Hi," said Chad, and stood just inside the door until Sybille turned from the four blaring television sets, each tuned to a different channel.

She frowned. "What are you doing here?"

"I thought you'd like some company. Can I come in?"

"Company," she repeated. "Why?"

"I, uh, I saw ... I was watching ... Can I come *in?*"

She shrugged, and Chad took that as permission. He sat in one of the huge chairs, trying not to slide on the smooth leather all the way into its depths. The butler came in with a tray holding a glass, a variety of soft drinks and a plate of cookies. He set it on the coffee table, near Chad's chair, and left as silently as he had come. Chad slid forward and poured ginger ale into the glass. He took ice from Sybille's ice bucket. He took two cookies. "Thanks," he said.

Sybille was watching the television sets, her eyes sweeping in an arc across them and then back. Chad waited, nervously crunching cookies, trying to pick up the crumbs that fell on his lap. "You were watching what," Sybille said at last. She still looked at the screens, but she touched a button that cut off the sound.

"Lily. On television. I thought you'd feel bad if you saw it, 'cause she said—"

"I know what she said. Why did you come here?"

"I just said. I thought you'd feel bad."

"And what did you think you could do about that?"

"Just..." Chad squirmed. He wished he were somewhere else, anywhere else. He couldn't stand the stiff way his mother held her head, because it looked so unhappy, but he was afraid of it, too, because it also looked fierce and unapproachable. "Just tell you I was here!" he blurted. "I hate it, being alone when something awful happens, and I thought you'd hate it, too, and I didn't, uh, I didn't want you to be lonesome!"

Sybille's mouth worked. "That's very nice."

Love me, Chad begged silently. Please love me, please, just a little bit.

She sat still, looking at the screens. "You're getting to be a big boy. You'll be as tall as your father."

"Yeh. Or taller. He says." His shoulders were slumped. I guess she can't, he thought. Maybe nobody ever taught her to love anybody. Except... I didn't know you had to learn that.

"She lied," Sybille said flatly. "They all lie about me. Remember I told you people did that?" Chad was silent. "Remember?"

"Yeh," he said.

"I took her from nothing. I made her one of the most famous preachers in the country. And I took a small part of the money that came in for Graceville; that was my due. I told her all about it; she said I should do what I wanted, even take more if I needed it, because I deserved it. She knew what she owed me. We understood each other. But somebody kidnapped her and poisoned her with lies. She said she *thought* she loved me! She said it on television!"

"Yeh," said Chad. "Well, I just wanted you to know, you know, that I'm around. I mean, I don't think anybody's poisoned, but if you wanta talk or anything, or have dinner, or whatever, you could call and we could go somewhere. I mean, I could listen if you just feel like talking. 'Cause you're not, uh, like, alone. Whenever you feel like it. You know."

Sybille seemed to be watching an automobile chase on one of the screens. "We never have very much to talk about."

"No. I mean . . . I guess not. But we could, like, learn."

"I'll be in jail," she burst out after a moment. "I've lost everything I've worked for, my whole life, did you know that? I don't know how it happened, it started perfectly, but it just . . . fell apart. And now I'm going to jail. You'll hate me there."

"Could you, uh, could you *look* at me?" Chad asked.

Slowly, Sybille turned her head.

There was a long silence as they looked at each other. In that over-size chair, his mother looked small, Chad thought, as if she'd shrunk. Her hair wasn't as neat as usual, and she was wearing a terrycloth bathrobe. He'd never seen her in a bathrobe; she was always dressed in something with fur or gold buttons or something. She looked lonesome, he thought; with just those tvs to keep her company.

Chad felt a terrible pain. He ached with it, and it took him a minute to realize it was pity. His throat was full of tears; he thought he was going to throw up. He jumped out of his chair and stood beside Sybille. Without planning it, he put his hand on her hair, as if she were a child. "I wouldn't hate you, I couldn't. You're my mother and I'll take care of you. Or, you know, do whatever I can. Like visit you, and call, and send you books and flowers and stuff, and . . . you know, whatever you want. I just . . . I just wish . . ."

She looked at him; she had to look up to do it. She fixed him with her pale-blue eyes, and perhaps she wanted to tell him she loved him and perhaps she didn't. Chad never knew, because even though he never stopped wishing for it, he never heard her say it.

"I'll call you, okay?" he said at last. His voice was choked and sad. "Like, every day, if you want."

"If you want to," Sybille said.

"But, do you *want* me to?"

"Well, why not? You can tell me about the world when I'm in jail."

"Maybe you won't be, though."

She was silent. She could not say the words *attempted murder* to her son.

"Well," Chad said. "I guess I'll go."

She nodded and turned back to the television sets. She had never asked how he got there.

"I'll call you."

"Fine." She paused. "Thank you for coming." She struggled a minute. "I'm glad you did."

Chad beamed. She really was happy to see him. She really needed him. He bent down and kissed Sybille's cheek, twice. "I'll talk to you tomorrow." He grabbed another cookie from the plate, and sprinted from the room and down the stairs. The butler was waiting at the front door, to let him out. As he did, Chad heard the sound of four television sets begin again.

Lily was asleep when they returned. They had stopped along the way to get Chad a hamburger, and when they walked into the hospital room Valerie was reading in her armchair. She looked up and saw Chad's sleepy face. "That was a good thing you did," she said, going to him. "I'm so proud of you."

Chad put his arms around her, nuzzling his face into her neck. "It wasn't fun."

"I'll bet it wasn't. But it's no fun to ignore people in trouble, either. You don't like yourself much if you do." She held him away from her, his face between her hands. "I love you, Chad. I'm awfully glad to know you want me to be part of your family."

"Yeh. I love you, too, Valerie. I love you, I love you, I love you." In a burst of energy, Chad made love seem real again after his confusion with Sybille. It oughta be easy to love, not hard, he thought, but he was too sleepy to pursue it. "Are we staying here?" he asked Nick. "I'd kind of like to go to bed."

"We're leaving this minute," Nick replied. But when they turned to go, they saw that Lily was awake.

"Was it all right?" she asked Chad. "It must have been hard."

"Yeh, but it was okay. I'll tell you about it sometime, if you want."

"I'd like that." Half sitting in the hospital bed, wearing the same blue robe she had worn on television, Lily looked at Valerie and Nick, close together, their arms around each other. "I wish I could marry you. Wouldn't that be wonderful? But I can't, not after what's happened. In a few years, maybe . . . but you don't want to wait that long."

"No," said Nick emphatically. "We've waited fourteen years. Not another day, if I can help it."

"But you could give us your blessing," Valerie said, and looked at Nick.

He smiled at her. "Yes. That would be wonderful. After so many storms, we'd like very much to begin with your prayers."

Lily's face was radiant. She sat up and stretched out her arms. Still holding each other, Valerie and Nick put their hands in hers.

"May the Lord bless you and keep you," said Lily softly. Her voice was steady and confident; the voice of a woman who had begun to find her way.

"May the Lord make his countenance shine upon you . . .

"And give you peace."

MY NEW
AMERICAN
LIFE

Francine Prose

MY NEW AMERICAN LIFE

WILDERNESS BRANCH LIBRARY
6421 FLAT RUN ROAD
LOCUST GROVE, VA 22508

HARPER

An Imprint of HarperCollins*Publishers*
www.harpercollins.com

HarperCollins books may be purchased for educational, business, or sales promotional use. For information, please write: Special Markets Department, HarperCollins Publishers, 10 East 53rd Street, New York, NY 10022.

FIRST EDITION

Designed by Fritz Metsch

Library of Congress Cataloging-in-Publication Data has been applied for.
ISBN: 978-0-06-171376-7
11 12 13 14 15   ov/rrd   10 9 8 7 6 5 4 3 2 1

To Howie

MY NEW
AMERICAN
LIFE

Chapter One

———⦿———

THE DAY after Lula's lawyer called to tell her she was legal, three Albanian guys showed up in a brand-new black Lexus SUV. She had been staring out her window at the drizzly afternoon and thinking that the mulberry tree on Mister Stanley's front lawn had waited to drop its last few leaves until it knew she was watching. Obviously, this was paranoid and also egocentric, but in the journal that her immigration lawyer and her boss had suggested that she keep, she wrote: "October, 2005. Does a leaf fall in New Jersey if no one is there to see?"

Don Settebello and Mister Stanley would go nuts for a line like that. They were always telling Lula she should write a memoir about her old Albanian life and now her new one in the United States. Don even had a title, *My New American Life*. Lula had a better title, *Stranger in a Strange Land*, but she'd already seen it in the public library. Maybe she could still use it. Maybe no one would notice.

Raindrops beaded the SUV as it trawled past the house where Lula lived and worked, taking care of Mister Stanley's son Zeke, a high school senior who only needed minimal caretaking. In fact Zeke could do many things that Lula couldn't, such as drive a car. But since Mister Stanley believed that teenagers shouldn't be left on their own, and since he went off to Wall Street at dawn and didn't return until late, he had hired Lula to make sure that Zeke ate and slept and did his homework. Mister Stanley was very safety-conscious, which Lula found very admirable but also dangerously American. No Albanian father would do that to his son and risk turning him gay.

Lula's duties included making sure there was food in the house. Most afternoons, Zeke drove Lula to the supermarket in his vintage 1970 Oldsmobile. Considering how little they bought and how much of it was frozen, they could have shopped once a month, but they enjoyed the ritual. On the way, Zeke gave Lula driving tips: who went first at an intersection, how to speak the silent language that kept drivers from killing each other like they did constantly in Tirana. Zeke might have been explaining the principles of astrophysics, but Lula appreciated the gesture, just as Zeke liked feeling superior to Lula and better about having a nanny only nine years older than he was. The word *nanny* was never mentioned. Lula explained to Zeke that in her native country only party bigwigs were allowed to own the black deathmobiles that sped through Tirana in packs, and then the economy tanked and no one could afford a car, so now Albanians drove their hot or secondhand Mercedes like kids who'd had their licenses for about five minutes.

As had Zeke, who still wasn't legal to drive at night. But he'd grown up in a car culture, driving was his birthright. Every country had problems, but when Lula saw how Americans drove, how American *children* drove, she couldn't help feeling cheated for not having been born here. Her dad used to borrow her uncle's car, and then he sort of stole it and smuggled it over the border from Albania into Kosovo, where both her parents were killed in a car wreck. Lula had never mentioned this sad fact to Mister Stanley or Zeke. It would only have upset Mister Stanley and made Zeke suspect that his driving lessons might not be enough to put Lula on the road.

Mister Stanley said Zeke could have the gas-guzzling-pig Olds if he hardly ever drove it. If he had to drive at all, his dad preferred him in a tank. Zeke was so in love with the Olds that he kept it in the garage and rode the bus back and forth to school, and Mister Stanley parked his seven-year-old Acura minivan at the end of the driveway. Officially, Zeke was only allowed to drive to The Good Earth Market, which his father liked, because it was close and had organic choices, and which Zeke also liked (it was practically the only thing he and his father agreed on) because he believed in staying small and locally owned and off the corporate grid, though his actual food tastes ran to mesquite-flavored corn chips and microwavable ramen. Zeke didn't notice the other shoppers looking down their rich straight suburban noses at what he and Lula bought. Probably theirs was the only household in which the Albanian girl let the American teen decide. Lula had cooked vegetables, many times, but Zeke refused to eat them. Let his wife worry some day.

After she and Zeke got back from the market, Lula mixed them each a mojito, a splash of alcohol in Zeke's, a healthy splash in her own, heavy on the sugar and mint. Zeke sat on a kitchen stool and watched Lula make dinner. Most nights they ate pizza with frozen crust, tomato sauce from a jar, and mozzarella that, refrigerated, would outlive them both. Sometimes Lula unpeeled tiny ice-dusted hamburgers, which, steamed in the microwave, were surprisingly delicious, surprisingly like a street snack you could buy in Tirana. Bad food made Zeke feel rebellious, which every teenager needed. The better Zeke felt about himself, the more secure Lula's job was, and the likelier her chances of staying in this country, though Mister Stanley and Don Settebello had made it clear that their helping Lula was not about her working for Mister Stanley and being good for Zeke.

And now, hooray, she was legal! Lula inhaled and shuddered, half at the shiny black Lexus still patrolling the block, the other half at her daily life. The life of an elderly person!

Last night, like every weeknight, Lula and Zeke had eaten dinner in front of the TV. Lula made them watch the evening news, educational for them both. The president had come on the air to warn the American people about the threat of bird flu. The word *avian* was hard for him. His forehead stitched each time he said it, and his eyelids fluttered, as if he'd been instructed to think of birds as a memory prompt.

"At home," Lula marveled, "that man is a god."

"You say that every night," Zeke said.

"I'm reminding myself," she'd said. Her country's love affair with America had begun with Woodrow Wilson, and Clinton and Bush had sealed the deal by bombing the Serbs and rescuing the Kosovar Albanians from Milosevic's death squads. Even at home she'd had her doubts about the streets paved with gold, but when she finally got to New York and started working at La Changita, the waitstaff had quickly straightened her out about the so-called land of opportunity. And yet for all the mixed feelings shared by waiters and busboys alike, the strongest emotion everyone felt was the desire to stay here. Well, fine. In Lula's opinion, ambivalence was a sign of maturity.

Yesterday night, as always, she'd felt sorry for the president, so like a dim little boy who'd told a lie that had set off a war, and then he'd let all those innocent people die in New Orleans, and now he was anxiously waiting to see what worse trouble he was about to get into. He seemed especially scared of the vice president, who scared Lula, too, with his cold little eyes not blinking when he lied, like an Eastern Bloc dictator minus the poufy hair.

"There is no bird flu," Lula had told Zeke. "A war in Iraq, Hurricane Katrina, sure. Maybe one chicken in China with a sore throat and a fever."

But by then the city police chief had appeared on the screen to announce that the alert level had been raised to code orange because of a credible terrorist threat against the New York subway system.

Lula said, "There is no threat."

"How do you know everything?" Zeke asked. "Not that I don't agree it's all bullshit."

She'd been about to tell Zeke—again!—about having grown up in the most extreme and crazy Communist society in Europe, ruled for decades by the psycho dictator Enver Hoxha, who died when Lula was a child, but not without leaving his mark. The nation was a monument to him, as were the seventy thousand mushroomlike concrete bunkers he'd had built in a country smaller than New Jersey. But before she even had a chance to repeat herself, she'd been distracted by an advertisement for the new season of *ER*.

"Look, Zeke," she'd said, "see that gurney rushing in and doors flying open and all the nurses throwing themselves on the patient? Other countries, no one rushes. No one even looks at you till you figure out who to pay off."

As a reward for sitting through the news, Zeke got to watch his favorite channel, which showed grainy reruns of a cheap black-and-white 1970s series about a small-town mom and daughter both in love with the same cop who grew fangs and bit girls' necks. Zeke was obsessed with vampires and with the 1970s. He predicted that vampires were going to be huge.

"One problem with vampires," Lula told Zeke, "in my part of the world, harmless people are always being burned at the stake because their neighbors think they are blood-sucking bats." She hated lying to Zeke. But vampire lynchings had happened. She'd just changed one little phrase, *always* instead of *used to*, and put it in the present tense. She never, or hardly ever, used to lie at home, where for decades mass lying had been a way of life, where you agreed that day was night if you thought it might help keep your children safe. She'd almost never lied at all until she'd applied for her U.S. tourist visa. But ever since she got here, she couldn't seem to stop.

Zeke said, "Why would people do evil shit like that?"

"Because they wanted their neighbor's house or husband or wife?"

Zeke said, "That doesn't happen here. Vampires are a metaphor."

"A metaphor for what?" Lula asked.

"For everything," Zeke replied.

After dinner, Lula plastic-wrapped the leftover pizza in case Mister Stanley came home hungry, which he never did. She'd worked for Mister Stanley for almost a year and still had no idea what he did for food and sex. Maybe he was a vampire. Mister Stanley's milky skin was so translucent that, until she tired of it,

Lula liked standing where she could see him backlit so that his bat ears glowed like a pair of night lamps.

NOW AS SHE watched the brand-new SUV prowl the suburban street, she was sure, or almost sure, it had nothing to do with her. For one thing, she didn't know anyone in this snooty town, and no one knew her. Mama dead, Papa dead, may their souls rest in peace, not that she believed in the soul. She hoped they were in a heaven (which she also didn't believe in) that was as little as possible like Albania. But would they have wanted that? When her dad drank, which was constantly, he said he would die for his homeland, and in his own way, he had.

Lula still had a few aunts, uncles, and cousins sprinkled around Albania and Kosovo, but they'd lost touch. An Albanian without a family was a walking contradiction. Of course she hadn't said this to the embassy officer in Tirana who'd approved her tourist visa. She'd brought in pictures of neighbor kids, whom she'd claimed were nephews and nieces she could hardly bear to leave for that last-fling vacation before she came home and married her childhood sweetheart. She said "Christmas wedding" a dozen times so the guy wouldn't suspect she was half Muslim. Dad's mom, her granny, was Christian. Wasn't that enough? Anyway, Muslim meant nothing in Communist post-Communist Albania. An American wouldn't know that. Muslim meant Muslim to him.

She'd said, "I want to see the world, starting with Detroit, where my aunt lives." The officer smiled. How cute! His heart flopped for the Albanian girl so innocent she thought Detroit was the world. One look at Detroit, she'd jump on the first plane home and shrivel into a raisin before she was thirty-five. Lula crossed and uncrossed her legs. On the visa officer's wall was a poster of the Statue of Liberty. Give me your tired, your poor, your huddled masses. Lula had to convince him that she wasn't planning to stay. Everyone lied to the embassy. It didn't count as a lie. Since 9/11 they made you lie, but that hadn't stopped one Albanian girl or boy from wanting to come to New York.

The Lexus turned and passed the house.

Mister Stanley had given Lula a cell phone that he liked her to keep charged, though she never called anyone, and no one had called her, not since her best friend Dunia had left the country and gone home. Mister Stanley had programmed in their home phone number, Mister Stanley's cell and work phones, Zeke's cell phone, and Don Settebello's office. She was the only person on earth with five numbers on her phone!

She was like the girl in the fairy tale. The princess in the tower. One of the made-up "traditional" folk stories she'd written for Mister Stanley and Don Settebello was about a beautiful maiden imprisoned in a castle. A prince sees her at the window, falls in love, and, unable to reach her, transplants a strong, quick-growing vine from his native region. The good news is, he climbs the vine and rescues her; the bad news is that the vine grows and grows and wipes out the local farmers, their punishment for locking up the princess in the first place. Don especially liked that one, which, he said, proved that indigenous folk cultures foresaw the threat of species importation and genetic engineering.

Next fall, Zeke would leave for college, and Lula would have to figure out the next phase of her new American life.

That is, if things went according to plan, though Lula couldn't have said what the plan was, or who'd designed it. She'd saved fifteen hundred dollars, which was reassuring, though hardly the astronomical sum she might have thought before she saw the drink tabs at La Changita. She kept the money in cash in the secret compartment of the old-fashioned desk in her room, the so-called guest room, though Zeke said they'd never had guests. Next September was the cutoff date, her target day for leaving. By then she would have spent almost two years at Mister Stanley's, a fact she tried not to dwell on. She was too young to have her life fall away in chunks like the glaciers crumbling nightly on the Nature Channel.

Deep autumn had already come on when she'd answered Mister Stanley's ad on Craigslist. Dunia was still in the country, their tourist visas were expiring, they were waitressing illegally at La Changita, near Tompkins Square. All evening, Lula and Dunia drank what the loud, young, undertipping Wall Streeters left in the sweating pitchers painted with happy monkeys. After the owners, Rat Face and Goggles, went home, Luis the cook fed the waitstaff his special *ropa vieja*, and everyone got drunk and bet on who'd get deported first.

They knew it wasn't funny. The day after Eduardo the busboy didn't show up for his shift, his wife came into the restaurant, crying. Eduardo had gone to settle a parking ticket, and now he was somewhere (his wife hoped) between New York and Guerrero. Tears bubbled through the curtain of her little son's lashes. Bleeding heart Lula and Dunia had to talk each other out of adopting Eduardo's family and bringing them home to share the tiny Ludlow Street walk-up that wasn't even theirs.

By that point Lula's visa problem was keeping her up at night. She told herself not to worry, the government had plenty of people to deport before they got around to her. Busboys like Eduardo, Arab engineering students, hordes of cabdrivers and cleaners. On the other hand, who would a bored horny INS dude rather have in detention: Eduardo, some Yemeni geezer in a skullcap, or two twenty-six-year-old Albanian girls with shiny hair and good tits?

Lula and Dunia had shared a one-bedroom on the Lower East Side with a Ukrainian girl, an unemployed dental assistant who was never home, and a beanpole from Belarus who wanted to be a runway model and gave them a break on the rent if they pretended not to hear her puking in the bathroom. Lula said they had to do something about their immigration status, but Dunia said if they did nothing, something good would happen. Dunia's mother was a Christian Scientist, a rarity in Albania, and sometimes Lula heard the mother's soft prayerful voice under the daughter's raucous smoker's croak. Lula believed in watching out, in contingency plans, common sense. Dunia had often told Lula that she should try being a half-full-glass person instead of half-empty-glass person. In Lula's opinion, she and Dunia traded off, half-emptiness and half-fullness, but you couldn't argue with Dunia, so she'd let it go.

When Lula showed Dunia Mister Stanley's Craigslist ad, "Divorced man looking for companion for teenage son, Baywater, New Jersey, ten miles from downtown Manhattan," Dunia said ten miles if you swam. Dunia also said that a Slovakian girl she knew answered an ad like that, and it was an escort service. Genius Dunia was back in Tirana now. Or so Lula hoped. Not long after Lula moved to New Jersey, Dunia phoned, yelling above the La Changita racket, babbling in Albanian (which they'd mostly stopped speaking by then) that two men in black suits had come looking for her at the restaurant, and she was going home before they deported her. Since then, Lula's e-mails had bounced back, and no one answered when she called Dunia's mom in Berat. She'd looked on Facebook and MySpace, but Dunia wasn't there. She tried not to think about the things that could have happened to her friend. What if the men in black suits were worse than INS agents? Lula didn't know how to look for Dunia, short of going back to Albania and hiring a detective.

Lula and Mister Stanley had arranged to meet for the first time in the Financial district, for coffee. Even in the Starbucks gloom it was clear that Mister Stanley wasn't looking for a girlfriend or even occasional sex but, like his listing said, for a responsible person to watch his kid. From a distance, Lula had tagged him as a depressed mid-level accountant, but up close he turned out to be a depressed something higher up, which meant he could pay Lula very well for doing almost nothing. At the interview, Mister Stanley explained that his wife had left—abandoned— him and Zeke and traveled to the Norwegian fjords because she wanted to start over, somewhere clean and white.

"Ginger," he said. "My wife." His voice had the pinched, slightly nasal timbre of a chronic sinus sufferer.

"That's a scream," Lula had said. It was funny, a woman named Ginger, like being named Salt, and funny that a woman would want something whiter than Mister Stanley.

Then Mister Stanley had told her that just before Ginger left, she'd developed—she'd *begun* to develop—some serious mental-health issues. He'd tilted his head toward Lula to see if she knew what he meant, if what he was saying translated into whatever Lula spoke. Lula knew, and she didn't know. She'd found his unspoken doubts about her comprehension, like so many things in this country, at once thoughtful and insulting. An illness, Mister Stanley had said, for which no one had managed to find an effective medication, or even a diagnosis.

Christmas Eve, said Mister Stanley, would be a year since his wife's departure. They'd managed, him and Zeke. But he worried about his son, alone for so many hours. Then he'd asked what Lula *was*. Meaning, from what country. He said he wouldn't have thought Albanian. He seemed to find it amusing.

Lula said, "I grew up in Albania. But my parents were visiting my dad's cousin in Kosovo, and they got stuck there when the war broke out and the Serbs came and tried to murder everyone. They couldn't get home to Tirana. They were killed in the NATO bombing." The smile dribbled off Mister Stanley's face. It was the perfect moment to mention that her visa was running out. Mister Stanley said he had a childhood friend, Don Settebello, a famous immigration lawyer. There'd been a profile of him in the *New York Times*. Don was a miracle worker.

A few days after the interview, Mister Stanley drove Lula out to meet Zeke and see his brick battleship of a house with wavy leaded-glass windows and a curved porch bulging from one side, like a goiter. A gnarled tree in the front yard had purpled the sidewalk with berries. She hadn't thought there were houses like that so near the city, nor fat crows that sat in the mulberry tree and warned her not to take the job.

"Mind your own business," she told the crows.

"Excuse me?" said Mister Stanley.

"Albanian superstition," a lying voice explained through Lula's mouth.

Zeke's hair was as black as the crows, but duller, and a thick octagonal silver bolt emptied a space in one earlobe. Zeke's excessive smile was a mocking imitation of someone forced to communicate pleasure or harmlessness or just simple politeness. Zeke shook her hand, his long body slumped in an S curve, checking her out even as he acted too annoyed to see her. Veto power was all he had. It was easier if he liked her. And Lula was hardly the wicked-witch prison guard he'd imagined his father hiring.

Mister Stanley had left the two of them in the living room.

"What do you do now?" Zeke said.

"I'm a waitress. In the Mojito District. So is Zeke your real name?"

"Why do you ask?" Sunk in the couch across the room, Zeke peered at her from beneath his inky slick of hair.

"Because it sounds like someone frightened. *Zeek ʒeek ʒeek.* Or like a little bird."

"It's my name. How did you learn English?"

"In school. In Albania."

"You speak perfect English. You sound like a British person."

"Thank you. Our teacher was British. Plus I took private tutoring from an Australian." No need to tell this innocent kid she'd paid for those lessons with blow jobs. "The next generation younger than me, they all learned English from Sponge-Bob SquarePants."

"SpongeBob is gay," said Zeke.

Lula said, "So what?"

"Ezekiel," said Zeke. "Like in the Bible."

Lula said, "I never read the Bible. I grew up atheist. Half Muslim, half Christian." Normally, she never mentioned the Muslim part, so already she must have felt that Zeke could be trusted not to think she was plotting to wage jihad on McDonald's.

Zeke said, "There's an Iranian kid in my class. He kept getting his ass kicked in public school, so they put him in my school where everybody's super tolerant. His dad's a famous eye surgeon. They live in a mega-mansion."

"Albania is the most tolerant society in the world," said Lula.

"Good for it," said Zeke. He turned on the TV, and together they watched a hard-looking Spanish girl make out with male and female contestants, deciding which she liked better. Lula sensed she was being tested, not on her response to the show, but on her response to Zeke watching the show. What was her reaction? Boredom passed the test.

Zeke heard his father in the hall and switched off the TV. "What restaurant did you say you worked at?"

"La Changita," Lula said. "The little monkey."

Zeke asked if she could make mojitos.

She'd said, "We'd need fresh mint."

Mister Stanley appeared in the doorway. "I see we've found plenty to talk about."

Mister Stanley often said "we" or "one" when he meant "you" or "I." Sometimes Zeke imitated him, but only under his breath, so his father could pretend not to hear Zeke say, "One would one might one should," in Mister Stanley's voice. At first Lula wondered if this usage was correct, if there was something wrong with *her* English. None of the younger Wall Street guys talked like that. The mystery of Mister Stanley's career was solved when Zeke explained that his father used to be a professor of economics until he let himself get recruited by a bank, which he seriously regretted, even though he made lots more money than he had as a teacher.

Maybe nobody else applied for Lula's job. Maybe no one wanted to live with the sad-sack father and son. Maybe Mister Stanley thought Lula was a war refugee, which strictly speaking was true, and that he was doing a good deed, which strictly speaking was true. Lula wouldn't have hired herself to take care of a kid. She would have asked more questions, though Mister Stanley asked quite a few. It was unlike him not to require notarized letters of reference. But she had turned out to be good with Zeke, so maybe Mister Stanley had sensed some maternal feeling burbling up inside her, or the decency that Lula prided herself on maintaining despite her many character flaws and the world's efforts to harden her heart.

Lula was twenty-six. Old, she thought on dark days. Only twenty-six, on bright ones. She had time, but she had more time if she stayed in this country. She wanted to learn that American trick, staying young till forty. Some American girls even got better looking. Not like Eastern Europeans, who started off ahead but fell off a cliff and scrambled back up a grandma. Maybe the pressure to marry aged them before their time. But there was no pressure on Lula. If her ancestors wanted grandchildren, they were keeping quiet about it.

To make everything official, Mister Stanley had taken her into his so-called library, the dank, mildew-smelling, manly lair where he hardly ever went except to pay bills. The shelves were empty but for a few rows of dusty books that Mister Stanley must have used in his university courses. He said, " 'Come into my parlor,' said the spider to the fly. I suppose we should talk about terms."

Over Mister Stanley's desk was a framed antique print of an exploding volcano. Lula had watched its sparks fly as Mister Stanley spelled out the rules. Be there when Zeke got home from school. No drinking or smoking in the house. No driving in bad weather. In fact no driving anywhere except to The Good Earth. Make Zeke eat an occasional vegetable. No overnight guests, except relatives, with Mister Stanley's approval. Always lock up when she left. Mister Stanley used to subscribe to a burglar alarm service, but he'd had it discontinued when it turned out that the service was robbing houses.

When she'd asked Mister Stanley to pay her in cash, he assured her banks were safe. She'd said she was sorry, but Albanians had such bad history with banks . . . her voice trailed off into the economic catastrophe and massive social unrest that came after Communism, like those last scenes in the horror films when the maniac pops from the grave. "You've heard about our pyramid scheme? Offering investors fifty percent. What was anyone thinking? The government was in on it, too, everybody got wiped out."

Mister Stanley had nodded tiredly. He said, "Of course I remember. Scary stuff. It could happen anywhere. Sure, we can do this in cash." Probably it was wiser, seeing as how Lula didn't yet have a work visa, though Don Settebello would fix that. Mister Stanley said, "If I ever get tapped for a government job, you'll have to deny you know me."

"Sure," said Lula. "We never met."

"Joke," said Mister Stanley.

Lula knew that some Americans cheered every time INS agents raided factories and shoved dark little chicken-packagers into the backs of trucks. She'd seen the guys on Fox News calling for every immigrant except German supermodels and Japanese baseball players to be deported, no questions asked. But others, like Mister Stanley and Don Settebello, acted as if coming from somewhere else was like having a handicap or surviving cancer. It meant you were brave and resilient. And being able to help you made them feel better about themselves and their melting-pot country. Their motives were pure, or mostly pure. They liked power and being connected, they liked knowing which strings to pull.

Now Lula would be able to stay. Everyone would be happy. The Balkans had no expression for "win-win situation." In the Balkans they said, No problem, and the translation was, You're fucked.

WATCHING THE BLACK Lexus SUV turn and crawl down the block, Lula wondered if Zeke was in trouble. In her opinion, he was just a semi-depressed American teen, but American TV survived on the blood spilled by semi-depressed teens. As the shooters' neighbors always said, Zeke was a good boy. Quiet. But that unlikely piece of bad news would arrive in a police car.

Her next thought was immigration. Then she thought, with joy and relief, Since yesterday I'm legal! Then she remembered, Big deal. This was Dick Cheney America. Native-born citizens worried. It was just a matter of time before someone on Fox News got the bright idea of sending back the Pilgrims who'd landed on Plymouth Rock.

Lula's lawyer, Don Settebello, had grown up in the same apartment building as Mister Stanley. The first time Lula went to Don's office, she gave a long impassioned speech, all true, about how she loved this country and how badly she wanted to stay here. Don held up his hand. Time was not money but something more precious than money. Time was time. All his clients told him how much they loved it here. He could make it happen. And he had. He'd called in favors, done the impossible. Lula had a visa. Heroes could do that, said Mister Stanley, who several times said he worried that Don would push too hard and ruin his career, or worse.

Probably everywhere was the same. You paid and paid, and when you stopped paying, the favors stopped. Also this was New Jersey, the Mafia's home state. Lula watched *The Sopranos* with Zeke and Mister Stanley. Maybe the black SUV had come because Mister Stanley or Don quit paying a few months early.

The SUV reached the end of the block and pulled into a driveway. Lula watched it turn again and head back down the street. She wished she weren't alone in the house. Why was she so edgy? Could it be the residue of her Communist early childhood? Blame her delicate nervous system on growing up under a system that thought the Soviet Union was too liberal and was best friends with China until the dictator decided that China was too liberal, and China cut them loose. Blame it on the neighbor woman in Tirana who got sent away because her son rotated the roof antenna so he could hear a chesty Italian girl sing his favorite song. The reception was too fuzzy to see, but the audio was enough to get his mom dragged off in broad daylight. It was one of Lula's first memories. Everyone was afraid. Her dad was taken away for one night. But the next day, he came home.

Even though Lula's immigration status was secure for now, she felt her future depended on the web of lies she had started spinning the first time she'd met Mister Stanley. It was Mister Stanley's fault for asking her a question he could have answered, though she knew it was something any prospective employer might wonder.

"Why did you leave Albania?"

She'd gazed into her Frappuccino. "Listen. Mister Stanley, you have to understand."

"Call me Stanley."

Of course. Stanley. Mister Stanley had to understand that in the part of Albania where Lula grew up, blood feuds still raged for generations. Revenges. Bride kidnappings. Their idea of courtship was still the fireman-carry and rape. Her Cousin George was involved in one such case. The couple holed up in a cave and the girl's relatives blocked the mouth of the cave with stones, and the lovers suffocated. Lula thought it was smart to emigrate while she was several rungs down the hit list.

"Dear God," said Mister Stanley.

So it really was his fault, falling for such a story. Hadn't he been a professor? Shouldn't he have known better? She did have a Cousin George. But the story happened in the time of her great-great-grandfather, when the family slept in the same room with their donkey on a mountaintop in Shkodër. Her actual Cousin George had one of the bigger Mercedes dealerships in Tirana, and when she imagined him holed up in a cave, she saw him yelling about bad cell phone reception and blaming his wife, who looked like a fatter, older Donatella Versace. Besides, no one considered a woman or child worth the bullets and ill will. A woman's blood was worth less than a man's. Now the blood feuds were all about real estate. Very unromantic.

Mister Stanley should go to Albania if he wondered why she'd left. Who would choose Tirana over a city where half-naked fashion models and their stockbroker boyfriends drank mojitos from pitchers decorated with dancing monkeys? The land of opportunity. Hadn't Mister Stanley heard? But America was like Communism and post-Communism combined. You weren't supposed to be materialistic until you got successful, after which it was practically your duty to flaunt it in every-one's face.

The lie about the blood feud had been a mistake. Mister Stanley asked if those vendettas ever carried over here. Lula said her clan was superstitious about crossing water. Anyway, her family hadn't lived in that part of Albania for generations. Her great-grandparents, rest in peace, had left the north for the capital, where she'd studied English at the university. When her parents got caught in Kosovo, she'd stayed behind at school in Tirana. After they died in the war, she'd graduated from university and lived with her aunt and uncle and taken more English lessons until she'd figured out what to do next.

Mister Stanley complimented her English. He'd said, "That story about the cave . . . you should write it down."

Lula said, "That's what I should do when your son is at school."

Maybe that was part of the reason she was hired. Mister Stanley got a babysitter and his own private art colony for the same low price. The Lorenzo de Medici of Baywater, New Jersey.

Mister Stanley was all business, working and doing his job. He slept through most of Saturdays, which Zeke spent with his friends, girls and boys, all with dyed black hair and facial hardware. Neither Mister Stanley nor Zeke was big on family life, but Lula felt it was only friendly to offer to cook them Sunday breakfast. Mister Stanley said, Thank you, that would be nice, but no bacon, egg whites only. Cheerios or oatmeal. His bad cholesterol numbers were high.

No one talked at these Sunday meals. Zeke's chair was not even a dining room chair but an armchair pushed to the table, so Zeke could nod off, or pretend to. It was awkward, eating egg-white omelets with silent Mister Stanley and his snoozing son. It was as if there were two Zekes: the agreeable boy he was with Lula, and the furious troll he became around his father. Lula told Zeke he should be nicer to his dad, and Zeke agreed, but he couldn't. It would have meant going against his culture.

Sometimes Mister Stanley got annoyed at his son. But his impatience or disappointment or hurt (it was hard to tell) expressed itself as sadness rather than anger. By Albanian standards and even, Lula suspected, by American ones, Mister Stanley had a narrow emotional range. Nothing in Lula's past had prepared her for his baby-bottle lukewarmness. Especially when they'd been drinking, her father and her uncle believed that pointless yelling was not just the prerogative but the proof of maleness. Because they did so much shouting, no one paid attention, so the end result wasn't so different from the end result of Mister Stanley's composure.

At home, family parties always ended in fights, but never once was there anything like a family gathering at Mister Stanley's. Wasn't there an Albanian-style widowed aunt or grandma who could have moved in with the dad and son and kept house? Mister Stanley had neither parents nor siblings, and on those rare occasions when Ginger's parents phoned from Indiana to speak to their grandson, Zeke instructed Lula to tell them he was out.

On Sunday afternoons, father and son did father-son things—baseball, tennis, the park—inspired, Lula sensed, by their need to prove something to the disappeared mom: how well they were doing without her. Mister Stanley had a boyish love for buying sports equipment, and he was at his most cheerful (not very) when he and Zeke left to try out a new racket or catcher's mitt. Each time they returned, Zeke had sustained some minor injury that required a bandage or ice pack, which his father seemed to enjoy providing. The happiest moment of the week arrived on Sunday nights when Lula and Zeke and Mister Stanley watched Tony Soprano and his even more messed-up family drive their gigantic vehicles through neighborhoods flatteringly near Baywater.

Mister Stanley had mentioned his Sunday outings with Zeke at Lula's job interview. Meaning he wasn't adopting Lula, she shouldn't expect to be invited. That was fine, Lula said. That was when she mentioned that she didn't drive. Mister Stanley had said *that* was fine, but she might feel trapped in the suburbs, and she'd said, No, that was fine, she was a big reader, it was how she'd learned English, and Mister Stanley said that was excellent. Zeke wasn't much of a reader, maybe it would rub off. The sweet little public library was within walking distance.

Lula worried she would be expected to have books around the house. She was reassured when Mister Stanley didn't ask what she liked to read.

Lula had told Mister Stanley she wanted structure. Well, structure was what she'd got. Walls, a roof. A front yard. Be careful what you ask for.

Sometimes on weekends Lula went into the city. The happy shopping couples, the giggly groups of girlfriends, could see how lonely she was. Sometimes she thought they were laughing at her. Stranger in a strange land. She was always happy to get back to New Jersey.

Another problem with lying was how often lies came true. Now, for example, since the public library was one of the few places she could walk to, she had become a reader. She'd looked up Albania and spent hours reading the novels of Ismail Kadare, her country's greatest novelist, who until now she'd only pretended to have read. Trying to imagine the words back into Albanian was good for her English. Not having gotten one piece of mail—let alone a utility bill—at Mister Stanley's, she couldn't apply for a library card. But now that she had her work visa, maybe she'd try again.

She had also started writing, another lie come true. Zeke let her borrow his laptop when he was at school. He made her promise not to look at his files. Touched by his trust, Lula never mentioned the beautiful girls who kept popping up, asking Zeke to get back in touch. Who knew if they even looked like that, or how old they thought Zeke was? Lula e-shopped for luxury items—garden furniture, scented candles, motorboats—she would never buy, priced itineraries to places she would never travel.

Eventually, Lula buckled down and wrote a story in English, with the help of a dictionary and a thesaurus she found in Zeke's room. In the flyleaf was an inscription. "To Zeke, Happy Birthday from Mom, may words give you wings!" What heartless witch gives a teenage boy a thesaurus for his birthday?

Trying not to think too hard, Lula wrote a story about the blood feud in her great-great-grandfather's time. She pretended that her Cousin George was the bridegroom's brother and added a long poetic passage about the bride walled in, stone by stone. There was also a lot about muskets, information that came easily, her dad having been a gun nut, and finally lots of folkloric stuff, curses and proverbs she found on Albanian online forums. She put in everything but the sound track of Albanian folk songs.

Mister Stanley liked her story so much that it became part of the package they gave Don Settebello, who now listed writer among her skills, along with translation and childhood education. Independently, or maybe not so independently, Mister Stanley and Don suggested she write a book. Lula couldn't imagine why a country would want a citizen from a long line of blood feuders. So to tip the scales in her favor, she wrote a sad story about the day she heard that her parents had been killed in the NATO bombing.

"I'm so sorry," Mister Stanley said.

"I'm okay," Lula assured him.

It was true, they'd died in the war. So what if they hadn't really got stuck in Kosovo when the war broke out, but had sneaked across the border when it was almost over? Thousands of refugees had been fleeing from Kosovo into Albania, from the Serbs and from NATO. Only her crazy father had stolen his brother's car and, fueled by drink and misguided patriotism, driven himself and her mother in the wrong direction. His Kosovar brothers needed him! Her dad had gotten it into his head that the Kosovo Liberation Army could use his collection of tribal muskets. So what if it wasn't the NATO bombing that got them, but an auto crash, and her dad was driving drunk? They'd hit a NATO tank. Lula's private opinion was that he'd been on a suicide mission. The six years since her parents died sometimes seemed like an eye-blink and sometimes like forever. Some days Lula could hardly remember them, some days she couldn't stop seeing their faces. She still cried whenever she thought about her dad's funny porkpie hat, a style increasingly popular with hipster boys in Brooklyn.

"You should write a memoir," Mister Stanley had said, that first conversation.

"Maybe short stories," said Lula.

"I don't know," said Mister Stanley. "Don says nonfiction sells better. A memoir of immigrant life. Coming from the most backward Communist country and moving here—"

"Not the most backward," said Lula. "You're forgetting the stans. Turkmenistan. Uzbekistan."

"Sorry," said Mister Stanley. "That was thoughtless."

"Don't mention it," said Lula.

BY THE TIME the Lexus had passed the house four times, Lula had progressed from being sure it had nothing to do with her to thinking it was no wonder that the car had come to punish her for lying.

The Lexus stopped. Three guys got out and ambled toward

Mister Stanley's. No double-checking the address. They acted like they lived here. All three wore black jeans streaked with white dust. Maybe they were in construction. Had Mister Stanley hired someone to fix the house and not told her?

One of the men wore a red hoodie appliquéd with the black double-headed Albanian eagle. Not exactly regulation INS business wear. So it made sense, of a kind. How many Albanians were there in the metropolitan area? The odds were against this being a random home invasion. Which wasn't to say that her fellow countrymen wouldn't rape and kill her for fun. But the odds were also against their doing that to an Albanian girl they didn't personally know.

Had Mister Stanley called Albanians to work on his house? Surely he would have said. Lula sometimes watched a TV show that warned you about the latest dangers—phone scams, dust mites, black mold, carjackings. But the series was in rerun, so you couldn't tell if the threat was current. Not long ago she'd seen a segment about a gang that went door-to-door and offered to fix your roof, and if you refused your house burned down.

The three guys were like a comedy act. Two of them looked like twins. Same body type, black cop shades, overly gelled spiked hair. Stocky, big hips, fat asses. She'd gone to high school with guys like that. Maybe she even knew them. The one without the hoodie wore a long black leather coat.

The third was taller, red-haired, and fell in behind the other two. Cool, both hands in his pockets. Cute. He glanced up at the window and saw her. He had a mustache and longish hair. He reminded her of a boyfriend with whom she'd sniffed glue when she was young and crazy and going to raves in the bunker fields. Now that the Cute One had seen her, pride wouldn't let her lock herself in the bathroom and pretend not to hear the doorbell.

The third time they rang, she opened the door but kept the chain on. She looked at them hard, each in turn. Strangers. She would have remembered.

"*Miremengyes*," they said. Good morning.

"*Miremengyes*," said Lula.

"Lula," the Cute One said. "Little Sister."

How had these guys found her? How did they know her name? Maybe they knew Dunia. Had she sent Dunia her new address? Oh, Dunia, Dunia, where was she? Best not to think of that now.

"Whassup?" said Leather Jacket. On the street they might speak Albanian, their secret code, but on this American doorstep, they showed off for each other in the street slang of their new country.

"Remind me how we're related," Lula said.

"All Albanians are related," said Hoodie. "Brothers and sisters." His eagle sweatshirt was half unzipped. Around his neck, on a silver chain, hung a double-headed silver eagle.

The Cute One gestured at the SUV. "We're good friends and customers of your Cousin George." Then he curled his lips in a way that transformed his pretty mouth into Cousin George's fat liver lips. Lula laughed, partly because it was funny and partly because it was nice to meet someone who could imitate her cousin.

"Brothers and sisters," said Hoodie.

"Okay," said Lula. "Got it."

Leather Jacket said, "Congratulations. Congratulations on your work visa."

"How do you know about that? My cousin doesn't know yet."

The Cute One's smile uncovered a gold tooth. "Don't worry how we know. My girlfriend works in immigration."

Lula said, "I have a great lawyer. My boss—" The quick sharp looks the men exchanged made Lula sorry she'd boasted. Her Balkan survival instinct had been blunted by the spongy atmosphere at good-guy Mister Stanley's.

Lula undid the door chain. Please don't let them steal Mister Stanley's television and Zeke's computer. But who would want Mister Stanley's ancient Motorola, or Zeke's student laptop? Maybe that would make Mister Stanley finally buy a flat screen, which would make Zeke happier than the therapist he'd seen weekly when she'd first got here and then decided to stop seeing, a change that inspired Mister Stanley to give Lula a little raise. There would be no more little raises if Mister Stanley found she'd invited these guys into his house. And maybe no green card, no citizenship. Disaster. On the other hand, they were Albanian. They called her "Little Sister" and knew her Cousin George. The Cute One was cute. And nothing else remotely this interesting was going to happen today.

The men brushed past her, then turned and, one by one, shook her hand. Two of the handshakes were ceremonial. The Cute One's was a caress. How long had it been since anyone touched her, not counting the restaurant customers grabbing her ass? She could always tell which guy it would be, and after how many mojitos. The last time she'd had sex was with a waiter, Franco, who took her to his loft in Long Island City, which he shared with three roommates. He'd showed her the sculptures he made from mattress springs he'd found on the street. She'd said they looked like space aliens, apparently the right answer, and then he told her he called it his Bedbug Launching Pad series, very nice considering that they were about to get in his bed. Mostly she remembered her surprise that a guy that drunk could get it up at all. She'd drunk quite a bit herself, or she wouldn't have been there.

"I thought you guys were brothers," said Lula. "Up close not so much." The same way of muscling into space was the main resemblance.

"You think I look like this guy?" said Hoodie. "Are you kidding me, or what?"

"Brothers with different mothers and fathers. Blood brothers." Leather Jacket slashed a finger across his upturned palm. "No joke."

Hoodie said, "Every Albanian is related by DNA."

"So we're family," Lula said flatly. Then she waited to find out what her three long-lost brothers wanted.

The Cute One hung back, scanning the living room as if searching for a place to hide something or a place where something was hidden. Only when Lula looked through his eyes did she see what a dump it was. Heaven, compared to Albania. All the creature comforts. Still, it was sad to have come this far and to have wound up here.

She could have made the house more pleasant, or at least less musty and smelly, but Lula wasn't the type to redecorate someone else's space. Everything from Ginger Time remained as Ginger left it—the puffy grandmother furniture, the piano no one played. Lula had developed a wary and disapproving relationship with Ginger, based on her examination and appraisal (negative) of Ginger's stuff, and on what little she'd heard (more negative) from Mister Stanley and Zeke. One bleak morning, Lula had gone through Ginger's dresser, holding the baggy cargo pants and roomy dashikis up against her body. The stretched-out granny underwear explained a lot, though not the question of why Ginger had been the one to leave. How could a woman—a mother—walk out on two helpless babies like Zeke and Mister Stanley? Mental health issues. What did that mean? Mister Stanley hadn't said.

The Cute One looked around and sniffed. What was he comparing it to, his sumptuous walk-up in downtown Bayonne? Or maybe some shack in Durrës? Why should Lula feel protective of Mister Stanley's home?

"What's that smell?" said Leather Jacket.

"The grave, I think," Hoodie said.

"It's my boss's house," said Lula. "My job is watching his kid."

"We know that," said the Cute One.

Lula hoped he wouldn't go over to the fireplace. She hoped he wouldn't look at the family photos. If she couldn't change the lamps or move the end tables, what were the chances of her saying, Mister Stanley, Zeke, are you sure you want to keep a mantelpiece full of mementos of your life with a lunatic who left you for a glacier?

The family had traveled a lot. Many of the snapshots were posed against natural wonders, mountain peaks and canyons. Their smiles were frozen, and they always looked cold, even in the desert. Apparently, they weren't the type to ask strangers to snap their photos, which showed Mister Stanley and Ginger,

Zeke and Ginger, but never Zeke and Mister Stanley. Ginger seemed not to take pictures, but the travel was her idea. Lula couldn't imagine Mister Stanley and Zeke going anywhere on their own.

The Cute One held a picture toward her. From across the room, Lula saw Ginger and Mister Stanley posed against rocks at a beach. For the first time she noticed that their arms were around each other's shoulders.

"My boss, Mister Stanley," Lula said.

"Tarzan!" The Cute One curled his lip.

"And her?" the Cute One asked.

"Ginger. His wife. His former wife."

"Ginger the person? Ginger the cookie!"

He handed the picture to Leather Jacket, who said, "Ginger the Spice Girl. Hah!"

In a soft voice, Hoodie started chanting Albanian names and their English translations. "Bora snow, Era wind, Fatmir lucky. Beautiful Albanian names, ugly words in English." He took a deep breath and resumed, rapping himself into a trance. "Jehona echo, Lula flower—"

"Shut the fuck up, you fucking idiot," said Leather Jacket.

"Guys," the Cute One said warningly.

Hoodie emerged from his name-trance like a child waking up cranky. He said, "So you and the boss . . . ?" He joined his left thumb and forefinger and poked his right index finger through. The Cute One shot him a look.

Leather Jacket said, "Sister, disregard this ignorant donkey bent over one too many times for the Greeks."

The Cute One said, "Okay, guys. Cut it out. I'm Alvo."

"Pleased to meet you, Alvo," said Lula.

"This is Guri," said Alvo, pointing at Hoodie. "And Genti." He indicated Leather Jacket. "Better known as the G-Men."

Lula said, "So . . . what do you guys do?"

"Listen to her," said Hoodie. "Already asking her brothers the rude American question."

"Contracting," Alvo said.

"And you're here because . . . ?"

Their expressions were like conversations reaching back to her childhood. She said, "Would you like some coffee?" If there was ever a moment to be Albanian, this was it. A shift in the pitch of their shoulders told her she'd done the right thing.

Hoodie—that is, Guri—and Leather Jacket Genti rearranged the furniture so the comfortable chair, Zeke's chair, was at the head of the table. Alvo sat in the soft chair, the others on either side. They reached into their pockets and pulled out cigarettes.

She said, "Please don't smoke. My boss—" Zeke wasn't supposed to smoke or drink. Tobacco was disgusting. Lula's father's machine-gun cough still interrupted her dreams, less so after her hair stopped smelling of smoke, as it had when she'd worked at La Changita. She didn't think Zeke's super-weak mojitos counted as drinking. Lula bought the rum with her salary, not with the food allowance Mister Stanley gave her.

"Please," she repeated. "If I get fired . . . what then?"

Hoodie said, "One cigarette each. Trust me. No one will know."

Lula plunked down a soup bowl for them to use as an ashtray and stomped off to the kitchen. She ground a lot of coffee. Mister Stanley wasn't picky about much, but he did like his whole Starbucks beans. This was not a job for the timid electric coffeepot. She boiled the coffee in a pan. She had to wash off a coating of grime, but Ginger's Zen tea set would do nicely. Lula decanted the tarry sludge into delicate Japanese cups.

She brought four cups on a tray. The men thanked her. She sat in her Sunday breakfast seat, next to Leather Jacket and across from Hoodie. Leather Jacket took a bottle of clear liquor from his pocket and splashed some into the men's cups. When he looked at Lula, she nodded. The alcohol burned deliciously. Spiked coffee at ten in the morning!

"Delicious," Lula said.

"Raki," said Leather Jacket. "From my grandfather's mulberry trees in Gjirokastra."

"*G'zoor*," they said. Enjoy. Good health. Long life. They drained their cups.

If Lula had hoped for a rush, she was unpleasantly surprised when the caffeine and alcohol melted her into a puddle of self-pity. How pathetic her life must be if she was ecstatic because three Albanians had home-invaded Mister Stanley's and dosed her coffee with lighter fluid.

"Thank you," Alvo repeated. "Little Sister, the reason we're here is we need to ask you a teensy favor."

Lula braced herself. *Teensy favor* could mean fly to Dubai and back, coach both ways, with a dozen condoms full of heroin up her ass.

"We need you to hold on to something for us. It's nothing." As Alvo leaned toward her, his handsome smile emphasized that it was nothing.

Lula pictured columns of shrink-wrapped white bricks

stacked in Mister Stanley's garage. Good-bye sweet library walks, good-bye innocent cocktail hours with Zeke. From now on, she would constantly be looking out the window.

Lula said, "You don't even know me—"

"My point exactly," said Alvo. "There is no Reese's Pieces trail for ET to follow from us to you. Except for your Cousin George and my aunt in the immigration office."

His aunt? Five minutes ago it was his girlfriend. But who was Lula to judge someone for not keeping his story straight? Better an aunt than a girlfriend. She was pleased to hear it.

"Hold on to what?" she said.

"A gun," said Alvo. "A little gun."

Lula sighed. She should have known. Maybe the white dust on their jeans was an illegal substance. Who drove SUVs like that except coke dealers and pimps? Contractors so rich and successful they had to go around armed?

Lula said, "What kind of little gun? I know about little guns. Also bigger guns."

"Seriously?" said Guri. "No insult, you're a girl."

"Seriously." Lula ignored the girl remark. At twenty-six, she liked it.

"My dad was a gun nut," she said, then decided to leave it at that. For weeks they lived on polenta, but Papa got his semi-automatic. She knew each gun's uses. Assassin guns, hunting guns, snake guns. Her father was a pussycat, but he could get reckless when he drank. Then her mother would lock up his guns, and they would yell about that. They'd wrestle over the car keys, and sometimes—this had turned out to be the fatal part—sometimes her father won.

He used to borrow her uncle's car and, not having a son,

take Lula for target practice in a garbage dump or picnic spot, depending how hard you looked. This was after Communism, when you could get Italian movie magazines, from which he'd tear photos of Madonna and nail them onto a plank and teach Lula to aim for the heart. He had nothing against Madonna, he just had a strange sense of humor. He'd probably thought it was funny to aim his car at the NATO tank and stomp on the gas. He'd lost all their money and their house in the pyramid scheme and sneaked over the border to sell guns, as if all the Kosovo Liberation Army needed was a middle-aged guy hawking tribal muskets and broken Nazi pistols. Lula had grown close to her Aunt Mirela, with whom her family lived before, and with whom she moved in again after university. When Aunt Mirela died of a kidney ailment that could have been cured somewhere else, Lula spent her tiny inheritance on a ticket to New York.

Alvo said, "Small enough for a shoe box. Easy."

"Easy," Lula said. "Famous last words."

Leather Jacket said, "Easy is one word."

"Shut up, asshole," said Hoodie.

"Easy," Alvo repeated.

She wished she knew what the gun had done and why they needed to hide it. Why couldn't they just throw it down a storm drain? But why waste a good gun when they could find an Albanian girl to sit on it like a hen until it hatched baby guns? The Americans had laws for everything having to do with guns. Her father would hate it here. He would have been one of those who said all the wrong people had guns. If someone found the gun, Lula could get deported, visa or no visa.

She said, "I'm hiding your gun because——?"

Alvo rose out of his chair.

"What good would it do for you to know? Would it be better for you? Or me? The less you know about us, the better."

"Suppose I need to get in touch with you?"

"You won't," said Leather Jacket. "We'll be in touch."

"Okay," Lula said. "I'll keep it. But I don't know how long I'll be living in this house."

"No offense," said Alvo. "But I don't get the feeling you're going anywhere soon." He twitched one shoulder at Leather Jacket, who produced a brown paper lunch bag and set it on the table. They all stared at the bag. Alvo nodded, and Hoodie took out an evil-looking snub-nosed revolver. Then they all stared at the gun. For Lula, it was as if her father's spirit had entered the room and given his ghostly approval to her new American life.

"When will you come get it?" Lula said and promptly burst into tears.

The men couldn't have looked more shocked if she'd picked up the gun and shot herself. Lula hadn't planned on crying, no more than she'd planned on not being able to stop. Maybe it was the eagle on Hoodie's shirt, or the taste of raki, or some magnetic force that dragged her back to her granny's house, when Granny was alive, telling that story about the woman who went around collecting women's tears and selling them in vials, the ultimate high-end cosmetics, until a neighbor denounced her and she was about to be sent away, but a party official's wife asked for a sample, and the dealer in tears was pardoned in return for a steady supply. Most likely the gun made her cry.

All this time Lula was sobbing. How she missed her mother and father, and especially her grandmother! She would never see her again. There was no one here who knew these stories, who knew Lula or her granny. Lula cried for her granny and her parents and her childhood, for her home, all lost, for Communism, good riddance, for the lawlessness, the riots, the violence, the problems grinding on. For her once-beautiful homeland now in the hands of toxic dumpers and sex traffickers and money launderers. She cried for missing her country, for not missing it, for having nothing to miss. She cried for the loneliness and uncertainty of her life among strangers who could still change their minds and make her go home.

She blinked. The three guys were staring at her, as if through a rainy windshield.

"Get over it!" Guri yelled. Lula stopped crying, instantly cured, as if from a case of the hiccups.

"We'll come check on you," Alvo said.

Squeegeeing her tears with her hand, Lula couldn't help asking, "When?"

"Don't worry," said Leather Jacket. "You'll see us when you see us."

Chapter Two

———— ∞∞∞ ————

Lula watched her three new brothers ease themselves, like fragile cargo, into the SUV. Leather Jacket in the driver's seat, Hoodie beside him. Alvo in back.

"See you soon," she bleated.

The house swam into focus. In two hours Zeke would be home, and the site of a tough-guy sit-down would have to be restored to the suburban haven where a responsible dad was raising his son in the wreckage of his marriage.

Lula took the gun upstairs. She paused in her bathroom door-way. One advantage of living here was having her own bath-room. How quickly she'd switched from making do with a filthy communal apartment-block latrine to needing her middle-class personal space. She was glad not to have to use the same toilet as Mister Stanley, nor to have to wait while Zeke did whatever he did, locked in for an hour every morning. Lula liked being able to keep her bathroom clean and modestly stocked with the beauty products she'd bought in the East Village with Dunia, and which she grudgingly replenished after hoarding every precious squirt of shampoo.

She thought of that scene in *The Godfather*: the gun taped inside the toilet tank. No need for such contortions to hide something at

Mister Stanley's. Her impulse was to put it in the same drawer with her money. But not even sensible Lula was that unsuperstitious. "Don't keep your gun with your money" was probably, or should be, an Albanian saying.

Finally she slipped the gun in her underwear drawer. In a normal house with normal men, that would have been the last place. But neither Mister Stanley nor Zeke would look there. It was very American, following the rules of privacy and respect designed to help men and women have happy, healthy relationships. At home, there were different rules: You pretended to be fascinated by everything your boyfriend said until you got the ring, and he pretended to listen to you until you agreed to have sex. After marriage, you could go back to ignoring or putting up with each other and leading separate lives. For now, it was exciting to keep Alvo's gun in her underwear drawer. Almost as if it were Alvo.

Given the state of her underwear, she was glad the gun *wasn't* Alvo. Mostly she wore cheap synthetics from outdoor bins on Fourteenth Street, except for one fancy bra and silk panties, lavender laced with dark pink ribbon. The bra alone had cost her a week of tips at La Changita. She'd read in a magazine that one of the top ten secrets of successful women was wearing expensive underwear under their business suits. I wear it for myself, explained one female CEO. It's my secret message from myself to myself. Lula bought the costly underwear, but had never worn it or gotten the secret message, which might have been: Who do you think you're kidding? She hadn't bought the underwear for corporate success, but for the future boyfriend. Buy it, and the boyfriend will appear. But the boyfriend had never appeared. Maybe it would work magic if she wrapped the Cute One's gun in her good lingerie. It was nice to have a reason to wish she believed in magic.

Downstairs, Lula dragged the dining room chairs back to their usual places. But furniture wasn't the problem. How could three little cigarettes have left so much of themselves behind? Hoodie and Leather Jacket smoked black cigarettes that reminded her of her grandpa, who'd grown his own tobacco. Alvo smoked Camels. The basement furnace wheezed and complained as Lula pumped the front door until the chilly house smelled like the Tirana train station in the dead of winter.

At four, when Zeke got home from school, Lula was in the kitchen.

"You're cooking?" he said. "What's with that?"

Lula watched the bubbles of steam leave ragged craters in the thick red paste. Every fall, her granny used to simmer bushels of red peppers down to a sort of ketchup from which she made delicious sandwiches with cream cheese. It was destiny that, on Lula's walk home from the library yesterday, she'd spotted a box of red peppers outside the corner grocery that ordinarily never sold anything fresh, except a few shriveled lemons and cucumbers halfway to being pickles. Maybe Granny, wherever she was, had sent Lula the peppers with their witchy power to trump tobacco.

Zeke said, "How come it smells like cigarettes in here?"

Lula said, "Gas, not smoke. Matches. I had to light the burners. The pilot light went out."

"Did you start smoking? I wouldn't blame you for needing something to cut the boredom."

The boredom? If Zeke only knew! She'd spent her day with guys whom Zeke would pay money to meet. She said, "You

think I'm crazy enough to start smoking when cigarettes are fifteen dollars a pack?"

"Seven dollars. Oops. Was that a trick question?"

"Please don't smoke," said Lula.

"I don't," Zeke said. "One cigarette a week."

"That's too much."

"Okay. One cigarette a month." Zeke picked up the newspaper. "Awesome old lady."

This morning, Lula had walked into the kitchen to find the
newspaper left open to a feature story about Albanian sworn
virgins dressing and living like men to support their widowed
mothers. The pretext for the article was that the custom was
dying out, but really it was an excuse to run a photo of a butch
Albanian lady in cowboy drag, her knees apart and a rifle slung
across her lap.

Lula said. "Every time the paper has something on Albania,
your dad leaves it out for me to read."

"Do you think my dad has a crush on you?"

"No," Lula said. "I think he misses your mom."

Zeke said, "I don't know. Mom calls every so often and asks
for money, and he sends a fat check wherever she is. So he must
still care or feel guilty. Or something. Did you know any old
ladies who dressed up like that?"

"No," said Lula. "But I had this great-aunt . . . once someone
stole some of our firewood, and she shot the guy."

"Did she kill him?"

"No. But she popped the guy in his kneecap from ten meters
away." The firewood had been a good touch. So had the shattered kneecap. If Zeke asked if her story was true, she'd confess
she made it up.

Zeke said, "How long is a meter?"

"Look it up. You're a senior. Don't you study math?"

Zeke said, "Do you think you got her DNA?"

"She never married. Nobody got her DNA."

"Don't you know anything about DNA? You could both have Genghis Khan's DNA. Didn't you study science?"

Was it Hoodie or Leather Jacket who'd said all Albanians had the same DNA? Would sex with Alvo be incest?

"What's the matter?" Zeke said.

"Why?" Lula said.

"You looked weird for a minute."

Lula said, "It's hostile to tell people they look weird. Or tired. This waitress at La Changita was always telling people they looked tired and ruining their whole evening. Every time she said it, they had to run look in the mirror."

"Does weird always have to mean bad? Couldn't someone look weird good?"

Lula said, "Do you want a sandwich? Red pepper paste and cream cheese."

"No thanks," said Zeke. "I don't eat anything the color of blood."

"Pizza is the color of blood. Ketchup is the color of blood."

"They're the color of tomatoes."

"What kind of vampire are you?" Lula said. "Okay, I'm making pizza."

Stewed peppers and microwaved tomato sauce canceled out three cigarettes. All the same, Lula kept sniffing the air. When Mister Stanley got home, his nostrils didn't so much as flutter. Lula leaned against the counter while Mister Stanley sipped a glass of cold water into which he had squeezed the juice of a lemon he cut into wedges and kept, plastic-wrapped, in the fridge. Lula liked Mister Stanley, who was kindhearted and decent, who only wanted the best for his son, and who always treated Lula with perfect consideration. So the fact that she was sometimes revolted by the sight of him drinking his nightly glass of water filled her with guilt, and also with anger at herself that spilled over onto Mister Stanley, like the droplets that sometimes dripped down his chin.

"How was work?" asked Lula.

"Uneventful," said Mister Stanley. "Another day of wishing I'd never quit teaching."

"You could go back," said Lula.

Mister Stanley said. "My life is very expensive, as my wife was quick to point out before she made it more expensive. One only hopes she's getting the help she needs, though she never seems to stay in one place long enough to . . . Well, on a brighter note, how's Zeke?"

"Fine."

"Homework?"

"Done."

"Did you read that article?" Mister Stanley said. "About those Albanian women dressing like men? Imagine wanting to—or being forced to—live like that."

"People do what they have to." It was the kind of gloomy statement Lula counted on to silence Mister Stanley when she was tired of talking. But why was she feeling sullen? She'd had an interesting day! She briefly considered mentioning the sworn virgin in Shkodër who was a Party official responsible for the deaths of many innocent people. But it was a long ugly story she didn't feel like telling. She said, "My granny was a ball buster. Except that she got married and had kids and wore a dress."

A smile wobbled on Mister Stanley's face. "Where did you learn an expression like . . . *ball buster?*"

Lula knew some English expressions that Mister Stanley probably didn't. It was touching that he'd found it hard to say. But how could he work on Wall Street and be so clean? She'd learned the phrase at La Changita, from young guys who were probably angling for Mister Stanley's job. You learn a word the first time you're told not to *be* that word, implying you already are.

"I don't remember," said Lula.

Mister Stanley said, "You were saying about your grand-mother?"

"She loved pro wrestling. She made my grandpa get an ille-gal TV antenna so she could watch the matches from Bavaria. He could have gotten sent away for that." That part at least was true.

"Write it down," said Mister Stanley. "Another terrific story. I'll pass it along to Don. Speaking of which, I almost forgot the most important thing. You and I and Zeke are having dinner with Don on Saturday night to celebrate your work visa com-ing through."

Lula said, "Don't you think that's bad luck? Can I get you a snack? I made this delicious red pepper paste my granny used to cook."

"No thanks," said Mister Stanley. "I'd love to, but red pep-pers give me heartburn. What's bad luck?"

"Celebrating," said Lula. "Celebrating anything."

Mister Stanley said, "Lula, when you apply for citizenship

and you go for your interview, do me a favor. Don't say you think it's bad luck to go out to a pricey restaurant in Manhattan and raise a glass to a positive change in your immigration status. And have someone else pick up the tab. It's deeply un-American."

Lula said, "Sorry. I know. I'm grateful. I can't believe that you and Mr. Settebello would do this. I mean, in addition to—"

"Please," said Mister Stanley. "We're happy for you. In fact, what about a little bonus in case you want to buy something to wear to the dinner? Only if you want to . . . only if . . . I wouldn't—"

"Thank you," Lula said. "That's so nice of you. I'll go into the city this week."

"Be careful," said Mister Stanley. "Watch out."

Had Mister Stanley gotten a secret tip from Don? Was there some kind of crime wave? Had the code level been kicked up to red in honor of Halloween? Lula and Zeke had watched the terror threat level rise before each holiday, as if suicide bombers thought that blowing themselves up on Presidents Day would put them on the fast track to the Garden of the Martyrs. Lula often told Zeke how governments loved keeping people scared, how Enver Hoxha had built all those bunkers for people to defend themselves against an attack by . . . whom, exactly? The Greeks? The Serbs? The United States? No one ever said. It didn't matter. All that mattered was fear. The bunkers had turned out to be indestructible, just as the dictator promised, which meant that seventy thousand cement cow pies remained, plopped along the roadsides and on people's lawns.

Lula had been in Tirana on 9/11, which she'd watched on blurry TV with tears streaming down her face. She and Dunia had wept again as they stood on the platform above Ground Zero. Dunia said that at home the hole in the city floor would already have become a picnic site. Picnic site, toxic dump site. Shit happens, Dunia said. Lula and Dunia used to compete in acquiring American slang.

At the site Dunia had tried to pick up a good-looking cop, but it stopped being fun when he told them that leaving his shift early would dishonor the memory of the dead. When Lula asked Mister Stanley where he was on 9/11, he'd said, "Well, as you know, I work downtown. At first one talked about it a lot, but then I stopped, and I find I no longer want to."

"Be careful of what?" Lula asked now.

"I don't know," said Mister Stanley. "Just be careful is all."

EVEN THOUGH NEITHER Mister Stanley nor Zeke suspected that the three Albanians had paid Lula a visit, she was glad when, the next morning, Estrelia came to clean.

Lula had been relieved at the beginning when Mister Stanley said cleaning wasn't part of her job. Estrelia had been with them forever; she came every Tuesday. Don Settebello had been very helpful to Estrelia and her husband and son.

Butterball Estrelia radiated sweetness but hadn't learned much English, probably because she spent her days in empty houses. Had she talked to Ginger? Lula had no language in which to ask. She liked Estrelia but preferred to be out of the house while she worked. It was awkward, standing around, watching Estrelia shake her head at the stacks of newspapers and magazines Mister Stanley didn't have time to read, the papers and books Zeke lost track of, the wadded up T-shirts and single sneakers kicked into corners. Estrelia neatened the stacks and herded the shirts and shoes, glancing guiltily at Lula, whose shrug meant, I don't blame you.

Estrelia's vacuum purred, and Estrelia purred along with it. Let the crime scene detectives come now! Any skin flaked off Hoodie's ankle was just more dust to Estrelia.

After a brief conversation about Estrelia's son Sebastian (fine) and her husband (also fine, *gracias*), Lula and Estrelia played a translation game, exchanging basic vocabulary in English, Spanish, and Albanian. Estrelia knew all the furniture words, and they had moved on to colors. Estrelia picked up a cushion and pantomimed what green it was—trees no, birds no, river yes, dive in the river. Lula said Nile green, then in Albanian, river green, and Estrelia said something *verde*. Then on to the crocheted blanket, but there were no words in any language for the shades of acrylic in this item of hand-made Ginger decor.

Estrelia was finishing up in the dining area, and Lula was about to go to her room, because it was even more awkward loitering outside the bathroom and comparing the Spanish, Albanian, and English words for toilet brush. But just then, Estrelia poked the vacuum hose into the chair in which Alvo had sat yesterday. The vacuum coughed, and Estrelia extracted a scrap of paper she handed to Lula.

Lula smoothed it out on the table. In faint purple type was the address of a supermarket in Manhattan. One quart orange juice, 2.59. Cigarettes, 7.95. Unless Mister Stanley had started smoking (impossible) or Zeke had gone into Manhattan to buy cigarettes (unlikely) or the receipt had been here since Ginger Time (Estrelia was way more thorough than that), the only logical conclusion was that it had fallen from Alvo's pocket.

"Oh, thanks, it's mine," Lula said. What would she do with a sales receipt? Treasure it as a memento? Use it to stalk Alvo to his neighborhood market? "Thank you. I lost this. I need it. Taxes." Taxes? She put the receipt in her pocket, and motioned for Estrelia to follow her into the kitchen.

Estrelia froze. Did she think some subtle status shift had raised Lula from coworker to boss, no longer a friendly young person but a harsh taskmaster about to point out some neglected duty? Lula cradled Estrelia's elbow with a pressure meant to seem affectionate but which probably felt like the grip of a cop collaring a suspect.

Estrelia sat at the kitchen table while Lula made her a sandwich of red pepper paste and cream cheese on a sesame roll.

She said, "Zeke and Mister Stanley won't taste it. There's only so much I can eat." Estrelia nibbled at the bread and, nodding vigorously, smiled. Then she furrowed her penciled-on brows in a friendly question directed at the sandwich.

Lula would have liked to tell Estrelia about her granny. She would have liked to ask if Estrelia had a granny, if she was alive or dead. Lula didn't even know the Spanish word for granny. She pointed at the sandwich, then hunched over, pretended to walk with a cane, and rocked an invisible baby.

Estrelia got it, or got something.

"*Sabroso*," Estrelia said.

EVERY TIME LULA went into Manhattan, she could hear Dunia saying, "Ten miles if you swam." On dry land, you had to take the George Washington Bridge, the tunnel, or the train. The least miserable route involved two small buses and then a big bus that took you to midtown, from where you could take the subway to anywhere you might actually want to go. Lula would be lucky if she could find something pretty to wear and get back in time for Zeke's return from school. Zeke could take care of himself and would never tell his father if she wasn't there when he arrived. In fact he'd probably like a break from Albanian watchdog Lula. But being present so that Zeke wouldn't walk into an empty house had been one of the few promises that Mister Stanley had extracted from her, and Lula was determined to keep it.

New York had been fun with Dunia, shopping for items they couldn't afford, egging each other on to ask the price of luxury items they wanted and were scared to touch. Of course they'd gone shopping in Tirana, at street markets when they were teenagers and then at the boutiques that had started springing up in Blloku, the understocked, overpriced shops, still smelling of fresh paint, that Mafia guys were opening so their bored childless mistresses could buy stolen designer shoes from each other. New York had confirmed what Lula and Dunia had long suspected, that the nicest store in Tirana was a sandbox in the nursery school of real-world consumer culture. At first Lula had felt almost angry at the gorgeous variety and obscene profusion of stuff for sale. But being with Dunia had alchemized her anger into humor. Together, they were twice as strong and could pretend to be superior to all that unattainable splendor. They'd been each other's armor, protective gear against the serenity of the American girls letting strangers paint their faces, against the trancelike calm of the women pawing through swaying garments.

Oh, Dunia, Dunia, where was she? Every week the TV ran a

story about sex-trafficked girls, and though Lula was certain, or pretty certain, that Dunia was too smart to let herself get caught up in anything like that, Albania was Albania. Anything could happen. People fell down potholes in the sidewalk and were never heard from again.

Today, Lula missed Dunia with a particular pang as she performed the humbling yoga of trying on a sweater and skirt in the communal dressing room of the store whose designer bargains were legend even in Tirana. Like the women around her, Lula faked indifference to the range of female bodies in the mirrors. At home no one thought about weight so much. Poverty and fear kept you thin, though strangely, in this country, they had the opposite effect.

But no matter how hard Lula tried not to notice, she couldn't help surreptitiously watching the girl beside her stuff a blouse into her backpack while, as a distraction, her friend argued with the woman guarding the dressing-room door. Would the clerk get fired when someone found out the blouse was stolen? Probably not. She shrugged when another customer gave her a handful of antitheft devices she'd found in a jacket pocket. Lula could probably steal the sweater and skirt and keep Mister Stanley's money. But she'd just gotten her visa. How embarrassing to get deported for shoplifting an outfit to wear to a party to celebrate being legal.

Lula studied her reflection. She still looked okay in the street-bin underwear, a miracle considering her sedentary life, the nightly mojitos, the frozen burgers and prepackaged pizza. Granny would die all over again if she knew how Lula ate. She shifted from hip to hip, appraising the short black pleated skirt, the white V-necked sweater, schoolgirlish, cheerleaderish, just sexy enough to turn heads without going all-the-way slutty. Lula also decided on a deep Goth-purple sweater. Maybe Zeke would imagine she'd dressed in funeral colors for him, while Don and Mister Stanley would think her look was exotic Albanian.

The skirt and sweaters came to a hundred and thirty dollars, which left her with change and a pleasant feeling of sensibly saving for the future, plumping up the safety cushion in the secret compartment of the desk that, Zeke said, had belonged to Ginger's mother. The swing of the shopping bag on her arm filled her with optimism. Not only did she have new clothes, she had a future in which to wear them.

She knew how to live in New York, how to take the subway to the first of the buses that would take her home to New Jersey. One Sunday morning, she and Dunia had drunk a bottle of wine and memorized the subway map. The web of colored lines materialized before her eyes, like the chart of the veins and arteries on the poster of the skinless body that Zeke had tacked to his bedroom wall.

Every seat on the train was taken. Lula's heart ached for the souls damned to ride both ways, mashed together in rush hour. At least she had been spared that. Thank you, Mister Stanley.

Finally someone got up from one of the two-seaters at the end of the car. A little kid made a run for it, but Lula stopped him with a look. A woman whose skin seemed to have been baked from some rich flaky pastry shut her book, sighed theatrically, and slid over to make room for Lula, then sighed again and went back to reading *Daily Affirmations for Women Who Do Too Much*.

Across the aisle was a young Hispanic couple, a skinny

hypervigilant guy in jeans and a light sweater pushed up to reveal a muscular arm bulging with Maori tattoos. His heavily made-up transvestite girlfriend had nodded off on his shoulder, so the ends of her long glossy curls swung against his chest. You only had to look at them to know they were in love. It wasn't what they planned or wanted, but love was love, what could they do? Lula knew she shouldn't stare, but she couldn't help it. No one could, including the woman beside Lula, who glanced up from her book and shifted in her seat, sighing her critique of the sinner perverts doomed to burn forever in hell. Lula stared at her neighbor until the woman had to look back. Her eyelashes curled like a moth's antennae. What did she see in Lula's face that made her own face clench so tight?

Lula said, "We're all God's children, don't you think?"

Why had she said that? She didn't believe in God or Jesus or Allah or Buddha. Some new American language was erupting through her, the same language that had her cradling and rocking her arms as she tried to tell Estrelia about Granny's red pepper paste.

The woman regarded Lula coolly, then almost smiled, then decided not to. She said, "Maybe you're right. Jesus wouldn't have made them unless He had His reasons." With which she returned to her book.

The boyfriend gazed at Lula over the head of his sleeping beloved, and a flicker passed between them, almost as if he'd heard her above the roaring train. Maybe this was Lula's new role in her new American life, opening blocked channels of communication, bringing these strangers a gift from a country where tolerance was the best result of everyone forced to be the same.

Who cared if the three Albanian guys never showed up again? Here she was, in New York! How much friendlier the city looked when she had money and a mission. What she'd just witnessed would never happen at home. For one thing, there were no subways. For another, no Puerto Ricans. Or cross-dressers, for that matter, except for one club in Tirana where they still changed in the back room. No doubt about it, there was more freedom here. You just had to watch your back and not shoot off your mouth or do anything stupid that would get you locked up or kicked out.

How appealing her fellow passengers looked in those ingenious vessels—their bodies!—so brilliantly designed to contain all their hopes and fears, their dreams and experiences, bodies designed to change as their souls were changed by every minute on earth. She wanted to stay in this city with them, she wanted to have what they had. She wanted it all, the green card, the citizenship, the vote. The income taxes! The Constitutional rights. The two cars in the garage. The garage. The driver's license. The good sense to appreciate what Don and Mister Stanley were doing to help Lula belong to this crowded, overwhelmed, endlessly welcoming city, where sooner or later, like on the subway, someone would scoot over and make room.

Chapter Three

A_T THE_ very last minute, dressing for Don Settebello's dinner, Lula vetoed the knee socks that would have nudged her outfit over the line from college girl to role-playing escort-service college girl. She took the filmy black scarf she'd gotten last Christmas from Zeke, draped it around her neck, and tied it in a sort of noose, accentuating her pallor and giving her look a subtle vampire edge that Mister Stanley and Don might appreciate, if only on a subliminal level. Zeke would like it a lot.

Lula dreaded coming downstairs and finding Mister Stanley and Zeke waiting for her and feeling obliged to say how nice she looked. So she was preemptively ready, on the couch with her coat on, when Mister Stanley appeared in a suit and, twenty agonizing minutes later, Zeke clomped downstairs in a black shirt, black jeans, and a black bomber jacket.

Lula said, "You look good, Zeke."

"Doesn't he?" Mister Stanley said wistfully.

Zeke held his phony smile for so long that no one could mistake it for the real thing. Then he said, "Awesome! Lula's finally wearing the scarf!"

"Your Christmas present from Zeke," said Mister Stanley. "I remember! How sweet!"

The dead tree Mister Stanley lugged home last Christmas Eve bumped across Lula's visual field. By Christmas morning it had dropped its needles on the scarf, an envelope containing a hundred-dollar bill from Mister Stanley to Lula, an iPhone for Zeke, and two Banana Republic shirts Zeke would never wear. Lula had given Zeke the *Coumadin Rat Bleed-Out Live* CD he wanted, and for Mister Stanley, she wrapped up the stubby ceramic pitcher she'd tossed into her suitcase in Tirana. When she left, she would ask for it back. Zeke gave his father a card promising to be nicer in the coming year, a promise he broke (silently, for Lula's benefit) even as Mister Stanley read the card aloud to Lula.

All Christmas Day, Mister Stanley kept saying how nontraditional it was to have holiday dinner at Applebee's and catch a movie at the mall. They'd watched gladiator blood spurt across a giant screen and waited for the day to end. No one mentioned that it was the anniversary of Ginger's departure. When they got home the answering machine was blinking. "Merry Christmas, honey, it's Mom. Love from Ubud. Bali. I think. I meant to send you a present, but the post office was so . . . and these—" The machine buzzed, and Ginger's voice sank beneath the ocean between them. Mister Stanley had said, "Mom sounds better, don't you think?" and Zeke ran up to his room.

Now Zeke said, "I knew that scarf would look awesome. Let's go. We're late. Don will be waiting."

"That's my line," said Mister Stanley. But Zeke was already out the door.

In the months that Lula had lived here, the three of them had been in the car together so rarely that their seating arrangement hadn't been worked out.

Zeke said, "It's your party, Lula," and dove into the back seat.

Mister Stanley pulled onto the street, headed toward the highway, and merged into the onrushing traffic. How unlikely, that every driver should choose to observe the rules of the road over suicide and murder. Lights parted to let them through. Why should driving seem harder than escaping from a coffin underwater? Everybody drove. Everybody was born and ate and slept and had sex and died. And drove. It wasn't Lula's fault that she couldn't. Where she came from, driving was more of an extreme sport than an everyday method of transportation.

Eventually her father had aimed his brother's ancient Zastava at the armored personnel carrier, and that was the end of that. A cousin of a cousin had arranged to have her parents' bodies shipped back to Tirana along with the corpses of Albanian boys who'd gone to fight with the KLA. Lula and her uncle and aunt waited at the airport, together with the families of the dead freedom fighters. Lula knew better than to ask to see what remained of her parents. The image she wanted to remember was her father's stubborn potato face when Aunt Mirela yelled at him for heading into a war zone for no good reason. A very good reason, her father had said. I'm helping where help is needed. It was lucky that Aunt Mirela and Uncle Adnan didn't blame Lula when her father stole their car for her parents' final trip across the border to Kosovo.

The lunar glare of security lights in an office park strobed past, shocking Lula out of her melancholy reverie just in time to note the tipsy invitation of a tilting neon martini. Twice, they passed a black Lexus, and Lula turned around so sharply that Mister Stanley asked what was wrong.

"Lexuses are cool," said Zeke. "The company should make hearses."

If Lula had been alone with Zeke, she would have told him to knock on wood and shut up about hearses.

Mister Stanley said, "Zeke, these wet dead leaves are almost as bad as black ice. Not almost. As bad. Be careful."

Zeke made a snoring sound.

Mister Stanley said, "Your mom called. She telephoned me at work."

The fake snoring stopped.

This was when Mister Stanley informed Zeke that his mother had called? On the way to Lula's party? But really, it made sense. He didn't want to be alone with his son, or even looking at him, when he told him.

"So . . . what did she say?"

"She said she's doing better. She sounded less upset, or anyway, less angry."

Zeke said, "What's *she* got to be angry about?"

"I wish I knew, son," said Mister Stanley.

After a silence, Zeke asked, "Where is she?"

"Sedona, Arizona."

"What's there?"

"Red rocks. Indian spirits."

Zeke said, "Mom's kind of town."

"She said she wants to see you. She wants you to come visit." Mister Stanley tried and failed to keep the worry and begging out of his voice.

"That's not going to happen," Zeke said.

"Right on," said Mister Stanley. "I like your thinking on this. So okay, let's forget it, for now. This is Lula's night. Poor Ginger! I wish there were some way we could help. But she doesn't want our help."

"Let's have fun!" said Lula weakly.

"Definitely," said Mister Stanley.

The fleet of hired cars double-parked in front of the restaurant promised that the wine would be good. The wine and the steak. There were places like this in Tirana, where Party bigwigs went and later gangsters. Guns in every armpit. A guy in a tuxedo and a black bow tie sprinted toward the car. Mister Stanley shrank back, and the parking valet had to pry the keys loose from his fist.

"Dad," said Zeke. "Take it easy, okay? Valet parking is awesome."

Inside, a group of beauties flitted like moths around the glowing lectern that held the reservation book, a shimmering tableau shattered by the arrival of Mister Stanley's party. One girl split off from the rest to guide them toward Don Settebello, who had risen from a banquette and was waving as if to beloved passengers sailing into port.

Crossing the restaurant, Lula turned a few heads and was glad, for Don and Mister Stanley's sake. They deserved to have dinner with someone who made other men momentarily forget what they were saying.

Don gathered Mister Stanley and Zeke in one exuberant hug. In his office, Don greeted Lula with a formal handshake, but tonight he stood on his toes to kiss her cheek. This was a celebration! Don's round bald head and belly reminded Lula of a bowling pin for giants. Don had many qualities—intelligence, kindness, generosity, power—that women found attractive. Lula wished she were one of those women, instead of the kind who was drawn to the sort of guy who asked you to keep a gun for him and didn't let you ask why.

Peering around Don, Lula saw a child's head on a platter. Don's daughter had rested her head on her plate to express how depleted she was by the boredom of watching her stupid father welcome his stupid friends.

"Hi, Abigail," said Zeke.

Abigail thrust out her tiny pink tongue and licked the empty plate.

"Abigail!" said Don Settebello. "Be polite, please!"

"Nice to see you," Abigail droned.

Don and Mister Stanley dropped back as Lula and Zeke approached the table. Lula heard her lawyer tell her boss, "Betsy must think I'm stupid enough to believe that people get last-minute opera tickets on Saturday night. She loves to wait until it's too late to get a babysitter so I can't go out and commit all the chauvinist-pig misdemeanors she thinks I've been waiting to do all week. Heinous macho crimes against the female gender, which I obviously can't perpetrate if I have Abigail with me."

"At least Betsy calls you," said Mister Stanley. "Unlike Ginger." Hadn't he just said in the car that Ginger had phoned? Lula sensed competition over whose estranged wife was more exasperating. Mister Stanley admired Don, but they'd grown up like brothers, and there was an edge of brotherly rivalry, an odd note that crept into Mister Stanley's voice when he worried out loud about Don pushing his luck in choosing to fight Washington with every case he took on. It wasn't clear, exactly, what he feared might happen to Don, though several times he'd mentioned how shocking it was to think that his friend might be made to suffer for having a conscience and speaking out.

"How shall we arrange ourselves?" Don asked. Abigail wasn't budging from the center of the banquette. Zeke slid in beside her, Don sat on her other side, Mister Stanley beside him. Lula was exiled to the end, celebrating her party from the far edge of the children's section. Even though they liked Lula, the men would rather talk to each other.

"Of course you win," Don told Mister Stanley. "Ginger has always taken the cake." Lula couldn't ask what Don meant by "the cake" with Zeke and Abigail listening.

Lula had promised herself not to drink much, no matter how good the wine was. The watery mojitos had probably lowered her tolerance to the point at which she might say something that made no sense, or more sense than she wanted. But the seating arrangement was making her ill-tempered and reckless. Put her at the children's table, and she'd be the baddest child. When the waiter appeared with the wine, Lula beamed up at him and mimed upending the bottle into her glass. Unamused, he filled it to the precise level he'd learned in red-wine training. La Changita had a rum sommelier, a conga player whose English was so bad he could fake knowing one rum from another.

"To Lula and her new American life!" said Don, and all except Abigail raised their glasses.

"To peace in our time," said Mister Stanley.

"Amen!" said Don. "To bringing the troops home from Iraq!"

"That's not going to happen," said Lula.

"To our little Albanian pessimist," said Mister Stanley.

"Realist," muttered Zeke.

"*G'ʒoor*," said Lula.

"*G'ʒoor*," said Mister Stanley and Don.

"To whatever," toasted Zeke. He was bringing his water glass to his lips when Lula grabbed his arm.

"It's bad luck to toast with water!"

"What am I supposed to do now?" asked Zeke, horrified by the attention.

Lula pinked Zeke's water with a few drops of wine, ignoring Mister Stanley's dirty look. Two drops. Why couldn't he be charmed, as always, by her quaint Old World customs, instead of worried that he was paying her to turn his son into an alcoholic? Then Mister Stanley remembered—European!—and relaxed back in his seat.

"I already took a sip of water," said Zeke. "Does that count?" Zeke stared into his water glass as if he was watching bad luck rise from it like a genie.

"One sip doesn't count," said Lula, wishing it were true.

Lula's first mouthful of wine tasted like drinking velvet or pipe smoke or liquefied brocade. A cascade of flavors brightened the future enough that, if she didn't feel happy yet, she could imagine feeling happy before the night was over. To speed along the process, she drained her glass and signaled the waiter to refill it. Only a few times in her life had she drunk wine this good, always when a table at La Changita ordered from the top of the list and then got so blasted they left half the bottle, which Lula hid so that she and Dunia and Luis and Franco could finish the two-hundred-dollar Amarone.

"Jesus," said Don Settebello. "Speaking of bad luck. One of my clients, Salvadoran guy, he's just got his green card, the guy was a journalist back home and now he's got a job with CNN, he's on his way to sign his contract, crossing Broadway and Fifty-first, a taxi jumps the curb, the driver's first day on the job, the fucking stupid moron—excuse me, kids—runs over my client's foot."

"Nightmare!" said Mister Stanley. "That's why defensive driving is so critical, Zeke. The streets are swarming with nut jobs."

"Wait. It gets worse," said Don. "The guy's foot is smashed, they operate on him for hours, chewing-gum and duct-tape everything together, good as new, or practically. They're writing him a scrip for physical therapy when somebody notices he has no health insurance, and they deport him because no facility will take him."

"Deport him deport him?" said Mister Stanley.

"From the country," said Don.

"Can they do that?" asked Lula.

Don shrugged. "My dear, we all know goddamn well they can do anything they goddamn want."

"So where is he now?" asked Mister Stanley.

"Juarez, for all I know. They dump the poor bastards over the border. All my e-mails keep bouncing back, which is never a good sign."

Lula felt as if her wine had been replaced with some icy acidic punch. Instantly sober, she said, "I have this friend—"

"Health insurance," said Mister Stanley. "Who would bother working otherwise?"

"You would, Stan," Don said. "And you know why? Because you're the only guy in America still waiting for Wall Street to keep its promise. How long has it been now?"

"Twelve years," Mister Stanley said glumly.

"How time flies!" said Don. "Bill Clinton's first year in office, Good Guy Stan lets himself be lured down from his ivory tower by these headhunters—don't you love that expression?—who claim they're about to start a new program, a socially conscious Grameen-bank kind of thing, small loans to small businesses. Help the little guy. Good deeds and good money. Who could resist? Except that the good deeds part never happened, as I remember warning you. Remember what I said? I said, Lie down with the big dogs and you get up with the big fleas—in a corner office! So now you get to foreclose on the same little guys you thought you were going to help, and even now, even now some part of you still believes that things will turn around and you'll get to do some—"

"Badgering the witness!" Mister Stanley said.

"Lula," said Don. "Did Stan ever tell you that the young guys in his office call him the Professor? Did he ever tell you how when we were kids back in Rockaway, the neighborhood bully offered Stan ten bucks, a fortune back then, to steal a beer from the corner store? Stan did it, not so much for the money itself, which trust me his family needed, but because he believed the kid would pay him. Even then Mr. Big Heart thought that people did what they promised. So of course he got caught and his poor dad had to go in and apologize and pay off the owner not to call the cops and—"

"Dad, you stole a beer?" said Zeke. "That is totally cool."

"I was eight," Mister Stanley said. "Half your age. A child. I didn't know any better. Tell Lula what *you* did, Don."

"I tracked down the little bastard bully and beat the crap out of him. From there it was a hop skip and jump to the DA's office, until I got fed up with persecuting the poor and deporting the innocent. My point is, it's never too late to come over, or back, to the side of the angels."

"You would too, Don," said Mister Stanley, his pale cheeks pinking with every gulp of wine.

"Would what?" said Don.

"Keep working if it weren't for health insurance. Because you can actually do some good. You're helping people. Like Lula."

"*G'ʒoor* to that," Lula said. She toasted the air and drained her glass. It was semi-interesting, what Don had said about Mister Stanley, but her attention had been hijacked by Don's client with the broken foot. She hated stories about how if you'd only stopped to pick up that piece of trash or ordered that second cup of coffee, if your Metrocard hadn't failed to swipe, your whole life would have been different. She also hated stories about people being deported and stories about car wrecks. Lula would ask them about Dunia. They would know what to do.

"On second thought," said Mister Stanley. "I'm not so sure I would keep working without the coverage. Every day I ask myself why I get up in the dark before dawn and drive through the filthy smelly tunnel—for what? To transfer money from one pocket to another? Other people's pockets. And it's all going into the same pocket. Okay, the same five hundred pockets. What if I quit tomorrow? Whose life would it change but mine? Not the guys we turn down for loans, not the families—"

"Hear, hear," said Don Settebello. "My old friend Stanley discovers the pimply fat face of capitalism."

"The main thing that will change if you quit," said Zeke, "is that you won't be able to pay for my college."

"That won't change," said Mister Stanley. Then he put his head in his hands.

Don signaled the waiter for another bottle.

Lula said, "Something like that happened when I worked at the restaurant. There was this busboy, Eduardo . . . and I have this friend, Dunia."

The waiter loomed over Don's shoulder. "Ready to order, sir?"

"If we had menus," Don said.

The waiter stomped off and returned with a stack of leather-bound tomes. None of the entrees were under forty-five dollars. A hamburger was thirty, but Lula would feel embarrassed ordering a burger here. A plate of home fries—fifteen bucks! Lula knew that the waitstaff had nothing to do with the pricing. Even so, she felt as if they were conspiring to relieve Don of the maximum amount of his hard-earned cash. How odd to find herself on the customers' side of one of those undeclared wars that sometimes broke out between customers and waiters.

Mister Stanley said, "I'll have the rib eye."

"Me too," said Zeke.

"Make that three," said Lula.

"The porterhouse," Don said. "And I want to hear mine moo."

A wail went up from Abigail. "What about me? Isn't anyone taking *my* order? Am I not here?"

"What would you like, honey?" Don said. "Order anything you like."

"You know I'm a vegetarian. Dad, why did we even come here?"

"We have a very fresh swordfish tonight," the waiter said.

"Is swordfish a vegetable?" Abigail demanded. "Dad, is swordfish a vegetable? Does it have a face or a central nervous system? Because I'd really like to know if it has a face or a central nervous system."

Lula glanced at Zeke, who seemed delighted by Abigail's courage. Lula sent him a telepathic message. Don't be fooled. You can count on a vegetarian to eat little boys like you for breakfast.

"I'll have the creamed spinach," Abigail said.

"That's all?" Don gave Mister Stanley a searching look, asking for a ruling on whether Abigail was just messing with his head or if she'd developed a full-blown eating disorder. Mister Stanley shrugged. What did he know about girls?

"Appetizers?" said the waiter. "Sides?"

Defeated by his daughter, Don surrendered to the waiter. He said, "We're in your hands." Lula wanted to cry out, No!

"We'll bring some appetizers and sides," said the waiter, ignoring Lula's furious stare. *Ka-ching*, she thought. *Ka-ching*.

Don said, "What's up with that bottle we ordered? Sooner rather than later."

Mister Stanley put his hand over his glass. "I'm fine. I have to drive the family back to New Jersey."

The family? Lula was family? Sweet dear Mister Stanley!

"What about you, Lula?" said Don. "I'm not drinking alone, am I?"

Lula raised one eyebrow and nodded. Deal me in.

Don's smile conveyed a loopy familiarity, as if he and Lula had agreed to embark on some joint project. In Lula's experience, the end of that particular project—drinking—was usually sex, but she couldn't tell if that was what was on Don's mind. She'd known it was on Franco's mind, that night when, after La Changita closed, he stood behind her chair and pressed his groin into her back. What a gentleman! How did guys like Don Settebello signal erotic interest? Probably just like other guys, but Lula wasn't sure. Besides which, he was her lawyer. If they had sex, a principled fellow like Don would feel he had to recuse himself from her green card application, which would make having sex with Don a lose-lose situation. Unwelcome thoughts of Alvo crowded into her mind. Or maybe not so unwelcome. Lula picked up her glass and resumed her progress along the road to tipsy well-being.

A convoy of waiters closed in on them, thumping down shrimp cocktails, wooden boards draped with pâté and cured meats, cheeses, pickles, platters of tomatoes ripened in costly winter sunlight, every red slice bundled beneath its own snowy blanket of mozzarella. The plates would not stop coming. There was twice as much as they could eat. Half would go back to the kitchen. The waiters would eat well tonight. As they should, thought Lula.

She helped herself to a shrimp, amazingly firm and fresh and sweet, considering the season. Nauseating, nonetheless. Lula picked up her wine glass and put it down without drinking, glad now that she was sitting so far from Mister Stanley and Don.

Zeke and Abigail stared ahead as if they were at the movies. It was easy to get Abigail's attention, but hard to know what to do with it. Her laundry-bleach blue eyes scared Lula into asking, "How do you like school?"

"My school sucks shit," said Abigail. "My dad pays thirty grand a year so I can call my teachers by their first names."

"Every school sucks," said Lula.

Abigail was having none of it. "You want to know how bad mine sucks? Have you ever read *Macbeth?*"

"I read *Macbeth*," said Zeke.

Abigail said, "We had to memorize a section of the play and recite it in front of the class, and I did the witches' speech—"

"Obviously," said Zeke.

"Right? Except that my teacher said I was taking the easy way, because it rhymed, but she'd pass me because I said it with energy and passion. Energy and passion. How gross is that?"

"Extremely gross," agreed Zeke.

"Scum-sucking bitch." Abigail screwed up her face and croaked, "Double double toil and trouble."

Had Don and Mister Stanley heard that? It was not Lula's place to tell her lawyer that his precious little daughter cursed like a Hungarian.

Zeke couldn't stop looking at Abigail. Lula's plate, on which there was one lone shrimp tail, vanished before she had tasted the cheeses and pâtés. Annoyance turned to outrage and then, shockingly, to bereavement. She had missed the cold cuts at her own celebration. Platters of home fries and bowls of creamed spinach signaled the imminent arrival of the meat. It seemed like a mockery to set a bowl of creamed spinach down before Abigail, a separate portion identical to all the other bowls of creamed spinach she could have had, for free. But not for free, not free at all. This was costing Don a fortune.

Deliciousness steamed off Lula's steak, aswim in its pool of blood. Not having fun wouldn't save Don money or bring the cow back to life. It wasn't her fault if Eduardo the busboy and Don's client had been deported. Or if Dunia had disappeared. Lula too could disappear. Enjoy yourself while you can.

The conversation stopped as everyone chewed. Abigail masticated dainty bites of spinach with theatrical distaste. After a while Don Settebello asked everybody how their steak was, and everybody said good. Great.

Don said, "How's the writing going, Lula?"

"Great," said Lula. The same word she'd used for her steak. The last thing she'd written was, "Does a leaf fall in New Jersey if no one is there to see?" The day the Albanian guys showed up. She hadn't written one sentence since. She hated lying to her journal. It was the one place in her life reserved for unadulterated truth. But if she wrote the truth, she would have to mention how much time she'd wasted lately thinking about Alvo. If she couldn't write about that, best not to write at all. It would spare her the dilemma of how much to say or not, how much to admit to herself about being the kind of person who would hide a stranger's gun in her trusting boss's house.

She said, "I'm writing a short story now. It's about this government bureau that analyzes people's dreams, and everyone has to report their dreams, and they're on the lookout for any dreams that might indicate that someone is plotting against the state." Lula held her breath. Neither Don nor Mister Stanley showed any sign of recognizing the plot of a novel by Ismail Kadare.

"How does it end?" asked Mister Stanley.

Don said, "What are you thinking, Stan? Never ask a writer a question like that."

"I don't know yet," Lula said.

"See?" said Don Settebello. "I hate to imagine what would happen if that story got out. Can you picture FBI agents shaking down therapists?"

"Hell, yeah," said Zeke. "That shrink Dad sent me to would bend over for anybody with a badge."

Don said, "I never trusted those prying bastards, all that money changing hands, a whole economy based on helping the comfy middle class deal with their comfy middle-class problems."

"Not always so comfy," said Mister Stanley. "Ginger's doctor seemed like he was doing her a lot of good until she decided he wasn't."

Don said, "After the divorce, when I had that little fling with a younger, not *that* much younger woman, Betsy said it would impact Abigail. But I don't think it has. Do you? Anyway, that's all I need, some nervous-nelly doctor blabbing my secrets to some FBI goons who could then spread the lie that the country's ballsiest immigration lawyer is in treatment for pedophilia. It's sort of like what Lula said. I mean, the plot of her story. I bet Dick Cheney insists on personally vetting the videotapes of sessions with hot young starlets in therapy for sex addiction."

"Poor Lula," said Mister Stanley. "We shouldn't joke like this around her until she's got her green card."

"Who's joking?" said Don.

Mister Stanley said, "Let's leave her with a few illusions about the country where she's trying to stay."

"*If* I get my green card," Lula couldn't help saying.

"You will," Don said. "Trust me. Meanwhile you can think anything you want. But just to be on the safe side, you should probably watch your mouth. Do I sound paranoid? I *am* paranoid. We'd be insane if we weren't. By the way, how *is* Ginger? Excuse the mental leap."

"Better, I think," said Mister Stanley. "She called from Arizona. Only once did she allude to hearing holy messages from the red rocks in some canyon."

Lula and Zeke exchanged quick looks. Mister Stanley hadn't mentioned that part in the car.

After a silence, Mister Stanley said, "It must be tough for Lula. She sees what's happening to this country. But she comes from a culture where America is God."

In one corner of Mister Stanley's garage, two John Kerry/John Edwards placards leaned against the wall, and several times Mister Stanley told Lula that he'd donated serious money to get Bush out of office. Lula was impressed by his freedom to say this. She was impressed by the freedom of the American press to tell the world that their vice president accidentally shot his friend in the face. At home, it wouldn't have been accidental. And he would have succeeded. Still, you had to watch out and not criticize, same as anywhere else. You could never predict when Americans, even Mister Stanley and Don, would get all defensive and huffy.

"It's hard for everyone to see what's going on here," said Don.

Lula said, "Everywhere it's common sense to keep your mouth shut. Growing up under Communism wasn't such a picnic."

"Amen," said Mister Stanley.

Don said, "I promise you, Lula, this is a free . . . My God, I almost said free country. Knowing what I know." Staring into his wine glass, Don said, "The thing that kills me is . . . the beauty of the U.S. Constitution. I love that fucking document, it still makes me cry, the sheer goodness and purity of the Founding Fathers' hopes and dreams, their ideas about what humans deserve and how they should be treated. The way these guys in Washington are trashing it . . . Christ, I've got to quit drinking. Every night's the same. The fourth glass of wine, I'm crying about the Bill of Rights and ruining everyone's fun—"

Abigail said, "Oh? Were we having fun? I must have missed the fun part, Dad."

Lula said, "Mister Stanley's house is a wonderful place to write."

Don said, "It's adorable, Stan, the way Lula calls you Mister Stanley. Like some servant girl from the nineteenth century."

Mister Stanley shook his head. "I've begged her to call me Stan."

Lula shrugged. She didn't know what to call Don Settebello, so she didn't call him anything.

They went back to tearing at their steaks. Abigail ate one last dab of spinach and pushed her bowl away so hard it spun. The others watched till it stopped.

Don said, "It's a miracle when the system functions. More often it's like with my Salvadoran client—all your ducks are lined up, actually your clay pigeons, one of them gets shot down, and it's back to square one, the poor guy is sent back to wherever. If he's lucky. And then you have a case where it works, and a person with Lula's brains and heart and talent gets to live here."

Mister Stanley said, "Here's to Lula. And Don."

"And Stan." Don's swallow of wine lasted so long that even Zeke and Abigail watched his Adam's apple bob up and down.

Lula said, "Thank you. I'm happy and grateful to be here."

"We want you here," said Don Settebello. "Fresh young blood. You're what keeps our country young."

Zeke stage-whispered to Abigail, "Fresh blood? That's so vampiristic."

Abigail said, "Are you actually listening to Dad?"

"Shut up, young lady," Don told her. "Okay, here we go." Don clinked his spoon on his glass, and half the restaurant turned. Don waited till the eavesdroppers went back to their meals.

"Dear friends, I've got an announcement. This is a celebration for me, too. Just because my life isn't already busy and difficult and frustrating and overextended enough, I've decided to take on a new project. I'll be doing some Guantánamo work, going down there and trying to get those guys to trust me. Do whatever I can. Not that I have high hopes, or any hopes at all, but I can't just sit back and watch. Plus to be honest with you I was flattered. They've got the top guys on this. The sharpest habeas corpus guys, the heavy-duty death penalty guys, famous law professors from Germany and France. And who am I among these superstars? Don from immigration—"

"You're hardly Don from immigration," Mister Stanley said. "Not for ten, fifteen years now. You have a very public career. You're a hero."

"Stan," said Don. "Are you listening? Did you hear one word I said?"

"I'm still processing," Mister Stanley said. "Guantánamo. Jesus Christ, Stan. I don't know what to say. I mean . . . how did all this happen?"

"Actually, I was recruited. This old friend of mine from law school—"

"Amazing." Mister Stanley didn't want to think about Don having other old friends besides him.

Abigail said, "Don't do it, Dad. Don't go. We all know you can't keep your big mouth shut. They'll probably keep you there. They'll lock you up in one of those orange suits and say you're Osama bin Laden."

"Darling!" said Don. "It makes me so happy that you not only know where *there* is, you know what goes on there. Stan, Zeke, Lula, do you realize that this . . . child understands more than most adults. It makes me want to keep doing it, to preserve the beautiful country in which my daughter is growing up."

Abigail said, "Think about *me* for five minutes."

"And what's more," said Don, "she seems genuinely concerned about my welfare."

"God," said Abigail. "Do you think I'm stupid? If you get sent to jail, it goes on my permanent record. Fat chance of my getting into boarding school and getting away from Mom once they find out my dad is a terrorist."

"Let's raise a glass to Don," said Mister Stanley. Everyone's glass was empty. Mister Stanley waved over the waiter, who was so perturbed to be getting instructions from him instead of Alpha Don that he filled Mister Stanley's glass to the top. Mister Stanley spilled a few drops. Lula watched red flowers bloom on the white cloth as Mister Stanley said, "We're grateful to you, Don. As your friends, as Americans, as citizens of the world!"

Lula lifted her glass to Don Settebello, then to Mister Stanley, then Zeke. Abigail wouldn't look at her.

"Cheers," said Lula. "*G'zoor.*"

NOW THAT LULA's big night was over, Zeke grabbed the passenger seat, and Lula climbed in back. A few blocks from the restaurant, Mister Stanley ran over a curb on which, miraculously, no one was waiting to cross. Furious honking pursued them, but Mister Stanley didn't notice. Zeke turned around to Lula and pantomimed pouring something down his mouth. Wasn't he worried that his father would see? It worried Lula that his father didn't see.

"You want me to drive?" asked Zeke.

Mister Stanley said, "Are you kidding, Junior? Your learner's permit specifies no night driving."

"What learner's permit? I've got a license," said Zeke.

"No night driving," said his father. Lula was reassured that Mister Stanley was sober enough to remember. If only she could drive! But that was the red wine talking. Even if she had a license, she'd drunk twice as much as Mister Stanley and was probably half his weight. Drunk or sober, her father was always a terrible driver. He'd learned too late to have the reflexes. His whole generation had. And soon it would be too late for her as well. Lula fastened her seat belt and braced herself as they sped toward the tunnel.

"Dad, that's a red light!" Zeke cried.

Mister Stanley slammed on his brakes and fell silent until they'd passed the Newark exit, when he said, "Do you think Don could be developing a tiny bit of a drinking problem? Poor Don. Who could blame him for tying one on, with that daughter? All that great work he's doing, and that girl treats him like . . . Jesus, I hope we don't get stopped. I should have stuck to club soda. Let this be a lesson to you, Zeke."

Zeke said, "What lesson would that be?"

"I don't know," said Mister Stanley. "Maybe about the downside of living in the moment."

Again Zeke wheeled around in his seat. "Did you hear that?"

he asked Lula. "Dad thinks his problem is too much living in the moment."

"Fasten your seat belt," said Mister Stanley. "Or I'm pulling over."

Zeke said, "This kid in my school wound up in the ICU because someone told him if you eat mothballs you can pass the Breathalyzer test."

"That's a myth," said Mister Stanley. "Deadly deadly deadly."

"Concentrate, Dad," said Zeke.

Lula shut her eyes and thought of everything she'd ever done wrong, sins against her parents, boyfriends, girls whose boyfriends she'd slept with, every lie she'd ever told Mister Stanley, Don, and Zeke. She decided to count her sins, starting from the first, but she kept losing track and having to go back to the neighbor boy whose hand she purposely stepped on and broke his pinkie and almost got her whole family sent away because the kid's dad was secret police. Then Lula gave up counting and apologized for each one. Sorry, Granny, for not returning the change when you sent me to buy butter. Sorry, Papa, for telling Mama we used Madonna for target practice. Underneath were the real sins. The time she chose to play with her friends and refused to visit her dying grandpa. The secret gladness she'd felt when her parents left for Kosovo, and then after graduation when there was so much more room for her in Aunt Mirela's apartment. But why was she even thinking this way, when there were monsters at home who'd sent innocents to their deaths during Communism and never apologized, never felt guilty? What about the Dictator? Had he woken in the middle of the night, worried he'd hurt someone's feelings?

Against all odds, Mister Stanley seemed to be parking in front of the house.

"Thank you, Mister Stanley," she said. "Thank you, Zeke."

"Why are you thanking *me*?" said Zeke.

"Because we're alive," said Lula. "Safe."

"No one's safe," said Zeke. "Full moon."

LULA HAD TO grab the banister on her way upstairs. Maybe that was why the wine cost so much, for waiting politely until you got home to slam you against the wall. Lula sat on the edge of her bed. Beyond her tented fingers, the revolving room picked up speed. A bath would feel nice, a cold bath, shocking the dizziness out of her, boiling off the alcohol just to keep warm. Hand over hand, she made her way to the bathroom and sat on the toilet lid.

Something was wrong. Out of place. The shower curtain was drawn. Lula never took showers. Could Estrelia have left it that way? Lula had taken several baths since Estrelia cleaned. Why would Zeke or Mister Stanley rearrange her shower curtain? Was that a shadow moving behind it?

Lula pulled back the curtain. She must have closed it and forgotten. She was turning the knob that stoppered the tub when she noticed that her soap was not in its dish. Now that was strange. Lula was obsessive about her soap, hand-milled in France by monks consecrated to silent prayer and shampoo. The soap lay beached against the drain, in a milky puddle. A sudden rush of nausea felt like a new kind of thirst that could only be slaked by immersing her body in water. But how could she bathe in a tub in which a stranger might have been? *Might have?* The tiles were wet.

And what was this? A curly red hair inscribed in the gooey lavender skin of the soap. Oh, hideous. Disgusting! Lula grabbed a swatch of toilet paper, and, averting her eyes, swabbed the soap with the paper, which she flushed down the toilet. Pretend it was one of the Lower East Side water bugs, puny wimps compared to the roaches that used to chase her around Aunt Mirela's apartment.

She would have been more frightened if she hadn't been drunk. Alcohol was so skillful at widening the distance between the self that knew what was happening and the self that felt compelled to do something about it. This was not her imagination. Something had to be done. Lula flung open the closet doors, then crouched and looked under the bed. What about Zeke and Mister Stanley? What if the red-headed serial killer had showered as ritual preparation for stabbing them in their beds? It would be her fault. Those guys with the gun, who were they? She had no idea. But she'd let them into the house.

She stepped into the silent hall. Propping herself against the wall, she listened and heard nothing but the distant buzz of Mister Stanley snoring.

A sense of peace overcame her, a feather quilt of fatalism. Let what happens happen. Most likely, it would be nothing. She was tired. She needed her rest. Things would sort themselves out. If she was murdered in the night, it would mean she'd made a mistake. Just before she fell asleep, she had a disturbing dream in which she saw Don Settebello, blindfolded and in shackles, his head gleaming behind the window of a plane painted camouflage green and black, bouncing over the ocean.

Chapter Four

THE BURNING coin of pressure glowing between Lula's brows made it hard to remember why she was supposed to feel grateful to be waking up at all. Maybe because she hadn't been bludgeoned in her sleep by the killer who'd left his hairy signature scrawled across her soap. That is, she hadn't been murdered *yet*. It was only 4:00 a.m.

In the darkness, Lula ran her hands along her arms and legs. Unhurt, but for the hangover. Maybe the so-called intruder was a wine-fueled hallucination, a byproduct of rich beef protein and the frightening drive home. But she could picture the red hair, the winking copper wire. Someone's hair was that red.

Alvo's. It was Alvo's.

The possibility that Alvo had sneaked in and showered in her tub seemed marginally likelier than a quick cleanup by some random psycho. So it wasn't so scary. But troubling, she had to admit. And weirdly, sort of hot. It was foolish and stupid to have feelings for your stalker. As Lula got older, she seemed to be growing less mature about boys. At university in Tirana, her sensible younger self ended a brief romance with a guy just because she didn't like something she saw in his eyes during sex. Later Dunia's cousin went out with him, and he held a rotisserie skewer to her throat in bed.

Unless Alvo's late-night visit had nothing to do with her . . . Lula switched on the night lamp and vaulted across the room.

"Thank you," she whispered. Thank you? The gun was still in her underwear drawer. Then she remembered her money, and a fresh surge of adrenaline propelled her to the desk where—thank you again!—the envelope of cash was where she'd left it. She was deranged to think first about the gun and only then about her money.

They needed to put new locks on the doors. If something happened to Mister Stanley or Zeke, Lula would never forgive herself. In the morning she would have to figure out what to say. Mister Stanley, I made some new friends. I was so happy to meet Albanians, and one of them was cute, so I agreed to keep their gun. And now there's this little detail, they're breaking into the house when we're out. Showering in my bathroom. Bye-bye job, good-bye green card, farewell new American life.

She rolled onto her side and crossed her arms over her chest like a mummy. Both arms were numb when she awoke again at seven-thirty.

In the morning light, her imported soap was dry and smooth, her shower curtain open. Maybe she had dreamed it. No need to alarm Mister Stanley, especially if the hair belonged to Alvo, which it probably did. It was definitely his hair color. Maybe stalking was a courtship thing for him, a New World improvement on the old-school bride kidnap. She wondered if she could ever ask Alvo about it some day, or even make a joke. If she ever saw him again, unless she caught him creeping around.

It was Sunday, her day to cook breakfast for Zeke and Mister Stanley. She stripped off her slept-in party clothes, scrubbed the bathtub, rinsed it, and filled it again. She slid beneath the water to her chin and let the hot steamy bubbles melt away the soreness. By the time she got out, it was like any other Sunday. Sunday with a headache.

Lula threw on her jeans and a sweatshirt, then hurried downstairs, where she found Mister Stanley, drinking coffee at the dining room table, his back bowed over the Sunday paper. Lula made a quick tour, checking for shattered windows, busted doors, anything to track the route that Alvo, or someone, had taken. But there was only the usual mess, the usual sad Mister Stanley. How glad she was to see him. Mister Stanley wasn't hurt or even, it seemed, aware that anything unusual had occurred.

Maybe she could turn this into one of those cultural comparisons that Mister Stanley and Don so enjoyed. In her country, under Communism, if someone broke into your place and didn't take anything, it meant you were in trouble. Whereas after Communism, no one would bother breaking in unless they were planning to take something. Under Communism, there had been nothing to take. Every night, she and Zeke watched a news story about the White House insisting there should be more spying on private citizens. People acted shocked, as they should be, even if it was naive. In Europe, people admitted that the desire to spy on your neighbor was basic human nature. . . . They could discuss this in the abstract, but it wouldn't be long before Mister Stanley realized that Lula meant something specific.

Mister Stanley said, "I'm sorry, Lula. I overindulged last night."

"Sorry for what?" said Lula. "Nothing bad happened."

"The drive home couldn't have been fun," he said. "I shuffer . . . Shuffer? I shudder to think what could have happened. I will never do that again, I promise, never—"

Why was he looking to Lula, of all people, to absolve him? Because she was the only one here. She wanted to give him a consoling pat on the shoulder, but she never touched Mister Stanley, and she didn't want to start now, both of them weakened in body and spirit, both perhaps seeking relief from the damage that alcohol had inflicted on their bodies. Mister Stanley wasn't the type of guy to hit on the nanny, but every guy was a hangover away from being that type of guy. Even a friendly shoulder squeeze was a door best left unopened. Meanwhile, a surge of fondness almost persuaded Lula to tell him about her shower, the soap, her suspicions. It would be a relief to share her worries with him. And wasn't it her duty, as his employee? The impulse hovered in the air, spinning like a smoke ring. Lula told herself: No one's in danger. Relax and see what happens.

"We survived," she said. "No one got hurt. The car didn't even get scratched."

"I'll never do it again," Mister Stanley said.

Maybe she had imagined the incident with the soap. Her father used to say, My daughter Lula has some imagination. He'd made it sound like a genial way of calling her a liar. Imagination was part of what had gotten her this far. It was a tool in the arsenal that armed you for survival.

"Did you see this?" Mister Stanley slid the paper across the table. Another munitions dump had blown up near Durrës.

"Great," Lula said. "My country is practicing for the future nuclear reactor."

Mister Stanley said, "You know what it was? A factory full of little kids some gangsters paid to disassemble Kalashnikovs and stockpile explosives."

Lula said, "I told you things are bad there. You think it's all sworn virgins and blood feuds and paranoid dead dictators?" In case everything fell apart and she was deported for the crimes of her Albanian brothers, she wanted Mister Stanley to know what she would be going back to.

Mister Stanley glanced up. His face reminded her of how Estrelia had looked when Lula marched her into the kitchen to taste Granny's pepper paste. Lula said, "Everywhere seems romantic until you actually—"

Mister Stanley said, "One was never under the impression that Europe's most repressive dictatorship was romantic."

"It was the hangover talking," said Lula. "Sorry."

Mister Stanley's expression was uncharacteristically chilly and removed, as if he was looking at her and seeing someone else. Maybe Ginger.

He said, "You women always come at things from a crazy angle."

You women? This conversation had to stop before their hangovers exchanged one more word. Lula was heading into the kitchen when Mister Stanley said, "Anyhow, it was fun last night. Don's quite a guy. A hero."

"A hero," Lula agreed. "I wouldn't have the courage to do what he does."

Mister Stanley said, "I don't know. People do what they have to."

Where had Lula heard that before? She'd said it to Mister Stanley. A ribbon of pain cinched Lula's temples. She went into the kitchen and started separating eggs. The third yolk slipped into the bowl with the whites, and loudly, in Albanian, she cursed the eggs for fucking their mother.

Through the door she heard Mister Stanley say, "Good morning. Finally, Zeke!"

How could Mister Stanley and Zeke sit at the table without even making small talk? Maybe Ginger had been the talker. At La Changita, Lula had often seen mothers and girlfriends propping up the conversation, while the husbands and sons sulked or drank. It was easier in Albania, men and women divided, no one expecting the other sex to say anything much worth hearing. Lula brought in a bowl of Cheerios and an egg-white omelet for Mister Stanley, plates of scrambled eggs and toast for herself and Zeke.

Mister Stanley chewed his cereal. *Crunch crunch* pause *crunch crunch* pause. He said, "I want my low cholesterol back. I want to be young again."

Zeke said, "Dad, don't be depressing." The eggs were runny and undersalted, but Zeke seemed to enjoy them. Lula made a resolution to cook more. Kids appreciated it when adults made the effort.

Mister Stanley said, "Did you hear what Don's doing, Zeke?"

Zeke said, "I used to think Abigail's school was cooler than mine, but now it sounds like it sucks."

Mister Stanley said, "Don pays a fortune in tuition. Here's a guy who does nothing but good, who has nothing but decency in his heart, and that daughter of his, poor guy—"

"Abigail's awesome," Zeke said.

"What year is she in?" Lula asked.

"She's a senior, like me."

Lula said, "I thought she was twelve."

"Food issues." Mister Stanley contemplated his remaining Cheerios and wedge of egg-white omelet. "Tragic. Speaking of being a senior, Zeke, I got a call from a Mrs. Sullivan, the college counselor at your school."

Zeke said, "Do we have to do this now? I'm actually enjoying my breakfast. You want me to wind up like Abigail? I could quit eating too."

Mister Stanley said, "Not only have you not been to see Mrs. Sullivan, Zeke, but she thinks you haven't applied to one college, nor have you handed in the list of colleges you plan to apply to."

"I forgot," said Zeke.

"No one forgets something like that," said Mister Stanley.

"Okay, I was busy. Like you, Dad. And Mom wasn't here to help."

"You must be thinking of Old Mom. By the time New Mom left, she couldn't have helped anyone much, including herself." Normally Mister Stanley went overboard not to criticize Ginger. His tone made Lula suspect they might be headed for a dark place disguised as Zeke's college plans.

"I could have helped," said Lula. The idea that Zeke might not go away to school filled her with claustrophobic panic. No one was holding her prisoner here. She didn't have a contract. She could leave whenever she wanted, even if Zeke never left. Don Settebello and Mister Stanley had promised to help her become a citizen whether she worked here or not.

Zeke said, "No insult, Lula, but it's not like you know anything about the American college application process. You said Albanian girls got into the popular majors by blowing the professors."

When had Lula said *that*? Probably during an evening of mojitos, junk food, TV, and Lula speaking too freely. It was fun, trying to shock Zeke. Fun, but not very smart.

"You *said* that? You told *Zeke* that?" asked Mister Stanley.

"I don't think so," said Lula. "We had exams, like here."

"You did," said Zeke. "You told me that."

"You must have misunderstood," said Lula.

"These eggs are awesome," Zeke said.

"Have some more," said Lula.

"Watch the eggs, Zeke," said Mister Stanley. "You'll probably inherit my cholesterol numbers. It's never too early to develop healthy nutritional habits."

"That's what I mean," said Zeke. "This is exactly how Abigail got that way."

Mister Stanley said, "Mrs. Sullivan suggested we use the Veteran's Day weekend to visit a few New England colleges. She wrote down the names and Web sites. We're already late with this—"

"No freaking way," said Zeke.

"Lula could come with us," said Mister Stanley.

"I'd love to!" Lula said. A road trip was a road trip. America awaited her out there. She'd never been farther than New Jersey. She'd never even been to Detroit, where she'd told the visa officer she was going.

Mister Stanley said, "Come on, Zeke. We used to travel all the time."

"All right, fine," Zeke said. "Maybe we'll have a car wreck, and I can miss the rest of school."

"Knock on wood!" cried Lula.

"I thought Albanians weren't superstitious," said Zeke. "That's what you're always saying, but then you knock on wood."

"Be careful what you wish for," his father said. "Even Protestants believe that."

MONDAY WAS COLD but sunny, and Lula decided to take a walk. After a full weekend of Zeke and Mister Stanley, it would be pleasant to sit and read in the cozy library with the steam pipes clanking. And she didn't want to stay home. She knew the feeling would pass, especially if nothing else happened, but for now the idea of a stranger using her shower had spoiled her pleasure in being alone at Mister Stanley's. Most likely it was a one-time event.

Yet if the intruder was Alvo, maybe he would return. What if he came back today, and she missed him again? She weighed the odds, and chose to bet on the chance that Alvo might reappear. If the psycho stranger showed up, she would have calculated wrong.

Lula spent the day alternately looking out the window and trying not to look out the window. No one drove by, no one walked past but the mailman. The most exciting event was the *plop-crunch* of letters sliding through the slot.

How much mail Mister Stanley got, and how much went into the shredder! The three envelopes that arrived today—two invitations to upgrade credit cards and a charity solicitation—seemed destined for the same fate, but another item whispered to her as it skimmed across the floor. On the thick, hand-tinted, old-fashioned postcard two sepia rock formations rose like craggy penises. The caption said, "Red Rocks National Monument. The Scout and the Indian Maiden."

The postcard was addressed to Mr. Ezekiel Larch. Lula knew she should leave it for Zeke. But postcards weren't like letters or e-mail. Postcards dared you not to read them.

Written in brown fountain-pen ink and chicken-scratch handwriting, it said: "My dearest darling Zeke, I hear you're almost headed for college. There are some Great places out here where the air is clean and the magic isn't sick and filthy and Polluted. Or anyway, not Yet. Come here for school? College? Kindergarten? Seems like Yesterday. Keep in touch. Love, Mom."

There was no return address, the smudged postmark was illegible, and the capitalization was quirky, to put it mildly.

Lula put the card on the counter where Zeke couldn't miss it, then returned upstairs to resume her vigil, watching and not watching for the black SUV until she heard Zeke's footsteps.

By the time Lula got downstairs, Zeke was reading the postcard. She shouldn't have left it out. She should have put it somewhere he would find it after he'd fortified himself with juice and a snack.

Zeke said, "College between two penis rocks? I'd rather stay home. Forever."

"I don't think that's an option," said Lula. "Staying home forever."

Zeke said, "Dad would like that."

"Untrue," said Lula, reflexively, though maybe Zeke was right. Albanian eagle parents pushed their offspring out of the nest as soon as they could fly, but maybe that was just to make sure they flew back after their divorces. Lula had no nest to return to. Problems or no problems, Zeke was a lucky baby bird.

Lula said, "Are you looking forward to the college trip with your dad?"

Zeke said, "You're joking. Dad and I saw this *Sopranos* episode before you got here. Mom hated me and Dad watching it, but it was almost the only thing Dad insisted on. Tony killed this guy while Meadow was at an interview on her college tour. Something like that would be cool."

Lula said, "Something like that would not be cool. Come on. You get time off from school. I get out of the house. We both get a change of scenery. It's a win-win situation."

Zeke said, "You've never traveled with my dad." Staring into the refrigerator, he asked, "Do you want to hear about the worst summer of my life?" Lula's dad used to talk like that, addressing himself to the icebox. So did Mister Stanley. It was strange how men preferred deep conversation with a kitchen appliance.

Zeke said, "This was after eighth grade. We took a family cross-country road trip. From New York to Chicago Mom and Dad fought about the air conditioner. Dad said it couldn't be fixed, and Mom said that was Dad in a nutshell: Nothing could be fixed. Dad wouldn't let Mom drive, he did the crawly speed limit. We were in Nebraska for like twenty years. We only stopped to sleep or eat or piss until we got to the West, and then we'd stop at every national park, and I'd get out and kick some pebbles, and my mom would cluck her tongue and say weird spiritual shit about nature, and Dad would give me a lecture full of fascinating facts he'd learned in college geology, and Mom would look like she wanted to kill him. Then I took pictures of Dad and Mom against the natural wonders, and my dad took pictures of Mom and me. Then we'd get back in the car and drive fifteen hours to the next national park."

"That was your worst summer ever?" Lula said. "Everywhere in the world kids are being kidnapped and drafted as child soldiers. Or blown up in munitions plants. I'll bet when Don Settebello starts going down to Guantánamo, he meets kids—prisoners!—not much older than you."

Zeke said, "Don should stay home and take care of Abigail. Are you trying to guilt me or what?"

Lula said, "Okay. Sorry for the lecture. So is that why your mom left? Boredom?"

In all of Lula's time here, she had never asked Zeke directly about his mother's departure, and he'd never volunteered. It wasn't that she didn't care or wasn't curious, but she was afraid that Zeke would hate her if he told her. Men were like that, even young ones. Her first boyfriend in Tirana told her his uncle used to sneak into his bed and fondle him, and the next night he broke up with her. Another guy to whom she'd practically been engaged told her he'd stolen from the church when he was an altar boy, and then he left her too.

"I *wish*," said Zeke. "To say you're bored in this house is like saying the sun rises in the east. It *is* the east, right?"

Lula remembered a grade-school play about valiant Chinese people all working together to feed their population. She'd played the wife of a rice farmer, and in the end they all sang a Chinese song, translated into Albanian, about the sunrise.

"I was joking," Zeke said. "About the sun. My mom went

kind of nuts. One day, I was riding the school bus home, I saw her standing on the corner. From her expression I thought she'd come to tell me Dad was dead. She said she needed to ask me something private. She said, 'Zeke, pretend I'm a stranger, and you're walking home, and you see me. What do I look like?' "

"What did she look like?" said Lula.

"Like a bag lady," Zeke said. "But I couldn't say that."

"Good boy," said Lula. "Smart boy."

Zeke said, "Hey, are you wearing makeup?"

"Not really," said Lula. "Go on."

"After that she turned into a clean freak. She burned through two washing machines in a year. They were still under warranty, they just gave us new ones. I had to hide my T-shirts. She shrunk them into doll clothes. She started making Estrelia wear fluffy slippers when she cleaned the house."

"Poor Estrelia," said Lula.

"Poor me," said Zeke. "Poor Dad."

"Poor everybody," said Lula. No wonder Mister Stanley had hired her. They were lucky to get someone sane.

"Dirt and filth and pollution were all my mom ever talked about. Her face would get twisted up—" Zeke attempted to demonstrate. He got as far as clenching his teeth and narrowing his eyes until a shudder shook his features back into slacker default mode.

"She wouldn't like Albania," Lula said, just to say something. "For them a garbage dump is a clear mountain stream or the side of a country road."

"Not here," said Zeke. "Here you have to be a corporation to get away with that. Anyway, my mom stopped leaving the house except to go to this support group in the Lutheran church basement. Tree-hugging twelve-step crap. That's when she started talking about working her way back to cleanness."

"Didn't your dad make her see a doctor?"

"He did. She hated the guy. He put her on meds she refused to take. Finally one evening Mom sent us to the store for dish-washing detergent and laundry soap, and when we got back she was gone. I'm pretty sure she knew The Good Earth would be closed on Christmas Eve. We had to drive to the Shop-well, which was closed too, by the way. It gave her more time to escape. She took her passport and a big suitcase. Maybe she was nuts, but she was sane enough to write herself a huge check from my parents' joint account. Christmas Eve, did I say that?"

"You did," Lula said. "How do you know about the check?"

"I heard Dad telling Don," said Zeke. "Christmas Eve. Really nice. I wanted to call the cops, but Dad said give it a week. He said that's what the police would say. Sure enough, a week later, we got that postcard of glaciers in Norway."

Lula asked, "Do you miss her?"

"I think I miss a feeling from before she got sick. Dad says she has an illness."

"Sounds like one," Lula said. She tried to recall the message on the card Zeke was holding. Pollution had been capitalized, she was fairly certain. "Do you think she's happier now than before she left? Or less angry, like your dad says?"

"I think she's pretty cracked."

"Cracks get mended," said Lula.

"Some do, some don't," Zeke said.

"Now you sound like me," Lula said.

That night, when Mister Stanley asked how Zeke was, Lula told him he'd gotten a postcard from his mother.

"What did it say?"

"It said maybe Zeke would go to college out West, where she is."

"That's not going to happen," said Mister Stanley.

"That's what Zeke said," said Lula.

"Good." Without turning to face Lula, Mister Stanley glided from the refrigerator to the window and stared into the darkness.

After a while he said, "You know, there are some pictures one really wishes did not exist in one's head. The problem is, they crowd out all the other pictures, the good pictures, the memories from when one was young and happy. Or anyway, from when one was young. So one must have been happy. Do you know that Ginger taught second grade and, though I begged her not to, she quit to take care of Zeke? Do you know that Ginger used to be a beautiful, caring person?"

Lula shook her head. She didn't ask what Mister Stanley's mental pictures were, the good ones or the bad. She thought of Zeke's lip quivering when he'd tried to look like his mother, and of him saying he missed a feeling from before his mother got sick.

She said, "Young doesn't always mean happy."

Mister Stanley said, "One forgets sometimes. Thank you. Good night, Lula."

THE NEXT MORNING, the black Lexus pulled up to the curb. Partly from nervousness and partly from superstition, Lula ran through a series of disappointing scenarios, beginning with it being some *other* Lexus—unlikely!—and progressing through the scene in which Alvo waited in the car while Hoodie and Leather Jacket, Guri and Genti, came in and retrieved the gun.

Alvo and the G-Men ambled up the path. Lula straightened her sweater and skirt. She'd been putting on makeup since the first time they came. She ran downstairs, then waited to open the door until they rang three times. Hoodie and Leather Jacket shook her hand. Alvo gave her a brotherly kiss on both cheeks. He smelled like smoke and beach sand.

She said, "Can I get you guys coffee?"

The other two watched Alvo nod.

"Please," she said. "No smoking this time."

"We just smoked in the car," said Hoodie.

Lula took her time in the kitchen brewing the muddy coffee. They thanked her, then Leather Jacket said, "No one here smokes? No one in this house eats or sleeps or breathes or fucks? Or farts?"

Lula said, "They eat and sleep and breathe. No, wait. I don't know if the boss eats."

"What's their problem?" asked Hoodie.

"Shell-shocked. Before she left, the mom tried to poison them." Why had Lula said that? Because the true story of their loneliness, of Ginger's housewifely discontent shading into a mentally ill obsession with dirt, made the Larches seem even sadder and more pitiful than they were.

"No shit? What with?" asked Leather Jacket.

"Dishwashing liquid," Lula improvised.

"Stomach ache," Hoodie said. "Not fatal."

Alvo regarded his cup. "Maybe we should feed the coffee to the dog first."

"There is no dog," said Lula.

"Is the dog dead too?" said Alvo.

"I don't think there was a dog," said Lula.

"We know there's no dog," said Alvo. Had he factored that information in when he'd sneaked into the house? Or was he simply remarking that he'd noticed there was no dog?

Lula said, "You guys want your gun back?"

Alvo said, "Little Sister, we are not here about the gun. The truth is, we worry that you don't get out of the house enough."

Did she look pale? Tired? Sick? She needed to check herself out in the mirror.

Alvo said, "Because we are family, practically cousins of your Cousin George, we've come to take you for a ride, so you can breathe the fresh air."

Lula loved how he talked.

Hoodie said, "The fresh New Jersey air. You're a comedian, boss."

Lula said, "Is this the part where I wake up tomorrow morning in some sheik's harem in Dubai?" How could she joke about such things with Dunia out there, lost?

Ha ha, the three men laughed. Then Alvo asked Lula, "Is something wrong?"

Lula said, "I have this friend—"

"Those sheiks want twelve-year-old virgins," said Hoodie. "Little Sister is overqualified."

"Thanks a lot," said Lula.

"Shut up, shithead," Alvo said. "Come on, Lula. We've got errands. Business. Come for the ride."

What girl wasn't a sucker for male business errands? Not the former little girl whose papa had taken her into the homes of tribal warlords up north from whom he'd bought vintage muskets. Not the former teenager whose boyfriend had brought her to pick up an ounce of dirt weed he cut with wild parsley to resell at the bunker-field raves. It was pleasant to tag along, hardly noticed but there, subtly raising the temperature with your female physical presence.

She said, "I need to be back before Zeke gets home."

Hoodie looked exasperated. "You think we have all day for joyrides?"

They had places to go, people to see. Important things to do besides chauffeuring some loser Albanian nanny around northern New Jersey. But if they weren't kidnapping her, then what? That Alvo might want to spend time with her was too much to hope for.

"Let me get my coat," she said.

"Don't leave any notes," said Hoodie. "And we'll need to take your SIM card."

Lula knew he was kidding. Still, closing the door to her room, she had the sickening feeling she would never see it again. When you prepare for a journey, her granny used to say, prepare for death. What gloomy people she came from! No wonder her glass was half empty. But what if Zeke and Mister Stanley came home to find her gone? They would think it was their special curse. Or just something women did. Maybe Lula too had vanished in search of greater whiteness. In this case, the white sands of the emirates.

Hoodie paced as she took the coffee cups into the kitchen and washed them. Another mistake. In hiding the traces of her secret life, she had destroyed precious DNA evidence that might help the authorities find her. Get a grip, Lula told herself. Three friends of her Cousin George's were taking her out in a Lexus.

Leather Jacket and Hoodie lunged for the doorknob, but Alvo said, "After you." There was a pile-up, almost a scuffle, as the two guys stepped back and let Lula, then Alvo, through.

"Albanian cavemen," muttered Alvo. As Lula scrabbled in her purse, searching for her keys, Hoodie patrolled the front walk until Alvo said, "Cut that shit out," and Hoodie waited under the mulberry tree, where Leather Jacket joined him.

Alvo said, "Neanderthals. They still think women should follow five paces behind. Like my granny, rest in peace. Fifty years of eating my grandpa's dust."

"My granny too," said Lula. "My keys are in here somewhere." Did Alvo wonder why she was bothering to lock the door when guys like him could stroll in and shower whenever they wanted?

"Our friend Spiro," said Alvo, "he finds this high-powered Albanian girl, Columbia B-School graduate, no one believes such a smart girl would marry Spiro. But women are desperate, I guess. They get engaged, fly up to meet his family in Toronto, and he asks her if she could walk into the house behind him. Just this once. So this girl gets behind Spiro and takes off her nine-hundred-dollar Manolo Blahniks and smashes the high heel into his skull so hard he bled like a goat."

"I guess that ended the engagement," Lula said.

"They're married! They hold hands now. They both work on Wall Street. The modern Albanian couple. My granny should have done that. She didn't have the right shoes."

"I got the keys!" sang out Lula. Alvo was careful to walk beside her and not hurry ahead, a positive sign of reconstructed Balkan male behavior. That Lula should even register—and appreciate—this was depressing. But comforting, in a way. She liked being with someone who knew what it was like to watch your genius granny tag after your birdbrain grandpa. It was so hard to live among strangers with whom you shared no history, no knowledge of a way of life that went back and back.

Halfway to the car, Alvo put out his arm. "Let them get in first."

"In case the car blows up?"

Alvo's smile was all tolerance at her failure to appreciate his gesture of macho courtesy, making sure the vehicle was warmed up for the lady. Beneath the grin was a question. Why was Lula so jumpy? Lula's smile said, No reason. Really, no reason at all!

Alvo opened the door for her, and Lula slipped inside. On the dashboard was a TV screen, and as Leather Jacket left the curb, a blinking violet cursor imitated everything they did. Albanian hip-hop boomed out of the speakers.

"What group is that?" asked Lula.

"Keep It Bloody," said Hoodie. "You know them?"

"Sort of," Lula said. Regardless of the language, it was always the same guys yelling about how tough they were. The difference was the bitches whose asses these guys were going to kick were Serbs.

"Sort of?" said Hoodie. "Either you know them or you don't."

"Let it go, dumbass," said Alvo.

Lula said, "A bunch of guys driving a Lexus with black windows, and you play this music, this loud? How often do you get pulled over?"

Alvo said, "Good question. I like how this girl thinks."

Leather Jacket said, "Never. New Jersey's finest know better than to fuck with us." He took the prettiest streets, past mansions with white pillars and brick facades veined with dead ivy. They floated so high above the road they could have been in a balloon. Lula touched a button, and her window slid down to admit a gust of chill air, perfumed with leaf mold.

Leather Jacket pulled into a strip mall and parked in front of a supermarket with hand-lettered signs in the window.

"Need anything?" said Alvo.

"No, thank you," Lula said.

"Want to come in?" Alvo asked.

As Lula and Alvo crossed the parking lot, she felt buoyed by an updraft of something like exultation. Everything seemed natural, effortless, as if she and Alvo were a couple, young, in love, enjoying their courtship freedom before they had the two kids and bought the brownstone in Brooklyn. Where had *this* fantasy come from?

The few elderly shoppers stared at Lula and Alvo as if they were celebrities they couldn't quite place. The dying fluorescent light and sour-milk smell were happy reminders of Tirana. Alvo paced the aisles, checking out the cans and packages but also the walls and the ceiling. He said, "We are in construction. I mentioned that, right? I notice construction details."

"What kind of construction?" said Lula.

"Commercial only," said Alvo. "Residential is asking for headaches. First the client wants wallpaper, then she wants it ripped out. Businesses, they know what they want. Aisles, cash registers, shelves. Especially cash registers."

Alvo seemed to know what he was talking about, and the sound of the words—commercial construction—was honest, industrious, solid. And the gun? This was New Jersey. You'd be crazy to be in the building trades and not carry a weapon.

Alvo picked up a quart of orange juice and a carton of Camels. So that *was* his sales receipt Estrelia found in the cushions. Lula had saved it in her desk. Alvo's shoulder brushed against hers as they—ladies first—left the market.

But as they approached the SUV, Lula felt the temperature between them drop. She said something lame—testing, testing—about the weather, but Alvo didn't answer. This time he opened the door on his side and let her open hers. This time Hoodie took the wheel with Leather Jacket beside him. Alvo frowned into space. Lula had no idea what had gone wrong, or how she could fix it.

Hoodie's aggressive driving style matched the new mood inside the Lexus. The cursor on the GPS danced across the screen, and its female voice cried plaintively, "Reconfiguring, reconfiguring."

After a while, Alvo said, "My friend Spiro, the one with the stiletto heel in his head? That's why you don't want an Albanian boyfriend, Little Sister."

Little Sister. Alvo's fraternal romantic advice made her heart hurt. But why had she even thought that Alvo wanted to be her boyfriend? Maybe Lula was losing her charms. Welcome to twenty-six.

Lula said, "I dated this Argentinean guy, Franco, he was ten times crazier and more jealous than the worst Albanian shithead."

Alvo said, "What did he do, this Franco? For a living."

"An artist," Lula said.

Alvo glared at her. "Let me get this straight. You fucked an Argentinean?"

"No," lied Lula. "I said dated." First he'd told her not to go out with Albanian guys, and now he seemed ready to honor-kill her for dating an Argentinean.

"Glad to hear it. Dated." Alvo nodded at the front seat. "My gorilla pals here get very upset when they see Albanian girls going outside the community."

Lula said, "Good luck telling an Albanian girl what to do."

"Funny," said Alvo, mirthlessly. "Here we are. Home sweet home." How had Hoodie managed to find all new streets and arrive at her house without her realizing they were close? The SUV jerked to a stop. No one spoke. No one mentioned seeing Lula again, and the Lexus roared away before she'd unlocked Mister Stanley's front door.

Chapter Five

————— ⌘ —————

Days passed, then more days, with no sign of Alvo. What did Lula have to look forward to? The college trip with Zeke and his dad? Zeke's departure for school promised deliverance, of a sort. But Mister Stanley would find a reason to keep Lula around. He would pay to have another human watch him sip his water. How would Lula break away? Home comfort was seductive.

Oddly, the gun reassured her. But was that really so odd? Lots of people felt that way. For example, her father. Lula told herself that the three guys would return, if only to pick up the pistol. Handguns were costly, hard to obtain. Meanwhile her challenge was to keep busy and stave off worry about her future.

One morning, frustration drove Lula to travel into the city and check out the supermarket from which Alvo's receipt had come. Useless, as she'd known it would be. What did she think would happen? That destiny would deliver them both there at the same moment? What a coincidence, our meeting here like this! So now it was her turn to be the stalker in this romance.

Parked outside the supermarket was a construction van. From the door she could see that repair work was being done. She peeked through a gap in the plastic curtain. The workers were Chinese. Maybe her friends were in charge. She knew that a lot of

Albanian guys ran construction crews. She'd met some of them in a bar on Second Avenue on the night Albania competed in the World Cup.

She walked down the supermarket aisles, pretending to look at food, until she saw a checker watching her in the security mirror. She bought the costliest peanut butter, hand-shelled on a farm in Georgia, along with a jar of organic strawberry jam from Vermont.

She was taking off her coat when Zeke walked in the door.

"What's this?" Pointing accusingly at the peanut butter and jelly, he seemed upset that Lula had gone grocery shopping without him.

"I went into the city," Lula said.

"You went into the city to get peanut butter and jelly?"

"I got it especially for you. I read about this brand in the paper. Try it. Trust me, okay?"

Zeke said, "Did you get crackers?"

"Use a spoon," Lula said.

THE WEATHER TURNED even more dismal, and after a week of gloom, Lula powered up Zeke's computer and closed out a cascade of girls in bikinis wanting to chat. She imagined her own cascade, snapshots of lost keepsakes and loved ones gone forever. Back home in '97, when the economy tanked, everything went missing: doorknobs, letterboxes, public toilets, storm drains. Thieves would come in the night and steal the swings from the children's playground, the drinking fountains from the park. But who would want to read about that? Who would care about the neighbor who almost got lynched for stealing paper from the communal toilet?

The true stories of her childhood were tales of grubby misery without the kick of romance, just suffering and more suffering, betrayal and petty greed. It was nicer to mine the mythical past. Wasn't that the Albanian way? Five minutes into a conversation, Albanians were telling you how they'd descended from the ancient Greeks. The Illyrians. Those folktales had come from somewhere. Hoodie said they were all related. Every Albanian fairy tale was someone's great-granny's life story. Little Sister, they'd called her. For all Lula knew, it was true.

She could write the most famous legends and pretend they were family stories. For example, the tale of the heartless girl everyone called Earthly Beauty, who put her prince through hell before he could make her his wife. Lula wrote, "My grandfather's half brother fell in love with a woman known as the Earthly Beauty. She charged him money for peeks at her—a finger, a hand, an arm. He paid for every inch of flesh he saw, he spent his dead papa's fortune. And every inch, every beautiful inch, made him want her more."

Don and Mister Stanley were so good to her. It was sinful that fooling them should be easy and even entertaining.

Oops. Now came a part about the boy finding a hat that made him invisible. Lula would have to leave that out if she wanted her story to have any credibility whatsoever. The same thing went for the bottle from which genies appeared and threatened Earthly Beauty on our hero's behalf, genies whose power she turned against him by making them work for her. Lula imagined Earthly Beauty looking like Angelina Jolie. She turned the genies into thugs whom Earthly Beauty seduced, but ended the scene just short of her having gang-bang sex.

But still the tale had one final twist. The hero finds some enchanted grapes, red and green. The red grapes make horns grown on Earthly Beauty's face. The green grapes make the horns drop off. Magic cosmetic surgery. So the red grapes let the prince wreck his beloved's looks, and the green grapes turn her back into Earthly Beauty. After which she's so grateful she marries him, even though he was the one who destroyed her face in the first place. But then he fixed it. And he loves her.

She wrote, *My grandfather's half brother found some grapes.* No wonder there was such bitterness between Albanian men and women. This was their version of Cinderella. What do you do if the girl doesn't like you? Throw acid in her face, then pay for the plastic surgeon. If you believed the story, Earthly Beauty deserved it, stealing the guy's money for a glimpse of her hand. But that was how women were! That was why you took your girlfriend out for an expensive dinner and then refused to pay for your wife's dentist and let all her teeth fall out. If you still had any money left, you divorced her and found a younger wife who still had her own molars.

Lula deleted the last line. Then she typed it again. "My grandfather's half brother found some grapes."

She saved the file under "Earthly Beauty" and shut down Zeke's computer. She put on three sweaters and a coat and grabbed an umbrella and headed out the door.

The library was deserted except for nice Mrs. Beller, who had introduced herself early on and who always seemed personally disappointed that Lula could never provide the documentation required for a borrower's card. Were Mrs. Beller's tremors worse today, or was some bad news on her computer making her shake her head? She didn't acknowledge Lula. Had Lula offended her somehow? Could the librarian have unearthed some awful secret about her?

Lula went to the magazine rack and was soon engrossed in an article about a Texas dynasty literally and figuratively screwing each other for generations, when they weren't crashing cars into trees or jumping off the roof. The story cheered Lula. It sounded like a family you might hear about at home, though the money would have been different, as would the trees and cars and roofs. An hour passed, then another. Without the quiet welcome of this undemanding place, she might have fled Mister Stanley's long ago. Which might have been a good thing. Who knew where she would be now, how much better off, or worse?

Eventually, she made herself stand up and put on her coat. She was relieved when Mrs. Beller said, "See you soon, dear. Stay dry."

On the way home, Lula passed a drenched terrier guarding its owner's front porch. Ugly Dog to Earthly Beauty. What if the magic fruit didn't make you grow horns but created some more believable, less disfiguring problem? A bad mood. Bipolar depression. The magic green-grape cure could be some ancient folk pharmacology that would thrill Don and Mister Stanley.

Back in the house, Lula tossed her wet clothes into the laundry room and went up to her desk, where, she was surprised to see, she'd left Zeke's laptop on. She was always careful to shut it down, especially when it was raining. Many friends at home had had their hard drives fried by lightning.

Obviously, she was losing her mind. She'd left the Earthly

Beauty file open. The cursor blinked at the end of the text. Lula read through the final section.

My grandfather's half brother brought Earthly Butey the pretty red grapes, but they were poison. She fell ill and almost died while he searched the world for help. Finally he found an old heeler in the mountains who said, feed her green grapes. That wouldn't have been the guy's instinct, the red grapes had done enough bad. But he did what the heeler said, and Earthly Butey got better and fell in love with him and they married and had fifteen children and lived happily ever after, and she never complained when the guy had young girlfriends well into old age.

Lula hadn't written this. She knew how to spell *beauty* and *healer*. Her story wasn't about poisoning a girl and then curing her and she's yours. Fifteen children? The wife who doesn't mind the old guy having young girlfriends? What sicko male pig wrote that? A male pig who couldn't spell.

Or maybe someone was trying to make her think she'd lost her mind. She and Dunia had watched an old black-and-white movie on the Belarusian model's TV about an evil husband convincing his wife she'd gone mad so he could put her in an asylum and steal all her money. But Lula was sane enough to know that someone had sat here and read what she wrote and finished her story for her.

This was creepy in the extreme! Had Lula come home sooner, her chair might have been warm from her self-appointed ghostwriter's ass. Frantically, she searched the house for signs of alien presence. Nothing had been disturbed. She should run back to the library and throw herself on Mrs. Beller's mercy. But what would happen when Zeke came home to find the intruder still here? Lula should dial 911 and tell the police that someone had broken into the house to write fiction on her computer. She'd like to hear how that went. Anyway, no self-respecting Albanian called the cops for any reason, good or bad.

Lula checked the house again. She even went down to the basement, which scared her in the best of times. Really, it was fortunate she didn't believe in ghosts. When Franco, the waiter-sculptor, took her to his loft, he'd told her a story about angels finishing an artist's work while he was away. Franco must have believed that spirits worked on his crappy sculptures, assembling the rusty bedsprings into outer space creatures while he was off serving red beans and rice. It was one of those things guys said when they wanted you to get you in bed. Could Franco have tracked her down and done this? Franco was grateful that she'd never once mentioned their one-time-only drunken night of awkward sex.

Unless Lula had written some notes to herself and forgot, notes so rough she never bothered correcting the misspellings? She would have remembered. She had to be logical, look at the facts, be her own detective.

It had to be an Albanian person who knew about Earthly Beauty. It was Alvo. It had to be.

Maybe Alvo's ending wasn't so bad after all. Readers might prefer the randy Albanian codger with the fifteen kids and the harem. And what became of the Earthly Beauty? Whiskers, sagging breasts. Most people would think she got what she deserved for making her boyfriend suffer.

Lula corrected the spelling and grammar and printed out

the story, and that night asked Mister Stanley if he would mind looking at something she'd written. From across the kitchen, she watched him read. As he turned the last page, he said, "This is excellent. Can we share this with Don?"

"Naturally," Lula said.

THE NEXT WEEK, Don Settebello called and asked Lula if they could have lunch tomorrow. Just the two of them. During her work-visa application process, Don had several times taken her out for a burger to keep her informed about her case. All very proper and professional, the kindly hip avuncular lawyer reassuring the client in whom, he said several times, he saw his daughter, grown up. Surely he didn't mean Abigail, who had better start eating right now if she planned to turn into Lula. She'd assumed that Don meant his feelings for her were the purely paternal good wishes that a powerful older man feels for a bright, deserving young woman.

Don said, "Let's go to Mezza Luna. At the moment it's very hot, but I'm sure I can get in. The line cooks are all my clients. I need to ask you a little question. Maybe two little questions."

Lula couldn't say no, though it made her uneasy to recall that subliminal sexual thrum she'd picked up from Don at the steak restaurant. Dear God, don't let him hit on her and make life complicated. She had to admit it was flattering that an important guy like Don would knowingly violate the ethics of his profession for a shot at Lula, who lately had not exactly enjoyed an excess of male sexual attention.

"Two little questions?" repeated Lula. She hadn't meant

to sound provocative. Could one be: Will you blow me? Don would never say that.

Lula dressed up in her new clothes, this time without Zeke's scarf, and took the three buses that, against all odds, got her to the restaurant on time. Don rose to kiss her cheek. On the table were a glass and a half-empty bottle of red wine. Half full, Lula reminded herself.

"Something to drink?" asked the waiter.

Lula pointed at Don's bottle, and the magician-waiter produced a glass from thin air.

"Brilliant choice," Don said.

Don asked after Stan and Zeke. Fine, they were fine, everybody was fine. When Lula asked Don how his cases were going, he stared into his wine and was silent for so long she wondered if he'd heard her. He said, "I went to Guantánamo."

Lula said, "What happened?"

"It took me two days before they'd let me talk to anyone, and then another two days before anyone would talk to me. And then . . . the stories they told me, it was worse than you can imagine." Don closed his eyes for a few moments, leaving Lula free to look him in the face and see more anger and torment than she wanted to see in her lawyer's face, or in anyone's, for that matter. "You know what they call torture? Enhanced interrogation techniques. You know what they call a beating? Non-injurious personal contact. A suicide attempt? Manipulative self-injurious behavior. If I told you what I heard there, they'd have to kill us both. I could lose my security clearance, and my poor client would be fucked. Except he's already fucked. I'm not going to tell you his name, he's a Harvard-trained Afghan cardiologist, he went home to start a clinic, and some piece-of-shit neighbor got two grand for turning him in as a Taliban leader. The neighbor probably wasn't even a shithead, just some desperate slob who needed the money. Meanwhile my guy gets three years of torture. No sleep. No food. Constant loud noise. Made to eat his own shit. Shackled and hung from the ceiling. Razor cuts on his penis."

Lula put her hands over her ears and lip-read Don saying, "Fucked."

"It's great you're doing something," she said. "Or even *trying* to do something."

"Who knows what I'm accomplishing," said Don. "Making myself feel better. But what will they let me actually *do?*"

Why were Don and Mister Stanley always asking Lula questions that had no answers? She said, "During our dictatorship these things also happened—"

"Meaning what exactly?" said Don

"Meaning these things happen," said Lula. She hoped the food here was good. "Human nature, maybe . . ."

Don said, "I don't know what else to do. Once you know, once you've seen . . . So I take my life in my hands from the minute I get on that ridiculous toy plane with rust holes in the fuselage and nowhere even to piss. At least I give these guys some courage, some heart. Let the so-called Justice Department know that someone is paying attention. Then I come back and eat this fancy food and drink this fabulous wine, and maybe the guy gets tortured worse because I tried to help him."

"That's what happens," said Lula. "Like I said, human nature."

Don said, "You've got to stop saying that. I never said shit like that when I was your age. I was Mr. Idealism. I was the guy who was going to save all the little guys from the big bad bullies."

Lula shrugged, very Balkan. "You should have grown up where I did. We knew the truth from birth."

"And what truth would that be?"

"Put the little guys in power, and overnight they turn into the big bad bullies."

Lula stopped. Were they arguing? She didn't want Don to think she was calling him naive. But it never hurt to remind him where she came from and what her country had been through. Don knew she was half Muslim. He'd said, Don't make a point of it. Her visa application said Christian.

Lula said, "So what's the question you wanted to ask me?" If the question was about sex, let Don ask it now. Saying no would be harder after he'd paid for the meal.

Don shook his head like a swimmer with an earful of water. "Oh, right. About that story you gave Stan . . ."

"What about it?" said Lula.

For a moment, she considered telling Don that someone had sneaked into Mister Stanley's house and finished the story on Zeke's computer. She felt like a child with a secret she wanted a grown-up to know. But she wasn't a child, and if her coauthor was Alvo, Don Settebello's knowing would only make everything more complex. She trusted Don, but only so far. She would wait and see what happened between now and dessert.

"I thought your story was fantastic," Don said.

"Thank you," said Lula. The waiter appeared with a choice of breads. Don waved the waiter away.

"Hey, wait a minute," said Lula. The waiter returned, and

she helped herself to a crusty roll studded with raisins and olives.

"Nicely done," said Don. "I like appetite in a woman."

Lula buttered her roll and took a bite, and with her mouth still full in what she hoped was an unsexy way said, "You were talking about my story."

Don said, "Right. Your story. I took the liberty of showing it to a friend in publishing, and she gave it to an editor friend who, coincidentally, happens to be Bulgarian."

"Bulgarian?" Lula already had a bad feeling about this Bulgarian person.

"Bulgarian," said Don. "Anyway, she read your piece. She liked it very much."

"Thank you," said Lula uneasily.

"Don't thank me," said Don. "But she did suggest that . . . well, that story about the Earthly Beauty and the guy who wins her after going through all that abuse and the part about the grapes is a very popular Balkan folktale. So it seemed . . . strange that it happened to your grandfather's half brother."

Cousin, Lula wanted to say, except that she suddenly couldn't remember what she wrote. Maybe Don was right.

Don said, "She did say that the part about the fifteen kids and the harem was extremely Balkan. And not the traditional ending. I enjoyed that part too."

Lula said, "It's a short story."

Don said, "I thought it was true. Something from your journal."

"I've branched out," Lula said. "I thought you and Mister Stanley knew that. Anyhow, calling a character my grandfather's half brother doesn't mean he was my grandfather's half brother. I could call a character Don, and he won't be you. Have you read Ismail Kadare? The greatest Albanian novelist? He wrote about Egyptian pharaohs and medieval monks to hide the fact that he was writing about our dictator."

Lula shouldn't have mentioned Kadare. It was unlikely that Don would remember her passing off a Kadare plot as a story she was writing, but why take chances? She said, "Bulgaria was Disneyland compared to how we lived. How people *still* live in Tirana. Your Bulgarian friend should visit."

Don turned up his palms, and his fingers curled, groping for . . . what? He didn't care about Bulgaria. He didn't care about Lula's story.

Don said, "Camp Delta was a shock. You think you know, and you think you know . . . but when you see the real thing . . . I'm obsessed. I want to tell anyone who will listen. The loneliness, the pressure . . . Thank God for good friends and good food. I hope my daughter finds that out. Another bottle, please. Pronto!"

"No, thank you," Lula told the bottle pointed at her glass.

"Yes thank you for me," said Don.

Neither spoke for a while. Then something fell on Lula's hand so heavily that dishes clattered. At first she thought that a fat warm brick had landed on her fingers, but it turned out to be Don's hand, pinning Lula's to the table. Lula's instinct was to shake it off, but she waited without moving.

Don said, "You're a beautiful woman." He sounded as if he were shocked to suddenly find that out. He said, "Is it all right if I say that? If I compliment you like that?"

"A compliment is a compliment," Lula said, gracious but not flirtatious. "Always welcome, believe me."

Don looked at her over the top of his wine glass, and there was a moment, a split second, really . . . *lawyer client, lawyer client*, Lula chanted inside her head, telegraphing how much Don was risking merely by touching her hand. And for what? Human contact? Romance? Distracting himself from the pain and injustice of the world with a few hours of sordid, unprofessional, maybe actionable sex?

And then, for no discernible reason, or perhaps for a good reason indiscernible to anyone but Don, something broke the mood. Don removed his hand from Lula's and pushed his spectacles back on his nose. Don the lonely guy vanished, and Don the righteous lawyer replaced him.

Don said, "This morning I woke up and looked in the mirror, and my hair was gray."

Lula tried not to look puzzled. Don's hair, what there was of it, had been gray when she met him.

"I'm quoting Chekhov," said Don.

"I've read him," Lula said. "I don't remember about the gray hair."

"Young people never do," said Don. "Anyhow, by some divine intercession, or more likely thanks to some bureaucratic fuckup, they let me talk to another detainee. This one's a businessman from Mosul with the bad luck to have the same name as some al-Qaeda motherfucker. Of course they don't let me meet the big guns. The guys who actually did something or plotted something and are still entitled to protections, I don't care how Dick Cheney tries to fuck with the Constitution—"

Lula said, "If Hoxha and Milosevic had a baby, and the baby was a boy, it would look like Dick Cheney." She'd been waiting months to say this to someone besides Zeke, but she'd chosen the wrong moment. To Don, it was a nonsensical interruption.

"It's fine if I meet with the innocent guys. Nobody gives a rat's ass what they didn't do. This guy's been in solitary for months. The family found out and got in touch. The wife's going crazy. The three kids are crying for their daddy. The guy just came off his hunger strike. He's down to eighty-five pounds."

Lula said, "What's he accused of?"

Don said, "Nothing yet. The guy ran a charity. Funded religious schools. Helped out widows and orphans."

Lula said, "The KLA bought its whole arsenal that way, going from house to house in Detroit and the Bronx, collecting for widows and orphans."

Don said, "That's the kind of cynical shit everybody says." His scowl made Lula feel terrible for being one of those cynics. She made a mental note to tone down the Eastern Bloc pessimism, or realism, depending.

"I believed this poor bastard. I've been a lawyer for thirty years. I can tell when a client is lying."

Every lie Lula had ever told passed before her eyes, starting with the one Don knew about, her omitting the half Muslim part on her visa application. No one in her family had been religious for generations. That is, if you didn't count the third cousin who got born again and went to Afghanistan to wage jihad. Everyone had a third cousin like that. What if they traced him to her? If just one nosy agent found out, she could be back in Tirana tomorrow.

The restaurant's creamy light made everyone look healthy, rich, and happy to be having lunch with everyone else. How long could her comfortable life here last? She ordered the haddock with grapes and saffron.

Don said, "Thanks. I'm not eating." He gulped his wine like water. Lula wondered if she was going to have to help him into a cab. His office number was on her phone. She could call his secretary.

Don said, "A client of mine got deported."

"The one whose foot got run over?" Lula welcomed the chance to prove she had listened. She hoped it was the same client. The more of Don's clients who got sent home, the less optimistic she felt.

"Good girl," said Don. "But no, another one. Honestly, I start to wonder, Why am I even trying?"

"Don't blame yourself," said Lula. "You helped me get my work visa. You fixed things for Estrelia and—"

"This guy *had* a green card," said Don. "He's a contractor. Bangladeshi. His family's some bizarro evangelical Protestant."

"What did he do?" asked Lula.

"Illegal weapons possession. Unregistered handgun. To be honest, if I lived where this guy lived, on the far edge of Bushwick with two little kids and a wife, I'd find a way to protect myself, permit or no permit."

"Okay, sure, wow," said Lula.

"Is it too warm in here?" asked Don.

How could Don see the droplets beading up on the back of her neck? On TV, the suspects who sweated were either on drugs or guilty or both.

"Allergies," said Lula. She wondered which was more dangerous, ditching Alvo's gun and pissing off the Albanians, or holding on to it and worrying that someone would report her to the INS. The latter seemed less likely.

"It's not allergy season. You should get your eyes checked," said Don. "I was around your age when I started wearing glasses."

What age? she might have asked anyone else. But Don knew her age, to the day. It was on her application. Don already knew so much, she wished she could ask him about the gun. After all, he was her lawyer. But she knew what Don would say: Lose the sketchy Albanian pals, don't answer the door when they knock. She would pretend to take his advice, and she would ignore it.

Lula's haddock arrived. It could almost make you believe in God, or in some higher intelligence that had created this fish that, perfectly poached, flaked apart in buttery layers. She smiled at Don. "Would you like some?" Too much generosity! A remark like that could encourage Don to hold her hand again.

"No thank you," said Don. "I seem to be on an all-liquid diet. Go ahead, finish your lunch. I won't ruin it for you, I promise."

Don was as good as his word. He waited till Lula had cleaned her plate, then said, "It's worse than I imagined."

"Let's have coffee," said Lula. She and the waiter conspired wordlessly to get enough coffee into Don so he could ask Lula to calculate the tip—twenty percent—before he signed the credit card slip.

"Drink up," Lula kept saying, while she plied him with small talk about Zeke and Mister Stanley—the upcoming college trip, Zeke's B+ on a math test. Don drank all his coffee. From boredom, probably, but so what? The aim was caffeination.

Walking Don to his office, Lula glared at the few pedestrians rude enough to stare. It was an honor to hold a hero's arm as he lurched down the sidewalk.

Don could manage the elevator. They shook hands, then made an awkward attempt to hug. Lula took the buses back to Jersey.

She decided not to mention the lunch. But that night Mister Stanley asked, first thing, "So how was lunch with Don?"

"He seems a little . . . sad," Lula said. "He didn't eat much."

"Was he drinking?" Mister Stanley asked.

"Only wine," said Lula.

"I thought so too," said Mister Stanley. "I mean, about him seeming sad. Well, Jesus, Lula, who isn't sad with the state our country is in? This evening, driving home, I heard on NPR that forty thousand people are living in homeless shelters. And that's just in New York City! I worry about Ginger. I don't want her to suffer. Fortunately, she prefers the company of goofballs in Navajo sweat lodges to the company of drunks with the DTs picking bugs from under their skin."

"I'm sure she does," Lula said. "I'm sure she's fine." She went to the sink and devoted herself to washing a fork Zeke had left in the drain.

Mister Stanley said, "What did Don want to talk about?"

Lula said, "My story."

"He told me he liked it a lot."

"He did. But next time I think I'll wait before I let anyone read it."

"We didn't mean to rush you," Mister Stanley said. "I hope Don didn't upset you . . . He's been under a lot of stress."

"Don's a hero," Lula said.

"That he is," said Mister Stanley.

Chapter Six

———∞∞∞———

JUST WHEN Lula had given up hope of ever seeing the Albanian guys again, Alvo showed up. He had a gauze bandage wrapped around his hand, and he flinched when he shut the front door behind him. There was something sexy about his wince and the whiteness of the bandage. When Lula asked, he told her he'd cut himself when a saw blade snapped. Being in the building trades was an accident waiting to happen. He said, "The workman's compensation board loves it that nobody's legal anymore, so nobody files claims."

"I didn't know they had workman's insurance here," Lula said.

"They used to," Alvo told her.

"Coffee?" asked Lula. It was noon. She had been delaying the moment of making a sandwich from the last of Granny's red pepper jam and realizing that this would be the best part of her day, and that it was already over. She should offer Alvo something to eat. Zeke's leftover pizza? She could make an omelet.

Alvo said, "I was just in the neighborhood. You want to go get lunch?"

"Do I need to change?" Lula hadn't intended to make him look her up and down. Why had she quit dressing nicely and putting on makeup? Because she had no patience.

"Jeans are fine," Alvo said.

She'd expected to find Hoodie and Leather Jacket waiting in the Lexus. But the SUV was empty.

"Are you okay?" Alvo asked.

Why did everyone ask her that? Was every emotion so plain on her face for the whole world to see?

She said, "At university I played poker. Lots of times, I won enough to buy my friends drinks at this club where we hung out in Blloku."

"What club?" asked Alvo.

"The Paradise."

"I used to go there," said Alvo. "How come I never saw you?"

"I was there," Lula said.

Alvo started the SUV and pulled away from the curb.

"I wish I could drive," said Lula.

"I could teach you," Alvo said. "It's easy. Babies drive. Senile grannies drive. It would take one lesson."

"Two lessons," said Lula.

"One lesson," Alvo said.

Leftover drops from a morning shower sparkled on the fallen leaves and the brownish grass. They drove past a golf course on which there was a structure with three roofs, pointed like witch's hats.

"Look!" she said. "It looks just like that snack bar in the park in Tirana."

Alvo nodded. That he knew which snack bar she meant made her senselessly happy.

Eventually, Lula and Alvo slipped into something resembling a companionable silence, the calm married-couple happiness that Lula, despite the odds and the evidence, still hoped someday to experience. With Alvo? She was dreaming.

The silken GPS voice guided Alvo through a series of turns. Then it murmured: "Approaching destination." Alvo parked in front of a restaurant with a black curtain covering the window. Almost Albanian looking, except for the Asian lettering.

"Old Sam?" read Lula.

"Old Siam," said Alvo. "Old Sam. Very funny."

Lula said, "Go ahead, laugh. Nice guy. How do you know I'm not dyslexic?"

"Albanians don't get dyslexia. It's a disease Americans invented so they won't have to admit their kids are retarded."

"Maybe I caught it since I got here," said Lula. From this point it should have been easy to steer the conversation toward spelling. If only she could find out if Alvo could spell *beauty* and *healer*. That would answer a lot of questions. Or anyway, one big question.

Alvo said, "We should get out of the car."

"Sorry," Lula said.

There was a worrisome scarcity of vehicles in Old Siam's parking lot. Two sips of a sweet umbrella drink—next stop, Bangkok whorehouse. No wonder her social life was in ruins! Who would date a girl who couldn't tell being trafficked from a lunch date? As they crossed the asphalt, her fingertips and, weirdly, the surface of her scalp seemed to be responding, independently of her brain, to Alvo's lanky physical *thereness*. It was impressive, how a few nerve endings firing at once could silence Lula's sensible doubts about being alone with a man she'd met when he came to hide a gun in her house.

Alvo said, "This Thai guy from work told me about this

place. I love that about this country. Some people live here a lifetime, they only eat Albanian. But I like restaurants that serve the real deal from countries Albania never heard of."

"Me too," Lula said. She imagined herself and Alvo, brave culinary explorers, eating their way around the world without leaving the tri-state area. He'd said, A guy from work. Maybe he and the guys ran a crew. Maybe they had Thai workers.

"Queens is the best," said Alvo.

"I've never been to Queens," said Lula. "I'd love to go to Queens."

There were no other customers to spoil the pristine perfection of the tables set with yellow cloths and folded napkins. Someone switched on a sound system, and a girl with a baby's voice cooed and hiccupped her way through a song that sounded like a lullaby but was surely about lost love. If Lula ever had a child, she would play it music like that.

The Asian woman who came out from the back of the restaurant was so glad to see them that Lula was frightened to look directly into her joy.

"Water?" The woman smiled, setting menus before them. They nodded. "Beer? Thai beer?" Nod nod. More smiles. Lula watched her walk toward the kitchen door, where another Asian woman and two blond men in white shirts and ties waited tensely as if to debrief her after a top-secret mission.

"Mormons," said Lula.

"That's what I was thinking," said Alvo.

Lula said, "How did they get in? Even under heaviest Communism you saw Mormons in Tirana."

Alvo said, "Someone paid. Someone always pays."

The walls were covered with mirrors in which Lula saw herself and Alvo beside a canal in Bangkok. An optical illusion: A poster behind them pictured a temple with orange dragons coiled beneath its pincerlike spires.

Lula said, "Have you eaten here before?"

"Never. I like to change things up from day to day. Never the same thing twice." Alvo's tone was unsettling. He hadn't sounded like a laid-back, self-employed contractor wanting to maximize his fun, but rather like a gangster or politician describing security tactics designed to foil an assassination. Or was it a philosophical statement? Lula didn't feel she could ask. Maybe it was personal magic, a secret he had with himself, like the female CEOs wearing French underwear to board meetings. Alvo's gun was in Lula's underwear drawer, wrapped in those filmy garments that might not, after all, have been such a waste of money.

He said, "Also in private life. You don't want to be stupid. The place where lovers get blown away? It's always the lover's lane. The bench overlooking the Hudson. What sane person would go there? Some psycho sneaks up behind you. Blam. The perp's halfway to Pennsylvania before the ambulance comes."

He's paranoid, thought Lula. Another thing they had in common. *Paranoia* was English for Balkan common sense. Lula could live without making out on a bench above the Hudson. But what would it be like to have a boyfriend who never did the same thing twice? Sexually, it could be interesting. Where was she getting *boyfriend*? From one Thai meal? If lunch was a relationship, Lula and Don were married.

But wait. Was that a hair on her plate? No, a thread from her glove. Lula picked it off, but not before her lavender soap, inscribed with a copper hair, hovered like a disgusting mirage above the sparkling china. In seconds it vanished, but not before Lula was able to positively match its color with Alvo's.

She said, "Have you ever stalked someone?"

Alvo said, "Strange question, but okay. You want me to stalk you?"

"Look in the mirror," said Lula. "There we are. Eating lunch in Thailand."

Alvo looked. It didn't interest him. After that there was silence.

Finally Alvo said, "I wouldn't go there. I know this Sherpa guy. Buddhist. Hard worker. Never lies. He told me there's this dog at home that brings down yaks by reaching up their asses and pulling out their guts."

"Urban legend," Lula said.

"That's what I thought," said Alvo. "Then I saw it on the Internet."

"If it's not a hoax," said Lula, "why aren't those dogs the hot new pets for rap stars and Asian drug lords and Mexican narcos?"

"Good question," Alvo said.

The waitress brought their beers.

"*G'zoor*," Alvo toasted Lula.

"*G'zoor*," Lula said.

A few swallows infused Lula with a fizzy optimism. Life was not so bad. Back in Tirana no one was taking her out to lunch, and this place would be fancy, and it wouldn't be Thai. At home there was only Albanian. And Chinese, which was the same lamb, only candy-coated and orange. Just before she left Tirana, a Mexican place opened up, Señor Somebody's, where waiters in cowboy hats served melted sheep cheese and corn chips to missionaries from Missouri. Dunia and the Belarusian model had taken Lula to a Thai restaurant on Rivington Street for her twenty-fifth birthday, so she'd eaten Thai food. Once.

"Why the big sigh?" asked Alvo.

Lula said, "I was thinking about a friend."

"Friend as in boyfriend?" said Alvo.

"Friend as in homegirl. Last night, I couldn't sleep, I got up and went downstairs and turned on the TV and flipped through the channels. The best thing about my boss's house is, the walls are so thick no one hears anything."

"Excellent," said Alvo. "Let's say if you have guests."

Was Alvo flirting? It could be embarrassing to mistakenly assume he was.

"I never have guests," Lula said. "So last night on TV this Albanian girl was talking about marrying a rich mafioso and falling in love with his brother, who took her to Italy, where he beat her with a belt and turned her out as a prostitute until her uncle found her and an Albanian lawyer got her back. Two other girls were interviewed, both with similar stories, ghosts with smeary mascara running down their face. The thing was, I'd been lying awake worrying about my friend Dunia. She was here in New York with me, and she went back, but it's like she left the planet. She smart, she's tough. I tell myself she's okay. But maybe I'm just being lazy—"

"I've eaten lots of Thai food," said Alvo. "But I don't recognize hardly anything on this menu."

Lula said, "Pad thai is all I know. Why is this place so empty?"

Alvo said, "Maybe everybody in New Jersey is too retarded to know that Siam means Thai."

He waved the Thai woman back, then looked into her eyes so warmly he could have been her favorite son stopping by for lunch. The woman nodded and waved her arms, sign language for I'll-take-care-of-you, and disappeared into the kitchen.

"Nicely done," Lula said.

"Some people you can trust," Alvo said. "You know right away. Which we learned growing up, am I right? I read this book about bodyguards who work for the mob and the British royal family and Saudi diplomats. The Arab drivers are the brave motherfuckers. The ones who get sent to Guantánamo."

Lula said, "My lawyer has a client in Guantánamo."

"Too bad for him." Alvo crossed himself. "Too bad for his client."

"You're Christian?" Lula asked.

"I'm nothing. I'm Albanian. Like you."

"Like me. I mean, if there is a God, why is he so pissed off at Albanians?"

"Maybe God has a lousy personality," said Alvo.

"Could be." Neither had anything more to add on the subject of God. The conversation faltered until, even though it was a boring first-date question, Lula asked, "When did you come to this country?"

"1990, luckily for me. Or I'd still be there. You must have some hotshot lawyer to get a work visa after you're already here."

"He's famous." Lula tried not to think about Don's hand dropping on hers.

"If he's so good, why's he got a client in Guantánamo? Crazy country."

"It beats home," Lula said.

Alvo said, "The U.S. saved Kosovo from being ethnic-cleansed by the Serbs. No matter what else, we should be grateful. . . . But you know what? Sometimes I think this country's becoming like Albania, and Albania's becoming like this country. Like we're on opposite escalators meeting in the middle."

"In Albania's dreams," said Lula.

"We should be in the EU. Forget the trafficking, the drugs. If we had oil or even natural gas, we'd be in the EU yesterday! Then you get these deluded Albanian brothers sending the wrong message by plotting to blow up some army base in South Jersey. How does *that* make us look?"

"What plot?" said Lula. "What base?" Mister Stanley must have decided not to call her attention to that news item.

"Born-again jihadis," said Alvo. "It's a problem. No one in our family would go to my second cousin's wedding because he wouldn't allow alcohol or music. What kind of religion would even *think* about a dry wedding? Bad way to start off a marriage."

Lula almost mentioned that something similar existed in her family. Not that she knew her own jihadist cousin well enough to be invited to his wedding, or even to know if he got married. But something kept her from volunteering too much personal information. Who was Alvo, anyway? How had he found out her name? Cousin George? His aunt in immigration? Or was he an INS spy?

Lula said, "Would you know how to locate an Albanian girl if she went back home and vanished?"

"Why? You plan on vanishing?"

"My friend," said Lula. "Dunia. The one I'm worried about." Tears popped into her eyes. Alvo looked alarmed. In their brief acquaintance, he'd already seen her start crying and not be able to stop. He probably thought this was something she did all the time.

"Okay, look," said Alvo. "I know people. Here and there. Maybe I can find out something. No promises..."

He handed Lula his cell phone. "Write down her name and whatever contact info you have." Then he thought better of it, took back his phone, and swapped it for a ballpoint pen and a paper napkin, on which Lula wrote Dunia's name and Dunia's mom's address. Alvo read it and shook his head.

"Glad I'm not there." He put the napkin in his pocket, and Lula felt as if she were watching Dunia vanish into the linty darkness of Alvo's jacket.

The Thai woman returned and set down a platter of crunchy fried scraps. Lula helped herself to a mouthful of salty, oily, delicious ... what?

"Parsley," Alvo said. Lula liked it that he knew, and that he not only ate with gusto but made little smacky noises. Of all the lies people told about sex, about the ratio between hand size and penis size, about the pleasure-delivering capabilities of the circumcised versus the uncut, the only one that was true, in Lula's experience, was the correlation between liking food and being good in bed. The subject was pleasant to think about, only mildly spoiled when she remembered Don Settebello saying he liked a woman with an appetite.

The woman brought more food. Duck country-style, very authentic.

"Thank you," chorused Alvo and Lula.

"Every fall my grandfather shot a duck," Alvo said. "One duck per comrade per year."

Lula picked up a chunk of duck and, with her front teeth, pried the moist spicy meat from the bones. She put aside the crispy skin she planned on saving for last. She caught Alvo watching her lick her fingers.

"My father too," she said. "The annual duck. Wasn't there some national holiday when the comrades were all supposed to go out and get trashed on raki and fire away at game birds and shoot each other in the back?"

"I don't remember," Alvo said. "No one ever took me along. Hunters were always getting shot."

Lula said, "My father taught me to shoot." Bullet-riddled Madonna vogued in front of her eyes.

"I taught myself," said Alvo. "I had to."

Another missed opportunity. She could have sounded girlie, asking why a contractor needed a gun. She was sorry the subject had come up. What if Alvo wanted his gun back? "So what do you guys build?"

"All commercial. Supermarkets. I thought I told you. We renovate supermarkets."

"Maybe you did," Lula said. She was thinking about the supermarket to which she'd tracked his sales receipt. Someone was doing construction there. Maybe he'd bid on it and lost. Two and two were adding up. Adding up to zero.

"I wish you'd renovate *our* supermarket," said Lula. "It's very organic and expensive, but there's a nasty smell, like a dead rat in the basement."

Alvo said, "What's it called?"

"The Good Earth," Lula said.

"Near you?"

"Five minutes," Lula said.

Perhaps someday she would know him well enough to tell him about finding the sales receipt and going to the store, hoping to meet him. Alvo would be flattered, or pretend. They would agree it was funny and cute, and then they would have sex.

"Where do you live?" asked Lula.

"Astoria," Alvo said.

"With who?"

"Alone."

"I thought you had a girlfriend."

"Did. I don't anymore."

"Sorry to hear that," lied Lula. On a normal date, you could ask why he and his ex broke up and shift the conversation to a more intimate level. When things got really personal, maybe she could ask him about showering in her bathroom. Then perhaps they could talk about his finishing her story on Zeke's computer. She would tell him that his ending, about the fifteen kids and the harem, was the part her boss and her lawyer liked best.

The Thai woman replaced their plates with bowls, chicken curry for Lula, something meaty for Alvo. Not only did she know what they wanted, she knew when they wanted different things. Did the heat in Lula's chest come from the chilis or from Alvo reaching across the table and chopsticking a hunk of chicken from her bowl? She pushed her bowl toward Alvo. Take as much as you want!

She said, "So how did you get to this country?"

"Boring story," Alvo said. "My dad was an engineer."

Lula said, "Everybody from former Communism was an engineer."

"In Detroit he had a barbershop, another family skill. My grandfather cut hair in his village. He cut the mayor of Detroit's hair, the whole family got green cards. So you could say I've moved up from barbershop to construction, or down, from engineer to construction. Depending on how you measure."

Lula said, "We went down. Any way you measure. Right after Communism ended, my father was crossing Skanderbeg Square, and he saw a woman with a huge bird hopping around on the sidewalk. She said it was an eagle, but my dad knew it was a falcon, big as a three-year-old child. Gorgeous. The woman was starting a business, renting out our national symbol for soccer games and races, weddings and private parties. She already had more orders than she could handle. But she had to hire a staff, rent an office, a phone, there were vet bills to pay. In other words, massive overhead. If my father wanted to invest, he'd get fifty percent in six months. Do I have to tell you what happened?"

Alvo said, "To his investment? No. What happened to the bird?"

Lula flapped her hands in the air above her head.

Alvo said, "Too bad your dad couldn't have found an eagle with two heads. That could have been serious money."

"Too bad," Lula said. She had been alone when she saw the woman and bird. Her dad wasn't even there. Why had she lied to Alvo? Because it was a good story.

He said, "You people who stayed longer went through a lot we missed."

Lula found herself staring at Alvo's hands, wishing she could take both his hands in hers and place them over her heart so he could feel their two hearts thumping in the same Balkan rhythm. "What could I do? My father wasn't an engineer. He made shoes." In a manner of speaking. One of his jobs included fencing stolen Chinese slippers.

"Then how did you get here?" Alvo said.

Lula said, "My aunt inherited some money from an uncle in Detroit. She'd kept it in an American bank, and when she died, she left it to me."

"You got here on a tourist visa? How did you manage that?"

Lula smiled and fluttered her eyelashes.

"The old-fashioned way," Alvo said.

"Have you been back?" asked Lula.

"My mother moved back home," said Alvo. "She lives in Tirana now. She and my dad divorced. I guess his being a barber wasn't good for the marriage. I visit every few years to see her and eat her cooking. That's how I know about the Paradise Club. Where I never saw you."

"I was there," said Lula.

"I would have remembered," said Alvo.

The Thai woman brought sweet coffee and a wobbly orange dessert. "On the house," she said. Alvo took a few bites, smiled at the woman, then pushed the pudding toward Lula, who polished off the whole plate. Alvo drained the last drops of beer, and Lula did the same, though it tasted awful on top of the mango pudding. There was nothing left to eat or drink and no reason to stay.

Alvo said, "Will you be around next week?"

Where else would she be? She would try to fit him into her busy schedule of nothing. "Sure. No, wait a minute. Monday, Tuesday, Wednesday, I'm going on a college tour with Zeke and Mister Stanley."

"Like on *The Sopranos*?" said Alvo. "When Tony whacked the snitch?"

"I saw some episodes," said Lula. "But not that one."

"Before your time," said Alvo. "So you and the boss *are* fucking."

"Separate motel rooms." The question had never arisen. But she knew Mister Stanley. He and Zeke would share a room. She would get her own.

"My father wanted me to go to college," said Alvo. "The nearest community college was in ghetto Detroit. Fifteen percent white student body. The odds of not getting my ass kicked would have been better in jail."

Lula decided not to mention her career at the university in Tirana, though in other conversations—with the waitstaff at La Changita, and with Don and Mister Stanley—she'd taken every chance to boast about her education.

Alvo said, "So is that part of your job? Little Miss Make Everything Right. All you Albanian girls are the same. Mother Teresa was just the smartest."

"Mother Teresa?"

"The best at public relations. She worked a genius angle. Everyone in Albania is saving and scheming to move somewhere better than Albania. Which is basically anywhere. Only genius Mother Teresa moves somewhere worse than Albania. That gets you the Nobel Prize!"

"She's the most famous Albanian ever," Lula said.

"There you go," said Alvo. "Her and John Belushi. Everyone knows what famous people are like when the cameras stop rolling."

Lula had always admired Mother Teresa, cradling the dying,

cupping her wizened monkey hand around the last flicker of life. She said, "I can't picture Mother Teresa throwing her cell phone at a photographer."

"Check!" Alvo pulled out his wallet.

What had Lula said? She should have agreed with him about Mother Teresa. It probably wasn't personal. Alvo had somewhere to be.

"Thanks for lunch," said Lula. "What about the week after?"

"The week after what?" said Alvo.

"We could get together the week after I get back."

"I don't know," said Alvo. "Who knows if the world will exist by then."

"It will," said Lula.

"Why are you so sure?" Alvo said.

"Okay, maybe I'm not," Lula said.

They drove back in silence. As Alvo stopped in front of Mister Stanley's, he kissed her twice, switching cheeks. Very proper. Little Sister.

Lula touched his shoulder.

"See you soon," Lula said, at the same moment that Alvo said, "See you later."

THAT AFTERNOON, ZEKE came home with a bright new pimple flourishing on his chin. Lula tried not to notice, then gave in and stared. He was eating a vegetable tonight, no matter how he complained. Lunch with Alvo had left Lula feeling cross and oppressed by the compulsory niceness that had turned out to be such an important part of her job.

She said, "We're having pizza," without offering Zeke the frozen hamburger option. What a disgusting way to live, eating frozen dog food, when twenty minutes away people were feasting on roast duck and fried parsley. "And salad. You're having salad."

"I hate salad," said Zeke.

Lula said, "Let's go to the other market for a change. The faraway one." She could tell that Zeke heard the needling challenge in her suggestion that he venture beyond the borders Mister Stanley had circumscribed. His unteenage willingness to accept his father's limits made Lula suspect that Zeke himself had his own fears and hesitations. His father's rules provided a welcome excuse not to confront them. Though who could blame a kid for being reluctant to drive to the market where his mother sent him and his dad on the night she disappeared?

Zeke's smile looked less like a human expression than like an orangutan trying to make a rival orangutan back down. "I haven't got time. I have to write some crap paper for English."

"About what?" asked Lula.

"About crap," said Zeke.

Zeke drove them to The Good Earth, where delusional Lula imagined she might run into Alvo, there to ask if the owners wanted professional help eliminating the dead rodent smell from their basement. They bought mozzarella, tomato sauce, pizza crust. On the drive back, Lula said, "We should go to the other market sometime." What character flaw compelled her to keep probing this sad boy's sore spot?

"My dad would have a fit," Zeke said. "I think he checks the mileage."

"He can't check it every day," said Lula. Not until they were home and Lula was about to open the cheese did she notice that its package was puffed up and slimed with white.

Zeke said, "That mozzarella smells like when kids used to get sick on the grade-school bus."

Lula said, "I saw on TV how they take moldy hamburger and smush it around so the red meat is on the outside and the green in the middle—"

"You made me watch that story," said Zeke.

Lula dropped the cheese in the garbage, and Zeke followed her outdoors to put the plastic bag in the bin. Neither was wearing a coat, so Lula chattered to distract them from the cold. "Those bitches change the expiration dates, some poor kid eats a burger at the family picnic and winds up on life support so the supermarket can make . . . what? A hundred bucks, ten bucks, who cares how much. Human life is worth nothing to them."

"Corporate capitalism," Zeke said.

"Communism's no better," said Lula.

"Obviously," Zeke said. "Forget the cheese, okay, Lula? You can use tomato." He sounded so tragic that Lula rushed them back into the warmth.

"Mojito?" said Zeke.

"Definitely," said Lula. She made Zeke's light, as usual, but didn't hold back on her own and drank it quickly, then fixed herself another.

She said, "One night at La Changita these customers played musical chairs. They were the last ones in the restaurant, and they'd run up a giant bill and left a humongous tip. So the staff let them screw around before we kicked them out. The leader turned his iPhone up loud, and the customers danced around the chairs, and when the music stopped they scrambled. The homeliest girl was the first one out, and she burst into tears. They don't play that game in Albania. They play other sadistic games, but not that. Not enough chairs to go around was something we knew from life. No one would have understood what was supposed to be fun."

Zeke said, "Can I ask you something?"

"Sure." Lula drained the last of her drink.

"How come you don't have a boyfriend?"

Did Zeke imagine that was what her story meant? She almost said, I do have a boyfriend. "What kind of boyfriend would I meet here? Even the mailman's married. You want to fix me up with someone?"

"My friends are pretty young," said Zeke.

Lula hovered over Zeke as he ate three slices of pizza, then tossed the rest in the garbage because she didn't want Mister Stanley seeing the wretched meal she'd made for his son. After that she went up to her room. Let Mister Stanley drink his scrumptious glass of water solo.

That night, Lula woke from a dream in which Dunia's streaked face emerged from belching clouds of black smoke. How she longed for Dunia's counsel, her bad hair advice, bad fashion advice, bad boyfriend advice, bad immigration advice, bad life advice. Dunia was the only one with whom she could talk about Alvo. She could ask Dunia to read the tea leaves of bad-boy courtship. But how could Lula even think about her own problems when Dunia might be in danger? Probably Dunia was fine. People changed e-mail addresses. They moved back home and forgot you. Or they bounced back your e-mails as punishment for your staying in New York without them.

Or maybe Dunia wasn't okay. Maybe lazy selfish Lula was just telling herself not to worry. In the bar on Second Avenue at the Albanian World Cup game party, she'd met a woman who ran a nonprofit that rehabbed Albanian girls after they'd been trafficked. The woman gave Lula her card, and Lula checked the Web site, on which you could order pillowcases the rescued girls embroidered, which was not an encouraging sign of their reentry into their old existence, or any existence at all. Wasn't it time for Lula to tell Mister Stanley and Don about Dunia? What could they do? Alert Interpol and the CIA because her friend wasn't returning her calls? Don would pay attention only if Dunia was in some secret U.S. prison, which Lula doubted.

How could Lula find her friend, short of going back? A real friend, unlike False Friend Lula, would do anything necessary. She promised herself not to forget how lucky she was, living her comfy new American life in Mister Stanley's comfy house instead of selling her body to some tuna fishermen in Bari or hiking up her skirt on a service road beside a Sicilian *autostrada*.

Chapter Seven

———— ᘓᗒᗡᗢ ————

O N T H E morning of the college trip, Lula was ready early, dressed in her peacoat and the cheap secretary suit she'd bought for her very first meeting to discuss her case with Don. By the time Mister Stanley came down, Lula had made a thermos of coffee and packed a bag of low-fat cheese sandwiches, cut in half. Mister Stanley tasted a sandwich half.

"Delicious," he said, taking it along when he went upstairs to wake Zeke. Forty minutes passed before Zeke slouched downstairs. His hair was glued in two hornlike tufts, and his black T-shirt and jeans looked slept in.

Zeke threw on his jacket, opened the back door of his father's Acura, and lay down with his face pressed into the crease of the seat.

"You've got to put your belt on," said Mister Stanley. "We'll be on the highway."

"I'll sit up when we're doing forty," said Zeke.

"Crash test dummies implode at thirty," Mister Stanley said. "I've seen their heads fly off."

"Please, Dad," said Zeke. "I'm tired."

Mister Stanley said, "Of all the moments to regress."

"He'll be okay," said Lula.

Turning to watch Mister Stanley's house recede and vanish, Lula felt as if she were leaving a child who might grow so quickly as to become unrecognizable in her absence. How melancholy the house looked as it watched them go. She tried to see it through Ginger's eyes, as a prison she was escaping, a jail guarded by those tyrannical warders, Zeke and Mister Stanley. What if it were Ginger who'd sneaked into the house and bathed in Lula's tub? The hair in her soap was red. Ginger was a redhead, a clean freak, and probably cagey enough to misspell *beauty* and *heal* and to try to think like an Albanian male. But Ginger was in Arizona. It must have been Alvo. A warm rush melted the ice chip that had lodged briefly in Lula's heart.

Mister Stanley had printed out pages from MapQuest, which he handed Lula. "Ginger was the family navigator," he said.

Lula said, "You should get GPS."

"I wouldn't know how to work it." Mister Stanley tried to sound dismissive, as if a GPS system was a frivolous toy and anyone who used one was a frivolous toy person. But he couldn't carry it off. The Wall Street guys who'd eaten at La Changita were all about their gadgets.

"It's not that difficult," Lula said.

"How do you know?" asked Mister Stanley. "Do you ever use that cell phone—"

Lula said, "All the new cars in Albania, GPS comes standard."

"This car sucks," said Zeke. "I wish we could take the Olds."

"The gas would cost more than your first year's tuition," said Mister Stanley.

"Give me the money instead of school. That's what I've been saying!"

"I'm glad you're sitting up," said Mister Stanley. "Now please put on your seat belt."

One of the favorite after-hours conversations at La Changita concerned the spoiled brattiness of American children, a category in which the waitstaff included the customers. Everyone had a friend who worked as a nanny, everyone had watched some mom bribe her little monster into putting on his mittens. Lula didn't volunteer her opinion, which was that no one knew how to raise kids, they just screwed them up differently in different places.

"Turn that down," said Mister Stanley. "We can hear that racket leaking through your earphones."

"Ear*buds*," said Zeke. "Not phones."

The singer was screaming the same two words over and over. Back pray? Black pay? Mister Stanley gritted his teeth. Zeke disappeared into his music, and Lula felt as if she and Mister Stanley were coworkers trapped in an elevator between floors. She leaned her head against the cool window and let her mind drift back to her lunch with Alvo and its unclear conclusion. Kiss kiss. Little Sister.

"Please, Zeke," Mister Stanley pleaded.

Lula had resolved to stop comparing Mister Stanley to Albanian fathers, with their overly manly approach to raising manly Albanian sons. It was darling, the way Americans put so much faith in going to college, the way American parents bought their baby birds a dovecote in which to roost for four years before their maiden flight out into the world. In Tirana, university students were like neighbors in a roach-infested slum, six to a dorm room, all working the same shitty job, smoking pot, drinking cheap raki, waking up in bed with a guy you sort of recognized from English class.

The traffic thinned as they passed oily black trees and swamps choked with russet weeds. How bleak everything was, even the new mansions like hairless patches of mange scratched from the fur of the mountains. The cold window burned Lula's cheek. She shut her eyes and let the tires sing her to sleep.

When she awoke, Mister Stanley was exiting the highway.

"Some navigator," he told Lula. "Good thing I memorized the directions."

"Sorry," said Lula. Zeke's head was tipped back, and his breath whistled in his nose. They drove past some barns and a meadow. Though she'd always hated those shooting trips with her father, now the memory of them filled her with grief. Twice her dad had slapped her for missing the target. No wonder she'd refused his offer to teach her to drive. It would upset him to know she'd never learned. Alvo had said: one lesson.

"Zeke," said Mister Stanley. "Wake up. Do you really want these schools to catch their first sight of you passed out?"

"You see anybody looking?" said Zeke. "Dad, you're getting like Lula."

Lula said, "Meaning what?"

Mister Stanley said, "Here we are. Harmonia College."

"Great. The gay one," said Zeke.

"Mrs. Sullivan suggested that you and Harmonia would be a good fit," said Mister Stanley. "And that with your grades and SAT scores you'd have a decent shot."

"Mrs. Sullivan is gay," said Zeke.

Lula had expected something brick and ivy-covered. A college in a movie. This one looked like Albania. Windowless, half buried in sod like the dictator's bunkers.

Mister Stanley said, "This place had a rough time during the sixties. Prehistory to you guys. But when they rebuilt, they figured they'd skip the breakable glass. In case the students rebelled again."

"Rebelled against what?" said Zeke. "The skyrocketing price of weed and K-Y Jelly?"

Mister Stanley sighed. "Mrs. Sullivan mentioned that it used to have a reputation as a druggy school, but all that's long past."

Zeke said, "Let me get this right. We're begging them to let us blow one hundred and twenty grand so I can smoke grass and have gay sex."

"Look," said Mister Stanley. "There's the admissions office. Visitor parking."

"Should I wait in the car?" asked Lula. Two young women in identical parkas and jeans walked past the windshield, holding hands.

"What did I tell you?" said Zeke.

"You might as well come along, Lula," said Mister Stanley. "I don't think they'd mind if we bring a friend."

A friend? Was that what Lula was? Friend-of-the-family Lula.

Friend was not how the admissions secretary assessed Lula's situation. The girl in harlequin glasses and a pencil skirt gave her a long, icy stare. Was Lula the dad's young Russian mistress, the son's pedophile older girlfriend? Or was Zeke correct about it being a gay school?

"Ezekiel Larch," said Mister Stanley. The secretary asked if they'd taken the tour. Mister Stanley said no, they hadn't.

"They left about five minutes ago. You can probably catch them if you hang a left and head up the path toward the arts building."

"Thank you," said Mister Stanley, grabbing Zeke's elbow and hustling him toward the door, with Lula following close behind.

"Have fun," called the receptionist. "Let us know if Zeke is still planning to stay over."

Stay over? Zeke looked at his father as if he'd just heard he was being put up for adoption.

"Applicants can stay overnight," explained Mister Stanley.

Zeke said, "Thanks but no thanks. We're leaving right after the tour."

It was easy to find the gaggle of parents and teenagers shifting from foot to foot in the cold as they listened to a Viking maiden in a Peruvian poncho. A peaked, striped knitted wool cap with earflaps ended in hairy blue strings that vanished in the tangle of her yellow curls.

"Welcome," she said. "I'm Bethany. I'm a sophomore. Concentrating in theater."

Everyone in the group checked Zeke out, sizing up the competition and concluding that Zeke was unlikely to offer much competition, so they didn't have to bother checking out Mister Stanley or Lula, although some of the dads checked out Lula and then looked guilty in case she was Zeke's older sister.

Bethany said, "And you're——?"

Zeke tried to think of a way not to answer, but at last gave up his name.

"What a beautiful name. Welcome to Harmonia, Zeke. You'll love it."

"This is like science fiction," Zeke whispered to Lula. But within moments he'd surrendered, dazzled by the high beams of Bethany's smile.

Lula and Mister Stanley trailed behind as Zeke followed on Bethany's heels—sandals in this weather!—into the eggy smelling, overheated cafeteria, past the organic salad bar, the troughs of mystery chunks bubbling in thick ochre sauce, the plastic canisters excreting coils of peanut butter. They toured the sunlit art studios where a group of students were spraying newspapers with red paint, then a theater in which another group was painting a backdrop of a red desert crisscrossed with white picket fences, which, Bethany explained, was for a production of *Our Town* set in outer space.

Bethany extolled the range of vegan dietary choices, the enviable art careers of the faculty, the deep spiritual beauty of the ninety-year-old Egyptian poet with an endowed chair who had mostly quit teaching but who lent his super-beautiful spiritual vibe to college events. It seemed to Lula that Bethany was directing much of this at Zeke, interrupting her monologue with questions designed to draw him out.

"What kind of food do you like, Zeke?"

"Pizza." Nervous laughter.

"This one cook, Mario, makes this amazing three-cheese-and-pineapple pizza."

"Awesome," said Zeke.

"Do you paint, Zeke? Have you ever been in a play?"

"No, but I'd like to," Zeke said. The other kids glared at Zeke as if he'd pushed his way to the front of the line and had already been admitted.

After they'd trekked through a suite of rooms, each containing a grand piano, Bethany said, "Everybody at Harmonia is some kind of artist."

"I like music," said Zeke.

"What bands do you listen to?" Bethany asked.

The parents had begun making discontented clucking noises. Perhaps some sort of protest might have erupted, but Bethany or no Bethany, their kids might still want to go here.

"My Chemical Romance?" said Zeke. "Ever heard of them?"

"I totally love them," Bethany said. "There's this great jazz class here called Noise. Last year one kid put his drumsticks through the snare drum, and the teacher, Bob Jeffers, gave the kid an A."

"Bob Jeffers teaches here?" said one of the fathers. "I used to go hear him years ago—"

Bethany ignored him.

"A class called Noise?" said Zeke. "That is superior."

Lula tried not to wonder why Bethany had fixed on Zeke, hardly the most attractive boy among the prospective students. Maybe she saw something in him. His sweetness, his vulnerability. Love was strange, everyone knew.

Sure enough, at the end of the tour, as they stood before the chapel where, Bethany told them, Harmonia graduates were always returning to marry each other, she reminded them about the Day and Night at Harmonia admissions option, which enabled applicants to go through a day of classes and have dinner and stay in a dorm, if they'd reserved in advance.

"Did we reserve?" Zeke asked Mister Stanley.

"Actually, yes," said his father, for which he was rewarded with the first grateful look Lula had ever seen Mister Stanley receive from his son.

Was Mister Stanley really going to hand over his child to this predatory female? He wanted Zeke to go to college. And this might be the only college that wanted him, a fear that Mrs. Sullivan seemed to have planted in Mister Stanley's mind.

Three other kids, two boys and a girl, stepped forward. That they had also made arrangements to stay made Zeke's going with Bethany seem less like a kidnapping than like an admissions option.

"Everybody have cell phones?" asked Bethany.

Everybody did.

"Your kids will call you first thing in the morning. We'll take good care of them. Don't worry." Then she thanked everyone and repeated what an awesome school Harmonia was, and left with her captives in tow.

"Let's go," Mister Stanley told Lula. "Before Zeke changes his mind."

Lula thought, He won't.

MISTER STANLEY MUST have memorized this segment of the directions. Because without much trouble he found the chain motel by the side of the highway where they had reservations.

"Nothing luxurious," he told Lula. "But it's the only game in town."

Glass doors glided open, admitting them to the lobby. A nervous boy, perhaps a Harmonia student, regarded them fearfully from the front desk. Mister Stanley had reserved two rooms, just as Lula expected. The clerk apologized because the rooms were on different floors.

After they got their key cards, Mister Stanley said he needed a nap. Lula was probably tired too. In the elevator he mentioned that, if she wished, they could meet downstairs for dinner at seven. Well, yes, in fact she did wish. She hadn't eaten anything all day except for one low-fat cheese sandwich. Lula continued up to her floor, where her key card didn't work. Red light, red light. *Buzz buzz*. Don't panic, try again. Green arrow, green light. A chimpanzee could do it. Not until she entered her room did she realize it was almost dark outside. The best thing about the shortest days of the year was the promise that the days would get longer. There was nowhere to go but up. The key in a slot made the lights go on. Cheap energy-saving bastards! Be thankful, Lula told herself. They were trying to save the planet.

She flopped down on the spongy bed, grateful to be safe in this simple, more or less clean room among hundreds of simple, more or less clean rooms, a bed, a deadbolt lock, a phone, towels, TV. No flat screen, but big enough. And most important, all hers.

She took off the floral bedspread they couldn't wash between guests and lay down on the sheet that, she hoped, they could. The pillows were comfortable, and the remote was placed precisely where a mind-reader had imagined Lula's hand reaching. Lula clicked through the channels, pausing at a talk show on which today's subject was marriage. The middle-class couples confessed their infidelities and cried, the poor couples refused to confess and then got trapped into telling the truth when their lovers appeared onstage. Then they cried and shouted. Some of the poor women cried, but none of the poor men. None of the middle-class women yelled, but many of them cried. Had Mister Stanley cried over Ginger? One night, on her way upstairs, Lula had heard a sound like someone sobbing from Mister Stanley's room. Just the possibility that it might be Mister Stanley had upset her so badly that she'd convinced herself she must have dreamed it. But now she thought, Who wouldn't cry? No wife, no fun, no girlfriends, a job he hated, a son who seemed to despise him.

Lula must have slept. Stadium lights from the parking lot shone into her window. Trucks whined past on the highway. She switched on the news and watched a congressman apologizing for his adulterous affair, then a group of senators calling for an investigation into charges that U.S. soldiers tortured prisoners in Iraq, then the president telling the press that the United States didn't torture. It was interesting how everyone lied and only the adulterers got caught. She was lucky to be in this warm motel and not in a smoldering ruin in Baghdad. No sooner had she thought this than another story came on, about a family of refugees from Katrina still living, eight to a room, in a motel outside Denver.

In the desk drawer was a flyer from a pizza delivery chain. Lula hoped the restaurant served steak. At two minutes to seven she left her room and found Mister Stanley waiting at one of a few tables in an area lit by the glowing juice and milk machines. Very Eastern European. Mister Stanley raised his glass of something golden in an uncharacteristically effusive greeting.

"Good evening," Lula said.

On the wall a shrimp and a lobster wearing top hats and tuxedos were jitterbugging to the notes of a song whose lyrics were "Surf and Turf Tonite!"

"We're pretty far inland for the surf," Mister Stanley said.

"I was thinking that too," said Lula. But the pride they took in their wise decision to skip the catch of the day evaporated when the bruised-looking Harmonia-student waitress informed them that their only choice was between spaghetti Bolognese and fried shrimp. She thought the kitchen could do a vegetarian Bolognese, but she wasn't sure.

"I'll have the spaghetti," Lula said.

"Make that two," said Mister Stanley. "And bring us your best bottle of red. For once I'm not driving."

"The wine's forty-eight bucks," the waitress said. "For which it will suck, I guarantee."

"Bring it, please," said Mister Stanley.

Lula said, "There were places like this at home. In the mountains. The cook only prepares one thing, but it's always great, and there's usually a goat or even a cow turning on a spit out back—"

Mister Stanley said, "We can assume with some confidence, there is no goat outside."

The waitress brought the wine, already opened. That wouldn't have flown at La Changita. Lula wanted to object on Mister Stanley's behalf. But that would only make the situation more awkward. Mister Stanley poured Lula a glass, then filled his own and said, "No ceremony here." He seemed disappointed by the spaghetti's rapid arrival and gave the waitress a sullen look, which went unnoticed. She plunked down a shaker of grated cheese and stalked back to the kitchen. Mister Stanley let his pasta cool as he drank the wine, and Lula did the same.

"Have you heard from Zeke?"

"Why would I?" said Lula. "He's having fun."

"What did you think of that Bethany?"

"Super friendly," said Lula.

"It's so strange," said Mister Stanley.

"What's so strange, Mister Stanley?"

"Call me Stanley, please. It's strange how alone I feel. And Zeke isn't even gone yet. Maybe if my marriage had lasted, I could be looking forward to a new phase of life. Ginger and I could be traveling. Poor Ginger! I have nightmares about her drowning and not being able to save her. If she'd been happy with us and hadn't . . . fallen ill, I'd have someone to talk to, someone to share the heartbreak of losing the boy—the young man!—who five minutes ago was an infant in our arms. Have you ever had those dreams in which you're trying to walk or drive and everything's dark and you can't see?"

"I don't drive," said Lula, ungenerously. Of course she'd had dreams just like that.

"May you never have that dream, and may you never discover how closely it mimics real life. Groping around in the darkness, taking all the wrong turns. Don tried to warn me before I took this job with the bank. But I thought . . . I don't know what I thought. The money and the power . . . I thought the additional income would be good for Ginger and Zeke, and that I could somehow improve the lives of all those poor folks who needed my help."

This was more emotional intensity than Lula had heard from Mister Stanley in all their previous conversations combined. It could affect their relationship, and not in a positive way. Not knowing more than she needed to was a policy that Lula tried to follow, not only with Mister Stanley, but also with Zeke and Don. It was how you survived under Communism. Who said you had to be intimate with everyone's personal secrets?

He said, "I always imagined that on the day Zeke left for college I would cheer up Ginger with a surprise—two business-class tickets to Venice!"

Lula tried to picture Mister Stanley's head in Ginger's lap while the gondolier serenaded them with swoony Venetian ballads. She said, "It's not like Zeke's moving to another country."

"Losing is losing," said Mister Stanley.

Now was the time for Dunia's half-full-glass pep talk, but no matter how she tried, Lula couldn't see what was left in Mister Stanley's glass. He said, "After they leave the house, it's never the same. It's not supposed to be the same. *Then* you'd have a problem. Those kids who never leave home and turn into . . . I don't know what they turn into."

Lula said, "They turn into cannibals hiding body parts in the freezer." She stopped. Mister Stanley was looking at her strangely. "That happened in Albania. Also here. I saw it on TV."

"TV." Mister Stanley made a face. "The point is, no one prepares you. Empty nest? Just that word—*nest*—is a joke. Empty heart and soul is more like it. That's why it blindsides you. I know you probably think we're not much of a family, Zeke and I—"

"Family is family," Lula said.

"But what I want to tell you, Lula, and what you'll find out when you're a parent, is that every time I see my child, I'm seeing every moment that child has been alive, every stage of his life, the baby, the toddler, the older kid. Besides which I'm seeing my own life—"

Lula wanted to cover her ears. The sorrier she felt for Mister

Stanley, the harder it would be to leave. Lula was alone too, but she still had a chance to find someone with whom to take that gondola ride. How pathetic, to console herself by measuring the potential brightness of her future against the certain gloom of Mister Stanley's.

He said, "This college admissions process thing is an evil plot to make one hate one's last months with one's child. Even if you know it doesn't matter, you still get sucked in."

At least Mister Stanley was saying *one* and *you* again, instead of *I* or *me*. Lula twirled a forkful of crunchy pasta and tasted the afterburn of chemical tomato, harsh but with a comforting similarity to the pizzas she made for Zeke. She hoped Zeke was having fun.

What was that jangly music-box tune? Lula stared at her purse as if a small rodent was banging on a toy piano inside it.

"Answer the phone," said Mister Stanley.

"I can't find it," said Lula.

"Push the goddamn green button!" Mister Stanley said.

Zeke said, "It's me. It's me. It's Zeke. Tell my dad to come get me."

LULA DIDN'T REMEMBER the motel being so far from the college. Perhaps it only seemed distant, every mile lengthened by her lack of confidence in Mister Stanley's driving and by her terror that they would never find the dining hall entrance where Zeke had said to meet him.

"Where the hell is he?" said Mister Stanley.

Zeke emerged from the shadows and jumped into the back seat. "Let's get out of here. Don't even think about asking."

"Have you eaten?" said Mister Stanley.

"Let's go home," said Zeke.

"You need protein," his father said.

Some guardian angel of paternal instinct must have been guiding Mister Stanley, because after fifteen minutes on dark country roads, they pulled into the parking lot of a diner crowned with the feather headdress of a neon Indian chief. Zeke slid into a booth near the window. Mister Stanley sat next to him and Lula across the table.

Lula was glad she hadn't filled up on motel spaghetti. She ordered a tuna melt, a piece of lemon meringue pie, and a large Coke. No, make that coffee.

Mister Stanley ordered the burger deluxe, then changed his mind and asked if they had a plain can of tuna, no mayonnaise, which they did, though it clearly lowered the waitress's opinion of Mister Stanley. He said, "I'll have coffee too. The hard stuff. Caf."

"Coffee," the waitress said. "And you, hon?"

"I'm not hungry," said Zeke.

"You need a minute?" the waitress asked him. "You can tell me when I bring your mom and dad their coffee."

"How could Lula be my mom?" demanded Zeke, after she went away. "She would have had to have me when she was ten years old!"

Mister Stanley said, "Zeke, you can trust us. What happened?"

No one expected Zeke to answer. Lula was startled when he said, "We were each given a big sibling, you know, instead of a big sister or brother, which is so corny and sexist. Bethany was my big sibling."

The waitress brought their coffee. Sipping his, Mister Stanley watched Lula burn her tongue.

"Careful," he warned her, too late.

"We went back to Bethany's room and talked," Zeke said. "Really talked. She told me about her town in New Hampshire, and how she's the first person to go to college in her family, and I told her about us and Mom—"

"What did you tell her about us and Mom?" Mister Stanley asked.

"The truth. Nobody was trying to impress anyone. It was like we'd been friends forever. We went and heard these kids she knew in a band, practicing. We had dinner in the cafeteria. The food sucked, no one could eat it. But lots of kids came and sat with us, so it was fun, and then we went to her room and—"

"You don't have to tell us this part," said Mister Stanley.

"You *do* have to tell us this part," said Lula. How stupid was Mister Stanley if Zeke was willing to talk? Let Mister Stanley look daggers at her. "What happened in Bethany's room?"

"As soon as we got there, Bethany said she was going to the bathroom and she'd be right back, but after a while this other girl came in and asked where Bethany was, and the girl got all stressed and said she thought I knew, everyone knew, you had to watch Bethany constantly because she would try to kill herself the minute she was alone. Sometimes she got better, but she went through bad times. And this was one of them. Her friends had convinced the school to let her stay if they watched her round the clock. She told me they'd try to find her—"

"What kind of school is this?" interrupted Mister Stanley. "To allow such a thing! To permit a mentally ill girl to give tours of the college. And to put you in such a position! What happened to the poor girl?"

"What happened to *me*!" Zeke said. "I sat on the edge of her bed, thinking how lucky she was to have friends who cared about her so much. Also how weird it was, because Bethany seemed so cool and at peace with herself. Her friend told me to wait there, in case Bethany came back. And if she did I should hang on to her and find a way to let someone know. I started to get really nervous, thinking the whole college was probably searching for Bethany. She might be dead, and it would be my fault, even though no one had told me."

"It wouldn't have been your fault," said Mister Stanley. "It would have been the college's fault."

Zeke said, "Finally I went out into the hall, and I ran into this older dude, some kind of hall monitor. He asked me if there was a problem, and I told him everything. Like a scared little bitch. The dude said, 'Fuck me, are those bastard theater kids up to that shit again?' "

"That person was in authority, and he used language like that?"

Zeke ignored his father. "It turned out they'd done it plenty of times. They call it real-life serial theater. Punking, college style. They do it to kids who are applying. Kids they figure won't get in, so they won't have to deal with them later." Zeke's voice had thickened with tears.

Mister Stanley said, "How could a tour guide and her sadist friends presume to know who will be admitted?"

Lula longed to throw her arms around Zeke and hug him to her chest and promise that soon, sooner than he could imagine, all this would seem funny. Though it was equally possible that it never would. Once, some girls in Lula's neighborhood had locked her in a storeroom. It hadn't made her claustrophobic or done any lasting damage, but still sometimes a bathroom lock jammed, and it all came back. She wanted to tell Zeke that he would grow up and be happy and loved. Today, she'd been mistaken for his sister and his mother, and tonight she felt like both, wishing she could protect him from so much she couldn't control. Maybe that was what family meant: wanting, and not being able, to help the people you love. She used to wish she could get her parents a nicer place to live than a room in her aunt's apartment in Tirana. The biggest apartment in the block, practically a villa, was occupied by the family of the prettiest girl in Lula's class, a girl who early in life had pimped herself out to a Party official.

Mister Stanley said, "Someone should be informed. One can't have . . . I'm sure the college . . ."

"I wouldn't go to that school if they paid me. I want to go home. And if you tell anybody about this, I won't apply anywhere. I'll move to the West Coast and work in a photocopy shop. I'll go live with Mom in Arizona."

"Whoa there, big fella," said Mister Stanley.

The waitress reappeared. "Can I get you something, hon?"

"Ant and roach poison," said Zeke.

"Kids," said the waitress, over her shoulder. "God love 'em."

"That was terrible," said Mister Stanley. "What you just said to that waitress. Zeke, my God."

" 'Ant and Roach Poison' is a song," said Zeke. "A Sweat Bees song. Don't you know anything, Dad? Okay. Miss? When you get a chance? I'd like a cheeseburger deluxe and fries and a chocolate milkshake."

"You got it," said the waitress.

Zeke wolfed down his food and ordered another side of fries. Lula and Mister Stanley each drank several cups of coffee. Mister Stanley tried to persuade Zeke to visit the other two colleges, but Zeke said no way, not now.

Mister Stanley said, "Look on the bright side. Everyone's still alive, no one is sick or in danger, and whatever happens at the other two schools has to be an improvement."

After that, he kept quiet.

Zeke ordered a slice of blueberry pie. Slowly, his mood improved. Mister Stanley said, "The motel has movies on demand. You can stay up late and order in any movies you want."

"I hope it's flat screen," Zeke said.

Mister Stanley nodded.

THE NEXT MORNING they met in the motel lobby and drove home in the rain. Mister Stanley refused to start the car until Zeke fastened his seat belt. When they turned onto the highway, Mister Stanley said, "For the record, we never agreed that you could charge an adult movie."

Zeke said, "You were snoring, Dad. The motel said it wouldn't show up on the bill."

"You believed them?" said Lula.

Zeke said, "Dad promised me it was flat screen, and it wasn't. So who's the liar here, really?"

Mister Stanley said, "I'm sorry, Zeke. But this is a moral discussion I don't have the energy for right now."

"Fine," said Zeke. "Me neither."

The minivan's wheels on the wet road seemed to whisper *sad sad sad*. What if Zeke didn't go to college? Could they stay like this forever, aging year after year into a trio of ghosts haunting Mister Stanley's house? Mister Stanley should have thought twice before getting so upset about his son leaving home. Be careful what you wish for. Be careful what you fear.

When they got back, it was late afternoon. Zeke slammed the door to his room. Mister Stanley sat at the dining room table and began opening the mail. Lula asked if he was hungry, and when he said no, she went upstairs.

Her room smelled faintly of cigarettes. On her blanket was a small red cardboard box. "Little Charmy Puppy," it said, in Chinese-style letters. Lula took out the furry Dalmatian dog and flipped the switch on its belly. She set the puppy on the floor. It barked and waggled its rear, then rose up on its stumpy hind legs and yelped so piercingly that Lula clapped her hand over Charmy Puppy's mouth.

What an adorable present! She hoped it wasn't a thank-you gift. Thanks for taking care of the gun. Lula rushed to the bureau. She unwrapped the gun, to make sure. Did Alvo suspect it slept with her underwear? Let him meditate on that. She counted her money. All there. She switched off the puppy, lay down on the bed, and put the toy near her pillow. Watched over by her mechanical pet, Lula fell asleep.

Chapter Eight

In the days that followed, Lula rehearsed how she would thank Alvo for Little Charmy Puppy. It was nicer than imagining what she would say if Mister Stanley discovered that Albanians were creeping around his house when no one was home. When she noticed that she couldn't look at the mechanical dog without sighing, she shoved it into a drawer, as if it were Charmy Puppy's fault that Lula was attracted to a guy who would rather stalk her than see her. But then she took it out again and made it do its tricks.

Having lived with relatives in a cramped apartment, Lula had long ago learned how to construct an imaginary wall between herself and the pushy cousin brushing her teeth and spitting into the same sink. Brick by invisible brick she constructed such a wall between herself and Zeke, with whom she still grocery-shopped and ate and watched TV, though now it was as if they were living the same lives in separate buildings. Surely Zeke must have felt the chill. For once, Lula didn't care. She would knock down the invisible wall as soon as Alvo showed up. It wasn't Zeke's fault that Alvo hadn't called, but Zeke was the only one here to blame. She avoided Mister Stanley, except for the brief nightly exchange required to reassure him that his son was still alive.

To pass the time, Lula wrote a true story about having a crush on a neighbor kid and slipping notes under his door, but never having the nerve to write anything, so she'd doodle on the paper and hope he knew it was from her. Soon after, his parents moved out of the building, and later she heard they were terrified that the secret police were tormenting them with encrypted messages that said nothing.

One night, Mister Stanley told her that Don Settebello had asked if he could come for Thanksgiving dinner. "Little Abigail is going to be with her mom. I think that's why Don wants to be with us. His second family."

"I'll cook a turkey," Lula said.

"Have you ever cooked a turkey?"

"Many times back in Albania," Lula lied. Her granny's *peshest*, crumbled cornbread soaked with turkey gravy and baked crisp at the edges, was a legend. Anyway, all you had to do was turn on the Food Network, day or night, and learn some famous chef's holiday turkey secrets. Lula kept hearing a funny phrase: *a successful turkey*. How successful could it be, dead and eaten by people?

But either to spare Lula the effort or because they didn't believe she was qualified to produce this national ritual of the grateful Pilgrim stomach, Don and Mister Stanley agreed to split the cost of a caterer who specialized in festive dinners and whom Don heard was fantastic. Lula tried not to feel hurt. It was less trouble for her. Less trouble was very American, she might as well enjoy it.

No one cooked in this country, though they were obsessed with every mouthful and afraid of how it might harm them.

One bond between Lula and Zeke was the pride they felt in the market among the shopping-cart cornucopias of good-for-you citrus and leafy greens, wheeling their own fuck-you cart, empty except for pizza crusts and frozen burgers. Though maybe only she and Zeke imagined that anyone noticed. It occurred to Lula that her willingness to sign on to Zeke's diet might be an unhealthy sign of regression to someone else's childhood. Or worse, a symptom of depression, a disease that didn't exist when she was a child. Under Communism, suicide equaled a failing grade in the dead person's political education.

On the Tuesday before Thanksgiving, Lula worked beside Estrelia, straightening up, futilely trying to make the house welcoming or just presentable. Was Estrelia trying to say that she stuffed her family's turkey with chiles?

"*Pica*," Estrelia said, giggling as she pantomimed steam rising out of her mouth.

That night, Mister Stanley told Lula that Don was bringing someone. A woman. He said, "I couldn't be happier. Don deserves some fun."

"Great! Who is she?" Lula felt as if a fat cold raindrop had slid down the back of her neck. What was her problem? She didn't want Don Settebello. He'd come on to her, more or less, and she'd gracefully rejected him without anything getting messy. Maybe she should have turned her palm up. Played with his fingers, even. What if Don had been her last chance at romance? At home everyone knew some spinster who'd rejected a suitable guy because she thought she could do better, and no one asked after that. Lula thought of the game of musical chairs she'd witnessed at La Changita. She felt like that girl who'd lost the first round. But why would anyone want a hero like Don when she could yearn after a lowlife who stalked her and left her cute Chinatown mementos?

Thanksgiving dinner was at five, and at three a van full of Mexican guys in baseball caps arrived with a foil-wrapped turkey and plastic tubs of mashed potatoes.

"Microwave?" said one of them.

"I can do that," Lula said.

Mister Stanley seemed dismayed. Perhaps Don had led him to expect handsome unemployed actors.

He said, "I'll bet Don helped those guys with immigration."

One of the Mexicans gave Lula a page of printed directions.

"Microwave," he said.

Mister Stanley sighed.

"Don't worry," Lula said. "This will be great."

Unwrapped, the bird looked gelatinous. No way this buzzard could be cooked from within by agitated atoms. Lula put it in the oven, and, just as she'd seen on TV, took it out early so it could drink back its own juices.

Don showed up at five fifteen. The woman with him was very pretty, a few years older than Lula. Don introduced her as Something Something, the sharpest lawyer who'd worked for his firm in years, maybe the sharpest ever.

"Tell me your name again," said Mister Stanley. "I'm getting old and deaf."

"Untrue, Stan." Don glared at him.

"Savitra Dasgupta," the woman said. The ends of her beautifully cut black hair brushed the shoulders of the pleated man's shirt she wore, tucked into pressed jeans. Lula felt sluttish and frumpy, a bread dumpling neatly sliced by the knife-edge of Savitra's pleats. Lula had gravy stains on her skirt, and she hadn't even really cooked.

The guests stalled in the front hall. Mister Stanley was supposed to ask them in, but that must have been Ginger's role. Mister Stanley should have hired someone else, someone unlike Lula, someone with the domestic talent to make him and his son a real home. Lula saw their pretend home through Savitra's eyes, just as she'd seen it through Alvo's. It was amazing how fast you got used to things and stopped seeing them at all. Where was Alvo spending Thanksgiving? Eating turkey and cranberry sauce? More likely, bellied up to a bar in the Bronx with his homies and ESPN and a keg of homemade raki.

Lula studied Savitra, taking lessons in the art of assuming a posture so regal that by the time they drifted toward the living room, where Lula had set out salami and cheese and sliced apples already edged with brown, Lula and Savitra had swapped places, so that Savitra was the hostess, and Lula the anxious guest. Lula hated these girl-on-girl dominance games, especially now when her hands were tied, because she was not about to repay Don for the miracles he'd worked on her behalf by being bitchy to his new girlfriend.

Savitra gazed at the cheese and wilted fruit.

"How autumnal," she said.

Like an expensive brooch pinned to the edge of Ginger's sofa, Savitra sparkled as she told Mister Stanley about her rise to the top of her class at Georgetown and the cases she'd worked on at Don's firm. Savitra subtly conveyed the fact that she had turned down big corporate money to "give back" to the country that had provided her family with a chance for a better life. Don beamed as if Savitra were his own prodigious child. And indeed he treated her like a delicate, moody girl. Like Abigail, in fact. He kept asking, Was she too hot? Too cold? Was everything okay?

Mister Stanley poured the drinks. Wine for Lula and Savitra, cold black coffee for Zeke. Scotch for himself and for Don.

"A light one, please," said Don, whose hasty glance at Lula was the only sign he gave of remembering their lunch.

Mister Stanley asked Savitra where her family came from.

"Great Neck," she said curtly.

Don said, "Savitra's grandfather is from Bangladesh. Her family owned a textile plant."

Savitra said, "My great-grandfather made silk for Christian Dior." It took Lula a few seconds to understand the conspiratorial smirk Savitra flashed in her direction. As a fellow immigrant, Lula was marginally less white than Don and Mister Stanley.

"I like your shirt," Savitra told Zeke. Zeke was charmed, as were the two men. As was everyone but Lula.

"Dog Breath?" Zeke read aloud, looking down as if to see what his shirt said. "Ever heard of them?"

"No," Savitra said. "But I hope you'll play their music for me sometime."

"Any interesting new cases?" Mister Stanley asked Don.

"Why spoil our dinner?" said Don. "Same psychotic freaks in the White House. Same al-Qaeda maniacs. Same innocent civilians trapped in the middle."

"Sorry to hear that," said Mister Stanley.

Don said, "But listen. Our brilliant Savitra may have found a loophole that could crack open one of our Guantánamo cases."

Lula could hardly bear it! Don's girlfriend was not only

pretty and sexy but a legal genius. Couldn't Lula just be happy for Don and Savitra and the Guantánamo detainee?

Savitra said, "Don's the brilliant one."

Don said, "And Savitra obviously has a mind of her own."

Savitra said, "Don's the one who could wind up in Gitmo."

"If I do, Savitra has promised to bring me samosas," Don said.

The two lovebirds nestled on the couch. Zeke walked behind the sofa and mimed gagging so only his father and Lula could see. Lula asked Zeke to come help her in the kitchen.

"Open the oven," she told him.

"Awesome turkey," said Zeke.

"Big strong boy," Lula said. "Bring this to the table. Make everybody sit."

Zeke picked up the platter with a weightlifter's grunt. Lula scurried in and out the dining room with bowls of mashed potatoes and a basket of rolls she'd made from tubes of dough. It had been fun to watch through the oven door as the gummy blobs swelled into perfect crosshatched grenades.

"Can I help?" asked Savitra.

"Sit," said Lula, which no one had done, no matter how many times Zeke told them. Lula had gone to great trouble to create an attractive holiday table. Organic beeswax candles from The Good Earth, Ginger's best china. She'd even ironed a tablecloth.

"Didn't I tell you, Stan?" said Don. "Aren't those caterers terrific?"

Savitra said, "Shouldn't we call Zeke back? He seems to have given up on us and disappeared."

Mister Stanley frowned at Lula. Wasn't Zeke her job?

Zeke made them suffer a long, tense wait before they heard his footsteps.

"Welcome back," Savitra said.

"Everybody begin," said Lula. "Start eating. I forgot to make the gravy. It will take two minutes."

Savitra called after her, "Are you sure I can't help?"

"No," said Lula. "Please." But Savitra, with that mind of her own, followed Lula into the kitchen, where she posed like a temple goddess with one hip thrust out and one elbow against the refrigerator door. Making gravy was tricky enough without Savitra saying, "May I ask you a personal question?"

"Sure." Lula was glad she could focus on whisking flour into the drippings.

Savitra took a sip of wine. "Did you ever fuck Don?"

"Of course not!" Lula said. How pleasant it was to tell the truth, and how false it sounded. "He's my lawyer."

Savitra said, "So Don claimed. I just needed a reality check. We'd been dating for two weeks before he bothered informing me he was married and had a daughter. This guy's a human rights hero, but when it comes to women—"

"He's separated, I think."

"Married, actually. Legally married. I know what legal is."

"Don's a good guy," said Lula.

Savitra said, "I hear you're a writer."

"Look," said Lula. "The gravy's ready."

When Lula and Savitra emerged from the kitchen to find that the others had started eating, they exchanged a surprisingly friendly and rich communication. Both were thinking that an American girl would have been pissed at the rude American men. But Lula and Savitra came from older cultures that

assumed men ate first, after having been waited on, like royalty or babies. They knew better than to expect a hollow show
of chivalry from the greedy pigs, though the look that passed
between them said, We're American now. The greedy pigs
should have waited.

Mister Stanley was telling a story about a guy at his job who
rode a motorized scooter to work and everyone in the office
thought it was really cool, but last week the guy fell off his
Segway and broke his collarbone in two places. Zeke and Don
hated Mister Stanley's story, each for a different reason. As Lula
and Savitra filled their plates, the three men watched.

"Savitra! Is everything all right?" said Don.

"Lovely," Savitra said, gently squeezing Don's arm.

"How's business, Stan?" asked Don. "Who would have
thought that my childhood pal would rise to become a Master
of the Universe?"

Mister Stanley shrugged. Seeing Savitra touch Don had so
deflated his spirits that he seemed to have lost the will to ever
speak again.

Finally he said, "Actually, I wouldn't be surprised if the
market goes the way of that hotshot's Segway. This housing
bubble, the derivatives, the subprime lending . . ." Everyone
watched his pale fingers glide along the table like a scooter and
plummet off the edge.

"Are you joking?" asked Don.

"I don't have your sense of humor," said Mister Stanley. "I
never did."

"Please," said Don. "Don't—"

Mister Stanley said, "Does the word Enron mean anything
to anyone here? Are our memories that short? If I were Joe

Average, I'd be cashing in my pension and buying gold and stashing it in the mattress."

Lula looked around to see how the others were reacting. Having had some experience with economic meltdown, Lula wanted to tell them: Don't think it can't happen here. But Don and Savitra were looking at Mister Stanley as blankly as if he'd just suggested that they might be in danger of running out of mashed potatoes. Nor did their expressions change much when Mister Stanley said, "What we saw with Enron was just the tip of the iceberg. Risk management is a fancy term for what the lemmings do when they hold hands and jump off a cliff."

"Lemmings don't hold hands, Dad," said Zeke. "Lemmings don't have hands."

"You sound like Abigail," Don told Zeke, then glanced worriedly at Savitra to see how she'd responded to his mentioning his daughter.

Savitra asked Zeke what his favorite subject was.

"Subject?"

"In school," Savitra said.

"None of them," said Zeke.

Don said, "Did I tell you, Stan, I was back in Guantánamo last week? The UN guys called off their inspection visit because they're not being allowed to talk to the detainees one-on-one. Oh, and the hunger strike's started up again. The strikers are being force-fed with gastric and nasal feeding tubes. They're reusing the same tube for every guy up and down the line, strapping them into these horrible chairs so they can't vomit up their food—"

Savitra said, "My God, Don! Reusable nasal feeding tubes?

We're eating Thanksgiving dinner. You need to give yourself a break—"

"A break," said Don. "Only the prisoners don't get a break. And those poor kids fighting our wars."

Mister Stanley shook his head. "We do have a lot to be thankful for."

"Name one thing," said Zeke.

"That we're not in prison," Mister Stanley said. "That you're not in the army."

"Not yet," said Zeke.

"When we were your age, there was a draft," said Mister Stanley.

"You told me that," singsonged Zeke. "And you burned your draft cards and went out onto the street and stormed the Pentagon and—"

Don said, "All over the country, American families are giving thanks. As we should, for the privilege of living in this country. We should be offering up our prayers of gratitude for our precious freedoms. It's not about the cranberry sauce. Nor is it about what the indigenous people taught us to grow before we slaughtered them all."

"Not in the Northeast, Don," said Mister Stanley. "Not so much slaughter went on here."

"Stupid fucking wrong-way Columbus thought they were Indians," Zeke said. He caught himself, horrified to have said "Indians" in Savitra's presence.

"Marvelous turkey," said Savitra.

"Thank you," said Lula.

Don said, "I really will have to thank the guy who turned me on to those caterers."

Don and Savitra left early.

Afterward, Zeke and Mister Stanley helped Lula clean up. Mister Stanley said, "Poor Don! Betsy was a piece of work, but this one's going to put him through the wringer." Lula made room for Zeke as he cautiously transferred the gravy pan from the stove to the sink.

Zeke said, "Dad, you just wish a girl that hot was putting you through the wringer. What's a wringer, anyway?"

Mister Stanley said, "Can you two finish up without my help?"

"We're good here," Lula said.

Chapter Nine

THE SNOW seemed apocalyptic, not falling so much as hurled. Bulletins came from the silent world: Zeke's school was closed, and so, more unexpectedly, was Mister Stanley's office. New rules, emergency measures, enabled Mister Stanley to turn on the early-morning TV news. Batting at snowflakes, as if in playful combat, a reporter puffed her cheeks and chafed her arms, while, behind her, a rickrack of broken trucks zigzagged across the highway.

"Record breaking," Mister Stanley said several times to make it clear that he was being kept from work by severe climate change and not by unmanly squeamishness about inclement weather. Zeke faked jubilation when in fact Lula suspected he would rather be at school than home with her and his dad.

The endless day stretched before them. How would they get through it? Everything grated on Lula's nerves. The rumble of Zeke's music, Mister Stanley's footsteps. How could anyone live with anyone else, unless you were tied by blood or sex and didn't have any choice? How tiny the large house had become, and how she longed to escape it.

She said, "I'm going back to bed."

"I don't blame you," said Mister Stanley.

Months ago, Lula had found three sleeping pills in Ginger's

medicine cabinet, and though she was wary of any Ginger-associated medication, she'd saved them for an emergency, which the news had assured them this was.

Lula's sleep was racked by nightmares, most of which she forgot, except for one in which she was visited by her dead parents and Granny, and another dream—or was it the same dream?—in which she sat in a stadium and watched truckloads of pastry flour dumped on Dunia. Lula somehow understood that this was a fundamentalist country in which adulterers were executed by being baked into apple pies.

When she awoke, it was still snowing. The sky was battleship gray. An alarming jingle was blaring from Lula's phone.

"Lula?" said a voice. "Did I wake you up? Wake up! It's afternoon."

Lula said in Albanian, "I was just dreaming about you!"

Dunia said in English, "I hope I was having fun."

"Where are you?" Lula said.

Dunia said, "Twenty miles from you. In Maplewood, New Jersey."

"I thought you were in Tirana. You always talked shit about New Jersey."

"I never got there," said Dunia. "I'm here. Like you."

"I didn't hear from you, I didn't hear from you. I started thinking you'd been trafficked."

"Very funny," Dunia said. "Though in a manner of speaking I was. Ha ha. I'm joking. I'm married. I married Steve. A rich American plastic surgeon. Very romantic story."

"Why didn't you answer my e-mails?"

"That's the unromantic part," said Dunia. "I'll tell you when I see you. Want to meet for coffee? Have lunch? Go shopping?"

"Now? Have you looked out the window? I don't have transportation. I'm stuck here."

"I've got a driver," said Dunia. "I'll come to you."

"A driver?" Lula repeated.

"A driver!" Dunia shouted. "What's wrong with this connection?"

Dunia sounded the same and different. Well, Lula had changed too. Even if nothing happens, you get new cells every seven years, so technically the former best friends were now one-seventh strangers.

"I didn't mean today," Dunia said. "I meant a week from today! See you then. Kiss kiss."

Lula walked to the window. Mister Stanley had shoveled the walk without the help he always asked, and never got, from Zeke.

Zeke was playing like a child in the snow, a big child with no one to play with. He'd made a snowman self-portrait, three white snowballs, the middle one in a ripped leather jacket and with something—shoe polish?—trickled down the sides of its lumpy spherical head to give it vampire hair. Its eyes were two silvery CDs that caught the last light of day. The snowman had its back to the street, an unusual choice. It seemed to be looking at the house, and one silver eye winked at Lula.

LULA HAD PICKED up, from Mister Stanley and Zeke, the good habit of not worrying too much about the neighbors, a welcome change from Tirana, where for many reasons, none of them good, the neighbors were the first thing you thought of after food and money and sex, and often before. Inhabited entirely by schoolchildren and their parents, and a few old relicts, Mister Stanley's block came to a sleepy sort of life only on summer weekends when someone held a yard sale. Today it was deserted except for cleaning ladies, delivery guys, and an occasional handyman blowing snow from one lawn to another.

No one saw the Range Rover pull up in front of Mister Stanley's house, and though Dunia moved as if on stage, Lula and the driver were the only audience for Dunia's theatrical scowling at each crumb of snow that menaced her beautiful boots. Where had Dunia gotten such shoes, or the stylish black coat, understated and, Lula could tell, terrifyingly expensive? How had Dunia skipped a step from servant maid to queen, from an illegal-alien East Village mojito-joint waitress to a rich New Yorker, or at least New Jerseyite?

Dunia was always a fast learner. It was Dunia who'd taught Lula how to navigate the fitting rooms and cosmetics counters. Lula told herself not to be jealous. Lula probably had many things that Dunia didn't have, though right now she couldn't think of one. Watching her friend's halting progress up Mister Stanley's front walk, Lula felt simultaneously overjoyed to see her and sick with love for Dunia's clothes. Lula's happiness should have been pure. Dunia was healthy and safe.

The two friends hugged in the doorway.

"You smell great," said Lula.

"Specially blended," said Dunia. "From roses that bloom once every twenty years."

"You're kidding," said Lula.

"Half kidding," Dunia said. "Once every decade."

They hugged again, and Lula pressed her face into Dunia's

cashmere shawl. Only when the danger was past did Lula realize how worried she'd been.

Dunia said, "Can we go inside now? I'm freezing my you-know-whats off."

"Sorry," Lula said. "Coffee?"

"American," said Dunia. "If you have it."

"Starbucks," Lula said.

She started off toward the kitchen so she wouldn't have to witness Dunia's response to Ginger decor and by extension Lula's life. Dunia was an emissary from another world, a messenger bearing a mirror. Meanwhile Lula noted with relief that Dunia's roses had already overpowered the musty dead air of houses like this, where everything fun had already happened in the distant past. Why should Lula make excuses for herself? Let Dunia do the talking.

Dunia followed Lula into the kitchen, perched on a stool, and leaned both elbows on the counter. Her pale breasts scalloped the empty space inside the V of her dove-colored sweater.

"Sweet scene," Dunia said. "Homey."

"It's a job," Lula said. Mister Stanley's house was a step up, many steps up, from the skinny Belarusian girl's walk-up. But the purse that Dunia plunked on the counter was many steps up from Mister Stanley's. They were friends, they loved each other. Why should a pocketbook matter?

"Please don't smoke." Lula's upturned palms cradled the fragile ecosystem around her.

Dunia shook her head but put her cigarettes away. "I'm used to it. It's American. I told my husband I quit smoking. Steve used to bring home photos of cancerous black lungs."

"Tell me about Steve," said Lula.

Dunia said, "What's to tell? Steve is nice. Steve is positive. Steve knows what he wants. Steve is rich. Is Steve hot? No, Steve is not hot. If I met him for the first time, I'd think he was gay. That's what I thought when I met him for the first time. Mistake. Steve is not gay. He's American. He wants me to be American. When I talk about my old life, he looks bored, so I quit. At the beginning, he was fascinated by all the Albanian stuff. But now he wants me to be newborn, he wants my life to have started on the day we met. No past, no friends, English only, except—"

Lula said, "Is that why you disappeared?"

"Not exactly," said Dunia. "But sure, maybe yes. I was trying. I thought, I'll give the marriage a shot. Steve is very controlling. He throws tantrums, but they're easy to avoid. Don't leave the alarm system off or the faucet running. Otherwise, no problem. I get to shop till I drop in return for sex that's always short and always the same. Two, maybe three times a week. Of course his family assumed I was a Russian hooker. A million times his mom and sister and aunts interrogated me about how we met. Obviously they were thinking online, or some ad in the phone book. So now I'm like the Earthly Beauty. I make Steve pay every time he sees me naked."

Lula leaned across the counter and kissed her friend on the cheek. It was too complicated to explain that she'd written a story about Earthly Beauty, but it made her happy to even consider explaining and to decide against it.

"What was *that* for?" asked Dunia.

"I'm glad to see you," said Lula. "So how did you meet Steve?"

"At the airport." Dunia reached again for a cigarette, then

remembered. "I was having a problem with my ticket home. I should have known. I bought it from a bucket shop behind a realtor in the Bronx. The guy at the ticket counter hated me on sight. Our discussion got hot. I called him an asshole. Big deal. He was an asshole. Also a baby. Big Baby Asshole Airline Agent called for backup. I thought, Here we go. I'm traveling to Guantánamo on a one-way ticket."

Lula said, "My lawyer has a client in Guantánamo."

"Sad," Dunia said. "Poor him. Steve was in the business-class line. He got out of line and saved me. He had time before his flight. That's the kind of guy Steve is, gets to the airport three hours early. He was going to Nassau for some plastic surgery convention. We sat at one of those little round tables with high stools. God must have commanded me to travel in a short skirt instead of a sweatsuit. After two whiskeys Steve asked me: If he canceled his trip, would I go home with him right then? The next morning he said he'd take care of everything. Everything. And he did."

"That must have been some night," Lula said.

"For Steve it was," said Dunia. "End of story. He knows people. I'll be a citizen soon. Married to an American doctor. It's a dream come true."

"Nice." Lula chafed her palms together, dusting off the obstacles that ordinary people went through to get where Dunia was. She shivered with self-pity. Everyone else had it easy, everybody but her, everyone got the lucky breaks that whisked them along the road down which Lula was trudging, step by difficult step. She told herself, Have patience, or at least some pride. She had a work visa, she'd have a green card, she'd become a citizen maybe, and all on her own, without having to marry some guy she didn't love. On the other hand, everything could still go wrong. She could be deported back to Tirana, and Dunia would be in her fancy house, shopping for fabulous clothes.

"Nothing's easy," said Dunia. "Tonight at dinner he'll tell me about some brilliant rhinoplasty or challenging butt reduction. But if I say anything, anything at all, he picks up a magazine. Any time I want some body part tightened or tweaked, he'll do it for free. His business partner gave his wife a permanent smile and a killer cleavage."

"So why did you call me now?" Lula said.

"I missed you," said Dunia. "I'm bored."

"It can get boring here," Lula said. How good it felt to say so. From time to time, Mister Stanley and Zeke suggested that Lula must be bored, and Lula always protested. No, not at all, she was finding plenty to do. Alvo and his friends had implied that Mister Stanley's house was a tomb. They'd said it smelled like the grave.

"Anywhere can get boring." Dunia frowned at her pearly lip print on Mister Stanley's coffee cup. Licking her fingertip, she dabbed at the stain like a mother wiping another woman's kiss from her child's face. "So many minutes in a day! At some point Steve will ask the driver—in Spanish—what I did today, so it's good my driver can tell Steve about you, and Steve won't get jealous thinking I went to see some boyfriend. It's like living under Communism. Okay, I know it's not like Communism. The shopping is better. The sex is worse."

"A driver!" Lula said.

Dunia smiled lewdly. "Jorge. Dominican. Twenty-two. Drop-dead handsome."

"I can't even drive," said Lula. "Most of the time I'm stuck here. Unless I take the bus."

"I told you," Dunia said. "Ten miles to downtown if you swam."

Lula said, "You still have an accent. How does American Steve like that?"

Dunia made a face. "He likes to talk during sex. *Then* he likes the accent. He even likes me to talk Albanian. He thinks I'm begging, Fuck me up to my eyeballs! When what I'm really saying is, Tomorrow I have to tell Gladys the maid to clean the refrigerator. Out of bed he doesn't like the accent so much. He says the more American I speak, the more Americans I speak *to*, the more American I sound."

Lula said, "It's the opposite here. Everybody wants me to hang on to my roots. They love all the fairy tales and the sayings and folk songs and crap. You know what? I've started writing little stories about home."

"You always were a creative person. What an imagination! I remember you getting drunk one night after our shift at La Changita and making up some crazy shit about your dad teaching you to shoot Madonna in the heart. Whatever happened to Franco the waiter? He wasn't so cute, but still . . ."

"That was true about Madonna," Lula said. "A *picture* of Madonna."

Dunia said, "I missed you. But listen, no shopping today. I don't have the time I thought. The cleaning guy is coming to pick up the living room curtains. Also I have to go home and talk dinner with Gladys." Dunia kissed her fingertips. "Fried chicken. She worked for Steve before I got there."

It was a sign of power, having somewhere you had to be. In

the same article in which the female CEO advised buying fancy underwear, another successful corporate woman said her secret was to always give the impression that she had even less time than she actually had. Lula too had somewhere to be—right here—and someone who needed her: Zeke.

"We have Estrelia," said Lula.

Dunia slipped back into her coat. "Call me. Call me soon. Meantime you can stop worrying that I'm a sex slave in Dubai."

They hugged and kissed, then hugged again. And then Dunia was gone, leaving Lula feeling more hopeful and less alone, but so physically exhausted that she drifted into the living room and sank into the couch, where she remained until the last trace of Dunia's perfume had followed her out of the house.

DUNIA'S SAFETY AND good fortune were a relief, and yet her visit was like a spray of ice water, shocking Lula out of the coma in which she'd been snoozing at Mister Stanley's. Wake up! Girls found rich husbands or married men they loved. They didn't hide out in a Jersey suburb dreaming that Alvo would find some tough-guy-contractor language in which to tell Lula that he thought about her as much as she thought about him.

It was a welcome distraction to sit at Zeke's computer. Would anyone go for a story about a man who tried to build an apartment house that kept collapsing until he dreamed that the solution was to wall his beloved wife into the foundation? The house stayed up, but the foundation was always wet, soaked with the woman's tears. Mister Stanley and Don Settebello obviously believed that the laws of physics no longer applied once you crossed the Albanian border. It was fortunate that she'd mentioned mixing fiction and nonfiction. When she'd written enough for a book, they would sort it all out, but for now her two American guardian angels could think what they wanted about her pretending her stories were true.

Lula was writing the scene in which the builder explains to his wife why his real estate needs demand that she be buried alive, and when she refuses, he shoves her into a crawl space and, sobbing, mixes the cement. Lula was so lost in her story that when the doorbell rang, she heard it as the clang of the husband's shovel, smoothing out concrete. She ran downstairs and opened the door to find Leather Jacket on the front steps.

"Little Sister, why so sad?" Leather Jacket—Genti—kept glancing back over his shoulder. The unforgiving winter light pooled in his pitted cheeks. Lula told him to step inside, where he seemed even more uneasy. Had he come to ask her out behind Alvo's back? Was Alvo passing her along to his friend, a sick male custom she'd heard of but never experienced firsthand? Did they think she was a hunk of roast lamb to be tossed to the next guy down the table? More likely Genti had come for the gun. Let him stand in the hall and mumble.

"What?" said Lula.

Mumble mumble.

"I can't understand you!"

"Mumble mumble Christmas Eve? My boss? . . . not busy Christmas Eve? He wants to know, Do you want to go out?"

Why was everything a question? Genti sounded like a teenage girl. Gradually she understood. The guy was playing Cupid! It was all Lula could do not to throw her arms around him and squeeze till his jacket crackled. How touching that Alvo hadn't wanted to risk rejection in person. At the same time, how thoughtless and conceited of him to assume she wouldn't have plans. Christmas Eve was only two weeks away, and she had no plans.

What would happen to Leather Jacket if she told him to tell Alvo she was busy? Most likely the messenger wouldn't get killed if the bad news was about dating. As if Alvo cared enough to give his friend a hard time. He would just send one of the G-Men to ask another girl.

Lula said, "Tell him yes, I'd be happy."

"He'll be here at eight? He said dress nice?"

"Dress nice?" said Lula. "I always do. As opposed to what?" Where did Alvo get the nerve? But maybe it wasn't male arrogance. Maybe it was semantics. Maybe *nice* meant *up*, dress *up*, maybe they were sparing Lula the embarrassment of arriving at a formal event in a T-shirt and jeans. Obviously, she would dress up. It was Christmas Eve. But before she could ask for details, Genti shook her hand and left. Mission accomplished, he could go back to being a busy guy with important business elsewhere.

TWO WEEKS UNTIL Christmas. The winter days were too short and bloodless to sustain the weight of thought required to fathom the meaning of "dress nice." Nice by Dunia standards? Or Albanian nice: too shiny, too tight, too synthetic, and above all, too leopard. Nice like the big-haired singers who traveled the Balkan circuit with their big-haired manager husbands? Alvo was way cooler than that. He'd mean what Lula meant by nice.

Lula had patience and goodwill to spare, especially for Zeke.

On their drives to The Good Earth, they mixed high school metaphysical talk about the purpose of life (Lula assured him that life had a purpose) with the usual chitchat about driving and the other drivers, who, according to Zeke, were getting crazier and angrier as the holidays approached.

"What do you want for Christmas?" Lula asked.

"I don't know. Nothing. Wait. There's a DVD, this vintage vampire film called *Nosferatu*."

"Write it down," said Lula, who had no intention of spending money to feed Zeke's vampire obsession. She'd already bought him a leather belt on St. Marks Place, with rows of studs and grommets, and an iPod Nano for Mister Stanley.

Against her better instincts, she'd been letting Zeke drive to the market even when the weather was bad. She didn't tell Mister Stanley when the Olds slid into a snowbank, and Zeke and Lula had to dig it out, ruining Lula's boots. It would be hard enough explaining that she was going out Christmas Eve, abandoning Mister Stanley and Zeke on the anniversary of Ginger's departure.

She waited for a Saturday afternoon. Zeke had gone somewhere with friends. Christmas shopping, he'd said. Lula found Mister Stanley in the living room, reading the weekend sections of the Sunday paper. Tomorrow's news today. He was wearing his chinos, a cardigan, and a knit shirt, in which he managed to look more stiff and uncomfortable than he did in a suit. He looked like Mr. Rogers, the first American Lula ever saw on her granny's contraband TV.

"I need to talk to you," Lula said.

Mister Stanley said, "I have a wild idea. Let's go for a walk."

"Too wild," Lula said. "It's cold out."

"The air does one good," he said. "You'll turn into Dracula, entombed in this dark house."

A funny remark from the father of a vampire son. He was making a Mister Stanley joke. Trying to be helpful.

"Ha ha," Lula said. "Okay, let me get my coat." Outside, she pointed accusingly at the plumes their breath made in the air.

"Just around the block," said Mister Stanley. "No one is going to freeze."

Lula and Mister Stanley had the street to themselves, unless you counted the inflated plastic reindeer and carolers on the neighbors' lawns. Every so often a car passed, but no one slowed to watch the two of them drift from house to house, pausing to gaze at the Christmas displays, each of which, Lula thought sourly, consumed enough electricity to power all of Albania. But surely the lights were low-wattage. Why couldn't she just enjoy this harmless American custom instead of going straight for the dismissive immigrant envy? Because the decorations were intended to make outsiders envy the happiness inside.

No matter how much Lula had learned about American family life, she still longed to have participated in those family trips to the big-box store, the assembling of the decorations, with Dad and Junior following Mom and Sis's cheerful creative suggestions. Under Communism, one of the few foreign texts they'd been allowed to read was a translation of Hans Christian Andersen's "The Little Match Girl," which was taught as an illustration of class brutality in the West. Like everyone, Lula believed it. But in her new American life, she had learned about nuance. Mister Stanley came from the same class as the living rooms into which they were staring. An alternate title for her memoir could be *On the Outside Looking In*.

When Mister Stanley paused before a plastic sleigh the size of a tractor-trailer, Lula said, "I need to tell you something. I won't be spending Christmas Eve with you and Zeke. If that's okay with you."

"Of course it's okay," said Mister Stanley, too quickly. "So. What are you doing instead?"

"Going out," Lula said. "With friends." If Mister Stanley asked which friends, she would say friends from La Changita.

"Well, that's excellent," said Mister Stanley. "We want you to have your own life." He walked ahead to the next lawn, on which there was a crèche with a life-size camel whose plaster had chipped off so that hunks of flesh appeared to have been clawed away in a fight.

"It shouldn't make any difference," he said. "I think Zeke would be just as happy if we did away with the tree and the trimmings and the holiday cheer."

Holiday cheer? Had Mister Stanley forgotten that last year he brought home a dead tree, and they'd spent Christmas at the mall?

"Are you sure?" asked Lula.

"I don't know," said Mister Stanley.

Lula said, "When they outlawed religion under the dictatorship, people still celebrated. They'd pile up pyramids of baklava that looked like Christmas trees." Her granny had made baklava on Christmas. The pyramid part was extra. "The dictator ignored it because he loved pyramids so much he had himself buried in one. Until they dug him up."

"They dug him up?" said Mister Stanley.

Lula nodded. "And reburied him."

"That's awful." Mister Stanley chuckled, then caught himself. "A little-known fact, I guess."

"Every Albanian fact is a little-known fact," Lula said.

Mister Stanley smiled at his cute Albanian pet.

He said, "You're priceless, Lula. Enjoy yourself while you're young. Okay, let's go home now. You were right. It's freezing."

"LULA, *ESTE* JORGE," said Dunia, wrapping one flawlessly manicured hand around the wrist of the driver who had beeped for Lula to come outside and spare Dunia and her boots another damaging encounter with Mister Stanley's snowy walkway. "Jorge, *esta* Lula. *Mi amiga.*"

"*Buenos dias.*" Jorge's smile lit up the rearview mirror.

"*Buenos dias*," said Lula, glumly. Lazy Dunia could have come inside long enough for Lula to give her the history of her relationship, if you could call it that, with Alvo. Describing her fantasy romance was embarrassing enough without having to do it in the presence of New Jersey's most handsome driver. Even so, she was grateful that Dunia had, without hesitation, agreed to take Lula shopping. Despite everything, they had stayed friends, holding hands across the Grand Canyon of money and class that seemed to have opened between them.

"Don't worry about Jorge," Dunia said. "He speaks fifty words of English, all having to do with local highways. I've been teaching him Albanian. Our secret language, right, Jorge?"

"*Si,*" said Jorge. "Yes."

"Come to think of it," Dunia said, "speech is not his language."

"How is Steve with that?" Lula said.

Dunia slashed her forefinger across her neck and laughed. "I'm joking. Steve doesn't want to know what Steve doesn't know. Very incurious person. So what's the desperate situation?"

"I didn't say desperate. I said serious."

"You said desperate," Dunia insisted.

Maybe Lula had said desperate. "Okay, I meant serious. I need something to wear."

Dunia raised one eyebrow. "That's desperate? Baghdad is desperate. Hurricane Katrina was desperate. Ten-year-old Albanian kids working in a factory disassembling old Kalashnikovs is desperate. Did you hear about that?"

"My boss told me," Lula said.

"Nice boss." Dunia looked Lula up and down. She said, "Okay. Desperate."

"Short Hills Mall," she told Jorge. "*Gracias. Por favor.*"

It was easier once they were moving. Less intimate, in a way. Lula tried to talk without thinking, to just let the story of Alvo and his G-Men roll out. Or as much as she knew of the story. When she finished, Dunia was silent for so long that Lula had no choice but to contemplate the ridiculousness of what she'd just said.

"Let me get this straight," said Dunia. "You're spending Christmas Eve with a guy who takes you to some Thai joint and screws with your head and sneaks into your house and takes a shower and writes shit on your computer—"

"On Zeke's computer. Plus he left me a present." Lula

missed Little Charmy Puppy and its unconditional affection. She'd made it bark so often that it broke and couldn't be fixed.

"What present? You didn't tell me that part."

Lula smiled. Let Dunia imagine.

"Presents mean nothing," said Dunia. "Take it from someone who knows."

After that they rode in silence. Dunia said, "Bravo, Jorge! We're here. This is the only decent mall, the others are big wasters of time."

"Wastes of time," said Lula.

Dunia shrugged. "Look where perfect grammar's got you. So let's be clear about this: You want to make sure Mr. Psycho knows he can fuck you if he wants to. Take it from me, he wants to."

"You're one to talk," said Lula. "You've had some pretty strange boyfriends."

Dunia's pearl-dusted eyelids fluttered. Lula wondered if she was thinking of the tough little stockbroker who'd refused to do it in bed and who was always leading Dunia, flushed and dreamy, back from the men's room and the alleyways near La Changita.

"Don't change the subject," Dunia said. "Stop here! Forget the macho parking two steps from the entrance." She flung open the door and trotted across the lot. Lula rushed to catch up. Was Dunia running away? Possibly from the idea of Lula's romance with Alvo. True love and hot sex, even the chance of true love and hot sex, was the only thing that could compete with the standard of living that came with Dunia's boring marriage to Steve. Love, or even the hope of love, gave you status, in a way.

But if so, this slight edge was lost on the women who watched

Lula and Dunia from the mirrored fortresses of the cosmetics counters. Under their scrutiny, Lula's coat turned into a jester's rags, in which she skipped after Dunia, distracting her friend from the saleswomen's grown-up claims on her attention. They sized up Lula and looked away, as if from someone disfigured. Then they trained their come-to-me gazes on the one in the ostrich boots.

"I need a new outfit," Lula said. "Something sexy but elegant."

"Perfume," Dunia told her. "Trust me. Forget the outfit, the short skirt, the fishnet stockings, the unbuttoned blouse, the fuck-me shoes. More wastes of time and money. Dab something expensive in a few secret places, and their testosterone pumps. Steve brought me home a study from a medical journal. Certain scents increase guys' blood flow and give them massive hard-ons. Better than Viagra. Call a doctor if your erection lasts longer than four hours. The problem is, a different smell works on each individual guy. So Steve does his own research and comes home with this million-dollar vial of oil, probably illegal, he says it's extracted from poppies that grow in the kitchen gardens of Afghan warlords. God knows where it really comes from. If I put it where he wants me to, it gives me a hideous rash. So now I have to smell like a hooker and pretend to talk dirty in Albanian. How much fun is that?"

Did the women smiling at the two girls from their glittery counters suspect that the rich one was complaining about her sex life?

"Pheromones," said Lula. "Like with the insect family. That funny odor when you crush a beetle. To another beetle it's the irresistible sex smell."

"The death smell," Dunia said. "The day I met Steve in the airport I was wearing a bucket of Chanel No. 5."

Lula said, "How nice for the person sitting next to you on the plane."

"There was no person next to me on the plane," said Dunia. "No plane. I figured I might as well wear it. If I tried to bring it home to Albania, some customs guard at the airport would have stolen it for his girlfriend."

Dunia trawled the counters, eyeing bottles, raising and dashing the hopes of women who had spent the day seducing an empty department-store aisle. Grasping Lula's forearm, Dunia said, "Concentrate. Focus on this guy. Be him. Figure out what he'd like. Let your instincts guide you."

Now all the women were looking at them. How confident it made Dunia and Lula to stand there deep in conversation, suspended in time and space, feeling no compulsion to get on with the business of shopping. Lula couldn't be this brave alone. No one could. How she needed and loved her friend! Dunia flitted from counter to counter, spraying perfumes on tissue squares and writing, with a stubby pencil, the names of scents until she'd narrowed the selection down to three or four squares. In what exclusive rich-girl school had Dunia learned to do this?

"Smell them. But think about the guy."

"They're all starting to smell the same," Lula said.

"My God, you're hopeless." Dunia kissed Lula's cheek. The perfume ladies goggled. Did they think that Lula and Dunia were Russian hookers spending a stolen lesbian afternoon? She could see why Steve's parents worried about Dunia. How wrong they were, how little they knew. But the lie they believed about her friend was another lie come true. Somehow they'd transformed her into the ambitious Natasha climbing the social ladder on which their son was the bottom rung.

"I think musky," Dunia was saying. "A guy who stashes his gun with you and pretends to be in construction—"

"Pretends? He's in construction."

"Pretends," Dunia said. "Probably the fastest way to his heart is to pick up your skirt and show him. Look, no underwear."

"That's not going to happen," said Lula.

"I understand," said Dunia. "That's why we're doing perfume. Concentrate. Start again."

Lula sprayed and sniffed and tried to think about Alvo. But try as she might, she couldn't conjure up the scenario in which one whiff of something spicy or sweet gave him no choice but to jump her.

"Check out this one." Dunia sprayed a cold mist on Lula's wrist. "Give it a minute. Okay, sniff."

Lula closed her eyes and inhaled.

In the littered courtyard behind her housing block in Tirana had been a glorious flowering tree that thrived on garbage, weeds, cigarette smoke, and the fried food aerosol that fell on it from the windows. Luckily it bloomed around May Day, so the tree was left alone by the neighborhood committee, which usually ruled that anything pretty or pleasing was Western bourgeois mind poison. The May Day tree bloomed for a week, and people would come downstairs in the evenings and gather in groups or stand alone to breathe in the scent of the blossoms. No one stole the branches to have inside their homes. It was the only time when Communism worked like it was supposed to. After the blossoms fell, it was understood that the kids could stay out late and have battles, flinging the slimy petals and hard stamens at each other. The perfume Dunia had sprayed on her wrist smelled like those warm spring nights.

"This one," Lula said thickly. The bottle—sapphire blue, like the pharmaceutical vials in which Granny used to keep her gardenia water—reminded her of Granny's story about the woman who went around collecting tears and marketing them as a skin care product. Just thinking about that story seemed like asking for bad luck. Lula decided to keep the perfume in the drawer with Alvo's gun. Let her new smell and his pistol spend some time together.

A voice said, "Shall I wrap it up?"

"My treat," Dunia said.

"I can't let you do this," Lula said.

Dunia brandished her credit card. "Steve's treat," she told the woman.

Chapter Ten

—⊶⊷—

Mister stanley took the day before Christmas off and spent the morning rooting through the closets for some important item that turned out to be a package of tinsel that he draped, strand by strand, over the picture frames. When Zeke woke at noon, Mister Stanley, apparently having forgotten his plans to ignore the holiday, asked if Zeke wanted to go help pick out a Christmas tree.

Zeke said, "What kind of sick trees do you think will be left on Christmas Eve?"

Mister Stanley said, "Probably plenty. There will be plenty of choice."

Zeke said, "Then you don't need me."

Mister Stanley said, "What the heck, does one even need a tree?"

Zeke said, "What the heck, does one even need a tree?" and turned on the TV. Was he trying to exhaust the patience of his patient American dad? No, he was trying to remind his guilty American dad that his mother had abandoned them on Christmas Eve.

At six, when Lula decided to start dressing to go out with Alvo, Zeke was lying on the couch watching the Yule log burn on TV, while Mister Stanley sat in a chair, watching his son watching.

"Oh, look, it's just like Communist TV," Lula said in the grating warble she heard in her voice whenever she tried to brighten the dark air between them. "The newscaster would read us statistics of people starving to death in the West, and a clock would tick on the wall."

Mister Stanley said, "Zeke, do you think we could possibly watch something more compelling?"

"No," said Zeke. "I like this. It's totally compelling."

Mister Stanley struggled visibly not to ask, then asked, "Are you high on something, Zeke?"

"On holiday cheer," Zeke said.

Beckoning Lula into the kitchen, Mister Stanley said, "I think he misses his mom."

"I'm sorry," Lula said, meaning sorry sympathetic but sounding like sorry apologetic. In Albanian they were different words, and the difference could mean life or death.

Mister Stanley tented his fingertips like a priest. "Quite honestly, it was a challenge not to notice the symbolism and anger in the timing of my wife's departure. I told you it was Christmas Eve."

"You did," Lula said. What a heartless monster Ginger was. Yet somewhere in Lula's own heart she understood Ginger's panic. She was sure, or almost sure, that the remorse she felt for leaving tonight would vanish the minute she left.

"I'd better get ready," she said.

Even as Lula told herself that her date with Alvo would be nothing special—really, you couldn't say enough for low expectations!—she not only used all her creams and soaps but every one of the free bath-product samples she had hoarded from her first days in New York. There was a reckless glee in opening the tiny vials and anointing herself with substances so potent that the store had bet those precious drops on making her want more.

She walked naked across the bedroom, opened her underwear drawer, and gently unwrapped Alvo's gun from its cocoon. She held the silk in one hand, the pistol in the other, hesitating as if she were weighing them, deciding. She lay the gun on a hastily gathered nest of polyester and stepped into the silk panties, fastened the bra, and went to the mirror, braced for a vision of decrepitude and horror. But in fact she looked fit. Like a girl! Her ass hadn't sagged all that much, amazing when you considered how much time she'd spent sitting on it at Mister Stanley's. For a moment she drifted out of herself and floated into another perspective, the warmer, more admiring view of someone like . . . someone like Alvo. She imagined, as she hoped he would, slipping off the lace and silk. The physical symptoms of desire were unmistakable, even after a long remission. Like riding a bicycle, Lula thought, not that she'd ever learned to ride a bike.

Lula needed to calm down. It would be unwise to start out on her first real date with Alvo in a state of high arousal.

Given that Dunia had talked her out of spending money on a new outfit, "dress nice" had better mean her black dress and the heels that made her calves look thin but which she could dance in, if she had to. She put on her makeup, American subtle but heavy enough to convince an Albanian guy she'd made an effort. Even after she'd wiped off three different shades of blush and sprayed on the precise dose of perfume that, she'd learned through trial and costly error, communicated erotic interest without being too aggressive, she was ready twenty minutes early.

Which was lucky, because so was Alvo. Her phone chirped, and a text appeared. *Parked outside*. Short, to the point, and now his number was on Lula's contact list.

She had rehearsed her exit, and it went smoothly, as planned. She grabbed her coat and let the door close tenderly on her "Merry Christmas!" This time she added, "See you soon," to reassure them that she wasn't leaving forever. As she walked down the path, her knight in his shining black charger beeped his horn—honk, honk, hello. The guy had a few rough edges. Maybe he was nervous.

Lula slid across the seat and kissed Alvo on the cheek.

"Merry Christmas," he said.

All Dunia's painstaking olfactory research results were instantly corrupted by the unforeseen variable of Alvo's strong cologne. Despite the fortune Dunia had spent, Lula was glad to let the scent of those long-lost summer evenings surrender without a fight to the peacock pheromones of Alvo's preparations for the evening, which happily did not include the tight, shiny synthetics that so many Albanian boys favored. His black shirt set off the red of his hair, and in his black jacket and jeans, he could have passed for one of the guys who'd blown their trust funds on rum drinks at La Changita. Lula hadn't wanted to go out with those guys, so why did she want Alvo to look like one? Because she didn't want to be the bossy know-it-all, tutoring her fresh-off-the-boat boyfriend in the fashions and customs of their adopted country.

They rode in silence, struck dumb by the awareness that they'd altered their smells for each other. That had to signify something, if only the likelihood that Alvo had calculated the probability of his getting laid this evening. Lula's stomach fluttered. Dunia and her bright ideas. How much harder the perfume made it to pretend this was just a platonic friendly night out, Older Brother and Little Sister reeking like a pair of sex fiends.

"Where are we going?" Lula asked.

"The Bronx," said Alvo. "Where else?"

They crossed the George Washington Bridge, its bright loops improbably strung above the silver cord of the river. Down below, glittering hives of mist swirled around the streetlamps on the snowy banks of the Hudson.

Alvo said, "So how are the boss and his kid spending their Merry Christmas?"

"Watching the Yule log on TV," Lula said.

Alvo said, "Bleak. Very bleak."

"Please. I feel guilty enough," said Lula.

Alvo took the exit for the Whitestone Parkway. Then he said, "Are you sure you're not fucking the boss?"

"Jesus Christ!" said Lula. "How many times do I have to—?"

"Sorry," Alvo said.

Lula said, "What's the point of Christmas, anyway? We never had Christmas at home."

"Now we do," said Alvo. "Now it's a big travel season for Albanians. Everyone's got to come here. To do what, I don't know. Go to Radio City. Sit on Santa's lap. Right now I've got three cousins from Vlorë sleeping on my bedroom floor."

So much for the option of ending the evening at Alvo's apartment. But since when had Lula needed to do it in a proper bed? She'd grown so middle-aged and conservative since she and her boyfriends used to sneak out and rip off their clothes and roll around in the dictator's bunkers.

Alvo said, "I wonder if they ever took a survey: How many Albanian guys and girls had their first sex in a bunker?"

Lula said, "Did you just read my mind, or what?"

"Really?" said Alvo. "That's beautiful." Without taking his hands off the wheel, he bumped his elbow against hers. "You know what? One of my cousins brought me this little vial of water from a spring somewhere in Bosnia. Male water, they call it. Supposed to be Balkan Viagra."

"Do you need it?" Lula asked.

"Not the last time I checked," Alvo said.

Lula saw searchlights raking the sky above an industrial wasteland, beacons to guide their smooth landing in front of a one-story building on which red and green and silver lights spelled out "Merry Christmas, Happy New Year." Another string of bulbs outlined a double-headed eagle over the door.

"I've heard of this place," said Lula.

"Who hasn't?" Alvo said.

Two guys in bow ties lunged for the doors of the Lexus, but Alvo waved them off until he and Lula got out and he surrendered the keys.

"Valet parking sucks," Alvo said. "Paying some stranger to screw with your seat adjustment and mirrors. But in this neighborhood you need somebody to kneecap the junkie before he smashes your window for the pocket change stuck in the seat."

A squad of gigantic bouncers guarded the entrance, checking IDs and exuding random intimidation. One of them recognized Alvo and cleared a tunnel through which Alvo led Lula, a gauntlet of arm-punches and shoulder thumps that Alvo good-humoredly endured while Lula succumbed to the dizzying high of specialness and privilege. Which other girls had Alvo come here with? It almost spoiled her good mood to think about Alvo's life before her.

Lula saw a security guard holding a girl at arm's length, laughing as her flailing arms and fists bounced off his puffed-out chest.

"Spit on me?" he was saying. "What kind of way is that for a nice Albanian girl to behave?"

The coat check girl looked hard at Lula to see how she'd wound up with Alvo. Lula wanted to tell her: chemistry. For some reason she thought of Savitra asking if she'd had sex with Don Settebello. What did Lula know about Alvo's past? She knew nothing about his present.

A blast of noise blew these reflections straight out of Lula's head. As Alvo guided her into the crowd, Lula remembered why this feeling—too many people, too much sound, not enough oxygen, not enough room, a barrage of intense sensation bombarding your heart and belly—was something you might want. Sparks leaped from body to body, each body in a bubble yet paradoxically hyperaware of every other body nearby. It was a highly diluted but still arousing version of the wordless language two bodies speak when they are about to have sex.

As they moved away from the door, the space was less tightly packed, and indeed the dance floor had the forlorn air of a wedding before the party gets rocking. An invisible DJ shouted, "Let's slow it down!" as if it weren't slow enough already, and a soul singer crooned a ballad. A few couples, newlyweds or newly engaged, danced closely, half entranced and half convincing the world and themselves of their passionate future together.

"Let's get a drink," said Alvo, again reading Lula's mind. He found an empty corner and told Lula to wait. He'd forgotten to ask what she wanted. Or maybe it was a guy thing, profoundly cave man and Bronx. You not only ordered for your date but you told her what she liked.

Alvo vanished into the strobe-swept darkness. What if he never came back? How long did Lula have to wait before she called a taxi? There were plenty of single guys here. She could dance, have fun, maybe even find another guy to take her home. But there was no one she wanted to meet. She wanted to be with Alvo. He wouldn't do that to her on Christmas Eve. No one would stoop that low. No one, that is, but Ginger.

At last she spotted Alvo bobbing toward her with a shot glass in each hand. "Sorry it took me so long. I ran into this crazy dude who wanted to start a big fight. He claims we installed his air conditioner backward, and it blew dirt and soot and garbage all over his little baby. Now he wants us to reinstall it—"

"I thought you did commercial construction," Lula said.

"We do," he said. "Like I told you. The dude's hallucinating. This one's yours. *G'zoor.*"

"*G'zoor.*" Lula took a sip. Raki, the drink of good-bye and hello, of congratulation and consolation. Lula didn't think of herself as a nationalistic person. Mostly, in her experience, country was like religion, an excuse to hate other people and feel righteous about it. But then there was raki. Raki *was* Albania, it had that special taste. Even Albanians with no sentimental attachment to their home country brightened and got teary-eyed when the talk turned to raki. They got high just hearing the word.

"Mother's milk," said Alvo.

"Delirium in a glass," Lula said.

"Hell, yeah. Whoever said money can't buy happiness never got into the top-of-the-line mulberry raki."

"I like the walnut," Lula said.

"That works too," said Alvo. "Expensive."

Lula was trying to figure out what else to say about raki when a blare of static rattled the loudspeakers, and the music turned Albanian. A man sang about a woman he couldn't forget, while behind him the clarinets tried to cheer him up. The volume climbed, while the sinuous thumping of the electronic drum cast a spell on the crowd and dragged the enchanted ones toward the dance floor.

"Another drink?" Alvo asked.

"I've still got some." But oddly, Lula's glass appeared to have emptied itself. "Sure, why not?" She smiled.

"That's my girl." Alvo plunged off toward the bar against the incoming tide of merrymakers.

His girl? Had Lula heard right? It meant nothing besides approval of the pace at which she was drinking. He could have said, My man. Yet she no longer worried that he wouldn't return. She leaned against a wall that seemed to be keeping time with the drum and watched people approach the dance floor as if it were a pool into which they were either about to dive or venture one big toe.

It had been so long since she'd seen Albanian dancing. She'd forgotten how it made you want to join the line even if you were cool and modern and over Albanian dancing. So much individual soul was poured into the simple steps, men and women, young and old, married, single, fat, thin. No one wore the stiff mask of vacancy or anxiety that Lula had so often seen on the faces of Americans inventing their own dances, trying to seem unself-conscious even as they labored to telegraph a message about confidence, sexuality, and whether they were available or taken. How stressful it was when Americans paired off in Noah's ark couples, performing rhythmic preludes or aftermaths to sex, or danced in groups of girls, never groups of guys, writhing, distanced from the bodies they were showing off. Albanians just grabbed the last hand in line and let the music take charge.

Lula was dancing in place when Alvo returned with more raki. As they toasted each other, Alvo smiled so widely that his gold tooth sparkled at her, only at her. Alvo eased in beside her and bumped ever so slightly to the music. When his hip brushed hers she longed to rub against him like a cat.

Luckily, they had double rakis to finish before they had to decide whether to join the dancing, which, as luck would have it, stopped, giving them more time to figure out what to do next. A set of curtains opened, and a guy in a white suit bounded onto a low stage. His first "Good evening" in English and Albanian elicited manic applause. He slipped between languages, playing to both sides, the older people who clung to their native tongue and the kids who'd never learned it. But everyone understood and loved his patter about old friends and new friends, brothers and sisters, all family here tonight. More applause for the names of the stars who'd be entertaining them this evening, and for each of the beautiful cities in which the talent had performed. The applause built as two men, also in white suits, tried out the keyboards, one of which sounded like a clarinet and the other like a drum. The host whipped the audience into a frenzy of welcome for the singer, who strutted out nonchalantly, as if frantic clapping was the background noise of her everyday existence. Then her bright red mouth exploded in smiles, and she bowed from the waist and blew kisses.

Black as Zeke's, but varnished to a high gloss, the singer's hair framed her face in question marks. Curls spilled over the shoulders of her white dress, which had gauzy sleeves and pearl flowers like a wedding gown, only with a miniskirt stretched tightly across her belly. White boots rose up to meet it, exposing a long expanse of thigh, fit and tan in the dead of winter, though her face and hands were pale.

"Miss Ada Culpi!" yelled the MC, and the singer curled her arms, palms up, asking, asking. She sang to each person in the crowd, begging each kind soul to advise her, to tell her what to do about the man she loved but who didn't love her. No one believed this guy didn't love her, but her voice reminded them of every time they'd felt what she was pretending to feel. Lula had never felt that way. Then she remembered Alvo and thought she might be about to start now. She glanced at Alvo, steeling herself for the sight of entranced, hormonal male rapture. Instead he shook his head and shrugged, eloquently conveying his adorable opinion that Miss Ada Culpi was a little much. His shrug said he preferred more normal, less outrageous women like . . . well, like Lula!

Ada Culpi reached for the audience, grabbing them, pulling them in, signaling that the only way they could soothe her broken heart was by dancing. A few people, then a few more, formed a line, and the line of dancers grew long enough to coil once and then again. By now there were two rows, a men's line and a women's line facing one another.

Lula took Alvo's empty raki glass, set both glasses on a ledge, then led him onto the dance floor. The women's line grabbed Lula just as the men's line, led by a guy twirling a red scarf embroidered with a double-headed eagle, yanked Alvo the opposite way. Lula had drunk precisely enough to feel loose but not too loose as the steps came back to her, as natural as walking but less isolated and boring. Why should this seem so pleasant to a person like herself, a person who hated chorus lines, military parades, anything in lockstep? She liked the music, and she liked knowing what to do with her body in response to the drum beat and the hysterical clarinet.

A girl with purple eyelids held one hand, a middle-aged woman the other. The woman smiled, but not the girl. Lula trusted them both enough to briefly close her eyes. Alvo was out there somewhere. No need to fear he'd left the club or found a prettier girl to dance with. They were all dancing together, Lula and Alvo among them. As the lines spooled and twisted, Lula caught sight of Alvo, taller than most of the men. Alvo could dance, it turned out. Confidently, but not arrogantly, his back straight, his head held high. How handsome he was, and how glad she was to be here with him. Why should she care about a gun, some moody weirdness, a certain lack of clarity about what he did for a living? And okay, some low-level stalking.

Did Alvo see her? She couldn't tell. She watched his line snake closer until he was opposite her. He saw her. They looked at each other. That was that. Nothing needed to be discussed, not even inside her own head. Lula loved how the voice of sex drowned out all the other voices, the naggings of reason and common sense, shyness and hesitation. Desire and inevitability were the only voices left, and their interesting questions were the only questions: How and when? When and where? Would it be easy or awkward?

Alvo and Lula danced past one another and looked back, not caring who was watching. Alvo's line turned a corner, so that his back was to Lula, who peered around the dancers between them. There was nothing to do but keep dancing.

At last the music ended. The singer said, "*Falemenderit.* Thank you thank you thank you," and a storm of blown kisses rained down on the dancers, who regretfully dropped each other's hands so they could applaud.

Alvo found Lula and put his arm around her shoulders and steered her toward the exit. He produced a bill and a claim check and gave them to the coat girl, who sensed that this was not the moment for another competitive whole-body appraisal of Lula. They headed out into the cold night, which warmed up when Alvo grabbed Lula and kissed her right in front of the door. The bouncers whistled and cheered. Alvo handed over the parking ticket, then drew Lula into the shadows and kissed her with such force that it took several horn blasts from the valet to detach them long enough to get into the SUV.

Before leaning over to kiss her again, Alvo considerately pushed the buttons that heated the seats, and the warmth beneath Lula flowed into the warmth inside her. It must have started snowing, because Lula was dimly aware of the sigh of the windshield wipers.

"Merry white Christmas," Alvo said.

"Merry white Christmas to you," said Lula.

Alvo shook himself like a wet dog as he separated from Lula. As he drove, he yanked at his clothing with a shy embarrassed smile at some secret he had with himself, a secret that, Lula concluded happily, must be a massive hard-on. After a few blocks, he pulled over and parked on the formerly scary industrial street that now seemed private and romantic.

They kissed and pressed against each other as closely as the console between them allowed. Pausing for breath, Lula watched, from a momentary remove, passion locked in a heated argument with her sensible reluctance to have sex for the first time with Alvo in a vehicle, even one as roomy as this. It was awkward enough in bed, with every creature comfort helping you over the various hurdles, zippers and bra hooks and first seeing the other person naked.

"Not here," her sweet Lancelot murmured.

"No, not here," agreed Lula.

"My place," Alvo said. Then he slapped himself on the forehead and said, "Look how you've messed with my head. I forgot the Vlorë cousins."

Lula had messed with his head. His desire for her—for her!—had erased three entire cousins. Lula waited for Alvo to suggest a hotel. It couldn't seem like her idea, even if it was. She didn't want to look like a degenerate slut who did this all the time.

Typing into the GPS, Alvo said, "She'll tell us a hotel." Then he said, "Motherfucker. I don't have a credit card. This friend of mine got his wallet boosted at a club. Five round-trip tickets to the DR charged before he called it in. So now I only bring cash and my driver's license. I could pay you back—"

"I don't have a credit card," Lula said. "I don't even have cash."

"Big problem," said Alvo, then kissed her again, as if that

might solve the problem. After a while Lula heard herself say, "We could go to Mister Stanley's."

"And what?" Alvo said. "Introduce myself? Hi, I'm a friend of your nanny's?"

Lula said, "They'll be asleep. But we'll have to be very quiet."

"Silent as death," Alvo said. Lula wondered if it was possible to literally faint from desire. Probably not if you were sitting down. As Alvo started the motor again, Lula rested one hand on his thigh. Brushing against his groin, the backs of her knuckles confirmed her pleasant suspicions. She would have to make sure that Alvo left before Mister Stanley woke up.

Alvo groaned softly. "Wait. Slippery weather. I need to concentrate on the road."

Lula sat back and closed her eyes. That last double shot of raki had affected her more than she'd realized. Probably it would sober her up to focus on the challenge ahead: finding the quietest route to her room and figuring out what she would say if by some chance Mister Stanley or Zeke was still awake, waiting to catch Santa Claus squeezing down the chimney.

Alvo said, "Tonight is why God invented four-wheel drive."

The alcohol almost persuaded Lula that this might be the time to broach the subject of Alvo breaking into Mister Stanley's when she wasn't there. This time we'll sneak in together, she'd say.

Only at the last minute did better judgment prevail. Suppose it hadn't been Alvo? He might change his mind about getting naked and defenseless in a house where stalkers wrote Balkan stories on computers and showered, uninvited. As Alvo sped down the icy highway, Lula reminded herself to observe how he acted at Mister Stanley's, to see if he gave any sign of having been there before and knowing how to get to her room without her having to show him.

ALVO TOOK THE Baywater exit, then parked, and they kissed some more. By the time he started the car again, Lula's hesitations had vanished.

Mister Stanley's windows were dark, except for the outside light he'd left on for Lula. She told Alvo to wait behind the tree and crept around to the window to make sure that no one was sipping delicious cold water at the fridge.

All clear! She gave Alvo the thumbs-up sign, unlocked the door, and pushed him away so he wouldn't be groping her till they were safe in her room. Stealth came easily to Alvo. For such a forceful guy, he could be quiet as a kitten. Lula forgot to watch and see whether he knew the way.

She opened the door to her room. What was that smell? Musty, yeasty, with an edge of organic rot. Mice died in the walls in Tirana. Did that happen in New Jersey? Of course. But why now, why here, why on this night of all nights when she had found a guy she liked and was bringing him home? What would Alvo think of her? Maybe he wouldn't notice. She pulled him inside and shut the door. Light shone in from the street. Lula lowered the shade and switched her night lamp on low. She knew men liked to see. In the dark, the costly underwear would have been for nothing.

"What's that smell?" asked Alvo.

Lula said, "The kid's pet rabbit escaped and had babies inside the wall."

Alvo said, "I always wondered how bunnies have so many babies."

"Let's find out," said Lula.

"Not the baby part," Alvo said warily.

"Of course not," Lula said.

Alvo sat on the edge of the bed, spread his knees, and eased her toward him. The sweetness and the expertise Alvo put into his kisses made Lula feel hopeful about the immediate future. Of course there was fear and nervousness, that was part of the high. The silk panties were a brilliant touch. A nice surprise for Alvo.

By the time Lula surfaced for air, the smell had gotten stronger.

"Hey, where are you?" Alvo said.

"Right here," said Lula, demonstrating how right there she was. She had reentered the state of steamy bliss when Alvo pulled away.

"What the fuck?" he said.

Lula turned. A dripping-wet woman, naked except for a towel wrapped around one hand, stood in the bathroom doorway. Lula turned the lamp on full. The woman was smeared with some brown substance that Lula hoped was mud. She was backlit against the bathroom glare, her shadowed face surrounded by a bright nimbus of reddish gray curls. Then she stepped into the light.

"Ginger," Lula said.

"Who the hell?" Alvo said.

"The mom," Lula said. "The mother and the wife. The wife of Mister Stanley. I know her only from pictures."

"You stay away from my pictures," said Ginger.

"Pleased to meet you, Mrs. Stanley," Alvo said.

"Go back to hell, hog boy," said Ginger.

"Nice," Alvo told Lula, as if it was her fault. "Nice manners your roommate has."

"She's not my roommate," said Lula.

"Your boss," said Alvo. "Your boss's wife."

"I told you, I never saw her before!"

"Then what's she doing in your room?"

Ginger took a step forward. Proximity and lamplight were spectacularly unkind. Lula didn't know where to look first, or where not to look ever. Not at the tires of soft flesh stacked around Ginger's middle, not at the sunken loins and sparse pubic hair, the pouched thighs streaked brown, and certainly not at the grotesque mask of the face in the family snapshots.

"It's chocolate," Ginger said. "I had to cover myself with candy to get rid of the sour vibe you've brought into this house, miss."

What exactly did Ginger mean by "sour vibe"? The psychic residue of Lula helping Ginger's husband and son sweep up the ashes after Ginger had burned down their happy home?

"Chocolate," Lula said. "I hope so."

"Disgusting," said Alvo.

"You shut up, asshole." With a dramatic flourish, Ginger shook the towel from her hand, revealing, underneath, a butcher knife that she brandished, first at Lula, then at Alvo. Lula recognized the knife. The last time she'd tried to cook Zeke broccoli, it had sliced through the stem in one stroke. How had Ginger found it? It was Ginger's knife.

"Put that down, lady, please," said Alvo.

"Please, Mrs. Stanley," said Lula.

"Call me that one more time, and I'll cut your face off. I'll kill you both and let you bleed out on the floor."

"For your husband and son to find?" Lula said.

"Fuck them too," said Ginger. "The kid's a fruitcake like his dad."

Where was the Ginger who had sent her son those cheerful postcards implying that the red rocks and the clean Western air were healing her spirit? Where had Ginger really been during her circular pilgrimage to and from New Jersey? What had she done with the money Mister Stanley sent, and how had she convinced him that she was getting better? Lula should have been watching the knife, but instead her thoughts ranged through space and time, until the fog finally parted, revealing an unobstructed view of the truth that had been there all along.

It had always been Ginger. Ginger had a key. How could Lula not have realized that Ginger was letting herself into the house, showering in her tub, writing on Zeke's computer? The morning of the college trip, it had crossed her mind. But she'd instantly dismissed it. She'd wanted to think it was Alvo. And besides, Ginger was sending postcards from all over the country! Little Charmy Puppy had thrown her even farther off, as Ginger doubtless intended. Why would her employer's wife be leaving her cute wind-up toys? The obvious was now obvious, as it always was, sooner or later.

"The crap you let my child eat," Ginger said. "Frozen hamburgers! Pizza. You think a mother doesn't know? You think I didn't look to see the toxic slime you stashed away in the freezer?"

"We got what Zeke wanted," said Lula. "We bought what he would eat."

"First of all, what gives you the right to even say my child's name. Or to feed him poison."

"He's not a child," said Lula. "And it wasn't poison."

"To the mother he's always a child," Alvo said.

"Shut up, you Balkan boy toy." Ginger waggled the knife at Alvo. Why didn't Alvo grab it? He was as big and male and strong as Ginger was female and weak. Perhaps he doubted, as did Lula, that the substance with which she'd painted herself was chocolate. For now, squeamishness trumped mortal fear.

"What kind of house is this?" demanded Ginger. "I'll tell you. A whorehouse. It's Christmas Eve, and there's not even a Christmas tree downstairs!"

"Please, lady, give me the knife," said Alvo.

"In your fat gut I will," replied Ginger.

"We won't hurt you," Lula said, illogically, considering who had the weapon. But Ginger was so vulnerable, so old and crazy and naked. Ginger came several steps closer, smelling like chocolate, but with an undertone of shit.

"Hurt me? You already have. Sleeping with my husband, turning my child against me, undermining everything I worked for—"

Alvo said, "So you did fuck the boss!"

Lula said, "I told you. I never had sex with Mister Stanley."

"Mister Stanley," said Ginger. "Listen to you. Stanley got himself a real servant maid. A real Transylvanian goat girl."

"I'm not Transylvanian," Lula said.

"She's Albanian," said Alvo. "So am I."

"Bully for you," said Ginger. "I'm from Indiana, but I don't go around reminding people every five minutes."

"Albania isn't Indiana," said Alvo.

"Enough!" said Ginger. "This is making me sick! I'm not discussing politics with some camel jockey."

"Hey!" Alvo shouted. "Take that back!"

"Pipe down," Ginger said. "Wake my son and husband up, and it's your jugular, pal."

Lula pictured Mister Stanley and Zeke slumbering in their beds. Her heart contracted with pity for them. For all of them, Ginger included.

Alvo said, "Give me the knife. Slowly and calmly. Nobody panic."

"Where did you learn English? Watching *Law and Order*?" Ginger stepped closer to Alvo, pointing the blade at his neck.

"Why are you threatening *me*?" he said.

"Because you're the threat," answered Ginger. "What could this bitch do that she hasn't done, except two-time my husband under his own roof? Maybe she's done it already."

"Have you?" Alvo asked Lula.

Really, that was it.

"Button your pants," Lula told Alvo. "If you're going to die, you'll want your fly zipped to give a more dignified impression of your last minutes on earth."

"No one's going to die," Alvo said.

"Everyone's going to die," said Ginger.

"Would you like a robe?" Lula asked Ginger. "You must be freezing cold."

"I wouldn't wear your slut clothes," Ginger said. "I've seen what's in your closet."

For a split second, Lula was outraged. But it was only fair. Lula had held Ginger's dashikis and fat pants against her body.

"It's comfortable. Warm," Lula said. "My granny made it

for me." Anyone would forgive her for lying about her granny. Granny would forgive her. She would want her to save her life. Lula cringed at the thought of shit or even chocolate smeared inside Granny's robe. She needed to keep it firmly in mind that there was no Granny's robe.

There was, however, a gun. That Lula remembered it only now proved she wasn't a violent person. Loaded or unloaded, guns trumped knives. Her papa used to say, You don't ever need to use a gun, you only have to show it. What if Ginger had found it? Ginger hadn't found it. She'd be waving it at Alvo.

Not even Ginger could resist the offer of Granny's warm love against her cold skin.

"Sure," she said. "A robe would be nice."

Lula said, "I'll get it."

Lula looked back over her shoulder at Ginger menacing Alvo. A stifled sob leaped from her throat at the sight of Ginger's droopy behind. Some day Lula's would sag like that. Young people weren't supposed to know this, but Lula always had. Even her ass depended on her staying in this country. If she signed up at a decent gym, her muscle tone would hold up twenty years longer than it would in Tirana.

Alvo shot Lula a meaningful glance. He probably thought her plan was for him to grab the knife as Lula helped Ginger into the robe. Which would have worked, if there was a robe. He knew there was a gun, but not where Lula kept it. Because, unlike Ginger, he'd never been in this room with the time and motive and opportunity to look through Lula's stuff.

Ginger was too busy with Alvo to wonder why Lula would keep Granny's robe in a bureau drawer. With all her snooping around, how could she not have found the gun? Maybe Lula's underwear had created a magic force field. If so, it was worth the money, even if the silk against her breasts and the tops of her thighs was now a shaming reminder of her ruined hopes.

Lula aimed the gun at Ginger.

"Drop the knife," she told her in her most persuasive, and, she hoped, least cops-and-robbers tone.

Ginger tilted her chin at the gun. "Right. I'm dying laughing. Shoot me and explain it to my husband and son, then catch a one-way ride to the deportation center." With a shrug, she turned back and waved the knife at Alvo. "You know what? I'm sick of your face. Your face in its present form."

What was Lula supposed to do now? Nothing was going according to plan. A moment passed, another moment.

Lula squeezed the trigger.

The retort knocked her backward. Her papa would be furious to see her stumble and nearly fall. The room began to glitter, as if the walls were mirrored, the air bright with flakes of mica. The last thing Lula saw before she succumbed to a sudden, overwhelming need for sleep was Madonna smiling while a little girl riddled her with bullets.

OPENING HER EYES, Lula smelled incense. No. Gunpowder. Smoke. Ginger was slumped against the wall, stunned but evidently unharmed. No one had been hurt. The knife lay across the room. A trickle of plaster dust sifted from a charred hole in the wallpaper. Alvo grabbed a blanket and gently covered Ginger.

"What the hell?" said Ginger. "Where's my fucking robe?"

"There is no robe," said Lula.

"Liar," said Ginger. "Lying whore. Murderer. You almost killed me."

The door opened. Mister Stanley saw everything in five seconds.

"Jesus Christ," he said. "Jesus fucking Christ."

"Stanley," said Ginger. "Look at me! Your nympho trollop tried to kill me."

"She had a knife!" protested Lula, childishly.

"Hello, dear," Mister Stanley told Ginger. His bending over to kiss his wife on the top of her head was the saddest thing Lula hoped ever to see. He picked up the knife and took the gun from Lula, going from weapon to weapon liked an exhausted mother gathering toys after a playdate. With the gun in one hand and the knife in the other, he went into the bathroom, where he left the weapons and shut the door behind him. For such a safety-conscious guy, Mister Stanley seemed awfully calm. But why should Lula have been surprised? That was how he was. His composure was admirable, but she could see how it might have been part of what drove Ginger crazy.

"Hello, dear?" The cruel precision of Ginger's mimicry reminded Lula of Zeke. "That's what you say? Hello, dear? Stan, you are so *autistic!*"

"Are you a friend of Lula's?" Mister Stanley asked Alvo.

"My cousin," Lula said. "Mister Stanley, this is my Cousin Alvo."

"Cousin my ass," said Ginger. "She and the so-called cousin were getting ready to fuck."

Alvo rose off the edge of the bed and extended his hand to Mister Stanley. "I'm Lula's Cousin Alvo."

Just at that moment a voice in the hall said, "What's going on?"

"Don't let Zeke in," cried Lula.

"Mom," said Zeke. "What's that stuff on you?"

"Chocolate," Ginger said. "Remember we used to have so much fun baking cookies?"

Zeke wore a black T-shirt and plaid boxers. He screwed his fists into his eye sockets like a sleepy child. Look at him! Lula wanted to cry out. But what exactly did she want Zeke's parents to see?

"It stinks in here," Zeke said.

"You're shivering, Ginger," Mister Stanley said. "Your mom is shivering, Zeke."

"I'm freezing inside," said Ginger.

"This is gross. I'm out of here," Zeke said.

"Somebody stop him," Ginger said.

"Let him go," said Mister Stanley. "He doesn't need to see this. Are you comfortable down there, dear? Wouldn't you like to sit in this nice soft chair?"

She's filthy! Lula almost pointed out. But it was Ginger's chair.

"Nobody come near me," Ginger said. Propped against the wall, she pumped her legs under the blanket, and ten dirty toes wriggled against the satin border.

"I didn't know it was loaded," Lula said.

"I didn't know it was loaded," mocked Ginger.

Alvo looked from one of them to the other in such innocence and wonder, no one would have suspected that it was his gun. His loaded gun. He went into the bathroom and returned with the pistol.

"I'll take care of this," he said.

"Thank you," said Mister Stanley. "How did the gun get in the house in the first place?"

"I think it was your wife's," said Lula.

"Fucking liar!" Ginger yelled.

"And the knife?"

"From the kitchen," Lula said, nodding at Ginger again. The crazy wife had come heavily armed. She wasn't taking chances.

"Lying scumsucker," Ginger said, more resignedly this time.

"Thank God no one got hurt," Mister Stanley said. "My God, what a terrible illness."

"I'll say," Ginger said. "And you know what the fatal part was? Being married to you."

Mister Stanley sighed. Then he went to the phone and dialed without having to look up the number. He said, "Is this the doctor's service? This is Stanley Larch. Ginger Larch's husband. I'm sorry. I know it's Christmas Eve. But could the doctor call us back? My wife has come home unexpectedly, and we're having a bit of a crisis."

"A bit of a crisis?" Ginger said. "What kind of faggot talk is that? And isn't it just like my husband to send for that fetal pig, that Wannabe Sigmund Doctor Fat Fuck Freud who did such a fabulous job of curing me the last time?"

"You need to get dressed," Mister Stanley said.

"If you touch me I'll explode," said Ginger. "If you come near me I'll scream murder and rape and all your zombie neighbors will rise from their graves and come running. Hey, listen. Did you hear that?"

"Hear what?" said Mister Stanley.

"The front door slamming," Ginger said. "Elvis has left the building. By which I mean our son."

"Is that true?" said Mister Stanley. "Did Zeke go out?"

"A mother knows things," said Ginger.

Lula was sent to look for Zeke, and when she'd searched everywhere and couldn't find him, Mister Stanley asked Lula and Alvo if they would mind locating his son, who probably hadn't gone far, and make sure he got back.

"Your coats are on the floor," Ginger pointed out helpfully. "Dropped on your stumblefuck way to bed."

"Ginger and I will be fine," Mister Stanley said. "Just make sure that Zeke's okay."

Alvo hurried out to the car, and Lula tagged after him. The SUV still smelled of Lula's perfume mixed with Alvo's cologne. When Alvo put the gun in the glove compartment, Lula felt a deep sadness, as if she and the gun were breaking up after a long romance. Starting the ignition, Alvo said, "Poor kid. I have a little brother that age. He stayed behind with our aunt in Durrës. Big boy surfer didn't want to leave the beach."

"I'm an only child," Lula said.

"Too bad for you," said Alvo.

"Let's check the bus stop," said Lula.

"The buses don't run at this hour," Alvo said.

"Just check it." Lula told him how to get there, and sure enough, they found Zeke huddled on the bench in the shelter.

"Get in the car," Alvo said. "It's cold."

Zeke obeyed without argument. Lula wanted to tell him that he'd be all right, but Alvo's presence inhibited her, and besides she felt dwarfed by the magnitude of what Zeke must be feeling.

That crazy woman in Lula's room was this poor kid's *mother*. Zeke had rushed out in his T-shirt and shorts. Lula heard his teeth clatter.

"I'm blasting the heat," said Alvo. "You'll be broiling in a minute."

As the temperature rose, the mood inside the SUV grew relaxed and mellow, as if they were old friends or even family. Mama, Papa, Zeke. And though Lula was the one who was close to Zeke, the one paid to watch Zeke, the one who cared about Zeke, Papa was in control. Let Alvo have the power. It was a relief to have someone help her carry the weight. Only now could Lula admit how heavy it had been, only now as she pretended that she and Alvo were sharing the responsibilities of raising a teenage son. Borne along on the current of this convivial warmth came the chilling certainty that she would never see Alvo again.

"Better?" said Alvo.

"Nice ride," Zeke said.

"Thanks," said Alvo. "Lula's Cousin George hooked me up with a guy who got me a break on the vehicle."

"Is that how you guys know each other?" asked Zeke.

"Want to drive?" said Alvo.

"Are you serious?" said Zeke.

Alvo hadn't bothered asking if Zeke had a license, nor did Zeke bother mentioning that he wasn't allowed to drive at night. Mister Stanley would kill them. He would especially kill Lula. But eventually he would forgive her for having found his son.

"Would I ask if I wasn't serious?" Alvo said. "I don't joke about my car."

"Then sure. Definitely," Zeke said. "Awesome."

Alvo motioned for Lula to get in the back. And though it would have been simpler for Lula to sit behind Alvo, she went around to Zeke's side so she was standing there, waiting for him when he got out.

"Be careful," she said. "You know what your father—"

"My *fodder*?" demanded Zeke. "What about my *fodder*?" Was Lula's accent so thick? The first time Lula met Zeke, he'd complimented her English. Since then he'd never once corrected or criticized her. Lula might have asked what she'd done to deserve this if she hadn't just seen his mother naked and raving.

"Have fun," Lula said and kissed Zeke's cold cheek, something she'd never done. He shrank away. By the time Lula had fastened her seat belt, Alvo was asking Zeke if he knew where everything was on the dashboard.

"It's a little new to me," said Zeke. "My ride is a 1970 Olds."

"Sexy beast," said Alvo. "They don't make them like that anymore."

If only Alvo could read Lula's mind now as she beamed him the information that Zeke had never driven at night and was doing so for the first time on an icy Christmas Eve in a sixty-thousand-dollar vehicle with a gun in the glove compartment.

"The brights, the dims," Alvo said.

"Got it," Zeke said. "All systems go."

Zeke drove slowly. The streets were empty. At least it had stopped snowing. Lula began to enjoy it. She was disappointed when they reached Mister Stanley's and glad when Alvo said, "Keep driving."

As they passed, Lula stared into the brightly lit windows. Was Mister Stanley still there? Had he managed to get his wife cleaned up and dressed? Mister Stanley's Acura was in its usual spot, but there were no silhouettes on the shade that Lula had pulled a lifetime ago when she and Alvo sneaked into her bedroom.

Zeke didn't leave the neighborhood. Though he was breaking one big rule, he wasn't ready to break them all, and he stayed within the borders his father had drawn. They made a ten-block circuit and twice passed the house. The third time they saw an ambulance parked outside. Zeke drove a few blocks, rounded the corner, stopped, and switched places with Alvo.

"Nice parking job," Alvo said.

"Let's go home now," said Zeke.

Mister Stanley was starting his car and preparing to follow the ambulance. Its unhurried beacon spun a thread of light that spooled out and snapped back, like the string of a yo-yo.

Lula rolled down her window and asked Mister Stanley if he wanted her to go with him.

He said, "That's very kind of you, Lula. But I think we've got things under control. I'd rather you stayed with Zeke."

Zeke yelled, "Merry Christmas, Dad. How's Mom?"

"Merry Christmas, Zeke," said Mister Stanley. "She'll be fine. Are you sure you guys will be okay?"

"We're sure," said Lula.

"They will," Alvo said. "I'll check everything out before I leave."

"I appreciate that," said Mister Stanley. "I locked the front door."

"I've got my keys," said Lula.

The ambulance flashed its lights, and the two-vehicle cortege began its mournful crawl down the street.

"Good luck, Mister Stanley," called Lula.

"I'll let you guys say good night," said Zeke. Lula and Alvo watched him go into the house.

Alvo said, "The badass runaway rebel took his keys."

"The kid is smart," said Lula.

Alvo said, "The dad's gonna turn him gay if he doesn't give him some slack. Do you and the kid really need me to come inside and check the closets and look under the beds?"

"Of course not," Lula said. If only she and Alvo had done that the first time. The last time.

"It's been quite a night," said Alvo.

"First it was fun," said Lula. "Then it wasn't fun."

"Next time, all fun, I promise," said Alvo. "I'll call you."

But he wouldn't. Lula couldn't have said how she knew. But she knew. There wouldn't be a next time, let alone *all fun*. Alvo had the gun back. He wouldn't call. In the end he had decided: She was bad news and bad luck.

"See you soon," said Lula.

"Happy New Year," said Alvo.

Chapter Eleven

⊷≋⊶

Lula awoke to a grainy cold light and a sky the white of tomb-stones. The inside of her skull felt like her childhood jack-in-the-box, a clown that popped from its tin cube, banging its drum in terror. Now the pounding played a demonic duet with the clang-ing church bells. Happy Birthday, Jesus!

All over America, children were hyperventilating with joy, grabbing their mattresses to keep from racing downstairs and rip-ping open their presents. Lula knew that this was the made-for-TV version of American life, that half the population was sick and alone or homeless, conscious of the holiday only as some-thing they wanted to end, preferably after free turkey in a steamy, malodorous shelter. But how many households were recovering from a Christmas Eve when Mom showed up naked and smeared with chocolate and shit, a night when the lady of the house held hostage, at knifepoint, the Albanian nanny and her date?

Now Lula remembered why her room was so cold. She'd left a window open in an unsuccessful effort to eliminate the lingering stench of Ginger's madness.

Her fingers still reeked of gunpowder. She remembered her father describing one of their neighbors as the kind of guy who fired off one shot and spent the next three days sniffing smoke on his fingers. That's how her dad got sent away. The smoke-sniffing neighbor had been a police informer. Say something like that, it gets back.

Her papa had gone to jail until he promised one of the prison guards a tribal musket, and they let him go. He'd been away for slightly less than twenty-four hours, but from then on he referred to himself as a former political prisoner. Though Lula had been very young, she remembered that day, counted off in seconds and by the nonstop cups of tea her aunt prepared for her mother, who sat at the kitchen table, veering between extremes of panic and resignation, motionless but for the raising and lowering of the tea cup. The memory of those hours had merged in Lula's mind with the Communist TV news, the maddening tick tock of the clock behind the drone of the stern newsreader. And now the clock had slowed again in Mister Stanley's house, marking off the minutes until a father and son awakened to the reality of last night's visit from Ginger. It could happen anywhere, the nasty twist of fate that turns time into your enemy, implacable, mean, and patient, dragging its feet to torment you.

She was surprised to find the presents she'd bought for Mister Stanley and Zeke, still in their Christmas wrapping at the top of her closet, survivors of Ginger's search-and-destroy. No one would feel like celebrating. But even so it seemed wrong to have spent the money and effort and not try to help Mister Stanley and Zeke enjoy their sorry Christmas. She averted her eyes, as if from a wreck, as she bent to pick up her fancy underwear. She stood too fast, and a slosh of bile slapped the back of her throat.

Lula brought the boxes downstairs and placed them beside the other presents on the kitchen counter: an envelope with

Zeke's name on it, a small package addressed "To Dad from Zeke," and a large box, wrapped in silver paper with a card that said, "For Lula, Merry Christmas from Stanley and Zeke." The presents looked stranded and ashamed to have been left on the counter where everyday objects congregated: the mail, the groceries, the newspaper. Even without the tree, couldn't Mister Stanley have arranged the gifts near the fireplace? Everywhere parents were telling their kids that Santa had read their letters and heard their prayers and rewarded them for being good American children by bringing them the latest Barbie, the must-have video game. Not at Mister Stanley's. Their Christmas Eve visitor could hardly have been less like the jolly grandpa flying in from the Arctic.

How would Lula face Mister Stanley, and how would that conversation begin? Good morning, Merry Christmas, sorry about your wife. Her fear of discomfort, awkwardness, and an incapacitating rush of sympathy for her boss warred against her desire to hear what had happened with Ginger. Curiosity won out, and Lula ran the coffee grinder hard. Soon she heard the murmur and splash of Mister Stanley's shower.

Sunday Casual Mister Stanley walked into the kitchen.

"Smells good," he said. "Merry Christmas, Lula. Are you feeling all right?"

"I don't know," Lula said.

"You look a little pale," he said. So did Mister Stanley.

"It's the light," she said.

He poured himself a cup of coffee and, with his back to her, said, "Sorry about last night."

The sadness was almost too much to bear. The sadness and the pity.

"It's not your fault," Lula said.

"I know. But it must have been upsetting. And naturally one worries that a person might reasonably decide not to continue working in a house where this sort of thing occurs."

Where did Mister Stanley think she would go? And who did he think Lula was? A person who would abandon him and Zeke at a time like this? And why was he apologizing to a girl he'd caught in his house on Christmas Eve with a "cousin" who obviously felt so comfortable around a gun that he'd taken it with him, for which Mister Stanley had thanked him? And what was "this sort of thing"?

"How is your wife?" Lula didn't know what to call her. Not Mrs. Ginger. Not Mrs. Larch.

"We were lucky. Despite what my wife believes, her doctor's a human being. He was able to recommend an excellent facility. We were lucky they had a room."

Lucky. Someone had dressed Ginger. Someone had bathed her, or not. But yes, they were lucky that no one had been shot. Lucky that Zeke hadn't disappeared forever into the night. Lucky that wherever Ginger had gone was a five-star resort compared to the least hellish Balkan asylum.

"Well!" Mister Stanley said. "Between Ginger's care and Zeke's college, we're not going to be retiring any time soon."

We? Lula could hardly breathe until she realized that Mister Stanley meant *I*. She was about to make some chatty remark about how this was like Albania, where doctors treated you differently depending on how much you paid. Or maybe she should mention how, under the dictatorship, mental hospitals often doubled as political prisons. People used to say, You meet the most interesting people in the nuthouse. Or anyway, the purest. Normally Mister Stanley enjoyed comparisons between Albania and here. But maybe not at the moment.

"Thanks for looking after Zeke," he said. "Thanks for finding him. Jesus. I hate to think—"

"He wanted to be found. He was worried about you." It was true, it was easy to say, it made Mister Stanley feel better, and it gave Lula a break in which to recover from the memory of Alvo letting Zeke drive his SUV. Nothing could have been better for Zeke. How much heart Alvo showed! She would never see him again. But the breakage of her romance was a hairline fissure compared to the chasms that must have opened last night for Zeke and Mister Stanley.

Lula turned to hear Zeke say, "Is this Christmas? Is this *it*?"

"Zeke," said Mister Stanley. "What a pleasant surprise. We didn't hear you come downstairs. Good morning. Merry Christmas."

Lula scrutinized Zeke's features but couldn't see much difference between his crumpled frown and the face he showed his father every weekend morning. If you didn't know Zeke, or even if you did, you might not conclude that this was a kid whose mother had just had a breakdown in front of the nanny and a cool Albanian dude who let him drive his Lexus. Maybe it would hit Zeke tomorrow morning, or the next day, or maybe in twenty years. If there was one thing Lula had learned from Balkan history and from American TV, it was how long memories could stay bottled up before the cork exploded. Another cloud on the bright horizon of Zeke's future wife.

Mister Stanley said, "Lula, open your present."

Lula said, "Zeke first. It's Christmas. Zeke's the kid."

"Ladies first," said Zeke.

Having only one gift to unwrap, Lula exaggerated the drama of removing the paper, opening the box, and lifting the laptop from its Styrofoam nest. Chromosomes or maybe hormones worked in tandem so that both Zeke and Mister Stanley turned away at the same moment, with the same gesture, ducking as if from a blow, so as not to see Lula cry. The tears were real, but she faked a sob to prolong her time to float on the swell of pleasure and gratitude for this perfect gift, this generous investment in her future. She would deserve it, she would be worthy. She would work like a dog. She would make up beautiful stories and not pretend they were true. She would devote herself to the journal she'd neglected since she met Alvo. There was no reason not to, now. She had nothing to hide. Her authentic new American life would start fresh from today.

"Thank you," Lula said. "Now you, Zeke."

Zeke opened the envelope from his father. "Thanks. I can always use cash." He unwrapped the belt from Lula and slung it around his waist.

"Awesome studs! Thanks, Lula!" She'd underestimated his skinniness. Even on the last notch, the belt slipped down his hips. She had also underestimated the ferocity of the metal grommets that turned the belt into armor, the perfect fashion accessory for the collapse of civilization.

"It can be fixed," said Mister Stanley. "We can punch another hole—"

"You think everything can be fixed, Dad," said Zeke. "Nothing can be fixed."

"Hmmm . . . " said Mister Stanley. "Let's see what Santa brought *me*." He thanked Lula for the Nano even as the earbuds popped out of his ears. Saying he'd figure it out on his own, he stuffed it back into the box from which it would never emerge again.

"To Dad," read Mister Stanley. Zeke's quiet snort was intended for Lula, but Mister Stanley heard, and an echo seemed to linger until Zeke said, "Hope you like it, Dad."

Mister Stanley unwrapped a book. "*The Diamond Sutra!*"

"Buddhist meditations," said Zeke. "Helpful when you're . . . stressed." The last word created a depression in the air that slowly filled with disturbing images from the previous night.

Mister Stanley paged through the book. "That's very thoughtful of you, Zeke. Very unexpected. I'm touched."

"It wasn't my idea," said Zeke. "Abigail picked it out."

"Abigail? *Don's* Abigail?"

Zeke nodded.

"I didn't know you two were in touch."

"She meditates instead of eating," said Zeke.

"That's not smart," said his father.

"Abigail and Shirley and I—"

"Who's Shirley?"

"Another friend."

"But it's such a geriatric name," said Mister Stanley.

"What does *geriatric* mean?" Zeke asked Lula. Why was he asking her? Last night, switching places outside Alvo's car, he had made fun of her accent.

"Elderly," said Lula.

"Shirley's a kid in my class. I'm tired. I'm going back to sleep. I didn't get a lot of rest last night. Merry Christmas. Thanks." Zeke took the belt but left his dad's check on the counter.

"Do you want to go visit your mother?" his father called after him. "I thought I'd—"

"Next time," Zeke said. "Or maybe the time after that."

"Probably just as well," Mister Stanley told Lula.

"Excuse me too," said Lula. "I'm also really tired."

Mister Stanley said, "Before you go, can I ask you one question, Lula?"

"Anything," Lula whispered. Then louder, "Anything."

"How *did* that gun get in the house?"

"You asked me. I told you. I guess your wife brought it with her. I never saw it before. She must have picked up the knife in the kitchen. For backup." Ginger should have thought twice about what she did to her son. Now among the things she had lost was the right to say what had happened. Who would believe Ginger's story, even if it were true?

Mister Stanley said, "That Buddhist book he got me . . . you don't think it might be a sign of . . . I don't know . . . something he inherited from his mom?"

"Some girls convinced him it was cool. He explained that. Remember?"

"Right. I suppose that is a relief," said Mister Stanley. "Be sure and drink lots of water."

Lula sat at her desk until she heard Mister Stanley leave. She watched him shuffle out to his car and drive off. Then she got her new laptop and carried it up to her room. Moments later Zeke knocked and asked if she wanted help connecting to the Internet. Lula said she needed help powering it on.

It made for a pleasant afternoon, sitting on her bed and letting Zeke play with her new computer. For the rest of Christmas Day, neither said a single word that wasn't about electronics.

.   .   .

THE NEXT MORNING, Dunia called to ask about Lula's date. Had the perfume worked? Lula said her date was . . . interesting. She would tell Dunia more when she saw her. Dunia asked what Lula was doing New Year's Eve. Lula said she wasn't sure, her guy might be out of town on business.

Dunia said, "He's your guy now? And he's away New Year's? I thought you said he was in construction? What kind of contractor goes away on business on New Year's? Is he cheating on you already?"

"We're still in the getting-to-know-you phase," said Lula. "Everything's very new." Lula tried to freight that *new* with unfolding romance and passion. What a good little actress she'd become since she'd found it so hard to tell the visa officer about returning home to marry her fiancé on Christmas. If the fiancé had existed, yesterday would have been their anniversary.

"I see," said Dunia gloomily. "Steve says he wants a private New Year's Eve, the two of us quietly sharing a bottle of great champagne. Just the idea of it makes me want to kill myself and vomit."

Lula made her promise she wouldn't kill herself. They smooched their phones and hung up, swearing to get together soon. It was nice to have a friend, even one she had to lie to. The next time she saw Dunia, she would tell her the truth about her date with Alvo and about Ginger's visit.

In the days that followed, Lula got to know her new computer. She had plenty of time, the weather was cold, she tried not to leave her room. Zeke and Mister Stanley were still on vacation, though Mister Stanley was gone a lot, visiting his wife. A new side of Mister Stanley emerged: the considerate dutiful husband. Once, Lula heard him ask Zeke if he could think of anything his mother might want. Zeke's silence was like a finger poked into his father's chest. It was sad they couldn't help each other through their family hard time.

Instead, Mister Stanley and Zeke argued about Zeke driving the Olds in bad weather. Mister Stanley said they should order in, The Good Earth would deliver. Zeke let his father win after Mister Stanley described how road salt would eat away at the chassis of a vintage sedan and how he didn't intend to pay for body work. Zeke said he wasn't hungry, anyway, and Mister Stanley said everyone had to eat.

The bitterest fight was about New Year's Eve. Mister Stanley wouldn't let Zeke go to a friend's party with the slightly older boy who would be driving. Mister Stanley said he didn't know the boy, Zeke never brought his friends home. Zeke said that maybe now he *could* bring kids home, now that Mom was safely locked up. Lula heard doors slam and howls of murderous rage, sounds that must have reminded Mister Stanley of the place where he'd left his wife.

New Year's Eve came and went. All three of them went to bed early. Lula wouldn't have known it was New Year's if the newspaper hadn't featured a photo of confetti. Probably it was bad luck not to get drunk or have sex or eat some special food supposed to bring you money or luck in the coming year. Maybe it was too late for that. What worse luck could befall them? Lula knocked on her desk.

Lula was under house arrest, room arrest more like it, and she used the wintry hours to write a story about a farm that lay under a curse. Her granny had said there were places like that, dwellings whose tenants all died suddenly, suspiciously, and young. In Lula's story, a guy appeared in Berat one day, claiming his grandpa had left him the farm. He didn't care about the curse. Against all advice, he moved there with his beautiful wife and their beautiful kids, and they began to grow apples, tomatoes, and lettuce and to raise ducks and lambs. The place was their private paradise on which no one would set foot for fear the curse was contagious, though this didn't stop anyone from buying their produce at the market. Not one bad thing happened. And when a series of animal and vegetable plagues devastated the region, their farm alone was spared because they were quarantined by their neighbors' superstition.

Lula spent days trying to think of how the curse finally got them. But she'd grown to like this plucky family, and her imagination refused to conjure up the disastrous fire or flood or earthquake. Instead they lived to a healthy old age, their beautiful children had more beautiful children, and each year the farm grew more productive, its lambs fatter and more playful, its apples more delicious.

Lula spent more time on this story than on anything she had written, and she hated it the most. Because she didn't believe it. If the farmland was that fertile, the government would have seized it long ago, and the family would still be in court trying to get even one apple tree back. Also she wasn't buying the lesson it seemed to preach: Ignore the crowd and go your own way and life will turn out all right. In her experience, you could follow the rules or refuse to bend and you were still at the mercy of the same wicked cosmic dice-roll.

But regardless of what she thought, Mister Stanley and Don would adore it. Virtue, integrity, courage, hard work rewarded——that was the story they wanted to hear. Lula decided not to show it to them. Their approval would only annoy her. She didn't feel strong enough for their praise. On the other hand, the story might be just what Zeke could use right now. Do the right thing, follow your heart, keep on keeping on, and you get the happy family, the juiciest lamb chops, and the sweetest apples.

She printed out the manuscript and knocked on Zeke's door, then eased it open. Zeke lay on his bed, fully dressed, hooked up to his iPod. Lula had to kick the bed twice before he opened his eyes.

"Fleas Bite Dogs," he said. "I love this song. Want to listen?"

Lula said, "Why are you shouting? You should be listening to Buddhist chants. Helpful for stress."

"That was bullshit," Zeke said. "I knew Dad would fall for it big-time."

"He asked me if your giving him that book meant you were getting like your mother." Lula caught herself, too late. She'd always made a point of not telling father and son what they said about each other. Maybe she'd just wanted an excuse to say *mother*, in case Zeke wanted to talk about his.

"Not a chance," said Zeke.

Lula said, "Want to read something I wrote?"

Zeke took the manuscript. A short time later he came to her room.

"Did this really happen?" he said.

Lula nodded gravely. "In my granny's village."

"That is awesome," Zeke said.

. . .

LULA KNEW NOT to take credit, but she couldn't help noting: Just a few days after reading her story, Zeke appeared at Sunday breakfast and announced that he wanted to go to college. He said, "I guess it's the only way I'm ever going to get out of this dump alive."

"Dump" made Mister Stanley flinch, but he rapidly recovered and said that college involved more than escaping the family dump. In any case, he was pleased that Zeke was making the right decision. Then the two of them disappeared into the "library," where they remained until late afternoon.

"Progress," announced Mister Stanley, when at last they reappeared.

Lula's job now included helping Zeke fill out his college applications, a tedious and complex task he performed with such rare perseverance that Lula tried not to feel hurt by how badly he wanted to leave. But it wasn't just that. He wanted to grow up. Everyone did. Or should.

When Zeke asked Lula's advice about the application essays, Lula told him to go on the Internet and read the colleges' home pages and figure out what each one wanted to hear. Then he should write that. She was glad he'd asked her and not his father, who would have given him the wrong advice: write what was in his heart.

Zeke showed Lula a draft that began, "I want the freedom to express my full individuality while at the same time being an integral part of a larger community."

Lula said, "Zeke, put on your thinking cap! What teenager sounds like that? You can't just *copy* what they say. I thought you wanted to get in."

The second draft began, "Everything I've read about your

school makes me think it's a place that would let me be my authentic self and still work hard and learn from my fellow students who are also there to grow and learn."

"You nailed it," Lula said.

Now, when Zeke came home from school, he asked if there was mail, and now when the letters slipped through the slot, Lula searched for the fat envelope stuffed with good news. The college that accepted him would be setting both of them free.

The envelope arrived on a Saturday morning. Zeke ripped it open, skimmed the letter, punched the air, and said, "Okay!" Mister Stanley and Zeke high-fived each other.

"Congratulations," said Lula.

The only good-news letter had come from Alice Ames College, across the Hudson and forty-five minutes north. It sounded like a girls' school, but Mister Stanley said it had been coed for years. It wasn't too close, but close enough for Mister Stanley and Zeke to attend the accepted-students tea.

"Will you come with us? It seems only right after all the help you gave Zeke." Mister Stanley must have thought that attending the tea was some kind of reward. Which it was. Going anywhere was better than going nowhere. He was asking for Lula's company and support and trying to make it seem as if he was doing her a favor.

"I'd love to," Lula said.

Chapter Twelve

LULA HAD studied the brochure, the photos of attractive students of every body type, gender, and race, pausing for amusing, educational conversations as they strolled through the handsome stone cloisters. The pictures had looked real enough, but still she half expected Alice Ames to be a boarded-up storefront in a mall. She'd seen a TV program about a fake online college that promised to prepare kids for medical school and stole their parents' life savings. It had tickled her to see Americans taken in by the sort of scam people thought happened only in Eastern Europe. If she had a dollar for every La Changita customer who told her about not being allowed to drive his rental car to Prague because it might get stolen, she wouldn't have had to work there. But now that she'd come to care about Zeke and Mister Stanley, she'd lost the ironic remove from which she watched Americans get conned, and she hoped that Alice Ames was not a dirty trick cynically named after some grifter's favorite hooker.

They were halfway to the college on the day of the tea when Mister Stanley slowed down and said, "Wait. I'm remembering something. The college had some problem. A very public problem . . . not so long ago . . ." Lula and Zeke sat very still, neither liking his tone, the same tone in which he had forbidden Zeke to go out with his friends on New Year's Eve. But Mister Stanley couldn't seem to recall what the problem had been, and when they picked up speed again, Lula's sense of well-being returned, intensified by its close brush with disappointment.

A perfect meringue of snow glistened on the rolling lawns and filled the crenellations of the castle turrets. The cold seemed cleaner and sharper than the cold in New Jersey, and it made you want to go inside where it would be warm and smell of wet wool, and where young minds would be humming like air conditioners in summer.

At the edge of a parking lot a sign said, "Welcome Class of 2010." Lula refused to calculate how old she would be then. Zeke nodded at a purple balloon bobbling against the sign.

He said, "I hope this isn't a super-expensive mistake."

"It's a godsend," said Mister Stanley. "It will be worth every penny."

A *lot* of pennies, said the pillared veranda overlooking a meadow, a lot more pennies, said the stained glass windows along the staircase that led to a wood-paneled hall. Two girl students, bouncers in party clothes, sat at a table and power-smiled guests into writing their names on sticky labels. Mister Stanley and Zeke complied, but when Lula said, "I'm just a friend," the girls were so flustered that Lula got away with not having to wear a name tag.

The school should have chosen a more intimate space, where the students, parents, and teachers would have looked less lost as they tried to fill its rejecting vastness. The minority students in the brochure must have decided to skip the party. Two long tables held platters of fruit slices and ziggurats of cheese cubes, already in ruins, plus bottles of water, orange juice, and several industrial-size samovars.

Tea, Lula thought despairingly.

Sipping their tea, the parents assumed the hunched, vigilant postures required to balance a fragile cup of hot liquid while chatting with other nervous strangers. Lula noted how often they checked their watches and how hard they tried to conceal it. A few older students scanned the crowd. Would their glances have looked so predatory if not for Zeke's recent experience with Harmonia Bethany?

"Stay away from those girls," Lula whispered.

"Believe me," Zeke said. "I've learned."

A woman with a shiny domelike forehead charged toward them, her proffered handshake so aggressive that Lula's impulse was to jump out of her way. Unnerved, Lula missed the name of the assistant admissions director, who was thrilled— she checked Zeke's name tag—that Zeke might be coming to Alice Ames.

She said, "You'll probably think I'm prejudiced if I babble on and on about how much I love it here."

Lula took this opportunity to slip away and pour herself a cup of tea and find a corner from which to fake interest in the proceedings. But wait. This could be interesting. A man was walking toward her.

"I'm Carl," he said. "Carl Levin. I teach in the philosophy department."

Even better, a Jewish guy. At home girls said that Jewish guys made outstanding boyfriends. To hell with Alvo and his air-conditioner scam, if that was even what it was. Stay cool,

Lula reminded herself. What was her recent past if not a warning against excessive imagination? Besides, this event was not about Lula and her sordid love life, but about the bridge that Zeke was about to cross from his childhood into the world. And it was part of Lula's job to make sure that bridge was sturdy.

"Are you one of the incoming students?" the professor asked. Did she really look that young, or did he say that to all the second wives here with the college-age offspring of the rich husbands' first marriages?

Lula said, "I already went to university in Albania. My friend . . . I mean, my friend's son is enrolling here in the fall."

"Wait!" he said. "You're the Albanian friend! How many could there be?"

Lula said, "What do you mean?" This was how it happened. They knew who you were. They were waiting for you. You thought it was a college tea, but it was an INS sting, the kind where they promised illegals anything from amnesty to a pair of free tickets to a baseball game. And when you showed up, they nabbed you. But Lula had nothing to worry about. Thanks to Don, she was legal.

The professor's lips were moving.

"Excuse me?" Lula said.

This time he seemed to be saying, "Everyone loved Zeke's essay."

"What essay?"

"The one about the family that inherits the cursed orchard, but they keep their eyes on the prize and nothing unlucky happens and they raise the best lambs and apples. Zeke had a sentence at the end about how he'd heard the story from an

Albanian friend, and how it made him realize how important it was to work hard and keep the faith and do what you think is right, and how glad it made him feel to live in a country where people don't believe in curses. The sentiment was so positive. And it was so well written."

Zeke had copied her story. Sooner rather than later, Lula needed to tell him that plagiarism was wrong.

"To be perfectly honest," said the professor, "Zeke's wasn't the strongest application in the pool. But this isn't the sort of place that bases its decisions solely on grades and test scores. That essay got him in."

Mister Stanley hadn't wasted a cent of the salary he'd paid Lula. And was it really so bad if Lula had given Zeke some basic instruction in the relationship, however regrettable, between deception and survival? Once Zeke got where he wanted to be, he could sort out the moral issues. And how did a little all-in-the-family intellectual-property theft stack up against the fact that Lula's story had gotten Zeke the one thing he seemed to want? By the time Professor Carl finished raving about Zeke's essay, Lula had almost convinced herself that Zeke's submitting her work under his name wasn't plagiarism, but collaboration.

The professor said, "One of my colleagues read it aloud. It got passed around the committee. It was by far the most interesting essay we got. I work part-time in admissions, even though I was hired to teach the second half of the beginning survey course. From Machiavelli to Marx. When you don't have tenure, you agree to whatever they ask."

Lula said, "That's the beginning of philosophy right there."

"And also, as you doubtless know, these are unusual times."

Lula didn't know. His unspoken question (what had Lula heard?) made her recall Mister Stanley's reference to some trouble at the college.

"Unusual how, exactly?"

"Obviously, the shooting."

"What shooting?" Lula said.

"It's always the science students. Even here, where we have no science program to speak of. I never taught the kid, but his advisers said he was wound pretty tight. I know that's what they always say. Obsessed with grades. High-strung. No one knows where he got the rifle. He started blasting away at the gatehouse—"

"When was this?"

"Year before last."

"Was anyone killed?" Lula held her breath.

"No, thank God. The guy couldn't aim. A couple of minor flesh wounds. The security guard wrestled him down. The shooter weighed about ninety pounds. Very bloody and messy. Traumatic. But fortunately, not lethal."

"What happened to the kid?"

"Deported back to Singapore. Meanwhile, the freshman applicant pool dried up completely. Parents get nervous. No one believes that lightning never strikes the same place twice."

Lula made a mental note to tell Mister Stanley the part about lightning in case he remembered what he'd heard about Alice Ames.

The professor said, "One more year like this one, and our jobs are on the line. I think that's one reason Zeke's story was such a hit. It was exactly what everyone needed to hear just around now: If you keep on doing what's right and doing it well, the bad weather clears, and the curse gets lifted."

No wonder this place was so eager for students willing to step over some fading blood stains in return for no one fussing about their test scores. Lula felt vaguely injured on Zeke's behalf. If Zeke was going to steal her work, it should earn him something better than a college that no one else wanted to attend. But hadn't she read her own story? The cursed farm grew the tastiest apples. This college was pretty, the students looked happy, the professor was handsome and nice.

She said, "Why do school shootings happen so often in this country?"

"They happen everywhere," Professor Carl said. "And not as often as you'd think. But the media loves them."

"Going postal. Ha ha . . ."

"Your English is flawless." He smiled. "So what do you do now?"

"Okay. I'm not the Albanian *friend*. I work for the family. I take care of Zeke. Until he leaves for college."

"And then?"

"Good question. Any suggestions, Professor?"

"Please," he said. "Call me Carl." In Lula's experience, only a few steps separated "Call me Carl" from asking for her phone number.

"Any suggestions, Carl?" Lula tried to make "suggestions" sound lewd.

"Actually, my wife runs a terrific program that just started here, funded by the school. It helps women, recent immigrants, underemployed single moms with child-care issues, find their way into the workforce. She's a lawyer, she's amazing, she does this pro bono, part-time—"

Lula was still stuck on those two little words. *My wife.* There were many ways in which men signaled availability, but *my wife* was not among them, at least not in that proud voice of ownership, within the first few minutes.

"Let me go find her," said Carl.

"Nice to meet you." Good-bye forever. Oh, where was Mister Stanley? How soon could they leave this crime scene soaked with student-faculty blood?

Before Lula could find her boss and ask when they could go home, she saw Carl returning with a dark-haired woman who looked familiar. Lula struggled to place her, and at the same time to use every bit of sexless body language to communicate that not for one moment had she dreamed of stealing the familiar-looking woman's husband.

"Savitra!" Lula said.

"You two know each other?" said Carl.

"Small world," said Savitra glumly.

"She works with my lawyer," said Lula. How often did it happen, a coincidence like this, meeting the same person twice under such different circumstances? Probably more frequently than Lula might think. In Tirana there were also coincidences, but they usually involved ties of family and blood. The guy she'd sort of recognized from her English class and slept with one drunken night had turned out to be her uncle's nephew by his second marriage.

"Don Settebello is your lawyer?" Carl said. "No wonder! The guy's a hero."

Savitra said, "I met Carl my first day here at the school. We were married New Year's Day."

"Very sudden," Carl said. "A *coup de* you-know-what."

"His head is still spinning," said Savitra. The sweetness with which she smiled at Carl suggested the existence of a loving soul that had been absent or in hiding when she'd come for Thanksgiving with Don.

"Congratulations," said Lula.

"I loved Zeke's essay," said Savitra. "Carl showed it to me, but I never made the Albanian connection. Not until I saw you just now and put two and two together. How beautiful that Zeke should write down the stories you've told him. And write them so well! You've done so much for that kid. It just proves that education can happen in so many different ways. So outside the box."

Had Savitra read Lula's stories when she gave them to Don Settebello? It was amazing, how many secrets you could share with someone you'd met only once before. She and Savitra could have been best friends with years of sworn confidences between them.

Savitra said, "I don't know how much Carl told you about my work here. We've only just started, but I think we're about to accomplish great things, helping women find their way into the mainstream."

"I could use a job." Lula caught herself. She had a job. What if Savitra told Don, who told Mister Stanley?

"I understand, believe me." Savitra mimed a merry, conspiratorial agreement. Then she wrinkled her forehead, pantomiming concentration. Lula used to laugh when Granny warned her against frowning. Once again, Granny turned out to be right. Savitra had better be careful.

Savitra said, "When I see a woman who comes from a place that . . . well, not everyone comes from, and when that person is fluent in both languages, and when one of them is hardly a language everyone speaks, the first thing I think of is a court interpreter job."

"Brilliant!" Carl gazed worshipfully at his wife.

Lula said, "How much work could there be for an Albanian translator?"

"You'd be surprised," said Savitra.

"My God, yes," said Carl. "The coke trade and the heroin traffic and now, I was just reading, organized burglary rings—" He stopped himself in midsentence. Had he insulted Lula's homeland? "Listen to me. I'm sorry. It's like assuming every Italian has ties to the mob—"

"Not at all," said Lula. "Don't worry. Anyway, if our Albanian crime rate means more work for court interpreters—" She smiled so they knew she was joking and would be charmed by her lack of hypersensitivity about her native land.

Savitra's women's group met in the evenings. When Lula explained about not driving and the late-night buses, she was excused from going. It seemed like bad luck to sit in a room with women whose problems were worse than her own, though she knew that many Americans believed this was how your luck improved.

Savitra said she would e-mail Lula about the court inter-preter position. Lula wrote down her e-mail address as if she were a person who was constantly fielding messages about job opportunities.

In the car going home Zeke said, "Considering how many

bands there are, what's the statistical probability of finding kids who listen to the exact same music I do?"

A hundred percent, thought Lula. Hadn't Harmonia Bethany liked, or pretended to like, Zeke's favorite group?

Zeke said, "What kind of coincidence is that?"

Lula said, "Speaking of coincidence . . . Guess who I met? Remember that girl Savitra whom Don brought to Thanksgiving? She married a professor at the school. A philosophy teacher."

"I saw you talking to that young couple," Mister Stanley said. "I thought the woman looked familiar, but . . . married already? Thanksgiving was just six weeks ago. I wonder why Don didn't mention it. Though why should he? He's got more important things on his mind."

Lula thought she detected a faint note of satisfaction, possibly because Mister Stanley's fellow single dad had lost his girlfriend to a more age-appropriate husband.

Mister Stanley said, "I'm very glad you met some nice kids, Zeke. But liking the same bands is no reason to go to a college."

Zeke said, "It is, if it's the only school that accepted me. And when did I say that the kids were nice?"

"You chose the school," said his father. "We chose it together."

"It's fine with me!" yelled Zeke. "I like it! Now please leave me alone!"

"You know," said Mister Stanley, "the funny thing is, architecturally, it looks a little like the place where your mom is staying right now."

"Great," said Zeke. "My college looks like a mental hospital."

"A treatment center," said Mister Stanley. "And I'm talking about the buildings, not what goes on inside."

Lula imagined a student staggering from the recoil of a gun and another holding her forehead as blood poured through her fingers. Lightning doesn't strike twice. Lula had to find another job before she turned into Mister Stanley.

The next morning, when Savitra's e-mail arrived, Lula was astonished. "Hi Lula!" the message began. Savitra sent Lula a link to a site with information about New York and New Jersey court interpreters. It wasn't exactly a real job; you only worked when they called you. It was the first time Lula had come across the phrase *independent contractor*. What an appealing expression, with its dual associations of freedom and construction, though *contractor* made her think of Alvo, which she tried to avoid. All you needed to be approved or semi-approved or conditionally approved was to demonstrate that you were fluent in both languages and could speak and read English, especially the English that Americans used in courts. In New York there was an oral exam. You had to watch a film in which actors played witnesses from your home country, and you had to interpret, showing you knew all the technical terms like *plea bargain* and *bail bond* and *plaintiff*, which Lula had learned from TV crime shows.

She puzzled over the Web site's suggestion that would-be applicants attend trials to familiarize themselves with court procedures. No one in Albania went near a court unless they were in handcuffs or were suing to get back their land. Here, except for family court, trials were open to the public. Lula asked Mister Stanley to tell Don that she was curious about how a democratic legal system functioned, and Mister Stanley reported that

Don was delighted by Lula's interest. In his opinion, the Lower Manhattan courts would offer her more than Newark. Mister Stanley also approved of Lula's project, but he still hoped she could get home in time for Zeke's return from school.

"I promise," Lula said.

Chapter Thirteen

LULA WAITED patiently to send her purse along the conveyor belt and pass through the metal detector. It was relaxing to shuffle forward along with her fellow creatures, even the resentful ones who didn't want to be here. The guards didn't care how inconvenienced the prospective jurors were. They cared if their cell phones took pictures. Lula's phone did not take photos, which she announced—boasted, really—as evidence of her innocent intentions. She imagined that the look that passed between her and the guard was fraught with something more personal than his appraisal of her level of terrorist threat. The molecules in the overheated air seemed to thrum with the excitement of this intriguing alternative to watching the timid winter light do its cameo turn on Mister Stanley's lawn.

She gathered from the elevator conversations that her fellow passengers would be shocked to learn that she was voluntarily doing what they so wished to avoid. When the crowd turned in one direction, she headed the opposite way and found herself in a room not unlike the one in which they'd held Zeke's college tea. There was plenty of space on the benches. No one noticed Lula as she found a seat.

The judge's little gray head looked like a smoky bauble balanced on the edge of her desk as she instructed the jury about the seriousness of their duties and how the job they'd been asked to perform reflected the beauty of democracy and of their judicial system. She told them how grateful their country was for the sacrifices they were making. Lula tried not to be cynical, tried not to think the judge was just trying to make everyone feel better about missing work. When the judge asked the jurors to take care of themselves for the duration of the trial, to be careful crossing the street at lunch—at which they were not allowed to discuss the case—she wasn't threatening them with certain death beneath the wheels of the speeding Mercedes that would run them down if they even thought about voting to convict.

An African guy was being tried for resisting arrest after he was caught selling fake designer purses. Everywhere it was a crime not to do what the police said, just as everywhere cops could throw you in jail if they didn't like your face. But this vendors' license thing—that was really too much! The world's sidewalks were clogged with people selling hot dogs and halal lunches, bananas and bracelets. In Tirana you bought everything on the street, from olive oil to tampons. The moment her friend Dunia had fallen in love with the United States was the moment when she'd bought a knockoff Louis Vuitton satchel from a guy on Third Avenue.

The defense lawyer wore a pinstripe suit and a bouquet of dreadlocks, a fashion choice that suggested a proud idealistic character but an unrealistic nature and perhaps a deficient desire to win. Twice he quoted Descartes, maxims with an unclear relevance to the case. Lula imagined everyone speaking Albanian and tried to decide what she would and wouldn't translate in order to keep the African guy from going to jail for grabbing an armful of imitation Guccis and taking off when the cops demanded to see his vendor ID. But her opinion wasn't the point. She'd read on the Web site that the job was to translate without judgment, editing, or interpretation. It would be soothing to shift from language to language without the constant mental yakkety-yak about what was true or false.

The prosecution's first witness was a cop who appeared to be chewing gum even when he wasn't. He was sorry to have to say that the defendant threw a punch. Mr. Descartes asked how someone could throw a punch while running, and the cop explained, as if to a child, that first the defendant threw a punch and then he ran. The second cop, a skinny Asian kid, corroborated his partner's story, which he would have done if his partner said that pigs flew out of the defendant's ass.

There were no witnesses for the defense. No one who'd seen the incident came forward. The judge said, "Mr. Mamdani, do you wish to testify on your own behalf?"

Mr. Mamdani shook his head no.

The lawyers gave quick summations. No one's heart was in it. After more instructions from the judge, the jury retired for deliberations. Lula wanted to find out how the story ended. A guard came over to her and said, "This might take a while. You can go grab lunch."

Lula said, "I hurt my foot at the gym." No one had sworn *her* to tell the truth.

"You take it easy then, baby," said the guard. Lula closed her eyes and rested until the courtroom filled again and the judge asked the foreman to read the verdict.

"Not guilty," said the foreman, a gangly hipster whose wrists showed beyond the frayed cuffs of his sweater. How had they chosen him as their leader, and more surprisingly still, how had they reached the right verdict?

The lawyer hugged his client, who recoiled from his embrace. Only then did the defendant turn and look back at the court. Lula saw that he was crying. What satisfying drama! Justice served, a life saved, the capricious abuse of authority subverted once again. Was there another case that Lula could watch and be home in time for Zeke?

In the next courtroom, a kid was on trial for selling a joint to an undercover cop. In his opening remarks, the elderly defense lawyer informed the jury that though they might not know it, and though he was legally enjoined from saying so, he thought they should be aware that they might be voting to send his client—this boy—away for life. The judge sighed and told counsel he didn't care how close to retirement age the lawyer was, he had half a mind to cite him and he could go to jail instead of his client, because he had sworn an oath to uphold the legal system, whether he agreed with it or not and regardless of the frustrations that must come with being a public defender nearing retirement. The way the judge made "public defender" sound like a synonym for "loser" made Lula think that the two men had a history that preceded this case. When Lula left, the judge was still berating the lawyer.

On Tuesday, Lula watched a consumer protection group's suit against a Chinese manufacturer of toxic baby bottles. In theory it should have been interesting, the health-conscious ideas of one country versus the cowboy production goals of another. But there didn't seem to be any actual people involved;

none of the lawyers were Chinese, nor was there an actual baby who had been harmed by the bottles. So she found a courtroom in which a doctor was being sued for botching a woman's gastric bypass surgery. Lula was transfixed by the woman's narrative of what food did on its way from her mouth to the bag hidden beneath her parrot-green dress, but it depressed her to wonder what she would do if the plaintiff was Albanian, and she had to find the English terms for all the digestive parts.

The next morning, the ice flowers on her window almost persuaded Lula to stay home. But she put on her warmest clothes and a hair-ruining woolen hat and submitted to the three buses and the biting wind. As she came in from the cold, the courthouse lobby seemed especially steamy and vibrant. The briefcases and purses jittered along the conveyor belts like amusement-park patrons waiting for a ride to start. Even the metal detectors looked as benign as garden trellises, and the guards on duty smiled.

Already Lula felt as if she were going to a job she was good at, and loved. A golden aura surrounded the passengers jammed into the elevator, and in its glow she marveled at each person's particular beauty. What a gorgeous variety these American faces had! This morning, at the very moment when she was debating whether the warmth of her hat (which she pulled off, running her fingers through her flattened hair) was worth the insult to her vanity, these people had been in their homes, perhaps in front of their mirrors, making all the tiny choices and adjustments that would determine the faces they showed the world. How wondrous it all was, how mystifying in its vastness and strangeness! What had caused her to feel this sense of promise and even of joy? Did there have to be a reason? Or could you wake up one day and see the world differently without it signifying a brain tumor or the onset of mental illness?

Lula wandered into a courtroom where a woman was suing the owner of a corner grocery because she'd slipped and hurt her leg on a broken jar of pickles. The woman overdid the limp with an aggressive swagger that made it seem as if she were about to shake her cane at the jury—evidence of bad advice, or no advice, from her lawyer.

Why should Lula stop at translator? She was smart, she'd been a good student, she could be a judge! Don and Mister Stanley would help her, and someday she would repay them, not just financially but in ways they would value more than money.

The store owner's lawyer asked why the plaintiff hadn't produced one medical expert, which seemed like a good question, until the plaintiff's lawyer asked if his colleague was aware that expertise cost money, which his client didn't have. Which also seemed like a good question.

With no idea who was telling the truth, Lula was glad to leave it to the jury, another American grab bag, men and women, old and young, black and brown and white, all listening intently and occasionally asking for things to be repeated. When the trial broke for lunch, Lula felt like celebrating.

Luckily, lunch was the number-one topic in the elevators, and even in this short time she'd overheard several debates about where to find the best Cantonese noodle soup. What better way to honor her affection for this country than in an affordable restaurant surrounded by fellow immigrants from all over the globe, gathered at communal round tables to warm their faces in fragrant saunas of chicken broth?

Lula should have known better than to be seduced by soup. If she'd stayed put, as she had yesterday, she wouldn't have been part of the lunch crowd filing out of the building. She wouldn't have spotted Leather Jacket—Genti—on his way in, stalled in the security line, anxiously monitoring the basket in which his beloved coat was about to roll on without him. Genti didn't see Lula, which gave her a moment to decide whether to ignore him and keep going. The flame died under the noodle soup, the healing broth stopped bubbling.

She had to call Genti three times. Finally he heard her. He almost smiled, then looked worried.

"Little Sister, what brings you to this lowest circle of hell?"

Just being in this American palace of justice made her feel simultaneously emboldened and protected. She grabbed Genti's arm and yanked him toward the door, an awkward ballet made clumsier when Genti stopped to rescue his coat from the conveyor belt and shimmied into its narrow sleeves as they crossed the lobby. Lula tried to telegraph the fact that she and Genti were old friends, meeting by happy accident, instead of Albanian terrorists recognizing each other by some prearranged code signal.

She said, "I'm applying for a job in court. And you? Why are you here?"

Genti raised one eyebrow. "Arkon's in serious trouble. His trial starts today."

"Arkon?"

"I mean Alvo."

Lula hadn't even known her fantasy boyfriend's real name. "What did he do?"

Genti checked to see if anyone was listening. "Nothing. Guilty in the first degree of the crime of being Albanian."

"I get that. But what are the charges?"

"The guy fell on his sword for us. Me and Guri are not even implicated in their made-up lies. Even so, little bitch Guri is shitting his pants. He's hiding out in Allentown, Pennsylvania, pretending his granny's deathly ill. If his granny dies, it will be his fault."

"Made-up *what* lies?" asked Lula. Let it be a civil case. Let the guy whose air conditioner Alvo installed backward be suing.

"I told you. Nothing," said Genti. "Not paying off the right guy. Come listen. Our brother's facing serious jail time."

Serious jail time was not about an air conditioner. "What's he charged with?" Lula asked twice more, the first time almost inaudibly, the second time louder than she intended. Fear flashed across Genti's face. The fear of being embarrassed.

"Breaking and entering. Possible sentence fifteen years or more of—" Genti's fingers puppeted violent anal rape. Now it was Lula's turn to look around, embarrassed.

"A dog got injured in one of the break-ins. One of the break-ins we didn't do. A scratch. The dog probably cut itself shaving. Is that even a crime? But they found a bullet in the wall."

"From the gun?" asked Lula.

"What gun?" asked Genti.

"The one you left with me."

"Who remembers?" said Genti.

"I do," Lula said. "Let's go."

Genti peeled off his jacket again, and together they rejoined the line filing toward the metal detector.

The near-empty courtroom seemed like a hopeful sign. Alvo's case wasn't drawing the yelping packs of reporters.

"Where is he?" Lula whispered.

"There," said Genti.

"Where?"

"Over there, goddammit!" said Genti. A few people turned. Was this how it was going to be for the rest of the day, she and Genti embarrassing each other like an old married couple, squabbling and talking too loud as they watched their Albanian brother get put away for so long that when he got out he would be an old man wanting a twenty-year-old girl or probably, after jail, a twenty-year-old boy? Lula imagined visiting him, their palms pressed against the glass. Someone would have to tell her the right name to give the guards.

Everyone faced forward. None of those heads was Alvo's. Or Arkon's. They were in the wrong courtroom. Genti was a moron.

"I don't see him," she insisted.

"There," said Genti. "Look again. The dude dyed his fucking hair."

That was the missing puzzle piece. Alvo's hair was as black as Zeke's.

"His lawyer told him redheads always lose. Statistics. Hair color is everything. Natural blonds are the winners. After that comes gray."

"Where did he find this lawyer?"

"The Bronx," said Genti. "Where else?"

Alvo's lawyer wore a pale suit with a cripplingly tight skirt. Combed in a flawless upsweep, her silvery curls gleamed softly in the harsh institutional light. She approached the judge's bench and whispered in his ear. The elderly judge leered besottedly at the lady lawyer.

"Defense has informed me that a translator has been found for his client, who is insufficiently comfortable in English."

"My man's a genius," Genti whispered.

"Are you aware of that, Mr. Capone?"

You couldn't make up a district attorney named Mr. Capone! Lula felt another surge of love for her adopted country. Mr. Capone pointed out that when the accused was apprehended, he'd shown an excellent command of English. English curse words in particular. When this got a laugh from some cops up front, Mr. Capone mock-saluted them.

"Assholes!" Genti hissed.

The guard who materialized at the end of Lula and Genti's row informed them: One more outburst, and he'd have to ask them to leave. He himself spoke softly yet managed to create a rumbling in the atmosphere that got the whole courtroom's attention.

Alvo-Arkon turned. He looked haggard, but still handsome, even with the bad dye job. Poor guy! For Lula to assume she'd been rejected was pure self-centered pride. Alvo hadn't been thinking about her. A possible fifteen years in jail trumped a catastrophic first date.

Alvo spotted Genti and raised one shoulder in that corny way that always yanked his friends' leashes. Then Alvo noticed Lula. No surprise. No nothing. You wouldn't buy a fish with those eyes. He didn't know her, he didn't want to know her. Why was she even here?

"Sorry," Genti told the guard. Then he said, "I fucked your fat slut of a sister," pleasantly in Albanian so only Lula could hear.

The translator was a parched, round-shouldered gentleman

in a boldly checked suit. Not much competition there. What red-blooded court clerk would call this sad sack once Lula was an option? However long it took to get the job, she could still wear short skirts. The translator kept raising his forearm as if to ward off the hail of English. "Please, more slowly, slowly," he said.

"Mistrial!" Genti whispered.

The clerk read the charges. Not one burglary, but many. All groceries and supermarkets. A firearm had been involved. Lula put her head in her hands. Alvo was also charged with funneling money to terrorist groups in Kosovo.

"Objection!" yelled Alvo's lawyer.

"Objection sustained," said the judge.

"Now he's screwed," Lula whispered.

"That part is definite crap," said Genti. "That I swear on my daughter's life. In my opinion, Arkon could be a lot *more* patriotic."

"You have a daughter?" Lula said.

"A daughter and a son. The lawyers know it's horseshit too. Why are you closing your eyes?"

To read the print on a sales receipt. Orange juice and cigarettes.

Genti elbowed her. "Pick up your head. Sit straight."

Mr. Capone called Mr. Aziz. Yes, he was the owner of Sunrise Market at 411 Avenue C. Tears trickled down Mr. Aziz's cheeks when he described how his employee had called at dawn to tell him that there had been a break-in. Thank you, Mr. Aziz. Did the defense have any questions? Come on, thought Lula, no one got hurt, it was only money and minor property damage. Most likely the guy was insured. So who got stung? Some rich insurance company? Alvo was the Albanian-American Robin Hood.

Was there a camera? An alarm? A guard? No, sir, there was neither. There was a dog. A dog? Mr. Aziz's German shepherd had bitten the intruder. The dog had been shot. To death? No, sir, Rex survived. Lula recalled the bandage on Alvo's hand when he'd come to take her to lunch. Even then. But of course even then. He'd asked her to hide a gun.

"They got nothing on no one. Purely circumstantial." Genti must have watched the same crime shows as Lula.

Alvo's lawyer suggested that her client had been bitten earlier in the day by the dog, which had viciously attacked him, unprovoked, when he'd walked into Mr. Aziz's store to buy a quart of juice. Out of the goodness of his heart, her client had declined to press charges, and now his forbearance was being repaid by this trumped-up case against him.

"Brilliant," Genti said. "Is that brilliant or not?"

"Not." Lula looked at the jury. Disbelief on every face.

The lawyers approached the judge, and the next part played out in hushed voices. The judge declared a recess. *State of New York v. Jashari* would resume tomorrow at nine.

"Jashari," Lula repeated. This judge didn't warn the jurors to be careful crossing the street.

Lula watched Alvo confer with his lawyer until the guards came to take him away. He turned and looked at Lula. This time Alvo saw her. His jaw went slack with longing, and the look they exchanged was almost as good as the sex they never had. With all his heart, he regretted not having gotten back in touch.

Lula almost cried out his name. Passion rose from the embers of their awkward dating history. Maybe things could still work out. Maybe Alvo would get off on a legal technicality. Having realized that he loved her, he would reform, and they would start over, two strangers whom that trusty matchmaker, grand larceny, had brought together in a courtroom.

RATHER THAN FACE the buses and the cold, Lula accepted Genti's offer of a ride home. But even before she climbed into the SUV that Genti retrieved from the garage, she realized that riding with him would have its own discomforts.

"Why supermarkets?" she asked, as Genti darted in and out of the traffic that grew thicker and meaner as they headed up the West Side.

"How would I know?" said Genti. "We didn't do it."

"But why would anyone?" asked Lula, more diplomatically.

Genti's answer was loud music. Fuck you up, Serb bitches. Every boast and threat and off rhyme intensified Lula's gloom.

Genti took the Lincoln Tunnel. The minute they saw the light of New Jersey, his cell phone barked like Charmy Puppy.

"That cop's looking straight at you," Lula said.

"Let him look straight at my ass," said Genti. "Hey, boss, how's it going?" Genti switched into Albanian, but mostly he made noises, humming and clucking the international language that signified too bad, not good, we have a problem. "Okay, not to worry, boss, everything will be fine."

"Was he calling from jail?" Lula asked. "I thought you only get one call."

"Money works everywhere," Genti said. "But only so far. The boss says things don't look great. New charges, new evidence. They're trying to connect him to every unsolved break-in in

New York and northern Jersey. Little Sister, we need to ask you one last tiny favor. We know you have a good lawyer. The one who got you that work visa overnight."

"Not overnight," said Lula.

"Yes, overnight," insisted Genti. "We remember that first time, your bragging about this legal genius. So now the boss is wondering if you could talk to your boy. Get him to pull a few strings. We would never ask such a thing unless it was life or death."

Lula said, "My guy's in immigration. It's a whole different field."

"Lawyers know lawyers," Genti said. "Just like people know people. Kinship patterns, right?"

"Kinship patterns?"

"I'm taking an introductory anthro course at LaGuardia Community College."

"Improving yourself," said Lula. "Hey, watch it! You cut that guy off!"

"I saw the stupid bastard," said Genti, swerving. "One more thing. The boss said for me to tell you that what happened between you wasn't nothing. That's what he told me to say. Look, I don't know what *did* happen, but the boss said to tell you it—"

"Was not nothing. I heard. I'll do what I can. Are you going to the trial tomorrow?"

"If it's still going on. The whole thing could be over, and not in a good way, by this afternoon. Not to put any pressure on you. But we think your time would be better spent going to see your lawyer."

"I told you. There's nothing I can do," Lula said.

"There's always something," said Genti. "Call him. We'll go back into the city. I'll drive you there. I'll wait and take you home."

Staring out the windshield, Lula recalled the look on Alvo's face as he'd left the courtroom. Had his hungry stare been for her—or her lawyer? "I'll think about it. I'll call my guy. He's out of town a lot. He works in Guantánamo, where people have *real* problems."

"Little Sister, trust me. This is a real problem. Tomorrow's too late. I'll take you to his office."

Lula could have said no. She could have tried to say no. Instead she got her phone and pressed Don Settebello's number. Lula told his secretary she needed to see Don in person. Now. For only ten minutes.

"You're in luck," said the secretary. "He's just back from Cuba. His schedule opens up around two, two fifteen. He can give you five minutes tops. This better be important."

"It's life and death," Lula said.

DON SETTEBELLO LIKED to give the impression of a guy who worked out of a dusty back office, like a detective in an old movie. But Lula had long since discovered, not entirely to her surprise, that Settebello, Reitman and Leiber was a huge intimidating law firm with a huge staff instructed not to intimidate clients. The scrubbed young receptionist picked up the phone, and a scrubbed young man whisked Lula through a labyrinth populated by other scrubbed young people, all working for Don, not one of them looking up long enough to envy or even notice Lula, the family friend who could breeze into Don's inner sanctum. She was no ordinary supplicant, come to beg Don's help. She and Don and their families had spent Thanksgiving together.

Don's kiss on the cheek said, Hi! I have five minutes.

"I was in the neighborhood," Lula said.

"What are you doing, Lula?" said Don.

"I've been going to court, watching trials. I like your legal system. Very fair, very humane. I saw a judge tell the jurors to be careful crossing the street. At home that would mean she was threatening them, but here—"

"We try," said Don. "Some of the time we succeed."

"Some is better than never," said Lula. "I was thinking of becoming a court interpreter."

"Good! I heard you met Savitra. Crazy overachiever, but you have to give her credit. I mean what are you doing *here*?"

"How's Abigail?" asked Lula.

"Fine," said Don Settebello. "I've got her this weekend. So what's so life and death?"

Lula said, "I know there's probably nothing you can do, but I need to ask you a favor. I have this cousin from home, he's being framed for robberies he didn't commit."

Don said, "Is this by any chance the cousin who was in your room the night Ginger showed up?"

Ordinarily, Lula admired how quickly Don's mind worked. But this was a little too quick.

"So what have they got on the innocent cousin?"

Lula said, "Some grocery store dog bit him. There was blood at the crime scene. His blood. A guard dog. Actually, the dog bit him earlier in the day."

It was suicidal to lie to Don. But it was worth a try. She and

Alvo were friends. They'd been through something together. Their lives had been threatened—by Ginger. They came from the same place. Blood loyalty was the upside of the tribal psychosis that made people kill nephews and grandsons for fifteen generations.

Don said, "Please. Don't tell me any more. I don't want to know."

Lula said, "It's political. He's an Albanian patriot." Was that even true? Or was it something the court made up? Genti had said that Alvo—Arkon—wasn't patriotic *enough*. "He's innocent. I swear. I mean, about the break-ins."

Don returned to his desk and motioned for Lula to sit. He shut his eyes and massaged his eyebrows. "You know what the most painful part is, Lula? What hurts is how stupid you must think we are. I'm just curious: Do you think all Americans are that dumb, or only me and Stan? Do you think we didn't know you made up those stories you passed off as family history? So fine, everybody takes liberties. Famous writers, as we all know. But now do you really imagine that Don the Dummy is going to believe that your boyfriend or hookup or one-night stand or green-card husband or whoever the fuck he turns out to be is an innocent Albanian patriot framed on a bogus burglary rap?"

"He isn't my boyfriend." If only she hadn't worn that stupid woolen hat! Maybe if her hair looked better, Don would agree to help her.

Don said, "You know what, Lula? If you'd come into my office and said, Hey, Don, I've been screwing this Albanian dude who's gotten popped for B and E. You know anyone in criminal? Is there something you can do? I still wouldn't have done anything. I mean, I would still be horrified that you would ask me to waste my time fixing—refusing to fix—a case like this when the secret jails and black sites are jammed with water-boarded beat-to-shit miserable motherfuckers, a certain percentage of whom have done nothing wrong except be named Abdullah. But at least if you'd said that, if you'd said that, Lula, I would not have felt, as I do now, personally insulted."

"I didn't mean to insult you," said Lula. No wonder Don was famous. He must be a genius at badgering witnesses into saying what he wanted. Lula tried to imagine Don's wife Betsy, whom she'd never met. Then she thought of Savitra, and of Don's hand thumping heavily down on her hand at lunch. A woman would have to be crazy to marry, or even have sex with, a man who would prosecute every lover's quarrel like a criminal case.

Don said, "I haven't gotten where I am without being able to read a situation, and quite frankly, Lula, my reading of this situation makes me feel . . . I don't know what it makes me feel. Tired. Disappointed. It depresses me, Lula. You know that? As we used to say back in the day, it brings me down. You work in the home of my oldest friend. You're family, in a way. You know what I've chosen to do with my life, the problems I've made for myself, the sacrifices, not that they're sacrifices. Someone has to do it. The daily shoveling shit against the tide of government lying, military lying, pointless social lying. And now you're adding your own pathetic little lie about a guy who shouldn't even have been in your room that night Stan's wife went apeshit."

Why not? Lula wanted to ask. Why shouldn't Alvo have been there? Was jealousy the problem? Was it Alvo's criminal past? Alvo's criminal present? Lula's lying was the problem. Did Lula's minimal alteration of the truth make Don think that she didn't know why he'd chosen a hard life over an easy one, or what was at stake for him and this country? Did Don believe that her efforts to help a guy she had a little crush on was a threat to the Founding Fathers and the American way of life? Don was a hero. Case closed. Lula respected him for being brave and honest and always ready to help the underdog. Would Don refuse to keep working on her green-card case because she told a tiny white lie to save her Albanian brother? Don would go on helping her. Don was in every way—well, in most ways—a saintly human being.

"Look," said Don. "I know. People do crazy things for love. If this is love. Is it love, Lula?"

No! Lula wanted to say. Or was it? She didn't think so. This was hardly the moment to analyze the depth of her feelings for Alvo.

"You know a concept I've been having trouble with lately?" Don said. "No, why should you? Well, the fact is, I've been having trouble with simultaneity."

"Simultaneity?" said Lula.

"Two things happening at once," Don said.

"I know what the word means," said Lula. It was maddening that at this late date Don should question her English. Did he correct Savitra's grammar? Savitra grew up in Great Neck.

"What I mean," said Don, "is that at this very moment, this kid I met down there last week, this boy, this child, younger than Zeke, for fuck's sake, the usual story, they confused him with some jihadist piece of shit, they don't believe he's four-teen, the warrant says he's twenty, he looks older than his age. Now he looks like a little old man. They grab him off a Yemeni street and fly him blindfolded and shackled to Guantánamo, where he's been tortured and starved. He spit bacon back in a guard's face, he started acting up. They gave him electroshock until he seized so badly he's paralyzed down one side of his body. He's a kid. He's alive right now, Lula, and maybe right now he's being punched around after days and nights without sleep, at the exact same moment that you and I are sitting in this comfortable high-rent office and you're bullshitting me to save the ass of some loser whose only saving grace is that he comes from your country and at some point you wanted to fuck him."

"Losers are human beings too," said Lula.

Don said, "He's not your cousin. He's not political. And he did the crimes."

Lula said, "I don't know what he did. What if he stole something? Everybody steals. Compared to the crimes you deal with, what's theft? In grade school we learned that property is theft, and then they stopped teaching that, they said it was too right-wing. By the time I got to university, property was good, the more property the better, preferably real estate. Not having property was theft, or anyway, it gave you a reason to steal. Someone emptied a cash register? Okay. No one got hurt! The dog recovered! Let my cousin pay back what he stole. I'll make sure he does. Why take away fifteen years of his life? His whole life is what it will be. What kind of justice is that? Supermarket-owner justice. Aren't you the one who talks about the big lies and the small ones? You Americans and your freedom to give speeches about the truth. You don't know how free you are. In another country, you could piss me off and I could turn you in, or I could turn you in because I wanted your real estate, and they'd send you away to a labor camp, and that would be that."

Don said, "Are you finished, Lula?"

Lula shrugged.

Don looked at his watch. "I'm sorry about your friend. But I've got enough on my plate. I could do twenty years of non-stop habeas corpus before I got around to a breaking and entering case. Unless it was Watergate, maybe. But look, Lula, I've always liked you. And you've done wonders for Stan's kid. That poor boy was a basket case before you arrived. Or anyhow so Stan says. I don't doubt him. You're talented, smart, you're a scrapper. The country needs people like you. We'll forget this whole incident happened. Everyone makes mistakes. We'll just forget it and never mention it and work on your legal status. Then you can become a court interpreter or a lawyer or whatever, and the next time your boyfriend robs a store, you can defend him yourself."

Lula said, "It's not so easy to forget."

"You're young," said Don. "You'd be amazed at how much you can forget in twenty years. I hate to bring this pleasant chat to an end. But our five minutes are up. I'll call you if I hear anything about your green card. It'll be a while. Be patient. Give my love to Stan and Zeke."

Lula wanted to ask him not to tell Mister Stanley. But she couldn't ask, and besides she knew he would tell Mister Stanley. The whole story would come out. Mister Stanley would be furious, and this part of her life would be over. More proof, as if she needed it, of how your secret hope for a change in your circumstances could turn around and bite you. She shook Don's hand and thanked him, and though she assured him that she could find her way out alone, he remanded her into the custody of the same scrubbed boy.

Only in the elevator did she remember that Genti was waiting. The SUV slithered across the street, and she climbed into the passenger seat.

"What did your boy say?" Genti asked.

"He says he'll do what he can," said Lula.

"Good work! Should I pick you up tomorrow? We can go to court together."

"I have errands to do on the way," Lula lied. "I'll meet you there."

"See you in court, ha ha," Genti said.

"Funny joke," Lula said.

That night, she waited for Mister Stanley to mention the phone call from Don. But the subject never came up. How was Zeke? Had he done his homework? Hadn't Don said that he and Lula could just forget it? Maybe there was still a chance that everything could work out all right.

THE NEXT MORNING, Lula got through the line fairly quickly and hurried to the courtroom, where two elderly Filipino gentlemen were shouting at each other, while the judge shouted at their lawyers to make their clients quit shouting. What had happened to Alvo? Despite what Genti said, Lula never imagined his case would be settled so fast. Why hadn't Lula let Genti drive her into the city?

Lula left the court and rushed down the hall, looking in other courtrooms, searching for someone she could ask about Alvo. A guard sent her to another guard, who sent her to a desk, where a woman sent her to an office, where someone gave her a number to call. Exactly like Albania.

It was possible that she would never know how Alvo's story ended. Possible that, for Lula, the story would end here. When she called Alvo's cell phone, a recording apologized: The number was no longer in service. Lula looked around wildly, further alerting the guards who'd already noted her terroristic dash from courtroom to courtroom.

She left the building and went home. Maybe Genti would stop by and give her an update. By now, they had probably figured out that Don hadn't lifted a finger on Alvo's behalf.

No one stopped by. No one called.

Late in the afternoon, Zeke came home. His posture annoyed her. His fake smile annoyed her. The cigarette ash on his black jeans annoyed her. The way his hair sucked up all the light in the room annoyed her. Poor Zeke. Poor little baby. Ginger was his mother. How Lula's heart must have hardened for her to feel anything but love and kindness and compassion.

She said, "You want some hot chocolate?"

Zeke said, "Did I do something good that I don't know about?" His gratitude was depressing. It was scary how easily he could grow up to be Mister Stanley. Under the black dye and piercings was his father's son. But what was so bad about that? Mister Stanley was a decent, well-intentioned person.

"You didn't do anything especially good," said Lula. "You *are* good."

"My dad pays you to say that," said Zeke.

"This is me talking, not him." A voice inside Lula's head seemed to be giving some sort of speech about how grateful she felt for the time she'd spent with Zeke and for how much he'd helped her adjust to a new country. Why was the voice so solemn? Because she was hearing herself deliver the eulogy for her life with Zeke. Lula went to the window, where, she knew, the desolate sprinkle of snow would make her feel even more unhappy.

She said, "We have extra pizza in the freezer. We don't have to go out."

"Are you all right?" asked Zeke.

"I'm catching a cold," Lula said. "Dr. Lula prescribes hot chocolate."

Lula recalled seeing cocoa mix at the back of the kitchen cabinet. The packaging was designed to look vintage, and by now the contents probably were. But thanks to the scientific miracle of preservatives, the hot chocolate was delicious. Had Ginger made cocoa for Zeke? Zeke was not about to let the memory of his mother ruin his precious hot-chocolate moment with Lula.

A little later, Lula heated a pizza and left it out for Zeke. Mojitos were too much work. She could live without one. She went to her room and lay down. She slept and woke in her clothes. She thought it was nine in the morning. It was nine at night. She couldn't face Mister Stanley. They could skip the nightly check-in. Sooner or later Don would tell Stan about this guy Lula was lying about, and how she'd tried to make Don lie too. Her luck wouldn't last forever. It was already leaching away.

She took the last of Ginger's pills. After a while she checked her watch. Hours had gone by. Had she been lying awake in the dark, or had she fallen asleep? She felt achier but less stupid. Smart enough to register the fact that someone was knocking on her door.

"Lula," yelled Mister Stanley. "Can we talk downstairs?"

·   ·   ·

MISTER STANLEY WAS disappointed in her. Mister Stanley had been deceived. Mister Stanley had expected more of her. How could Lula have so betrayed his confidence and trust, consorting with thieves and criminals, endangering the welfare of the innocent boy he'd hired her and paid her generously to protect?

Over and over Mister Stanley said, "You brought a criminal into my home!"

The worst part was that Lula could see it from his point of view. She'd been naive and reckless. She should never have let the three guys into the house. She would have liked to tell Mister Stanley that, but another drawback to habitual lying was that no one believed you when you switched to the truth.

Apparently this was too serious for a kitchen conversation, which revealed a flaw in Mister Stanley's thinking. Nothing was too important for the kitchen. Her granny had died at her stove. But tonight Mister Stanley summoned her into the bookless library, the workless office, the dank ceremonial chamber where she hadn't been since he'd hired her and took her there to tell her the rules. Be home in time for Zeke, no drinking or smoking, no driving farther than The Good Earth, make Zeke eat vegetables, etcetera. Lula had broken every rule except the one against smoking, which Zeke broke himself. And the rule against letting him drive farther than the market, which there was still time to break. Mister Stanley had never thought to make a rule against driving Alvo's Lexus.

The library smelled like old people, like old clothes in old closets. It was the principal's office, where bad children were sent. Americans, with their big houses, their special rooms for special events. If her father wanted to have a talk, which he never did, he'd have taken her out to their favorite garbage-dump shooting range. How she missed her papa! There was no one to defend her against Mister Stanley's charges. So what if they were justified? Lula was only human. Humans made mistakes. She hadn't meant to hurt anyone. She'd just been unable to resist the lure of risky entertainment.

Lula watched Mister Stanley pace the room, ranting. If he would only shut up and listen, so much could be explained. Alvo and his friends had practically home-invaded her, practically held a gun to her head and made her ask Don to help. Alternately, she could confess. The gun was Alvo's. Lula had lied when she'd said it was Ginger's. She'd been afraid the truth might involve police and trouble with immigration. But Alvo wasn't a killer. Zeke was never in danger. Ginger had been the danger, sneaking around the house. And Lula had been so forgiving after Mister Stanley's wife had threatened them with a knife. How could Mister Stanley reduce Lula's loving relationship with Zeke to the cheap materialism of a service he'd paid for? Had he paid her extra for making Zeke hot chocolate? She cared about Zeke, she'd been kind to him. Zeke had been a basket case before Lula arrived.

And while Lula was numbering the wrongs committed against her, how could Don have betrayed her to Mister Stanley? What about attorney-client privilege? Did Don think that Lula never watched TV? Wasn't Lula entitled to this legal or basic human right, if not yet as a citizen then as a human being? There were probably grounds for a lawsuit here, if she'd had a green card and a hefty American trust fund.

Lula would have felt worse about her boss's accusations, but she kept being distracted by the way that anger had created or perhaps just unleashed a whole new Mister Stanley. Purple instead of mushroom white, outraged instead of apologetic, he seemed to have expanded into a physically larger presence. Had he occupied this much space with Ginger? It was shocking how long you could live with someone and know nothing about him. Who would have suspected that Mister Stanley could devolve into a jungle creature driven wild by animal instinct to protect his lair and his young? Not once in his tirade did he say "one" instead of "me," and with every word his voice descended from his sinuses deeper into his chest. The idea of Mister Stanley as an untapped reservoir of unsuspected qualities filled Lula with regret. She wouldn't be here long enough to discover even one more hidden aspect of his character.

But Zeke was the one she would really miss. Maybe she and Zeke could stay friends. She could visit him at college. An abyss opened beneath her, a landslide set off by her inability to picture the place from which she'd leave to go see Zeke.

If the mild Mister Stanley had a problem with eye contact, his spitfire incarnation's gaze was a high beam directed at Lula. But at last Mister Stanley blinked and stopped and waited for her to respond.

Lula put everything she had into the ultimate Mr.-Stanley-pleasing shrug. She tried to infuse her rising shoulders with a thousand years of Balkan history, with the what-else-is-new of invaders, murder, pillage, and exile, the what-can-you do of failed monarchies, empires, promises, and scams, the what-do-you-expect of Communism, of decades when you couldn't know anything, couldn't do anything, couldn't say anything, when all you could do was shrug and teach your children to shrug. She turned up both palms with the you-can't-tell-me-anything-I-don't-already-know world-weariness of a person who'd spent the formative years of her childhood under the paranoid leadership of a psychotic dictator, a person who had seen economic collapse and rioting and chaotic violence and everywhere gangsters in control, in the open and from the shadows.

She said, "Zeke was never in danger. Not from Alvo, anyway."

"How can you be sure?" Mister Stanley wanted her to have been sure.

"I'm sure," said Lula. "Trust me."

"I wish I could," said Mister Stanley.

"Then fire me," Lula said.

"Not so fast," said Mister Stanley. "We've had enough drama in this house. Let's think about alternatives. Take our time. Mull things over."

The way he'd said "mull things over" filled Lula with despair. She said, "I should probably quit."

"What makes you think you can quit?" Mister Stanley said, his voice rising again. "Have you considered your chances of finding another sponsor after you asked my childhood friend to sacrifice his integrity, to risk his career, to help some thug you let into my home while my son and I slept?"

"He's not a thug," Lula said. "Are you saying you won't sponsor me if I don't work here?"

"No," said Mister Stanley. "I'm not saying that at all. Though it might be more tricky. Legally speaking. Let's sleep on it. Let's revisit the subject tomorrow night when I come home. There's nothing like twenty-four hours to clarify one's thinking."

Chapter Fourteen

—⊗⊗⊗—

THE NEXT morning, Lula waited until eleven, an hour by which even the most pampered plastic surgeon's wife was certain to be awake. Still, Dunia sounded groggy when she answered the phone. A more thoughtful best friend might have asked how Lula was.

Dunia said, "Please God, somebody shoot me now. I am so hung over."

"Be careful what you wish for," Lula said.

"Old school," mumbled Dunia. "You sound like my granny."

"You and Doctor Steve been partying?"

"What Doctor Steve?" said Dunia. "Doctor Steve was another lifetime."

"Excuse me?" Lula said.

"The marriage is over. It's going to be annulled. Which makes everybody happy. Steve's family included. Steve's family especially. No ugly divorce courts, no bloodsucking lawyers, no scandal. Just a big cash settlement direct-deposited into my bank account. It turns out that Doctor Steve and the versatile Jorge my driver were having a little extramarital something on the side. I don't even want to think what special perfume Steve brought *him*. How could I not have known? Remember I told you that Steve liked me to talk Albanian during sex? The part I didn't mention was that he made me talk Albanian in a low growly voice. Pervert Steve wanted to imagine he was having sex with an Albanian guy! Speaking of which, whatever happened with that Albanian guy you went out with Christmas Eve?"

"Not much," said Lula.

"It's probably better," said Dunia. "Anyhow, no more Steve. What do they say? If it looks too good to be true, it probably is too good to be true? If it looks like a fish and smells like a fish, it probably is a fish. You know me. I'm an honest person. I'm not the blackmailing type. Steve was thrilled when I agreed not to ask for half of everything he's got. Which I probably could have gotten, if I was scheming or greedy."

"Congratulations," said Lula uncertainly.

"Thanks," said Dunia. "Anyway, I was going to call you. Guess where I am now? Twenty-fourth floor, Trump Towers. Overlooking the Hudson. Like Jesus told Peter from the cross, I can see your house from here. I rented a two-bedroom. I was thinking you could move in. Don't worry about the rent, at least for now. I'm bored. I want someone to hang with. Hey, it's your ticket out of New Jersey. We'll max out Steve's credit cards. Then we'll figure out what next."

"There's a job I want," said Lula. As if she had to convince Dunia, of all people, that she was an upstanding future citizen of the United States. "A court interpreter, to start with . . ."

"Fine! I already said I won't charge you rent. When do you want to come and check the place out?"

"I don't know. When would be good for you?"

"Right now," Dunia said.

. . .

BY THE TIME Lula got back that afternoon, she was already seeing Mister Stanley's house with the tender detachment of someone who used to live there. Or from the more objective perspective of someone else who used to live there. She wasn't the same person who, only a few months before, had gazed out her bedroom window and monitored the arrival of an SUV full of trouble.

The last remnants of that foolish girl had been blown away by the winter wind off the Hudson, the ice needles and face slaps of cold she'd fended off on her way from the subway to Dunia's overheated lobby, so like a cross between a Las Vegas casino and a grand hotel in Moscow. The uniformed doorman handed Lula over to another uniformed guard, who showed her to the elevator, where yet another lieutenant in Dunia's private army whisked Lula into the sky.

Dunia was waiting outside her door, perhaps to watch Lula admire the depth to which Dunia's high heels sank into the hall carpet. Welcome to America! Finally! They'd come a long way from Tirana. Dunia planted smoky kisses on Lula's cheek, then showed her into the apartment and stepped back to watch her friend's response to the Hudson River and half of New Jersey flinging itself at their feet.

"This works for me," said Lula.

"Look out the other direction," said Dunia, grabbing Lula's arm as they contemplated the skyscrapers poking their glittering heads through clouds of dusty sunlight.

"It's a sublet," said Dunia. "In six months I will have spent every last penny I got from Steve. But worth it, don't you think?"

"I've got sixteen hundred dollars saved up," Lula said.

"Don't make me laugh," said Dunia.

"I like what you've done with the place," Lula said.

Dunia said, "All the little personal touches ordered and paid for before I left Steve. I was thinking ahead."

"Thank you, Doctor Steve," said Lula.

"I thanked Steve, believe me," Dunia said. "Jorge the driver thanked him, too. I think Steve's living with Jorge now."

"The driver was cute," said Lula.

"The driver *is* cute," said Dunia. "Can you believe I put this place together, all by myself, in two weeks?"

"You should have called me," Lula said.

"I called you now," said Dunia. "We'll have fun. Let's wind the clock back a couple of years."

"We deserve it," said Lula.

"We earned it," Dunia said.

NOW THAT SHE was leaving, Lula welcomed the three bus rides home, which gave her plenty of time to figure out how to word her resignation. She knew it would be more professional to inform her boss before she told his son, but she wanted Zeke to hear the news directly from her.

As always, Lula was home before Zeke arrived, and as always she said, "Let's go get some food," exactly as she had every weekday afternoon for, God help her, more than a year. Their drama would play out less tragically in the car. Zeke would be at the wheel of the vehicle that he loved more than anyone, including Lula. He would not be looking at her, and his mind would be partly on the road. Better to tell him en route to the store than on the way home, because if he was upset, he would have to pull himself together before they went into the market full of strangers for whom he would have to wear the mask of unshakable teenage cool. The Good Earth was only a few minutes away. Lula had no time to spare.

They were barely out of the driveway when Lula said, "We'll always be friends. But there are going to be some changes. I'm going to work as a court interpreter, and I found a place to live, nearer downtown Manhattan."

Zeke said, "That's bullshit about your getting that job. So are you moving in with that guy who was here when . . . You know. The guy you said was your cousin. Like anyone believed *that*. The guy who let me drive his Lexus."

"Not at all!" said Lula. "I think that guy's in jail."

"I liked that guy," said Zeke.

"So did I," said Lula.

"What's he in jail for?"

"For being an asshole."

"I didn't know that was a crime," said Zeke. "Especially in New Jersey."

"It can be," Lula said. "The point is, I'm not moving in with him. I'm living with my friend Dunia. She's got a place in Trump Towers."

"That is awesome," said Zeke. "Can I move in with you too?"

"Maybe someday," Lula said.

"So you're just leaving us? Disappearing just like that?"

"You're going to college," Lula said. "You don't need me. You're practically grown up. You can pour your own cereal into a bowl."

"I don't eat cereal," Zeke said.

"Well, you should," said Lula.

Zeke, who had been slumped behind the wheel, pulled himself up to his full height. He said, "Will I ever see you again?"

"Constantly," said Lula. "You'll get sick of me. I'll visit you at college. I'll be your embarrassing old auntie. You and your friends can stay with me and Dunia when you come into the city." Would Dunia still have her apartment by then? They would worry about that later.

"Here we are," said Zeke. "At the store."

"Park close, it's icy," Lula said.

"I always do," said Zeke. "I'm a guy. Anyhow, the parking lot's empty."

Deserted except for a pickup truck, The Good Earth was closed for repairs. A worker wheeling out a cart of broken drywall told them, "Some dirtbags broke in and stripped the place clean. I don't know how those dumbfucks think they're going to fence a truckload of organic cauliflower."

"Let's get out of here," said Zeke. "Everything here is cheesy."

Lula's head felt swimmy. Another supermarket break-in? Alvo was in jail and couldn't possibly have been the dirtbag behind this one. Which proved he was innocent if, as the DA claimed, the robberies were all committed by the same person. Was there someone Lula should tell? Should she mention this to Don? She'd mentioned enough to Don.

From the edges of her consciousness came a sound like a cat choking on a hair ball. Zeke was crying. Gelid tears slipped down his chalk-white cheeks.

"Everything sucks," he said. "Mom going crazy. Now you're leaving. I think I might be gay."

"You'll be fine," said Lula. "I promise."

"Sometimes I wish I was a vampire," said Zeke.

"Why would you want that?" said Lula.

"Because you don't have to live and you don't have to die. It's easy."

"Not for a vampire," said Lula.

"Probably not," said Zeke.

Lula put her arm around him. A stranger driving past might have mistaken them for teenage sweethearts. Lula tried to beam concentrated rays of friendship and reassurance directly from her brain into his, and from moment to moment she felt a warm rush flowing back in her direction, so that it almost seemed to be working.

She said, "Let's try the Shopwell. I know it's further, but the drive would be fun."

Zeke looked at her. "It's too far."

"Don't worry," she said. "No one's going to tell your dad."

"I know that," said Zeke. He smiled his frozen fake smile, and then, as Lula watched, it slowly, slowly came unstuck and turned into a real one.

Lula put her head on Zeke's shoulder as he pulled out onto the street. And they rode like that, without speaking, all the way to the market and home.

IF THERE WAS one thing Lula should have learned from living at Mister Stanley's, it was the folly of comparing your life with how you imagined someone else's life, based on their real estate. Once, passing a house like Mister Stanley's, she might have envied its inhabitants their American happiness, complete with all the American creature comforts. Now she knew better. But still she found it a challenge of the spirit not to sink into the quicksand of envy that lay in the gap between the suitcases into which she was stuffing her possessions and the apartment full of designer furniture that Dunia had earned by being a sex worker of sorts, if not the sort Lula once feared. Well, at least Lula was mobile. She could move across the river without the twenty-foot van that, she hoped, Dunia could still afford when they got evicted from Trump Towers. Lula was like her ancestors, strapping all their worldly goods onto the backs of donkeys and migrating to higher pastures.

The real trouble with packing was that it left so much of her mind free and undefended against the cringe-inducing memories of last night's conversation with Mister Stanley. Lula flinched when she recalled Mister Stanley suggesting they go into his study. Come into my parlor, said the spider to the fly. And Lula, fearing that she might lose her resolve, announced that she was leaving while they were still in the kitchen. Even now, her face flushed when she remembered how Mister Stanley had struggled to turn his shock and disappointment into the legitimate concern of an upper-middle-class single dad dealing with an all-too-common domestic-help emergency.

"One would think you might at least give notice," Mister Stanley said huffily. "After all this time, two weeks seems the least that—"

"I would stay, if you needed me," Lula said. "If you needed someone to replace me. Mister Stanley, no insult, but Zeke is leaving for college in the fall. There's nothing I actually do. He can go to the market and microwave dinner by himself. I'm sorry, but he's growing up. And I'm not sure that it would be the best thing for Zeke to have me here for two more weeks when he knows I'm leaving."

"The best thing for Zeke" were the magic words guaranteed to vanquish Mister Stanley. He said, "I suppose I should have expected this after our conversation last night."

Lula said, "Zeke's a great kid. A very strong and beautiful person. You've done a terrific job with him in a difficult situation." She believed every word she was saying, and at the same time she was aware of how desperately she needed to keep Mister Stanley on her side. The green card was only part of it. Mister Stanley was her sponsor. Sponsor was only part of it. Mister Stanley was family. Mister Stanley would always be part of her new American life.

Mister Stanley said, "You've done wonders for him. We all have to thank you for that."

"Thank *you*," said Lula, inadequately.

"You're an inspiration, Lula. Not just to Zeke but to us all. Watching how you live, your nerve and determination. The courage to leave one life and start a whole new one, somewhere else . . . It almost makes one think one could—"

"You could!" said Lula. "You could quit your job and go back to teaching, if that's what you want. I'm sure a million colleges would jump at the chance to hire you! You could . . ." They both waited for Lula to imagine another positive life change that Mister Stanley could make. "You could . . ."

"I suppose I could," said Mister Stanley. "And given the likelihood of a financial crisis, or let's say a correction, I probably should." Lula and Mister Stanley stared at each other across the kitchen, a look in which, it seemed to Lula, they exchanged more pure unvarnished truth than in all the time she'd worked here. Mister Stanley wouldn't quit his job. He would stay on until he retired or until the crisis he predicted occurred. Zeke would leave home, and Mister Stanley would live here alone, dutifully visiting Ginger, who would get better or not, relapse or not.

Lula looked away. She felt as if the word *hopeless* was tattooed across Mister Stanley's forehead. In Albanian, *pashprese*. *Pashprese* meant an orphan begging on the streets of Tirana. *Pashprese* meant a family of eight crammed into one room of someone's aunt's apartment out near the Mother Teresa airport. *Pashprese* meant seeing your country run by dictators and gangsters and murderous politicians. *Pashprese* was not the same as *hopeless*. *Hopeless* was American, *hopeless* was Mister Stanley alone in his big comfortable house, working and making money so his wife and son didn't have to live with him.

Lula walked around so that Mister Stanley stood between her and the lamp. She memorized his glowing ears so the image would be available in case she needed it to light her way through some dark corridor in the future.

Lula said, "Mister Stanley, you saved my life."

"Call me Stanley," he said. "Please."

"Thank you, Stanley," Lula said.

"You're welcome," said Mister Stanley.

THE NEXT MORNING, as Lula folded and layered her sweaters in a suitcase, she heard herself make a sound somewhere between a sigh of grief and a grunt of self-loathing. But why should she feel ashamed? She had meant it one hundred percent when she thanked Mister Stanley for saving her life. And now it was time to *have* that life. When a door opened, you had to go through. Was it paranoid or realistic, half empty or half full, to assume that the door, any door, might not open twice?

Lula surveyed her baggage, her new laptop in its case. In fact, she wasn't so mobile. When she moved here, Mister Stanley had driven her from the city with all her things, but it seemed cruel to ask him to transport her stuff to Dunia's. Could she find a taxi to take all this? Or did she need a truck? She would have to ask Dunia. Could someone come today? Or would she have to live like this, rooting around in boxes of clothes, breathing in the gritty sorrow and shame swirling around Zeke and Mister Stanley, abandoned yet again? How long would it take to find someone to get her out of New Jersey?

Tires screeched against the curb. Lula ran to her window and saw two vehicles draw up, an old-model American car painted a shiny eggplant color, driven by Guri, and behind it the black Lexus. The perfect timing of the G-Men appearing at the perfect moment inspired Lula to imagine even more unlikely events. For example, Alvo waiting for her in the back seat of the Lexus.

Okay, that was too much to ask. Lula watched the two men lock their vehicles, Guri with a key, Genti with a stagy flick of the remote.

It might be fatally stupid, her being happy to see them. She'd assumed they were the same guys from before. The friendly burglars whose boss had taken her dancing Christmas Eve. The appreciative ones who thought she could save him from jail. The grateful ones who could help her move to Dunia's. But for all she knew, the two bruisers hustling up the front walk were the thugs they'd always been, the violent sons of bitches come to punish her for letting them down. They were here to blame her for their boss being sent away. How ironic, how like the corny stories she wrote for Don and Mister Stanley: In the end, the two villains reveal their true natures. Just when things are finally starting to go her way, they beat her to a bloody mess no man will ever want again. Once you let the devil in . . . She tried to remember Granny's saying. Once you let the devil in . . . then what?

But neither Guri nor Genti was talented enough to fake the bright amiable faces they showed her when she cracked open the door.

"Little Sister," Guri said. "Great to see you! Open up."

"How was Pennsylvania?" Lula said.

"Connecticut," said Guri. "Business trip to Norwalk. Open the door, please."

"You missed all the action," said Lula.

"Let us in." Genti's shoulders were up to his ears. "Come on. It's chilly."

"Why?" Lula asked. "What do you want?"

"To thank you," said Genti. "I swear on my children's lives."

Lula unfastened the chain. She said, "As a matter of fact, you guys couldn't have come at a better time."

Genti said, "That's what I told this lazy fuck. You can thank me for dragging his sorry ass off the couch."

They waited for Lula to ask them in and offer some refreshment. But it was no longer Lula's house. She was visiting too.

"What happened to Alvo?" she asked. "I mean Arkon."

"Whatever your boy did, it worked," said Genti. "The boss isn't going to jail. He's being deported instead. Too bad for us. But he's fine with it. For him it's a free ticket home, where he'll have his pick of Albanian girls. Plus his mom's a dynamite cook."

"Glad to hear it," said Lula. "I wish I could take credit." Had Don made a call, after all? Lula doubted it. Things had taken their course. Some judge came up with a better alternative to the American taxpayer housing and feeding a big strong Albanian boy for the next fifteen years. For the first time since she'd been in this country, everyone was overjoyed about someone being deported.

"Who can say who did what?" Genti said. "Who wants to know? The outcome is what matters. And we want to thank you. Maybe there is a favor we can do for you in return—"

"There is," said Lula. "You can give me a ride. I'm moving to my friend Dunia's place in the city."

"How much stuff do you have?" said Guri.

"Not much. It could fit in the Lexus, easy."

"It's about time," said Guri. "Don't take it wrong, but we always wondered how long our Little Sister could go on living in this tomb."

"It's not a tomb," said Lula.

"It is," said Guri. "It's the house of the dead."

Genti said, "Shut up, idiot. A ride is the least we can do. I'll take you and your stuff in the SUV. Guri will follow behind."

Lula led the guys up to her room, trying not to think about the night she'd brought Alvo upstairs. He had his pick of Albanian girls. His mom was a dynamite cook. The two men loaded their arms with suitcases and boxes. It would only take one trip. Lula grabbed her new computer. If she forgot something, she could get it. She'd meant what she'd said about staying in touch with Zeke.

With the two guys waiting outside, there was no time to get sentimental. Lula went through the house, checking for . . . what? Always when she'd imagined this scene, she'd planned on reclaiming the pitcher she'd gotten from Granny and given Mister Stanley last Christmas. But she couldn't do it. Not that Mister Stanley would notice. But it would feel wrong.

She was saying good-bye to the pitcher when Granny's spirit called her attention to something she might otherwise have missed, an envelope with her name on it, on the kitchen counter. In the envelope were five one-hundred-dollar bills, and a note from Mister Stanley that said, "Not as much as we might have liked, but with all our best wishes, good luck. Keep in touch. Warmest best wishes, Stan and Zeke."

Dear, dear Mister Stanley. Lula hadn't wronged him, really. She had helped his son. She couldn't stay here forever. She was sorry she had let Genti call Mister Stanley's house a tomb. Even if it was a tomb. Which it wasn't. She wished she'd thought to tell him that living human beings lived here.

Lula climbed into the Lexus.

"Got everything?" asked Genti.

"Everything," Lula said.

He pulled out, and Guri followed in his eggplant-colored sedan.

"We're both going into the city," said Genti. "We'll carry up your things. Then we'll be on our way." Lula pictured Genti and Guri trekking through Dunia's lobby as the doormen watched. She looked in the rearview mirror. Being followed made Lula nervous, even when she knew who was trailing her and why.

A few blocks from Mister Stanley's house Genti said, "Another thing. We remembered you don't know how to drive."

"Alvo was going to teach me," she said.

"That was then," said Genti. "This is later. But I can give you a lesson. You have to drive. You need it to be American. You need it more than you need to know who was the first president and how many stars were on the Pilgrim flag."

"You need it to be a human," said Lula. "What human doesn't drive?" She knew better than to tell him, an Albanian man, any man, that there was no Pilgrim flag.

"You'll learn fast," said Genti.

"When?" Lula said.

"Now," said Genti. They were still on a quiet residential street. He parked in front of a house and reached across and opened Lula's door. He said, "Get out and go around and get in."

"Here?" said Lula.

"Where else?" Guri had parked behind them. Through his windshield he gave Lula a hearty wave—of encouragement, she assumed.

"Don't you need a learner's permit?" Lula knew from Zeke that you did.

"No," said Genti. "Don't worry. It means nothing. In this country, you need a license to take a shit."

Lula got behind the wheel. Genti said, "Press on that pedal. Lightly! Okay, now the key." Her hand shook as she fumbled with the key. Lula screamed when the engine kicked in.

"Lesson one, don't scream," Genti said.

"I won't," promised Lula. "I mean I won't again."

"Turn the wheel, ease away from the curb. Good. Little Sister has talent."

Maybe she did have talent, because it wasn't a problem, going straight and sensing the width of the street. Genti found a parking lot and told her to pull in. Guri followed and waited while Lula started and braked and did figure eights.

"You got the hang of it," said Genti.

"I don't," Lula said.

"You'll get it now," Genti told her. Lula turned onto the street. "Look in your mirror. Our brother is behind us. You can brake if you need to. Our brother has your back."

The road fed into a bigger road, more heavily traveled. Genti said, "Don't worry, I'm here. I'm here."

It was what you'd want God to say if you believed in God. Lula didn't worry; she slipped into the stream of traffic, calm even though the sensible part of her knew she could get arrested, she could kill herself, or worse, she could run down an innocent person. A child. But if nothing too terrible happened . . . she was starting to think she could do this. Genti was watching out for her. He would lean over and grab the wheel if she did something wrong.

"Turn right up there," said Genti.

"Onto the highway? I can't!"

"You have to," Genti said.

And then, amazingly, Lula did. She was driving a vehicle! She was very careful, and the other drivers saw that, and they spoke the silent language, the language she'd learned from Zeke when they'd both thought she wasn't paying attention.

She signaled and glanced and gestured like a person, driving. She found a place between two cars and folded the SUV into traffic.

"The law of the jungle," Genti said. "Little cars move over for bigger ones. Survival of the biggest. It's why you want a big one."

It had begun to feel like one of those dreams in which she was driving a car and didn't know how, only this time she did know how. Like one of those dreams in which the airplane turns out to be a safe winged bus that never leaves the ground.

"Take that exit," said Genti.

"No," said Lula. "Not the bridge."

"Take the bridge," said Genti.

Before her was the George Washington Bridge. How majestic it looked, as solid and grand and permanent as the Great Wall of China!

"I can't," said Lula. "I'm sorry."

"Don't be sorry. You can do it. You can trust me," Genti said. "Just watch out. Take it slow."

The traffic was dense, which was fine with Lula, because she could crawl along and concentrate on keeping the greatest possible distance between herself and the car ahead. Let the other drivers cut in front of her. They had a lifetime of practice. She had enough to do, getting the knack of the play between the brake and the gas.

Genti said, "Take the far lane, the far lane!"

Someone honked, but not loud. Lula drifted from the slow lane into a slower one.

When the traffic came to a complete halt, Genti said,

"Good-bye and good luck. If I were you, I'd find somewhere to leave the car. You don't want anyone asking questions. If you know what I mean."

Lula said, "Is the car stolen?"

"Of course not," Genti said. "I'm insulted you would ask. Fully legal and paid for. The papers are in the glove compartment, signed over to you. Sold to you for a dollar. Have you got a dollar?"

"I think so," Lula said. She had twenty-one hundred dollars, counting Mister Stanley's bonus. It made her feel so hopeful that for a moment she felt a rush of friendliness toward Genti, though the feeling wasn't warm enough to tempt her into disclosing the reason for this upsurge of good will.

"Can I get the dollar from your purse?" Genti said. "Just to make it official."

"No, please!" Lula said. The traffic moved again. A station wagon swerved into her lane, and she hit the brake.

"Nicely played," said Genti. "I was just pushing your buttons. A lady's purse—I would never! Forget the dollar. You'll owe me. Okay, we're stopped again. No one's moving for a while. Gridlock. This is it."

"It?"

"This is where I get off."

"Where are you going?" asked Lula, plaintively. "I thought you were going to help me move my stuff to Dunia's."

"Someone there will help," said Genti. "I'm getting into my associate's car. You're on your own from now on."

"In the middle of the bridge? Someone will see you switch cars. How can that be legal?"

"The traffic's stopped," said Genti. "Our brother is right

behind us. Everybody's got their own problems. No one will notice me moving from car to car. If anyone asks, the wife and I had a difference of opinion, and I decided to ride with my friend."

Then, before Lula could say anything else, Genti got out of the SUV and slammed the door behind him.

"Wait a minute!" Lula cried, as the traffic picked up. Guri's car, with Genti in the passenger seat, passed her on her left. Both men waved and saluted her. When she looked again, they were gone.

The smartest thing, the most responsible thing, would be to stop and ditch the car. But she didn't want to do that. She could go very slowly (everyone was) and be extremely cautious. She would finish crossing the bridge and drive into Manhattan. That would be enough for one day. Tomorrow she could do more. She would get her green card. A job. She would get a driver's license. But what would she do with this big car when she was living at Dunia's? She didn't need a car. She could sell it and keep the money. The money would help her move on. But first she would ask the doorman to watch her fancy vehicle while the other doormen helped her move into Dunia's apartment. Lula would be arriving in the car of a person who belonged there.

Genti had said that the papers were in the glove compartment. But still it would be complicated, explaining to a dealer how she came to be in possession of a fancy new SUV. She would think of something. She would say, I have this Cousin George, a car dealer in Tirana with connections in the States. She would say "connections" or "relatives," depending on who was listening. She would say, I come from a tribe of people to whom such crazy things happen. If you ask around enough, eventually you find someone who doesn't ask too many questions. Flirtation and charm worked everywhere, second only to money.

Rehearsing exactly what she would say, Lula, who couldn't drive, drove across the George Washington Bridge in the brilliant winter sunshine.